Acclaim for Colleen

"Colleen is a master storyteller."

—Karen Kingsbury, best-selling author of
Unlocked and *Learning*

"*The Lightkeeper's Daughter* is a maze of twists and turns with an opening that grabs the reader instantly. With so many red herrings, the villain caught me by surprise."

—Lauraine Snelling, best-selling author of
A Measure of Mercy

"Suspense, action, mystery, spiritual victory—Colleen Coble has woven them all into a compelling novel that will keep you flipping pages until the very end. I highly recommend *Without a Trace*."

—James Scott Bell, author of *Deadlock* and *A Higher Justice*

"Coble's books have it all, romance, sass, suspense, action. I'm content to read a book that has any one of those but to find an author like Coble who does all four so well is my definition of bliss."

—Mary Connealy, author of *Doctor in Petticoats*

"*The Lightkeeper's Daughter* is a wonderful story filled with mystery, intrigue, and romance. I loved every minute of it."

—Cindy Woodsmall, *New York Times* best-selling
author of *The Hope of Refuge*

"Coble captivates readers with her compelling characters. Action-packed . . . highly recommended!"

—Dianne Burnett, Christianbook.com, for *Dangerous Depths*

"Coble wows the reader with a fresh storyline. Readers will enjoy peeling back the layers and discovering this is more than your average romance book."

—Romantic Times, 4-star review of *The Lightkeeper's Ball*

"Coble's historical series just keeps getting better with each entry."

—Library Journal, starred review of *The Lightkeeper's Ball*

THE MERCY FALLS COLLECTION

The Lightkeeper's Daughter, The Lightkeeper's Bride, The Lightkeeper's Ball

THE MERCY FALLS COLLECTION

The Lightkeeper's Daughter, The Lightkeeper's Bride, The Lightkeeper's Ball

COLLEEN COBLE

THOMAS NELSON
Since 1798

NASHVILLE   DALLAS   MEXICO CITY   RIO DE JANEIRO

Published in Nashville, Tennessee, by Thomas Nelson. Thomas Nelson is a registered trademark of Thomas Nelson, Inc.

Thomas Nelson, Inc., titles may be purchased in bulk for educational, business, fundraising, or sales promotional use. For information, please email SpecialMarkets@ ThomasNelson.com.

Scripture quotations are taken from the KING JAMES VERSION.

Publisher's Note: This novel is a work of fiction. Names, characters, places, and incidents are either products of the author's imagination or used fictitiously. All characters are fictional, and any similarity to people living or dead is purely coincidental.

ISBN 978-1-4016-8949-0

Library of Congress Cataloging-in-Publication Data

CIP data is available

Printed in the United States of America
13 14 15 16 17 QG 5 4 3 2 1

CONTENTS

THE
LIGHTKEEPER'S
DAUGHTER

For Ami,
I'm so glad you encouraged me to write this book!
Thanks for always being my champion.

PROLOGUE

1884

THE SHIP'S DECK rolled under his feet, and he widened his stance to protect his balance and the toddler in his arms. Where was she? He'd been from one end of the steamer to the other. Laura was nowhere to be found. He shifted the sleeping child and eyed the black clouds hovering low on the horizon. A lighthouse winked in the darkening seascape. The wind whipped the waves into a frenzy and tore at the masts. The boat fell into a trough, and the stern rose as the bow tipped. He grabbed at the railing for support. A rumble came to his ears. Thunder? Deckhands rushed by him, and he caught the faint stench of smoke.

"Fire!" a man shouted. "There's been an explosion!"

He turned to see smoke pouring from the hold. People milled on the deck, and crewmen rushed to lower the lifeboat. He grabbed the arm of a passing crewman and shouted over the howling wind. "The pretty woman with the red hair in a pompadour. Have you seen her?"

"She's gone. Left first thing this morning before we left the dock. This ship is going down, mate. Get on the lifeboat now!" The man jerked his arm away.

He watched the crewman rush to help panicking passengers into the lifeboat. Gone. How could she leave without a word? Laura would never leave her child. Other people streamed by him on their way to safety, but he stood rooted to the deck until the little girl in his arms whimpered.

"Mama," she said. "Papa."

He studied her eyes, so like her mother's. "We must get you to shore," he said. His purpose found, he strode to the lifeboat. Wide-eyed passengers crammed every seat. Some had other people on their laps. There was no room. Not for him.

He held up the little girl. "Please, someone save her!"

"Hurry, mister!" a crewman yelled. "Throw her into the boat."

A woman held out her arms. "I'll take her."

Julia clutched him and wailed. "It's okay, darling," he soothed. He kissed her smooth cheek, then lowered her into the woman's arms. The woman had barely settled the child when the steamer lurched and shuddered. It began to break apart as the lifeboat hit the roiling waves. He watched the men in the boat strain at the oars, but the waves swamped it, and it was making little headway.

He couldn't stay here or he'd go down with the steamer. Shucking his morning coat and shoes, he climbed to the rail and dived over-board. Cold salt water filled his mouth and nose. He struggled to the surface and gulped in air before another wave caught him. The fury of the current took him under again, and he lost track of how many times he managed to snatch a breath before being thrust toward the ocean floor once more. A dozen? A hundred?

Finally his knees scraped rock, and a wave vomited him from the sea to the shore. Nearly unconscious, he lay gasping on blessed ground. He swam in and out of darkness until his brain regained enough function to remember Julia. His stomach heaved seawater onto the sand, and the retching brought him around. He managed to get on his hands and knees and stayed there a few moments until his head cleared and he could stumble to his feet. He gawked at the devastation scattered across the beach.

The sea had torn the lifeboat to splinters. Bodies and debris lay strewn up and down the coast. Shudders racked his body, and he lurched along the rocks. "Julia!" he called. The wind tossed his words back at him. She had to be alive. He ran up and down the littered shore but found no trace of the little girl he loved nearly as much as he loved her mother.

ONE

1907

ADDIE SULLIVAN'S STIFF fingers refused to obey her as she struggled to unbutton her voluminous nightgown. The lighthouse bucked with the wind, and she swallowed hard. Her room was freezing, because they'd run out of coal last week and had no money to buy more. Her German shepherd, Gideon, whined and licked her hand. She had to get dressed, but she stood paralyzed.

A storm like this never failed to bring the familiar nightmares to mind. She could taste the salt water on her tongue and feel the helplessness of being at the mercy of the waves. Her parents insisted she'd never been in a shipwreck, but throughout her life she'd awakened screaming in the night, imagining she was drowning. In her nightmare, she struggled against a faceless man who tossed her into the water from a burning ship.

Thunder rumbled outside like a beast rising from the raging waves, and the sound drew her unwilling attention again. "The LORD on high is mightier than the noise of many waters, yea, than the mighty waves of the sea," she whispered. Her agitation eased, and she reached for her dress.

The front door slammed, and her mother's voice called out. "Addie, I need your help! Get your kit."

The urgency in her words broke Addie's paralysis. She grabbed her dressing gown. The medical kit was in the bottom of her chifforobe cabinet. "Come, Gideon," she said.

Carrying the metal box of bandages, acetylsalicylic acid powder, and carbolic acid, she rushed down the steps with her dog on her heels. She found her mother in the parlor. The patient lay on the rug by the fireplace. Her mother, lighthouse keeper Josephine Sullivan, stepped back when Addie entered the room. The woman's overalls and jacket were drenched from the rain and surf.

"You took long enough, girlie," she said. "I suppose you were hiding in your room."

Addie eyed her mother's set mouth, then knelt by the man. "What's happened? Where is he injured?"

"His arm is swollen. I think it's sprained. He has several cuts. I found him at the foot of the stairs to the lighthouse. I think he fell. He passed out as soon as I got him in here." Her mother stepped over to turn on the gaslights. Their hiss could barely be heard above the storm.

"I'll get you some tea after I tend to our patient," she said to her mother.

The wind had whipped her mother's hair free of its pins. Her gray locks lay plastered against her head. The wind rattled the shutters and lashed rain against the windows. "And food. You should have brought me something."

Addie clamped her mouth shut. The last time she'd tried to take food to her mother as a storm rolled in, her efforts were met with a tantrum. She turned her attention back to her patient. He was in his fifties and had little color in his face. Judging by his clean-shaven jaw, she guessed him to be wealthy and following the fashion of the day. His expensive suit, though shredded, bore out her speculation.

"Help me get his coat off," Addie said.

Her mother reached for the scissors from her sewing basket. "Cut it off. The clothing is useless anyway."

"But what will he wear?"

"Something of your father's."

Addie choked back her objections and took the scissors. The man's tie was missing, and blood showed through the white shirt under the jacket. She cut the shirt to gain access to his swollen arm. "I think it's only sprained."

Her mother dropped into a chair and pushed her wet hair out of her face. "As I said."

"It's God's blessing that he's unconscious. He might need the doctor."

"The isthmus is covered. I'd have to wait until low tide to reach the mainland."

"I'll secure his arm in a sling. He'll be fine in a few days," Addie said. He flinched and moaned, and she knew he'd awaken soon. She pulled out a bandage and secured his arm, then sprayed the cuts with carbolic acid and bandaged the worst of them. "Was there a shipwreck?" she asked.

Her mother shook her head. "Not that I know of. Just this man lying by the steps."

Addie silently prayed for him while she immobilized the arm in a sling of muslin. He moaned again. His eyelids fluttered, then opened. He blinked a few times, then struggled to sit up.

"No, don't move," she said.

He squinted into her face. "Where am I?"

"At Battery Point Lighthouse. Outside Crescent City," Addie said. "California," she added in case he was a bit addled. She touched his clammy forehead.

"The steep hillside," he muttered. "I fell."

"The steps are treacherous in this kind of weather. But you're going to be fine in a few days. I think your arm is sprained, but that's the worst of it."

His eyes lingered on her face, then moved to the locket nestled against her chest. He frowned, then struggled to sit up as he reached for it. "Where did you get that?"

Addie flinched and clutched the locket. "It was my grandmother's." She looked away from the intensity in his face.

"Laura." He clutched his arm. "My arm hurts."

Laura? She touched his head to check for fever. "Let's get you to the chair."

She helped him stand and stagger to the armchair protected with crocheted doilies. He nearly collapsed onto the cushion, but his attention remained fixed on her locket.

She was ready to escape his piercing stare. "I'll make us some tea."

In the kitchen she stirred the embers of the fire in the wood range, then poured out hot water from the reservoir into the cracked teapot. The storm was beginning to blow itself out, and she no longer saw the flashes of lightning that had so terrified her. She ladled vegetable soup into chipped bowls from the pot she'd kept warm for her mother. The sound of her mother's raised voice came to her ears and nearly caused her to spill the hot tea.

"You have no proof!" her mother shouted.

"What on earth?" Addie placed cups and the teapot on a tray, then rushed to the parlor. The man and her mother were tight-lipped and tense when she entered.

"Is everything all right?"

When neither the man nor her mother answered her, Addie set the tray on the fireplace hearth and poured tea into the mismatched cups. What could they possibly be arguing about?

She stirred honey into her mother's tea, then handed it over. "Honey?" Addie asked their guest.

He shook his head. "Black, please." He took the cup in his left hand, which shook. The tea sloshed. He didn't take his eyes off Addie. "I didn't believe it until I saw you."

"What?"

He set his tea down and glared at her mother before turning his attention back to Addie. His lips tightened. "The way you stand, the shape of your eyes. Just like your mother's."

Addie's eyes flitted to her mother. "Is your vision blurry?" she asked. Addie had often coveted the lovely brunette hair she'd seen in photos of her mother as a young woman. It was so straight and silky, and quite unlike her own mop of auburn locks that reached her waist. She actually looked more like her grandmother, the woman in the picture held by her locket. "What is your name?"

"Walter Driscoll. From Mercy Falls."

"Near Ferndale," she said. "There's a lighthouse there."

"That's right."

"What are you doing in Crescent City?"

"Looking for you," he said. His voice was still weak, and he was pale.

He must be delirious. She noticed the swelling in his elbow had increased. "Is your arm paining you?"

He nodded. "It's getting quite bad."

She reached for her medical supplies and pulled out the acetyl-salicylic acid. She stirred some into his tea and added honey to cover the bitterness. "Drink that. It will help." She waited until he gulped it down. "Let me help you to the guest room," she said. "Sleep is the best thing." He wobbled when she helped him up the steps to the spare room across the hall from hers.

Her mother followed close behind with Gideon. "I'll help him prepare for bed," she said. "It's not appropriate for a young woman."

Addie studied her mother's face. The woman's mouth was set, and Addie could have sworn she saw panic in her eyes. "Of course, Mama. Call if you need anything."

Closing the door behind her, she went to her bedroom and shut herself in with Gideon. The dog leaped onto her bed and curled up at the foot. She petted his ears. The foghorn tolled out across the water. The fury of the waves had subsided, leaving behind only the lulling sound of the surf against the shore. She left the dog and stepped to the window. She opened it and drew in a fresh breath of salt-laden air. The light from the lighthouse tower pierced the fog hovering near the shore. She saw no other ships in the dark night, but the fog might be hiding them.

The voices across the hall rose. Her mother quite disliked nosiness, but Addie went to the door anyway. Gideon jumped down from the bed and followed her. Addie wanted to know the reason for the animosity between Mr. Driscoll and her mother. She caught only a few floating words. "Paid handsomely," she heard her mother say. And "truth must be told" came from Mr. Driscoll.

What did her mother mean? They had no wealth to speak of. Many times since Papa died of consumption, they'd had little more for food than fish they could catch or soup made from leeks from their garden. The small amount of money Addie brought in from the dressmaking helped her mother, but there was never enough. Someday she wanted to walk into a shop and buy a ready-made dress. New shoes were a luxury she hadn't had in five years.

"She's not your child," she heard Mr. Driscoll say.

Addie put her hand to her throat. Did her mother have another child? Gideon whined at her side. "It's okay, boy." She had to know the truth even if it made her mother furious. She opened the door and stepped into the hall.

"If you don't tell her, I will," Mr. Driscoll said. "She has the right to know about her heritage."

Heritage? Who were they talking about? The door opened, and she was face-to-face with her mother.

Her mother's shoulders were back, and her mouth was stiff. "Spying on me?"

"No, Mama, of course not. I heard arguing. Is something wrong?"

"It's none of your business, girlie."

Mr. Driscoll's shoulders loomed behind her mother. "It most certainly *is* her business. You must tell her."

Her mother scowled over her shoulder at the man, then turned back to Addie. "Oh, very well," she said. "Come downstairs."

"Of course." Addie still wore her dressing gown, so she followed her mother down the stairs. Gideon stayed close to Addie, and Mr. Driscoll brought up the rear.

"Sit down." Her mother indicated the armless Lady's chair.

Addie's eyes were gritty and burning with fatigue. She obeyed her mother's directive. She glanced at Mr. Driscoll. He wore her father's shirt and pants, the blue ones with the patches on the knees.

Addie turned her attention back to her grim-faced mother. "What is it, Mama? What's wrong?"

"Wait here." Her mother went down the hall and into the office. She returned with a metal lockbox in her hands. "Your father never wanted you to know. I told him this day would come, but he wouldn't hear of it."

Addie's muscles bunched, and her hands began to shake. "Know?"

Her mother thrust a key into the lock and opened the box. "Perhaps it is best if you simply read through these items." She laid the box on Addie's lap.

The papers inside were old and yellowed. Mr. Driscoll stood watching them with a hooded gaze. "Mama, you're frightening me," Addie said. "What are these papers?" She didn't dare touch them.

Mr. Driscoll's Adam's apple bobbed. "They deal with your heritage, Addie. This woman is not your real mother."

TWO

ADDIE CURLED HER hands in her lap. Where was her fan? She was suffocating. "You're my stepmother? Why did you never tell me?"

"You are the most irritating child," her mother said. "Just read the things in the box."

Addie glanced at the yellowed papers. "Can't you just tell me what this is all about?"

Her mother chewed on her lip. "The nightmares of drowning you've suffered all your life? You experienced a shipwreck when you were about two. Roy found you on the shore and brought you home. He insisted we tell no one how we'd found you."

Addie examined her mother's words. Surely she didn't mean Papa hadn't been her real father. "You're jesting." She pressed her trembling lips together and studied her mother's face. The defiance in her eyes convinced Addie she spoke the truth.

Roy Sullivan had not been her father? He'd saved his pennies to buy her every Elizabeth Barrett Browning book that lined the shelf in her room. He'd bought her the treadle sewing machine. Even the stacks of fabric in her sewing room were purchased by him to give her the start she needed. She'd seen him make many sacrifices for her over the years on his modest lightkeeper's salary.

Pain pulsed behind her eyes. And in her heart. She needed air. She started to rise to go outside, then sank back to her chair when her muscles refused to obey. "What do you have to do with this?" she asked Driscoll.

"I believe I'm your uncle," he said. Cradling his sling with his good hand, he settled on the sofa.

Her hand crept to the locket at her neck. "My uncle?" She rubbed the engraved gold. "I don't understand."

Gideon thrust his head against her leg. She entwined her fingers in his fur and found a measure of comfort. "Is Addie even my name?" she managed to ask past a throat too tight to swallow a sip of water.

Her mother looked away as if she couldn't hold Addie's gaze. "Not if my suspicions are right," Mr. Driscoll said.

"Then who am I?" Addie pressed her quivering lips together.

He smoothed the sling. "I believe you're Julia Eaton, daughter of Henry and Laura Eaton. There are newspaper clippings in the file that lead me to that conclusion." He nodded at the metal box. "Laura was my sister."

Addie focused on the woman standing by the fireplace. Josephine Sullivan. Not her mother. No wonder Addie had always sensed a wall between the two of them. It explained so much. She'd often wondered why her auburn hair and green eyes didn't match either of her parents' features. Her mother had cruelly teased her about being left by fairies until her father put a stop to it.

"Why didn't you tell me?" Addie asked.

"Roy refused to allow the truth to come out. You were his little darling."

"You never loved me," Addie whispered. "Even before Papa died."

"Your disobedience killed him," Josephine said. "If I'd told you once, I told you a thousand times not to go swimming out past the breakers."

Addie dropped her gaze. "And it's something I'll have to live with the rest of my life."

"What's this?" Mr. Driscoll asked. "She killed her father?"

Josephine hunched her shoulders. "He took this post hoping the sea air would cure his consumption, but it never happened. The stress of saving Addie from her own foolish behavior sent Roy into a decline he never recovered from."

Addie bolted to her feet. "I need air."

Josephine caught Addie's arm and forced her back into the chair. "It's time the truth came out."

Addie rubbed her throbbing arm. "If you hate me, why did you keep me?"

"I don't hate you," Josephine said. "But you were a constant reminder of my failure to have our own child."

"Then why keep me?" Addie asked again.

Her mother shrugged. "Money. Someone pays for your upkeep. We receive a monthly check from San Francisco. The attorney who sends the funds would never tell us who his client was, so don't even ask."

"You were *paid* to keep me from my real family?" She struggled to take it in. "So the sewing machine was paid for by someone else? The books, the fabric, my clothes?"

"Roy was much too generous with you. I wanted him to save it for our old age. We earned every penny. He saved some, but not enough. Instead he bought you fripperies you didn't need."

"But we've been paupers since Papa died. Did the money stop?"

"With Roy gone, I was able to save it, as we should have been doing all along."

"That money belongs to Addie," Mr. Driscoll put in. "You'll hand over the bankbook or I'll file charges for kidnapping."

Josephine tipped her chin up. "I raised that girl. It belongs to me."

"I don't want it," Addie said, tightening her grip on Gideon. How foolish she'd been to stay here and try to earn her mother's love. "You should have told me."

"There was no need for you to know," Josephine said.

Addie turned her attention to Mr. Driscoll. "Why are you so sure I'm this Julia Eaton?"

He pointed with his good hand to the locket. "I gave my sister the locket you're wearing. She died right offshore here. The woman in the picture is her mother, your grandmother Vera. You look much like both of them."

"How did you find me?"

"A friend passed through here a couple of months ago. She came out to the lighthouse to take pictures with her new Brownie camera and happened to snap a photo of you fishing. When she showed it to me, something in your posture and the way you smiled reminded me of Laura. I knew she'd died nearby, so I decided to come. I never expected . . ." He swallowed hard.

"The Holy Scriptures say we may entertain angels unawares," Addie said. "I think that is the case this night."

His laugh was uneasy. "I'm hardly an angel, Miss Adeline."

Her father had always told her that truth never stayed hidden forever. God laughed at mankind's plans. What would her father say if he were alive today to face the revelation of the lies he'd told her? Everything she thought she knew about her life was in ashes.

She rubbed her forehead. "I don't understand anything. Why would someone pay you to care for me?" she asked her mother.

"Roy suspected the person wanted you out of the way. He became obsessed with finding out more and collected these clippings and other evidence." Her tone made it clear she'd never understood her husband's obsession.

Addie buried her face in her hands. "Who am I?" Gideon pushed his cold nose against her cheek. When she lifted her head to stare at Mr. Driscoll, the pity on his face stirred her. "What do you want from me?"

"I want to reunite you with your family." He hesitated. "Henry searched for weeks, desperate to find you and Laura. He'll be overjoyed to find you alive."

The thought that her real father had loved her stirred Addie out of her pain. A gust of wind and rain rattled the panes in the window, and she raised her voice over the din. "Reunite us? You mean you want me to go with you?"

He flexed his swollen fingers. "I hadn't thought of that. Perhaps you should stay here until I find out who paid to keep you away, and why."

"I need to help my mother." *My mother.* The familiar words mocked her, but surely the devil she knew was better than the one she didn't.

"That's right," Josephine said. "I depend on your assistance."

Mr. Driscoll looked at Josephine. "I suspect you have milked every drop of sweat possible from the poor child over the years. You deserve nothing more from her."

Though his words made sense, Addie shied away from the idea of leaving the life she knew. "I'd rather not face them until I know they want me."

He studied her face. "I can't introduce you as Julia until I get more proof. I don't want to subject you to possible scrutiny until we're sure."

She picked up the metal box. "The things in here don't prove it?" She skimmed through the articles about the shipwreck. One article mentioned the Eaton family's desperate search for Laura Eaton and her child, Julia.

He shook his head. "Your father collected articles about the shipwreck, but that's hardly proof of your identity. It's enough for me when I see the locket and look at your face, but Henry will demand more than that."

She slumped back against the chair. "Why wouldn't he see the resemblance as you do?"

"Henry Eaton is wealthy beyond your imagination. Better men than I have tried to hoodwink him without success. He is skeptical of any unproven claim."

She lifted her necklace. "But the locket?"

He chewed his lip. "Yes, he might believe the locket." He glanced at Josephine. "Where was it found?"

"It was around Addie's neck when Roy rescued her."

He nodded. "There are many questions about how you came to be here and why. Henry will want a logical explanation of how this happened. I'd like to have something more to prove your claim. When he realizes you're his darling Julia, you'll be showered with love and material possessions."

"I don't really care about money." Loneliness had dogged her all her life. The lighthouse stood on a rocky cliff that was an island most of the time. The only access to the mainland was an isthmus at low tide. Even then, her parents had rarely allowed her to go to town, and she'd longed to fit in, to find friends to laugh with and share with.

Addie stared at him with fresh eyes. Pain etched his mouth and left pallor on his face, but his blue eyes held keen determination. How had he gathered her true need so completely no longer than he'd been here? "Is the Eaton family large?" she asked. "Have I any siblings?"

"Not living," he said. "Your sister, Katherine, died in a streetcar accident three years ago. She was your half sister. Closer, really. After Laura died, Henry married our sister, Clara."

"Can you tell me more about the family?"

"There were three of us. Clara and I have the same mother. Our mother died in childbirth when Clara was born. Laura is the daughter of our father's second wife, so she was our half sister."

"So you're the oldest, then Clara, and my mother was the youngest?"

He nodded. "There are three years between Clara and me, and two years between her and your mother."

Addie's eyes filled. An entire lifetime of belonging had slipped from her fingers. "Katherine was my only sibling?"

He nodded. "But you have a nephew. Edward. He's five."

"A nephew! Do we look alike in any regard?"

"More than a bit," he said. "I have a thought. I can't just take you into Eaton Manor and announce you are Julia. However, Edward's father, John, has mentioned his need of a governess for Edward. Henry is raging about it. He dotes on the boy—being his only grandchild— and has had the care of him since Katherine was killed."

For the first time she was tempted to actually do this thing—to go to this family where Mr. Driscoll claimed she belonged. "Why hasn't Edward been with John?"

"Henry persuaded him that the boy needed his grandmother as he worked through the grieving process. Besides, John is a naval officer and was out to sea when Katherine died."

"The poor child. I would become his governess?"

He nodded. "If your education passes muster."

"I love studies. I obtained a degree through correspondence."

"So you wish to accompany me?"

Did she? She chewed her lip, then slowly nodded. "I'll come."

"You will not!" her mother said.

Mr. Driscoll fixed her with a cold stare. "You have no say in this." He turned his attention back to Addie. "You'll enter the household as my ward, the daughter of a friend. That way you'll be part of the family."

"Then what?"

"I plan to hire a Pinkerton investigator in San Francisco. I'll have him talk to this attorney and ferret out who hired him and why."

Addie hadn't been thinking about the faceless person who had contrived to keep her out of the family. "Why would someone do that?"

"It's something we must discover. Henry hasn't risen to prominence without making many enemies along the way. I have several people in mind."

"Who?"

He rose. "A couple of years before Laura's death, there was some scandal about one of Henry's rivals. When he went broke, his son committed suicide. Perhaps he sought to exact revenge. A child for a child."

She gulped in air. "This person might be dangerous. Are you sure of my identity?"

"Read the papers in the box, Addie. You'll see there is no doubt." He went toward the steps. "I'll leave you alone to absorb this news, my dear. I'm utterly exhausted, and my arm is a misery." His shoulders were stooped as he climbed the stairs.

There was no sound in the living room except the hiss of the gaslight. Addie stared at her mother. No, not her mother. Josephine Sullivan. Addie wasn't a Sullivan. Her entire identity had been stripped away.

Josephine sipped her tea. "You're about to be dropped into the lap of luxury. I expect you could send money to help me out from time to time."

"Did you ever love me at all?" Addie said, her voice barely audible.

"Let's not talk anymore tonight." Josephine moved from the fireplace and went up the stairs.

Addie sat frozen on the chair with the metal box in her lap. She dropped it to the floor, and the papers scattered. With a cry, she fell to her knees and buried her face in her dog's warm coat.

THREE

THE OFFICES OF Mercy Steamboats squatted on the corner of Main and Redwood. A three-story brick building, it presented an austere front to the world. Naval Lieutenant John North paused at the door long enough to remove his hat, then stepped into the entry.

"Good afternoon, Lieutenant North." Mrs. O'Donnell smiled from behind her typewriter. "Mr. Eaton is in his office. He asked me to send you in when you got here."

John walked down the tiled hall to the first door on the left. The imposing walnut door was closed. He gave a brisk rap on the polished surface. He'd slept little on the steamer from San Francisco, and his eyes burned.

"Come," Henry's voice called.

He'd rather go. John entered and closed the door behind him. "Good afternoon, Henry." When John had married Katherine, she'd insisted he call her parents Mother and Father, but it had never been natural for him. After she was gone, he'd been glad to revert. He suspected Henry felt the same way.

Henry regarded John over the top of his spectacles. "The ferry was late?"

"A few lingering storm swells slowed us down."

John settled in a chair and studied his father-in-law for clues to his mood. Henry's expression was as dark as the clouds rolling in from the west. A tall man, he had a thick head of brown hair that held only

18

a few streaks of gray in spite of being in his midfifties. His brown suit—impeccably cut, of course—fit his muscular frame perfectly. His waxed mustache suited his angular face.

"Have you been to see Edward yet?"

John shook his head. "That's my next stop. I'll set the nurse to packing his things."

Henry leaned forward. "What the devil are you thinking to yank him from the place he's been secure?"

"Henry, you knew all along this arrangement was temporary. I appreciate all you've done, but Edward is my son. Not yours. Not Clara's. He belongs with me."

Henry banged his fist on the desk. "You were happy enough to leave him with us when Katherine died."

"That's rubbish and you know it. I had no choice. I *do* have a choice now. My new assignment is at a desk, and Edward can be with me."

"You have no one to care for him."

"Actually, I do. Walter rang me, and the daughter of a good friend of his is seeking a position. He is bringing her in today to see if she will suit."

Henry's mouth grew pinched. "Can't the child at least stay until after my birthday ball? You too. You're on leave for a month. There's time to ease him into new arrangements."

Perhaps it would be best to let Edward get used to the idea, used to his father and the new governess. The last thing John wanted was to inflict more trauma on his boy. "Very well. But let's not argue about it anymore, Henry. It's bad for Edward."

"You don't care about what's best for the boy or you wouldn't be yanking him away from us. In the city, people might make fun of him. He's known and loved here. Have you ever thought of resigning, son?"

Henry's genial tone warned John to be on his guard. "The navy is my life."

"Mercy Falls is a charming town. Edward is happy here. I saw a house that would be perfect for you and Edward."

"The navy is all I know."

"You've managed naval supplies for years. You're detailed and organized. I'd put you over my companies without a qualm. Perhaps you could pull the steamboat business out of its slump."

"Henry, the steamboat travel is faltering all over the country. The train is more convenient. You need to be prepared for the coming decline. Perhaps invest in a train."

Henry held up his hand. "You know how I feel about the trains. Noisy and smelly."

"But profitable. You can't hide your head in the sand, Henry. The world is changing."

"Not in my lifetime." He wagged a finger at John. "I see what you are doing. Changing the subject. Think about Edward. Considering his challenges, he'll do much better here than in the city."

Heat rose along John's neck. "Edward is very bright. He'll have no trouble with school or with adjusting to a new place."

"He has fits, John. We must do whatever we can to help him."

"His epilepsy won't hold him back. He has spunk."

The last comment brought the faintest twitch of a smile to Henry's face. "Let's put aside our differences and think of the boy. I want to show you my new automobile, so I'll run you home."

If only Henry would take his own advice and think of Edward. Henry believed his solution was the only possible choice, and it wasn't one John was willing to consider.

❧

The stage passed a picturesque lighthouse on the coast. "Who mans it?" Addie asked Mr. Driscoll. He hadn't spoken since they'd boarded the stage. She and Driscoll were the only passengers since the last stop north in Trinidad.

"I believe it's unmanned at the moment. They're looking for a new lightkeeper, according to the paper."

The coach left the seaside and traveled up the hill. The vehicle rounded a curve and began to slow as it neared a town. Addie craned her head out the window at the charming valley. Milk cows grazed on the hillsides until the redwood forest encroached again. The stage rolled through Mercy Falls slowly, and she took in the small shops and brick buildings of the bustling town.

She gathered her valise from the floor by her feet. "Are they expecting me?" she asked.

"I called John. As I thought, he was only too happy to have help finding someone suitable. He's expected from the city on the afternoon ferry. May already be here by now."

"And my father?" She was unable to keep the eagerness from her voice.

"He knows as well. But remember, say nothing. I sent a telegram to a Pinkerton agent in San Francisco, and he is investigating. Once I have proof, we'll talk to your father."

Gideon laid his muzzle on her shoe. She rubbed her temple. The stage jerked to a stop. Moments later, the driver opened the door. Mr. Driscoll disembarked first, then extended his hand and helped her alight. She'd just completed the pale-green dress she wore, and the boots were new, a gift from Mr. Driscoll. Her hat, decorated with tulle, was a concoction she'd created to give herself courage, though she found it failing now.

Placing her hand on her dog's head, she stared up and down the sidewalk and smiled at several passersby. Such an interesting town.

"Shall we walk, or is there a carriage to greet us?" she asked Mr. Driscoll.

"The carriage is there." He indicated a grand brougham across the street. "But I need to run in to see Henry a moment. Will you be all right by yourself?"

"Of course." She watched him walk away, then glanced up and

down the busy street. Through the open windows of the building to her right, she heard the familiar clatter of sewing machines. Gideon growled and strained at his leash.

"Is something wrong, boy?" She allowed the dog to lead her toward the sounds of sewing. The austere brick building sat on the corner. She peeked inside the open door and saw rows of sewing machines. Women bent over their machines, and their feet pumped the pedals furiously. Addie had never seen machines sew so fast. How did they manage to keep their fingers unharmed?

Gideon led her to a small, sobbing girl. She stood to one side of her machine and held her left hand in her right. Addie saw the child's finger welling with blood. Gideon nudged the little girl's leg and whined. The child leaned against the dog.

"Honey, are you hurt?" Addie asked, hurrying to reach her.

A man in suspenders over his short-sleeved shirt approached. He gripped the girl's shoulders roughly. "You're being ridiculous, Bridget! Get back to work or I'll have to dock your wages." He thrust the child toward the vacant sewing machine.

She couldn't have been more than eight. She wore a rough dress made from a flour sack. Her dark-blonde hair hung in strings around her face, and she had a smudge on her cheek. Who knew when she'd last been bathed?

"What's going on here?" Addie asked. "Where is this child's mother? She needs attention."

The man narrowed his eyes at her well-made dress and black shoes. "You're not one of my workers."

Most of the machines had slowed or stopped, and Addie realized she had the attention of all the workers. "No, I certainly am not. This child is much too young to be working with a sewing machine. She belongs in school."

The man put his fists on his hips. "Look, lady, this is none of your business. Run along and let me tend to my workers."

"Where is this child's mother? I want to speak to her."

"My mama is sick," the little girl said. Her tears had stopped, and her eyes were big as her gaze traveled from the foreman to Addie. She had one arm looped around Gideon's neck.

Addie squatted in front of her. "Where do you live, honey?"

"Across the street on the top floor," the child said. She leaned forward and whispered, "My mom has consumption."

Addie winced at the family's lot in life. She well knew the pain of the illness. "What's your name?"

"Brigitte."

"That's a pretty name. Where is your sister?"

Brigitte pointed. "She's over there."

Addie saw another child only slightly older than this one. "How old is she?"

"She's nine. I'm eight."

Much too young to be working here, both of them. Addie inched closer and held out her palm. "I'd like to look at your hand."

The foreman grabbed the girl and drew her away from Addie. "Lady, this is not your business. I'm going to call the owner if you don't get out of here."

Addie stood. "Why don't you do that? Let's talk to the owner of this place and see what excuse he has to offer for forcing a child to do an adult's job."

"Mr. Eaton is across the street," the foreman said. "I'll go get him, and he'll toss you to the street."

Addie barely restrained her gasp. "Mr. Eaton?"

The foreman's cocky grin straightened. "You know him?"

She held out her hand again. "I'm taking this child with me. Her sister too. What's her name, Brigitte?"

"Doria."

Her skirts swishing, Addie marched between the rows of sewing machines to the little girl. "Come with me, Doria," Addie said.

The child's brow wrinkled. "I'll lose my job, miss. We can't afford to lose our jobs."

"I'll talk to the owner." She held out her hand. "Come along."

Doria took her hand, and Addie led her to where the foreman stood with Brigitte. "I'm taking these children home."

"If you go with her, girls, don't bother coming back." He nodded toward the front of the building. "Here comes Mr. Eaton's brother-in-law now. We'll let him sort it out."

Addie turned to see her uncle coming in the door. A man in a navy uniform was with him. Mr. Driscoll wore a thunderous frown that only darkened when his gaze clashed with hers. She straightened her shoulders and set her jaw.

"What is going on here?" Mr. Driscoll asked.

Addie tipped her chin higher. "Are you aware this business employs children who should not be near these machines?"

He blinked. "I have little to do with this place. It's one of Mr. Eaton's pet projects." He frowned at the girls. "These children work here? They surely don't run a machine, do they?"

"They do. Look at Brigitte's hand. She injured it under the needle."

The uniformed man stared at the foreman. "Is this true?"

He shrugged. "Mr. Eaton arranged it. We have about ten kids, some from the orphanage and some from the community."

"I'll have a word with him," the man said. "Did you care for the child's injury?"

"It's just a little prick. She'll be fine."

"Her fingers are bloody," Addie said. "It's still bleeding. With your permission," she asked her uncle, "I'd like to clean her up."

Mr. Driscoll nodded. "By all means."

"Where is the ladies' room?" she asked.

The foreman jerked a dirty thumb behind him. "In the back."

"Where are first-aid supplies to be found?" she asked.

"I'll get them," he said grudgingly. He stalked off toward a small office that had a window facing the work floor.

She eyed the navy man. Her uncle had mentioned that her new employer was an officer. If this was that man, she might find herself out of a job before she started.

FOUR

JOHN STOOD IN the shop and watched the workers disappear when the quitting whistle blew. "Who is that young woman?" he asked Driscoll. While her beauty had stunned him, her fire and compassion impressed him even more.

"Edward's new governess."

Aware his mouth had dropped open, John shut it. "Miss Adeline Sullivan?"

"Indeed. I do wish she hadn't gotten involved in this. Henry will be livid."

"Someone should have gotten involved long ago."

The foreman had vanished into his office after handing Addie the first-aid box and didn't return. John glanced at the other little girl. Doria stood off to one side with her hands clasped. Her lips quivered and she stared at the floor.

He saw a movement. "Here they come now." John watched Miss Sullivan and Brigitte weave through the sewing machines and tables of fabric. The child chattered to Addie, who seemed to be paying grave attention to the little girl. He studied her neat attire and the fiery lights in her hair.

"Ready to go?" Driscoll said when she reached them.

"I'd like to explain to their mother what happened," Addie said, her voice pleading for Driscoll's understanding. "She lives just across the street."

The husky, feminine voice had a confident quality that gave John pause. Her auburn hair glowed with vitality. Her eyes caught his, and he nearly gasped. Thick lashes framed eyes as green as a lily pad, and the flecks of gold in their depths lit them from within. Or maybe it was the compassion that shimmered there. Such purity, such empathy.

"Miss Sullivan? I'm Lieutenant John North."

She put her hand to her mouth. "My employer? I suspected as much. I'm afraid I'm not making the best first impression on you."

"On the contrary. I'm quite taken with your desire to help these children." He held the door open for them, then stepped into the slanting light of the sun. "It's good of you to care." Katherine had never noticed the poor around her. And why was he comparing Miss Sullivan to his dead wife? "You needn't trouble yourself," he told Driscoll. "I'll handle this."

Buggies clattered down the cobblestone street, and he waited for an opening before guiding the governess and the children to the other side. The five-story tenement was down a dark alley. Mortar had chipped from between some of the bricks, and one of the chimneys lay on its side on the roof. The faded paint and gouges in the door attested to the building's age and lack of upkeep.

He held the door open for Miss Sullivan and the children. Though he didn't say anything, he frowned. Addie shrugged and went past him up the stairs littered with paper and dried mud. The place stank of body odor, tobacco, and stale food. The banister wobbled when he touched it, and he opted to ascend without its assistance.

Brigitte and Doria scampered up the stairs like squirrels. Brigitte kept turning to see where the adults were, then dashing ahead a few more steps.

"How far?" he called.

"One more floor. We're on the top," Brigitte said.

He shouldn't be winded climbing five floors, but the stairwell had no ventilation, and the odors intensified as they rose. The last few steps left him breathless and longing for the cleansing coolness of the redwood forest.

The stench of cooked cabbage hung in the air. Doria's face grew pinched as she approached the first door on the left. The latch plate was bent, and he wondered if someone had kicked in the door. It wasn't locked, and the knob turned when the child laid her hand on it.

"Mama?" Doria called. "I have visitors." She held open the door. Her sister had grabbed Addie's hand and clung to it as they paused on the threshold.

He took Brigitte's hand and brushed past Miss Sullivan but left the door open. This place needed all the fresh air it could get. She followed with the dog, who rushed past her to the parlor.

Doria beckoned to him. Her face brightened when he stepped into the tiny parlor. "Mama's getting up. She was in the bedroom."

He glanced around the room. Sparse, threadbare furnishings, no decorations, paint that was streaked with soot. He heard a sound and turned to see a gaunt woman hurrying toward him. She wore a dressing gown that might have been white once but was now a blotchy gray. Her hair hung untidily from her bun, and she shoved it out of her face as she came.

The dog padded forward to greet her and licked her hand. She patted his head. "Is Brigitte all right?" she asked in a tremulous voice.

"She had a puncture from the needle," he said. "Please don't trouble yourself. Brigitte said you'd been ill. I'm sorry. I didn't introduce myself. I'm John North."

"I'm Nann Whittaker. Thank you for bringing my girls home, Lieutenant North." Her gaze went past him to Miss Sullivan, who had retrieved her dog's leash.

"I'm Addie Sullivan," the young woman said. "I tended to Brigitte's wound. It's quite minor. The iodine should stave off any infection."

"You're too kind," Mrs. Whittaker murmured.

He put his hand on the child's head. "They're much too young to be working on machines."

Mrs. Whittaker's smile faded. "If there were any way to put food on the table without them working, I'd take it. My husband was killed in a logging accident last year. We got by okay with my job at the sewing factory, but then I took sick."

"Consumption, Brigitte said?" Miss Sullivan put in.

The thin woman nodded. "The doctor says I need to get into the country, but that's not possible. I've got three other children, all younger than Brigitte."

Five children and no husband. The knowledge pained him. "Both girls are polite and hardworking. You should be proud of them."

"Oh, I am!" The woman pressed her trembling lips together. "I'll go back to the shop myself just as soon as I'm able, and they can go back to school. They are so smart."

"I can see that," John said, noticing Brigitte's bright, curious eyes.

"Brigitte made top grades in school." Mrs. Whittaker's hand made a sweeping motion toward the room. "I want more for my children than . . . this."

John nodded, unable to speak past the boulder in his throat. What chance did this family have? He wished there was something he could do, but he hesitated to bring her into his own house. She might pass her disease on to Edward.

He saw Miss Sullivan's eyes swimming with tears. He had to help. He dug into his pocket and pressed all the cash he had into her hand. Fifty dollars. "I'll see what I can find for the girls that isn't so dangerous," he said.

"God bless you," she whispered, her voice hoarse. "I had no food in the house."

"Can I pick up something for you?"

She shook her head. "The girls will fetch groceries for me."

"I must go," he told Mrs. Whittaker. "Good-bye, girls." He fled the stink of sickness.

Miss Sullivan and her dog followed him down the stairs. He noticed she was still fighting tears. "There's no choice but to let the girls work in that shop," he said, "but I'll talk to Henry about finding a job that doesn't involve the sewing machine. Mrs. Whittaker needs a good sanatorium for a few months. She might be able to work once she's stronger, but she'll never get well breathing in this air."

Addie kept her hand on the dog's head. "God is always sufficient. We must pray for them."

"I fear God isn't listening much of the time," he said.

"God is always listening. Sometimes things don't turn out the way we want. But even when they don't, God is always sufficient."

When they reached the first floor, she quickened her steps to exit the tenement, and he watched her draw in a lungful of air devoid of the smells permeating the building. The alley held other structures just like this one. How many other heartbreaking situations resided on the floors of these dwellings?

Mr. Driscoll met them on the sidewalk. Addie gauged his expression and realized he wasn't angry, just distracted.

"Everything is arranged?" he asked.

Lieutenant North shrugged. "Not really. It's a sad situation."

Mr. Driscoll turned toward the carriage. "Might I offer you a ride to the manor?"

His dark eyes never left Addie. "Thank you, but no. I have business at the bank to attend to before I leave town. Henry offered me a ride." He tipped his hat to her. "I'm sure we'll get a chance to get better acquainted tonight," he told her.

"Of course," she said faintly. She watched him walk away and wished she could stop him. Nothing in her life had prepared her for the onslaught of emotion that churned inside her from the first moment she'd seen him.

Mr. Driscoll offered his arm, and she took it. The streets were a muddy quagmire after the rain, and she lifted her skirt to clear the muck. A driver helped her into the carriage. She let herself imagine she was Elizabeth Barrett Browning about to embark on a journey. Or maybe Alice Roosevelt. She so admired the president's courageous daughter. Someday she wanted to see far-off places like Alice did, and dig her bare toes into distant sands. In her daydream, the man at her side matched the man who had just left her.

Josephine had worked to squelch Addie's romanticism, but Addie couldn't help it anymore than she could help the color of her eyes. "How far to the estate?" she asked Mr. Driscoll.

"At the edge of town. Five minutes," he said, settling onto the leather seat beside her. He cast a doubtful glance at Gideon. "You should have left that dog behind. I don't know how I'll explain it to Henry."

She tipped up her chin. "I wouldn't come without him."

"Which is the only reason I finally agreed. But it was most unfortunate. Henry is sure to be put off."

"I thought Lieutenant North was my employer."

"He is, but Henry's wishes are generally considered."

She watched the scenery as the carriage rolled through town. A drugstore and ice-cream shop looked interesting. She noticed a sign that said Mercy Stagecoach Company. Before she could ask, Mr. Driscoll pointed it out as belonging to her father. There were several dress shops and haberdasheries in town.

"Henry owns half the town," Driscoll said. "The bank, the creamery too."

Addie shrank back against her seat. "I fear I'll be out of place."

"You'll be fine. As my ward, you'll be treated like one of the family."

The carriage slowed at two large stone columns that anchored a wall taller than Addie's head. A massive iron gate barred the way. The vehicle stopped until the guard opened the gate, then it turned into a long driveway.

"Why is it gated?" she asked. "Are they in danger?"

He laughed. "You have much to learn, Adeline. The Eatons don't mingle with the lower class other than to employ them. It's better that way."

"Better for whom?"

His smile faltered and he turned away. "There's your new home."

Addie caught her breath at the sight of the mansion. Three stories high, it rambled in so many directions she had to crane her neck to take it all in. Five or six colors of paint emphasized the architecture's features. The porch encased two sides of the manor, and the railing made her think of toy blocks. The red trim accented the medium gray-green siding. The door and shutters were black. The home had so many gables and dormers, it made her dizzy to take them all in. Numerous outbuildings peeked from the coastal redwoods that shaded the yard. The forest began barely ten feet from the back corner of the house.

"It's quite lovely," she said.

"Henry attends to every detail," Mr. Driscoll said. "You'll see many homes such as these in town. We call them butterfat palaces, since most were constructed from money made from dairying. Henry's is the grandest by far."

"Did Mr. Eaton make his money in dairying too?"

"In the beginning. He owns many other businesses now, as I mentioned." He stepped from the carriage and helped her down. "Remember, mention nothing to anyone. It might be dangerous to reveal your identity."

"Dangerous?"

"Someone took great care to keep you from Henry. Whoever did this must hate him very much. That level of hatred might be dangerous. If Henry finds out who has done this, that person's life would be ruined. Henry would see to that."

"My father sounds formidable."

"He doesn't suffer fools gladly, and he expects those around him to be loyal."

She accepted the arm he offered, and they walked past banks of blooming goldenrod and salvia. Gideon followed at her heels. "How about you, Mr. Driscoll? How do you feel about Mr. Eaton?"

"He's a loyal friend to those he trusts. He's been good to me for my sisters' sakes, and I've made my home in the manor for many years." They reached the front door. He opened it and motioned for her to enter. "Stay," he told the dog.

She repeated the command and stepped into the entry. The first thing she noticed was the scent of something baking. A berry pie, perhaps. Then she saw the opulence of the hall. Her mouth dropped as she took in polished walnut floors and woodwork, richly colored wallpaper, and an Oriental runner down the entry and up the six-foot-wide staircase. Through a doorway lay a parlor with lovely red upholstered furniture and fine pictures.

She craned her head to look at the art that lined the walls. A woman's portrait caught her eye. "My mother? I'd like to know more about her."

"That's not her. It's your grandmother Vera."

She clutched her necklace. "The one in my locket. She's much older in this portrait."

"Yes."

She glanced at her shoes and realized she was tracking mud on the carpet. "Oh, dear me," she muttered. She quickly retraced her steps to the porch and removed her shoes. "Might I have a rag to clean up the mess?"

"Molly shall get it. Come along," Mr. Driscoll commanded. "I'll show you to your room, then introduce you to your charge."

Her pulse leaped at the thought that her new life was about to begin.

FIVE

ADDIE STEPPED INTO the room at the end of the long hall. The tiny space held only a dresser and a single bed covered with a blue and yellow quilt. A bowl and pitcher had been placed atop the doily on the dresser. Beside the bed lay a plain rag rug on the oak floors. The scent of beeswax hung in the air. Pleasant. And lavish compared to her stark bedroom at the lighthouse. The window in this room looked out into the deep shadows of redwood forest, and she shivered at their imposing height.

She dropped her valise on the floor. "What about my trunk?"

"The driver will bring it up. Will this suit?"

"Of course. Where is my charge's room?"

"Across the hall. I shall show you." Mr. Driscoll stood aside for her to exit, then stepped in front of her and led the way. Her slippers sank into the plush runner in the hall. The green wallpaper appeared new. Portraits of people lined the walls, and she longed to linger over the images to see if she could find a woman with red curls.

He motioned to her, and she followed him into the room opposite hers. Tin soldiers, a wooden train, and a stack of books on a small shelf proclaimed the space to be a child's room. A small table with two chairs was under the window. The other furnishings included a cot, a chest of drawers, and a chifforobe. This room had wallpaper in a tiny blue print that matched the blue quilt on the bed. A rug covered the unpainted floor.

"He's not here" she said.

"He's likely in the side yard with his nurse." He motioned to her and exited the room.

She hurried to fall into step. "If he has a nurse, does he really need me?"

"He's five. It's time he began to receive instruction in reading and sums. Come along, my dear." His clipped words urged her to hurry.

She quickened her pace. So many new relationships to learn. After a lifetime of loneliness, she was about to discover a family. Her pulse stuttered, and she wasn't sure if it was fear or anticipation. She followed him down the steps.

Gideon greeted her on the porch and pressed his cold nose against her hand. She rubbed his ears. "What about Gideon? He's used to sleeping with me."

"Gideon will sleep in the barn. It's clean and dry."

"Yes, sir." She stepped across the spongy grass to the side yard. A small boy gripped a baseball bat in his hands and squinted into the sun. An older woman in a gray dress prepared to pitch a baseball at him.

Addie drank in the curly dark hair and his quite adorable cowlick. He was a miniature version of his striking father. He wore knickers and a white shirt. He bit his tongue as he concentrated on the nurse preparing to pitch the ball. She wanted to run to him and scoop him into her arms. She longed to hear him call her Auntie. After a lifetime of wanting a large family, here was part of all she'd longed for.

The child saw Gideon. "A dog!" He dropped the bat and called the dog to him.

Gideon trotted forward, and the boy rubbed his ears. "He likes me," Edward said, his voice eager.

"Of course he does," Addie said. She knelt beside him. Her fingers itched to bury themselves in his curls. She wanted to put her nose in his neck and smell his little-boy scent. He was adorable, and she was already in love.

"Does he like to play ball?" he asked.

"I'm sure he'd like that very much," she said. She stood and watched the boy throw the ball to Gideon for a few minutes. Then Edward dropped the ball and stood staring. "Edward, are you all right?" she asked.

Gideon lunged toward the boy. When he reached him, he grasped Edward's sleeve in his teeth. "Gideon, down," Addie called, starting after him. The dog tugged the child down to the grass. She gasped and put on an extra burst of speed. She'd never known her dog to attack. He was the most mild-mannered canine. Edward slumped to the ground. His limbs began to twitch.

The nurse reached him. "He's having a seizure!" She pulled a hankie from her pocket, rolled it up, then thrust it between the child's teeth as though she'd done it before. "He has the falling sickness," she said, peering up at Addie.

"Epilepsy," Mr. Driscoll said, his tone sharply corrective.

The nurse inclined her head and glanced at Gideon. "What a blessing your dog pulled Edward down so he didn't fall, Miss."

"I have never seen him act that way," Addie said. "It was almost as if he knew what was coming."

"Nonsense," Mr. Driscoll said. "He was practically attacking the boy."

"Gideon has never attacked anyone." Addie petted the dog's head. "Look at him, Mr. Driscoll. He's worried about Edward." Gideon lay near the child. His dark eyes never left Edward's face. He whined and licked Edward's cheek.

The man studied dog and boy. "Nonsense," he said again, but his tone lacked conviction.

A *putt-putt* from behind caused her to turn. A most unusual contraption came rolling up the drive. It resembled a buggy, but there was no horse pulling it. The sun glimmered on shiny red paint and black leather seats. The wheels turned around red spokes. An oily stink roiled from it. The man in the seat behind the wheel wore a leather coat and beret, and a scarf around his neck. And a huge smile. Beside him sat a familiar set of wide shoulders encased in a navy uniform.

"Is that my father?" she whispered.

"It most certainly is. In his new Cadillac."

Henry. Her father. Her legs twitched and adrenaline surged, but she forced herself to remain still and watch him maneuver the vehicle over the potholes until it stopped with a final *putt*. Lieutenant North leaped out, then the automobile rolled on to the carriage house. Neither of the men noticed the boy on the ground.

❧

John spotted Miss Sullivan the moment he dismounted the automobile. She stood to one side with Driscoll, and he caught a gleam of auburn hair under her large hat. She was just as attractive as she'd been in town and inspired the same leap in his pulse. He'd hoped his reaction had been a temporary insanity.

She and Driscoll and Edward's nurse, Yvonne, faced a form on the ground, and it took a moment for the scene to register. When he recognized his son, he ran toward his boy. "Edward!" He knelt beside him.

The boy's eyelids moved, but he didn't awaken. At least no seizure contorted his features. "He had a seizure?" he asked, glancing up at Yvonne. She nodded. He touched Edward's forehead. "Edward. Wake up, son."

There was still no response and likely wouldn't be for a few more minutes. Edward would be tired for hours. John clenched his fists. If only he could fix this for his son. He took a deep breath, then smoothed his son's hair. "It's all right, Edward. I'm here."

"He collapsed so quickly," Miss Sullivan said in that compelling, husky voice.

He rose and nodded. "Were you here when Edward's attack occurred?"

"Yes, Lieutenant North." Her worried eyes never left the boy. "We'd just come out to meet him when he fell."

He lifted his son in his arms and carried him toward the house. The young woman fell into step beside him. The dog started to follow her, and she made a hand gesture that stopped it in its tracks.

"Is there anything I can do? If I'm going to be with him most of the day, I need to know how to handle this when it happens."

At least she wasn't flustered by the incident. She'd taken charge here the same way she'd done in the sweatshop. His deceased wife had dissolved into hysterics every time Edward had a "fit," as she called it. She'd never reconciled herself to the idea that her son had a chronic problem.

"Come with me," he told her.

He carried his son into the house and up the staircase to his bedroom. He laid the boy on top of the quilt and stood staring down at him. He ached to take the ailment on himself, but all he could do was stand by.

Miss Sullivan stepped closer to the bed. "Why isn't he waking?"

"He'll be up and around soon. But he'll be tired. He had a seizure."

"What can be done to help him?"

"I've had him to the best neurologists in the country, but there is no treatment for it."

"So he'll always have to deal with this?" Her gaze softened even more.

He nodded. "The main thing to remember when he has a seizure is that he needs to be kept safe. Help him to lie down, and put something soft between his teeth so he doesn't bite his tongue, then wait it out."

She caressed Edward's hair. "Poor child."

John warmed to her empathy. He thought it was sincere. "He's a good lad. Never lets it get him down." He folded his hands across his chest. "You were most confident in the sewing factory. I think it would be difficult for anything to get the better of you. I liked that."

Color stained her cheeks. "Thank you, sir. I was thankful for your protection."

"You're much younger than I expected." *And prettier*, he could have added.

Her green eyes held a challenge. "I'm nearly twenty-five."

"I merely remarked on your youth. If Walter thinks you are suitable, I'm sure that's the case."

She dropped her gaze to the floor, and her cheeks went rosier. "I'm sorry for my tone, Lieutenant North."

It wasn't his fault he liked her appearance entirely more than was proper. "Forgive me, Miss Sullivan. I don't mean to make you feel uncomfortable in your position. Take care of my son, and teach him well, and you'll hear no complaints from me."

"I will do my very best," she said. She turned toward the bed. "He's awakening."

Edward yawned, and his eyelids fluttered, then opened. "Papa? I did it again."

John sat on the edge of the bed and slipped his arm under his son's head. "It's all right, little man. You're fine now."

Edward bolted upright. "Where's the doggy?"

"What dog?"

"The one that helped me," the boy asked Miss Sullivan. "Was it your dog?"

"Yes. That's Gideon."

"He knew I was getting sick and helped me sit down."

John hid his smile. And his skepticism. "What did he do?"

"He jerked on my arm until I sat," Edward said.

John glanced at the woman. Her expression was soft as she stared at his son. "Did you know the seizure was coming?"

Edward shook his head. "I was going to toss the ball for him. Can the dog sleep on my bed?"

"You know your grandfather doesn't allow dogs in the house."

"But this is a special dog. He helped me. I'll ask Granddad myself." Edward scooted to the edge of the bed. He staggered when he gained his feet but quickly straightened.

"You're the only one Granddad might listen to," John muttered after his son disappeared through the doorway.

Glancing at the new governess, he wished he would quit feeling as though the undertow were carrying him out to sea.

SIX

ADDIE COUNTED EVERY tread as she walked back to the entry. Twenty-one. She kept track of every time she put her foot down on the entry and porch, and on each of the front steps. Thirty. And she prayed. The austere man she'd glimpsed sitting in the automobile next to the lieutenant wasn't what she'd expected.

The yard was empty except for Gideon and Edward. Smiling, she approached the boy and dog. "He likes you, Edward." She couldn't resist touching his hair again. The soft locks curled around her finger.

"Can I have him?" The question was asked with the innocence of a child who had never been denied.

Addie inhaled as she tried to decide how to answer. She'd raised Gideon from a puppy and would never give him up. "I'll be happy to share him," she said finally. "But he's my dog."

Edward's lip thrust out. "I want him to be *my* dog." He began to sob.

Addie wanted to gather him in her arms and soothe his cries, but she knew it wasn't wise to give in to every demand.

"How did you get him to do that?" a gruff voice demanded from behind her. "The dog, I mean. Yvonne informed me the canine appeared to have anticipated my grandson's fit."

She turned to see Henry Eaton approaching. He'd removed his cap and scarf. Flecks of mud dulled the sheen of his boots. "I don't know, Mr. Eaton. I've never seen him do anything like this before."

Edward had his arms around Gideon's neck. "He seemed quite attuned to the lad," Mr. Eaton said.

"He's always been intuitive. Whenever a shipwreck occurred at our lighthouse, he knew before we did. He would have plunged into the raging sea if I had allowed him to do so."

"He must stay with my grandson at all times," Mr. Eaton said. "You're the new governess, is that right?"

"Yes, sir," she said, raising her voice above Edward's hiccupping sobs.

He studied the dog again. "We should breed him. His pups might have his magical ability as well. I'll find a female at once. Where did you find him?"

"In Crescent City. My father bought him from a neighbor."

"Give me his name, and I'll see if he has any other dogs with this one's ability. What's the dog's name?"

"Gideon."

"This is a lucky day for us, young lady. We must do all in our power to make sure you and the dog stay with us."

The note of approval in his voice brought the truth to the front of her tongue. How much greater would his welcome be if he knew she was his daughter? She had to get away before she blurted out the story. "I believe God brought me here for a reason, Mr. Eaton. I'll do my part to follow the Lord's guidance in all ways."

"Such simple faith," he said. "Very quaint."

His condescending tone squared her shoulders. "If you'll excuse me, I need to unpack."

The intensity of his demeanor softened. "I've come on too strong with you. Please accept my apology, Miss Sullivan. We all indulge the child too much. It's his af-affliction, you see."

His heartfelt stammer tugged at her heart. "No need to apologize. "I've already fallen in love with Edward myself. I'll protect him with my life. After all, God has arranged this for Edward's benefit."

Eaton tipped his head to the side. "You look familiar. Have we met?"

She turned her head. "I don't remember meeting you, sir. I grew up much north of here."

"Strange," he muttered. He put his large hand on Edward's head. "Enough of these histrionics, Edward. The dog will be here for you. Miss Sullivan has graciously agreed to share the animal with you. Stop the wailing."

Her charge sniffled, then swiped the back of his hand across his wet face. "Can he sleep with me, Granddad?"

"You know I quite dislike animals in the house, boy," his grandfather said.

"But he helped me!" Tears filled Edward's eyes.

Eaton sighed. "Very well. But keep him out from under my feet. And out of the kitchen, you hear? It will be your job every morning to put him out for the day. He's not to lie around on the rugs."

Edward's eyes began to shine. "Yes, sir!"

Addie hid a smile at the boy's deft manipulation. She would have her hands full with him. He'd been coddled all his life. While she pitied him his affliction, it would be her job to see that he developed into a man, not a namby-pamby without backbone. At least her father showed love and compassion.

A movement caught her attention, and she watched Lieutenant North approach from the carriage house where the automobile was stowed. Warmth crept into her skin. When they'd talked over Edward's bed, she'd had the most peculiar sensation, as if something inside her had recognized him—the timbre of his voice, the way he looked at her as if he really saw her. He possessed everything she'd dreamed of when she read Elizabeth Barrett Browning's poetry: wide shoulders that tapered to a trim waist, unruly black hair, and dark brown eyes that pierced right through her defenses. She'd read about love at first sight and assumed it was the stuff of dime novels, but when she held this man's gaze, she could almost believe in it.

Her gaze went to her dog. Had he really sensed Edward's approaching seizure? Often she'd thought Gideon could sense pain and despair. He'd proven it again today when he'd led her to the garment factory. What if he possessed some innate ability to predict the seizures? He could be a great boon to the child.

She told herself not to be so silly. It was a childish fancy that had taken Edward. He'd soon outgrow it and move on to a new obsession. Children always did. She turned toward the driveway as a carriage turned in at the gate.

⌒⁕⌒

John turned his back on Miss Sullivan and approached his mother-in-law's carriage as it rolled to a stop. He extended his hand to help her alight. Would Katherine have aged as well as Clara? Her creamy skin was unlined, though he knew she had to be fifty or a little older by now. The smile he greeted her with was genuine. "Clara, it's good to see you."

She touched a gloved finger to his cheek. "John, when did you arrive? You look quite handsome with that tan."

He brushed his lips across her cheek and inhaled her rose perfume. "Just this afternoon."

"Fetch my parcels from the driver, would you? I am perishing for tea." She swayed off toward the house without waiting for his answer.

John shrugged and did as he was told. Henry never begrudged her any of the funds she spent on her fripperies. Katherine might have paupered him in following her mother's example. Carrying the parcels, he strode to the house, where he handed off the purchases to Molly, then followed the sound of voices to the parlor.

Miss Sullivan stood with her back to the wall and her hands clutched in front of her green dress. She faced his mother-in-law. Driscoll stood off to one side with Edward.

"Yes, ma'am," she said. "I studied three years of Latin, though I don't think Edward is quite ready for another language."

"I agree, Miss Sullivan." Clara made a sweeping survey of the younger woman. "Your dress is quite well made. Where did you find it?"

"I made it, ma'am."

"How refreshing to find such an industrious young woman. How did you learn to sew such a stylish garment?" Clara stepped nearer and examined the waist of the dress. "The way the waist dips is very becoming. And the stitches are invisible."

The young woman shifted, and the color leached from her cheeks. "My mother taught me to sew when I was a child. She thought the income would help the family, but I discovered a real love for textiles and design."

To John the dress appeared ordinary, but then, what did he know of style? He noticed how long Miss Sullivan's lashes were and averted his gaze. She was his employee.

Miss Sullivan touched Clara's hand. "Are you feeling all right, Mrs. Eaton? A headache perhaps?"

Clara pressed her other hand hard on her forehead. "My head does ache. How did you know?"

"I saw it in your eyes. Let me rub it for you," Miss Sullivan said. "I have some peppermint oil that will help ease the pain."

"What a dear you are," Clara said. "We have a few minutes before dinner, and anything you might do to help would be most welcome."

"I'm sure it will comfort you," Miss Sullivan said.

"Over our meal I wish to know more about your dressmaking skills. I'm planning a ball for Henry's birthday in two weeks, and I must have a new dress. I have an idea in my mind's eye, and perhaps you can bring it to life."

"I'll be happy to do whatever I can, Mrs. Eaton," Miss Sullivan said. "But I need to start immediately if I'm to have time to complete it."

John glanced at the young woman, then at his mother-in-law. Both of them were smiling. "What about Edward?" he asked. "Miss Sullivan was hired to teach my son."

Clara tapped her closed fan on her son-in-law's arm. "Don't be such a stickler, John. I'll make sure my dress doesn't cut into Edward's lesson time. Come along, my dear. Get your oil, and meet me in my salon."

John's mouth dropped as Clara took Addie's arm and escorted her out of the room. He'd never known the older woman to bother with those she deemed beneath her. After a falling-out with Walter over the young man's shenanigans of drinking and gambling, their father had bequeathed to her one of the most lucrative logging operations in the West. She seldom let anyone forget that she came from power and money. She must have been inordinately impressed with Miss Sullivan.

He called Yvonne and had her take Edward for his meal. When the boy protested, John stepped to the front door and called the dog in. Gideon's nails clicked across the wood floor, then he went up the stairs after the boy and his nurse, and John made his way to the dining room, where he found Walter pouring himself a glass of claret.

Walter set the decanter back onto the sideboard. "I hope Miss Sullivan is to your satisfaction."

"She appears competent." John noticed Walter's sling. "You never mentioned what you did to your arm."

"I sprained it in a fall down some steps. Near Crescent City. I shall dispense with the sling in a day or two." Walter turned to pour another glass of claret. "Miss Sullivan is a lovely girl, is she not? Edward is crazy about her dog. Hauling all her books here nearly broke my back."

John grinned. "I doubt you carried them yourself with your injury."

Walter smiled back. "You caught me. She's quite the scholar though." He went to his place at the table as the ladies joined them.

Clara seated Miss Sullivan beside John. The young woman's eyes took in the gleaming silverware and china, then the napkin ring holding the linen. She'd likely never seen a place set with twenty-four pieces of silverware. She bowed her head and closed her eyes. Her lips moved. Was she praying? The rest of the family gave her but momentary notice, then turned back to their plates. When she raised her head, she kept her hands in her lap. John nudged her discreetly, then slipped the ring off the napkin and placed it in his lap. A faint smile curved her lips, and she imitated his action. When the servants brought in the first course of raw oysters, he selected the proper fork.

She took only one oyster from the footman's tray, and he noticed her pale when she managed to gulp it down. "It's not my favorite either," he whispered. "But soup is coming too."

Henry appeared not to have noticed Miss Sullivan's discomfort. "I stole my cook from the Vanderbilts," he said. "I went to one of their parties, and after dinner, I slipped back to the kitchen and promised Mrs. Biddle double the salary and her own house on the grounds. She's been with us for three years."

John had never heard the story, but he could well believe it. When the footman brought the next dish, broiled salmon, he again deliberately selected the fish fork. Miss Sullivan was a quick study and selected the proper one as well. She took a larger portion of the fish from the tray and ate daintily as the conversation flowed about his new assignment at the base and the places he'd been with the navy. By the time the spring chicken arrived, she barely picked at the meat with the proper fork. At the salad course, she managed only a few bites, though he hid a smile as he noticed how quickly the bonbons disappeared when the footman brought them around.

All through the meal, Walter kept a sharp eye on Miss Sullivan. The longer the meal went on, the more his attention irritated John. Walter was much too old for an innocent girl like the new governess. John sprang to his feet when the meal finally came to a close two hours later.

Miss Sullivan rose as well. "Thank you for a wonderful meal, Mrs. Eaton," she said. "I'm blessed and honored to be here with you."

Clara colored. "What a lovely thing to say, Adeline. We shall enjoy having you join us at every meal."

How did Miss Sullivan do it? Any other governess would have been ignored at the end of the table. She drew everyone with her charm and naiveté. He found he didn't mind the thought of staying at the manor for the next three weeks.

SEVEN

ADDIE RUBBED HER tired eyes. All she wanted was to fall into bed, though she'd required the assistance of a chambermaid to find the way back to her room after dinner.

"Here you be, Miss," Sally said. She appeared to be about Addie's age. Combs held her wispy blonde hair to her head under the white cap.

"Thank you, Sally. This place is so big and intimidating. So are the people. Have you enjoyed working for the Eaton family? I'm not sure what to expect."

Sally ducked her head. "They be nice enough. Generous too."

"How long have you been here?"

"Two years, Miss."

"Do you have time off? I'm not sure how much to request. This is my first employment experience."

"Thursdays be my day off. So you'll be a servant, Miss? Not a guest?"

"I'm Edward's new governess."

"A working woman like you, you should come to the suffrage meeting next week!" Sally smiled as she warmed to her subject. "We be so close to getting the vote!"

Addie hadn't heard much of political issues at the lighthouse. "I might do that." Lieutenant North's penetrating gaze seared her memory. "Do you see much of Lieutenant North?"

Sally shook her head. "He be gone most of the time on his ship."
A smile played at her lips, "Lawdy, he be handsome. Those eyes." She
sighed. "But don't be setting your cap for him, Miss. Mr. Eaton dis-
courages mingling between the family and the likes of us."

Addie nodded, but her mind churned. Maybe when her real identity came out, her father would look kindly on a match. If the handsome
lieutenant would deign to notice her.

❦

Addie worked to feel more at home in the first two days. The meals
still baffled her, but Edward was a delightful boy, inquisitive and energetic, though a trifle spoiled. He responded well to correction and had
a quick mind. They hadn't started lessons, as she wanted to assess his
needs. The real problem was his father. Addie admitted to herself that
she was more intrigued with getting to know her employer than with
her real reason for coming here. She needed to focus on the goal.

And yet, Mr. Driscoll had told her his Pinkerton agent was on the
case. They'd soon have proof enough to tell the family of her true identity. Addie longed to see her father's reaction to her reappearance, but
she had to remind herself that patience was a virtue God was cultivat-
ing in her.

After lunch Wednesday, while the nurse took charge of Edward for
his nap, Addie grabbed a book from her room, then slipped outside
with Gideon. The mighty coastal redwoods towered over the impressive mansion. She picked up her skirts and ran for their cool serenity
behind the manor. Moss clung to the rocks along the path that led into
the dimness of the forest, and she breathed in the moist freshness.

She paused where a shaft of sunlight slanted through the canopy
of giant trees. A faint impression in the moss and vegetation led her
along, and she began to hear the sound of running water. She followed it and came to a waterfall. This must be the Mercy Falls that

the town was named for. The falls towered a hundred feet over her head, then thundered into the clear pool. Breathtaking. Gideon immediately plunged into the water.

A flat rock called to her, and she sank onto its gray surface. Prayer would calm her. She let the beauty of the waterfall and forest surround her and lifted her spirit to the Lord. She murmured the words to the Twenty-third Psalm, and peace reigned over the chaos she'd been feeling.

Her calm restored, she flipped open her book of Elizabeth Barrett Browning poetry. The pages fell open to "A Man's Requirements." Though she'd read it many times, this time she understood the words. She pondered the first stanza.

> Love me Sweet, with all thou art,
> Feeling, thinking, seeing;
> Love me in the lightest part,
> Love me in full being.

It explained exactly how she'd felt the moment she saw John North. Every innermost thought of her heart had been ready to spill from her soul into his ears. Every moment of the past two days that she'd spent in his presence had deepened her fascination with him. She found herself watching for him every moment and waiting for him to arrive home when he was gone. When his dark eyes turned her way, heat enveloped her.

Her head ached, and she took the combs from her hair and shook it loose to her shoulders. She uncapped her fountain pen and jotted some thoughts in the margin. They were the silly thoughts of a romantic girl, but she couldn't help her mooning over him.

"There you are."

She peered through the gloom to see Lieutenant North walking toward her. Her book fell into the ferns as she scrambled to her feet, smoothing her dress. She grabbed for her hair combs, but there was no time to make herself more presentable. "Is Edward awake already, sir?"

He stopped three feet from her. "He's napping. You can easily become lost in this forest. Every tree looks alike, and the lighting is poor."

She felt through the ferns for her book, and her hair fell forward to obscure her face. "I don't have a very good sense of direction, but I have Gideon."

"Lost something?"

"My book." Her cheeks burned when he reached into the ferns and retrieved it.

"Browning?" He flipped it open.

She caught her breath. If he saw what she'd written . . . She held out her hand for the book.

He shut it and handed it back to her. "I haven't read her since I was in school."

Her fingers closed around the book, and she clutched it to her chest. Now he'd think her a hopeless romantic and even less capable of caring for his son.

"I also came to discuss Edward's education with you. How is he doing?"

"Quite well. He's very bright."

"Are you going to have the time to devote to him and also see to Clara's new dress?"

She caught a whiff of his cologne. Something spicy. "Edward is my first priority."

"Unless Clara begins to demand more of your time."

Before she could think how to answer his concerns, she heard a scream from the direction of the house. Lieutenant North turned and sprinted back toward the manor, and Addie followed him. The terror in the shriek gave wings to her feet, and she had no trouble keeping up with the man.

A branch from a shrub slapped her in the face, and she shoved it out of the way, but it slowed her down. Lieutenant North disappeared ahead of her. She put on an extra burst of speed but still saw no sign of his back. The scream came again, and the sound galvanized her even more.

She leaped over a rock in her way, but instead of landing on her feet on the other end, something hard hit her back. Her breath whooshed out of her. Her arms pinwheeled out, but the heavy weight bore her to the ground. Her head plowed into the ferns, then her face pressed into moist moss. The fecund scent of the forest filled her head, and she struggled against the weight squeezing the breath from her lungs. A burlap sack smelling of oranges came around her head, and the suffocating darkness gave her new reason to fight. She flailed until someone grabbed her arms.

"Don't move," a voice hissed in her ear.

A cold blade touched her throat, and she froze. She didn't recognize the voice behind the threatening tone. It was a man, but that was all she knew. Calloused hands roped her wrists together behind her back, then the pressure atop her was gone. She heard steps swish through the vegetation. The normal sounds of the forest resumed—birds chirping in the trees and insects humming. She rolled to her back, then sat up. With her hands tied, she had to make two attempts before she gained her feet. The burlap sack was still over her head. She stumbled to a tree, then moved her head against the rough bark until she managed to rub off the offending burlap.

The scent of the forest washed the orange aroma from her nose. She would need help getting the rope off. And what about the scream she'd heard? Gathering her strength, she ran for the house.

❧

The rope chafed her wrists, and Addie was near tears by the time she emerged from the shadows of the redwoods. She stood blinking in the brilliant wash of light until her eyes adjusted, then she started toward the back door of the house. She hurried in case her attacker was still watching. Was someone else hurt? The scream she'd heard reverberated in her head.

"Lieutenant North?" she called.

The backyard appeared empty, but she called again. She longed to have her hands free again and to feel safe. A woodpecker's *rat-a-tat-tat* echoed in the open yard. The sound unnerved her, and she broke into a run. Perspiration moistened her forehead as she rounded the side yard and saw Mr. Driscoll lying on the ground. Mrs. Eaton stood nearby, wringing her hands. Lieutenant North knelt beside Driscoll on his right, and Mr. Eaton was on his knees on Driscoll's other side. Several servants with pale faces clustered on the porch.

"Lieutenant North?" she said in a faltering voice. "What's happened?"

Lieutenant North glanced up. "There has been a vicious attack on Walter," he said. "Someone struck him in the head, then vanished."

"Will he be all right?"

"The doctor is on his way."

She drew nearer. "I was also attacked."

"You are unharmed?"

"Yes, though my hands are tied." She turned around so he could see her bonds, then faced him again.

Lieutenant North had her turn around, and he struggled with the knot at her wrists. His hands were cool and dry, but her skin tingled where he touched her. Her gaze lingered on Driscoll. The poor man lay motionless and pale on his side. His eyes were closed. She saw no blood, so perhaps the blow was only enough to render him unconscious. Moments later, the rope fell to the ground by Addie's feet.

"Thank you," Addie said. She rubbed her wrists and turned back toward the group huddled around Mr. Driscoll. "How badly is he hurt?"

"He hasn't moved," Mr. Eaton said.

She inspected Driscoll's pale face. "Is there anything I can do?"

"Not unless you hold a medical degree," Lieutenant North said.

"I've often tended to shipwreck victims until the doctor arrived," she said. "I'm quite competent."

He moved back. "Very well, then."

She pushed past him and knelt beside the older man. When she touched his face, she found it cold. "He needs a blanket," she said.

"I'll get it," Mrs. Eaton said, rushing for the door as if eager to flee the scene.

She felt along Mr. Driscoll's head. "There is a lump here," she said, probing the spot. "He's bleeding." She wiped the blood on her fingers onto the grass.

Mr. Driscoll stirred, and she realized he likely felt the pain of having the wound depressed. He moaned and tried to push himself erect.

"Please lie still, sir," she said.

Mrs. Eaton returned with a quilt in her arms. She tucked it around her brother, then backed away. "Oh dear, where is the doctor?" she muttered.

A horse neighed, and Addie saw a carriage come rushing up the drive. "Is that the doctor?"

"Yes." Lieutenant North waved to the white-haired man holding the reins. "Here, Dr. Lambertson."

The man leaped from the seat with a black bag in his hand before the buggy had fully stopped. He wore black pants and a white shirt under a vest. His bowler was askew as if he'd grabbed it and jammed it on his head without looking. "Mr. Driscoll was attacked?"

"He's unconscious. We didn't move him."

The doctor's expression grew more sober as he knelt beside his patient. "A good decision, but I'm going to have to roll him over to tend to his injury. I shall require your assistance. Slide your hands under his buttocks, and I'll do the same with his shoulders."

Lieutenant North complied, and the men gently rolled Mr. Driscoll onto his stomach. The large lump on the back of his head oozed blood, and his hair was matted with it. She heard a sigh and and turned to see Mrs. Eaton crumple.

Addie sprang forward but was too late to catch her aunt. "Bring me a wet handkerchief," she called to Molly. The maid nodded and rushed for the house.

Addie pulled Mrs. Eaton's head onto her lap. "Mrs. Eaton?" she whispered, stroking her hair. Poor woman. Molly returned with the wet hankie, and Addie dampened the prostrate woman's pale face with it.

Mrs. Eaton's eyelids fluttered, then she opened them. "My brother," she murmured. "Is he dead?"

"No, no. The doctor is tending to him." Addie stroked the wet cloth across Mrs. Eaton's forehead again. The doctor worked at staunching her uncle's blood.

Maybe she shouldn't have come. She already cared about her new family, and the last thing she wanted was to thrust them all into danger. Someone wanted to keep her away, and it appeared that person was dangerous.

EIGHT

THE SUN HAD touched the tops of the redwoods by the time the doctor announced that Mr. Driscoll could be moved inside. After John assisted his uncle-in-law to a four-poster bed, he strode down the sweeping staircase in search of Miss Sullivan. Two attacks in one day disturbed him.

He found her in the solarium by Clara's prize azaleas. The greenery framed her and complemented the red glints in her thick hair, now sedately contained with pins and combs. Her face was turned toward the window, and he stood a moment and studied her. There was more to her arrival than he'd been told. Unidentifiable currents pulsed between her and Driscoll. He couldn't get past the thought that she might be Driscoll's doxy even though he couldn't quite see this fresh-faced girl in the demure gown on Driscoll's arm. Nor could he see the straitlaced Driscoll carrying on with such a young woman. The pharmacist took pains to conduct himself respectably in the community.

She put down the book in her hand. "Lieutenant North," she said, her voice wary. "How is Mr. Driscoll?"

"Resting." He dropped into the wicker chair opposite her settee. "I wanted to find out more about the attack on you. What happened after I left you?"

"I started back toward the manor right behind you. Someone tackled me from behind and jammed a burlap sack over my head so I couldn't see."

"A man?"

She nodded. "It was a man's voice."

"What did he say?"

"He told me not to move. When he put a knife blade against my neck, I obeyed."

John frowned and leaned forward to look at the ivory skin above her blouse. "He cut you?"

She shook her head. "No. He merely tied me up, then ran off."

"Seems strange two attackers would be on the property at the same time," he muttered.

"Perhaps it was the same person. He struck Mr. Driscoll, then ran into the woods and attacked me."

He nodded. "Likely scenario. But for what reason?" He studied the curve of her cheeks and that lustrous hair. He wondered what it would feel like.

"There you are," Eaton's jovial voice broke into their conversation. "How is Walter?"

"Recovering, with Clara's solicitous attention," John said.

Eaton pulled up another wicker chair. He glanced from John to Addie. "Is something wrong?"

"Miss Sullivan was attacked today as well."

Eaton's eyes widened. "You are all right?"

"Yes, sir. He encased my head in a burlap bag, then tied my hands." She held them out. A faint red line still showed on the translucent skin.

John noticed the color had drained from her cheeks. "Are you frightened, Miss Sullivan?"

She tilted up her chin. "Not exactly afraid, Lieutenant North. I am concerned for Edward, though, if there is even the remote possibility something dangerous is going on."

"I've been considering that myself. Perhaps we should go home, where we have close neighbors and the police are within minutes of the house."

"Where is home?" she asked.

"Near the naval base in San Francisco. I'm only staying until after Henry's birthday in order to allow my son to adjust to the changes."

"I'll be leaving with you?"

Why did she sound dismayed? He studied her downcast face. "Of course. It would be difficult to teach Edward from here."

"Mr. Driscoll didn't mention it," she said.

"I don't think we should assume there is any ongoing danger," Eaton said. "There's no need for you to take Edward and leave. It might simply have been a robber who attacked Walter. When he fled, he ran into Miss Sullivan."

John frowned at his father-in-law. "We have no way of knowing what really happened. I'm not sure I want to run the risk to my son."

Eaton picked up a paperweight and tossed it from hand to hand. "There is no need to react and change plans at this late date. Walter is injured. I'll need your assistance more than ever. Besides, Miss Sullivan is needed to help Clara with her gown for the ball."

"That's hardly my concern," John said. "Edward is my priority."

"As he is mine. I want only the best for my grandson. That includes having him here where I can care for him."

"Whatever you decide is fine, Lieutenant North," Miss Sullivan said.

He wondered again about her relationship with Walter. "Very well, Henry, I'll stay for now. But if anything else out of the ordinary happens, I will pack up Edward and take him home." He kept eye contact with Eaton.

Eaton's jaw clenched, but he didn't remark on John's tone. "Fair enough," he said, rising from the chair. The sound of his footsteps faded on the redwood floors.

John turned his attention back to Addie. She glanced out the window at the dark yard. "I'd hoped to retrieve my book from the woods. It's too dark now."

She was still pale. Her wide eyes revealed her stress. "The book will survive the night. You should get some rest."

"Mr. Eaton seems more concerned that you might leave than he was about Mr. Driscoll's injuries."

"He does love the boy," he said. "Even if his condition embarrasses him at times."

"The epilepsy is not Edward's fault!"

"No, but that doesn't mean he doesn't wish his grandson were whole and normal."

She winced. "I wish I could help him."

"So do I."

She locked eyes with him. "I'd like us to be friends. A team committed to doing what's best for Edward."

He smiled at the innocence of her remark. While he sensed something more going on than what he knew now, he didn't doubt her naïveté. "A friend is always welcome," he said.

When had he ever heard a woman be so open with her feelings? He couldn't help it. He liked Miss Adeline Sullivan.

⌒❧⌒

A smile hovered on Addie's lips when she left Lieutenant North. He might not completely trust her, but she would prove herself to him. She rubbed her sore wrists, and her smile faded as she looked at the red marks still on the pale skin.

She hadn't had time to consider the assault and what it meant. Nor the attack on Mr. Driscoll. Could her father's enemy have recognized her already and be trying to drive her away? And to silence Mr. Driscoll? She sighed and opened the door to her room, but the empty space repelled her. Gideon didn't come to greet her with his wet nose. Retreating, she retraced her footsteps down the hall to Edward's room. The lad lay on top of the covers in his nightshirt. She pulled the sheet over him and beckoned her dog.

Gideon rose from his post on the rug by the bed. He yawned, then trotted to her side. She petted him until they were both soothed, then tiptoed out. Mr. Driscoll's door was open when she passed, and she peeked inside to see him propped on pillows.

He gestured for her to come in. "I just sent the maid to ask you to come see me."

"Is everything all right?" she asked.

"Come closer so I don't have to raise my voice."

She peered down the hall, then stepped into the bedroom. Logs had been laid in the fireplace but weren't lit. She seated herself on the chair beside the hissing gaslight. She folded her hands in her lap and prayed for this to be over so she could retire. She was unutterably weary.

"I heard someone attacked you also, child. Is this true?"

"Yes, sir. In the woods. He put a burlap bag over my head and tied my hands." She showed him her wrists.

He fingered his temple. "He didn't hit you?"

"No."

"What did he say?"

"He said, 'Don't move.' But he put a knife blade to my neck."

"That's all?"

She turned up the wick on the gaslight so she could see better. "I suspect it was the same man who attacked you, and he happened to stumble into me. I believe he wanted only to slow me down so he could escape."

Mr. Driscoll blinked, and his hands dropped back to the sheet. "Have you talked to anyone at all about your past?"

"No, sir. When would I have had time?"

"The attacks must be related," he said.

"Is this normally a safe area?"

"Very safe. We've never had a break-in at Eaton Manor."

"Did your attacker take your wallet or anything else?"

He shook his head. "It's all accounted for."

Addie studied his pallid face. He could easily have been killed. "Do you have any idea what was behind the attack?"

He pointed to the glass on the bedside table. "May I have a drink?"

Was he stalling having to answer her? "Of course." She lifted the glass to his lips and let him take a sip.

"Thanks." His head fell back against the pillow. "I didn't tell Henry, but I think the attacker intended murder. He had a knife, as you know."

She put her hand to her throat. "How did you escape him?"

"I kicked the knife out of his hand. He shoved me, and I fell back into the tree. Clara came out onto the porch and began to scream as he came toward me. I think her presence prevented him from finishing the job. He grabbed his knife and ran off into the forest."

"You think the attacker wanted to kill you because you brought me here?"

His intent gaze held hers. "I'm a pharmacist and well liked. No one has so much as held up my drugstore."

"Why didn't the man try to kill me, too, then?" she asked, her head spinning with questions. "He merely threatened me until he could tie me up. I was an easy mark if he intended murder."

He picked at the sheet. "I don't know," he said after a long pause. "Maybe he thought it would cause the police to dig into your background and the truth would come out."

"There's nothing to be found if someone investigates me. Even those in Crescent City know me as the lightkeeper's daughter." She rubbed her eyes. "Have you heard from your investigator yet?"

"I received a call this morning. The attorney's office that processed the funds sent to your parents was destroyed by the Great Fire. All records were lost, so my investigator can't find out anything by examining them. I'd hoped he could bribe someone to let him look at the records without involving the attorney."

"Oh no! Will we be able to find any proof?"

"If he can locate the attorney, my agent might be able to persuade him to reveal the story, but that's a long shot. If not, the locket and your resemblance will have to do."

"What resemblance?"

He pointed to a painting over the fireplace that she'd paid little attention to. "Look at that picture of Laura."

She rose and stepped to the painting. Her mother. Addie had longed to see what she looked like, but she hadn't yet found a photograph. She drank it in. "Her hair is redder than mine. And she has green eyes." The woman's demure smile said she knew she was beautiful. And she was. Lustrous red hair lay coiled at the nape of her neck. The turquoise gown she wore accentuated the depth of her eyes.

Some dim memory struggled to bubble to the forefront of her memory. Soft hands, a sweet voice. Words of love. "She's much more beautiful than I," Addie whispered.

"Look beyond her more vivid coloring. Notice the shape of her nose, the fullness of her lips, the dimple in her right cheek. The similarities are subtle, but they're there if one knows where to look."

"Many people have dimples." Her fingers pressed the outline of the locket under her bodice.

"Perhaps it's easier for me to see because I loved Laura. You have her smile."

"But why would anyone want to prevent me from being united with my father?" She could look into the woman's laughing eyes no longer. She went back to the chair. "Do you have any idea who would have paid for my upkeep? You mentioned one of my father's rivals. Is there anyone else?"

Mr. Driscoll sipped his water. "I have some ideas."

"Such as?"

"You are nearly twenty-five, correct?"

She nodded. "My mother said I was about two when my father rescued me."

"I suspected Clara in the beginning. She met Henry first, and he sought her hand until he met your mother."

Addie liked her aunt, and the thought she might be behind her situation disturbed her. "Clara? What would be her reason to keep me away?"

"She might have wanted to wipe away all traces of Laura and her relationship with Henry."

She leaned back in the chair. "That seems so Shakespearean."

"He wrote about human nature. Jealousy is a powerful motivator."

"I suppose. What about an inheritance?" she asked.

Driscoll pursed his lips. "Laura's grandfather Francis died about two years ago. You are the beneficiary in his will. The will dictated the estate would go to you on your twenty-fifth birthday. In the event of your death, it would go to Clara, who intends it to be Edward's."

"Why Clara? This wouldn't be her grandfather, right? You and Clara had a different maternal grandmother."

He nodded. "That's right. But Laura was his only living relative at the time he drew up the will. He liked Clara, and when the attorney recommended a contingency bequest, Francis decided to leave his estate to her. I believe Henry forgot about the inheritance until recently. When he realized the passing of ownership was due to take place, he realized he had to have you declared dead."

"Just me? What about my mother?"

"He had her declared dead before he married Clara. I assume he thought it wasn't necessary for a child."

"And maybe he thought my great-grandfather would change his will."

He nodded. "The legal step has taken some time, and it's not yet completed. When that happens, the land will pass to Clara, who has drawn up papers for Edward to receive it."

"A great-grandfather." Addie clasped her hands together. "I always wished for grandparents."

"He was a remarkable man. He doted on you."

Yearning tugged at her heart. She'd missed out on so much love. "But all this still doesn't tell us who had anything to gain by keeping my presence a secret all these years."

Mr. Driscoll set his glass of water back on the bed stand. "We need to find out."

"What difference does it make now? I don't want anything from the Eaton estate. All I want is to make my father love me."

"I mentioned I feared for Henry's safety. The other possibility in today's attack is that he was the intended target, and the assailant didn't try very hard to hurt me when he realized he had the wrong man."

"I see," she said slowly. "You think whoever paid for me to be kept away is now about to move against Mr. Eaton."

"And perhaps you."

She gulped. The sensation of cold metal against her throat had been terrifying. But nothing was enough to drive her from the family she was just coming to know.

NINE

ADDIE SLEPT POORLY, startling awake at the slightest creak of a floorboard or the hoot of an owl outside her window. When she finally pulled back the curtains, the sun had crested the tops of the redwood trees and streamed through her back bedroom window. From the other window to the front, she could almost see past the town to the ocean's waves.

She'd thought leaving the lighthouse would be exciting, romantic. Now she longed for the roar of the waves outside her window and the cry of a seagull diving for a fish. The familiar held more appeal than she'd ever imagined.

Turning from the view, she washed at the pitcher and bowl on her dresser, then pinched a bit of color into her cheeks. She selected a white blouse detailed with tucks, and a gray skirt. When she stepped out of her room, her nose caught the aroma of sausage. She could just hurry down the back stairway and find her book before breakfast. Once she got back, she'd braid her hair and put shoes on, but for now, she wanted to talk with the Lord and dangle her toes in the water at the falls. It would almost be like standing at the ocean's edge. If she went down the back way, no one would know.

On the way out, she checked Edward's room and found it empty, then went down the back staircase to the first floor. Where was the rear door? The manor easily comprised forty rooms, and the labyrinth of halls and doorways confused her. It would take weeks before she could find her way easily. She went toward the back of the hall and found the smell of food stronger. Following her nose, she walked past a study, another drawing room, a ladies' lounge, and a library before seeing Mrs. Eaton in her study.

The kitchen had to be nearby. That's where the back door would be. She started past the study, but Mrs. Eaton called to her. Addie turned. "Yes, ma'am?"

Mrs. Eaton sat on a chair, with her gray silk skirt spread around her. "Come in, dear."

Addie looked down and spied her bare feet. Maybe Mrs. Eaton wouldn't notice if she scooted slowly into the room so her feet didn't show. She entered the room. Various needlepoint projects lay on a table, and smaller furniture pieces matched a female's size. She tucked her feet under her skirt as she sank onto a pink brocade chair beside a plant stand that held a fern.

Mrs. Eaton laid down her needlepoint. "I would like to discuss the ball with you." She pointed at Addie. "That blouse. Did you make it, Adeline?"

"Yes, ma'am."

Mrs. Eaton slipped her glasses onto her nose and inspected the garment. "The pin tucks and embroidery are quite lovely. You're very talented."

"Thank you, Mrs. Eaton. How might I help you?"

"What ideas have you come up with for my gown?"

Addie gulped. Sally had mentioned that the woman had already tossed aside one gown made by a top dressmaker. Mrs. Eaton had said no more about the dress in the last couple of days, and Addie hoped she'd abandoned the idea. "What if you hate it, Mrs. Eaton? I want to please you, but I admit I'm fearful."

The woman's brows rose. "Are you saying I'm hard to please, Adeline?"

"We met only days ago, and I have no way of knowing that," Addie said.

Mrs. Eaton laughed. "You certainly speak your mind, child. I rather like that."

"My father always told me I was the lightkeeper's daughter. God's child. And only truth would do." She winced at the words. Her father hadn't followed his own advice.

Mrs. Eaton picked up her needlepoint again. "You listen to him. The world could use more honesty. Now, what about that dress?"

"If I know clearly what you want and start right away, I can get it done. Provided I can find the proper material," she added.

Pink bloomed in the matron's cheeks, and her eyes sparkled. "I'd like something in chiffon. Very elegant and flowing, with lace framing my face. Maybe in white."

Addie feared she knew exactly what Mrs. Eaton was talking about. "You wouldn't prefer something in brocade or silk?" Something more suited to her age.

Mrs. Eaton shook her head. "I want the latest fashion. Brocade is so matronly." She picked up a magazine and thumbed through it. "Like this."

Addie rose and took the magazine from her employer's hand. It was as she suspected—something much more suited to her age than to Mrs. Eaton's.

Truth. The truth in love. "Ma'am, I fear this would not suit you well. Would you give me leave to try a pattern I saw in the latest *Godey's*? It's quite elegant, and no one else in town would have anything approaching its magnificence. It has a matching turban that's all the rage in Paris."

"Paris?"

"It would highlight your splendid eyes," Addie said. "They are a beautiful shade of green. I've never seen such lovely eyes."

The older woman preened. "Very well, Adeline. I'll trust your judgment. Don't disappoint me."

"I'll do my best," she said.

The work would be constant. Addie had very little experience with frills and lace. Her designs tended toward good lines and quality fabrics, not lavish trim and ruffles.

She rose. "I need to run to the falls and find my book. I dropped it yesterday."

"Very well. Breakfast will be ready in a quarter hour. And do put up your hair and come in shoes."

Addie hurried from the room. She had to find the book, get back, and finish her toilette in fifteen minutes.

⟆✣⟆

A mother quail and her babies ran through the morning fog across John's path. He waited for them to pass, brushed aside the towering ferns, and entered the redwood forest. The air smelled heavy with the scent of vegetation and pine. Birds chattered overhead, and insects hummed by his ears. He strode toward where he'd left Miss Sullivan yesterday to see if any evidence of her ordeal remained.

He reached the roaring Mercy Falls and peered through the mist curling around the water. There, the matted grass showed their path back to the manor. He followed the faint trail until it widened into a more flattened area. This must be where she'd been tackled. A burlap sack lay near a tree. He picked it up and caught the scent of oranges. Using his foot, he prodded the vegetation for anything else that might illuminate the incident.

The toe of his shoe struck something in the weeds. He parted the greenery and saw a book on the ground. Miss Sullivan's book of poetry. When he picked it up, it fell open, and his gaze was drawn to the scrawled words in the margin of a poem called, "A Man's Requirements."

John North. What a strong name. I was lost the moment I gazed into his eyes. So dark. So compelling. As if he knew me and I knew him.

Is that not strange? Did Elizabeth Barrett Browning feel this pounding in her blood the first time she saw Robert? Must pray and see what God would say about this.

He blinked and read the words again. His first inclination was to laugh at her naïveté. So innocent and childlike. Then he read the words of the poem.

> Love me Sweet, with all thou art,
> Feeling, thinking, seeing;
> Love me in the lightest part,
> Love me in full being.

Something in the words stirred him. Had he ever been the focus of a heartfelt longing? Not even Katherine had thought of him as her hero, nor, for that matter, had wanted to share her innermost thoughts. She certainly hadn't loved him with all her being. What might it be like to be loved like that?

Something rustled in the grass behind him, and he whirled with the book in his hand. Addie stepped into his line of vision, with her dog tagging along. She was singing "When the Red, Red Robin Comes Bob-Bob-Bobbing Along" in a clear, sweet voice. Her bare toes peeked from under the gray skirt she wore. He couldn't look away from her long hair, which caught a shaft of light that slanted through the leaves.

Her smile came as soon as she saw him. And dimmed when she spotted the book in his hand. The open book.

Pink rushed to her cheeks. "You found my book."

He shut it and held it out to her. "I stumbled across it when I was looking for clues that might point to your attacker."

Her fingers closed around the book, and she clasped it to her chest. She didn't meet his gaze, and her color heightened. He was sure she wondered if he'd seen her notes. The truth would embarrass her further.

Her gaze finally rose to his face. "You read it, didn't you? I can see it in your eyes."

"You're very direct," he said. His own face burned, a sensation he didn't think he'd ever felt before.

She lowered her lids and twisted a long curl through her fingers. "I'm sorry. It's not very ladylike to say what I think, is it? You must forgive me. I grew up with only my parents for company."

"Your honesty is refreshing," he said. If she didn't ask again whether he'd read her note, he wasn't going to offer up the information. "Is Edward up yet?"

She nodded. "He's having his breakfast, and I came out to find my book." She fell silent and bit her lip. "I should explain about the note."

He held up his hand. "Please don't. It might dilute the pleasure I took in knowing you find me somewhat attractive."

Her face turned a brighter shade of pink. "You're mocking me," she said in a choked voice.

"That's not my intention," he said before falling silent.

How could he clear the air between them? Right now he'd like to ask her to dinner and the nickelodeon. He suspected most women who flirted with him at a social event were more interested in his bank account or the fact he was a naval officer. Women found the role strangely dashing and romantic, but few really saw him for who he was. No one had ever remarked on his eyes. He studied her down-turned face. She was no more capable of subterfuge than the moss under his feet was.

He removed his bowler and rubbed his thick thatch of hair. "Can we start over? You mentioned earlier you'd like to be my friend. I'd like that too."

She stared at the ground, and he followed her gaze to her bare toes.

He'd never seen a woman's bare feet except for Katherine's, in the privacy of their bedroom. The young woman was unlike any he'd ever met. He wanted to find out more about her, hear her views.

"Please?" he said, putting a plea into his voice.

She smiled, a timid curve of her lips. Her long lashes swept up, and those green eyes smiled too. "Do you promise never to bring up this book again?"

"I promise," he said.

She rested her chin on two fingers, and her dimple flashed. "If you break your promise, you have to jump in the waterfall."

"Deal."

But he was talking to the wind in the trees. She had turned and fled the way she'd come, her auburn hair flying behind her.

⊱✦⊰

Addie pumped cold water over her feet. What was she thinking to have gone out without her shoes and with her hair down? This wasn't the beach. There were standards here she needed to abide by. She sat on the edge of the rock garden and dried her feet with the hem of her dress. The ugly wet spots on the fabric looked terrible. Now she'd have to change her skirt as well.

"Addie?"

She glanced up to see Mr. Driscoll approaching. "Good morning, Mr. Driscoll," she said.

He'd discarded his sling and wore a gray jacket and waistcoat. "You're out and about early."

She held up her book. "I dropped this in the forest yesterday after that man knocked me down."

"I'm glad you found it."

She noticed his eyes shone, and a smile tugged at his lips. "Do you have news?"

"You're a very bright girl," he said. "I do indeed. I received a call from my investigator. He's located the attorney."

She held her breath. "And?"

"The lawyer refuses to reveal his client, but he told my agent where the money is located. My agent managed to discover that there's quite a sum in the bank in San Francisco."

"I told you I don't care about the money. Ma—Josephine can have it." In spite of her word choice, Addie realized she still thought of Josephine as her mother.

His smile flickered and went out. "She cannot, Adeline. It's not right. That money belongs to you, and I mean to see you get it."

She stood and shook out her skirt. "I just want the proof so we can tell my father the truth."

"I want that as well. And we're getting close. Another couple of days, I suspect."

"I want to know more about my mother and the rest of my family. It's hard to ask questions without appearing nosy."

"Check out the attic. Some of her old dresses are probably packed away in trunks. Maybe pictures and diaries as well. There are traces of Laura around."

Addie wanted to run straight to the attic and see what treasures it contained, but she restrained herself. She was expected at the breakfast table. "Won't the family wonder what I'm doing poking around in the attic?"

"I doubt they'll notice. No one but the servants ever goes up there."

"I'll find a time to slip up there, then. What about the attack on you? Any word from the police?"

"No." He offered his arm, and she took it. He led her toward the back door. "I discovered the name of Henry's rival. The one whose son committed suicide. Samuel Tuttle. He lives in Crescent City now."

She stopped just shy of the door. "Near our lighthouse. Is it mere coincidence, or something more?"

"My question too. I think I'll travel up to speak to Mr. Tuttle personally. He might be the culprit."

Addie shuddered. "Revenge is so pointless. It can't bring his son back."

Mr. Driscoll held open the door for her. "Revenge can be sweet if the offense was grave enough. At least that's what I've heard. Maybe that's Tuttle's view as well."

"If he'll admit it, at least we'd have our proof." And her family would welcome her with open arms.

TEN

BACK IN HER room, a smile lifted Addie's lips as she braided her hair. While she might be naive of the ways of men, John clearly had not been offended by her ridiculous note about him. What had possessed her to write such a thing? Anyone might have seen it. She pulled on socks and shoes and coiled her braid around her head, then hurried down the steps. After she checked on Gideon, who waited patiently on the porch, she started toward the dining room.

She went down the hall past the salon where she'd talked with Mrs. Eaton. The dining room was down another hallway. She passed a large, airy room. Its bay window looked out onto a formal garden with clipped hedges, a labyrinth, and several fountains. Exploration would have to wait until later, but she was eager to see what delights the garden held.

She stepped into the dining room and approached the long table. "Good morning." The handsome lieutenant's eyes still held the warmth she'd seen in the forest. She'd never thanked him for his kindness in showing her which utensil to use the first night she'd arrived.

"Come sit by me." Mrs. Eaton indicated the seat to the right of her at the far head of the table.

Addie walked through the gauntlet of stares. Things were much more formal here than she was accustomed to. She didn't think she would ever get used to this lifestyle. She slid into the chair and picked up the linen napkin. She swallowed hard and prayed she wouldn't embarrass herself by clinking her fork on her plate or spilling her tea. This time, John couldn't easily show her how to proceed.

Mrs. Eaton passed her a bowl of fluffy scrambled eggs. "How are you adjusting, my dear? Are you sleeping well?"

"It's a strange place, Clara. Of course she doesn't sleep well yet," Mr. Eaton said.

Addie's smile faded at his tense tone. She turned to face Mr. Driscoll. "How are you feeling, sir?" She should have asked him outside.

Mr. Driscoll spooned scrambled eggs onto his plate. "Other than a slight headache, I am none the worse for wear."

"I told him he should have stayed in bed, but he insisted on getting up," Mrs. Eaton said. "His arm heals, but then he's nearly killed by an intruder."

"I need to open the drugstore," he said.

Addie took a bite of egg, but she barely tasted it. Mr. Driscoll was attacking his food with gusto.

"How are you, Adeline?" Mrs. Eaton asked. "I neglected to inquire after your health when we spoke earlier."

"I'm fine, ma'am."

"Not sore or bruised?"

"Perhaps a bit. But I feel nothing a long walk along the beach wouldn't cure."

John glanced at his pocket watch. "I would have time to take you and Edward to the beach if you'd like. He could use some exercise."

"There are bicycles in the carriage house," Mr. Eaton said. "You're welcome to use them."

Addie put her hands to her cheeks. "You have bicycles? I've always wanted to learn to ride one."

"Bicycles are out for today, then," John said. "Tonight I'll give you a lesson. You'll need to be able to get around at your leisure."

"Does Edward have a bicycle? Once I learn, we might go together. It would be excellent exercise for him." The family grew silent, and a rock formed in her belly when she realized her gaffe. "Oh, of course not. What was I thinking?" Her face burned, and she fixed her attention on her plate.

"Edward does have . . . challenges," Mrs. Eaton said. "But there is much he is able to do."

"Of course." Addie put her napkin down. "If I might be excused, I'll get Edward ready for our excursion."

"I'll direct the cook to prepare a lunch for you," Mrs. Eaton said. "And I'll send Wilson to fetch you around two. Would that suit?"

"That's perfect," Addie said.

John rose as well. Addie followed him out. "I'll only be a moment," she said. "Thank you for your offer."

His smile and easy manner returned. "My pleasure. I assume you want to take the dog?"

"Oh yes. Edward will have great fun with him at the water." Dressed in a navy blue sack coat and matching trousers, the lieutenant was just as handsome as he'd been in his navy uniform. "You have nothing else to do today?"

He shook his head. "I'm on leave for a month. It's been much too long since I had the opportunity to play with my son." He took his bowler from the hall tree and donned it. "I'll have the buckboard ready." He exited through the front door.

She took the stairs two at a time with a smile on her face. A day at the water and a drive with John, followed by lunch at the beach! She wanted to dance, but she forced herself to assume a sedate pace. She stopped off in her room to change into her bathing costume, tights, and bathing shoes. When she fetched Edward, she nearly danced into the room. She changed him into his bathing costume, then packed his sailboat, pail, and shovel in a bag.

"I forgot my hat," she said. "You take your things out to the buckboard, and I'll be right there."

Edward skipped off, and she darted into her room. When she

returned to the hall, she found Mr. Driscoll waiting for her. His somber expression wiped the smile from her face.

"Is something wrong?" she asked.

"You seem very chummy with John."

"We are related," she reminded him.

"By marriage only. Don't let your guard down around him. For all we know, he's the one who arranged for the attack on you and me."

"That's impossible," she said. "He was with me in the woods when you were attacked."

"He could have paid someone."

"For what reason?"

"Addie, you must use your head. If your identity becomes known, his son will no longer be Henry's immediate heir. He has the most to lose of anyone."

She found it difficult to breathe. "I believe he's an honorable man."

"The women all like him. I should have guessed you would be taken in by his good looks. He never stays with any woman long. Katherine was going to leave him."

"For seeing other women?" Bile burned her throat.

Mr. Driscoll patted her shoulder. "The reasons are too numerous to go into. But hold him at arm's length, my dear." He walked off.

Addie swallowed hard. Had she been duped by John's smile and dark eyes? She didn't want to believe it.

❧

A stone lodged somewhere in Addie's midsection as John helped her down from the buckboard. The sea breeze tugged at her hair, and she lifted her face to the salty tang on the wind. The temperature along the northern California coast ranged from fifty-five degrees in the winter to sixty-eight in the summer, but the sun heated the sand under her feet even on the coolest day. Today the air was close to seventy.

Edward raced after Gideon, who ran into the white caps rolling to the shore. Could Mr. Driscoll be right? She didn't want to believe John might have orchestrated the attack on them, but it made sense. Who else stood to lose so much if her identity became known? But how could he possibly know?

She chose not to believe it. Not until she could verify his lack of integrity.

John retrieved the basket of food, the quilt, and the toys from the back of the buckboard. "You're wearing a serious frown," he said. "Is everything all right?"

"Are you a philanderer, Lieutenant North?"

His brows rose, and he laughed. "You're a constant surprise, Addie. What a question. Is this a joke?"

"I'm quite serious," she said, grabbing her hat when the wind threatened to send it tumbling across the sand.

His grin faded. "Why would you ask such an insulting question?"

She dug the toe of her shoe into the sand. "I meant no insult. I have no experience with men. I thought perhaps . . ."

"You thought I was toying with your emotions."

She nodded. The dark intensity in his eyes made her shiver. This was no cold, passionless man, but one who felt things deeply. His lips flattened, and his nostrils flared. His eyes sparked with some emotion she couldn't name. Then it winked out as his control tightened.

When he smiled, it was a cold grimace. "I like you, Miss Sullivan. Do you think I play with your emotions because I want to become better acquainted?" he asked.

"Not unless your intentions are less than honorable."

He shifted the basket in his hand. "Less than honorable. I doubt you even know what it means for a man to behave dishonorably toward a woman."

She tipped her chin up. "My knowledge of such things might be a bit vague, but there's no need to mock me. I grew up around animals. I know what should be reserved for marriage."

The darkness behind his eyes lightened, and his lips curved in a genuine smile. A bark of laughter escaped. "We don't dare turn you loose in town. You'll tell the mayor he's too fat."

"Is he?"

He grinned. "He weights four hundred pounds or more."

"Maybe someone should tell him."

All trace of anger was gone from his face. "You're one of a kind, Miss Adeline Sullivan. The Eaton family may never be the same after your sojourn with us. No one says what they mean in that house. I'm afraid I've become accustomed to it." He glanced toward his son, who was throwing a ball for the dog. "Let's get our things settled." He turned his back on her and strode across the sand with his burden.

The wind tore the hat from his head and sent it sailing straight at Addie. She snagged it in midair. He slipped in the sand, then his legs flew out from under him, and he landed on his backside. The items he carried scattered in a circle around him. She gasped and ran to help. A seagull cawed overhead, and a white blob dropped. It landed squarely on the shoulder of John's jacket.

Addie stopped, observing first the mess on his suit, then the sand on his pants. His face reddened, but she wasn't sure if it was from embarrassment or anger. His lip curled when he spied the bird droppings on his jacket.

A giggle erupted from Addie's lips. And another one. "I'm sorry," she gasped through her laughter. "But if you could see your face. Such disgust. It's only a little offering from the gull to show his affection."

He stood before she reached him and bent to brush the sand from his trousers. "I think you were more deserving of that deposit from the gull."

Her giggles rose again, and she squelched them. She pulled her hankie from the inside of her sleeve at her wrist and stood on tiptoe while she dabbed at the gunk on his jacket.

His fingers caught hers. His intense gaze held her in place. "I should like to take you to dinner one night. Would that be acceptable?"

"Yes," she said, struggling to maintain her composure. "I would like that very much."

His grip tightened. "They'll try to change you, Addie. I should dislike to see that happen."

"Who will?"

"The Eaton family. Society. They'll shush you when you speak your mind." His hand went to a loose curl hanging down her back. "They'll tell you it's more proper to put your hair up."

"Mrs. Eaton already suggested I wear my hair up when she saw me with it down." Warmth gathered in her midsection at his touch. "I'm sure there are many things I need to learn."

He leaned close enough for his breath to mingle with the salt air that caressed her skin. "I like you just the way you are." His hand trailed from her hair to her cheek. "Promise me you won't change."

"How can I promise such a thing? God wants each of us to grow."

"Let's have a talk with him and ask him not to mess with perfection."

She managed to find enough moisture in her mouth to swallow. If he didn't take his hand from her cheek, she was going to throw herself into his arms. If there wasn't such a thing as love at first sight, she was in so much trouble.

ELEVEN

ADDIE'S HANDKERCHIEF DID little to remove the gull doo on John's jacket. He'd long since removed his jacket and rolled up his shirtsleeves. Popcorn clouds filled the blue bowl of sky overhead. He reclined on the blanket and watched Addie splash through the white-caps with Edward in her arms, both of them squealing at the cold waves. The dog chased them both.

"Come in with us," she called.

The moist sea air caused her auburn locks to curl. The thought that there might be an opportunity to kiss that smiling pink mouth nearly prompted him to obey. The slim tights of her swimming cos-tume showed off the shape of her legs, and he couldn't take his eyes off her.

She put Edward down, then stood with her hands on her hips. "Roll up your trousers. At least let the waves break at your ankles."

"I didn't bring a swimsuit," John said. He grinned. "Besides, don't you know that sailors drown in an inch of water?"

"Coward!" She staggered out of the sea, then paused to wring the water from her skirt.

He stood as she neared. She smelled enticingly of brine and sea-weed, an intoxicating scent to a man who loved the sea. It was all he could do not to nuzzle his face in her neck and kiss her smooth skin.

"I'm quite starving," she said. "What do we have for lunch?"

He forced himself to step to the lunch hamper and peer inside. "Egg salad sandwiches, cranberry scones, and apples. A veritable feast."

She dropped onto the blanket. "I might eat the whole thing."

Edward and Gideon frolicked on the sand. Edward kicked a ball, and the dog ran to pounce on it. She lifted the plates of sandwiches wrapped in wax paper. The kitchen maid had packed enough scones to feed an army.

"Edward, your luncheon is ready," she called.

Had John ever seen Edward so happy and carefree? The boy's curls were tousled, and his cheeks were as red as the apples Addie was lifting from the basket. She'd been good for his son. The dog had helped too. It was amazing how confident they all felt in the dog's presence. If not for Gideon, John would have been fearful of allowing Edward in the water.

He could do worse than courting Addie. The thought came out of the blue, but he quickly realized he was getting ahead of himself. But he acknowledged his willingness to go where this relationship might lead.

Henry and Clara would be gone tonight. When Edward was in bed, John might be able to get to know the intriguing Adeline Sullivan a little better. When was the last time he'd been this interested in a woman? Not since Katherine, he realized. And maybe that should be a warning to him.

But no. His relationship with Katherine had been a very different situation. She'd flirted, then backed off, then flirted and backed off again. She'd played a cat-and-mouse game that led to marriage before he realized what was happening. She'd offered her family name and beauty to escape an older suitor her father had selected, and John snapped it up because he thought she really loved him. Reality had soon set in.

This young woman was different. He bit into his sandwich. "There is no subterfuge in you, Miss Adeline. Why is that?"

Color came and went in her cheeks. "Everyone has layers. Even me."

He leaned closer as his son neared and allowed a curl to wrap his finger. "I look forward to peeling back those layers."

Her blush was charming. What would she think of living on a naval base?

❦

Addie glanced at John a few times as the buggy pulled away from the beach. Edward and Gideon slept as they traveled back toward town. "Thank you for a lovely day," she said.

"The pleasure was all mine."

Lassitude encased her limbs, and her eyes were heavy. The next thing she knew, she heard voices call and the rumble of more buggies. She opened her eyes to find her head resting on John's shoulder as the buggy rolled through Mercy Falls.

"I'm so sorry!" she said, startled. After she jerked upright, she brushed her hair out of her face.

He smiled at her. "I didn't mind."

Heat seared her cheeks, and she turned, pretending to scrutinize the stores and shops they passed rather than his amused eyes. Ahead, Mr. Driscoll stepped from the darkness of an alley onto the street and approached a woman who was holding a baby. "There's Mr. Driscoll," she said. She called out to him and waved. He flinched at the sound of his name but waved back when he caught sight of them.

"He should take care in that neighborhood," John said. "If a fellow is going to get mugged, it would be there. Thugs and gamblers haunt these streets."

"He's probably delivering medicine to someone," she said.

"It's no place for a woman and infant. He should escort her home."

They left town and entered the coolness of the forest. She smelled wildflowers and the scent of deep woods. The trees were so high and the trunks so big that all she could do was stare. She would never get used to it. "Is this virgin forest?" she asked.

"Yep. One of the last tracts left."

The beauty and serenity of the place drew her. The branches nearly touched the blue sky. "Why is it still unlogged?"

"Laura's grandfather left it to her daughter, Julia. When the child died, it went to Clara, and she signed it over to Edward. So this will be Edward's as soon as the paperwork declaring Julia deceased comes through."

Addie's throat convulsed. He was talking about her. This land belonged to her. She couldn't take it in. "So it belongs to Edward now? Or will soon?"

He nodded. "I intend to use it to increase Edward's net worth."

"What are you going to do with it?"

He hesitated. "I haven't decided. I've had a lucrative offer from a logging company, but it seems a shame to destroy something so beautiful."

In her mind's eye, Addie saw a lovely home for tuberculosis patients in a grove surrounded by clean air and nature. For someone like Nann Whittaker. If Roy Sullivan hadn't had the stress of the light-house, he might have recovered from his illness in a place like she envisioned, with paths for the patients to walk and babbling streams to nap beside. Such a pipe dream. Where would she find money for something like that?

"I would hate for it to be ruined," she said.

"I must be practical." He picked up the reins again. "We'd better be getting home."

"What time is it?" She tried to gauge the sun, but it was behind clouds.

He pulled out a gold pocket watch. "Nearly three."

Addie held to the side of the seat as the buggy made a turn onto the paved road. "Is Henry's birthday ball terribly exciting?"

John slapped the reins on the horse's rump, and the animal broke into a trot. "It's the most boring affair of the year, but Henry likes the illusion of a happy family gathered to celebrate."

"You sound as though you don't like him."

A muscle twitched in his jaw. "I admire him, and he's been good to me. But his demands can be hard to deal with."

"Demands? About Edward?"

"He thinks he owns my son." He slanted a smile her way. "I'm sure you've seen it."

She laid her gloved hand on top of his. "It's already clear to me that no one owns you, Lieutenant. You are the kind of man a woman can depend on with her life."

"I haven't had very good luck with relationships," he said. "Women seem to put a lot of stock in money and property. I'm not very good at figuring out the gold diggers."

"I don't care about money." But would he believe that when he learned the land he wanted for Edward belonged to her? She might give it back to him, but not if he would sell it. There were bigger and better things to do with it. She studied him. "Your wife, Katherine," she said. "How long has she been gone?"

His shoulders tensed. "About three years. She was struck by a street-car in San Francisco. Typical Katherine, she was trying to beat the vehicle across the street."

"I'm so sorry. She was shopping?" She knew the question was out of line the minute she saw his fingers tighten on the reins.

"So she said," was his only response.

Addie pondered the cryptic answer. Had Katherine lied to him about what she was doing? Or had he disapproved of the money she spent? She couldn't decipher the undercurrents.

He sighed. "You'll hear the rumor soon enough, so I might as well tell you. She was leaving me. Running off with some fellow who was teaching her to golf."

Addie smoothed the curls away from Edward's face. "She was leaving her son too?"

He nodded. "His illness was more than she could handle."

She wanted to pick up the child and hold him close. "It's not his fault."

"She thought it was mine," he said grimly.

Addie knew better than to probe that wound, but oh, how she wanted to heal it.

⌘

Addie's feet barely touched the floor after the day at the beach. When they reached the manor, she turned Edward over to his nurse for a bath while John took the motorcycle to the bank. The house seemed quiet without the very large presence of her father and Clara. She paused in the hallway outside Mr. Eaton's office.

No one would know if she slipped inside to look for pictures of her mother. The only one she'd seen was the one in Mr. Driscoll's bedroom. If Mr. Eaton loved her and her mother so much, surely he would keep some memento of their lives in his private domain. Glancing down the hall to make sure no servants were prowling about, she stepped into the office and closed the door behind her.

The late-afternoon sun slanted through the bay windows flanked by floor-to-ceiling bookcases. The chandelier over the desk sparkled with crystal, and heavy velvet drapes hung at the two windows. A spittoon was in a corner by the heavy chair, and a row of pipes was on one corner of the desk. A frame stood on the other corner, its back to her. It was a man's room, thick with the scent of tobacco. The gleaming redwood desk was clear of papers. She stepped around to the other side and frowned to see the picture was of Clara and another woman. Katherine perhaps? What had she been expecting? Of course Mr. Eaton would have his wife and daughter on his desk. He had no idea Julia still lived.

Addie picked up the picture and stared into the smiling face of the beautiful young woman. Katherine's hair was blonde and elegant. She had her mother's patrician nose and full lips, and the gown she wore must have cost the earth. Addie's bubble of happiness burst. John couldn't possibly be interested in her after having been married to the lovely girl in the photograph. She set the frame back onto the polished surface, then turned her attention to the bookcases. The shelves held gleaming leather books, and she wondered if she might be allowed to choose some to read. But she found no other photographs.

She turned back toward the door and stared at the drawers on the desk. Might he have any mementos tucked away from Clara? The thought of rummaging through his private papers held no appeal, but she longed to know more of her mother and the little girl once known as Julia. She wanted to find something that showed the love her family had once showered upon her. After a slight hesitation, she settled in the chair and pulled out the top drawer. It held a stack of papers. When she lifted them, a note fell from between the pages. She picked it up and saw several words in a feminine scrawl.

Only a payment of ten thousand dollars will prevent me from telling the world about your child.

Addie studied the note. There was no name to identify the author, and she wasn't certain Henry was the intended recipient. Maybe it had nothing to do with Henry, but if not, how had it come to be in his possession? She dropped it back into place and closed the drawer before going on to the next.

It was only when she pulled open the lap drawer that she found what she'd hoped to discover. She lifted a small scrapbook from the drawer and laid it on the desk. The leather cover was tattered and torn, but the photographs inside made her throat close. The beautiful woman she'd seen in the portrait stared into the camera. In her arms was an infant. Addie recognized the child as herself. In the next photograph she appeared to be about a year old and stood next to her mother. They were both dressed in white.

Her vision blurred, and a sob lodged in her throat. If only she could snatch the faint trace of memory lingering in her mind. Every time she strained to grasp it, it sifted through her fingers.

She finished flipping through the scrapbook. The last image was the same one she'd seen in the metal box at the lighthouse. Her life as an Eaton had been brief. She closed the book and replaced it, then shut the drawer when she heard John's motorcycle rumbling up the drive.

TWELVE

TWILIGHT WAS FAST approaching. John sat on the porch and watched his son play with the dog. He smiled at the camaraderie between the boy and Gideon. The dog barked and ran after the ball. The day at the beach had left him more relaxed than he'd been in a long time.

The dog changed directions and raced toward the front porch. John turned to see Addie exiting the house. She stood poised on the top step with an expectant expression. She'd changed from her bathing costume into a shimmery green dress. Her thick hair was wound on top of her head again. He much preferred it down.

"Have you come to call us to dinner?"

She nodded. "Mrs. Biddle said it would be on the table in five minutes."

"I haven't seen Driscoll. I think it might just be us."

"He mentioned he had to make a trip up the coast." She approached with graceful steps, pausing only to pet the dog and direct him back to Edward. "When would you like to go over Edward's lesson plans?" she asked when she reached John. "I'd like to ensure I'm doing what you expect."

He waved Edward over and told him to go get washed up for dinner. When the boy complained, then finally ran off to the house, John gestured to the wicker lawn furniture. "Have a seat and we can talk about it."

She gathered her skirt and sank onto the chair. Her clear green eyes focused on his face. "Edward is very bright. Is there a reason he is not attending school?"

"I would think it is obvious," he said.

Her eyebrows winged up. "His affliction? But surely that doesn't prevent him from school attendance."

"Kids can be cruel. I don't want him laughed at or ostracized."

"You sound as though you know this from personal experience."

He shied away from the memories of kids mocking his English accent when his family had first immigrated. He'd worked hard to overcome it. "Doesn't everyone?"

"I wouldn't know. I've never been to school," she said, her tone wistful.

"Never?"

She shook her head. "My father taught me, and I obtained a degree by correspondence."

"Admirable." He meant it. Not many women cared so much about education.

Her cheeks bloomed with delicate color. "Edward has to learn to live in the real world. Better now than to coddle him so much he doesn't know how to face adversity as an adult."

"He's five years old. There's plenty of time for him to face the hard knocks of life."

She inclined her head. "He's making great progress in just a few days on his numbers and letters."

"Excellent." He found himself watching her as conversation lagged. She was so innocent and sheltered, yet intelligence and fortitude glimmered in her eyes. He'd told her more about his feelings for his son than he'd even discussed with Katherine. Interesting. His wife's tactic had always been avoidance and tears.

Addie's slipper-clad feet, peeking out from under her green dress, moved in a rhythmic way, and she was humming "Maple Leaf Rag."

A carriage rolled down the driveway. The groom rushed to help with the horse, and John watched Lord Carrington clamber down and toss the reins to the groomsman. John rose to greet him and noticed the arrival had caught Addie's attention as well.

"That's Lord Thomas Carrington, one of Henry's friends from England. I haven't seen him in quite some time."

A bowler perched atop his head. Once upon a time, a black, curly beard had burst furiously from his cheeks and nearly encased his nose and mouth. John had often wanted to suggest Carrington follow the newer fashion and become smooth shaven, if only to see what lay beneath that mass of dark hair. Someone must have told him, because he'd shaved the beard into a trim mustache.

Carrington nodded as he passed. "John." He stopped when his gaze landed on Addie.

John extended his arm to Addie and waited until she took it. "Miss Sullivan, this is Lord Carrington. Thomas, Miss Sullivan is a friend of the family and has arrived to take charge of Edward's education."

The big man moved closer. "Delighted to meet you, Miss Sullivan," he boomed. "I hope you'll forgive me for remarking on how fresh and pretty you look this evening."

Addie blushed. "Thank you, Lord Carrington." She withdrew her hand from John's arm. "I'd better make sure Edward gets his hands clean. If you'll excuse me." She stepped through the front door.

Both men watched the graceful sway of her skirt. "Pretty girl. Yours?" Carrington asked.

"Of course not," John said.

Carrington bared his teeth in a smile. "Excellent. I have a mind to call on her."

"She's thirty years your junior, Carrington!"

"And pretty and fresh as a flower."

John barely managed to hold his temper. "If you're here to see Henry, he's gone to a concert."

"A fine reason to call again tomorrow." Carrington tipped his hat and strode to the buggy.

John stood slack jawed, emotions reeling. That man couldn't be allowed to get his hands on her.

❧

Addie eyed the bicycle John rolled from the carriage house. "Are you sure I can do this?"

"Of course. It just takes practice."

"Can I ride too?" Edward asked. He sat with the dog on the grass, watching them.

"Not tonight, little man," John said.

It pained her to see the light go out of Edward's eyes. She ran her hand down the gleaming paint. The metal warmed to her touch. "It's lovely. What do I do first?"

"Put your, uh, right lower limb through to the other side and perch on the seat. I'll hold the bike steady."

She lifted her skirt just enough to stick her leg through the opening, then sat. Just gripping the handlebars made it seem more real that she was about to have her first lesson on riding a bicycle. She was conscious of John's nearness as he held the vehicle steady.

"Now put your feet on the pedals," he instructed.

She propped her shoes on the platforms. "Do I move them?"

He nodded. "Let's go. Don't go so fast I can't keep up."

She began to push. John ran beside her on the brick drive, his breath warming her ear. A grin stretched across her face as the wind lifted her hair. "I love this!"

She rode up and down the driveway with John jogging beside her. At the top of the drive, she circled and began to pedal back toward the house. The bicycle rolled and maneuvered as if it were a part of her. She turned her head to tell John again how much she enjoyed the experience and realized he wasn't beside her anymore. She was balancing by herself. Her initial reaction was to jerk the handlebars, and the bike wobbled, but she regained control and pedaled on down the driveway. She made the final approach to the house on a sweeping curve.

It came more quickly than she'd mentally prepared for. She swerved too far, too fast. The bicycle rocked, and she jerked on the handlebars again to straighten it out. The cycle tipped, and she and the bicycle went down in a tangle of limbs and metal. Addie felt no pain at first, just the shock of taking a tumble. Then her elbow throbbed to inform her that she'd scraped it. Her forearm too. She pushed herself upright as John came running toward her.

"Miss Addie!" Edward, too, rushed to her side, but Gideon reached her first and pranced around her.

"I'm all right," she said as John arrived.

He knelt beside her and slipped his arm around her. "Are you injured?"

She had no idea of her true condition with him so close. Assessing the pain level, she leaned her head against his shoulder. His presence was the best medicine. "I-I don't think so."

Edward threw himself atop her, and she pulled him onto her lap when she realized he was crying. "It's okay, darling."

"You're bleeding," the child wailed.

John moved away, and she hugged Edward, relishing the little-boy scent of grass and dog. "It's merely a scratch, Edward. Proof of valor." John was still near enough that she could smell his bay rum hair tonic.

"I should call the doctor," John said. He placed his hand on her shoulder.

"No, no, I think I can get up with your assistance." Aware she was showing more of her leg than was seemly, Addie flipped her skirt into place. She brushed a kiss across Edward's cheek and scooted him onto the grass. "Papa's going to help me up." She grasped John's arm and allowed him to lift her to her feet.

"Does anything hurt?" he asked.

She smiled into his face. "Only my pride."

"Let's get you inside."

She glanced at the heap of wheels and metal. "No, I want to get back on the bicycle."

His mouth gaped. "You aren't afraid?"

"I'm terrified. But if I don't get back on now, I might never do it. The fall will expand in my mind. I want to learn this."

She released his arm and stepped away, though she preferred to stay close to him. "The bicycle appears unharmed."

"But you're not. You're bleeding."

She bent her elbow up to have a look. "As I said, it's merely a scratch." She straddled the bicycle again. "I believe I need your assistance."

"Against my better judgment." He steadied the bicycle.

She put her feet on the pedals and began to move up the driveway, though her chest was tight and her breathing labored. Chances were, she wouldn't fall again. Even if she did, she meant to master this skill. She loved the freedom she felt on the conveyance.

John ran beside her again, and she knew he wouldn't let go unless she forced him. Maybe it was safer to ride with his assistance. But no, playing it safe wouldn't help her learn to ride by herself.

"You can let go now," she said, keeping up a steady pressure on the pedal though her pulse began to thump.

He stepped back, and his hands dropped away. "You can do it!" he shouted after her as the bicycle picked up speed on the slope toward the house.

Addie gained confidence as the wheels turned easily and the bicycle handled well. She was beginning to understand how to handle it, and her balance didn't waver. She reached the front steps and braked. When the bicycle rolled to a stop, she put her feet down and sighed. She'd done it.

"Bravo!" John said, running to her side. "Your form was excellent. Now try to start it by yourself, without my assistance."

She smiled back into his animated face. What was this relationship that was developing between them? He'd never answered her question about philandering. Maybe he treated every woman as if she were special. Mr. Driscoll had warned her to be careful, but it was hard to think of such things when she looked into John's face.

His smile faded when she didn't move. "Miss Adeline? Are you all right?" he asked.

"Fine," she said, hastily putting one foot on a pedal.

She gave the bike a push with her right foot, then put her foot on the pedal and began to rotate the wheel. Her balance became steadier as the bicycle picked up speed. She was doing this alone! When she reached the top of the driveway, she turned in a circle and rode back to the house.

Her cheeks were warm from the ride. "I'll put the bicycle in the carriage house. Thank you for teaching me to ride. It was most exhilarating."

"One of the stablemen will do it." When she dismounted, he leaned the bicycle against the porch. "I should put some iodine on your scrapes."

"I can do it."

"It's hard to do by yourself. You can barely see if it's clean." He caught her arm and steered her toward the house, then down the hall to the parlor. "Wait here. I'll get water and iodine."

She rolled up her sleeve while he went to get the iodine. When had anyone tended to her so lovingly?

Dirt caked her elbow and arm where she'd grazed it on the driveway. Blood oozed from the abrasion. When John returned, he knelt and set the basin of warm water on the floor. Wringing out the washcloth, he touched it to the blood. She didn't flinch.

"Nasty scrape," he said. He washed the area as gently as he could.

"I can't see it well."

"As I said." He smiled and set about cleaning the injury. The only time she winced was when he applied the iodine. "Sorry," he said.

"The sting will ease in a moment."

He rose and stepped back. "I wouldn't hurt you if I could help it," he said.

Addie's eyes flickered, and she sobered. "You never answered my question at the beach," she said. "About your intentions. Were you avoiding a straight answer?"

He grinned. "You are so direct." He grew serious and held her gaze. "No, I'm not a philanderer, though Henry believes I need a new wife. He's been on a crusade to find me one."

"What do you think about it?"

"I have no desire to enter the matrimonial state again. Or at least I didn't."

"What does that mean?" she asked, her voice soft.

"There is something between us, Miss Adeline. I don't know what it is, or where it will lead."

"I don't either."

"I would like to find out," he said. "In fair disclosure, let me mention that I've been seeing a young woman in the city. My commander's daughter, Margaret. But I give you my word that I won't be seeing her again."

She bit her lip. "Have you been dating her long?"

He hesitated, then shrugged. "We've gone out four times."

Her expression softened. "Oh, Lieutenant North. That poor woman. What will she think when you don't ask her out again?"

"She's beautiful and sought after. I'm sure there are many men who will be glad to step into my shoes. I shall call her tomorrow and inform her of my interest in you."

Her eyes shimmered with moisture. "I don't like that she'll be hurt."

He laughed. "Miss Adeline, there isn't a woman alive who would find it in her heart to empathize with a rival as you do." That's what drew people to her, he decided, the compassion that emanated from her. Was it the result of her faith or something else?

"Did you love Katherine too much to replace her?"

He smiled. "What a romantic you are, my dear. Our marriage was less than warm."

"I'm sorry," she said, resting her hand on her chin. "I saw a photograph of her. She was very beautiful."

"And spoiled." John's smile faltered. "Edward embarrassed her. I fear at times I embarrassed her more."

Addie appeared so small in the large chair as she propped her chin on her hand. "You?" she asked.

Her tone implied it was beyond her comprehension that anyone wouldn't be honored to be on his arm. No one in his life had ever treated him with so much respect. No wonder she intrigued him.

"I didn't have enough ambition. Or perhaps I had the wrong kind." Such an honest woman as Addie deserved the truth from him. "And I know I wasn't the husband I should have been. I was away often, working hard to be the man she could look up to. I didn't handle the stress well. We drifted so far apart that we were strangers in the same house."

Addie shuddered. "I'm so sorry. Poor Edward, to lose his mother at such a young age."

If she only knew how much better off his son was without the mother who hardly acknowledged his existence. "He barely knew her. She avoided him when she could."

Her eyes glistened again, and she blinked quickly. "Poor child." She rose. "Thank you for tending to my wounds."

"My pleasure. Good night."

"Good night," she echoed.

He watched her walk away, her gown swishing with every step. Something about her made him want to be better than he was. When he saw the admiration and respect in her eyes, he could feel himself straighten and walk taller. Not many women caused that kind of reaction in a man.

So many women simpered and danced around the truth. Addie was exactly what she seemed. Being around someone so honest was a refreshing experience.

THIRTEEN

MONDAY MORNING, ADDIE surveyed her domain again. The schoolroom lacked a proper desk. The existing chair and table were too small for Edward. Such circumstances gave her the perfect excuse to go to the attic. She'd been itching to find more of her mother's possessions.

She touched the lad's head. "Edward, you practice writing your *A*. I'll be right back."

The boy put his arm around the dog's neck. "What about Gideon?"

"He can stay with you."

She told Gideon to guard the boy, then went in search of Molly and found her scrubbing a bathroom. "Molly, I hate to disturb you, but would there happen to be any school desks in the manor?"

Molly pushed a tendril of damp hair that had escaped her cap out of the way and leaned back on her haunches. "I'm not sure, miss, but there might be something in the attic. I could check for you." She started to get to her feet.

"Oh, don't get up. I'll do it if you direct me to the attic access."

"It's the door at the end of the hall by your bedroom."

"Thank you." Addie walked briskly through the labyrinth of halls and doorways, then found the attic door where Molly had indicated.

Light from the dormer windows shone dimly down the steep stairway. A lantern would help her see better, but she was in no mood to retrace her steps and bother Molly again. Perhaps there was a gaslight. She gathered her courage along with her skirts and ascended the stairs.

More light was the first thing she sought. Too many shadows dominated the space. She found a gaslight on a table, along with matches. When its hiss filled her ears, the warm glow from its globe made the attic appear less unfriendly. She glanced around and saw dressers, tables, trunks, and chifforobes. In another corner lay rolls of rugs. The other side held several desks and showed promise for what she needed. She picked her way through the jumbled furniture.

How would she know what furniture had belonged to her mother? She recognized the value of several lovely pieces under their drop cloths. She went through a stack of portraits but found none of her mother. In the back of the stack, she paused at the sight of a child, then realized it was too old to have been of her two-year-old self. The little one had long blonde curls and appeared to be about four. Perhaps it was Clara?

Addie left the paintings and began to look over the desks. Most of them were beautiful but built for a man, not a five-year-old boy. She removed protective covers from several pieces until she uncovered a woman's desk. The desk was so lovely an exclamation escaped her lips. A white pastoral scene was painted on the doors that hid the drawers. She admired the delicate turned legs and the scrollwork on the front and top.

She had to see inside the dainty piece. The doors refused to open, and she realized it was locked. The key must be here somewhere. Kneeling, she ran her fingers over the legs, then under the desk. A key had been taped to the back edge. She peeled it off, then fitted the key into the keyhole. The hardware clicked, and she opened two doors to reveal two shelves and three drawers in a pale wood tone.

She wished she could claim it for her own. Never had she wanted something so badly. She touched the smooth wood, then pulled open the drawers. The two on top were empty. The bottom one ran the width of the desk and held bundles of letters in a woman's script. Her hand hovered over one letter that was loose from the rest. Would reading this be prying? But surely whoever owned this didn't care, not if she'd left the letters in the desk.

Addie decided to take a peek and see whom this exquisite desk had belonged to. The paper was heavy and stiff in her fingers. She unfolded the letter and made note of the address.

Dear Laura,

A gasp escaped her throat. Her mother's letters? Her gaze roamed the desk. Did all these letters belong to her mother? She scooped them up and stuffed them into the waistband of her skirts. Once she reached the privacy of her room, she would read them. Perhaps they would reveal who was behind the events that had shaped her life.

She heard a creak on the steps and whirled to see John's dark head appearing through the floor opening. She feared he could read the guilt stamped there and turned back to the desk.

"You startled me, Lieutenant North." She closed the doors on the desk and placed the cloth back over it.

He stepped onto the attic floor. "What are you doing?"

"Trying to find a desk for Edward. The table is much too small."

He joined her. "Will this work?" he asked, pointing to a desk.

She examined it and nodded. "It's much like the one I used at the lighthouse."

He gave the attic a quick appraisal. "Lots of useless stuff up here."

"Beautiful things," she said. "Did you notice the desk I covered up? It's so lovely."

"I didn't see it." He lifted its cloth. "A woman's desk," he said. "I don't remember Katherine using it. But then, she didn't want anything old."

Addie ran her hand over the painted front. "It's exquisite."

"I'm sure no one would object if you used it while you're here."

"Oh, I couldn't." She took a step back. "I'm sure it's very valuable."

He shrugged. "It's just an old desk. I'll have one of the servants bring it down with this one for Edward. Do you want it in your room?"

"I'd rather use it in the schoolroom. Shouldn't we ask permission first?"

"I'll check with Clara, but I'm sure it's fine." He offered her his arm. "Lunch is in an hour. Henry will be back soon. I overheard you tell Sally you were itching to try the grand piano, and I'd like to hear you play."

She put her hand on his arm. She could get used to attention from this man.

❧

Addie sat on the bench at the grand piano. The ragtime music that poured from the instrument made John tap his foot. Edward cavorted with the dog on the wood floors, and John was of half a mind to join them.

"Who taught you how to play?" he called.

Her pensive smile faded. "My father taught me. He studied music and had thought to be a concert pianist before consumption changed his plans."

Her mouth grew pinched, and he wondered about the relationship with her mother. There was pain there. He stood and walked over to lean on the piano lid. Before he could ask more questions, he heard a bellow behind him. The music tinkled to a stop and faded to an echo of its vibrant energy.

Henry's broad form filled the doorway. "What is the meaning of this?" he shouted.

Addie's hands still lay on the keys, and she turned to face Eaton, her green eyes wide. "I was told I would be allowed to play the piano," she said.

"Not trash like that. This isn't a bordello." Henry's face reddened. "Pardon me for mentioning something so indelicate to a lady, but Miss Sullivan, that kind of music is most unsuitable for my grandson and for anyone to hear echoing from the Eaton house."

She paled even more. "I meant no harm, sir. My father paid for lessons, and these are the tunes I learned. To me, they express the joy I find in the Lord."

Henry's feigned smile was more of a grimace. "Well, you must unlearn them. Hymns will do more to connect you to God than that drivel can. There is suitable sheet music in the piano bench." He turned and stomped out.

Watching Addie's stricken face, John realized she was already feeling the pressure to conform, as he'd feared. He extended his hand. "I believe luncheon should be ready. Shall we go?"

She took his hand and rose, releasing it once she was on her feet. "I didn't mean to offend him."

"He'll get over it." The scent of Addie's honeysuckle cologne smelled better than the aroma of roast beef, which grew stronger as they approached the dining room. He stopped in the doorway when he saw Carrington at the sideboard, dishing compote onto his plate. If John had realized the man had been invited for lunch, he would have made his excuses. He'd respected Carrington until his attention to Addie had commenced.

When they were seated, he turned to Clara. "Miss Adeline and I were in the attic looking for a desk for Edward."

Clara stirred sugar into her tea. "Adeline? You've moved to first names?"

"A slip of the tongue," he said hastily.

Her gaze slid to Carrington, who was obviously besotted. "You appear to have some competition, John."

He resisted the impulse to tug on his tie. "About the desk?"

She took a sip of her tea. "Did you find one? There should be something suitable up there."

"Yes, we did. We also stumbled across a writing desk. I told Miss Sullivan I saw no reason she couldn't use it."

She stilled. "A white one? With a painted scene on the front?"

"That's the one."

She directed a gaze at Henry on the other side of the table. "Henry, dear. Adeline would like to use Laura's old desk that's in the attic. That's quite all right, isn't it?"

Laura's desk? John heard the taunting tone of her voice under the sugary sweetness that lay over it. He glanced at Henry and wasn't surprised to see red running up the older man's neck.

"Of course she can use it. Might as well get some good out of that old thing," Henry said in an overly hearty voice.

Addie's expression was stricken, and John knew she had caught the undertones too. It was clear to him that Clara had always known she was Henry's second choice. Pictures of Laura and baby Julia were in Henry's study somewhere, and he still wore the cuff links Laura had given him as a wedding present.

"I'll have one of the servants bring it down," John said. He noticed the Englishman was about to engage Addie in conversation again. "Miss Sullivan, since you're finished with lunch, I wonder if I might have a word with you. About Edward," he added when he saw a frown gather on Carrington's face.

"Of course." She put down her napkin and rose. "It's been a pleasure, Lord Carrington."

Carrington half rose. He took her hand and kissed it. "I look forward to seeing you again, Miss Sullivan."

She withdrew her hand and moved away from the table. John wanted to believe it was relief he saw on her face. He'd like to think she was too smart to be taken in by Carrington. She took his arm, and they stepped out of the dining room. Once the clink of silverware was behind them, he stopped in the hall.

"Is something wrong, Lieutenant North?"

"Beware of Carrington," he said.

"Mr. Carrington was very kind," she said. "He made no untoward remarks."

"He's already got you lined up in his mind as his next wife. He's buried one already."

Her breath came fast, and spots of color lodged in her cheeks. "What happened to his other wife?"

Surely she wasn't interested! "She died in childbirth."

"Recently?"

He dropped his gaze. "No," he muttered, struggling to maintain his temper. "About ten years ago."

"The poor man," she murmured. She removed her hand from John's arm. "But I'm not interested in becoming wife number two."

"I'm relieved to hear it," he said.

She tipped her head. "Are you? Why would that concern you?"

"He's much too old for you," he said.

She smiled, and her dimple appeared. "Surely he's not more than fifty."

"As I said. An old man." He put her hand on his arm and steered her to the staircase. "I'm sure Edward is finished with his lunch by now. I'll arrange to have the desk brought to you."

Her impish smile faded. "I thought Mr. Eaton seemed not at all fond of the idea."

"He said it was fine."

She swept up the stairs beside him. "It was what he didn't say that concerns me. It belonged to his first wife?"

"Clara's half-sister."

"Clara seemed somewhat jealous."

"She always has been. Have you noticed the pictures of a beautiful redhead around the manor? That was Laura. Henry would be wise to take them down. Everywhere Clara turns, she sees the reminders of Laura."

"I've only seen one."

He stopped and thought. "You're right," he said, nodding. "Clara must have succeeded in relegating them to the attic."

"He must have loved his first wife a great deal," Addie said.

"It seemed quite the grand passion." They reached the top of the staircase, and he turned her toward the schoolroom. "Katherine was always curious about the daughter, Julia. She'd wanted a sibling."

"Julia," she said, her voice strangled.

John hadn't missed the change in her voice. "Is something wrong?"

She shook her head violently. "You were saying?"

"She was around two. She and Laura went down in a shipwreck. I heard Henry didn't eat or sleep for days. He searched for them for weeks, but there was never any sign of them. There were no survivors."

"How sad," she whispered.

He touched her chin and turned her liquid eyes toward him. "Don't cry. It happened a long time ago. I'm sure Henry is over it all by now."

"Love like that never dies."

He smiled. "Such romanticism. No wonder you read poetry."

"Does he ever talk about them?"

He released her chin and shook his head. "Clara would be in tears if he did. The servants tell how he raved like a madman when he heard the news. Molly said she'd never heard a grown man cry like that."

Her fingers tightened on his arm as they moved toward the schoolroom. "Don't talk about it anymore or I shall cry myself. It's too sad for words." Her voice broke.

"As you wish. I was just answering your questions." He led her down the hall.

Edward's empty plate lay on the table in the schoolroom. John stepped to the window and looked down into the side yard. "He's tossing a ball to Gideon."

"They'll both burn off some energy."

He turned toward her. "You haven't asked how my call to Margaret went."

She smiled. "*Now* who is very direct?"

He raised his brows. "You're rubbing off on me."

"I hope not. You'll be reprimanded like me."

"Someone has reprimanded you?"

She waved her hand. "Nothing serious. Mrs. Eaton told me not to be so forthcoming about where I am from. That I must maintain the position."

He put his hands on her shoulders. "I told you not to let them change you." Her scent filled his head.

Her dimple appeared. "I promise not to change too much." She gazed up into his face. "What about your call to Margaret?"

He shrugged and let his hands fall back to his side. "It was fine."

"Did you tell her you wouldn't be calling on her again?"

"I did. She took it graciously, then asked when I would return to the city. I told her it would be several weeks."

Color stained her cheeks. "Do you intend to see her again?" she asked, her voice low. She turned toward the window.

He turned her back to face him. "No, Miss Sullivan, I do not. I should not have mentioned her question, but I must admit I wondered if you cared enough to be jealous. My remark was quite ungentlemanly."

Her expression warmed. "I care entirely too much, Lieutenant North."

No, he was the one who was smitten, and it was much too soon to be so taken with her.

FOURTEEN

ADDIE FOUGHT TEARS all afternoon. Hearing how her father had searched for her and her mother had done something to the fences she'd put up around her emotions.

"You did a wonderful job on your letters today, Edward," she told her charge.

His small face brightened. "Can I take Gideon out to play ball as a reward?"

"It's nearly time for your dinner."

His face puckered. "I don't like lessons when I have to stay inside. Gideon has been waiting for me to play all afternoon."

She glanced at her dog, who stared back at her with hopeful eyes as though he understood. And he probably did. *Play* was his favorite word. "Very well," she said. "I'll go down with you."

It was a sacrifice, because she wanted nothing more than to shut her door and go through the letters she'd stuffed under the mattress. What might she discover in those pages? The identity of the man who had attacked her? The reason behind the events that had changed her life?

She took Edward's small hand and led him and Gideon outside. Clouds swirled overhead, and a drop of rain plopped onto her face. "We won't be able to stay long," she warned. "It's going to rain."

She settled on the wicker chair and watched the boy throw the ball to her dog. Gideon was enjoying it as much as Edward was.

The dog wasn't used to being cramped up in the house. He'd roamed the island at their last station all day, then wandered home at night. The stress of the day had taken its toll, and her eyes drooped. A cacophony of wild barking opened them again, and she leaped from her chair to see Gideon crouched and barking at Edward. The dog lunged forward and grabbed the boy's arm. Was he attacking the child?

"Gideon!" she shouted, rushing to intervene.

The dog succeeded in tugging Edward to a sitting position. The boy's staring eyes did not respond to Gideon's agitation. The child swayed where he sat, then he toppled onto his back. Gideon pranced around the boy.

She knelt beside the boy. "Good boy, Gideon," she crooned as she checked out the lad. "You saw what was happening to Edward, didn't you?"

Addie pulled Edward onto her lap and held him. He jerked, and his eyes rolled back in his head. She pulled her handkerchief from the sleeve of her dress, rolled it up, then thrust it between his teeth.

Someone else needed to know about this. "Help! Lieutenant North, someone. Please help!"

At first she thought no one had heard her, then the door opened and a figure stepped onto the porch. She recognized John and waved to attract his attention in case he didn't see her in the twilight. As he started toward her, the heavens opened up with a gush of rain. She huddled over Edward and tried to protect him from the worst of the water.

❦

John reached them. "An attack of epilepsy?" he shouted over the pounding of the rain hitting the trees.

She nodded. "Is it safe to move him?"

"Yes. Here, let me." He lifted his son from her lap and rushed with him toward the house.

She splashed through the widening mud puddles. Gideon loped along beside her. When they reached the porch, she snapped her fingers at her dog. Mrs. Eaton would go into vapors if Addie let the muddy dog onto her redwood floors.

"Stay, Gideon," she said. The dog whimpered but lay down. "I'll get some rags to dry you and come back," she promised.

When she stepped inside, she found the household in an uproar. Both grandparents hovered over the unconscious boy. John had laid him on the leather sofa in the smoking room.

Clara wrung her hands. "Oh, why does this happen to our sweet lad?" she moaned. She caught sight of Addie. "What happened, Adeline? Was he upset?"

Addie shook her head. "He had a good day of studies. I gave him permission to toss the ball to Gideon, and he was having a good time."

"Maybe he got too hot," Mr. Eaton said.

"I don't think so," Addie said. "Gideon was doing the running. I heard the dog bark and saw Edward standing still, just staring. Gideon grabbed his shirtsleeve and pulled him down. A few seconds later he fell back."

John glanced up from his vigil beside his son. "The dog sensed it before it happened? Just like the day you arrived?"

"I think so. I watched it with my own eyes."

"Amazing," Mr. Eaton said. "Edward claimed it was so from the very first." He fixed his gaze on Addie. "What magic is this, Miss Sullivan?"

"Gideon seems to sense these things," she admitted. "He has often led me to injured animals or children."

"Did he lead you to the child in the garment factory?" John asked in a low voice.

She nodded. "He's a remarkable dog."

"We must breed him and see if this trait can be duplicated. I did some checking with a neighbor who has a shepherd. She'll have a female in heat in a few weeks. With her permission, I'd like to see what kind of pups we might get." Addie's cheeks went red, and Mr. Eaton stuttered. "Pardon me, Miss Sullivan. I should not be discussing something so indelicate. Have I your permission to, uh, mate Gideon?"

"Please do, sir," she said. "I'd love to have some little Gideons running around."

John was thinking more about a little girl with Addie's magnificent eyes.

Addie leaned against her closed door and let the pent-up air escape from her lungs. Every moment in the handsome lieutenant's presence left her more infatuated. When should she tell him about her identity? She longed to reveal it to him. As soon as Mr. Driscoll returned, she planned to inform him she couldn't keep the truth from John. She loved his name. Such a strong, manly sound encompassed by that one-syllable word.

She turned on the gas lamp, closed her curtains, then slipped into her white nightgown. In Gideon's absence, the room echoed with emptiness. He was so necessary to Edward, but she missed her companion. If the puppies were found to have his innate sense of compassion, Edward could have his own puppy.

They were much alike, she and Gideon. Ever since she could remember, she'd been able to sense another person's pain. When her father had a headache, Addie knew where to rub. When her mother broke her ankle, Addie's had throbbed as well. This was the first time in her life that she knew the right thing to do was to gift her dog to the child, but she couldn't quite summon the will.

Adrenaline still raged through her. The letters under her mattress awaited discovery. Standing by the gaslight, she realized she hadn't prayed in two days. No wonder her day hadn't gone well. That was usually her first thought, and the realization it had been her last thought struck her hard. She dropped to her knees by the bed and poured out her distress to the Lord. The agitation faded, and peace warmed her like a blanket.

It would be all too easy in this environment to forget her roots. To lay aside what was truly important. She had to be on her guard.

While she was on her knees, she thrust her hand under the mattress and found the bundle of letters. She rose and carried them to the chair by the lamp. Her hands trembled as she held them under the warm glow of light and tried to decide which letter to read first. Chronologically made the most sense. She sorted them by postmark. Some had the bold slash of a man's handwriting.

Once they were sorted, she laid the stack on the table and lifted the first one. It was addressed to her mother in a delicate handwriting.

Laura,

You simply must come to tea next week. Wednesday at 2:00 p.m.? Bring Clara if necessary, but come! Mr. Henry Eaton has confessed that he is quite smitten with you. He says Clara knows they are friends only. He asked me to intercede on his behalf.

Most warmly,

Inez

Addie noticed the date. October 19, 1875. The first meeting between her parents. She could imagine how it played out: her father, slimmer and with his hair still dark, bowing over her mother's hand. Was it love at first sight? And what about Clara? Had she known Henry felt nothing for her but friendship?

She picked up the next letter and saw a man's bold scrawl. From her father perhaps? She opened it and held it under the light.

My dearest Laura,

I am the happiest man on earth now that you know my feelings. Your face, your form, haunt my dreams. I am a man obsessed. Would you honor me with your presence on a ride along the shore next Saturday? I will be sure to bring a carriage with enough room for Clara if she could be persuaded to act as chaperone.

Your humble servant,
Henry

Addie drew the back of her hand across her damp eyes. The love her father felt was clear. She suspected her mother had the same experience. Reading their exchanges was like reading an Elizabeth Barrett Browning love poem. Totally enthralled with the relationship unfolding in the letters, she picked up the next one.

Laura,

I'm thrilled things are so wonderful between you and Henry. I'd be honored to be your bridesmaid for the wedding in June. I completely understand that your stepmother would insist that Clara be the maid of honor.

Warm regards,
Inez

Addie gave a blissful sigh. John's face flashed through her mind, but she pushed it away and picked up another envelope. The next five letters were all invitations to different parties and teas. The last was addressed in her mother's handwriting. It was in an unaddressed envelope with only the name Henry slashed across the front.

My dearest Henry,

I know you do not understand, but I must be gone for a few weeks. I still love you very much, but when I overheard the awful truth, it was more than I could bear. I will be in touch when I'm settled in the hotel. Don't try to make me come home yet. I need some time.

Laura

Addie folded the letter and put it back in its envelope. "Awful truth," her mother had said. What would cause a wife who was clearly devoted to her husband to flee with her daughter? Addie needed to talk to Mr. Driscoll. He'd said he would be home tonight. Maybe he was in his room. She snatched up her dressing gown.

FIFTEEN

JOHN TUCKED THE sheet around his sleeping son, then stepped over the dog and tiptoed out of the room. He started across the hall to his own bedroom and heard the murmur of voices. A man and a woman were arguing. Or at least it sounded like an argument. In case the woman was in distress, he followed the sound around the corner to the other wing of rooms. As he neared, the voices became clear enough to identify.

Driscoll and Addie. They were in the schoolroom.

He stopped before he turned into the final hallway. He'd listen a minute to make sure things were all right, then head to his bed. If she needed him, he wanted to be there.

"Why would she leave so suddenly?" Addie asked, her voice raised.

"You should have told me before you read the letters," Driscoll said.

"I have to know the truth."

Frowning, John sidled nearer while staying hidden around the corner.

"And we'll find out the truth," Driscoll said. "But we have to work together, Addie."

"I want to find out what happened," she said. "Who I am."

Driscoll cleared his throat. "You should have told me the minute you found the letters."

"You've been gone, Mr. Driscoll. Did you discover anything?"

"Unfortunately no, child. Tuttle died six months ago."

"He still might have been the one behind it." Desperation tinged her words.

"The money would have stopped."

"Unless he made arrangements for it to carry on in the event of his death. I want to tell Mr. Eaton now. And John."

John's gut clenched at the way her tone went soft when she said his name. At least keeping the secret from him hadn't been easy for her. Whatever it was.

"We have to be careful, Adeline. Someone has already attacked you. You're making yourself a target if we announce why you're here."

"I think it would be worth it. I'm tired of the charade." Her voice dropped to a near whisper.

"I advise patience."

"My whole life has been turned upside down since you appeared on our doorstep, Mr. Driscoll. It's easy enough for you to advise patience when you're not the one whose future hangs in the balance."

"I'm sorry, Addie." Driscoll's voice grew gentle. "I know this has been hard for you. Get some sleep. Let's talk about it tomorrow."

"Very well. I can see you are not going to budge. Good night, Mr. Driscoll."

"Good night, my dear."

Driscoll's footsteps neared, and John slipped into an empty guest room until the noise of his passage faded down the hall. Driscoll had brought Addie here for a reason, but the import of it escaped John. The rock in his gut grew heavier. The discussion John had overheard made one thing clear. Addie wasn't the innocent he thought. Just as much pretense ran through her veins as through all the other women he'd known. He'd been sure she was different. He'd been ready to pursue her. He'd even stepped away from a good match because of her. Addie's directness had been all a front. How very clever of her.

When he stepped back into the hall, he nearly ran down Addie. He caught her before she stumbled back against the wall.

"You startled me," she said. Her bare feet peeked out from under her green dressing gown, and her hair was down.

A visceral emotion hit John in the gut. His fingers itched to plunge into that thick mane of auburn hair, to examine the red tints in the firelight. He imagined lifting that heavy curtain to place a kiss on the warm skin of her neck. Resisting the liquid warmth of her eyes, he released her arm and thrust his hands in his pockets.

Neither spoke for a long moment. A blush colored her cheeks, and he eyed it. Figuring out how to blush on command must have taken some training and practice. It gave her an innocent air that had completely fooled him.

"Is something wrong?" she asked, clutching the neck of her dressing gown.

Would she tell him the truth if he asked why she was really here? He could tell her he'd overheard her conversation with Driscoll.

"No, nothing," he said abruptly. "You're up late. Can I help you with something?"

Her dimple flashed. "I couldn't sleep and thought I'd get some warm milk."

"You're going the wrong way."

"I get so turned around in this big place."

More lies? Probably an excuse to explain her presence.

He led her down the hall until it teed to the right, then to the end of the next hallway. "Careful, the stairs are steep."

He went down the steps ahead of her. Even in the kitchen stairway, the Eatons had spared no expense. Flocked wallpaper covered the walls, and the stairs and handrail were redwood. John and Addie emerged in the large kitchen. The wooden counters were clean and ready to be used in the morning.

He took a glass down from the cupboard and went to the ice chest. "Would you care to have it warmed?"

She held out her hand for the glass of milk. "You don't need to wait on me. I don't want to keep you from your bed."

He handed it over and watched as she poured hot water from the kettle on the woodstove into a bowl, then set the glass of milk in it to warm. "I'm a little hungry. Would you care for some jam and bread?" Her smile came. "I admit I'm a bit peckish myself. Let me get it. Sit down."

He sat at the kitchen table and watched her cut thick slices of bread and spread them with jam and butter. The intimacy of the moment swamped his resolve not to look at her hair.

He had to remember she had a secret agenda.

❦

The warmth John had shown for days was replaced by a chill demeanor that tightened his lips and hooded his eyes. As Addie layered on the toppings, she cast her mind back over the day and couldn't think of anything she might have done to offend him.

She placed the food on a plate and slid it in front of him. She slipped into the seat across from him and propped her chin in her hand. "I fear I was too honest about my feelings, Lieutenant. I've frightened you with my boldness, perhaps?"

"Candor is never misplaced, Miss Sullivan. Falsehood, on the other hand, is something I despise."

"Falsehood? Surely you know me well enough by now to know I say what I think."

"The problem is not what you say but what you *don't* say."

She studied his cold, dark eyes when he finally raised them. "You know," she whispered. "I wanted to tell you right from the start, but Mr. Driscoll forbade me to say anything."

"I heard you talking to him a few moments ago."

She thought about that conversation. Nothing had been said about her identity. All he knew was that she had some purpose for being here, but she couldn't endure his coldness. "You don't know all of the story, but I want to tell you."

"Will it be the truth?"

"Have I ever lied to you, Lieutenant?"

"Right now, I'm not really certain. I thought you were the clearest pool of honesty I'd ever peered into. I admit I'm most disappointed in you."

She winced. "I'm exactly what you see. The only thing I haven't revealed is my purpose in coming here."

"I thought it was to teach Edward. Or is that a lie as well?"

"The moment I heard about Edward, I wanted to meet him," she said. "He's very important to me, and I loved him from the first."

His eyes softened only a fraction at the mention his son's name. "So what other purpose brought you here?"

"I want to discover my heritage."

He frowned. "I don't understand. How could coming here help you learn that?"

"I was born here. To Laura Eaton." She waited until the light began to dawn in his eyes. "I believe I'm Julia Eaton."

"That's impossible! She drowned years ago."

She pulled her locket out from under her dressing gown and opened it. "Then explain this."

He leaned over and peered at the picture in the locket. His fingers grazed hers when he cradled the necklace in his hand. She shivered with the overpowering urge to touch his hair. If he didn't move, she wouldn't be able to resist. When he finally leaned back, she was able to breathe again.

"It's Vera," he said. "Where did you get it?"

"I think I must have been around five when my father gave it to me. When Mr. Driscoll showed up, my mother admitted it was around my neck when my father found me on the shore. I was about two."

"Julia's age when the shipwreck occurred."

"Yes." She willed him to believe her. "My mother showed me a metal box full of clippings my father had collected about the shipwreck. And someone paid my parents for my upkeep all these years. They were instructed not to turn me over to the authorities but to tell everyone I was their natural child. They were able to do that because my father had just taken the post at Battery Point a few days before the shipwreck. My mother hadn't joined him yet but arrived a few days later."

The coldness began to fade from his face. "You're really Julia Eaton?" He rubbed his forehead. "Does Henry know?"

She rubbed the warm metal of her locket. "Not yet. Mr. Driscoll is searching for more conclusive evidence."

"What role does Walter play in this?"

"A friend of his took a picture of me at the lighthouse, and he happened to see it. Something about my appearance made him think of my mother, so he came to see for himself. When he saw the locket, he knew for sure."

"It might have washed ashore and had nothing to do with you. And your resemblance isn't overt."

She pushed her hair back from her face. "That's why he's searching for more proof. If he can find out who paid for my upkeep, he'll go to Mr. Eaton then."

"Why would someone want to keep you from your family?"

"That's what we want to know."

He reached over and took her hand. "The attacks on you and Walter might be related to this."

The press of his fingers comforted her. "That's what Mr. Driscoll fears. He's hired an investigator, but the records of the attorney who paid the stipend were burned, and so far the attorney is not revealing his client."

"Henry will want proof, though the locket will have an impact. Still, it's not conclusive."

"Perhaps I should tell Mr. Eaton anyway. If we all work together, we may discover the truth."

"I'm not so sure," he said. "Someone had a powerful reason to keep you away from him. What if that's who attacked you and Walter?"

"If the truth comes out, that person won't have any reason for another attack."

"Or it might force him into a more desperate move."

"Or her," she said before she could stop the words.

"Her?"

"Mr. Driscoll suspects Mrs. Eaton."

"I can't see Clara involved in this."

"Jealousy? She was in love with Mr. Eaton before he dropped her for her my mother."

"I have heard that story," he said slowly. He pushed his half-eaten bread away. "We should retire, Miss Sullivan. This will take mulling over."

She rose when he did. When he avoided her gaze, she laid her hand on his arm. "Are you angry with me?"

"Maybe. When we drove past the property, you knew then all the plans I had for it would come to nothing, didn't you?"

She willed him to see the truth in her eyes. "You can keep the land. Money isn't the reason I came. Please don't hate me for it. I couldn't bear it."

His warm fingers lifted her chin, and he stared into her face. "I fear I could never stay angry with you for long." He brushed the back of his hand along her cheek, then stepped to the stairs.

SIXTEEN

LAST NIGHT'S LITTLE tête-à-tête was the first thing Addie thought of when she awoke. They'd eaten their bread and she'd drunk her milk by the dim glow of the gaslight. How strange to think that a few weeks ago she didn't even know John. Now he was all she could think about. The dear man had been understanding when she revealed her identity. She rubbed her eyes and yawned. She'd worked on Mrs. Eaton's dress until after midnight every night.

A knock came at her door, and she leaped from the bed. "Yes?" she called, grabbing for her dressing gown.

"Miss?" Molly said from the other side of the door. "A telegram has come for you."

Addie unlocked the door and opened it. Molly held out a silver tray with an envelope on the lace doily. Addie hesitated to pick it up.

"Miss?" Molly asked.

Addie collected herself and picked up the envelope. "Thank you, Molly. Is Edward awake?"

"Yes, miss. He has had his breakfast and is out back on the swing."

"Alone? Or is his nurse with him?"

"She's poorly this morning and stayed in bed. He wanted your dog to go, but Gideon refused to budge from your door." She pointed to the dog lying on the floor in the hall.

"Oh dear, Gideon should have gone with him. I'll be right there." She thanked the maid and called Gideon to her. She gave him a quick pat, then hurried back into the room.

Selecting a white lace blouse and a black skirt, she quickly dressed. On her way down the back stairway, she tore open the envelope and scanned it. She froze on the middle step when she realized it was from Josephine.

Have taken position at Mercy Falls Lighthouse. Stop. Will be there today. Stop. Want to see you. Stop.

Addie's first instinct was to rush to the lighthouse and embrace her mother, but she knew it would be fruitless. She'd tried to earn Josephine's love for twenty-three years and had never succeeded. Still, what was behind the summons? She stuffed the note in her pocket and stepped into the warm kitchen with the dog on her heels. Oatmeal bubbled from a pot on the stove, and the scent of bacon hung in the air. Her stomach growled, but she didn't have time for a real breakfast, not with Edward outside alone.

She stepped to the back door. "Go find Edward, Gideon." After the dog glanced up at her, then slowly went out, she shut the door behind him.

"Breakfast?" the cook asked.

"Might I take a few pieces of bacon with me? I need to be caring for Edward."

"But sure, let me get that for you." The cook forked four pieces of bacon onto a thick slice of bread and put it on a plate.

Addie scooped off the sandwich and left the plate. She thanked the cook, then hurried into the backyard. Nibbling on her sandwich, she scanned the yard for the boy, but the swing hung empty. Maybe he was in the front yard. She hurried around the back. No Edward. She shouted for Gideon, and he came running back to her side.

Maybe Edward had gone back inside through the front door. She took the last bite of her sandwich, then stepped into the front hall. "Have you seen Edward?" she asked the butler.

"No, miss. Not since he went outside."

She checked with the cook, and Edward hadn't come in the back door. Trying not to panic, she went back to the front. Still no Edward.

John came down the steps. "Is something wrong?"

"I can't find Edward." Aware her voice was rising, she made a conscious effort to modulate her tone. "I checked outside, and all around the house. Is there anywhere else he might have gone?"

John reached her side. "There's the falls. I've told him never to go there alone, though. And another pond that's a little closer. Let's try there first." He held open the door for her, then hurried down the steps. "This way."

She and Gideon followed John along a brick path through the large redwood trees. Trunks big enough to drive a buggy through reached for the sky on both sides of the path and blocked out the sun. Insects hummed around her ears, and she heard the sound of trickling water.

John strode ahead of her but paused long enough to point out their destination. "It's in the grove ahead."

As she quickened her steps, she prayed they'd find the boy happily skipping rocks. They broke through the towering trees into a clearing where water lilies floated on a clear pool. Wildflowers formed a blanket and perfumed the air.

"He's not here," John said, an edge to his voice. "How did he get outside without you or his nurse?"

"He went out before I was out of my room, and his nurse is ill," she said evenly. "We need to instruct the servants not to allow him outside without supervision."

"My fault," he said. "I should already have done that. I didn't take the attacks on you and Walter seriously enough." He raised his voice. "Edward!"

Gideon bristled, and a low growl rumbled from his chest. "What is it, boy?" Addie placed a hand on his head.

His ruff stood at attention, and he focused on a patch of bushes on the far side of the pond. She saw the vegetation flutter.

"It's probably just a deer or a squirrel," John said. He shouted for his son again.

Gideon's growl intensified. "I don't think it's an animal," Addie whispered. "He's not typically alarmed at animals."

"Could Edward be playing hide-and-seek?"

The back of her neck prickled. "He wouldn't growl at Edward."

Gideon walked on stiff legs toward the thick vegetation. She and John followed. The green leaves went into violent movement. A man with Edward under his arm broke from the cover of shrubs. A muffled shriek came from Edward, who had a rag in his mouth.

"Get him!" Addie shouted to Gideon.

The dog broke into a run and reached the fleeing man in seconds. He leaped onto the back of the criminal and knocked him to the ground. Edward rolled away, and the dog jumped between the man and boy. Baring his teeth, Gideon stood guard over Edward.

John rushed toward his son and the would-be kidnapper, but before he reached them, the man leaped to his feet and vanished into the forest. John dropped to his son's side and snatched the gag from Edward's mouth as Addie reached them. She knelt beside them as Edward burst into noisy sobs and flung his arms around his father's neck.

She exchanged a grim glance with John. None of this made sense to her.

The army of servants had been called together and questioned, but no one had seen anything. Though John had threatened to remove himself and his son back to San Francisco, he was reluctant to do so. If the kidnapper had penetrated the Eaton estate, how easily could he bridge the defenses of John's house? He had only a housekeeper and cook to defend his son while he was at work. Both were middle-aged women. Though he could take Addie with him, he wasn't sure if her arrival had plunged all of them into the fire with her.

What could Edward have to do with Addie's true identity? There was no clear connection he could see.

Henry had called a family meeting in the drawing room. Beside him on the sofa, Clara dabbed her eyes with a hankie. Addie stood by the window to the formal garden. Driscoll was in the easy chair by the fireplace, and John dropped into the matching seat.

Henry took out a cigar and chewed on it. "I'm going to hire a Pinkerton agent to investigate this," he announced. "They've a branch right here in Mercy Falls, and plenty of guards for hire."

"I'd feel immensely better if they were here," Clara said. "Abraham Lincoln employed Pinkerton's for his own protection. Did you know that?"

"I'll secure some guards to stand watch around the property," Henry continued. "I intend to find out who dared touch my grandson."

"What about enemies, Henry?" John asked. "Are there any pending acquisitions or touchy contracts that could be at the root of this?"

"If you mean someone who might kidnap my grandson to force me into a position I've refused, then no," Henry said. "Things are going remarkably well in the office. What about you, John?"

"Me?" John shook his head. "I'm a navy man. I simply carry out my duties day to day."

Henry's eyes narrowed. "Could this have been an attempt to kidnap Edward and demand a ransom?"

"I considered that, but it doesn't explain the attack on Walter. Or Miss Sullivan," John said.

The sun from the window highlighted the young woman's slim figure. The dog wasn't with her but was with Edward as he rested from his ordeal. John needed to protect her as well as his son.

Molly appeared in the doorway. "Sir, Lord Carrington is here."

"Send him in. Maybe he can make sense of this," Henry said.

A few moments later, Carrington strode into the room. His smile faded when he glimpsed their somber faces. "Has there been a death?"

Henry pointed to a chair. "Have a seat, Carrington. Someone tried to kidnap my grandson. The dog foiled the attempt."

Carrington's jaw dropped, and he sank into the chair. "Who was it?"

"If we knew that, he would already be in jail," Henry said with an edge to his voice.

"Ransom?" Carrington suggested.

"That's what we were just discussing. It seems to make the most sense," John said. He was unable to stop the instinctive roil in his gut when Carrington's eyes raked over Addie.

"I'm surprised nothing like this has ever happened before," Carrington said. "The recession has made men desperate, and it's well-known that you control the wealthy in northern California."

Clara fanned herself. "What's next? A holdup on my way to town? You must do something, Henry."

"I am," he said sharply. "As I said, I will hire Pinkerton's. They're as numerous as the redwoods. You can have one for your own carriage if you like." Henry sat back in his chair. "What are you doing here, Carrington? I didn't expect you today."

"I came to see if Miss Sullivan would care to go for a drive," Carrington said, turning hopeful eyes toward Addie.

Her cheeks grew pink. "I'm flattered, Mr. Carrington, but I'm sorry to say I must decline. Edward needs me, and I have other work I must attend to."

Carrington huffed and turned to John. "You surely aren't going to work Miss Sullivan all the time, young man."

"Of course not. She's welcome to take off any afternoon she pleases, and one whole day a week," John said, glancing at Addie. "Just please clear it with me, Miss Sullivan."

"You're very generous," Addie said, standing. "Thank you for your offer, Lord Carrington, but I'm going to be much too busy for the next few weeks for a social life. I need to devote all my free time to Mrs. Eaton's wardrobe. Now, if you'll excuse me, I need to tend to Edward."

Was that an appeal in the gaze she sent John's way? He rose and stepped to the door.

"I'll go with you," John said. He followed her out of the room and down the hall, where she stopped before they ascended the staircase. "Running from Carrington?"

She put her hands on her cheeks. "I'm sure he's a very nice man, but I have no interest in seeing him socially."

"He's considered a very good catch," John said before he could stop himself. He stood close enough to smell her honeysuckle cologne.

Her quick intake of breath told him he'd offended her. "I'm sorry. That was uncalled-for." He preceded her up the stairs. When he reached the landing, he turned and saw tears in her eyes. "I never thanked you for protecting Edward," he said.

She grasped his hand. "I already love Edward."

It was sheer force of will that kept him from showing his emotion. Her fingers tightened on his, and he could feel calluses on her palms before she pulled away and stepped into the schoolroom. She was no soft society princess, but a woman who knew what work was. So very different from Katherine.

SEVENTEEN

THE LATE-AFTERNOON SUN slanted through the windows and heated the schoolroom enough that Addie raised both windows to get a cross breeze. She was used to being outside more and being cooped up indoors so much made her long to be able to take a walk in the forest.

"Look, Miss Addie, I made an *E*," Edward said, holding up his paper. He still clutched the fat pencil. Gideon woofed his approval.

"Very good, Edward," she said. "You're doing an excellent job. I'm very proud of you." She touched his dark hair, so like his father's. It was soft and silky. Would John's feel the same?

"Make me three more of them," she said. She turned at a tap on the door and saw Molly standing there. "Good morning," Addie said, smiling at the woman.

"I brought a bit of food for you and the lad," Molly said. She carried in a tray loaded with boiled eggs, cheese, and tea.

"You're so thoughtful, Molly, thank you." Addie cleared a spot on the table, and Molly set down the tray. "How long have you worked here? I know so little about this place."

"Thirty years, miss. I came as a girl of sixteen."

"Goodness, you've been here all your adult life!"

Molly nodded. "That I have, miss. The Eatons have been good to me."

"You knew the first Mrs. Eaton," Addie said, deciding to throw out the question.

Molly stilled and took a step toward the door. "I were her personal maid when she married Mr. Eaton."

"So you knew her better than anyone else in the house," Addie said. "Who was her friend Inez?"

Molly's dark eyes looked Addie over. "How are you knowing these things, miss?"

Addie wished she could reveal it all, but did she dare? She'd felt a kindred spirit in Molly, but would the maid be quick to run to Mr. Eaton with the news?

"I found a letter in the desk," she said finally. "From Inez."

Molly's palpable tension eased. "Mrs. Inez Russell. They was best friends."

"Does Mrs. Russell still live here?" Addie asked, a plan beginning to form.

"That she does. Her husband is the haberdasher, and they live on Ferndale Street. She doesn't come here no more, but I sometimes see her at the market, and she always says hello."

"I saw a picture of Laura Eaton. She was lovely."

"She was, miss. And just as lovely inside. Always laughing and quick to help others. She volunteered at the hospital two days a week, even over Mr. Eaton's objections." She put her hand to her mouth. "I'm talking too much." She started toward the door.

"Please don't go, Molly. I'm very interested."

The woman stopped and turned back to Addie. "It don't matter now. Miss Laura has been dead and gone nearly twenty-three years."

Addie bit back the confession that bubbled up. "She had a child, didn't she?"

Molly nodded. "Little Julia. She were the sweetest baby ever borned. Red curls, dimples. Hardly never cried."

"Did you care for her?"

"Miss Laura hardly let anyone touch that child. No wet nurse, no nanny. She doted on that baby."

The hollow space in Addie's chest grew. The dim memory of soft hands and a sweet voice singing a lullaby was all she had. "She sounds quite lovely."

"Miss Laura didn't deserve—" Molly bit her lip and turned toward the door.

"Didn't deserve what, Molly? To die?"

"Don't say nothing to Mr. Eaton about my big mouth," Molly said in a low voice. "He'd fire me on the spot for gossiping like this." She stepped into the hall and pulled the door shut behind her.

What had Molly meant to say? It would have been easy enough to say Laura didn't deserve to die, but Addie sensed the maid's words had nothing to do with Laura Eaton's death. If only she had more letters. Addie had checked every drawer, and all were now empty.

Edward tugged on her sleeve. "Teacher?"

She smiled at the child. "Are you hungry, Edward?"

He shook his head. "I have to go potty."

"All right. Wash your hands when you're done, and I'll fix you a snack."

He nodded and tugged the heavy door open by himself. Addie studied the desk. She'd heard of such things as hidden drawers. Could this little desk have something like that? She pulled out the chair and seated herself in front of the desk, then opened the cabinet doors to reveal the drawers. No matter how much she pressed and tugged, the top drawers contained nothing but the velvet lining. She took out each one and checked to see that the bottom of the inside matched up with the outside. No hiding spaces here.

The remaining large drawer was what it seemed as well. She pulled it out and examined the bottom. Nothing. Before she put it away, she peered inside the cavity, but it was too dark to see much but the back. She ran her hand into the opening and traced the shape of it with her fingertips. She touched a small slit. She caught her breath and leaned forward to try to see better. If only she had more light. She managed to wedge a fingernail into the crack and tugged. It flexed but didn't open. She needed a letter opener or something with more leverage. There was nothing useful in the schoolroom, but she'd seen a letter opener in Mr. Eaton's den.

She heard Edward coming back down the hall, so she quickly slid the drawer back into place and shut the desk doors. It would be hours before she could check this again.

John paused outside the Pinkerton's branch office on the corner of Ocean Boulevard and Ferndale Street. He'd never hired a detective before, and he wasn't eager to have to do it now. He squared his shoulders and pulled open the door.

A man stood at a set of filing cabinets. A large desk took up most of the rest of the space in the room. "Good afternoon," he said. "May I help you?"

"I certainly hope so," John said, closing the door behind him. The place smelled of cigars. He put his hands in his pockets. "I need an investigation run on a young woman."

The man shook his hand. "Nathan Everest," he said. "Have a seat." He indicated the wood chair across from the desk.

"John North." John released Everest's hand and seated himself on the chair.

"Ah, Mr. Eaton's son-in-law." Everest moved to the other side of the desk and sat down. He pulled a sheet of paper to him and picked up a fountain pen. "Let me just get some information. The subject's name?"

Addie's face flashed into his mind. Was this the right thing to do? His instincts indicated she'd told him the truth about why she was here, but if he was going to protect her and Edward, he had to know more.

"Sir? The name?"

He collected himself. This would be best for everyone. "Adeline Sullivan. She came from Crescent City. I think her father was the lightkeeper up at Crescent City. It's called Battery Point. He's dead now, and her mother took over the station."

"Any other information on Miss Sullivan? Birth date, any other particulars you are aware of?"

"She's in her midtwenties, I'd guess. Right now she resides at the Eaton manor."

"What is it you suspect the young lady to be guilty of?"

"Nothing really," John said. "I just want to know more about her."

"Has she committed a crime?"

"Not to my knowledge. Though since her arrival at the manor, Walter Driscoll was attacked, and so was she. Also, someone attempted to kidnap my son this morning."

Everest's hand paused with the pen. "Do you need a bodyguard for the family?"

"I think that's been arranged. How soon do you think you'll have some information for me?"

"I have a man up that way. I'll place a call. I should have some preliminary findings in a few hours. Stop by the office in the afternoon and I'll tell you what I've learned. Will that suit?"

"Perfectly." John rose and shook the man's hand. "Thank you for your discretion."

"That's my middle name. Our business is between us only." Everest walked him to the door.

Back in the sunshine, John walked on toward Henry's offices. The transaction had left him feeling slightly unclean, though the man was pleasant and obviously competent. Pinkerton's reputation was of the highest quality. The franchise employed more investigators and guards than any other agency in the nation—some said they employed more men than the United States Army! With such a network, the agent would be able to dig out any information to be found.

At the Mercy Steamboats office, John ducked inside to ensure Henry had a bodyguard on the scene. Mrs. O'Donnell had the telephone earpiece to the side of her head and waved him past, so he walked down the hall to Henry's office.

A few feet from the office door, he heard a man say, "You won't like the consequences if I don't get my money."

Henry's shout carried loudly to John's ears. "I don't care what you do. This is not my problem. Now, get out of here."

"There are scary things that happen in the world, Eaton. Even children can get hurt."

"What?" Henry's voice rose. "What did you say?"

"You heard me. Consider yourself warned."

Moments later, a seedy-looking man in a rumpled jacket nearly bumped into John. The man's eyes glared from above a nose that appeared to have been broken many times. When he brushed past, John caught a glimpse of a gun under his jacket. He'd seen some shady organized-crime individuals in the city, and his intuition vibrated at the roughness of the man.

John couldn't imagine that his father-in-law would get involved with organized crime. When John poked his head into the office, he found Henry standing at the window and staring out over the bustling street. "Who was that man?" he asked.

Henry turned with a scowl on his face. "Nothing to be concerned about."

"It sounded as though he were trying to extort money from you."

Henry snorted. "It will be a cold day in purgatory when I give money to the likes of him." His expression cleared, and he dropped into his chair. "What brings you to town, son?"

"I wondered if you'd arranged for the Pinkerton agent. I'd thought to do it if you didn't have time."

"I made arrangements as soon as I arrived. The man should be at my estate by now."

John's brow puckered. "Could the fellow who was just here have had anything to do with Edward's attempted kidnapping?"

"I'd wondered about that myself, which was the only reason I spoke with him."

"And what was your conclusion?"

Henry picked up a pipe and chewed on the end of it. "Frankly, I don't know, but I mean to get to the bottom of it." He turned a genial smile on John. "I'm glad you're here. I'm in need of your assistance."

John had learned to be wary of Henry's congeniality. "In what way?"

"The bank is all a muddle. My manager quit without giving notice and left the books in a sorry state. I need someone with organizational skills to get it straightened out. Now that you've been here a few days, I'm hoping you're a bit bored and wouldn't mind helping me out with it. It shouldn't take you more than a few days."

"I manage supplies for the navy. I'm not a banker."

"But you know numbers and how things have to match up. You're an excellent manager. You could whip this into shape in no time. In the meantime, I would be interviewing applicants for the job."

John considered the request. He was intrigued, because working at the bank might give him the opportunity to find out what was behind the attempted extortion he'd just overheard, which might lead to whoever had dared to lay hands on his son.

"Very well," he said. "I'll help you out for a few weeks, but I have no intention of staying here permanently."

"Excellent! Let's head over there now, and I'll explain the job." He held up his hand when John opened his mouth. "I understand it's temporary, but I'm very appreciative of your assistance. Come along."

John followed him across the street and down one block to the bank. He followed Henry past the wooden counter to the hall of offices. Henry pulled out a stack of ledgers, then launched into an explanation of logging deposits and verifying withdrawals that left

John's head spinning. He jotted everything down and followed Henry to the vault, where he explained the procedures for locking it up at night. By the time his first training session was completed, it was nearly five.

"Come along, son. I'll give you a ride home."

John had seen nothing that would explain the stranger's demand on his father-in-law, but he meant to find out.

EIGHTEEN

THE FOLLOWING MORNING, Addie worked until ten on Mrs. Eaton's dress. Just before bedtime last night she had requested this afternoon off so she could go see her mother, and she had much to accomplish before noon. The basic outline of the gown hung on a mannequin, waiting to be finished. Cream lace overlaid the lilac silk that Addie had drawn up into an empire waistline. More lace fluttered from the V-neck to frame Mrs. Eaton's face and peeked from a cutout in the side of the gown and from under the hem.

The sophistication matched Mrs. Eaton's style, and the older woman was delighted with it. She'd also asked Addie to create a seaside dress and hat for the yacht race coming up in a few weeks, as well as several merry widow hats and a lingerie hat. It would be challenging to find the time to do all her benefactress wanted and still attend to Edward. She wished she'd never admitted to making her own dresses and hats.

Addie left Gideon in the schoolroom with Edward, who was copying his letters with a fat pencil. Mrs. Eaton had sent a request for her to come to the salon to discuss the final details on her dress. The telephone rang as Addie passed it in the hall. No one came running, so she picked up the candlestick phone and detached the earpiece. "Eaton Manor," she said into the mouthpiece.

A young woman's voice spoke in her ear. "This is Central. Mr. Eaton's secretary asked me to call and tell him she'd made the arrangements for his trip to Fort Bragg."

"Fort Bragg."

"He goes there twice a year," the friendly voice said. "Though it's a little sooner than usual this fall."

Addie smiled. "You must know everything, working for the switchboard."

"Oh, honey, the things I hear," the girl said.

"I'll tell him," Addie said.

"Are you new there?" the woman asked. "I don't recognize your voice."

"I'm Addie Sullivan, the new governess."

"Oh, so you're Addie. I've heard a lot about you. I overheard Mrs. Eaton tell Countess Bellingham that you make the most divine hats." The girl's voice grew eager.

"I rather like making them," Addie admitted. "From the time I was a little girl, I was making up hats with the bark from trees and ferns."

"I quite adore hats. I'm Katie Russell."

Russell. "Are you related to Inez Russell?" Addie asked, curling her fingers tightly around the phone.

"She's my mother. How do you know her?"

"Someone mentioned her name. She used to be friends with the first Mrs. Eaton."

"That's right. I've heard her talk of Laura." There was a pause. "Oh dear, I have to go. The switchboard is going crazy. I'd like to meet you sometime, Addie."

"Nice to meet you, Katie." The phone clicked off before Addie could say good-bye.

She hung the earpiece back and set the phone on the stand. So Mrs. Eaton had been talking about her. Maybe she could use the contact with Katie to meet Inez Russell.

❦

Carriages and buggies crowded the street, and Addie craned her neck to look to her heart's content. With no one along, she was free to express her wonder at all the people, shops, and excitement. It was a far cry from her former isolated life. Today she could forget that Friday was Henry's birthday ball. She dreaded having to appear.

Her afternoon off stretched in front of her with all the anticipation she used to feel waiting for her father to come from the mainland with a promised Hershey's bar. So many shops to browse through, so many plate-glass windows to gawk at!

She could try to find the Russell house.

Her anticipation died at the thought of walking up to a stranger's door and asking questions. She'd rather forget her past and enjoy the day, but the nudging desire wouldn't go away. Was it from God? She'd learned to listen to such promptings.

"Fine, God, I'll do it," she muttered. But how? All she knew was they lived on Ferndale Street. She stopped the buggy in the parking lot of the mercantile. Someone here might direct her. Lashing the reins to a hitching post, she walked across the parking lot to the side door as a man exited.

"Excuse me," she said. "Could you direct me to Ferndale Street?"

The man pushed his straw hat to the back of his head. His moon-round face was pleasant, with hazel eyes. "Sure, miss, it's the next crossroad to the south. It only goes right, toward the water. You looking for a particular house?"

"The Russell home?"

He nodded. "It's the last one on the road. Overlooks the sea. Big, gray one."

She thanked him and went back to her buggy. Driving down Ferndale Street, she noticed the houses were large and comfortable but not as lavish as Eaton Manor. The buggy slowed as the horse struggled through the potholes along the macadam road. At the top of the hill, she could see all the way out to the sea and could even catch a glimpse of the Mercy Falls Lighthouse.

Her mother was there by now. A stone lodged in her midsection at the thought of facing Josephine's disapproving stare again. She was going to have to go see her this afternoon too.

The last house was on the right. A large gray Victorian with white shutters and an L-shaped porch, the home hunkered amid a few straggly shrubs and trees. The salt and wind prevented the manicured look of the Eaton residence. She turned the horse into the dirt lane and sat there a moment trying to summon the courage to go to the door.

How would she announce she'd come to learn about Laura Eaton? What possible excuse could she give for her curiosity? "You'll have to give me the words, Lord," she whispered, clambering down from the buggy.

She smoothed her gloves and squared her shoulders before approaching the beckoning red door. A seagull squawked overhead and swooped low over evergreen huckleberry. Maybe they weren't home. She planted her foot on the steps and marched to the door. There was no bell, so she rapped with the knocker. Moments later she heard the sound of light footsteps.

A young woman about her age opened the door. Dressed in a light-gray skirt and white pin-tucked blouse, she wore a smile that welcomed Addie. Her dark hair was in a fashionable pompadour. Very Gibson Girlish.

One brow lifted. "Hello. May I help you?" Her eyes darted over Addie's shoulder to the buggy.

"I'm Addie Sullivan."

The woman's blue eyes widened along with her smile. "Addie! We spoke on the phone this morning. I'm Katie. Come in." She opened the door wider. "I assume Mrs. Eaton sent you? She could have called, but I'm so glad you came instead."

Were they expecting a message from the Eatons? "Not exactly," she said. Oh, she shouldn't have come.

"Mama will be so pleased you've come by."

Addie stepped onto the wood floor. A staircase in the entry rose to the second story. There was a doorway off the hall on both sides, and one at the back.

"We're just about to have some tea. I do hope you'll join us." Katie led her to the room on Addie's right.

Wasn't Katie going to ask why she had come or how she'd found the house? She hadn't called ahead to find out if this was their at-home day. She followed the young woman into a parlor decorated with a blue velvet settee and chairs arranged around a fireplace. The Eastlake tables were a bit heavy for Addie's taste, considering the delicate chairs. A piano occupied one corner of the room.

The woman on the settee had a throw over her legs. Her smile was as warm as her daughter's. She wore a pale-blue gown, and her hair was up in a French twist.

"Mama, this is Addie Sullivan," Katie said. "The new household member at the Eaton estate."

"I recognized the name the moment you said it," Mrs. Russell said. She put her feet on the floor and patted the space beside her on the settee. "What a delightful surprise."

Addie perched on the cushion. "I know this is quite an imposition," she began.

"Nonsense," Katie said, pouring tea into a cup. "Sugar?"

Addie nodded. "One, please." She accepted the tea after Katie stirred in the cube. "I'm sure you're wondering why I'm here," she said. There was an awkward pause, and Addie searched for a way to ask the questions burning on her tongue. "I was allowed the use of Laura Eaton's desk," she said. "It's so beautiful."

Neither of the other women remarked at her comment, and she knew it was going to be difficult to explain. Mrs. Russell might be an ally. She'd been best friends with Laura. An inner conviction grew that she needed to be honest. There was no other way to explain her appearance here.

"Maybe I should begin at the beginning," she said.

NINETEEN

ADDIE TOOK A gulp of tea so hot it scalded her tongue. Her heart hammered loud enough she was sure they had to hear.

Tell them.

She resisted the impulse to pour out her circumstances, but the compassion in Mrs. Russell's eyes held her riveted. The entire story surged to her throat. She set her tea on the table beside her. "I'm not here because Mrs. Eaton sent me. She has no idea how I'm spending my afternoon off."

The two women exchanged glances. "Is something wrong, my dear?" Mrs. Russell asked.

Addie clutched her gloved hands in her lap. "You must set aside all you think you know," she said.

"About what?" Katie peeked at her mother. They both wore puzzled frowns.

"About what happened twenty-three years ago."

Mrs. Russell's brows gathered, and she stared at Addie. "Twenty-three years ago," she said. "My daughter was born. My best friend drowned. It's a time I remember quite vividly."

Surely Laura's best friend wouldn't betray her daughter. Addie so desperately needed a friend, someone she could lean on. She held Mrs. Russell's gaze for a long moment. "I believe I am Julia Eaton."

Mrs. Russell's eyes seemed to swallow up her face. Her hand wadded up the throw on her lap. "Julia died. Drowned with her mother.

How dare you come here and say such a thing?" She searched Addie's face, and her tone lacked conviction.

"I assure you I was shocked as well," Addie said.

Mrs. Russell rubbed her forehead. "Julia. Julia was only two wh-when it happened."

"My father found a baby onshore after a horrendous shipwreck," Addie said. "He believed that baby was Julia Eaton."

"Why would he believe that?"

"Someone paid him to keep the child. Me. And he was curious enough that he subscribed to the San Francisco newspaper to read about any missing persons. I have the article about the boat going down, about the search for Laura and Julia Eaton."

"Is this some kind of plan to blackmail Henry? You should know he's a hard man to cross."

Addie shook her head violently. "I just want the truth, Mrs. Russell. You loved my mother. That's why I'm here. I have nowhere to turn, no one to help me find out what happened."

Mrs. Russell's eyes softened and grew luminous as she studied Addie's face. "You have the look of Laura in some vague way I can't put my finger on. The dimple, the eyes. Your hair color is different, but . . ." She put her hand to her mouth. "What of Laura?" she whispered.

"I don't know."

Mrs. Russell winced. "My poor Laura," she said. "She loved her baby so much."

Addie's eyes burned. "That's what I've heard. I want to know about her."

"Laura was a lovely girl. Just lovely. Full of life and fun. All the men were quite mad over her. She was invited to a party nearly every night."

"What about my father, Mr. Eaton?"

"Henry was smitten the moment he laid eyes on her. I was surprised when Laura responded to his pursuit."

"Why?"

Mrs. Russell took a sip of her tea. "He was a tradesman, and she was from money. But Henry always had big dreams, and he inspired her with his goals and plans."

Addie's pulse leaped, and she leaned forward. "My mother had the money? Not my father? I knew he didn't come from money, but I thought he had amassed a fortune by the time he met her."

"Oh my, no. But Henry knew what he wanted."

"Did he marry her for her money?"

"No, no. He was crazy in love with her. There was never any doubt about that."

Katie picked up her tea. "Where have you been all this time, Addie?"

"On a lighthouse station. North of here. My father was the light-keeper. My mother took over the job when he died of consumption five years ago."

Katie sipped her tea. "When did you find out that you were really Julia?"

"Not yet two weeks ago. The day before I came here." A lifetime ago. All she thought she knew, the memories, the heritage, was gone. Her future was just as uncertain.

"Does Mr. Eaton know?" Katie asked.

Addie shook her head. "No one knows but Mr. Driscoll. And Lieutenant North."

"Why haven't you told Henry?" Mrs. Russell asked.

Addie bit her lip. "Mr. Driscoll wants to find out who had paid for my upkeep all these years. He thought keeping quiet would be best, until we found out what was going on."

Mrs. Russell stared into space. "Laura came to me the day before she left. She said she'd discovered something terrible. Something she couldn't live with."

"Did she say what it was?"

Mrs. Russell shook her head. "She refused to tell me. She promised to write, but I never heard from her after that." Her voice grew choked, and she pulled a flowered hankie from her sleeve and wiped her eyes. Her lips thinned. "Rumors went around town that she was crazy. That girl was the most sane person I knew. Something dreadful happened. You can count on us, my dear. We will defend you with our last breath. Isn't that so, Katie?"

"Absolutely," Katie said. Her blue eyes glowed.

Why had Addie even questioned the Lord's prompting? He had always guided her. Having friends infused her with new strength.

⌒⁂⌒

What a way to end a day off. Addie would rather not have had to face her mother. The foghorn sounded as the sun sank over the ocean, and it would have been a lovely sound to Addie if she'd been sure of her welcome. The glare from the lighthouse washed out over the white foam hitting the rocks. She inhaled the salty air.

Her stomach plunged. She turned and glanced at the lighthouse. Addie waved. What would she call her now? Mama? Josephine? Addie wished she'd never come.

Her mother waved back and navigated the rocky path from the lighthouse to the buggy where they stood. "Girlie, you don't look any the worse for wear."

"I'm not," she said, hugging her mother before she could help herself. Josephine held herself stiffly as always, her arms at her sides.

"Come along," her mother said, stepping away almost before Addie had a chance to inhale the familiar scent of kerosene that clung to her mother's clothing.

Neither she nor her mother spoke until they were settled in the parlor with a plate of cookies and milk. The cookies were fresh, and she knew Josephine had made them just for her. The cold milk left a creamy taste on her tongue that banished the bitterness of facing a mother who disliked her.

"What have you discovered, Addie?" her mother asked. "Do you know yet who paid for your upkeep?"

"Not yet. Mr. Eaton is a man who demands his own way. He's married to my mother's sister, Clara." She wanted to call back the title "mother" when she saw Josephine wince. Though the woman had hurt her, Addie didn't want to cause any pain. "She enjoys the money and privilege. Lieutenant North was married to her daughter, Katherine. She died in a trolley accident three years ago."

"Does anyone suspect who you are?"

"I told John two days ago. My employer," she added.

Josephine gave her a sharp look. "John? He has given you permission to use his first name?"

She bit her lip. "Not exactly." She rushed on to change the subject. "Did you want to see me for a special reason?"

"You're my daughter. Isn't that enough?"

"You've never really accepted me as your child. That much is finally clear to me."

Josephine's lips tightened. "And I regret that. I was too harsh, girlie. Your father frowned at me from heaven."

"I tried everything to make you love me." Addie's throat closed.

Her mother sniffed. "Love can't be forced. We are too different. You have a tender heart. I fear the Eatons will try to mold you into one of them. Your father would hate that."

"I'll still be his daughter. They can't take out what he put in."

"Power has a way of corrupting, and few people are immune."

She laughed. "Power? That's hardly a situation I'll discover myself in. When Mr. Eaton finds out the truth, he'll be more likely to discharge me."

"You're his flesh and blood, Addie. That means a lot to a man like him."

"Edward is much more likely to be the apple of his grandfather's eye."

"What is your evaluation of Henry Eaton?"

Addie stiffened. What was the point of all this questioning? "He is nothing like Papa. He's loud and flamboyant. Likes all the toys his money can buy. Why, he even has an automobile! The house is filled with things. Expensive paintings and figurines. Silk lampshades and sofas. Rugs that cost the earth."

Josephine gave a disapproving *humph*. "Sounds too grand for the likes of you. Do you feel out of place?"

She considered the question. "Not really. I've been too busy trying to see what I could find out."

"It doesn't appear you discovered much."

"I will, though."

Josephine glanced at the clock, then rose. "Need to wind the light," she said.

"I'll come with you." Addie followed her out the back and to the door leading to the light tower. The metal steps clanged under their feet as they ascended. Josephine checked the kerosene light and filled it, then pulled the chain on the clockwork mechanism that rotated the lens.

"All set for two hours," she said. She squinted in the twilight. "That railing needs to be secured better. It's about to fall off."

Addie studied Josephine's face. "Why did you really ask me to come?"

Josephine pressed her lips together. "Someone broke in before I left Battery Point. Whoever it was riffled through Roy's desk. I fear it had something to do with you."

Addie raised her hand to her throat. "Was anything taken?"

Josephine shook her head. "Not money. I think some of the things Roy had saved about your situation are missing, but I'm not sure."

"They took no valuables?"

Josephine laughed. "What was there to take? I have no valuables, girlie."

"Your wedding ring and Papa's watch."

"They were in the lap drawer. The intruder left those."

The wind picked up as the sun sank in the west. Addie's dress billowed as they started back to the front of the house. "So it didn't appear to be a normal break-in," Addie pressed.

Josephine gripped her arm. "I admit I'm frightened."

"You weren't harmed?"

"I wasn't home. That's why I decided to take this station. It's closer to town and has a few more neighbors."

Addie had never known Josephine to show fear, not even in the face of a howling storm. She prayed for Josephine's safety as they walked through wisps of fog swirling about their feet.

TWENTY

BY THE TIME Addie returned to Eaton Manor, it was time for Edward's evening meal, but he wasn't in his room. Addie checked the playroom, then the bathroom. No small boy. After yesterday's scare, he wouldn't be outside. The servants now guarded the doors. Her fingers trailed along the smooth redwood of the banister on her way to the first floor. She stopped his nurse, who was carrying a basket of Edward's laundry toward the back kitchen, and asked if she'd seen Edward. The nurse told her he was in his grandfather's study.

Mr. Eaton was in the salon, having his evening claret. He would not take kindly to his grandson's intrusion. Addie went past the drawing room to the third door on the left. Mr. Eaton's study. Peeking past the open paneled door, she saw Edward seated behind the polished desk. "Edward, what are you doing in here?" she asked, approaching.

"Looking for Gideon," the boy said. "I couldn't find him anywhere." He stood and clapped his hands, and Gideon padded to him.

She held out her hand. "Come, dear, before your granddad finds you in here. I suspect he wouldn't be pleased."

A picture on a shelf of the bookcase caught her eye, one she hadn't seen last time she was in here. She picked it up. A young woman in a white dress sat on the porch steps with a small girl in her lap. Addie caught her breath and stared into the child's face. The curly hair, the wide eyes, even the dimple in the right cheek told her she was looking at herself. She saw the same dimple on the woman's face, but her hair appeared lighter and straighter, her face more rounded.

Her mother. The certainty grew along with the lump in her throat.

A locket around the woman's neck caught her attention, and Addie's fingers outlined the one nestled inside her dress. She tugged it out, and the heat of her skin warmed it in her hand. Every flourish, every detail, was as familiar to her as the lines in her palm.

Gideon whined, then began to bark. She turned from the desk in time to see the dog take hold of the waist of Edward's pants and tug him to the ground. "Edward, are you all right?"

The dog licked Edward's face, and the boy giggled. When he started to get up, Gideon nudged him, then put his paws on the lad's chest. Edward lay down, and his smile faded.

"I don't feel good," he mumbled.

She dropped to her knees beside him. "Edward?" His hand grabbed at her as his eyes rolled back in his head.

"Help! Somebody help!" she shouted. With the boy cradled in her lap, she breathed a quick prayer. Was this another episode of epilepsy or something else?

Footsteps pounded in the hall. Mr. Eaton careened through the door with his hair tousled. "What is it?" His gaze went to his grandson. "He's having a fit!" He fell to his knees and pulled the boy off her lap to lie flat on the floor.

As Mr. Eaton slid Edward away, Addie felt a pain in her neck and realized the child had her locket clutched in his hand. The chain gave way, and the pain subsided, but the necklace dangled from Edward's clenched fingers.

"There, my boy," Mr. Eaton said, smoothing the hair back from his grandson's forehead. "Wake up, Edward."

The child's eyelids fluttered, but he didn't awaken. His hand flailed, and the gold chain hit Mr. Eaton in the cheek. Addie gasped and tried to grab it, but the man's fingers pried it from the lad's fist first.

Mr. Eaton stilled as he examined the locket. "Where did he get this?" he demanded.

Addie put her hands to her throat, where the skin burned. She couldn't force a word past her dry lips. Waves of heat rose in her chest.

"It's yours?"

"It was my mother's," she said.

His fingers clenched around the locket. "Your mother's," he echoed. "Who are you?"

"Addie Sullivan."

He pried open the locket to reveal the picture inside. "This is Vera's picture in your locket." His voice was hoarse.

His eyes widened, and his gaze went back to her face. "Where did you come from?"

Should she tell him everything she knew? She eyed his tight mouth. He might throw her out. "The man I know as my father was a lightkeeper. I grew up at Battery Point." She caught herself before she revealed Mr. Driscoll's involvement. "My mother recently revealed that my father found me after a shipwreck."

Mr. Eaton gasped and reared back. "Laura," he whispered. "My dear Laura." Moisture filled his eyes.

His obvious emotion brought tears to her eyes. Everything she'd heard was true. He'd loved her mother very much, but what about her? "That necklace was around my neck."

"So you're . . . Julia?"

She swallowed past the tight muscles in her throat and searched his expression for a hint of joy. "I suspect that is so."

Sternness replaced the longing in his eyes. "Is this a scheme to take my money?" he asked. "How did you get this locket? The truth, now!"

"I told you everything I know, sir," she whispered. "My mother swears it is so. I myself have no memory of that night, though I have a dreadful fear of storms."

"It might be true," he said. He glanced at the still-sleeping Edward, then stumbled to his feet. "Your father. I must speak with him."

"He died of consumption five years ago. My mother took over for him, but she transferred to Mercy Point Lighthouse this week. Her name is Josephine Sullivan." She touched Edward's warm cheek. "What of Edward?"

"He will awaken soon. I'll send his grandmother to him. I want you to come with me."

"Yes, sir," she said. "Might I have my locket back?"

His features hardened, then he dropped the necklace into her outstretched palm.

Did his passion for her mother extend to her? She prayed it was so. Her pulse galloped at the thought that she might finally be welcomed into the bosom of the family she longed for.

⟳�֍⟲

The automobile rattled over the potholes in the dirt road that led to the lighthouse. Addie held on to her hat when the bottom of the machine dipped and swayed. Riding in this thing wasn't as much fun as she'd expected. She felt bounced like a badminton birdie. The car tore along the street at such a fast clip that she'd been hard pressed to keep the wind from ripping her clothes. She suspected they were traveling more than twenty miles an hour.

She sneaked a peek at Mr. Eaton. His jaw was grim, and both hands gripped the steering wheel. She caught him stealing glimpses of her from the corner of his eye. Perhaps he suspected she was an imposter.

He cleared his throat. "You have th-the look of Laura," he said.

"So Mr. Driscoll said."

He lapsed into silence again. The automobile lurched around a corner, then down a hill before stopping at the footpath to the lighthouse. He clambered from the automobile and extended his hand to help her down. She prayed she wasn't reading too much into the way he held on to her fingers a few moments longer than was necessary.

"This way," she said. She led the way up the hill past purple wildflowers blooming on the slopes. The waves crashed against the shore, and she drew a deep breath of salty air. In an instant, the tension in her shoulders eased, and her erratic breathing evened out. The rocky path led to the house, and she opened the door.

"Josephine?" she called.

Mr. Eaton turned to stare at her, and she realized how odd this was. She'd just told him about her parents, yet she called her mother by her Christian name. Turning from his questioning eyes, she led him across the painted board floors to the parlor. "Josephine?" she called again.

The stillness confused her. After rising at three in the afternoon, her mother was usually bustling around, polishing the lenses and preparing for another long night of tending to the light. The parlor was empty. So was the kitchen. She hurried up the steps and checked the bedrooms. No sign of her mother.

After returning downstairs, she stepped through the kitchen to the back door. Mr. Eaton followed her onto the stoop. Sea spray misted her face. The tide was rolling in, leaving flotsam on the rocks as the waves ran back to the depths, gleaming in the moonlight. She cupped her lips and shouted for her mother. No voice replied except for the squawk of two seagulls soaring in the blue sky.

"Perhaps she went to town," Mr. Eaton suggested.

She shook her head. "Not at this hour."

"Could she be down at the water? Or in the tower checking something?"

She peered toward the light tower attached to the back of the home.

"It would be unusual for her to be there now, but not impossible. I shall check. Would you like to come with me or stay here?"

"I'll escort you."

The tower would likely be accessed from upstairs. She climbed the stairs and found the access door at the end of the hall. "Josephine!" she called up the steps. Her words echoed against the round walls. "I don't think she's here."

"Shall we ascend to make sure?"

"She would have heard me." Addie studied the open network of the iron staircase but could see nothing. Mr. Eaton put his foot on the first step, then glanced at her, as if seeking permission. She nodded and followed him up the circular stairway. The metal clanged as their shoes struck the treads. The noise reminded her of a mourning bell.

The air was close and stale. As they neared the top, the scent of kerosene grew stronger, but it was carried on the wind of some fresh air. Her steps quickened, and she lifted her skirts to prevent tripping. She came up against Mr. Eaton's broad back. His arm came out and prevented her from stepping onto the platform. "What is it?" she asked.

"You stay here a moment, Miss Sullivan." He planted his other foot onto the metal floor, then disappeared from her sight.

In spite of his admonishment, she followed him. At first his bulk blocked the view of the floor where he knelt. Then he stood, and her gaze fell on the still figure there.

Josephine lay face forward. The back of her head didn't look right. Addie put her hand to her mouth when she realized that blood matted Josephine's hair. A scream tried to escape from her mouth but lodged somewhere below her Adam's apple.

"Mama?" she finally managed to whisper. She moved closer.

Mr. Eaton blocked her from reaching her mother. "I'm most sorry, Miss Eaton, but I fear she's dead."

A wave of dizziness assaulted her. "Dead? You must be wrong. Let me tend to her. I can help her."

She evaded Mr. Eaton's hands and knelt beside Josephine. When Addie touched her, her skin was cold, so cold.

It was only then that the scream managed to rip free from her throat.

TWENTY-ONE

ADDIE SAT ON the sofa with her hands clasped together. So much needed to be done. Josephine's body would need to be prepared and a casket found. The lighthouse would need to be cleaned and the parlor readied for the funeral.

Who would come? Sadly, few people knew her mother, as she was new to the area. Perhaps she should arrange a quiet burial. Her fingers tightened. Money. It would take money to bury Josephine. She supposed she had money in a bank somewhere, but the thought of digging through the Sullivans' personal affairs made her shudder. Still, it had to be done.

A cup of tea might fortify her. In the kitchen, she put loose tea in a tea infuser, then dropped it into a cup and poured hot water from the teakettle sitting on the woodstove. While it steeped, she stepped to the back door and peered out onto the lawn, where the constable stood talking to Mr. Eaton.

Mr. Eaton had taken his automobile to the neighbors for help. They'd called the constable. Addie's mind didn't want to examine why a constable had been necessary, but she forced herself to consider the circumstances.

Murder. Josephine had been murdered. Someone had hit her on the back of the head. A sob escaped her lips. Through the window she saw Mr. Eaton follow the constable toward the back door. She opened it as they neared.

Mr. Eaton's expression was grim as he shut the door behind the constable. "Ah, tea. So thoughtful of you, my dear. Three sugars, please."

She lifted the infuser from the cup and added sugar, then handed the tea to him. Her own desire for a cup of tea had vanished. "Do you know who did this?" she asked the constable.

The man removed his hands from his pockets and shook his head. His round spectacles made him look like President Teddy Roosevelt. "We will investigate, but I have little hope. The lighthouse has no near neighbors. Did your mother have any enemies?"

So he suspected murder. She forced down her nausea. "Not that I know of. She just moved here."

He glanced around. "Is there anything missing?"

"I haven't looked." She rubbed her head. "I've not been thinking."

"Would you accompany me as I look around?"

"Of course." She sent a plea toward Mr. Eaton, who was sipping his tea.

"I shall assist as well." He drained his cup, then set it on the table. "Where did your . . . she keep her money?"

Mr. Eaton didn't want to call Josephine her mother. In other circumstances, it might have been funny. "The study is across the hall from the sitting room. I'll show you."

The house seemed so empty. Their footsteps bounced off the walls and floors in an eerie tattoo. She pushed open the door to the study and gasped. Papers lay strewn on the floor, and drawers hung open. She picked up her mother's favorite globe, chipped and broken, and held it to her chest. Words escaped her.

The constable adjusted the spectacles on his nose. "It appears the perpetrator was looking for something." He picked up a sheaf of papers and began to sift through them.

Addie's head swam, and she rounded the desk to drop into the chair. The left drawer hung open. Her father's money box still lay inside.

She lifted it out and turned the key. Inside, she found stacks of money and coins.

"The murderer wasn't after money," she said, holding the box out to the constable. "When I was here this afternoon, Josephine said this had been hidden, but it's in plain view now."

"It's all there?"

"I don't know how much she had, but there's over a hundred dollars here."

Another officer poked his head in the doorway. "Sir, the coroner is here."

The constable made notes. "I'd be obliged if you would make a note of anything you find missing. I need to speak to the coroner." He exited the room behind the officer.

Mr. Eaton lifted a paper from the floor and scanned it. "Is there anything here to validate your claim as my offspring?"

Could he not bring himself to say *daughter*? "Josephine showed me some newspaper clippings. They were here in the lap drawer." She yanked it out and riffled through the contents.

He moved to stand at her right arm. "Let me see."

She sorted one more time, then leaned back. "They're not here."

He sat heavily in the chair. "Then there is no proof of your claim."

She clutched the locket in her pocket. "There is this," she said.

He fixed a stare on her. "You wouldn't be the first pretty face to try to hoodwink me."

Heat ran up her neck, but she refused to let her gaze drop. "Sir, I know nothing beyond what was told to me."

"Which was?"

"That Roy Sullivan found me on the beach."

"What else?" he prodded.

"He was paid to care for me."

She heard Mr. Eaton's quick inhalation, and her pulse ratcheted up. Of course. The person who had killed Josephine had paid for her upkeep. It made perfect sense. The culprit feared being exposed and having to face her father's wrath. "The money is still here, but the newspaper article is gone." Where else might her mother have hidden proof of their story?

She leaned forward. "This desk has a secret drawer."

Once, her father had shown her how to find the spot, and when she was a child, she used to hide under this desk and press the access tab for fun. She'd never looked inside. Kneeling under the desk, she ran her fingers over the wood until she found the button. When she pressed it, the drawer sprang open. She lifted out the tray inside, then scrambled to her feet and laid it on the desk.

Mr. Eaton hovered over her shoulder as she sorted through the contents. On the blotter she laid out a bank book, some bills, an envelope of photos, and a copy of a birth certificate inscribed with the name Julia Eaton. The birth date was Addie's own.

~❈~

John glanced at his timepiece, then returned it to its home. "You have no idea where they went?"

Clara shook her head. "They rushed out and left a message with Molly that they'd return as soon as they could. It's been hours."

John put his hands in his pockets. He could go through some files in Henry's office while he waited. Some of the numbers at the bank weren't adding up, and he needed to talk to Henry about them.

The front door slammed, and Henry's voice called, "Clara, come here."

Clara started to get up, but John shook his head. "I'll help him." He stepped into the hall and found Henry holding Addie by the arm. She swayed where she stood, and even her lips were pale.

"What's happened?" John asked. "Has there been an accident?"

Henry hesitated. "Murder," he said. "Miss Sullivan's mother was murdered at the lighthouse today."

The young woman's eyes welled with tears. John stepped to her side. "I'm sorry, Addie," he said. "Is there anything I can do?"

Her reddened eyes closed, then she shook her head. "The police are investigating."

"Where is Clara?" Henry asked.

"In the parlor."

"Come with me. You all should hear this at once." Henry led Addie into the parlor, where he seated her in a chair.

"Henry, where have you been?" Clara demanded in an indignant voice.

Henry seated himself beside her and patted her hand without glancing at her. "It has been a most extraordinary day," he said. "In many ways."

A faraway expression dimmed John's father-in-law's eyes, and he kept glancing at Addie.

"A most extraordinary thing," Henry murmured. "It appears Miss Sullivan is my daughter."

John tensed as Clara shrieked and fainted onto the sofa. He sprang to her assistance. The maid rushed in with rose water, and he dabbed Clara's handkerchief in it and ran it over her face. "Clara." He patted her cheeks.

"She'll be fine," Henry said. "You don't seem surprised, John. Were you aware of this situation?"

John rose and propped Clara's head on a throw pillow and lifted her feet to the sofa. "I was. Miss Sullivan confided in me a few days ago."

Henry glowered. "So I'm the last to know?"

"No, sir," Addie said quickly. "Mr. Driscoll knows because he found me, but I've told only Lieutenant North."

"Walter knows and said nothing? Why did neither of you tell me?"

Her eyes flashed an appeal toward John, and he sprang to her defense. "Miss Sullivan wanted more proof. She knew you would demand something more than a locket."

"She's quite right too. And we found more."

He withdrew something from his inner jacket pocket and plunked it down on the coffee table.

Three sets of eyes pinned Addie to her chair. She tried to decipher the emotion she saw in John's eyes before deciding it was compassion. She longed to clasp his hand and draw strength from him for the coming ordeal.

Mrs. Eaton had been brought around. With her complexion pale and a light sheen of perspiration on her forehead, she lay back against the cushions, uttering an occasional moan and an "oh dear."

"Buck up, Clara," Henry said. "This is quite an unusual situation, and I shall need your full attention."

She brought her lace hankie to her nose. "What nonsense is this, Henry?"

Mr. Eaton removed his jacket and unbuttoned his vest. He filled his pipe and lit it. Drawing in two quick puffs, he sighed and turned back toward his wife. "Little Julia didn't die in the shipwreck." He gestured toward Addie. "There she sits."

Addie wanted to be anywhere but here. She was aware how it appeared—as though she'd sneaked into the household under false pretenses in order to gain something from them. All she wanted was a family.

"Is this what you're claiming, Addie?" Mrs. Eaton asked. "That you're Julia Eaton?"

"I think Mr. Driscoll should be here," Addie said. "He might be able to explain it better than I." Addie heard footsteps, then Mr. Driscoll stepped into the room.

"What's going on?" he asked.

Mr. Eaton puffed furiously on his pipe. "Addie here tells me that you brought her into the house, knowing she was my daughter. Would you care to explain yourself?"

Mr. Driscoll's gaze moved from person to person. "Someone paid the lightkeeper to care for Addie. To keep her from this house."

Mrs. Eaton gasped. "Paid to keep her away? What could be the reason?"

Mr. Driscoll shrugged. "That is what I wanted to find out. I kept her true identity hidden because I feared if I brought her here, her life might be in danger."

"Her life?" Mrs. Eaton scoffed. "No one would harm her."

"Walter has a valid point," Mr. Eaton said. "After all, someone attacked her. And now someone has killed her adopted mother."

Addie stood and clutched her hands together. "What if the attack on me in the forest was deliberate and had nothing to do with Mr. Driscoll's attack?"

"We don't yet know what happened to your mother," Mr. Eaton said. "Sit down, child. You're overwrought."

Addie had seen no real sign of joy from him. No warm hug. No tears of relief. He'd simply announced her existence to the family as if she were trying to shock them. She supposed it would take a while for the truth to sink in. The last time he'd seen her, she had been a child of two. How could she expect him to entertain warm thoughts of her when for all these years he thought she was dead? She glanced at John and found him studying her with troubled eyes. Did he harbor new questions about her motives, or would he trust that she wanted nothing more than to know and love her family?

Mrs. Eaton clenched her small fist. "So you slipped into the house to spy on everyone here?"

"No!" she said. "I mean, I want to know who I am. I wanted to learn about my mother. I had no idea I wasn't Addie Sullivan until Mr. Driscoll showed up."

John focused on Mr. Driscoll. "How did you come to find Miss Sullivan?"

Mr. Driscoll gestured to Addie. "Show them the locket."

Her icy fingers found the locket in the pocket of her dress, and she held it out.

"It's just a locket," Mrs. Eaton said.

"It was Laura's," Mr. Driscoll said. "I gave it to her myself." He took the necklace from Addie's fingers. "Look. Here is her mother's picture." He opened it and showed it to Mrs. Eaton.

Mrs. Eaton stared at it. "It is Vera," she whispered. Her hands shook when she handed it back.

"Exactly," Mr. Eaton said.

"How do we know this locket didn't wash up on shore? Maybe she found it and thought it would be a suitable way to insinuate herself into the family," Mrs. Eaton said.

"How could she have known of Vera's identity or her connection to us?" Walter asked. "Also, I discovered more proof today, but let me recap how I found Adeline. A friend showed me her photographs taken on her vacation along the north shore. She was so proud of them. I indulged her and flipped through them. This picture caught my attention." He handed a picture to Mr. Eaton.

The photograph shook in Mr. Eaton's hand. "She looks very much like Laura in this."

"The lighting favors that impression. But the way she stood, the curve of her cheek. They were enough to draw me to investigate. When I met Adeline, I saw the locket and was certain."

Addie saw the picture over her father's shoulder. She'd only heard about it until now. Mr. Driscoll must have been busy gathering proof. "What did you find today?" she asked.

Mr. Driscoll reached into his pocket. "Here are two pictures of Addie. One at age three and one at eight. Compare it to the picture of Julia at two. The one in the newspaper clipping."

Addie's mouth gaped. She hadn't been aware he had them. Josephine must have supplied them to him.

John reached for the photos. His brows gathered as he studied them. "There's no doubt it's the same child," he said, passing the photos to Mrs. Eaton.

She gave them a cursory glance and handed them to her husband. "What is it you want, Miss Sullivan?"

The older woman's stiff return to a formal mode of address signaled her displeasure, and Addie clasped her hands together once more. Any hope she had for a warm reception into the bosom of her family evaporated like the morning fog.

"I'd prayed for a warm welcome," Addie managed to say past the boulder in her throat.

Mrs. Eaton dabbed at her eyes. "Of course, if we were sure you really are Julia, it would be different. I fear I don't quite believe you yet."

Mr. Eaton glowered. "How can you argue with these pictures, Clara?" He turned toward Addie with a smile. "I don't quite know what to say, my dear. But I'm very glad you're home."

When he enveloped Addie in a hug, she hardly knew how to react. She inhaled the smoky scent of his pipe tobacco and the spicy hair tonic clinging to him, then put her arms around him and hugged him back. The awkwardness grew until he released her and stepped back.

"Might I see the pictures?" she asked. When he handed them over, she stared with fascination at her younger self. Any lingering doubt she might have had vanished when she saw her three-year-old self compared to two-year-old Julia. In the older picture, she stood in the front of the lighthouse with Roy. Her gaze lingered on the father of her childhood.

Mr. Eaton held out his hand for the pictures when she was done. "We must celebrate tonight," he said. "A night on the town! I'm taking you all to dinner."

"It's been an upsetting day," Addie said. "I really am not up to it." Though Josephine hadn't really loved her, Addie still mourned.

"We'll come home early," Mr. Eaton said. "We'll dine in a private room."

She couldn't bear the thought of more scrutiny, more questions. Her head throbbed, and she had never been so weary. "Very well," she said. She smoothed her plain gray skirt. "What should I wear?" she asked.

Mrs. Eaton rose. "Come with me. I shall find you something suitable. We can't have my niece not in the very top of fashion."

"Not black," her father called after them. "This is a celebration."

It wasn't a celebration for her. It was acceptance of a sort. Though not the homecoming she'd hoped for.

TWENTY-TWO

GASLIGHTS GLITTERED OVER sparkling crystal and fine china in the private dining room at the Colony Bay Restaurant. Through the large plate-glass windows, John watched the water on the bay reflect the lights along the boardwalk. He couldn't get his mind around the fact that the beautiful young woman beside him was his wife's half sister.

Addie took a sip from her water glass. The tension radiated from her shoulders and showed in the tight press of her lips. She hadn't smiled since they'd been seated. She was a true Eaton tonight. Her hair was piled onto her head, and a tiny beret perched on her curls. The emerald gown was lavish with lace and glitter.

Several men came up to talk to Henry. "Lord Carrington, please join us," Henry said.

John wanted to roll his eyes. He watched the English lord bow over Addie's hand. The man's interest was palpable. John couldn't gauge how Addie felt. When he couldn't take any more, he rose and held out his hand to Addie. "Would you care for an after-dinner stroll along the waterfront, Addie?"

She sent a relieved smile his way, then rose and put her gloved hand on his proffered arm. "We'll meet you at the carriage later," he told Henry.

He led Addie out past the soft murmur of laughter and voices in the main salon, to the doors, and onto the waterfront. The soft waves lapped at the shore but failed to drain away the anger that had built in him through the evening. There was no reason for it. She'd confessed to him before the news came out, but watching her step into the bosom of the Eaton family sickened him. And it was all about how they'd change her. He knew what was in store for her and wished he could abort it.

He stopped under a gaslight. "It's about to begin, Addie. They'll try to make you just like Katherine. She wanted the biggest house, the most glamorous clothes, the most expensive buggy."

"Money means nothing to me, but family means everything. I never knew my sister, so her behavior has nothing to do with me."

In the wash of golden light, he studied the curve of her cheek, the shape of her eyes. "Now that I know, I'm astounded I didn't see the resemblance. You're an Eaton through and through."

She winced. "You say that as though it's a curse. You're part of the family as well. As is your son."

He touched her cheek, so soft under his fingers. "A fact I would be swift to change if I could. You're too good for them." He dropped his hand and began to walk again. He steered her toward the pier. "How will all your talk of God and praying fit in with this family whose god is possessions?"

Her gloved fingers tightened on his arm. "God is the most important thing in my life."

"I expect that to change very quickly. Henry will have plans for you. You'll be expected to live up to the Eaton name."

"I'll always be Addie Sullivan," she said. "Nothing will change that. Can't you understand my desire to know my roots?"

"They'll make it more than that, Addie. Or should I say Julia?"

She shook her head. "I don't answer to that name."

She had no idea how her life was about to change. He clasped her hand tighter. "Henry will be quick to call you Julia."

He stopped at the edge of the pier. Lanterns glowed upon the yachts out for an evening sail. The slap of the waves against the boards under their feet should have been peaceful but only contrasted with the storm of emotion he somehow kept in check. Her perfume mingled with the scent of brine. Somehow he'd begun to care about her. That was the real reason for the emotion churning his gut. Things would change now. Henry would want her to marry money, a title. John could see it coming.

She was close, so close. Her eyes widened and grew luminous in the light. He saw her hitch in a breath. Her gaze dropped to his mouth, and he knew she felt the same attraction he did.

He took her shoulders and pulled her to him. Her palms lay against his vest. He bent his head. Her lips were soft and tasted of the cinnamon apples she'd had for dessert. Her hands stole around his neck, and he drank in the sweet taste of her, the way her softness molded against him. Taking his time, he pulled her closer and deepened the passion sparking between them. Her glove moved up and cupped his face, and her breath stirred his skin.

He broke the embrace and stepped away. "We should go back."

Her kiss was untrained, and he knew she was as innocent of men as she seemed. This might have been her first kiss. And he found himself wishing he could do it all over again.

❧

The household slept. Though Addie was exhausted, she kept replaying the kiss she'd shared with John earlier in the evening. She touched her lips and swung her legs out of bed.

Her mother's desk might distract her. She made her way quietly to the schoolroom. The white paint glowed in the shaft of moonlight slanting through the window. The thought of what was in the drawer hadn't been far from her mind all evening. It seemed even more important tonight, having lost the mother who had raised her. She needed a knife or a letter opener to get it open. She slipped into the hallway. It was pitch black, and she had to feel her way down the stairs. She found a letter opener in her father's desk drawer, then returned to the schoolroom.

She turned the wick of the gaslight higher when she entered. The light chased the shadows from the room. She sat in front of the writing desk, then fit the edge of the letter opener into the crack of the hidden drawer. Patiently, she pried at the panel until it gave a bit; then she used her fingers and managed to pop it open the rest of the way.

She reached into the cavity and felt around the space. Paper crackled under her fingers, and she released it from the tape holding it in place. A simple letter in an envelope. That's all. Why would this letter be important enough to hide away? She replaced the panel, then carried the letter over to the light. The envelope was addressed in her mother's familiar looping handwriting.

To Whom It May Concern.

She stared at the words. Was this her mother's last will and testament? Addie hesitated, not knowing whether she had the right to read it. Maybe she should give it to Mr. Eaton. Or Mr. Driscoll. She flipped it over. The flap was loose on the back. Either it had come loose with the passage of time or her mother had never sealed it. She lifted the flap. The letter was right there.

She couldn't resist the temptation. Her goal here was to find out who had paid for her to be kept from her family. This could be a vital clue. She slid out the letter and unfolded it. Her mother's legible writing filled the page.

To Whom It May Concern,
    If you are reading this, then I am dead. Or worse. I fear leaving all the evidence in one spot, so I've left it in three places. Sunshine,

dust, and pigeons. If you find this, tell no one in this house. Trust no one. Remember me.

Laura Eaton

What could it mean? Addie studied the words. Sunshine. The solarium, perhaps? She glanced at the clock on the fireplace mantel. Nearly midnight. No one would be up and about. Even John shouldn't be prowling around now. She could slip downstairs and search the solarium. It was on the backside of the manor, and she should be able to turn on the lights without alerting anyone to her presence.

She stuffed the letter back into the envelope, then put it in the pocket of her dressing gown. The door creaked when she opened it, and she froze and listened for any movement or noise from the hall. Nothing but silence. She moved to Edward's room and found him peacefully sleeping. He wouldn't miss her dog for a few minutes. Gideon would alert her to the presence of anyone else, though when she heard his nails click on the wood floor, she regretted her decision.

Downstairs, all was silent except for the ticking of the great clock in the entry. She felt her way along the dark hall, past the library and the music room. The door to the solarium stood open, and she stepped inside and turned on the gaslight. The illumination eased the prickles along her back, though the great glass windows reflected the light back at her so that she couldn't see out into the yard. Anyone might be out there watching.

She told Gideon to lie down, then surveyed the space. Where might someone have hidden something that would ensure its invisibility through decades of cleanings and new arrangements? The rattan furniture had cotton cushions that would have been beaten and even replaced in the twenty-three years since Laura ran from here. A couple of tables added style to the furniture. Pots of plants and plant stands lined the windows. There were even three full-grown potted palm trees. Anything hidden in the plants would have rotted.

She turned her gaze to the table and chairs. In the Eastlake style, their ostentatious ornamentation could maybe house a hiding place. She pulled out a chair and examined it. The cushions matched the settee and were removable. She lifted up the cushion to reveal the smooth seat. Nothing there. When she turned the chair upside down, she checked the legs and the underside of the seat but found no obvious hiding place. She examined each of the chairs in turn. Nothing. The table held no surprises either.

She should just go back to bed. Rubbing her eyes, she turned to go back to her room. She noticed a music box in the corner. The mahogany case was smooth and unscratched as though it was seldom used. She lifted the lid and it began to tinkle out the tune to the "Wedding March." She closed the lid and lifted the box from the table. Carrying it to the settee, she laid it on its top and examined the underside. There was a tiny cover over something. The clockworks that turned it?

Carefully prying the cover off with a fingernail, she removed it. At first all she saw was gears and wheels. She picked up the box and held it under the light, tipping it this way and that. The light revealed the corner of a piece of paper. She wiggled her fingers into the opening and managed to snag the paper between her index and middle fingers.

The tiny scrap was rolled up tightly. She unwrapped it to reveal two handwritten words.

Insane asylum.

What on earth? What did that have to do with her mother running away?

John couldn't sleep. He kept remembering how soft Addie's lips were, the scent of her breath. He was coming to love her in an intense way he never expected, and he doubted Henry would allow them to marry. With Addie's deep desire for a family, he feared she wouldn't stand up to her father's tyranny either. If she even saw it as tyranny.

He sat on the edge of the bed and noticed a glow through the window. John's room was directly over the conservatory, and there should be no light out there at this hour. He peered out the window and realized the illumination spilled from the house. Someone was in the conservatory.

He put on his robe and slippers, then snatched his pistol from the shelf at the top of his closet before going in search of the meaning of the light. When he reached the conservatory, he found it empty and unlit. But the faint odor of the gaslight still hung in the air, and the globe was warm.

Maybe a thief was on his way out of the house with his booty. John moved quickly toward the back door and found it locked. On his way to check the front door, he noticed a ribbon of light spilling from under the library door.

He brought his gun up and flung open the door. When he saw Addie whirl to face him, he dropped the weapon back to his side. A pile of books lay on the floor at her feet. She'd taken at least fifty from the bookshelves.

He advanced into the room. "Addie, is something wrong?"

She put the book in her hand onto the top of the stack. "You frightened me."

"I'm sorry. I thought someone had broken in. What are you doing down here so late?"

He watched her as the color came and went in her cheeks, and she put one bare foot atop the other. John crossed the three steps separating them to take her in his arms. She nestled against him, her head against a heart that felt as though it would leap from his chest. Her tiny feet stood on top of his slippers, and he bent his head and kissed her again. "I'm glad I came to investigate the light," he murmured against her warm lips.

She returned his kiss, then pulled away. "There's something I must tell you, John." She colored. "I'm sorry. You haven't given me leave to use your Christian name."

"I think the first time I kissed you gave you permission for anything," he said, resisting the urge to pull her back into his arms. He would never get enough of the sweetness of her lips.

Her smile warmed the room more than the gaslight. "I found something, John. In Laura's desk." She pulled a paper out of the pocket of her dressing gown.

He took it and read it. "Your mother wrote this. 'Sunshine, dust, and pigeons.' What does that mean?"

"I found the sunshine clue in the conservatory. It was in the music box." She reached into her pocket again and pulled out a tiny scrap of paper.

He read the two words. "'Insane asylum'? What could that mean?"

"I don't know. My mother said to tell no one in this house. She obviously feared for her life. I have to know what happened to her."

He embraced her again. "Darling Addie, that was a long time ago. What difference does it make now?"

She lifted anxious eyes to him. "It's not in the past, John. Someone killed the woman who raised me. Someone paid to keep me away from here for twenty-three years."

He pulled her against his chest again. "I won't let anyone hurt you, Addie. I'll help you find out who is behind this."

"I knew you would. That's why I told you," she said against his chest. She pulled back to stare into this face. "How did my father meet Laura and then Clara?"

"He was helping his father in the blacksmith shop and met Laura's father, the senior Mr. Driscoll, who took a shine to him. Mr. Driscoll hired Henry to work at the estate, and he met Clara there. He saw Laura from a distance and was smitten. He arranged for one of her friends to vouch for him."

"Did you meet Laura's father?"

He shook his head. "He died shortly after Henry married Laura."

"What about Laura's mother?"

"She died of childbed fever after Laura was born." He dropped his hands from her shoulders. "Why all these questions, Addie? And why are you poking through these books?"

"I came in here thinking the dust clue might be in the books."

"A good guess." He released her with reluctance, then stepped over to pick up a book. "How far did you get?"

She joined him in front of the bookshelves. "Through all of them. I found nothing."

"We'd better put these back and get to bed. Tomorrow we'll figure out where to look next. We're a team."

"A team," she echoed with a smile breaking out.

But maybe only until Henry got wind of their romance.

TWENTY-THREE

ADDIE CLASPED JOHN'S hand as he escorted her toward her room. She didn't know how to cope with how John made her feel, as though her heart would gallop right out of her chest. She noticed things about him too . . . like how his hair curled at the nape of his neck, and the clean masculine scent of his skin. She wanted to kiss him again.

He stopped outside her closed bedroom door, then reached up and caught a curl around his finger. "He'll try to stop us, Addie."

"Us?" she managed to whisper.

"You're not one to play games, and neither am I. We can't deny we have feelings for each other."

"My father will have to listen to what I want," she said.

He stepped closer. "Has his response been what you expected so far? His goal in life was to marry Katherine to royalty. He nearly had apoplexy when she married me."

"He's rich. What does a title matter?"

"Henry is nouveau riche. He wants the old name to go with it. He'll try to sell you to the highest bidder."

She shifted. Her father couldn't possibly be as bad as John said. "I won't be sold." She took a step back. "I'd hoped for a warmer welcome from him and Mrs. Eaton, though. Has she always been jealous?"

He continued to wind the curl around his finger. "Clara has had a full life with Henry. They raised a child together. You're an unexpected wrinkle from the past, disrupting things. I heard Katherine mention a few times that her mother always felt Henry loved Laura best."

"Why would she think that?"

"Well, he's refused to take down that portrait in the bedroom they used to share. Walter has it now."

"What would you do if you remarried?'" she asked. "Would you remove traces of Katherine?"

His bemused smile faded, and he dropped his hand. "I have Edward to think of. He would need reminders of his mother. And that she . . . loved him."

Why had he hesitated? Of course she loved her son. "You said his condition embarrassed her, but I'm sure she adored him."

He pressed his lips together. "What society thought was most important to Katherine."

"Does Edward remember her?"

"He sometimes mentions her. I think he remembers her good-night kisses. That's about the only time he saw her."

Addie tried not to show her horror. How could a mother not care for her child, especially a wounded one like Edward? She resolved to show him even more love and compassion. But firmness too. The lad needed structure and discipline.

John was so close she could feel his body heat radiating across the few inches between them. "I'm sorry if I seem too curious."

The tenderness returned to his eyes. "You can ask me anything, darling. I have no secrets from you."

He brushed his lips across hers, then stepped back before she had time to respond. "Sweet dreams."

"Good night," she murmured, watching him retreat to his bedroom. When his door shut, she stepped into her room with a smile lingering on her face.

She took a step back when she saw her uncle sitting in the chair by the window. "Mr. Driscoll, what are you doing here?"

He rose. "I think you should start calling me Uncle now, don't you, Adeline?" He smiled.

"Yes, sir. But what are you doing?"

"Waiting on you. I want to know what you were doing in the library."

"Looking for evidence my mother hid."

"Evidence of what?" he asked, his smile fading.

The note had said to tell no one, and though she trusted her uncle, she resolved to honor her mother's request. "About why she left when she did."

"I assumed it was for a trip."

Addie shook her head. "No. She discovered some kind of devastating news. Something she couldn't handle."

"What does that have to do with who paid for your upkeep, Addie? That's our real question."

"I only care about finding more about my mother," she said, choking out the words. "I want to know what happened to make her take that trip."

Mr. Driscoll turned a kind glance on her. "She's dead, my dear. No matter what you find out about her, you can't bring her back."

Her eyes burned, and her throat closed more tightly. "I have this vague memory of my mother singing." She hummed the song. "Something about hush-a-by baby. I remember her eyes. Green with thick lashes. Her voice was so sweet, and her hands were soft."

His eyes grew moist. "She sang that all the time. Laura was an excellent mother."

"So you must understand why I want to know about her."

He put his hand on Addie's shoulder. "All you need to know is that she loved you. What else matters?"

"Did she know God? I want to know what things were important to her. I come from her, and I want to make her proud."

His hand dropped away. "It's a useless pursuit, child. Help me find out who paid for your care, and we might discover who attacked us. And who killed Mrs. Sullivan."

"Where did you get the pictures you brought today?"

"The attorney. Though he still won't tell me who has retained him, he found the pictures in a file at his home. They were the proof we needed to tell your father, so the timing was perfect."

"Do you think my father was glad to find me? He showed so little emotion."

"He was crazy about you when you were a child. I think he was overjoyed. I can't say the same for Clara."

Addie's smile faded. She liked her aunt. "I'd hoped she'd embrace me like a daughter, since Katherine is gone."

"You're a tie to Laura, and she couldn't abide her sister."

She twisted the tie on her dressing gown. "Why not?"

"Clara met Henry first. He courted her before he met Laura, but one look at the older sister, and he never noticed Clara again."

"He married her, though!"

"I think that was Clara's doing. Henry was lost, aimless when he couldn't find Laura's body. He neglected his work, didn't shave for days."

"Poor man." So much love. She had only to stir the embers and he would love her like that.

"Clara came in and ordered him to bathe and get ready to take her to dinner. To my surprise, Henry obeyed her. She dragged him out of his depression by the sheer force of her will."

"She doesn't seem the dragon sort."

He laughed. "I love my sister, but she can be a bulldog when she wants something. And she wanted Henry. I think she was determined he wouldn't escape a second time."

"She must have really loved him to do that."

"*Obsession* would be a better word. She never went out with another man, not even when Henry married Laura."

The more she was around John, the more she understood obsession. "They seem happy."

"Clara is. Henry changed after Laura died. He was always laughing, joking around. After her death, he became all business and built the town with his money and power."

What must it be like to be loved the way Henry loved her mother? Addie imagined a life spent with John at her side. Pure bliss.

"Get that look off your face, Niece," Mr. Driscoll said. "I warned you about John. He's not for you."

"Why not? I care about him. I believe he cares about me."

"For one thing, Clara would never allow it. She plans to marry him off to money and a title."

"I can't imagine why Clara would care. He's not her son."

"He's her grandson's father. That says it all."

"You said he was a philanderer. That's untrue."

"I wanted to warn you off. If you think he'll escape the future mapped out for him, you're deceiving yourself. And your father will begin to play his queen on the chessboard of life. He won't let you deny him that pleasure."

"I think I'll wait and see what the Lord has planned for us," she said.

He snorted. "Your future is what your family makes of it. Nothing divine in that calculation."

She followed him toward the door. He was so wrong. God moved them about at his will. If her Maker intended her to marry John, it would happen. If that wasn't his plan, she'd have to find a way to accept it.

❦

After he left the bank the next day, John found Clara reclining on the davenport with a damp cloth to her face. "Headache?" he asked.

"It's quite abominable."

"I'm sorry. Is there anything I can do for you?"

"Shut the curtains, if you would. The light is stabbing my eyes."

"Of course." He pulled the heavy drapes across the windows. "I'm going to town with Addie and Edward."

She pulled the cloth away and winced. "Whatever for, John?"

"I'm going to take Miss Sullivan to see the constable, and I thought I'd take Edward to visit my parents. They were away on vacation and returned yesterday. They'll expect to see us as soon as possible."

"Please get used to calling her Julia, dear boy. Henry will insist on it." She peered at him through puffy eyes. "You're not . . . interested in her, are you? That will never do, you know. Henry has plans for her already."

John's elation at the thought of a few hours with Addie and his son vanished. "What kind of plans?"

"Lord Carrington," she said. She put the cloth back on her head. "Leave me be, John. I can't talk now."

Carrington. A man much too old for sweet Addie. But she would be influenced by her father's desires. When he reached the yard, he found Edward with Addie and her dog under a redwood tree. She was lying on her back with her slippers resting on the trunk. Edward's head was on her stomach, and the dog lay with its head on its paws. Her hair hung from its pins, and his eyes traced the silken strands looped on the grass.

"My nymph," he said.

She jerked to an upright position and began tucking her hair back into its proper position. Though she sprang to her feet, bits of mud and grass clung to her skirt as a reminder of the unladylike position in which he'd found her. His smile broadened.

Edward sat with his knees clasped, and John beckoned to him. He got slowly to his feet. "Are you ready for our visit to Grandma?"

Edward scuffed his feet in the grass and grimaced. "Do I have to go, Papa?"

He steeled his voice. "Yes. Grandma would be very disappointed if I didn't bring you."

"Her house stinks."

John winced. "That's very rude, Edward. Get in the buggy." He turned his smile on Addie. "Can you bear to spend the day in my company?"

Her dimple came. "I think I can endure the suffering."

He took her hand. "I'll take you to lunch to ease the pain."

Her eyes smiled. "What about Gideon?"

"We couldn't leave our guard dog behind." He clasped his hands around her tiny waist and assisted her into the seat. The honeysuckle fragrance drifted from her skin. He lifted Edward up beside her, then whistled for the dog to leap into the back of the buckboard. John sprang onto the front seat beside them and took the reins.

The buggy clattered down the cobblestone drive to the street. He reined in the horse, then pulled onto the thoroughfare. Weekdays were normally busy in Mercy Falls, and this Thursday was no exception. Buggies and automobiles jostled for position on the narrow streets. John and Addie passed street vendors hawking food.

He reined in the horse in front of the brick police station. "Why don't you wait here and I'll see what I can discover. I'm used to dealing with officials."

The animation had drained from her face. "Thank you."

He went inside and found the officer in charge of Josephine's murder investigation. There was little the man could tell John, and he said they wouldn't be able to release the body for a few more days. John strode back to the buggy and climbed to his seat. "He'll call when we are able to pick up the body," he said. "You'll have a few more days to make arrangements."

"I still can't believe it," she said. "It seems so pointless. She knew nothing."

"You're convinced her death is related to your identity?"

"Are you not?"

Was he? He picked up the reins. "I think it's likely," he admitted. "I'm sorry you're having to deal with this."

"God is in control," she said. "I rest in that."

He glanced at her from the corner of his eye. "What was it like growing up in a lighthouse?"

"I loved it. Helping my father maintain the light, working around the property. When a shipwreck happened, he would be called upon to rescue the survivors. There often weren't any, though, and that was hard to endure."

He winced at the woeful tone in her voice.

Her gaze wandered to Edward, who leaned against her with his eyes closed. "I've been meaning to ask you about Edward. How long has he had—this condition?"

"Since he was about two."

She pleated her skirt with her fingers. "What is the cause? I know little about it."

"No one knows. It's thought to do with impulses in the brain, but they are uncontrollable."

"Has his condition stayed stable? Does he normally have as many episodes as he's endured since my arrival?"

He slapped the reins. "It's worsened a bit this year." The truth of that was like having an injury probed with a knife.

"I'll try to find an herb that will help. I shall research it." Her voice held determination.

He smiled. "My little healer. You try to fix everyone. Can you fix my heart?"

"Has someone harmed it?"

"I fear it's been irretrievably ensnared by you."

Her smile widened, and she placed her small gloved hand on his forearm. "That's a perfect state for it. I shall endeavor to keep it that way."

"And what of the state of your own heart?"

She sobered. "I fear it is as entangled as yours."

"I pray it stays that way, no matter what your father plans."

"I'm sure he has more important things to worry about than the state of my heart."

"There is nothing more important than that." The buggy entered the city limits, and he slowed the horse. "Have you had any more thoughts as to the meaning of your mother's cryptic note?"

She withdrew her hand from his arm and adjusted her glove. "I did. *Dust* could be the attic."

"And pigeons?"

She shook her head. "That clue has stumped me."

"Perhaps the labyrinth in the garden. The pigeons love the bird-bath in the middle of it."

She clapped her hands together. "The very thing! I've been meaning to explore that labyrinth and haven't had the time."

"We'll explore it together if you promise me a kiss when we get to the middle."

Color stained her cheeks. "A lady never promises any such thing."

"I might have to steal one, then."

She opened her fan and waved it, but he could see the heat spreading up her face and grinned. Had he and Katherine ever indulged in romantic banter? He couldn't remember anything like this.

TWENTY-FOUR

EDWARD BEGAN TO stir on Addie's shoulder. He lifted his head, then flopped it down with a contented smile on his face. She glanced at John from the corner of her eye. She'd noticed how the child relished his time with his father, and seeing it, Addie ached for the same relationship with her real father. Things would change soon. Her new papa would love her unconditionally, just like God.

The springs on the buggy squeaked as John shifted in the seat. Wide awake now, Edward squirmed from her lap to sit between her and John.

"We're almost to Grandma's," John told Edward.

The boy's high spirits subsided, and he leaned back against the buggy seat. Addie knew better than to ask questions about the situation with John's parents. Edward had said the house was smelly. Did John come from folks like the ones in the tenement? He seemed much too lofty to have grown up in a place like that. His military bearing seemed innate.

The buggy rolled past a sea of women in the street. "What's happening?" she asked. She craned her neck to take in the banners, which said Votes for Women and Equal Rights. "Oh, it's a suffrage march. I wonder if Sally is here?"

"Sally?"

"One of the chambermaids. She invited me to come to a meeting." She saw men in the parade as well.

"I've been to a few."

"You're in favor of voting rights for women?"

"Certainly," he said, tossing her a smile. "No one can tell me you are incapable of knowing your own mind or comprehending the issues."

She smiled back at him. "My father always said too many people are afraid to speak the truth."

"He was right." The buggy stopped in front of a butcher shop in a block of town lined with aging storefronts and cracked sidewalks. John seemed distant as he got out of the buggy and lifted his son to the street. His big hands circled Addie's waist, and she was close enough to see the gray rim around his dark eyes. She followed him into the shop where two women turned at the tinkle of the bell on the door.

Addie glanced around. Meat hung from hooks around the perimeter of the small room entirely constructed in wood, even to the slatted ceiling. More meat lay on the counter. Hams hung in the windows. The man behind the counter wore a voluminous apron that used to be white over his vest and tie. The streaks of red made her stirring hunger vanish.

"Why, it's little Johnny," an older, plump woman declared as she waited in line. "I haven't seen you in years, Johnny."

"Hello, Mrs. Gleeson," John said. An easy smile lifted his lips.

"We're so proud of you, Johnny. On a submarine! My, what an exciting life. Are you home for good?"

"No, ma'am, I'm just on leave." He pulled Addie to his side. "This is, um, Julia Eaton, Mr. Eaton's daughter."

The woman stopped short, and consternation squinted her eyes. "I beg your pardon?"

Addie extended her hand. "I realize it's confusing, Mrs. Gleeson. I'm pleased to make your acquaintance. My father thought I'd drowned some years back, but as you can see, I'm quite well."

The woman's mouth gaped. "Oh my stars." Mrs. Gleeson took Addie's hand as the customer in front of her took her packages and exited the store. Mrs. Gleeson made an obvious struggle to recover her aplomb. "Is that your boy?"

From the way she eyed Addie, the story would be all over town by lunchtime. Addie stepped back and dropped her hand to her side. Would her father be upset? But no, he'd been introducing her last night as his daughter.

John put his hand on his son's head and pulled him away from Addie's skirt. "This is Edward."

"What a fine lad. He's the spitting image of you. Your mother and father must be so proud. Isn't that so, Leo?" she called to the butcher, who stood watching them with a cleaver in his hand.

"That's right, Evelyn," the man said.

Addie studied him and realized he was John's father. They shared the same ears, finely formed and close to the head. She sent a tentative smile his way, but he remained focused on his son.

Mrs. Gleeson turned back to the counter. "I'll have two pounds of that pork loin you mentioned, Leo. Then I'll let you visit with your boy."

Addie waited for John to address his father, and when he merely moved to a corner of the room and waited, she shuffled out of the way of the door and studied the meat in the display case. Flies buzzed above it, but the glass kept them out. Fresh steaks, ground beef, and lamb lined the trays inside. The air was heavy with the smell of meat, and she understood Edward's reference to the odor in the place, though it wasn't offensive to her.

Mrs. Gleeson took her purchases wrapped in white butcher paper, then placed a final pat on Edward's head. "Don't be a stranger, Johnny," she admonished. The bell tinkled over the door, and she was gone.

"Lock the door there, Johnny, there's a good boy," his father said.

He transferred the meat to an ice chest while his son complied with his request, then beckoned to them. "Your ma is upstairs. She'll be glad to see you. Supper should be on the table shortly."

"We can't stay for supper, Pa. I was in the neighborhood and thought I'd stop by and bring Edward over to say hello."

"It's your loss, boy. Your ma is making beef stew, your favorite." Mr. North wiped his hands on the bloody apron that swathed his generous chest and stomach, then whipped it off and rolled it into a ball.

"Edward might have a taste. I don't believe he's ever had beef stew." John took his son's hand and glanced at Addie as if to say, *Come along.*

She was eager to meet the people who had raised this man she was coming to love.

❧

John had walked these narrow back steps a thousand times. His mother made sure they were spotless, and the aroma of beef stew wafted down the hall. Edward's feet dragged, and John tugged on the boy's hand. "Come along, Edward. I bet your grandma has cookies. There are always cookies in the jar."

His son's expression lifted. "Oatmeal?" he asked.

"Probably. And with raisins." He led the way through the parlor to the doorway into the kitchen, then paused and listened to his mother sing the words to "Shoo, Fly, Don't Bother Me!" The tune brought his childhood rushing back.

His mother turned from where she stood at the stove, and her ready smile came. "Johnny!" Her smile widened when she saw the boy. "And Eddie. Come give your granny a kiss."

"My name is Edward," the child said, but he tugged his hand from John's and went to give his grandmother a kiss.

John's heart swelled at the sight of his mother clasping his son to her bosom. He joined them and dropped a kiss on the top of her head. "Hi, Ma."

She released Edward, who dashed to the cookie jar sitting on top of the icebox. "Can I have a cookie, Grandma?"

"I just baked them. Help yourself. I'd rather you call me Granny, sweetheart." Her bright blue eyes etched with lines caught sight of Addie. "And who is this, Johnny? Your girl?"

Heat encased his neck. "This is Miss Addie Sullivan, Ma. She's been teaching Edward his numbers." He hesitated, uncertain how to explain her real identity.

His mother's eyes sharpened. "This is the long-lost Eaton daughter? Julia Eaton?"

The news must have traveled already. "That's right." He turned to Addie. "Addie, this is my mother, Mrs. Ursula North." He watched his son open the cookie jar. "Just one for now, Edward."

Addie pulled her hands from behind her back and came forward to take his mother's outstretched hand. "Pleased to meet you, Mrs. North."

"What a pretty little thing you are," his mother said. "We need to fatten you up some though. Would you like a cookie?"

"I'd love one, thank you." Addie dug a cookie out of the jar, her eyes roving the dining room. "You have a lovely home."

John took another look at the room he rarely noticed anymore. His grandfather had made the maple table in the middle of the room. A red and white tablecloth hid the initials he'd carved into the top when he was five, and matching fabric covered the fronts of the base cabinets along one wall. The rose wallpaper was starting to fade, and the linoleum counter as well. But everything was spotless, including the rug on the painted wood floors under the table. The old pie safe was packed with dishes and pots. He noted the new wood cookstove.

His mother smiled. "Thank you, my dear. I've been telling Johnny's father that I want to redecorate. He hasn't agreed yet, but I'm wearing him down. Where's your father, Johnny?"

"He came up ahead of us. I think he's cleaning up."

"Good. I'm about to put supper on the table. Oh, and Mrs. Eaton called. She'd like you to stop by the mercantile and pick up an order for her. Something about hats."

"It's a good thing Addie is with me, then." John heard footsteps in the hall and tensed. "Here he comes now."

His father joined them in the kitchen. "Supper about ready, Ma? I'm starving."

"Sit down, Pa. John, you and Miss Sullivan sit down. Eddie, come help your granny get the food." She took the boy by the hand. "I've got apple pie afterward."

John didn't know how to get out of the meal without hurting his mother, so he did as he was told and pulled out a chair for Addie. Her green eyes were wide, and he knew she wondered why they were here. He had the same thought as his father took the head of the table. His dad would be needling him before an hour was up.

His mother set steaming bowls of beef stew and dumplings in front of both of them. Edward carried the freshly baked bread to the table. John's father lifted the boy to his lap once Edward completed his task.

"You're a fine boy, Eddie. You should have your papa bring you over for the day, and I'll show you how to carve up a chicken. That's the first thing you need to know if you're going to be a butcher like Grandpa."

Edward stared into his grandfather's face. "I'm going to be in the navy like Papa and go on the submarines. It smells funny here, Granddad. I don't like the butcher shop."

John's gut clenched, and he rushed to intervene before his father exploded. "Great stew, Ma. The dumplings are perfect."

"Thank you, son." His mother slid into her seat at the other end of the table. "Pa, let's not have any arguments at the supper table."

Her plea had no effect. John's father's brows lowered. "Always gone, never home with your family. Parenting is more than begetting a child, Johnny. You need a trade that takes you home to your wife and kids every night."

John set Edward down. "Go eat your stew."

John took a bite but barely tasted it. He heard Addie put down her spoon.

His mother's smile had faded, too, and her face bore signs of strain. "Leo, please," she said.

His father said nothing and began to eat his stew. The air thickened, and it was all John could do to continue to lift his spoon to his lips.

His father eyed Addie. "You're teaching the boy?" he asked.

She put down her bread. "Yes, sir. Just the basics, like his numbers and letters."

"He learning them all right? I mean, his—" He broke off and glanced at his son.

"Edward is a smart lad," John said, louder than he'd intended. "He's picking it up quickly."

"I've got a dog now, Granddad," Edward said. "His name is Gideon, and he lets me know when I'm going to fall."

The older man's brows rose. "Is that right?"

"Well, I'm sharing the dog," Edward said. "He belongs to Teacher too."

"What's this about, Johnny?" his dad asked.

"Ever since Miss Eaton arrived, he's been fixated on her dog. He thinks the dog warns him before an . . . episode," John said.

"That so?" His father turned curious eyes on Addie.

"I've seen it. Gideon does seem to sense when Edward might be having a problem," Addie said.

"Don't that beat all," his father murmured. "What about school?"

"He's not ready yet," John said.

"It's a mistake to coddle the boy," his father said. "If people are going to make fun, he needs to learn it and toughen up."

John gritted his teeth to keep back the retort. He took the last bite of his stew. "Great supper, Ma. We'd better go."

"I want my apple pie," Edward protested.

"Maybe next time." He grabbed his son's hand and escaped the censure.

TWENTY-FIVE

JOHN TURNED THE horse into a lot by the mercantile. "Here we are. It's nearly closing time." He alighted and held out his hand to help her down. His broad shoulders and bowler towered over her when he set her onto the street. She took his arm, and they entered the side door of Oscar's Mercantile. John removed his hat and tucked it under his arm. The scent of cinnamon, coffee, candles, and leather tickled her nose as soon as they were inside. A counter of fabric bolts caught her eye first, and she stopped to examine them. The quality ranged from common gingham to nicer satins and wools. She picked up a thimble painted with a rose and exclaimed over it, but John's interest had been caught by a display of saddles along the opposite wall.

A middle-aged woman approached John. Her skirts rustled, and the harsh black dress she wore did nothing for her pale skin. Her yellowish-white hair had been arranged in a thin pompadour that exposed her scalp in places.

"Lieutenant North, I assume you're here to pick up Mrs. Eaton's order?" she asked in a gravelly voice.

"I am," he said. He nodded toward Addie. "This is Miss Julia Eaton. Miss Eaton, this is Mrs. Silvers."

"Oh my," the woman said, her eyes widening. "Mr. Eaton's long-lost daughter! The news of your return has spread through town. What a wonderful surprise for your father."

Addie smiled. "A wonderful surprise for me as well, Mrs. Silvers. I've longed for an extended family all my life."

"And Mrs. Eaton raved about your dressmaking ability before your identity was known," Mrs. Silvers said, taking Addie's hand. "I'm very pleased to meet you."

Addie extricated her palm from the woman's overenthusiastic pumping. "I'm sure whatever she said was an exaggeration of my poor skills."

Mrs. Silvers's gaze roamed Addie's gown and hat. "If you created what you're wearing, I must say Mrs. Eaton didn't praise you enough."

Was this how everyone would react to her now that she was known to be an Eaton? "Thank you, Mrs. Silvers."

The older woman turned. "I expect you want to see the items. Come this way."

She led them from the dry-goods department past rows of jams and jellies until she reached the wooden counter. "Here we go." She lifted a box from the back counter and placed it by the ornate cash register.

Addie peeked inside and nearly gasped. "Are those egret feathers?" She saw a flash of red. "And is that a cardinal?"

Mrs. Silvers beamed. "Yes indeed. Aren't they lovely?"

Addie put her hand to her mouth. "I'm sorry, but I don't use bird feathers on my hats. Especially not egrets and certainly not stuffed cardinals."

She couldn't look away from the poor dead cardinal until John took her shoulders and pulled her away from the counter. Her eyes burned, and she gulped. "I'm so sorry for your trouble, Mrs. Silvers, but I could not bear to touch them."

Mrs. Silvers drew herself upright. Her lips were pressed in a tight line. She lifted the box and put it on the back counter. "I went to great trouble to meet Mrs. Eaton's specifications."

"I'm sorry," Addie said again. "I'll be sure to tell Mrs. Eaton the reason we return empty-handed."

She wanted to rush from the store so she didn't have to look at the box, but if this was what Mrs. Eaton had referred to when she said she'd ordered the final trim, an alternative must be found. Addie searched the shop, sighing in relief when she spied a fitting substitute. "The velvet rosettes are beautiful. I'll take three of them. And some of that tulle."

Neither would come close to what the woman had spent for the bird and feathers. John stood with his hands behind his back, obviously clueless to what had just happened.

"No matter. I shall be able to sell the feathers to other, less sensitive, women," Mrs. Silvers managed an ingratiating smile. "Is there anything else?"

Addie shook her head, miserably aware her aunt would be unhappy. John took the bag, and she followed him outside. With the purchases stowed in the back, he helped her board the buggy.

"What was the problem?" he asked as the horse pulled them onto the street.

Addie shuddered. "I never use birds on my hats. Have you read about the bird hunts? They trap the birds, kill them, then pluck out the feathers and discard the carcass. They're slaughtered merely to adorn a vain woman's hat."

"Some women often don't care who is hurt as long as they have what they want," he said, a slight smile lifting his lips. "I fear Mrs. Silvers will never get over the affront."

Heat swept up her chest to her neck. "I'm sure it's my fault. I've grown up among seagulls and fish. They'd done little to teach me proper manners."

He laughed, a short bark full of genuine delight. "I like never knowing what you're going to say next." He slapped the reins on the horse's rump. "You realize you won't be allowed to teach Edward when Henry has a chance to think about it. I'll have to find another tutor to go with me to San Francisco."

She smoothed the glove on her hand. "I'd wondered about that. I could ask to continue, but he might say no."

"He'll certainly say no to allowing you to accompany me to the city."

"I want to get to know my family better," she admitted. "But I find I want to know you better even more than that."

The buggy exited town and entered the shadow of the redwoods. "We must see what we can do about that," he said.

❧

The painted columns of the manor glistened in the sunshine, but the view of the massive structure made Addie shudder. She had to go in and tell Mrs. Eaton she had refused the bird and feathers the woman wanted on her hat and gown.

"Are you cold?" John asked, stopping the carriage. He stepped down and held up his hand to help her.

"Not at all." She accepted his assistance. "I'm dreading telling Mrs. Eaton about the feathers."

He set her on the ground, but his hands stayed on her waist. "I assumed you'd already prayed about it."

"I did. She might not be paying attention to God." She smiled to show him she was joking. "I enjoyed the jaunt very much."

He glanced at the house, then stepped back with obvious reluctance. "Not half as much as I did." He handed her the purchases. "We could search the attic later. Or the labyrinth."

More hours spent in his company. "It's won't be dark for several hours yet. Let's examine the labyrinth."

"I think we'd better face Clara first."

She walked toward the towering porch columns, whispering another prayer that Clara would accept her decision. She sensed John staring at her. Taking courage from his concern, she carried her box of tulle and flowers inside.

The grandfather clock in the grand hall struck six. At this time of day, Clara would likely be in her study poring over menus for tomorrow. Addie navigated the labyrinth of halls to the room. The door to the study was shut. She took a deep breath and rapped on it.

"Come in," Clara called.

Addie twisted the brass knob and pushed open the door. Clara looked up from where she sat at her rosewood desk. She wore a white serge dress with blue silk piping. "Ah, Julia, you have the things I ordered? Let me see!"

Addie stepped nearer. Her tongue refused to form the words she needed, so she let Clara take the box and withdraw the items from inside.

Clara frowned and looked up at Addie. "Where are the feathers? And the bird? I ordered a cardinal. The bright splash of color will be most becoming with my skin tone."

Addie wet her lips. "I'm sorry, Mrs. Eaton. I should have mentioned it sooner. I know bird feathers and stuffed birds are quite the fashion, but I can't in good conscience use them on my creations."

Clara's delicate brows rose. "What nonsense is this? Those egret feathers cost the earth! And I ordered the size of the bird most specifically."

"The mercantile had them in, and I saw them," Addie said. "But the willful destruction of birds for vanity's sake is something I can't endure. I bought these other things instead."

Clara stamped her foot. "I don't want other things!" She tossed the tulle and ribbon flowers back into the box. "I'll be a laughingstock to go out in plain tulle."

"I keep up on all the styles. The simpler things are all the rage in Paris. If you allow me to follow my vision, you'll be on the cutting edge of fashion."

The red in Clara's face began to soften to pink. "Simpler things? What do you have in mind?"

"Fashionable women in Paris are beginning to wear turbans for night. I mentioned that to you earlier. And the day hats are larger, to frame the face. I have so many ideas." She prayed silently for Clara to listen.

"Turbans? Truly?" Clara appraised the purchased items again. "Out of tulle?"

"No, no, the tulle is for the day hat I have in mind for you. The turban will be in velvet. It's quite unusual. No one else in California will have one like it."

Clara's blue eyes widened, and a glimmer of avarice shimmered in her eyes. "I am most intrigued, Julia. Do you have a sketch?"

Addie's sigh eased from her lips. God had answered her prayer. "I'd like you to trust me and let me make it for you. It looks so much lovelier on than in a sketch. The color will be most attractive with your eyes and fair skin."

"Will it be done in time for the ball?"

"Yes, ma'am. It's nearly done already. I just need to add final touches."

Clara drew on her gloves. "Very well. Carry on with your vision, Julia."

"Thank you, Mrs. Eaton. I won't let you down."

"I trust that is the truth, my dear. I hope you realize how important this ball is to me. And to Henry. His associates from San Francisco will be here and even one of his clients from New York. I'm counting on you to make sure that if anyone's toilette is discussed with awe, it is mine." She touched her closed fan to Addie's cheek. "And perhaps you should begin to call me Mother and Henry Father. Our friends will expect it."

"Yes, Mother," Addie said, the word rolling awkwardly off her tongue.

Clara started for the door, then turned. "Oh, and Julia, one more thing. Have you anything suitable to wear yourself?"

Addie had been expecting this. Her father would want her to meet the people of his social circle. "I'm afraid not, Mother. And I have no time to make a ball gown."

"I have too many to count. We're close to the same size. Have Molly show you my closet."

"This is a masked ball, isn't it? May I purchase a mask in town?"

"I have at least ten. You may take your pick." Mrs. Eaton swept out of the room.

Shaking, Addie sank onto the settee. While the thought of attending a ball was intoxicating, she dreaded fending off Carrington. John's chocolate eyes came to mind. Dancing in his arms would be worth dealing with Carrington.

Twenty-six

Henry stopped Addie as she headed toward the labyrinth in the garden just before dusk. "Your mother informed me that you needed a dress. There is no need to wear one of her cast-offs. I want you to be the talk of the state after the ball. Buy whatever you like, my dear."

"Thank you, Father." She managed the proper address, though it was still difficult to think of him as her real father. "I don't think there is much time to find one."

"If you'd like to go to the city, I'll be happy to take you." He wagged a finger at her. "Remember, there will be royalty at the ball. Men who might be interested in an alliance with the Eaton name."

"When I marry, I wish the man to love me for myself, not for your money."

He snorted. "Such romanticism, my dear. Infatuation never lasts. Only a solid alliance. Don't you worry your pretty head about it. I'll ensure you make a strategic match."

That's what she feared the most. She managed a smile, then escaped through the kitchen to the garden. Birds chattered from the manicured trees surrounding the garden. The wind tugged strands of Addie's hair loose from the ribbon that caught it at the back of her neck. The heavy scent of roses wafted on the wind, and she inhaled it with appreciation. She missed her dog, who now spent more and more time at Edward's side. It hurt her every time she had to order him not to accompany her, but the boy needed Gideon's help.

A twig snapped, and she turned to see John approaching. He'd removed his jacket and tie and rolled up the sleeves on his white shirt. His head was bare, and he wore an eager smile. Her mind flashed to his promise to steal a kiss. "Have you been through the labyrinth many times?" she asked

He offered his arm. "Only once or twice."

"Have you any idea where to search?"

"A few thoughts." They stepped through the opening of the six-foot clipped shrubs. Flagstones paved the wide path, which meandered past banks of flowers and rock gardens.

"I love this," Addie said. "I could stay here forever." She paused at a statue of a horse. "Should we examine everything that might hold a hidden compartment?"

"That particular statue was installed only three years ago, so I believe we can forgo a study of it."

With her hand on his arm, they strolled deeper into the labyrinth. "I hope you know how to get out," she said.

"I have a good sense of direction, but I wouldn't mind being stuck in here with you for a few days."

She lifted a brow. "You might change your mind when I grow grouchy from hunger."

"Oh you're that kind of lady, eh? One who demands food?"

"Especially sweets."

"I admit I noticed how you prefer the trifles."

"Don't talk about it or I might have to go back for food."

He led her into a circular area twelve feet across. Benches and iron chairs rimmed the grass. In the center stood a fountain with a stone hummingbird rising ten feet in the air. Water gurgled from the bowl to spill over colorful rocks in a lovely pool. Speechless, she stood and drank in the scene.

"I know what you're thinking," John said. "You're wishing you didn't have your shoes on. I don't mind if you want to go wading."

Addie turned an impish smile his way. "I fear my father would highly disapprove of my tendency to shed my shoes at a moment's notice."

He grinned. "It's one of the things that endears me to you."

She removed her hand from his arm and stepped nearer the fountain. "Was this here during my mother's lifetime?"

"It was installed when the labyrinth was built in 1860. So we should examine it closely."

She glanced at her feet, then back at the statue. "The only way to go over every inch is to wade into the pool."

Amusement lit his eyes. "I shall allow you the honor, since I know you want to do it so badly."

"I think you'll need to join me. It's much too tall for me to reach to the top of the hummingbird."

"Oh, the sacrifices I make for you." He settled on the bench and yanked off his shoes.

Smiling, she sat on the grass and reached under her skirt to remove her shoes and stockings. The moist grass cooled her feet when she stood. Her dress would get damp, but she didn't mind. She tried to hold the hem above the pool and waded toward the fountain. The water splashed onto her skirt, and when she reached the fountain, she gave up the struggle to stay dry, as she needed both hands to examine the statue.

John joined her, and they poked fingers into every crevice and ran palms over every surface. Nothing. She tried to hide her disappointment as he helped her from the pool of cold water. "Now what?" she asked after they'd donned their shoes again.

He was staring at the rocks. They'd been stacked and mortared as a support for the hummingbird. He walked around to the back, and she followed. "What is it?"

"Just checking for loose mortar. Ah, let's check this." He dug his fingers into the cracked mortar of a rock and wiggled it loose. The cavity was empty.

"If she'd hidden it in a loose rock, wouldn't it have been repaired by now?"

He nodded. "Quite possibly." He gazed around the circular park-like area.

"Where does that path lead?" she asked, indicating a trail leading out of the center.

"Out of the labyrinth eventually. A labyrinth isn't the same as a maze. There are no dead ends. It's a place for reflection and prayer. A few feet along that path, there used to be a small altar and prayer bench."

"Oh, I want to see!"

He clasped her hand in his. "This way."

Her fingers curled around his hand, and she was glad she'd neglected to draw on her gloves. The warmth of his skin connected them in a new way. She nearly asked him why he hadn't stolen his kiss. They reached a small brick archway. Stepping through it, she saw a matching bench and altar surrounded by flowers. Pigeons roosted atop it.

"It's so lovely," she said. A warm breeze enveloped her when she approached the bench. The back arched to match the altar. She sat and breathed in the fragrance of the flowers. "I must come here often."

He sat beside her, and silence descended. She heard only the chirping of birds as they searched for a good hiding place. Her gaze fell on a sundial. "What about that?"

"Maybe."

They approached the sundial. It stood on a stone column embellished with carved rosettes. She ran her fingers over the stone in search of any part that moved.

"Here!" John twisted on a rosette, and the ornamentation dropped into his hand. He reached inside and withdrew a piece of paper. "Our pigeon clue!"

Her fingers trembled when she took the paper he passed to her and unfolded it. "It reads, 'Father murdered,'" she whispered.

❧❀❧

Friday morning, the cranky motor on John's 1906 Harley-Davidson didn't want to start, and he had to fight with it before drawing out the familiar *putt-putt* of the engine. He rode it to Mercy Falls. As he reached the center of town, he realized a line had collected outside the bank. Frowning, he parked the motorcycle by the front door. He climbed off and strode toward the door.

"There he is!" Mrs. Paschal cried. She rushed toward him with her hands outstretched. "Lieutenant North, I want my money."

"What's going on here?" John asked. The line stretched down the block and around the corner.

"It's my money, and you have to give it to me," the woman said, clutching at his coat sleeve.

"Of course you can have your money, Mrs. Paschal," he said soothingly. "The bank will open in forty-five minutes. I have to run an errand and I'll be right back. The tellers will be along in a few minutes."

"I want my money now!" she shrieked, grasping at him.

He evaded her hands and rushed back to his Harley. He leaped into the seat and gunned the engine, then turned back the way he'd come. He realized he was sweating, and he wiped his forehead. "I think there's a run going on at the bank," he said out loud, though there was no one to hear. "A real run."

He turned the Harley into the Eaton Manor driveway. When he stopped the motorcycle outside the house, the door opened, and Henry rushed from the manor.

He reached John's Harley. "John, where have you been? There's a run developing at the bank."

"I saw. I just came from there. Do you know what's caused this?"

Henry scowled. "The Knickerbocker Trust Company just failed. I got a telegram about it early this morning."

John winced. "We should be all right. We've got plenty of reserves." He noticed Henry wasn't meeting his gaze. "We do have plenty of reserves, Henry. No need to worry."

Addie came through the front door with her dog by her side. She knelt and rubbed Gideon's head, but her gaze lingered on John. He could feel the waves of empathy rolling from her, and it gave him strength.

Henry leaned against the doorjamb. "I loaned ten million dollars to Knickerbocker just yesterday." His voice trembled.

A loan of that magnitude! John struggled to stay calm. "Without telling me? No wonder numbers weren't adding up." He struggled to maintain his temper.

"I was going to tell you. It was a temporary loan, and I expected to recoup it with 10 percent interest."

John did calculations in his head. "That leaves us with only 5 percent reserve. We might be in trouble."

"I'm aware of that," Henry snapped. "Get over to the bank and calm them down. Tell them you'll give them part of their money today and the rest later."

"That's hardly accurate. You did this, Henry."

Henry jabbed a finger in John's chest. "It's your job to make sure we're not bankrupt by the time this day is over."

"No. It's your problem, not mine. I was only helping you out, and you know it. Besides, you won't be bankrupt. There are the other businesses. The boats, the dairies." But the bank's failure would be catastrophic to the people who had entrusted Henry with their money.

He realized Henry hadn't answered him. "The other businesses are in no danger, right?" John asked.

Henry had gone white. "They're mortgaged, son. To the hilt. If the bank fails, I fail."

John couldn't breathe. The scale of this was too huge to take in. "I see." He straightened his shoulders. Addie's future was at stake. Edward's too. "I'd better see what I can do at the bank."

Henry clutched at his arm. "This doesn't affect only me, you know. It's you and Edward." He squinted into John's face. "Julia too."

"Is this why you asked me to help out? So I could take the blame if your risk failed?"

Henry's face reddened. "Of course not. You're family. I'd hoped your oversight would see us through. Obviously I was wrong."

John's fists clenched. Henry had set him up. "You didn't even consult me about the loan to Knickerbocker. I would have advised against it."

"Precisely why I didn't mention it. If this gamble paid off, I would have been able to reestablish myself."

"Instead you've brought your family to the edge of ruin."

And Henry would be out on the street. John had seen that crowd at the bank. There would be no talking to them. "I'd better get to the bank," he said.

TWENTY-SEVEN

PEOPLE SHOUTED AND shoved one another in the bank lobby. John fought his way through the crush, then slipped into the back rooms, where two of Henry's tellers cowered in the corner.

Paul Lingel swiped a lock of hair back into place over his bald spot. "What are we going to do?" he asked in a quavering voice.

John fixed a stare on both tellers. "We're going to do business as usual. I shall go out there and try to restore order and confidence. I want both of you to be smiling and confident."

Paul straightened his tie and knocked mud from his black pants. "Yes, sir."

John took a deep breath, then strode out to the oaken counter. "Good morning!" he called, stretching his mouth into a smile. "You're all out early."

"We want our money," a beefy man in overalls said at the front of the line.

John couldn't lay hold of the man's name. "Of course. No one is saying you can't have your money, but what are you going to do with it when you get it?"

"We'll have it in our possession," the man said.

"Then what? Hide it under your mattress?" He laughed and held up his hand. "Please, friends, there is no need for panic."

"I got a telegram from my uncle," someone yelled from the back. "His bank in New York closed down, and he lost everything."

People cried out and surged toward the counter. John tried to reason with them, but they shouted him down, demanding their money. He signaled to the tellers, who came forward. Their nervous smiles would only serve to inflame the crowd.

"Please, in an orderly fashion," he called. "Panic will make things worse."

His final statement pricked the bubble of agitation, and he saw the crowd visibly relax. He allowed himself a sliver of hope until the man in overalls thrust his fist into the air.

"This is no different from 1873!" he yelled. "Banks failed all over the world." His fist came down on the counter. "Give me my money!"

Just like that, the run started. Though John tried several times to restore order, no one paid attention. The tellers began to pay out money from deposits, and the line diminished, then ballooned again. He wished he'd asked Addie to pray before he left the house. It would take a miracle to get through the run and still be solvent.

Within an hour, Paul pulled him aside. Perspiration dotted the older man's forehead. "We're almost out of cash," he whispered, wiping the back of his hand across his damp face.

"Let me look." John strode back to the vault and slipped inside. Only two stacks of money were left.

The bank had failed.

His knees gave out, and he sank onto a nearby chair. Those poor families were about to lose their life's savings. Anger burned in his belly. Henry hadn't even considered the possible effects of his actions on the people of this community. How could John go out there and tell the people that the money was gone?

He considered the ways he might pull this out yet. He might announce the bank was closing for the day rather than tell them the money was gone. But that would only postpone the inevitable. No bank would loan Henry the cash, not considering the current situation. The people waiting out there—shopkeepers, factory workers, homemakers—were going to have to know sooner or later that their worlds had shifted.

He got heavily to his feet. While Henry might prefer to avoid the situation, John wasn't going to do it. He'd speak the truth today, even if it pained him. And it did. He dreaded the disbelief and disillusionment on the faces of these anxious people.

Carrying the last two stacks of money, he returned to the counter and distributed the funds into the tellers' cash drawers. "Carry on," he said. "Let me know when the money is gone."

He watched those in line jostle for position, then step to the windows and demand their money. Reddened, fearful faces waited and watched as their turn neared. Three people served, then seven. Five minutes. Ten. It wouldn't be long now.

Paul shot a desperate glance John's way and held up his hand. John stepped into the crowd and held up his hands. "Friends, I'm sorry, but the bank is going to have to close its doors. Our cash is gone. I'm going to do what I can to call in loans to pay you, but for now, I must ask you all to leave."

The din increased to a roar. People pushed the others around them. He heard more cries for money, actual sobbing, and his gut clenched. Someone shoved him, and he struggled to keep his balance before going down into a sea of feet. Someone yanked him up, then planted a fist in his face and another in his stomach.

He welcomed the pain. A kick landed against his thigh, and the agony spread up to his waist and down to his ankle. Then another slammed into his head, and fog rolled across his vision. He fought his way through the blurry vision and reached for support. A hand grabbed his and hauled him to his feet. He reeled, and a hand seized the back of his collar and pulled him free of the kicks and punches still aimed in his direction.

"Lieutenant North, are you all right?" Paul propelled him down the hall while the other teller blocked access.

John nodded, and sharp pain circled his neck at the movement. "Thanks, Paul."

"What are we going to do now?" the older man asked.

John buried his head in his hands. "Only God knows."

Edward's inheritance was gone. Addie's too.

⌖

Addie's hands perspired inside her gloves. When the policeman had called today to tell her they were releasing Josephine's body to the mortuary, she'd called Katie to accompany her. This visit wasn't one she wanted to make alone. Addie sat on the buggy seat beside her friend and adjusted her hat.

"Is there anything I can do?" her friend asked.

"Pray for me," Addie said.

"Of course." Katie gathered her skirts and clambered down from the buggy.

Addie did the same. "Stay," she told Gideon. Edward had a cold and was napping, so she'd been allowed to take the dog. The plate glass of the mortuary windows gleamed. When she stepped inside, not a thread or a crumb was on the carpet. A light scent hung on the air. Cinnamon perhaps? A man in a suit came from the back to greet them. His muted smile added to the atmosphere of quiet competence.

"Miss Eaton?" he asked, his gaze flickering from Addie to Katie.

"Yes," Addie said. "I'm here to pay for Mrs. Sullivan's preparation."

"Of course. The body is not quite prepared yet. We only received Mrs. Sullivan from the police this morning. But if you come back tomorrow, she'll be ready."

Addie couldn't restrain a shudder at what faced her. "My friends have offered to have the funeral in their parlor. Would you deliver the casket to the Russell home?" With the preparations for the ball in full swing, having the funeral at Eaton Manor was out of the question.

"Gladly." He handed her an invoice.

She counted out the money for the coffin and embalming. "What about a burial plot?"

"I've arranged for her to be buried at the church at the top of Mercy Hill, as you requested."

"Thank you. The viewing will be Sunday and Monday. I'd like the burial to be Tuesday."

"That's all been arranged," he said in a soothing voice. "Is there anything else I can do for you?"

"I think that's everything," she said. "I appreciate all you've done."

He gave a small bow. "I'm here to serve you, Miss Eaton. Let me know if there is anything else I can do."

She murmured her gratitude and escaped into the fresh air, with Katie on her heels. She stood on the sidewalk with her chest heaving.

Katie touched her arm. "Are you all right?"

Addie nodded. "I couldn't have borne it if you hadn't been with me."

"So many things hitting you all at once," Katie said.

Addie linked arms with her friend. "Papa always said when I'm blue to find something to do for someone else. I'd like to buy some food and take it to the Whittaker family."

"I love the idea! The market is down a block. Do you have enough money?"

"I have plenty." She'd found the bankbook for the money her adoptive parents had been paid for her upkeep. The vast sum in the San Francisco bank had left her speechless. Nearly thirty thousand dollars. Unbelievable.

She and Katie filled bags full of groceries, then packed the buggy and went to the tenement row. Lifting two bags of food, Addie whistled for Gideon, then went to the front door. Climbing five flights of stairs with her burden would be a challenge, but it had to be done.

With Katie behind her, she started up the steps. Gideon ran on ahead, turning to look back at her as if to ask why she was so slow.

Huffing, she finally reached the fifth floor. She paused to drag in a lungful of oxygen, then led the way to the door. It hung open, and the smell of cooked cabbage wafted out. A child's plaintive cry tugged on her heartstrings.

"Mrs. Whittaker?" she called. "It's Addie Sullivan. Can I come in?"

When the child only wailed louder, Addie stepped through the doorway. She saw the kitchen, so she carried the bags to the table and set them down. Katie unloaded the parcels while Addie went in search of the distressed child with Gideon at her side. The dog bounded ahead, his tail straight up and his ears alert.

"Mrs. Whittaker?" she called.

The older girls would still be at work, so the child must be one of the younger ones. Addie stepped into a small bedroom. The drapes over one tiny window blocked all light from the room, and she squinted to make out a small girl crouched by the side of the bed. Addie glanced at the bed and saw Mrs. Whittaker's pale face on the pillow.

Gideon rushed to nose the little girl. The child threw her arms around the dog and cried harder. Addie knelt beside her, but the girl flinched when Addie tried to touch her. She rose and touched the woman in the bed. Mrs. Whittaker's breathing was labored, and her eyes were closed. Her color was bad. Pasty.

Addie smoothed the woman's damp hair. "Mrs. Whittaker, can you hear me?"

When there was no response, she opened the drapes and struggled with the sash until she managed to raise the window. The woman needed fresh air. She went to find Katie, who was putting groceries away in the few cupboards and the ice chest.

"Did you find her?" Katie asked.

"She needs a doctor. She's unconscious."

Katie closed the cupboard door. "I'll fetch him."

When her friend was gone, Addie went back to the bedroom. There'd been no change in Mrs. Whittaker's condition. The little girl still had her face buried in Gideon's fur, so Addie sat beside her and began to sing "In the Good Old Summertime" to her. The little one began to sniffle, and the sobs stopped. She finally lifted her head and peeked at Addie.

"Hello," Addie said, smiling. "I'm Miss Eaton. This is Gideon. We came by to help your mama. Can you tell me what happened?"

"Mama won't wake up," the child said.

Addie guessed her to be about three. "How long has she been sleeping?" Probably a useless question. A child this young had no conception of time.

"A long time. She didn't fix me anything to eat. I'm hungry."

There was nothing Addie could do for Mrs. Whittaker until the doctor arrived. "I can fix you something to eat."

"We don't got no food. My sisters went to see if the neighbors could give us some bread and milk."

"I brought some."

Addie held out her hand, and after a brief hesitation, the little girl took it. Addie led her to the kitchen and prepared the child bread and jam, then poured milk from the glass bottle in the ice box. She pulled out the rickety chair and lifted the little girl onto it to eat.

"What's your name, honey?" she asked.

"Goldie." The little girl took a huge bite of her bread and jam. She looked like a squirrel with her cheeks puffed out.

"You eat while I check on your mama." Addie went back to the woman's bedroom, where Gideon stood watch.

No change. Five children. What could be done for them? Mrs. Whittaker was going to have to go to the hospital. She needed a sanatorium, though the nearest one was in San Francisco. Someone would have to care for these children. The oldest was ten. Addie could only imagine the expression on Mrs. Eaton's face if she brought home these dirty children.

Maybe Katie could help.

She turned at the sound of footsteps and saw Katie rushing through the door with the doctor in tow. He sped back to the bedroom without asking directions, and Addie knew he'd been here before. She followed him and stood back while he examined the unconscious woman.

"I've instructed the ambulance to come," Dr. Lambertson said without turning from his patient. "I've been trying for two weeks to get Mrs. Whittaker to go in for treatment. She's in a very bad way."

"What can you do for her?" she asked, turning to view the woman's white face. If Mrs. Whittaker wasn't struggling so hard to breathe, Addie would think she was dead.

"She needs rest, good food, clean air. She won't get it here. Not with five children to feed."

Addie bit her lip. She wanted to offer to stay with the children, but she had to get home. Her family would be enraged.

The doctor straightened. "The children will have to go to the orphanage overnight at least. Maybe several weeks. And Mrs. Whittaker may not survive."

He turned a kind eye on Addie. "You'd better run along, Miss Eaton. This isn't a healthy place for you to be. Your father would have my head."

"What about the children?"

"I'll take care of delivering them to the orphanage."

It wasn't what Addie wanted. She stood in the doorway, trying to decide if she dared buck the Eaton's expectations. She was trying so hard to fit in. To be part of the family. She couldn't risk it.

TWENTY-EIGHT

THE DOCTOR STEPPED back. "I think you'll live, John."

John wasn't so sure. Every muscle ached, and his gut throbbed from the kicks. "Thanks, Doc." He slipped off the examining table.

"I'll give you a packet of pain powder. Take it with food. And rest."

"I'll try."

The doctor's smile vanished. "How bad is it, John? The bank, I mean?"

"Bad." He still hoped to be able to call in some loans and stay afloat. He'd spent two hours going over the books and trying to find a way to avert further catastrophe. The chances were slim to nonexistent.

The doctor's worried frown deepened. "Did my wife show up?"

John buttoned his shirt carefully over the bandage. "Yes, sir. She was one of the first in line. Your money is safe."

The doctor leaned his head back and sighed. "Thank you, God."

"Hundreds more weren't so lucky," John said. He put on his hat and thanked the doctor again before limping out to his buggy.

People on the street glared and stepped around him. News traveled fast, especially bad news. He suspected Henry might have already heard by the time John got back to the manor. In fact, he expected his father-in-law to be waiting for him at the door. It astounded him that Henry hadn't come to the bank.

He left the town limits behind and breathed easier as the cool shadows in the trees fell across his face. Birds chirped overhead, and the babble of the river running beside the road soothed his spirit. He wanted to hold his boy in his arms and forget today had ever happened.

Not likely he'd be allowed that privilege. Henry would want a complete description of the day and a plan of attack for pulling them all from ruin. And though John could throw it back on Henry's shoulders, the reality remained that this disaster affected his son as well.

At the manor, he turned the motorcycle over to the groom, then strode inside. The servants scurried up and down the stairs with armloads of decorations and chairs for the ballroom on the third floor. The ball was tomorrow night.

Clara greeted him at the door. She was paler than usual. "Is it true?" she demanded. "Is our money all gone?"

"The bank failed," he said.

Her lids fluttered, and she sagged. He caught her and half carried her to the sofa in the parlor. "Sally, get some water," he called to a servant he saw passing by the doorway.

He fanned Clara with his hand until Sally returned, then held the glass to Clara's lips. She swallowed, then sputtered. Her eyes opened. Daze changed to panic when her gaze locked with his.

"What are we going to do?" she shrieked. Her hands went to her hair, and she yanked on it until it came free from its pins.

"Hush, Clara." He pulled her arms down. "Henry has more assets. You'll be fine. It's the common people in town who have lost their life's savings." Even if the other businesses were mortgaged, they were bringing in money. Henry's kind always made out.

He pushed her back against the sofa. "Rest. Where's Henry?"

"On his way home." She moaned again. "We must put on a brave front. It's too late to cancel the ball."

❧

Saturday night, Addie stood in a corner of the third-floor ballroom in her borrowed finery. The space glittered with gaslight from the chandeliers and sconces around the gilded room. The gleaming wood floor bounced back the brilliance. The tray ceiling rose to a skylight that allowed moonlight to filter into the room as well.

The luxurious fabric of the dress she wore rustled with every movement. Behind her black velvet mask, she could observe without fear of people watching. She tried to imagine herself as Alice Roosevelt, confident and in control. But no amount of mind trickery persuaded her to move from her corner. Her hands perspired inside the gloves that came past her elbows.

Laughing couples swung by as the live band played. None of them looked familiar in their fancy attire and masks. She hoped no one would ask her to dance until her nervousness eased. This was her first time at a ball, and she would likely embarrass herself and her family by stepping all over her partner's feet. A sumptuous display of food was spread on white linen-covered tables along the west wall. She scanned the crowd for John but knew she wouldn't recognize him if she saw him.

Just as well. Her thoughts kept going back to the plight of the Whittaker family. She should have done more. And the entire family was in an uproar about the bank failure. John had been grim and distracted when she got back from town, though she'd longed to share her day with him. She'd seen him and her father engaged in serious conversations throughout the day, but she'd been distracted with Clara's demands for final arrangements for the ball.

Every muscle tightened when she saw Lord Carrington approaching—without a mask and dressed in his suit. She glanced away from his determined face to see if she could find help from any quarter. Behind her was a door to the hall, so she turned and slipped through it.

She heard Carrington call, "Miss Eaton." She closed the door, then rushed away.

She should never have agreed to come. Her father was going to try to auction her off to the highest bidder. Her vision blurred, and she lifted her skirts to hurry. When she heard a male voice call out behind her, she put on another burst of speed. Then she recognized it as John's voice. She turned to see him striding toward her in a black tail coat and pants and white bow tie. He wore a black velvet mask, but she would have recognized those broad shoulders anywhere.

"Not leaving so soon, are you?" he asked when he reached her.

"Lord Carrington was in pursuit," she said.

He nodded, a smile tugging at his lips. "And you ran like a rabbit."

"Like a jackrabbit," she agreed, smiling. "How did you know it was me?"

He touched a curl hanging to her shoulder. "No one else has hair like that."

His comment brought her pleasure. "Thank you. I think." She smiled up into his face.

He put her hand on his arm and turned back toward the ballroom. "It's necessary for us to face our fears. I promise to protect you."

"How easy for you to say," she said. "You aren't out of your element like I am mine. I don't even know how to dance."

"We can remedy that." He laid his right hand on top of hers, where it rested on his left arm. "I'm not the best dancer in the world, but I can waltz without breaking your toes."

"I can't give you the same promise," she said. "You'll be risking your feet if you dance with me."

"I do believe it would be worth it," he said, leading her back into the crowd.

Her father hailed her before they'd taken three steps toward the dance floor. "Julia, come here, please." He stood in his tails with Clara on one side and Lord Carrington on the other. "Lord Carrington has been looking for you."

The Englishman bent over her gloved hand. His blue eyes shone. "Please, call me Thomas," he said. "You look lovely, Miss Eaton."

"Addie," she said without thinking.

"Julia," her father corrected with a warning glint in his eye.

"It will take me some time to get used to that," she said. She caught John's smile, then bit her lip and glanced away.

"Would you care to dance?" Lord Carrington extended his arm.

Before she could admit she didn't know how, John interrupted. "We were on our way to the floor when Henry called us over," he said. "Shall we continue?" he asked her.

She placed her hand on his arm, and he led her to the center of the room. "What do I do?" she whispered.

He slipped his hand on the right side of her waist and took her left hand in his. "Follow me."

The warmth of his hand penetrated the silk layers of her dress. His spicy scent filled her head. If she leaned forward, she could put her ear against his chest. Would his heart be pounding as hard as hers?

He counted off the rhythm in her ear. "One, two, three."

Awkwardly at first, she let him guide her around the floor. Her skirt billowed around her in a most delicious way, and she couldn't stop the smile that sprang to her lips as she figured out how to do it. "I'm waltzing!"

"And quite beautifully," he said, smiling down into her face.

She rested her head against his chest and felt him wince. "Did I hurt your bruises?"

"It was a most delicious pain," he said, smiling down at her.

She stopped in the middle of the dance floor. "I have a poultice to put on them. If I'd known of your injuries last night, I could have prevented much of your pain today."

His smile widened. "Being with you is the best medicine, but I'll allow any ministrations you want to make after this thing is over."

She allowed him to whirl her around the floor again. She was out of breath by the time the dance ended. Lord Carrington came to take his turn, then another gentleman, whose name she didn't remember. She kept an eye out for Lord Carrington's reappearance, but she saw him in conversation with John. John winked at her as she danced by, and she knew he'd occupied the odious man on her behalf.

She'd first thought her attraction to John was simply because she wasn't used to male attention. But she'd had plenty of it over the past two weeks, and she still sought him out. She loved him.

TWENTY-NINE

A LADY NEVER perspired, but Addie felt a definite glow on her face after the last dance. Mr. Eaton waved her to his side again. She was happy to oblige, since he stood alone. Her dream was to find their hearts were in tune, that she was the daughter he'd dreamed of.

"Having a good time?" he asked, smiling when she reached his side.

"It's lovely. And a little disconcerting. So much attention." She flipped open her fan and waved it over her face.

"It's because you're an Eaton, Julia. Always remember that."

She nodded, her smile fading. "I'll keep that in mind."

"Lord Carrington is quite smitten."

"He's nice enough, but a bit above me."

"You mustn't allow yourself to think that way. Thomas would be a splendid match for you."

"I'm not looking for a husband, sir."

"Call me Father," he said, his voice gruff. "I've looked for you for a long time."

"Yes . . . Father." The word didn't roll off her tongue as easily as she'd hoped.

"Now, back to the Carringtons. They're an old and established English family. And rich."

"I don't care about money," she said, when it was clear he was waiting for a response from her.

"I want you to marry into a title. That's the one thing the Eatons lack. We're self-made. But with you as an English lady, the Eaton reputation can only grow."

"As I said, I'm not looking for a husband, Father."

"Of course you are. It's what every woman wants. And what could be better than a husband like Carrington? What else could you do with your time but find a good man and bear children?"

"I'd like to become a nurse," she said. Saying it out loud made her realize how ridiculous it was. An Eaton tending to the sick. He'd never allow it.

"What the devil are you talking about?" he sputtered. "The Eaton name is not an asset to be squandered. I suspect Carrington will apply to me for your hand. And I'll be happy to grant it."

She took a step back. "Surely not without my permission!"

"A father knows what is best for his daughter. You need to trust my judgment, Julia."

She met his gaze and lifted her chin. "I want to love the man I marry."

"Love," he scoffed. "Don't be so naive, child."

"You loved my mother."

His voice softened. "That I did. And you'll come to love your husband."

She wanted to tell him of her love for John, but now wasn't the time. It would take some time for her father to realize she had a mind of her own. "Yes, sir."

"Father," he corrected again.

"Father." She managed to speak without breaking down, but she longed for her room and her dog.

"Good girl," he said, his smile breaking out again. "I'll make sure of a very good match for you, Daughter."

Daughter. It soothed her heart to know he loved and accepted her. To know she finally had an extended family. It was a whole new world.

"Father, that little girl who was hurt at your garment factory—Brigitte Whittaker?"

"I did as you asked. She and her sister are toting fabric now."

"I'm so grateful. I stopped by the tenement yesterday, and Mrs. Whittaker is quite ill with consumption. I'd like to do something."

"Consumption. There's nothing much to be done for that. I forbid you to go back to that place. Full of noxious vapors and sickness." He patted her shoulder. "Put it out of your head."

She nodded, but her frown remained.

It was after midnight when the last guests filed off to their bedrooms. Most had come in from San Francisco and would be staying for the weekend. She resolved to avoid the majority of them. Lord Carrington had pressed her hand and invited her for a yacht ride on the following Friday, and she'd been forced to accept, with her father's gimlet eye on her. Though the thought of a day on the water appealed to her, she prayed there would be others on the boat as well.

One lone hall light illuminated the back stairway to the second floor. She went down the steep steps to avoid a last-minute encounter with Lord Carrington. She stepped into the second-floor hall and moved toward the sanctuary of her bedroom. John's door was open as she passed, and his light was on, but she saw no sign of him in the room. Averting her eyes for her unseemly curiosity, she scurried toward the end of the hall.

He stepped out of Edward's room as she neared it. "Addie, hold on a moment," he said, grasping her arm. "Edward has had another spell."

"Oh no!" She started to enter the room, but he blocked her passage.

"He's fine now. Sleeping with Gideon at the foot of his bed."

"I miss him," she said. "Gideon."

His eyes softened. "I imagine Henry has forgotten about finding a mate for him. I'll see what I can do. Edward would be quite taken with a puppy, and perhaps Gideon could pass along his intuition."

"I hope so, because you'll be going back to the city soon, won't you?"

"I will. I'd hoped to take you with me."

She dropped her gaze. "I'm not sure my father will allow it."

"What do you want, Addie?"

At least John used the name her soul responded to. She raised her gaze from the carpet. "I want to be with you," she said. "Such a bold thing for me to say."

He reached out and wrapped a curl around his finger. "We must see what we can do about that."

Laughing revelers rounded the hall corner and approached. He dropped his hand back to his side, and Addie fled to her room. A choice between John and her family might be fast approaching. She wanted both, which wasn't likely to come about.

❧

The overpowering scent of flowers made Addie's head ache. "It's so good of you to host Josephine's funeral," she told Katie and Mrs. Russell.

Mrs. Russell patted her hand. "My dear, it was the least I could do for my best friend's daughter." She glanced around the parlor. "A respectable attendance from the Eatons and those who do business with them."

"They were very kind," Addie agreed. She started to say they'd come only out of duty but bit back the words. It was time she learned a little discretion in her speech.

Flowers nearly smothered the room. The casket containing Josephine's body was in one corner, and even more flowers surrounded it. A table of food, finger sandwiches, and desserts had been spread for the visitors. This day would soon be over, and the undertaker would arrive to take Josephine to the grave site.

She saw a familiar top hat approaching through the window. "Oh no, it's Lord Carrington," she said. "He's been pursuing me most relentlessly."

"He's a very nice man," Mrs. Russell said. "A trifle old for you, perhaps, but wealthy and generous. I know your mother thought most highly of him."

Addie's face burned at the rebuke. "I'm sure you're right," she said. "But I'm not interested in him."

"Lord Carrington pursued your mother most persistently. He was livid when she turned him down and married your father. Thrown over for a commoner."

"But he is pursuing me. He must be quite old if he was in love with my mother."

Mrs. Russell tugged at her glove. "I often wondered if he had something to do with your mother's departure."

"What do you mean?" Addie asked.

"He came to see her two days before she left. Laura sent a note to me that night."

"What did it say?"

"That she'd learned something dreadful." Mrs. Russell shook her head. "But when she came to tea the next day, I could not persuade her to reveal what it was she'd discovered."

"She might have learned this thing from Lord Carrington."

"I've often wondered," Mrs. Russell said.

Addie tried to control her excitement. "I'm going yachting with him on Friday. I shall ask him directly."

"You think that's wise?" Katie asked. "He may not want to drag up old conflicts."

"I'll press him."

"You're such an unconventional young woman," Mrs. Russell said. "I quite admire your forthcoming spirit. You should come to the next suffrage meeting."

"One of the maids invited me," Addie said. "I haven't had time, but I'll come soon."

Mrs. Russell smiled. "You've been too busy adjusting to your new position. And spending time with the dashing lieutenant. I don't blame you. He's quite handsome."

"He's a good man," Addie said. "I sense loneliness in him. He's like the missing piece of me."

"Such a poetic thought," Katie said. "I don't know if I'll ever feel like that about a man. Sh, here comes Carrington." She extended her hand. "Lord Carrington, so kind of you to come."

"I wouldn't stay away." He pressed Addie's hand. "Have the police found who did this thing?"

She removed her hand when he would have kept it. "Not yet. They are not optimistic that they'll find the criminal."

Another couple came through the door, and Mrs. Russell hurried off to greet them with Katie in tow. Addie wanted to call at least one of them back to help her deal with Lord Carrington.

He claimed her hand again and tucked it into the crook of his arm. He led her toward the table of food. "I'm famished, my dear. What can I get you to eat?"

"Nothing, sir. I've already eaten."

"Oh, call me Thomas."

"My father taught me to call my elders sir and ma'am," she said. She barely restrained a gasp when she realized how offensive what she'd said must sound to him.

The muscles in his arm tightened under her fingers. "I realize you have your cap set for young North," he said, stopping short of the food table. "You should know there was plenty of talk when Katherine died."

"What kind of talk?"

"She was leaving him, you know."

"I know."

"Such a freak accident to be mowed down by a streetcar. Some said John pushed her in front of that car."

"I don't believe that for a moment," she said, raising her voice. She withdrew her hand and restrained herself from slapping him. "If you'll excuse me, I'd better speak to the other guests."

Shaking, she stalked off to the door in time to see John arriving on his motorcycle. She stepped from the house and went to greet him.

He dismounted and put the kickstand down. "Is something wrong?"

"That vile Carrington practically accused you of murdering Katherine! He said people believe you pushed her under the wheels of the streetcar."

His brows rose, and his eyes flashed. "I've heard that rumor." He smiled then. "Nice of you to defend me, but it's not necessary."

"It was necessary. He spoke loudly enough for others to hear him." She took the arm he offered, and they strolled toward the house.

"Carrington must have noticed our relationship."

Her fingers tightened on his arm. "Do we have a relationship, John?"

"I don't know who else gets away with being so blunt with me," he said. A smile curved his mouth.

The words *I love you* hovered on her lips, but she bit them back. He might find her amusing. Intriguing, even. But he didn't love her. Not yet. She would do everything in her power to make that happen.

"How are you doing?" he asked, studying her face.

"I miss her even though she never loved me. Now she never will." Her voice broke.

John's other hand covered hers. "I'm sorry, Addie."

"I like to hear you say my name," she whispered.

He embraced her, and she laid her head against his chest. His heart beat fast in her ear. She let herself dream that in other circumstances he might have kissed her.

"We should go in," he said, drawing her away from him.

Thursday was to be a day beyond reach of the Eaton family's expectations. Addie relished the hours that stretched ahead of her as she took a family buggy to Mercy Falls. The last few days had been gloomy as the Eatons conferred about what to do. She'd heard her father say the estate would have to be sold unless she managed to land a wealthy husband. The weight of the responsibility nearly crushed her.

At church on Sunday, Katie had invited her to dessert today at the Burnett's Confectionery Kitchen, with a promise of chocolate. Addie had eaten chocolate only a few times in her life. Her papa would sometimes bring her a Hershey's Bar from the mainland, and she would eat one square a day until it was gone. But more than the promise of chocolate, the thought of sharing the afternoon with Katie lifted her spirits.

She parked the buggy in the lot, then walked down the sidewalk to the candy store. Through the plate-glass window, she saw Katie standing at the ornate glass and oak display. The bell on the door tinkled when Addie stepped inside. Her mouth watered the moment she smelled the delicious scents inside the shop.

Katie smiled when she saw her. "I took the liberty of ordering for you. I wanted you to try my favorite. A hot-fudge sundae with pecans."

"What is that?" Addie couldn't take her gaze from the tempting array of chocolates, pralines, and hard candies.

"Ice cream with chocolate and nuts."

"Ice cream?" She'd heard of it but never had it.

Katie led her to a small wrought-iron table and chairs. "You'll see." She sat and pulled off her gloves.

Addie did the same, though she wanted to buy an intriguing candy called a Tootsie Roll. A passing contraption caught her eye. "There's John on his Harley-Davidson."

Katie twisted in her chair to stare out the window. "It makes a most dreadful noise," she said, raising her voice over the rumble. "And it appears unsafe."

"I think perhaps that's why he loves it. It's the one place he can be a boy again," she said.

She became aware that Katie was staring at her with her mouth gaping in a most unladylike manner. "Is something wrong?"

"You're in love with him?"

"What? With whom?"

"Don't play the ingenue. With John North. It's as plain as the ribbons on your hat."

Heat rose in Addie's cheeks. "He's an intriguing man."

"You're blushing! It's true. You're in love with him."

Addie turned back toward the counter. Now would be a good time for their dessert to arrive. "I don't know what love is."

"Your heart pounds when he's around. You watch for him in a crowded room. You daydream about what it's like to kiss him."

The heat intensified in Addie's face. "That's infatuation. Even I know the difference. How does one know it's love?"

Katie laid her gloves on the table. "I'm no expert, since I've never been in love myself, but I've watched my friends get married. They say that the man they love makes them want to be better than they are. That he brings out the best in them and complements their weaknesses. And they do the same to their husband."

"I don't know if it's love," Addie said. "I care about him. I want to see him learn to enjoy life. He's always so serious."

"I hope you don't get your heart broken, Addie," Katie said, her smile fading. "Lieutenant North is a dangerous man."

"Dangerous?" He was certainly dangerous to her peace of mind.

Her friend nodded. "He has such a charming way about him."

"That's hardly a negative trait."

"Perhaps not. But that doesn't negate the fact that he may not be as interested in you as he seems."

She put her hands on her cheeks. "I never said he was interested!"

"How else could he have stolen your heart? He's paid you some attention."

Was that all her feelings were? An inexperienced girl's misunderstanding of a man's attention? The proprietor placed a mouthwatering dish in front of her, but she could barely concentrate on the amazing concoction of flavors.

THIRTY

FRIDAY MORNING, ADDIE watched Edward's form on the pinto pony. She was still exhausted from the events of the past week, and the last thing she wanted to do was go for a boat ride with Thomas Carrington.

"Back straight. Heels down," she called. The horse she rode was a quick and responsive mare named Whisper. Ferns as high as trees bordered the clearing where they rode. Addie kept an eye on Gideon to ensure Edward wasn't on the verge of an attack.

"Papa will be so surprised," Edward said, his cheeks flushed. "He never let me ride before."

"He was rightly worried about you. It would be dangerous for you to become ill while on a horse. It was all I could do to persuade him to let you try."

The boy's grin stretched wider. "I can do anything with Gideon."

It was true. Since she'd arrived at Eaton Manor, she'd seen Edward's confidence grow. This latest adventure was to be a surprise for John's birthday. She glanced at her watch, a gift from Mr. Eaton. It had once been her mother's, and Addie couldn't stop admiring the diamonds and the delicate workmanship. It was nearly ten o'clock, and she had to be ready for the dreaded yachting trip at noon. Lord Carrington's staff was preparing a picnic lunch for aboard the boat.

She opened her mouth to tell Edward it was time to head back to the house, when a flock of birds rose from a bush near him. The pony reared with its eyes rolling.

Addie rode forward and snatched at the reins, but the pony evaded her. "Edward, hang on!"

The boy's knuckles were white as he gripped the reins. Then the horse bolted straight for an opening in the thick ferns. Gideon barked and followed.

"Rein him in!" she shouted. She urged her horse after Edward. The ferns and towering trees blocked out the sun. It was like stepping into twilight. She caught a flash of white and saw the pony racing toward the stream. Edward still clung to his back, with Gideon on the pony's hooves. Once the horse hit the stream, Edward's chances of being seriously injured by rocks would increase.

"Rein him in, Edward!" she screamed, urging her horse faster. "Pull hard on the reins!"

The boy straightened from his hunch over the pony's neck. She saw him yank on the reins. "Don't let up. Pull!" she yelled. Edward continued to pull on the leather. The pony began to slow, then finally stopped, his sides bellowing with exertion. Foam flecked his sides.

Addie dismounted and ran to pull Edward from the pony. "Are you all right?"

His eyes filled, but he nodded. "That pony can run fast. But I did it, Teacher. I made him stop. And I didn't fall off."

She hugged him. "I'm very proud of you. You were quite the little man."

John's voice spoke behind her. "You are quite the little man, Edward."

"Papa!" Edward released Addie and ran to this father. "Did you see me? I didn't fall off even when the birds spooked the pony."

John lifted his son into his arms. "You were very brave." He kissed Edward's cheek. "You were right," he told Addie. "He needed to learn to ride."

She clasped her hands together. "Thank you for trusting me. I want him to enjoy being a child."

"So do I."

Edward wiggled to be let down. "Miss Addie said we could go wading in the stream!"

John raised a brow. "I'd rather you didn't, Edward."

Addie curled her fingers in Gideon's fur. "You could come with us."

"Yes, Papa, you come too!" Edward tugged on John's hand.

Addie nearly giggled at the consternation on John's face. She grabbed her horse's reins and led him through the redwoods and Sitka spruce. They passed rhododendrons, huckleberry, and redwood sorrel. The roar of the waterfall grew louder until its cold spray misted her face.

"Take off your shoes," she said.

"I-I have bank figures to go over."

She only hoped he found some way out of the overwhelming pressure on her to save the Eaton family. "Everyone deserves some time off. We won't be long."

Edward took off his shoes and pulled his knickers higher. "Hold my hand, Papa," he said, pulling on his father's fingers.

With a roll of his eyes, John sat down and pulled off his shoes and socks, revealing long white feet. No calluses. He'd obviously not been accustomed to walking barefoot on the beach, as she was. Gideon barked and ran ahead of her to the water. He jumped in and snapped at the small fish swimming in the stream. He eyed a frog until Addie commanded him to leave it alone.

She waded out into the stream. "Come on in, Edward." Her skin quickly numbed from the frigid water. Minnows darted between rocks in the clear water, and larger fish swam from her splashes.

"Ooh, it's cold!" Edward waded toward Gideon. He turned to face his father. "Come on, Papa."

"I'm coming," John growled. He rolled his pants legs up a little more, then gingerly stepped into the water. He grimaced. "Boy howdy, is it cold!"

Addie giggled behind her hand. "You'll get used to it in a minute."

He still wore his bowler, vest, and jacket, but with his pants rolled up and the wonder on his face, he reminded her of a little boy dressed in his father's clothes. She leaned down and flicked cold water at him. A dollop splashed on his cheek and rolled down his neck.

His eyes went wide, then he grinned and took off his hat. He scooped up a hatful of water and started toward her. Adrenaline kicked in, and she scurried backward with her hands out. "I give, I give!"

He advanced on her. "You're not getting off that easy."

"Do it, Papa!" Edward splashed water as he practically danced along beside his father.

Gideon barked excitedly as if he approved as well. "Traitor," Addie told him.

Her feet slid on the moss-covered rocks. She threw out her hands to try to regain her balance, and John caught her arm. She clutched at him, and in the next moment, she was in his arms, and they both tumbled into the stream. Cold water filled her mouth and nose and soaked her clothing. Her water-heavy dress dragged her down, but she managed to sit up. Laughter bubbled from her throat when she saw John. His wet hair hung in his face, and his suit was soaked.

"Hungry?" She picked a flopping minnow off his shoulder and tossed it back into the water.

"That was too small to keep anyway," he said.

The current caused by the waterfall kept trying to force her back down, and she only managed to resist its pressure by holding on to John. He had his arm around her back and his hand at her waist. She was close enough to see the flecks of white in his eyes—like starbursts. A rather comfortable position, or it would have been if not for the freezing water.

"I suppose we'd better get up," she said, her head buttressed by his shoulder.

"I'm in no hurry. The damage is done." He kept his left arm around her, but dumped a frog out of his hat with his right. "You're right. The water doesn't seem so cold now." He put his hat on his knee.

"I'm sorry your suit is ruined," she said.

"It's the most fun I've had since I was a boy." His tone was wistful. "No wonder Edward loves you."

Her pulse kicked up a notch when his face came closer, but he stopped, then scrambled to his feet and held out his hand to lift her from the rushing water.

"Are we still on for the concert tomorrow night?" he asked.

"I can't wait," she said.

"You're going with Carrington today, aren't you?"

"Yes. I don't want to, but my father insists."

"Don't let him force you into anything you don't want to do, Addie."

"What would you do if your family's future depended on you?" she whispered.

He sighed and rubbed his head. "Your father has brought this on himself. What if this is discipline from God?"

"I'd never thought of that," she said. "If I intervene to save him, I could be circumventing God's will." She would have to think about this.

THIRTY-ONE

THE SEA SPRAY hit Addie's face, and she adjusted her parasol. What she really wanted to do was toss it into the sea foam. Playing this new role of lady wasn't something she relished yet. The bow of the yacht rode the waves like a champion. The steam-powered vessel had two masts and stretched over two hundred feet along the waves. The lounge chair she reclined upon pointed her toward a stunning view of the cliffs along the coast.

She'd expected others to be on board when she saw the size of the craft, but only crewmen scurried along the deck. She and Lord Carrington were the only passengers, a gaffe she wasn't sure how to rectify. If she'd known beforehand, she would have invited Katie along to chaperone.

"Comfortable?" Lord Carrington asked.

"Quite. She is magnificent."

He beamed. "I had her built two years ago. She rivals anything in the Royal Navy."

Her nose caught a whiff of roast beef. The chef would soon have dinner ready, and she prayed they could eat on deck. She didn't want to be below deck and at Carrington's mercy. She shifted on the chair and stared at the passing coast.

"You seem ill at ease, Miss Sullivan. I assure you I'm completely harmless," he said.

She turned to face him. Distinguished mustache, salt-and-pepper hair at the temples, erect posture. He appeared honorable, but what did she know of men and their motives? If her journey to find her heritage had taught her one thing, it was that she was an innocent surrounded by people of murky motives.

"Why so serious?" he asked, a dimple appearing in his right cheek.

"I learned something interesting about you."

The amusement in his blue eyes faded. "About me?"

She twirled the parasol but kept her gaze on him. "I heard you wanted to marry my mother."

"You believe in going for the jugular, I see."

"Is it true?"

He nodded. "It is. You have the look of her, you know."

"I've only seen pictures. They do a poor job of capturing her essence. Her vitality, her spirit."

"Her hair was redder than yours, and she was very fair. Your eyes are like hers, green and sparkling with life."

"You must have loved her very much."

He broke eye contact. "Enough to let her go when she made her choice."

"Did you break off all contact with her then?" Addie held her breath while she waited to see if he would lie to her.

"Yes."

Her fingers tightened around the parasol. She should have expected less than the truth, especially if he had anything to do with her mother's disappearance. "No contact at all?"

He shrugged. "She sent me a note when I was in the city about a week before she left. She asked that I come to see her. I did so."

"What did she want?" she asked, careful to keep any judgment out of her voice.

"My help. She wanted to leave."

She barely bit back a gasp. "*You* helped her leave?"

He nodded. "I've never told any other person. Certainly not your father."

"He would blame you for her death."

His gaze veered to the distant shore. "And I feel somewhat responsible. If I'd urged her to stay, would she still be alive?"

"Did she say why she was leaving?"

He hesitated. "She felt her life was in danger."

Addie's gasp escaped her throat this time. "Did she say from whom?"

He took off his hat and rubbed his forehead. "Look, Julia, this is all such a long time ago. Why go dredging up these memories now? What difference does it make?"

She snapped her parasol shut and leaned forward to grip his forearm. "Thomas, what if she was murdered?"

"She was lost in a storm."

"Her body was never found."

His lips twisted. "That's hardly unusual on the ocean, is it not?"

"No," she admitted. "But I was found on the shore, wet but fine. So where was she? How did I get there?"

"The providence of God, I suspect. What possible proof do you have for such an outrageous thought?"

"I found some letters of hers. And she left a note indicating she was fearful." She bit back the information about the clues. "I think there would have been *some* evidence that she perished on the boat, if she did," Addie said. She couldn't explain her growing belief there was more to the story than a tragic shipwreck. There was no evidence to prove her mother had even died on that boat.

She considered who might have wanted to harm her mother. Her father? But no, he'd been possessed as he'd searched for her and had changed afterward. He was too cool and collected to feign that kind of passion. What about Clara? Her sister was a formidable rival, and Clara got what she wanted after Laura died.

Thomas rose and held out his hand "Let's go enjoy that lunch the chef has prepared for us."

His candor had calmed her fears about him. She accepted his

assistance and followed him to the dining room below. It was only later she realized he never answered her question about whom her mother feared.

John unbuttoned his jacket, then buttoned it up again. The new tuxedo was a bit loose and looked better closed. He combed his hair again, then tried it on the other side. No, it was better in the normal manner. He changed it, then rubbed his face. His shave had gotten all the stray whiskers.

He straightened his tie for the third time, then picked up his hat and exited his room. Edward was playing with toy soldiers on the floor with the dog. "Good night, son," he said. "Be good for Yvonne."

"I will, Papa." Edward kissed him. "You smell good."

John tugged at his tie when his neck heated. "It's just hair tonic," he mumbled, knowing it was more than that. The saleswoman at Oscar's Mercantile had assured him the cologne was the one the women asked for most often for their husbands.

"See you in the morning." Leaving his son, he strode down the wide staircase to the entry. Women liked to make a fashionable entry, didn't they? She wouldn't be ready yet. But when he reached the front door, he found Addie waiting on the entry settee with her hands folded in her lap.

When she saw him, she rose with a brilliant smile that stole his voice. "I didn't want to be late. I'm so looking forward to this. I quite adore Scott Joplin's music. I've never been to a nickelodeon."

He wasn't quite sure what he mumbled as he offered his arm and escorted her through the door. She would be the most beautiful woman there tonight. The emerald gown brought out the color of her eyes. Auburn curls peeked from under the velvet turban she wore. A swatch of something filmy protruded from the top of the hat. The same style on Clara the other night had looked attractive, but on Addie it was elegant and breathtaking.

The carriage was waiting. He helped her inside, then climbed in behind her. The driver set off as soon as John shut the door behind them. Her perfume made him dizzy.

"Did you make your dress?" he asked.

She smoothed the folds of the skirt. "No, there wasn't time. Clara loaned it to me. She's being very solicitous now that their future hinges on me."

"You look lovely," he said.

The dimple in her cheek flashed. "You seem to have survived the dip in the stream yesterday."

"My suit didn't." He watched the light dim in her eyes and cursed his poor choice of words. "It was worth it to see Edward's enjoyment, though."

The sparkle came back to her face. "You should do it more often."

"I should," he agreed. He'd nearly kissed her yesterday. Maybe he should have. He shifted on the seat. "I want no secrets between us, so I want you to know I've done some investigating."

"Of me?"

He nodded. "I made the decision before I knew you as well as I do now. I'm sorry if you find it offensive. I have a son to protect. And I find I want to protect you as well."

A cardinal flitted from a redwood tree, and she watched its path. "And what did you find out?"

"Everyone in Crescent City spoke of you and your parents most highly."

She put her hands to her hot cheeks. "I hardly knew the townspeople. What must they think to be asked such questions? What could they possibly have to say?" Straightening in her seat, she turned to stare at him.

"That you're an angel in skirts. Taking food to the poor, mending clothing for free, ministering to the sick when you weren't working hard on your parents' behalf." He smiled. "They say your father told glowing stories. Exactly my impression of you. I'm relieved. But I'm afraid it brings us no closer to helping you figure out who attacked you or paid for your upkeep."

Addie slipped her hand into his. "Tonight, let's think of happier things."

The happiest thing he could imagine would be to have her at his side for the rest of his life. The errant thought nearly made him gasp. He'd realized his attraction, but it was only now that he understood how deep it went.

The carriage pulled up in front of the nickelodeon. Women in colorful dresses on the arms of men dressed in tuxedos streamed toward the entrance. The driver opened the door, and John stepped down onto the street, then helped Addie out. He straightened when he saw the admiring glances other men threw her way. Her eyes were wide as she took in everything: velvet seats and curtains, gilded ceiling, ornately carved railings. The level of excitement in the audience created a rising hum of conversation.

He stopped to introduce her to the mayor, several society women, and a couple of Henry's employees before they found their box seat in the balcony. Once the drapes behind them were closed, he settled beside her and planned to watch her reaction to the ragtime music.

The audience thundered its approval of Willie Richards. The handsome man of color bowed, then took his place at the piano. He first thundered out "Maple Leaf Rag," and John's foot kept time to the music.

"He's quite extraordinary," he whispered to Addie, who was lost in the music.

She gripped the oaken railing in front of her, and he thought she might leap over the balcony. At least that's the reason he told himself it was all right to take her gloved hand. She only removed it long enough to clap at the end of the number, then slipped her hand back into his in a natural movement that touched him.

Her fingers tightened on his when Richards began to play "The Entertainer." "It's my favorite," she whispered.

John paid more attention to Addie than he did the music. The concert was over much too soon. He had her wait with him in the box until most of the crowd cleared out, then led her down to meet the musician. He stood back, smiling as she gushed her enthusiasm to the pianist. When John finally led her back to the carriage, her hat was askew, and high color lodged in her cheeks.

He helped her inside the carriage, then told the driver to take them for a ride along the seaside before heading home. When he settled beside her on the leather seat, she slipped her hand into his.

Her eyes shone in the moonlight. "Thank you for a night I'll never forget," she said. "It was quite wonderful, John." Her lips parted in a gleaming smile.

He leaned closer until their breaths mingled. "I'm glad you enjoyed it."

Her face was turned up to his. He shouldn't find her so tempting, but he did. He drew his fingers across her cheek. It was soft as the velvet in her hat. He bent his head and brushed her lips with his. She inhaled and went rigid.

"Don't be afraid," he murmured. "I won't hurt you." He kissed her again, pulling her more firmly into his arms.

One gloved hand lodged against his chest. The other arm stole around his neck. The sweetness and purity of her lips was like nothing he'd ever dreamed of or imagined. He deepened the kiss and realized how deeply he'd fallen in love with her. Not because she was an Eaton, but because she was Addie. Delightful, laughing Addie.

He pulled away and smiled into her half-closed eyes. The heady fragrance of her hair, her skin, filled his head. Words of love hovered on his lips, but he held them back. It was too soon. He might frighten her.

Her eyes came open, then her fingers crept to her lips. "You kissed me," she said. "I dreamed you might tonight."

His heart stuttered, then leaped to a steady rhythm again. "I should say I'm sorry, but I'm not."

She touched his cheek. "I wondered what love felt like," she said. "Now I know."

He crushed her to his chest again. There was no pretense with her. He kissed her again, not caring to hold back the depth of his love.

His breathing was ragged when he raised his head. "Oh Addie, Addie, what did I do before you came into my life?"

Tears shone on her lashes. "I don't think I lived before tonight."

"We must be married. Quite soon, darling girl. I can't wait for long."

"I'd marry you tonight," she said. "Right now."

He traced the curve of her cheek with his finger. "I'll ask your father for your hand tonight."

A shadow darkened the joy in her eyes. "What about Lord Carrington?"

"What about him?"

"Father seems quite set on a match with him." She wet her lips. "I've been thinking about what you said. That God might be disciplining him. You might be right."

The shadow didn't leave her eyes, and the fear in her face spread to him. Henry had to consent.

THIRTY-TWO

ADDIE KEPT TOUCHING her fingertips to her lips on the ride back to the manor. John loved her! She couldn't take it in. Her lips felt fuller, softer. Different. She was going to be married. Life could change just that fast. She couldn't wait to tell Katie. Her father had to agree. He just had to. His own daughter would be the new mother of his grandson. What more could he want?

John kissed her quickly when the carriage stopped in front of the manor. "I'll talk to your father now."

"I'd like to be there. Is that allowed?"

"It's not usual," he said. "But I can't deny you anything tonight."

Her heart would not stop its insistent knocking against her ribs. "I'm so happy," she whispered.

He clambered down and held out his hand. "I'll do my best to keep you that way," he said, his eyes smiling.

She looped her arm through his and allowed him to lead her toward the house. "That's Lord Carrington's brougham," she said.

"Perhaps he'll leave soon so we can talk to your father." He opened the door for her.

The flowers on the entry table perfumed the hall. She and John followed the voices to the drawing room, where she found Lord Carrington and her father smoking cigars. The claret was out on the table, and both were talking more loudly than usual.

Her father turned his head and saw her in the doorway. His face was flushed, but he bellowed out her name. "Julia, my dear, I have wonderful news for you. Come in. You too, John. You might as well hear this now."

She glanced at John, then slipped into the room. "What is it, Father?" She'd never get used to calling him Father.

His smile was expansive, and he preened. "Your future is all settled, my dear. Lord Carrington has graciously asked for your hand, and I've given my permission. The wedding is to be at Christmas." When she opened her mouth, he held up his hand. "I know that's not much time to arrange all the fripperies you ladies like, but Clara will help make the arrangements. You'll be Lady Carrington." He beamed at her.

The bright bubble of her joy burst in her chest. Instead of being upset at the denial of a proper proposal, Lord Carrington smiled.

"But Father, I hardly know Lord Carrington," she said.

Henry waved his hand. "There'll be time enough for that after the wedding."

She glared at the Englishman. "I don't know you well enough to marry you, sir. And you're much too old for me."

"Julia!" her father gasped.

She whirled toward her father. Her face was hot, and her hands shook. "It's true. He also wanted to marry my mother. How can you even think of allowing him to marry me? Did you know he came to see my mother before she died? What if he had something to do with her death?"

"Go to your room!" her father shouted. "You know nothing about this."

"I know more than you think," she said. "I'm not going to marry him."

Lord Carrington rose and stepped to where she stood. He took her hand and raised it to his lips. "I'll leave you to absorb the news, my dear. You're overwrought. I shall call on you tomorrow." His eyes held kindness. "I'll see myself out."

She stood mute as he walked from the drawing room. When the front door closed, she glanced at John. His eyes were steely. She took his hand, and he squeezed it.

Her father poured himself another glass of claret and drank the whole thing. "I realize you were caught off guard, but I'll not have my own daughter speak to me with such disrespect."

"I meant no disrespect, Father, but I'm not going to marry that man. Don't you even care that he might have had something to do with my mother's fate?"

"Oh my dear, you're being much too melodramatic." Her father leaned back. "Carrington is a good man."

Was her father being deliberately obtuse? "You don't know that!"

John dropped her hand and stepped forward. "Henry, I must protest this arrangement. Carrington is much too old for her."

He set down his glass. "What the devil, John? This is no business of yours."

"It is indeed, sir. I want to marry Addie myself. I love her, and she loves me."

Hearing John say the words brought back Addie's joy. She stepped to his side. "He's right, Father." She linked hands with John. "I love John. I want to marry him and be a mother to Edward."

Her father slammed his fist on the arm of the chair. "Ridiculous!" He shook his finger at John. "I gave you one daughter, whom you made miserable. I'll see Julia dead before I see her married to you."

John paled. "Then we'll marry without your blessing."

"You'll do no such thing!" Henry surged to his feet. "Go to your room, Daughter. We will discuss this between us."

"I won't marry Lord Carrington, Father. I won't!" She ran from the room and nearly tripped over her skirt in her mad rush upstairs. Sobs tore from her throat.

When she reached her room, she hurled her hat across the room, then fell onto her bed and wailed.

The grandfather clock in Henry's office chimed two in the morning. John's movements were jerky as he pulled open the desk drawers and went through them. He barely controlled his anger. Henry had no right to treat Addie like she was some kind of property to be bartered off. He knew what had to be behind this: money. Carrington was probably buying her the way he would a horse.

He heard footsteps in the hall, and he quickly killed the gaslight. The room plunged into darkness. The door opened, and a shadowy form filled the doorway, then moved into the office. There was no place to hide, so he sat motionless until the moonlight allowed him to recognize the figure.

"Addie," he whispered.

She gasped and turned toward him. "John?"

He rose from the chair and embraced her. "What are you doing up?"

She pulled away, then went to the doorway and shut the door. "Turn on the light."

"What's happening?" He lit the light and adjusted the glow.

She joined him at the desk. Her hair spilled onto her lilac dressing gown, and he couldn't take his eyes off the long curls that hung nearly to her waist.

"You've been crying," he said, noticing her reddened eyes. He took her in his arms again. "We'll convince your father."

Her head nestled against his chest and her fingers clung to his shirt. "I can't marry Carrington, but this is what I've longed for." She raised her head and stared at him with tear-filled eyes. "I wanted to be part of a big family. To have roots. If Father doesn't consent to our marriage, everything I've worked to find will be gone."

"Are you saying you won't marry me without his consent?"

She bit her lip. "I would rather have his blessing, but I can't marry Carrington." She glanced over his shoulder at the desk. "What are you searching for?"

He guided her to the desk chair. "I want to find proof of your father's mismanagement. I thought if I could show you that he's reaping what he's sown, you'll be able to let go of feeling responsible for his future."

"I already know he's done this himself."

He pulled out more desk drawers and lifted the contents onto the top. "Sort through these and see what you find."

She picked up the top sheet of paper. "What am I looking for?"

"Contracts. Legal notices. Bank accounts." He settled in a chair with another stack of paper. They read in silence for several minutes until he heard her gasp and saw her pale. The paper in her hand shook.

He rose and stepped to the desk. "What did you find?"

She held out the paper. "I think it's a will. My maternal grandfather's."

Not what they needed, but it had obviously upset her, so he took it and began to read. The first part detailed property and money left to Clara and Walter. Both were substantial. He read on.

To my daughter Laura I bequeath the bulk of my entire estate. In the event of her death, the estate shall pass to her daughter. If she leaves no heirs, the estate shall pass to any offspring Clara or Walter produce.

He rubbed his forehead and puzzled out the meaning. Edward was the beneficiary? He was the only descendant. No, wait, he wasn't thinking right. His gaze went to Addie's face. She was the legal heir. She was Laura's daughter. "He wasn't going to tell you this," he said slowly. "He's never told me that all this belongs to Edward, not him and Clara. All he's ever mentioned is the tract of land I showed you. It's all been a lie."

She blanched even more. "He's acted like this was all his." She straightened. "Not that it matters now. It's all gone."

"No it's not," he said slowly. "This is all in a San Francisco bank. It's still intact."

"Then why is he so desperate for me to marry Carrington?"

"It's the title he's always craved, not so much the money."

She winced. "He cares so little for me. How has he managed this? How can Walter and Clara not know?"

"Walter was abroad when your grandfather died. And Clara would have let Henry handle matters of the estate. He covered it all up."

"We have to find that other clue," Addie said. "Maybe it's all connected to my mother's disappearance."

"There's no time like the present."

He tucked the will into his pocket and led Addie up the stairs and down the hall to the attic steps. They creaked under his weight as the couple climbed to the attic. He lit the gaslight. "I'm not sure where to look first."

Addie scrutinized the attic's shadowed contents. "My mother loved music."

"And you. I know there is a trunk of your old toys around here, because Edward found it once. I think it's in the northwest corner." He stepped past shrouded furniture and stacks of pictures to the alcove. Two chests were under the window. "I think it was this one." The brass latches on the chest were battered. He lifted the lid. "Yes, this is the one." He began to lift out dolls, clothing, and a tiny tea set.

Addie picked up a rag doll and sat down on a rug. "I remember this! The eyes, especially." She traced the outline of the embroidered face.

John joined her on the carpet and put his arm around her. "I bet you were a beautiful little girl. I hope we have a daughter with your eyes and hair."

"I want another son, a brother for Edward too," she said. She leaned over and kissed him.

Her lips tasted of strawberry jam. She wound her arms around him. He deepened the kiss, and passion ignited between them. He couldn't get enough of her soft lips. Her body was soft beneath his, and he realized they were lying on the carpet instead of sitting on it, though he had no memory of how they got there. It took a monumental effort to roll away and sit up. His pulse hammered in his chest. He wanted to hold her again, but he knew he didn't dare. She was much too tempting.

She touched his arm. "John?"

He forced a smile. "We've gotten sidetracked. Let's see if there's anything else here."

The smile she turned on him stole his breath. Such trust and love. He'd nearly broken that trust. He bent over the chest and pulled out small items.

She picked up the tea set and peered inside each cup, then lifted the lid on the teapot. "John, there's something here!" She thrust her fingers into the pot and withdrew a tiny scrap of paper.

"Get it under the light," he said when he saw her squint at the tiny print.

She scrambled to her feet, and he followed her to the sconce on the wall. Her brow wrinkled as she strained to see the words. "It reads 'Fort Bragg.'" She stared at him. "The first time I talked to Katie was when she called to pass along a message from Father's secretary about having completed the arrangements for his trip to Fort Bragg. She said he went twice a year."

A memory surged to the forefront of his mind. "There's an insane asylum there."

Addie's hand went to the pocket of her dressing gown and

emerged with a paper. "This clue. The one about that reads 'insane asylum.'"

He knew what she wanted from her thoughtful expression. "You want to go to Fort Bragg." But his gut twisted at the thought of digging any deeper into this morass.

THIRTY-THREE

PEOPLE NOTICED WHEN she came to town. Monday morning, Addie could barely make it from store to store without being stopped with a smile and friendly hello. Before it became known she was an Eaton, people were friendly, but now that her identity was common knowledge, they gave her deference.

She knew her smile was lopsided as she spoke and went on her way down the street. Dawn had come with her still wide-eyed and sleepless over the revelations of the night before. Her father cared nothing about her and never would. All that mattered to him was more money and power.

She rounded the corner and saw her uncle outside a tavern. He was staring into the window with a faraway expression that cleared when he turned his head and saw her. "Julia, my dear, you look lovely. What are you doing in town today?"

She brushed a kiss across Walter's cheek. "I had some errands to run." Did he know about the will? She didn't see how he could and have a relationship with her father. He needed to know what she'd found though. She owed him so much. "I found some other things my mother hid," she said.

He took her arm and drew her off the main sidewalk. "What kind of things?"

"Notes. Clues. One reads, 'Fort Bragg' and the other one reads, 'Father murdered.'"

He blanched. "Did she mean *our* father was murdered?"

"I'm not sure, but that's what I'd assumed."

"Fort Bragg. Henry goes there on business a few times a year."

"So John said." It was all she could do to hold back the contents of the will she'd found. She had to find out more before she told him.

"I'll put my investigator on it," he said. "Thank you for keeping me informed. Now I must go, my dear. I have an appointment. I'll see you at dinner."

"Let me know if you find out anything," she called after him. She resumed her brisk stroll down the sidewalk and reached the hospital, a small brick building down the block from the garment factory. Mrs. Whittaker had been taken in more than a week ago, and Addie should have checked on her before today. Her only excuse was how unsettled her life had been.

She climbed the steps to the second floor and found the nurses' desk. After asking the nurse where to find the older woman, she went to the end of the hall. The scent of carbolic and alcohol hung in the air. The coughing of patients told her she'd reached the right ward. She pressed her hand against her diaphragm and took a deep breath. Pinning on a smile, she stepped into the ward.

She walked between the rows of beds. The stench of blood and sickness nearly gagged her. Gaunt, pale faces turned her direction as she traversed the length of the room, searching for Mrs. Whittaker. When a voice called out her name, she turned and saw the woman struggling to sit up in a bed she'd just passed. Mrs. Whittaker had lost weight and was deathly pale.

She lifted a limp hand to Addie. "Miss Sullivan, is that you?"

Addie rushed to the bed and pressed the woman back against the pillow. "Rest, Mrs. Whittaker. I stopped by to see how you are."

The woman fell back, panting. She dabbed at her lips with the handkerchief. "I'm better. Stronger. But my poor children."

"Have they been to see you?"

Mrs. Whittaker shook her head. "The county orphanage won't let them." She reached over and clutched Addie's hand. "Would you go see them? Make sure they're okay. It would mean so much to me to know they aren't being mistreated."

"I'll do what I can," she said. "Can I get you anything? Food, something to drink?"

"I'm fine, dear. Or I will be." Her violent coughing into the handkerchief left flecks of blood.

"I'd better be going, then. I'll pray for you." Addie fled the ward.

She raced past nurses pushing squeaky carts and a doctor walking at a fast clip. Out in the sunshine, she gulped in fresh air that had never smelled so sweet.

"Julia?"

She turned at her father's voice. He stood in his bowler with his suit buttoned and a flower in his buttonhole.

He glanced from her to the hospital. "What were you doing in there?"

"Visiting a friend."

His brows gathered. "Who would that be?"

She held his gaze. "Mrs. Whittaker."

"The mother of the girls who work at the garment factory. Julia, I expressly forbade you to get involved with that family. You could catch her disease. You're an Eaton. Good works are fine, but please limit them to something I approve."

She curled her fingers into fists in the folds of her dress. "I care about this family, Father. I want to help them."

He took a firmer grip on his cane. "Then give them money."

"I want to do more than that. Those children were taken to the orphanage. I can't bear to think of them there. Five children, Father." Her voice broke.

"My dear, there are children all over this country in orphanages. You can't take in all of them."

She put as much appeal in her voice as she could muster. "Maybe not, but we could take in these."

His brows rose, and his expression of horror said it all. "Absolutely not!" He took out his pocket watch. "I must go, my dear. I'll see you at home tonight. Lord Carrington is coming for dinner."

"Father—" But he was gone before she could object.

She walked on toward her buggy, then saw Katie on the other side of the street. Addie darted between two buggies to intercept her friend, who looked fetching in a blue dress framed with lace at the neck. She carried two bags in her left hand.

Katie shifted one of the bags from her left hand to her right. "Addie, I was just thinking about you!"

"Do you have time for ice cream?"

"Oh, I wish I did. I have some clothing to deliver to the orphanage. Why don't you come along with me?"

"For the Whittaker children?"

Katie nodded. "Mama and I canvassed the neighborhood for items. I have a nice assortment. The children would be so glad to see you."

Addie took one of the bags from her. "I could use your advice."

Katie's blue eyes widened. "Is this about John North?"

Addie fell into step beside her, and they walked toward the orphanage. "Not just John," she said.

"What's wrong?"

"I don't even know where to begin. John proposed Saturday night, and I said yes."

"Addie, I'm so happy for you."

"Don't be. When we arrived home, Father informed me that he'd given my hand to Lord Carrington."

Katie stopped on the sidewalk. "No!"

Addie nodded. "He won't listen to reason. He's insisting I marry Carrington."

"But he might have had something to do with your mother's death! And he's *old*, Addie. Old enough to be your father."

"I know."

Katie tipped her head and held Addie's gaze. "You've changed since I met you."

"In what way?"

"When we first met, you were like Gideon. Eager, happy. You said what you thought with never any guile. Now you're so eager to please your father that you're letting him mold you into some idea he has of the proper daughter."

Addie started to speak but wasn't sure if she even had a defense. Was Katie right? She thought about her recent decisions. She'd barely objected when her father forbade her from helping the Whittaker family anymore. "There may be some truth to what you say."

Katie held up the bag of clothes she carried. "Two weeks ago, you would have been the one gathering donations. You would have moved into the apartment and cared for the children yourself instead of letting them go to the orphanage."

Addie's eyes burned. "I wanted my father to love me."

"We all crave approval. But at what cost, Addie? I think this price is too dear."

Addie's knees nearly buckled. When was the last time she'd opened her Bible? She hadn't even asked God what he would have her do in this situation. "You're right," she whispered. "I have to go." She thrust the bag into Katie's hand and ran back the way she'd come.

❧

Addie fell face-first into the soft moss. The roar of the falls filled her ears and drowned out the sound of her sobs. Edward was eating his lunch under the careful watch of his nurse, so she'd been free to take her dog. Gideon whined and licked her cheek.

This perfect dream was crumbling in her hands. And she'd let it, because she'd allowed other people to become more important to her than God.

"I'm sorry," she whispered against the softness of the moss. "I wanted so much to belong."

You belong to me. I am the only Father you need.

The words impressed themselves on her heart. How easily she'd been enticed away from the things that truly mattered. "I thought I was strong, Lord. That nothing could shake my faith."

And nothing had. Only her willful decisions to let what other people thought matter more than what God wanted. Without so much as a backward glance, she'd dropped her desire for God's will and followed her own. Her life would mean nothing if she let the world creep in.

She groaned as she remembered the desperate face of Mrs. Whittaker. Addie had let her father's disapproval keep her from doing what she knew was right. And those children. She'd abandoned them to the orphanage. God had urged her to help, but she'd been afraid.

She sat up and swiped at her face, then opened the Bible she'd brought. Gideon crowded close and put his head on her lap. Her study of the names of God fell out. She picked up the pages. *El Shaddai. All-Sufficient God.* Why had she thought she needed any man's approval? Only God's mattered.

She flipped to Proverbs 3. "Let not mercy and truth forsake thee," she read. "Bind them about thy neck. Write them upon the table of thine heart." She shut her Bible. With God's help, she'd cling to the truth and follow him, not the whims of man.

She rubbed Gideon's head, then pushed him off. She rose and turned toward the path, but stopped when she saw John approaching through the ferns. Had he come here for solace or had he come in search of her? She waited for him to see her.

Brushing the ferns out of the way, he strolled as if he had all the time in the world. His head was bare, and he'd removed his jacket. His sleeves were rolled up to reveal his strong forearms. She thought of the scripture that mentioned God's strong right arm. This was a man she could depend on. A man who would be strong where she was weak.

Gideon bounded forward, then groveled on his back for John to rub his stomach. At the dog's appearance, John's gaze went toward the spring.

Their eyes met, and he stopped. A grave smile tugged at his lips. "Addie. There you are."

"Were you looking for me?"

"Yes. I knew you'd be here." He glanced at the waterfall. "This is your special place with God, isn't it?"

She nodded and stepped closer to him. "I feel him here."

He wound a curl around his index finger. "You've changed me, Addie. Sitting in church yesterday, I realized how far I'd fallen away from God. I want to remember what it was like to want to follow him."

His fingers in her hair caused warmth to spread out from her belly. "I haven't been a very good example lately," she whispered. "I let what everyone else wanted come first."

"I told you it would happen."

"You did. But no more."

His hand became more entwined in her hair. He glanced at her bare feet. "I'm glad. I love the real Addie. The one who plays ragtime on the piano, and the girl who splashes me with water and runs barefoot through the house."

He pulled her closer, then bent his head. She stood on tiptoes and wound her arms around his neck. Addie inhaled his breath, his essence, into her lungs. He was part of her. She was bone of his bone, flesh of his flesh. His lips met hers, and she tried to put how she felt into her kiss. Her surrender, her love. She would go anywhere, forsake anything, for him.

When his lips lifted from hers, he searched her face. "Will you defy your father and Carrington?"

"Yes."

"We might move back to San Francisco."

"I'll have you and Edward, no matter where we live. That's enough."

John glanced at Gideon, who still sprawled on his back, with his belly exposed. "That's one way to get the dog for Edward."

She poked him in the ribs. "So that's all this is? A ploy to get my dog?"

Gideon rolled over and looked on expectantly at the word *dog*. John laughed and prodded the animal with his foot. Gideon's expression turned blissful. "Whatever works."

Her smile died when he held her face in his hands. "I'd take you, dog or no dog. That spring behind us reminds me of you. I saw you described in the Bible this morning. It was in Isaiah 58. 'And the Lord shall guide thee continually, and satisfy thy soul in drought, and make fat thy bones: and thou shalt be like a watered garden, and like a spring of water, whose waters fail not.'"

She inhaled and pondered the words. "Which part is me? The fat part?"

He threw back his head and laughed. "No, darling. The spring of water. I was so jaded before you came into my life. You make everything new and fresh. Thank you for that."

She nestled against his chest again until she heard the sound of her father's automobile. "He's home. I have to tell him."

"Actually, he's leaving. For Fort Bragg. I came to get you so we could follow him—if it's still important to you."

She ran her fingers across the faint stubble on his cheeks. "Bless you for that. But yes, I want to know about my mother. What about his dinner guest? Carrington was coming."

"Your father canceled when he got home for lunch a few minutes ago."

He took her hand and they ran toward the house with the dog at their heels. Addie prayed this day would finally bring her some answers.

THIRTY-FOUR

THE RENTED COACH awaited John and Addie when they disembarked at the quay in Fort Bragg. Gideon stayed close on her heels. John had made the decision to bring him, because he might be of assistance to them, though they both worried about Edward. Molly had promised to watch him closely.

Addie could hardly think as they walked past the remains of gutted fish and heaps of fishing nets. Addie held her hankie to her nose, but it did little to block the stench of rotting meat. The pier bustled with fishermen, buyers, and travelers awaiting passage on the next boat to the city.

"We'll never find him," she said, once John handed her into the carriage and climbed in beside her.

"Our driver says he's taken Henry many times over the years. He goes to a home outside of town. So that's where we're heading." He took her hand. "We have to be careful, Addie. We can't go rushing in there demanding to know what he's doing."

"I know. And it's likely a dead end." She pressed her trembling lips together. "It's good of you to humor me."

"I'd do anything for you, Addie," he said, his eyes soft.

She squeezed his hand. "And I do love you for it." She craned her neck to stare out the window as the cab rolled through town. The bustling seaside port seemed to subsist on logging and fishing. They soon left the streets behind and rolled along a country lane that wound through Sitka spruce and wildflowers. The towering edifice at the top of the hill had to be the insane asylum. The stonework and shuttered windows gave it a secretive air.

John leaned forward. "Let us out here. Come back in two hours."

The driver nodded and pulled the horse to the side of the road. John helped Addie out of the cab, then paid the driver while she called Gideon to her. When the clopping of the horse's hooves faded, he took her hand, and they walked along the road to the side of the building.

"Why don't we go to the front door?" Addie asked.

"We can't walk in and ask why Henry comes here twice a year or why he's broken his routine and come here today. If there's anything unsavory going on with the residents, they are hardly going to admit it."

She clung to his hand and stared at the large home. Her silly vapors had brought them on a wild goose chase, and she would be embarrassed when they found out nothing. Hiring the boat and their lodging wouldn't have been cheap either.

The road wound around to the back of the asylum. A garden with a labyrinth and clipped hedges caught her eye. Stone benches and a small waterfall looked serene and inviting. Several people wandered among the flowers on the other side of the fence.

Her fingers tightened on John's forearm. "Isn't that my father?" She pointed toward a man sitting beside a woman on a bench.

John peered. "I think you're right. I can't make out much about the woman."

"Can we get closer without being seen?"

"I think so. There are so many huckleberry shrubs through the back field. We can hide behind them as we get closer. Mind your skirt, and hang on to me. The ground will be uneven."

She nodded and clung to his support. He led her down into the valley from the road. They moved from shrub to shrub until they stood five feet from the stone wall. The barrier was eight feet tall without a gate on the backside.

"We can't see anything now. We had a better view from up on the road," she said.

"We might be able to hear something."

He took her hand and led her to the wall. Holding his finger to his lips, he sidled down the stone structure in the direction of the bench where they'd seen her father sitting. She strained to make out the conversation on the other side of the wall.

"Are you chilled?" Her father's voice spoke. "I can get you a shawl."

He continued to speak of the weather, his day, and the news from the city. There was no response from his companion. John and Addie exchanged puzzled glances.

Addie peered through the gloom but couldn't make out the woman's features.

"I have to leave you now, my dear," her father said. "It's been good to see you."

Addie and John waited. She heard footsteps fade along the cobblestone path to the building.

"How do we get into the garden?" John asked.

"There might be an access near the building."

She followed him along the perimeter. Attached to the stone building was a small gate. Wild roses grew beside it and perfumed the air. He tugged on the padlock, but it didn't budge. He shrugged and dug out a pocketknife. He poked and prodded until he succeeded in popping the lock. Once the lock was removed, he twisted the handle and opened it slowly.

"Coast is clear," he said, stepping through.

She followed him with her pulse hammering in her throat. A six-foot-high clipped hedge blocked the rest of the garden from view. When they stepped past it, she realized they were in the maze. Finding their way out might not be easy. John led her down a few false paths, but they finally came out by a fountain that gurgled its welcome.

Addie's gaze fell on the woman who sat on the bench. Her breath came fast as she noticed the woman's faded red hair, high cheekbones, and green eyes. It had to be her mother.

❧❦❧

Addie knelt in front of the woman and took her cold hand. "Mama?" This lady was an older version of the portrait Addie had seen at the Eaton manor. She knew without any doubt that this person was Laura Eaton.

The woman's eyes focused on her, and a tiny frown crouched between her brows. "I had a little girl once." Her trembling hand touched Addie's hair.

"This woman is your mother?" John's voice shook.

Unable to speak, Addie nodded.

The woman's slurred speech and wide stare hinted at the reason for her compliance. "I think she's drugged." John said, glancing around the garden. "Looks like no one is out here." He checked the time. "We've got an hour before the cab comes back."

"We could start walking to town."

"Someone will be looking for her soon. It's nearly sundown."

She realized he was right. The quality of light had changed. "We could hide if someone comes." She grabbed his hand. "Please, John, I can't leave her here."

"I agree." He knelt by her mother. "Mrs. Eaton, it's time to go."

"Go," she agreed, her eyes vacant. She came to her feet when he tugged on her hand.

A bell chimed. "That's probably the dinner bell," Addie said. "We have to hurry. Someone will be coming." She took her mother's hand. "Come along, Mama."

Saying the words hit her. *Mama.* She had a living mother, even if she was damaged. She led her mother to the gate, and they stepped through. John pulled it shut behind him, then fiddled with the lock.

"It's broken," he said. "I'll have to leave it."

They hurried across the field. Addie was thankful for the darkness that now quickly began to fall. They would be harder to track when a search ensued.

"It's a big place," John said. "I expect they'll search the building first and won't realize for a while that she's missing."

"I hope so."

"Our hotel is on the edge of town. I'll register us while you stay outside with her. I'll come get you when it's safe to go to our rooms. She'll need to stay with you."

Addie tightened her grip on her mother's hand. "Of course."

They reached the road and began the trek toward town. Her new shoes pinched her toes, and she prayed she could endure walking until the cab came. "How much longer before the cab arrives?"

John checked his watch. "Forty-five minutes."

An eternity. "This road doesn't seem to be well traveled."

"A blessing for us," he said.

They trudged toward town. Head down, her mother walked slowly, pausing often to touch a flower or a tree branch. Addie watched her for any sign of coming out of her stupor. How long might something like that take? Hours? Days? She suspected an evening dose came with dinner.

"How could he do it?" she blurted out. "How could he put her in a place like that?"

"You don't know he did, Addie. Don't jump to conclusions."

"He let everyone believe she drowned, though he knew differently."

"Maybe he was trying to spare the family the shame of knowing she was in this state." He nodded to her mother, who was humming tunelessly.

Addie clenched her fists. "There's more to this, John. I feel it."

A light bobbed ahead of them in the road. "There's the cab," he said, relief highlighting his tone. He held up his hand, and the buggy slowed, then stopped.

The door opened, and her father stepped onto the road. His mouth was tight, and his eyes narrowed. His gaze went from Addie to her mother and back again. "Get in," he said.

Addie took a step back. "You locked my mother away. How could you?"

"There's more to the story than you know. Get in and I'll explain."

Addie glanced at John, who shrugged. There was nowhere for them to hide. She took her mother's unresisting arm and helped her into the carriage. Gideon leaped in after her.

"There's room for only three inside. I'll ride up top with the driver," her father said. "Make no judgment yet, my dear. You'll understand when you hear the full story."

Addie didn't reply. Nothing he could say would change what he'd done in her eyes. Even if her mother was quite mad, she deserved better than being hidden away for a quarter century.

The carriage set off with a jerk. It continued on toward the asylum. "He's not turning around," John said. He leaned forward and spoke through the open window. "Why aren't we turning around?"

Her father didn't acknowledge him. Addie stood and put her head through the window. "Father, why are we not turning around?"

"Your mother needs her medication," he said without turning to look at her. "You see the state she's in, my dear. Why else would she be here?"

The carriage lurched, and Addie fell back onto the worn leather seat. "We have to escape. I can't let her go back to that place." She held her mother's hand. The older woman had stopped humming, and her faded eyes showed a trace of awareness.

John pressed his lips together. "I wish I had my pistol," he said.

"When the carriage slows to turn into the lane, let's jump out," she said. "It will have to nearly stop."

He nodded. "I'll take your mother with me. You jump out the other door."

The vehicle slowed. Addie grabbed the door handle.

"Now!" John thrust open the door and grabbed her mother's hand. They both hurtled through the door.

Addie tried to do the same, but her door was stuck. She slid across the seat and prepared to leap from John's side.

"Oh no, you don't!" Her father grabbed at her from the front window.

She beat at him with her fists but couldn't tear free of his grasp. Gideon growled and leaped forward. He sank his teeth into Mr. Eaton's wrist.

Her father howled. "Get him off me!"

While he was thrown off center, she leaped from the carriage and hit the grass. Pain flared through her shoulder and back, and she bit back a moan. Holding her arm, she rolled until she saw the carriage stop. Gideon jumped from the coach and ran to her.

"Good boy," she gasped. She forced herself to ignore the pain and ran back to where John stood with her mother.

"Run!" he yelled. He grabbed her hand in his left one and her mother's in his right, and they plunged into the pine forest.

THIRTY-FIVE

THE DARKNESS PRESSED in on them. John stopped to let his eyes adjust to the lack of light. "He'll have trouble finding us in the dark," he said, groping. "I can't see my hand in front of my face."

"Let's hide under a tree," Addie suggested. "Maybe we can circle back and get to the road and hike out of here."

"Good idea." He swept his hand across the air and moved forward until his fingers touched the pine needles of the nearest tree. "Here. And hurry. I think I hear him."

He pushed Laura under the tree, and Addie followed. The dog belly-crawled to join her. John squeezed under the sheltering limbs with them. The dead needles were soft under him, and the tree above them released the scent of pine. He squeezed Addie's hand when something crunched nearby.

The sound grew nearer. It sounded like a hand brushing at every tree. He held his breath and lay with his cheek resting on the pine needles. The darkness was complete, but he sensed Henry was near.

"Kids, this has gone on long enough," Henry's voice was right beside him. "I know you're here somewhere. Let's talk about this. You're overreacting."

Addie's fingers squeezed John's. Hard. He couldn't hear her breathe either. The feet by his head shuffled, and the scent of pine intensified. Then the steps went farther into the woods.

"Julia?" Henry called again. "Come on out, Daughter. This is ridiculous. You don't need to fear me. I'm only doing what's best for your mother."

The footsteps moved deeper into the forest. Henry's voice grew distant until John couldn't hear it any longer. He strained to make out whether his father-in-law might be circling back to trick them. There was no sound but the wind in the tree boughs.

"I think it's safe," John whispered.

He rolled out from under the pine. When soft sounds told him Addie and her mother had done the same.

Addie clasped her hands together. "I knew he wouldn't find us. I asked God, and he wouldn't let me down."

Oh, how he loved her simple, childlike faith. His own faith seemed weak by comparison. He rose and held out his hand. He helped her to her feet, then raised her mother from her prone position. The poor woman moaned under her breath, and he wondered if her medicine was wearing off.

"This way," he told them.

He led them back the way they'd come. The moon was out when they stepped out of the forest's shadows. But it was only a sliver and cast very little light. He glanced up and down the road but didn't see the carriage.

"Where is it?" Addie asked.

"Maybe the driver didn't want to be involved in what was happening and went back to town."

She stepped closer and took his hand. "Could we go to the asylum and borrow a buggy?"

"They wouldn't loan us one."

"I was thinking we might borrow it without asking."

He grinned, though he knew she couldn't see him. "Why, Miss Adeline, how shocking."

"We wouldn't hurt it."

"It's a great idea. Let's see what we can find."

They set off toward the asylum. The ground was uneven and hard to gauge in the dark. Several times he caught Addie or her mother when they stumbled. The dog kept jogging ahead, then turning back as if to ask why they were so slow. John kept pausing and glancing behind them but saw no sign of Henry.

They reached the building, then wound around to the west, where a large barn stood. The door was unlocked, so he shoved it open and peered inside. It was dark, so he lit a lantern by the door and held it aloft to check out the resources.

A brougham was by the door, and two horses snorted in alarm at the lantern. "Come in," he told the women.

Addie led her mother inside, and he shut the door. "You hold the light while I harness the horse."

He soothed the nearest horse, a mare, then led her to the carriage and hitched her up.

"I heard something," Addie whispered.

He stopped and listened. Shouts, calls from the house. "They've realized she's gone," he said. "Get in. We're ready to get out of here."

He took the lantern from her and set it on the floor, then helped the women inside. He waited for the dog to leap inside too. With the door shut, he blew out the lantern, then shoved open the doors. There was still no one in the yard. He clambered onto the driver's seat, then grabbed the reins and guided the horse out of the barn. When he slapped the reins on the mare's rump, she took off at a lively clip for the road.

So far so good. The carriage reached the road, and he turned the horse's head toward town. With the straightaway in front of them, he prayed for a smooth journey. The horse broke into a canter, and he spared a glance back at the asylum. Men were running from the building toward the barn. They'd realize the horse and carriage were gone. He let the horse have her head, and her stride lengthened.

When he passed the area of the forest where they'd hidden, he stared but saw nothing. It was only when he saw the lights of the hotel that he began to relax. The question was, what were they going to do next? It probably wasn't safe to stay at the hotel. There weren't many in town. Henry would have no trouble tracking them down.

⊷❦⊶

Addie's mother made anxious noises and tugged at her skirt. Maybe she needed the medication her father had mentioned. It might not be safe to withdraw it all at once. Addie should have thought of that sooner.

"Who are you again?" her mother asked in a thin, reedy voice. She sat with Gideon's head in her lap.

"I'm Julia, Mama. Your daughter."

"I wish it were true," the older woman said.

Addie patted her hand. At least her mother seemed to be improving. Outside the window the moon gleamed on the water. The quay was just ahead.

"Why are we going back to the quay?" she asked John through the window.

"We've got to get out of town. Your father will track us down if we stay."

Addie leaned against the leather seat back until the carriage stopped and John jumped down to open the door. This felt like a bad idea.

"How are we going to get a boat at this hour?" she asked when he opened the door. "And what if Father comes here to stay on his yacht for the night?"

He lifted her from the carriage. "We have to try. I'm not sure what else to do."

The activity at the quay had changed to men laughing and drinking. She heard the occasional splash as someone threw something into the water.

"John?" A man's voice spoke out of the shadows. Lord Carrington stepped into view.

Addie's muscles clenched. She stepped down from the carriage and blocked his view of her mother. "Lord Carrington."

"Miss Eaton." He raised a brow. "Eloping?"

"Not exactly."

"Thomas. Is that you?" Her mother's voice was thin and weak.

Lord Carrington grew rigid. His eyes widened. "W-Who is that?"

Addie stepped out of the way. "My mother." She watched him come forward and peer into the carriage. She heard his gasp.

"Praise be to God, it is you, Laura." His voice trembled.

If nothing else, Addie knew he would help save her mother. There was no doubt how he felt about her. "We need your help, sir. Most especially, my mother needs it."

With obvious reluctance, he took his gaze from her mother and turned to her. "I am at your disposal, Miss Addie."

"My father had her locked away in an asylum. He's looking for us now. We have to escape. Quickly."

"Of course. My yacht is moored in the bay. My man is right here with the dinghy." He reached into the carriage. "You can come out now, Laura. No one will hurt you." He helped her down with the utmost tenderness.

Her mother stood blinking at the lights. "I'm so cold," she said, her teeth chattering.

Lord Carrington glanced at Addie. "Do you know what's wrong with her?"

"I think she's overdue whatever drugs they were giving her."

"Laudanum?" he asked.

"I'm not sure."

"I have some aboard ship in the medical kit. We'll wean her off it more gently."

"You sound as though you know of these matters."

He smiled gently. "You wouldn't want to know the things I've seen." He nodded toward the pier. "Come. Let's go." Still holding Laura's hand, he led her away.

John stopped a young boy and arranged to have the horse and carriage returned to the asylum. "I don't trust Carrington," he said as they followed the gentleman and her mother.

She pressed her fingers on his arm. "We have no choice, John. Where can we go?"

His nod was grudging. "I wish I had my pistol," he said again.

She followed him to the end of the pier, where a dinghy bobbed. John kept glancing behind them. When he went rigid, she turned to look also.

"It's my father," she said to Lord Carrington. "Hurry."

The deckhand helped them down into the boat. Gideon hesitated, then made the leap to the craft. So far, her father hadn't spotted them. But he'd seen the carriage. He opened the door and peered inside. As Addie sat down, she saw him emerge.

She grabbed the railing. "He's seen us!"

"He's too late," Lord Carrington said, shoving off.

The men took every available oar and rowed toward the yacht. Addie watched her father gesture and shout from the pier, but she couldn't make out his words. She prayed for the Lord to slow him down, to help them escape. Her father managed to commandeer a dinghy, but he nearly fell as he tried to maneuver into it.

Their dinghy reached Lord Carrington's yacht, and moments later they were aboard. The men lashed the dinghy to the side, and Lord Carrington hurried to the cabin to tell the captain to shove off. It seemed an eternity before the large craft began to move away from shore. There was no sign of her father, but his ship was fast. And he wouldn't give up easily.

Her mother was shaking uncontrollably now. Her teeth chattered, but perspiration dotted her forehead. Addie embraced her and led her to a lounge chair, where a throw lay waiting. She draped her mother's form with it.

"Mama, I'll take care of you," she said.

John eased her into the chair and lifted her feet onto the lounge. Her mother's eyes were clearer, even though she suffered from a condition Addie didn't know how to ease. Gideon sat at her feet.

"Who are you again?" her mother asked through her chattering teeth.

"I'm A-Julia. Your daughter, Julia."

Her mother's eyes widened. "That's impossible," she gasped.

Lord Carrington arrived with a small bottle. He administered some drops to her mother, and the shaking began to ease. "Not too much," he muttered. He had her sip coffee, then watched her head drop back and her eyes close.

"How long will it take for her to become lucid?" Addie asked.

"Hard to say. A few hours. A few days."

"I have so many questions to ask her."

"I can answer some of them," Lord Carrington said.

Addie curled her fingers around John's hand. "Why didn't you answer them the other day?"

"I wasn't sure what camp you were in. If you loved your father, it would be difficult for you to hear the truth about him. My priority was to get you out of that house. That's the real reason I offered marriage. I do hope you'll forgive my ungallant confession."

John's bark of laughter held relief. "Then you'll put up no objections to dropping your suit?"

"I'll not stand in the way of true love," Lord Carrington said.

"Why was I not safe in that house?" Addie demanded.

"Because your father is a murderer."

THIRTY-SIX

THE SALON BELOW deck was appointed with plush fabrics and comfortable seating. Lord Carrington had insisted on dinner before he continued with explanations, but Addie could barely eat the delicious food when all she wanted was to know what he'd meant.

"Tell me," she finally demanded as the men leaned back with their claret. She glanced at her mother, whose eyes were closed. Her color was better, though, and her chest fell up and down with reassuring regularity.

Lord Carrington put his wine on the table. "You asked me why your mother summoned me before she left."

Addie nodded. "But you didn't tell me."

"You weren't ready to hear it."

"We are now," John said, his voice grim.

"I'll tell you," her mother's reedy voice said. She sat up with her eyes open and clear.

Addie moved to her side. "Mama?" She took her mother's thin hand. It was cold as the waves. Gideon whined and nudged their linked hands.

Her mother held on with a tight grip. "Are you really my Julia?" she asked.

Addie barely managed to choke out the words. "I am."

Her mother's wondering eyes traveled Addie's form. "Praise God," she said. "I believed you'd drowned." She passed her hand over her forehead. "So many jumbled memories."

"Take your time," Lord Carrington said, moving to her other side.

"Thomas. You too. I prayed for rescue so many years. How many?" she asked. "How long was I locked away?"

"Twenty-three years," Addie said gently.

Tears flooded her mother's eyes. "A lifetime," she murmured. She swallowed hard. "It was all Henry," she said. "He orchestrated everything. I thought he loved me."

"I'm sure he did," Addie said, seeing her mother's distress.

"He did at first. I believe that. But he grew to love my money more. He killed my father to get his hands on all of it."

Addie gasped. So did John. Only Lord Carrington remained unmoved, and he'd surely heard this story before. Addie clung to John's hand. This was going to be worse than she'd dreamed.

"I can tell them about it," Lord Carrington said. "You don't have to do this, Laura."

"I want to." Perspiration beaded her forehead. "Could I have some tea?"

"Of course, darling." He sprang to his feet and went to the galley.

Addie swallowed down the massive lump forming in her throat. She wanted to bury her face in Gideon's fur and cry. Even when her father was after them, she'd held on to a shred of hope that there was an explanation for what he'd done. To discover he had a soul as black as Satan himself left her fighting tears.

"I'm here," John murmured against her hair. "We'll get through this. Just rejoice that your mother is alive."

Addie forced back her tears. "You're right."

"When did you find this out? That he'd killed your father?" John asked her mother. "Just before you left?"

She nodded. "He knew I'd discovered the truth."

"How did he do it?" John asked.

"Poison. It looked like a heart attack, but I found the poison in Henry's dresser before he disposed of it. When I accused him, he admitted it. He said he was tired of waiting for Father to die. He had a bad case of gout, and Henry claimed death would be a release. A release—from gout!"

"I'm so sorry," Addie said. She didn't remember her grandfather, but she could see her mother's pain.

"There was some reason Henry needed money quickly. He'd asked Father and was refused. So Henry killed him."

"And you fled," John said. "With Julia."

Her mother nodded. "He told me no one would believe me. That he'd put me in an insane asylum and I'd never see my daughter again. So I ran."

"After you hid the clues. We found them," Addie said.

"And you tracked me here?"

"We followed . . . Henry." Addie didn't want to call him Father. Not after what he'd done.

Lord Carrington returned with a cup of tea and toast. He offered it to her mother, who nibbled on the toast and took a sip of tea.

"Did you finish the story?" Lord Carrington asked, settling beside her.

She shook her head. "Not yet." She set her tea on the table. "Henry boarded the same ship as Thomas and I, but we didn't know it. He drugged me, and the next thing I knew, I was at the asylum. It was one he practically owned. I heard him warn them to keep me drugged at all times, because I'd killed my father and was extremely dangerous. That they shouldn't trust what they thought was lucidity. They were happy to do whatever he said because of the money he'd given them over the years."

"What about me?" Addie asked.

Her mother's eyes held grief. "I told him I'd left you at my grandfather's. I never dreamed he would sink the ship to cover my disappearance. I don't know how you were saved."

"I do," Lord Carrington said. "I'd taken you to my room so your mother could get some sleep. The next morning she was gone. I couldn't find your mother and feared Henry had thrown her overboard. A storm rolled in. I heard an explosion, then the captain yelled to get to the lifeboats. I overheard a crew member say it was a bomb."

"An explosion?" Addie asked. She rubbed her head. "I remember a man carrying me on a burning ship, then throwing me into the sea. That was you?"

He nodded. "I actually threw you into a lifeboat. It sank, though, and you ended up in the sea."

"Henry sank the steamer on purpose?" John asked.

Lord Carrington shrugged. "That's what I've always believed."

"But how did I end up at the lighthouse?" Addie asked.

"I'm coming to that." He picked up the tea and put it back in her mother's hand. "Drink, Laura. You must get something down. It will help fight the drug's effects."

She nodded and sipped at her tea, then took another bite of her toast.

"As I said, I ran to a lifeboat with you, but it was too full for both of us. I handed you over to a woman in the boat, then dived overboard. I thought I had a better chance of swimming on my own than going down with the ship."

"And you made it," she said.

"I did, but the lifeboat didn't. The storm upended it. The waves tossed me onto the beach farther up the shore, and when I came to, I thought you'd been drowned with all the others. A couple of days later, I came back to this area to search and saw you on the lawn with the lightkeeper. You were giggling and fine."

"So you said nothing?" she asked.

"I knew I couldn't raise you myself. For one thing, I had no visa, so I'd be unable to adopt you. I'd hoped to catch up with your father as well, and a child would slow me down. I arranged for one of my lawyers to offer Roy Sullivan money to care for you."

Addie's head whirled. "It was you! So you knew all along where I was?"

He nodded. "I was quite dismayed to find you at Eaton Hall a few weeks ago. I knew it was only a matter of time before your father eliminated you. He would never let you live to take his money."

Her chest constricted. "So you were trying to protect me for all these years. Why?"

He shrugged. "You should have been mine."

"I wish you were my father," she whispered. She turned and buried her face against John's shoulder.

❧

"What's next?" John asked Carrington.

The three of them stood on the stern of the ship watching the dark sea. Addie's mother had fallen asleep below.

John gestured to the water. "You realize Henry's yacht is one of the fastest. I'm sure he's chasing us."

"We're running with no lights, and it's a big ocean," Carrington said. "I hope to make Eureka and summon the police. We have Laura as a witness."

"Will he say she's insane and can't testify?" Addie asked.

Carrington's lips tightened. "He might, but the three of us know better."

John expected a battle. Henry wouldn't go down without a fight.

Addie gasped and put her hand to her mouth. "Josephine. The woman who raised me. Someone killed her. W-Was it Henry?"

He put his hand on her shoulder. "I don't know, Addie, but it makes sense that he might have. Or, more likely, ordered it done. I doubt Henry would sully his own hands."

"But what about the attack on Mr. Driscoll? And me? And the man who tried to take Edward? Are those incidents tied to Henry as well?"

She was trembling. John embraced her, his arm circling her waist. "I can see how he would think you and Driscoll were a threat, but Edward is his own grandson!"

"But he's also the heir to everything."

"Not while your mother lives. She is. And you after her."

"And he knew she was alive. So Edward would be the one he would want to eliminate perhaps?"

He shook his head. "For what reason? Henry won't live forever. Who would inherit if Edward were out of the picture?"

"Wait a minute," she said slowly. "I found a blackmail note in Henry's office right after I first came."

"Blackmail? Any idea what someone might have against him?" Carrington asked.

"The note demanded ten thousand dollars or the blackmailer would tell the world about Henry's child. At least I assumed it was Henry's child. There was no one named in the note."

"His child. Could that be you, Addie?" Carrington asked. "Who knew of your existence besides me?"

"No one that I know of," she said. "We lived quietly in the lighthouse." She paused, her brows gathering in a frown. "Oh wait. There was the solicitor you hired, Lord Carrington. But Uncle Walter was unable to find out anything from him."

"I suppose it's possible he told someone. An employee, perhaps, who deposited the money into Mr. Sullivan's account."

Addie stepped away from John's side. She paced the deck. "So my father knew of my existence before I came to the manor?"

"I suspect that's possible," John said. "If so, when you arrived, he would understand he had to work fast. There could be only one reason you were there—you'd found out the truth."

"And of course he would know of Driscoll's involvement, as he was the one who brought you," Carrington said.

Addie returned to John's side. Gideon accompanied her. "But if

I'm the child mentioned in the blackmail note, why would Edward be threatened? That piece still doesn't make any sense."

A splashing sound wafted over the water. John held up his hand. "Listen. I hear a boat. If that's Eaton, we may have a chance to capture him and get him to the authorities. Then he can explain it all."

An explosion battered his ears, and in reaction, he swung Addie behind him. Seconds later, something splashed in the waves off their starboard. "He's firing on us!"

Addie peered past him. "How could he do such a thing?"

Carrington ran to the helm. "If he sinks us, he's rid of everyone standing in his way." He yelled down into the hold. "Start the engine!"

A few moments later a rumble started under John's feet. The yacht picked up speed. It had been running silently on sails, but now that they'd been discovered, speed was all that mattered.

"Get below!" John yelled to Addie. "Your mother will need you." When she ran for the salon with Gideon, he turned to Carrington. "Do you have guns?"

Carrington shook his head. "I've never had any need of something so barbaric."

The yacht in pursuit fired on them again, and John realized it was getting closer. Why hadn't he brought his pistol at least? He paced the deck.

"More speed!" Carrington shouted.

The rumble in the bowels of the ship grew, and a bit more distance opened between the two yachts. "Is that Mercy Falls?" John asked.

"Yes," Carrington said. "If we can make it to town, he won't dare do anything to us there."

"You don't know Henry," John said. "He'll twist this around and accuse us of something atrocious." He strained to see through the gloom.

"I think we're leaving him behind. When we reach shore, I'll go to the constable, while you get the women to safety. We'll meet back up when I've finished pressing charges."

John shook his head. "Henry owns the town, and it was his influence that got the constable the position. I fear we'll be hard-pressed to convince the constable to arrest him."

"You might be right. We could press on to Eureka."

"It might be best."

Addie's head rose from the opening to the hold. "What about a decoy?" She stepped onto the deck. "My mother is terrified. Mr. Eaton can't be allowed near her. I want to take her to safety."

John folded her in his arms. He could feel the shudders that seized her body. "What do you have in mind?"

She glanced at Lord Carrington. "We have the dinghy. Mercy Falls lighthouse is just ahead. Mama and I could hide out in the lighthouse. I can padlock the door from inside, and we can go up into the light tower until you come for us."

"He'll follow Carrington's yacht."

"Yes. You can lead him away and find help so Mama never has to see him again. Once the authorities have him in custody, I'll unlock it."

"I don't like it," John said. He held her close. "I don't want anything to happen to you."

"We'll be fine."

"You could go with the women," Carrington said.

"I'd rather do that," John said.

Addie shook her head. "Lord Carrington, you need the strength of John's word with yours. Henry is too influential a man for a foreigner such as yourself to challenge alone."

John held her close. "I don't trust your father," he said.

She pulled back and gazed up at him. Her eyes were brilliant in the moonlight. "What could possibly go wrong? My father won't have any idea we're not on this boat."

He couldn't argue. The other yacht was distant enough that he could no longer hear the flap of its sails or the water on its hull. Eaton would never know a dinghy had left with the women.

"All right," he said. "But I still don't like it."

Carrington ordered the dinghy prepared, and the men helped the women into it. Gideon leaped into the boat with them. The hollow spot in John's chest grew as he watched it lowered into the sea.

THIRTY-SEVEN

ADDIE'S MOTHER WAS increasingly lucid, but chills still racked her body. Addie rowed for shore with all her might. The oars in her hands were like long-lost friends. She put her back into the effort and steered the craft toward the light winking on and off on the spit of land to her northeast.

"Are you okay, Mama?" she asked.

"I'm so c-cold," her mother whispered.

"You probably need more medicine," Addie said.

She should have brought the laudanum. What had she been thinking to leave it behind? She rowed harder until the dinghy bumped against the sand in shallow water. She leaped from the boat and dragged the craft onto the rocky shore, then helped her mother.

"Let's get you inside," she said.

Wading through calf-high flowers, she half carried her mother up the steep incline to the house. Gideon ran on ahead. The lighthouse beacon drew her attention. Who had wound the light? She hadn't stopped to wonder who was tending the light since Josephine's death. No lights shone from the home, so maybe neighbors had stopped by to help out.

Her mother trembled, and her teeth chattered. Addie steered her toward the back door that led to the kitchen. "I'll find chamomile tea. It might help you."

Inside, she settled her mother into a chair at the table, then lit the gaslight. The tea was in the pantry off the back porch. No fire warmed the wood cookstove, so she poked at it. No embers glowed in the cold ashes. She would have to start it from scratch. She found kindling and wood, then arranged it in the fire box. The match sputtered when she struck it, then the fire flared to life. She set the kettle on to heat, then turned around to check on her mother.

She wasn't at the table. "Mama?" Addie called.

She walked into the parlor and found her mother holding a picture of Addie up to the moonlight streaming through the window. Addie was about five. Tears rolled down her mother's cheeks. Addie embraced her, and the older woman clung to her.

"You're really Julia," her mother said, her voice hushed. Her hand caressed Addie's cheek, then she glanced back at the picture. "I recognize you. All these years . . ."

"I know. But I've found you now." Addie didn't like the way her mother trembled. It was more than emotion. "Come sit down, Mama. I'll get you some tea."

She snatched a throw from the chair as she passed and draped it around her mother's gaunt shoulders. The kettle shrieked as they stepped into the kitchen. She hurried to grab it from the range while her mother sank onto a chair. Steam rose from the cup of tea as Addie carried it to her mother. While her mother sipped the chamomile tea, Addie ticked through in her mind what she would need for a night in the tower.

Blankets, pillows, food, and water. It might be hours before the men returned.

"I'd like to go to bed now," her mother said.

"I wish we could stay here in the house," Addie told her. "But we're going to have to go to the light tower and lock ourselves in."

Her mother's eyes went wide, and the tea sloshed over the lip of her teacup. "He's not out there, is he?"

"I don't think so, Mama. But we can't know what's happening.

We're safest in the lighthouse. I can padlock us in until the men come back."

"Thank the Lord." Her mother's voice was stronger. She sipped at the tea until it was gone.

Addie heard something. A voice, a scrape. She wasn't sure what. She rose and flipped off the gaslight, then peered out the window. A light bobbed on the water.

"I think a boat is out there," she whispered. "We need to go up now."

She helped her mother to her feet. "Come with me."

She raced up the steps with Gideon and scooped pillows and blankets off the bed in the room at the top of the stairs. By the time her mother finished the climb, Addie had their supplies ready. She led her mom down the hall to the stairs that led into the tower. The light on the boat appeared to be onshore now. The men could be halfway up the slope by now.

"Very quiet," she whispered to her mother.

The stairway door hung open. Addie stepped inside and pulled her mother in with her. She shut the door and fumbled in the dark for the padlock. It wasn't on the door. Where was it? She dropped the bundle of blankets and pillows and felt along the floor for the missing lock. Her hand grazed the gritty floor, then something metal skittered away. She followed its trail and cornered the padlock. The key was in it. She took it out, then looped the padlock through the door handle and clicked it shut.

When she tugged on it, it stayed snug. "Let's get upstairs," she whispered. "As quietly as you can."

She led the way up the winding metal stairs. Wincing every time their footfalls clanged, she kept checking to make sure her mother stayed on her heels. They reached the top. Another door separated the stairs from the light room. It hung open as well. Looking past the Fresnel lens, Addie stared out past the glass enclosing the lamp. Lanterns bobbed on the hillside. One, two of them.

Her fingers tightened on the blankets. "They're coming," she said. Gideon snarled, and she quieted him with a glance.

Her mother grabbed her hand. "Who?"

"I don't know. It's too soon for John and Thomas to be back with the constable." She dropped the blankets into the corner and arranged a makeshift bed. "I'm sure it's nothing to worry about, Mama. Maybe neighbors arriving to wind the light. If it is, I'll ask one of them to call the police. Why don't you lie down and rest a bit?"

Her mother moved to her side. "I feel much better. The tea helped, but I'm so tired."

Her voice was stronger. Addie helped her lie down, then covered her with another blanket. Gideon lay down beside her. "I'll be here if you need me."

With her mother settled, she went back to her post at the window. She crouched beyond reach of the flashing light. The lanterns stopped at the house and winked out. Whoever they were, they were searching the house now.

❧

Carrington's yacht sped through the night seas. John kept an ear out for Henry's boat but heard nothing, saw no lights.

"How long until we reach Eureka?" he asked.

Carrington stood at the helm with the wheel in his hands. "A few more minutes."

"I haven't heard anything to make us think he's behind us," John said.

He paced the deck back to the stern. Water churned behind the yacht. Stars glittered overhead, and the moonlight gilded the railing with a glimmer of light. Still, he saw nothing behind them, heard nothing but the lapping of waves and the chug of their own engine.

He walked back to Carrington. "Could we shut off the engine and listen for anything out there?"

"Certainly. I'll see to it." Carrington yelled instructions to power down temporarily.

Carrington turned the helm over to his first mate, then walked with John back to the stern. Both men stood and listened.

John strained his eyes through the darkness but saw nothing. "I don't think he's following us."

"You believe he noticed the ruse and followed the women?"

John leaned over the railing. Nothing. "He's wily. He could have been closer than we realized but wasn't firing."

"If so, he would have seen the dinghy shove off."

It made horrible sense to John. "We have to double back."

"You're sure that's wise? We're nearly to Eureka and help."

"How long?"

"Fifteen minutes."

"And another forty-five minutes back. Explaining to the authorities will take at least another hour. We can't risk it. In two hours both Addie and Laura could be missing."

"I have an idea," Carrington said. "One of us could go to the constable, and the other could go back to check on the ladies."

"Addie pointed out they might not believe you."

"True enough, but Henry won't be there to fill them with his lies. I have some standing with my money and title."

"That's our best chance, then," John said.

Carrington gave instructions to his crew. When the yacht reached the dock at Eureka. Carrington leaped over the side into another dinghy and waved the boat on. John watched him row to shore as the yacht made a wide turn and headed back the way she'd come.

As the boat plowed the waves back to the lighthouse, he stood at the bow and prayed for the safety of the woman he loved and her mother. From here, he couldn't see the lighthouse winking its warning.

"Should we be able to see the lighthouse from here?" he asked the first mate.

"Not yet, sir. Another half an hour."

John gripped the railing. If he could swim there faster, he'd plunge into the dark water. He'd never had a premonition before, but his skin prickled and his breath came hard and fast. Something was very wrong.

THIRTY-EIGHT

ADDIE CLASPED HER knees to her chest and sat with her back propped against the wall. She glanced at her sleeping mother, then back out across the dark terrain. It was only a matter of time before the intruders tried the door to the tower. When they found it locked, they would suspect she and her mother were hiding up here.

The padlock might not hold determined men for long. Or maybe they'd think the lighthouse tower was locked because the lightkeeper hadn't been replaced. She prayed for God to blind their eyes, to distract them from their search.

She crawled to the metal stairs and peered into the darkness. It was too impenetrable for her to make out the door. Silence pressed against her ears. But they were down there. She sensed them. Easing back to the window, she gazed out again. Moonlight gleamed on the whitecaps and touched the rocks along the coast. Nothing moved, though.

If only they'd go back to their boat and shove off.

Her mother sat up. A scream tore from her throat. "No, Henry! Please, no!"

Addie leaped to her mother's side. Her heart hammered at her ribs. "Sh, Mama," she crooned. "It's okay. It's Julia." Gideon followed her.

Please don't let them have heard her.

Shouts echoed from below. "Up here," she heard a man yell. She hunkered beside her mother, who covered her face and moaned.

"I'm sorry, so sorry," her mother whispered. "I had a nightmare."

Addie hugged her. Perspiration soaked her mother's hair and the fabric of the back of her dress. She trembled violently.

"I think I'm going to throw up," she choked out.

Addie helped her bend over, then rubbed her mother's back as she retched. The stink of vomit made her gag, but she managed to control herself. "Let's move you over here."

Her mother nodded and dabbed her mouth with the hem of her gown. "Did they hear me?"

The answer was the thunderous pounding on the door from below. Mr. Eaton's voice came from the other side of the door. "Julia, I know you're in there. Open the door this instant."

Addie clutched her mother to her. "Don't answer. Stay very quiet."

It was hopeless to think he'd just go away. They'd all heard her mother. He knew they were there, but it would take time for him to break down the metal door and padlock. God would come through for them. She knew it, depended on it. He would be sufficient to this challenge.

"Get an ax," she heard her father say to his unknown partner.

Could an ax break down a metal door? She prayed not.

"Julia, this is your father. You must open this door now. I'm not going to hurt you. I just want to talk to you."

Hot words hovered on the tip of her tongue. Not hurt her? He'd tried to sink their yacht. If she said nothing, though, he'd have no positive proof she was on the other side of the door.

Her mother clapped her hands to her ears. "Go away, Henry!" she screamed. "Haven't you tortured me enough?"

Addie shrank back against the wall. If only she had a weapon. There was nothing up here but a wrench. It might come in handy, though. She groped for it, and her fingers closed around it.

A fierce banging commenced against the door downstairs. Gideon sprang to his feet and began to bark. The man must have found the ax in the well house. She and her mother covered their ears as the relentless battering continued. Addie wanted to scream at the horrific din. She imagined the metal denting and caving beneath the blows. When the noise ceased, the pressure on her chest eased, and she drew in a breath.

When no more demands came from her father for a few minutes, she eased onto her knees and peered out the glass. A movement below caught her eye, and she realized he was on the rickety catwalk. She'd forgotten about it. He sidled along the metal support. The moonlight caught a glint at his side. He had a pistol, and he'd be here in minutes.

"Get up, Mama," she said. "Let's go."

She led her mother through the door and to the top of the stairs, but before they could begin to descend, she heard the battering resume on the door below. There was no other exit. If Addie were alone, she could climb out onto the other side of the catwalk and outmaneuver her father, but her mother was much too weak to accompany her.

Addie gripped the pipe wrench. If she leaned out the window, she might be able to use it on the catwalk and loosen it enough that Mr. Eaton couldn't approach.

"Sit tight, Mama," she whispered.

She took the wrench and swung it against the glass. Her mother screamed as the window shattered outward. Gideon ran in circles and barked. A few shards rained onto the floor and crunched under Addie's feet as she knocked the last few pieces out of her way. Holding on to the window frame, she leaned out and began hammering with the heavy wrench against the metal catwalk. The metalwork trembled under the blows but held fast to the lighthouse.

"Julia, stop at once!" her father yelled.

Pain rippled up Addie's arm from the blows, but she continued to batter at the metal. She saw him draw his gun and ducked back inside as a bullet ricocheted off the frame where she'd been a moment before. He couldn't fire his gun while sidling around the building.

She waited a moment, then peered outside to see him on the move again. She leaned out and swung the wrench once more. This time she detected a weakening of the bolt holding the catwalk in place. With renewed vigor, she pounded at it again. Her father was moving faster now. He was within reach of the nearest window. He'd be inside in moments.

Glass shattered to Addie's left. Her mother had found a wooden box and swung it against the window. Henry's face was inches away. "You killed my father, Henry!" she shrieked. "I hate you!" She threw the box at him. "I won't let you hurt my daughter too."

He batted it out of the way. One foot slipped from the catwalk, but he recovered his balance and inched closer. "Laura, darling, you know I did it all for us. For our future. Help me in. We can talk about it."

Addie saw it coming. Saw her mother's dress flutter in the breeze as the older woman hoisted herself into the window. Saw her poised with both feet on the bottom stile. It seemed everything moved in slow motion.

"Mama, no!" Addie scrambled back from the opening where she perched.

Her outstretched hand grasped at her mother's arm. And missed. Her mother launched herself at Mr. Eaton. Gideon lunged and caught the hem of her dress in his teeth. She was far enough out the window that her body struck her husband's. The force of weight knocked him from his perch. They grappled with each other, then Mr. Eaton hurtled toward the ground.

Her mother's dress began to rip in Gideon's teeth.

"No!" Addie shrieked.

She leaned out the window and grabbed her mother around the waist. It was all she could do to get both of them back inside the light tower. The battering at the door began again, and she covered her ears.

CRAN

The minutes ticked by too slowly. John paced the deck and stared into the darkness. "Why aren't we seeing it yet?"

"We should be," the first mate said.

John squinted in the darkness. "There it is!" He ran along the deck. "Do we have another dinghy? There's no pier."

"Sorry, no."

"I'll swim." He shucked his jacket, shoes, and socks.

"Wait, sir. Let me get the yacht as close as possible and upstream a bit so the current will help propel you to shore."

John nodded but clambered to the top of the railing to be ready. When the first mate gave him the nod, he dived overboard. The cold water shocked him and gave him renewed purpose. He surfaced and gasped in air, then struck out for land. The tide carried him just past the lighthouse, but he struggled to shore, cutting his knees and hands on the sharp rocks.

He staggered from the ocean, with cold water dripping from his body. His legs trembled from the long swim, but he forced himself up the slope that led to the back of the lighthouse. He heard the sound of metal against metal. What on earth?

As he neared the lighthouse, he caught sight of something on the ground at the base of the tower. As he approached, he realized a body lay there. "Oh please, God, no." He started forward.

He ran to the heap of arms and legs and stared down into Henry's face, twisted into a grimace. John's eyes burned with uncustomary emotion. Where was his Addie?

The pounding of metal on metal had stopped, but he turned toward the back door. Addie had to be here somewhere. He strained his ears to hear her voice, but there was nothing. Not even a bark from Gideon.

"Just the man I need."

John turned at the sound of the man's voice. He squinted in the darkness. "Walter? Is that you?"

The man emerged from the shadows. "Hello, John."

The moonlight glinted on the gun in Driscoll's hand. John looked at it, then back at Driscoll's face. "What's going on?"

The gun came up. "Your fiancée is holed up in the lighthouse. You're going to get her down for me."

"I don't think so."

Driscoll gestured with the gun. "Through that door."

"Nope. I'm not going anywhere with you."

"I'll shoot you where you stand."

John clenched his fists. "Then do it."

The gun wavered in Driscoll's hand. "Addie!" he shouted. "I've got John down here. I'm going to shoot him if you don't come down."

John started to yell out to tell her not to listen, but he hoped if he kept quiet, she'd assume Driscoll was lying. He heard something overhead. He glanced up and saw moonlight illuminating Addie's face in the lighthouse tower. Their gazes locked.

"Stay there!" he shouted.

Driscoll fired, and a bullet zinged off a rock by John's feet. "I'll aim for his head next, Addie!" Driscoll screamed.

Addie's head disappeared. "Addie, no!" he yelled. He started toward the door to the house so he could gain entry to the tower, but a bullet plowed into the earth by his feet. Driscoll raised the gun to John's chest. All he could do was pray Addie wouldn't come down.

A few moments later she and Laura emerged from the house with Gideon. Her mother leaned heavily against her as they moved slowly.

Laura flinched when she saw her brother. "Walter?"

"Hello, Laura," he said.

"What are you doing?"

"Get over there by John," Driscoll ordered.

The women joined John, and he embraced Addie. Gideon whined and nosed at John's wet pants. Laura continued to stare at her brother.

"Let's take a moonlight stroll," Driscoll said. "That way." He motioned to the path that led to the cliff.

John put Addie behind him. "Why, Walter?"

"Why take a stroll? Because I said so."

"Why are you doing this?" Addie whispered, peeking around John.

"I have no choice," Driscoll said. "My creditors want their money now."

"The man in Henry's office demanding money," John said. "I overheard him tell the fellow it wasn't his debt or his problem. He was trying to get money from Henry for something you owed. Gambling?" He recalled seeing Walter two weeks ago, exiting the alley. "We saw him coming out of the alley where games are going on all the time."

"I remember," Addie said slowly. "I thought he was delivering medicine." She rubbed her forehead. "I found a note in my father's office, asking for ten thousand dollars to keep quiet about a child. I assumed it might be his indiscretion, but it was yours, wasn't it, Uncle Walter?"

Driscoll motioned with the gun for them to move along. "Henry had always bailed me out in the past, but he decided I had to face the music this time. I would have been ruined if the truth came out. I tried to get the money by gambling, but I only succeeded in digging myself into a deeper hole."

"Was that you pounding on the door?" Addie asked. "Why would you work with Henry when he wouldn't help you?"

"When you told me about the clues you'd found, I knew Henry had killed my father. I told him to pay what I needed, or I'd go to the constable. He agreed before he left for his trip to Fort Bragg. One of his men called me from Fort Bragg and told me to meet him here. He said that if I'd help him with a problem, he'd give me double what I needed."

"But why kill us now?" Addie asked, stepping out from behind John.

"It's because of your grandfather's will," John said, keeping his gaze on Driscoll for an opening to attack. "You saw it, too, didn't you, Walter?"

His lips thinned. "I never dreamed Henry would cheat me out of my inheritance that way. I should have had my share all along."

Laura held out her hand toward him. "Did you know Henry had me penned up?"

His eyes held regret. "Not until recently. But you've been dead to me for years. I can't let sentiment keep me from my needs. Now that Henry is dead, the Eaton estate is all mine, so long as I take care of this problem here. Very tidy, don't you think?"

John's muscles coiled. "So with us out of the way, you inherit what's left. Once you dispose of Edward too." He had to save them. His son's life depended on it.

Driscoll waved the gun. "Enough of this chatter. Move or I'll shoot the dog."

Addie cried out and reached for Gideon. "Come with me, boy," she said.

John clenched and unclenched his fists.

"Follow the little lady," Driscoll said. "I'd hate to shoot her dog."

John didn't have a choice. He caught up with Addie and kept his body between her and the madman. Driscoll marched them out to the edge of the cliff.

"Right there is fine," Driscoll said from behind him.

John turned quickly. For all he knew, Driscoll was going to shoot him in the back.

"Was this your plan all along?" Addie asked. "When you brought me to the manor?"

"Quite honestly, I wasn't sure how I might use you to get the money I needed. I had thought Henry might be so grateful to get you back that he'd give me the money to pay my debts. When my creditor attacked me before I had proof, I knew I had to move faster."

"You killed Josephine, didn't you? Looking for more proof," Addie said. "That's how you came up with the pictures of me as a child."

"I watched her leave, but she came back to the house before I was finished. She tried to blackmail me."

"Did you arrange to have Edward kidnapped?" John demanded, curling his hands into fists.

Driscoll raised a brow. "It was the syndicate. They'd thought to exert pressure on me and Henry to pay what I owed."

John saw Driscoll turn the gun toward him, then his finger tightened on the trigger. It was now or never. But before he could make a move, Gideon leaped silently out of the dark. His teeth fastened on the arm that held the gun.

Driscoll wrestled with the dog. "Let go, you mangy mutt!"

John jumped and tackled Walter. The man was wiry and stronger than he expected. John tried to get the gun, but the older man kept it just out of reach. Gideon continued to worry Driscoll's arm, but he hung on to the weapon in spite of all efforts to dislodge it.

"Let go of me," Driscoll panted.

John kneed him in the groin, and Driscoll groaned but fought back. He kicked out at the dog. Gideon yelped, then leaped into the fray again as Driscoll pinned John to the ground and began to bring the gun around. The dog bit into his wrist again, and Driscoll grabbed Gideon by the neck with his left hand and began to choke him.

John struggled to get his leg free so he could kick out. He reached for a loose rock by his head, but before he could bring it up, Driscoll slumped onto him. John lowered him to the ground, then glanced up into Addie's face. She still held the rock she'd used to strike Driscoll.

"Wicked arm you've got there," he said. He shoved Driscoll off, grabbed the gun, and struggled to his feet.

Addie collapsed into his arms, and Gideon came to nose at his hand. "I'm glad you two are on my side." He saw lights on the water. "Here comes the cavalry."

"A little late," Addie said.

"I don't think you need the cavalry. You're strong, my love. And you have a fearless sidekick in Gideon."

"And I have you," she whispered.

✿

Addie warmed her hands with a cup of hot cocoa in front of the fire at the Russell home. Gideon lay at her feet with a self-satisfied smile on his doggy face. She'd fed him until he could eat no more as a reward for being such a hero.

Mrs. Russell bustled in with oatmeal cookies, fresh from the oven. "Are you warm enough, my dear? You were shaking so."

"I'm fine now. It was shock, I think. Is John back yet?"

"I thought I heard his buggy stop outside. Katie went to let him in." Mrs. Russell put the cookies on a side table. "Katie and I will leave you two to sort things out."

Katie led John into the room. Addie drank in the sight of him. They'd nearly lost what they had. Her heart swelled at how good God was. He'd seen them through this valley. She waved back at Katie as she disappeared up the steps.

"Addie." John was at her side in two steps. He knelt and took her cold hands in his warm ones. "I couldn't wait to get back to you."

She took comfort from his grip. "What's happened with Mr. Driscoll?"

"The doctor says he'll live."

"He's in jail?"

John joined her on the sofa, but he kept control of one of her hands. "Yes, but don't feel sorry for him, love. He nearly killed you. And his own sister." He released her hand and slipped his arm around her.

She burrowed into the comfort of his embrace. The clean scent of him reassured her. "I'm so glad it's over. You saved my mother, John."

He kissed the top of her head. "We did it together."

"I'm too tired to think," she said. "I can't impose on my friends for too long. I'm not sure what to do."

He tipped her face up and brushed a kiss across her lips. "You'll marry me, of course. As soon as it can be arranged."

Her pulse skipped, and she pulled back. "Right away?"

His eyes were smiling and full of love. "I'd marry you tomorrow if we could arrange it that quickly."

The thought of being a family with him and Edward brought heat rushing to her cheeks. "I'd like that more than anything in the world," she said.

"Tell me what to do and I'll arrange it."

"There are so many things to do, I don't know where to start," she said, laughing.

The smile left his face. "When, my love?"

The possessiveness in his voice heated her cheeks even more. "I need at least two weeks. I have to make a dress."

"I'll buy you one."

"I want to make it. I'll only have one wedding day."

He released her hair from its combs and plunged his fingers into the mass of curls. As his lips claimed hers, she realized how God had given her every desire of her heart.

EPILOGUE

THE ROAR OF the ocean was music in Addie's ears. Her white lingerie dress, while simple, was the only wedding dress she needed. John insisted she appear barefoot to take their nuptials. Silly man, but how wonderful to be loved for who she was.

"Kneel there by Gideon. Our hero," Katie said. She had her Brownie camera on a tripod and was documenting the day. Her dark hair gleamed against the lilac bridesmaid dress Addie had made for her.

Smiling, Addie knelt on the grass with the lighthouse in the background. Gideon crowded close, and she put her arm around him.

"Just a moment. Don't move," Katie called.

Addie froze her smile until she heard a click. "Are we done?"

"Done!"

At her friend's announcement, Addie rose and stretched. Guests in buggies were beginning to arrive. Though Clara's offer to use the manor house had been generous, Addie belonged here, not in fancy drawing rooms or on manicured lawns. Her true home was by the sea, with the lighthouse winking overhead. The wedding would be at sundown, when the light could be wound.

"I see you watching for John," Katie said, linking arms. "You're not supposed to see him before the wedding."

Addie tucked a strand of hair behind her ears. "Do you think I should have put my hair up? John wanted it down, but it seems almost disrespectful on such a momentous occasion."

Katie held her at arm's length and studied her. "I've never seen a lovelier bride."

"You'd say that if I wore a flour sack."

"It would be true. You are just glowing. I hope a man looks at me someday like John looks at you."

Addie turned her friend toward the lighthouse. "It will happen."

"Uh-oh, John is here," Katie said. She grabbed at Addie when she would have turned toward the road. "Oh no, you don't. Inside with you, before he sees you."

"Katie!" Addie protested.

"No bad luck allowed." Katie steered her to the back door.

"I don't need luck. God has this all under control."

"I'd have to agree, after seeing all you've gone through."

The girls stepped into the kitchen. The yeasty scents mixed with cinnamon made Addie's tummy grumble. She'd been too excited to eat today. The neighbors had pitched in and brought the food. Clara had paid for cake and ice cream to be delivered. Everything was in order.

"Where's Gideon?" Katie asked as she affixed Addie's veil to her head, then added flowers.

"With Edward." Addie clasped her hands together and glanced at the clock. "It's time." The butterflies in her stomach took flight.

She peeked out the window. Guests had begun to mill around the yard. The tulle on the bower by the cliff rippled in the breeze. Piano music came to her ears from the instrument John had arranged to be moved to the yard. "The Entertainer" rang out, and she smiled. Who else was lucky enough to have ragtime played at her wedding?

Thomas Carrington poked his head into the kitchen. "Ready?" His eyebrows rose. "You look quite lovely, Addie."

She pulled her veil over her face and joined him on the back stoop. "Thank you so much for agreeing to give me away."

His eyes were moist. "I'm honored to be asked."

"How's Mama?"

"Excited. Still weak though. I have her on a lawn chair in the front row."

The music changed to another ragtime tune. Addie tucked her hand into the crook of his arm and stepped into the grass. As the piano music tinkled, she strolled between smiling friends and neighbors toward the bower. The Whittakers smiled and waved as she passed. Clara had taken the children into her house, and Mrs. Whittaker planned to join the children and take over as housekeeper as soon as she was well enough. Mrs. Russell dabbed at her eyes as Addie approached. She waved at Addie from her spot near the front, and John's father gave a grave nod.

Addie's eyes met her mother's for a moment. All the love and pride she'd longed for were in those serene green eyes. Her mother blew her a kiss, and Addie returned the gesture.

Then her gaze locked on the bower, where John awaited her. Dressed in a double-breasted frock coat and tan trousers, his dark eyes under the top hat caught and held hers. Edward stood beside his father, with his hand on Gideon's head. He tugged at the round collar on his shirt. The knickers he wore already had grass stains on the knees.

All three watched her approach, but she had eyes only for John. A slight smile played at his lips, and the love in his eyes brought moisture rushing to hers.

He stepped out to take her hands.

Lord Carrington stepped between them. "Not yet, son. She's still mine at the moment."

John's hand fell back to his side, and he smiled. "I've waited for her all my life, Carrington. No one's standing between us now."

Lord Carrington grinned and passed her hand to John's. His eyes stayed on her through the ceremony, which she barely heard as she repeated her vows. When he slid the ring on her finger, she caught her breath. She had a family. A husband who loved her. A son. God was so good. He'd provided every desire of her heart.

After the ceremony, John led her away from the crush of well-wishers. "I want to talk to you a moment."

They stood at the base of the lighthouse, which blinked out its warning every three seconds. He embraced her, and she nestled against his chest. His hand crept to her hair, and his fingers entwined in her curls.

"You're distracting me," he murmured.

She lifted her head. "Oh? You had something to say beyond telling me how much you adore me?"

"You have no idea how much." He bent his head to kiss her. His lips nuzzled her jawline and her neck. "Do you still think I'm your Robert Browning?"

Heat seared her cheeks. "You promised never to bring up that book. I shall take great pleasure in watching you jump over the falls."

He grinned. "I'm taking you with me."

"That wasn't part of the arrangement," she said, somehow managing to keep a straight face.

One eyebrow lifted. "Didn't you just promise whither so I goest? Or something like that?"

"You might have to remind me of that when we're at the top of the falls."

He chuckled, then sobered. "Now, back to what I have to tell you."

Her skin still tingled from his touch. She pulled away. "I'm listening."

"I've managed to keep Mercy Steamboat out of bankruptcy. The creamery too. Your mother and Clara should be all right financially."

"Mama has Lord Carrington too."

He nodded. "But I wanted to do what I could to help Clara and you." His gaze was troubled. "I need to talk to you about where we will live."

"We'll be in San Francisco, won't we?"

He shook his head. "I resigned my commission, darling. I can't take you from your mother. You searched for her so valiantly, and she fought for you so hard."

She swallowed over the constriction in her throat. "You did that for me?"

"I'd do anything for you."

She kissed him. "You're a good man, Lieutenant."

He smiled. "I'm not a lieutenant anymore. I'm a private citizen."

"Where shall we live, then?"

"There's a house I want to show you. It's down the lane and faces the water. I'll purchase that if you like it."

"I'll be by the sea! I know I shall love it."

He smiled. "I see the wheels turning behind those beautiful eyes. You're wondering what I'm going to do."

"You're going to run the Eaton holdings," she said.

He inhaled. "How do you do that?"

"Women's intuition," she said, brushing a kiss across his lips. "You're so good at organization. It makes sense."

"I'll never be able to keep anything from you."

"I hope you don't try."

He kissed the tip of her nose and exhaled. "I'll do the best I can with the other businesses. They're all struggling under Henry's mismanagement. Things will be tight for a while."

"We'll be fine. I'm not a spendthrift. And we have my money."

"I plan to support my family myself." His smile was tender. "I'm worried about the people who lost so much in the bank failure."

Her smile faded. "Me too."

"I have an idea that might help some. Clara has moved to a smaller place in town that her grandmother left her. The income from the creamery and the steamboat will sustain her. With your permission, I'd like to sell Eaton Hall to a group that wants to turn it into a sanatorium."

He was such a good man. She clung to him. "Oh, John, I'd like nothing better! But will that be enough to repay the people who lost their savings?"

He shook his head. "I wish it were. But I can repay some of the money at least."

"I've thought of another solution. I wasn't sure you'd agree, but I'd intended to talk to you about it tonight."

"What is it?"

"The land. We could sell it to the investors you mentioned. Surely that would be enough to give the bank customers their money."

His brows rose, and a smile lifted his lips. "Addie, you'd want to do that?"

"Of course. Would it be enough?"

"I believe it would," he said, pulling her close. "You are a remarkable woman. But I've also gotten an offer from a group who wants to turn it into a park area. It's nearly as much money."

"John, how wonderful! Let's do that."

"We'll have no resources to fall back on though."

"We have God. He'll see to anything we need. He always has."

Day-to-day dependence on God was all she needed to flourish. She laid her head against her husband's chest and listened to his heartbeat. Together, they formed a strong cord of three strands. There was nothing brighter in her future than that reality.

"Let's go home," she whispered.

ACKNOWLEDGMENTS

IT IS SUCH a privilege to do another project with my wonderful Thomas Nelson family. Publisher Allen Arnold (I call him Superman) is so passionate about fiction, and he lights up a room when he enters it. Senior acquisitions editor Ami McConnell (my friend and cheerleader) has an eye for character and theme like no one I know. I crave her analytical eye! It was her influence that encouraged me to write a historical romantic mystery, and I'm glad she pushed me a bit! Marketing manager Jennifer Deshler brings both friendship and fabulous marketing ideas to the table. Publicist Katie Bond is always willing to listen to my harebrained ideas. Fabulous cover guru Kristen Vasgaard (you *so* rock!) works hard to create the perfect cover—and does it. And of course I can't forget my other friends who are all part of my amazing fiction family: Natalie Hanemann, Amanda Bostic, Becky Monds, Ashley Schneider, Heather McCulloch, Chris Long, and Kathy Carabajal. I wish I could name all the great folks who work on selling my books through different venues at Thomas Nelson. You are my dream team! Hearing "Well done" from you all is my motivation every day.

My agent, Karen Solem, has helped shape my career in many ways, and that includes kicking an idea to the curb when necessary. Thanks, Karen, you're the best!

Erin Healy is the best freelance editor in the business, bar none. She sees details the rest of us miss, and it doesn't hurt that she's an amazing suspense writer. Thanks, Erin! I couldn't do it without you.

Writing can be a lonely business, but God has blessed me with great writing friends and critique partners. Kristin Billerbeck, Diann Hunt, and Denise Hunter make up the Girls Write Out squad (www. GirlsWriteOut.blogspot.com). I couldn't make it through a day without my peeps! And another one of those is Robin Miller, conference director of ACFW (www.acfw.com), who spots inconsistencies in a suspense plot with an eagle eye. Thanks to all of you for the work you do on my behalf, and for your friendship.

I'm so grateful for my husband, Dave, who carts me around from city to city, washes towels, and chases down dinner without complaint. Thanks, honey! I couldn't do anything without you. My kids—Dave, Kara (and now Donna and Mark)—and my grandsons, James and Jorden Packer, love and support me in every way possible. Love you guys! Donna and Dave brought me the delight of my life—our little granddaughter, Alexa! It's hard to write when all I want to do is kiss those darling, pudgy feet. She is the most beautiful baby ever!

Most importantly I give my thanks to God, who has opened such amazing doors for me and makes the journey a golden one.

READING GROUP GUIDE

1. Addie desperately wanted to belong to a family. How easy is it to change who you are to gain approval?

2. How do you gauge your self worth? How *should* it be gauged?

3. John wanted to protect his son from the world. What are the pros of this? The cons?

4. Addie is a romantic at heart and an optimist. What are consequences of looking at the world through rose-colored glasses?

5. It's said that opposites attract. Why do you think this is true?

6. The Bible says we are to respect our parents. Where do you think the lines are between respect and obedience?

7. God warns us that the love of money is the root of evil. What is it about wanting more and more that corrupts?

8. When I researched this book, I noticed a strong correlation between today's world and the turn of the 20th century. In what ways are they similar? Different? What can serve as a warning for us today?

9. Is it better to be a conformist or to be an individual? Are you always just one of these, or sometimes do you conform while other times you stand alone?

10. People treated Addie differently when her true identity became known. Why do people elevate those with money and power? Do you treat someone differently if they are wealthy?

THE
LIGHTKEEPER'S
BRIDE

For Jen
I treasure your friendship and constant support. Love you!

JEHOVAH-SHALOM—THE LORD OUR PEACE

ONE

THE LAPEL WATCH on her blouse read half past nine when Katie Russell removed the skates from her boots and dropped them inside the door of the Mercy Falls Telephone Company. She pulled the pins from her Merry Widow hat, then hung it on a rack. Smoothing the sides of her pompadour, she approached the switchboard in the room down the hall. "Has it been busy?" she asked the woman in front of the dangling cords.

Nell Bartlett sat with her stocking feet propped on the railing of the table that supported the switchboard. Her color was high and her voice clear and energetic as she answered a question then disconnected the line. A faint line of discontent lingered between her brows as she eyed Katie. "It's your shift already?"

Nell was unmarried and still lived with her ailing mother, though she was thirty-five. On the street she dropped her gaze and barely whispered a hello, but in front of the switchboard she came alive. Whenever she entered the office, she removed her hat, let down her hair, and took off her shoes.

"It is indeed," Katie said, approaching the switchboard. "Has it been busy?"

"Not too bad. I only received three calls last night." Nell's tone indicated her displeasure. "But the rings have increased quite nicely this morning." She rose and stepped away from the seat in front of the switchboard but kept one hand on the top with a proprietary air.

Katie settled herself in the chair and donned the headset. Nell slipped her shoes back on, wound her hair into a bun, then put on her hat. Out of the corner of her eye, Katie watched her scurry from the room, her mousy identity back in place.

Katie peered at the switchboard then forced herself to put on her hated glasses. She nearly groaned when the light came on at her own residence. She plugged in the cord and toggled the switch. "Good morning, Mama."

Her mother's voice was full of reproach. "Katie, you left before I could tell you that Mr. Foster called last night while you were out gallivanting at the skating rink."

Katie bit back the defense that sprang to her lips and kept the excitement from her voice. "What did he say?"

"He asked to speak with your father and they went to the library."

Such behavior could only mean one thing. Heat flooded Katie's face. "He asked Papa if he could court me?"

"He did indeed! Now you mind my words, Katie. You could not make a better match than this. You need to quit that ridiculous job and focus on building your social ties."

Katie opened her mouth then shut it again. Another light flashed on her switchboard. "I must go, Mama. I have another call." She unplugged the cord over her mother's objection. Her parents didn't understand how important this job was to her. She thrust the cord into the receptor. "Operator," she said.

"Fire! There's a fire," the man on the other end gasped.

Katie glanced more closely at the board, and her muscles clenched. The orphanage. "I'll call the fire department, Mr. Gleason. Get the children out!" She unplugged and rang the fire station with trembling hands. "Fire at the orphanage, hurry!" She rushed to the window and looked out to see smoke billowing from the three-story brick building down the street. People were running toward the conflagration. She wished she could help, too, but she turned back to the switchboard as it lit up with several lights. Moments later she heard the shriek of the fire truck as it careened past.

She answered the calls one by one, but most were people checking to make sure she knew about the fire. The morning sped by. She relayed a message out to the North house and managed to chat a few moments with her best friend, Addie North. One call was Mrs. Winston asking the time, and Katie realized it was after one o'clock. At the next lull, she removed her sandwich from the waxed paper and munched it while she watched the board.

The light for Foster's Sawmill came on. She plugged in. "Operator."

Bart Foster's deep voice filled her ears. "I'd recognize that voice anywhere."

Katie pressed the palm of her hand to her chest where her heart galloped. "Mr. Foster, I'm sorry I missed your call last night."

"I had a most rewarding chat with your father," he said, a smile in his voice. "Did he tell you?"

Her pulse thundered in her ears. "He did not."

"Excellent. I wish to tell you of our conversation myself. Might I call tonight?"

"Of course." She wasn't often so tongue-tied. All her dreams of respectability lay within her grasp. From the corner of her eye, she saw her boss step into the small room. "I won't be home until after seven. Will that be too late?"

"Of course not. I shall call at seven thirty."

"I look forward to it. Did you wish to place a call?"

"Someone must be there since you are not quite yourself." The amusement in his voice deepened. "Connect me with your father's haberdashery, please. I'll see you tonight."

"Of course." She connected the cord to the shop then turned to face Mr. Daniels.

"I just stopped by to commend you on the way you handled the fire call, Miss Russell. You kept your head about you in a most admirable fashion."

She stood to face him. "The children? Are they all out safely?"

He nodded. "I just came from the site. The building is a total loss, but everyone is safe, thanks to your quick call to the fire department that I was told about. Well done. I'd like you to consider more hours. You're the best operator I have. People like you, and you're most efficient."

She couldn't stop the smile that sprang to her lips. "Thank you, sir. I'm honored. I love my job."

"Then you'll increase your hours? I'd like you to work six days a week."

She realized the plum that had been thrown into her lap. These were tough times, and jobs for women were scarce. But her parents—especially in light of Bart's courting—would be less than pleased.

"Katie?"

"I would like nothing better, Mr. Daniels, but I fear I'm going to have to cut my hours instead. Nell will be delighted with the extra work."

❧

Will Jesperson brushed off his hands and surveyed the gleaming glass on the Fresnel lens in the light tower. Whether he'd done it properly was up for debate, but he liked the way the sun glinted through the lens and lit the floor of the tower. He glanced outside again. He'd found it hard to keep working when he would rather study the clouds and the waves from this vantage point.

Beautiful place, this rocky northern California shoreline. He still couldn't believe he had landed such a perfect job. Instead of pursuing his hobby once a week, he could do it every day. There were weather balloons in the shed just waiting to be used. He eyed the rolling clouds overhead and held up a finger. The wind was coming from the north. Was that common here? He'd have the time and equipment to find out.

He stepped outside and leaned against the railing. The beauty of the rolling sea transfixed him. Whitecaps boiled on the rocks poking up from the water at the mouth of the bay. Seeing them reminded him of his grave duties here: to save lives and warn ships of the dangers lurking just below the surface of the sea. Squaring his shoulders, he told himself he would keep the light shining bright—both here at the lighthouse and in his personal life. God had blessed him with this position, and he would do his best to honor him with his work.

He removed his pocket watch, glanced at the time, and then stared back out to sea when he heard a man yell. Were those shouts of alarm? Through the binoculars he saw a ship moving past the bay's opening. A puff of smoke came from a smaller boat trailing it—*gunfire*? The small craft caught up to the ship, and several men clambered up the mast.

Pirates. Will pressed against the railing and strained to see when he heard more shots across the water. Additional men poured onto the ship and were already turning it back toward the open ocean. He had to do something. Turning on his heel, he rushed toward the spiral staircase. The metal shook and clanged under his feet as he raced down the steps. He leaped out the door and ran down the hillside to the dinghy beached on the sand.

The pirates shoved men overboard, and he heard cries of pain. He clenched empty fists. No weapon. Still, he might be able to save some of the men thrown overboard. Shoving the boat into the water, he put his back into rowing, but the tide was coming in and the waves fought him at every stroke.

He paused to get his bearings and realized the ship was moving away. The smaller boat, attached by a rope, bobbed after it. Something whizzed by his head and he ducked instinctively. A hole appeared in the side of the boat behind him. The pirates were firing on him. His hands dropped from the oars when he saw several bodies bobbing in the whitecaps. Men were already drowned.

The wind billowed the sails and he knew he had no chance of intercepting the ship. But he could save the men that he could reach, then inform the authorities of what he'd seen. He grasped the oars and rowed for all he was worth.

⌒ᗢᖇᗢ⌒

At 3:03 a light came on and Katie answered. "Number, please." The caller, a man whose voice she didn't recognize, sounded breathless.

"Is this the operator?"

She detected agitation in his tone. "It is. Is something wrong?"

"Pirates," he said in a clipped voice. "Just off the lighthouse. They shot some sailors and dumped others overboard."

She sprang to her feet. "I'll contact the constable. Do you need further assistance?"

"I need a doctor at the lighthouse. I've got two injured men. The rest are—dead. I couldn't get their bodies into the boat, but they're washing up onshore now." His taut voice broke. "I had to leave the men on the shore to get to a phone, but I'm heading back there now. Tell the doctor to hurry."

"Right away," she promised. She disconnected the call and rang the doctor first. Saving life was paramount. The constable would be too late to do much about the pirates. With both calls dispatched, she forced herself to sit back down, though her muscles twitched with the need for activity. She reminded herself she'd done all she could.

The switchboard lit again. "Operator," she said, eyeing the light. The call originated from the bank.

"R-10, please."

She plugged in the other end of the cord to ring the Cook residence.

Instead, she heard Eliza Bulmer pick up the phone on the other end. "I'm sorry, Eliza, we seem to have a switched link somewhere. Would you hang on until I can get through to the Cooks?" Katie asked.

"Of course, honey," Eliza said. "I just picked up my wedding dress, and I'm trying it on. So if I don't say much, you'll know why."

"You're getting married? I hadn't heard. Congratulations."

"Thank you." Eliza's voice held a lilt.

"Just leave the earpiece dangling, if you please."

"I can do that."

There was a *thunk* in Katie's ear, and she knew Eliza had dropped the earpiece. Katie waited to see if the ring would be answered at the Cook residence but there was only a long pause. "There's no answer, Eliza. You can hang up," she said.

The other woman did not reply. If the phone were left off the hook, it would go dead. Katie started to raise her voice, but she heard a man's voice.

"You said you had something to tell me. What is it? I need to get home."

The voice was familiar, but Katie couldn't quite place it. It was too muffled.

"Honey, thank you for coming so quickly," Eliza said.

Though Eliza's voice was faint, Katie thought she detected a tremble in it. *This is none of my business*, she thought. *I should hang up.* But she held her breath and listened anyway.

"Would you like tea?" Eliza asked.

"No, Eliza, I don't want tea. What are you doing in that getup? I want to know what was so all-fired important that you called me at work—something I've expressly forbidden you to do."

Katie's stomach lurched as she tried to place the voice. Identification hovered at the edge of her mind. *Who is that?*

"Very well. I shall just blurt it out then. I'm out of money and I must have some to care for my daughter. I need money today or . . ."

"I won't be blackmailed," the man snapped.

A wave of heat swept Katie's face. She heard a door slam, then weeping from Eliza. She wanted to comfort the sobbing young woman. Numb, Katie sat listening to the sobs on the line.

The door slammed again. "Who's there?" Eliza asked in a quavering voice. She gasped, then uttered a noise between a squeak and a cry.

Katie heard a thud, and then the door slammed again. "Eliza?" she whispered. A hiss, like air escaping from a tire, came to her ears. "Are you all right?"

Only silence answered her.

She jerked the cord from the switchboard and broke the connection. Unease twisted her belly. She'd already dispatched the constable to the lighthouse. But what if Eliza was in trouble? Her fingers trembled so much she had trouble slipping the jack back into the switchboard. She muffled her mouthpiece with her hand and asked Nell to come back early. She had to make sure Eliza was all right.

TWO

WILL WATCHED THE physician minister to the two men on the parlor floor. "Will they live?"

The doctor nodded. "The bullets missed anything vital, but they lost a lot of blood. This fellow has a concussion." He indicated the younger man, who was still unconscious. "He nearly drowned, but I think he'll be all right."

The older man groaned and rolled over before vomiting seawater onto the carpet. Will rushed for a cloth and mopped up the mess. *Poor fellow.* He glanced out the window and saw the constable walking toward the lighthouse. "Excuse me a moment, Doctor."

The lawman was on the porch by the time Will exited the house. "Find anything?" Will asked.

Constable Brown shook his head. "No sign of the pirates. Before I came out I called the towns up and down the coast and told them to be on the lookout for the ship. So far, five bodies have washed ashore here. Terrible thing." He nodded toward the door. "Are these men able to answer questions?"

Will shook his head. "They're still barely conscious."

"I'll check in on them at the hospital tomorrow. Now tell me exactly what you saw."

Will relayed his first sight of the pursuing pirates and the actions he'd taken. "It sailed off to the north," he said.

"There's been no piracy in these waters for years. Odd. They were too far away to identify any of them?"

"Much too far."

"Pity." The constable turned to go back to his buggy. "Let me know if you remember anything else."

"Of course." Will watched him whip his horse into a trot, then noticed a figure walking along the water. He was almost upon the lighthouse. Was that Philip? The man waved and Will waved back then strode down to greet his brother.

They met at the base of the cliff to the beach. Will enveloped him in a hug and pulled back when he smelled whiskey on his breath. He quickly hid his dismay. "You're the last man I expected to see today. What are you doing here?"

"Can't I just show up to make sure my big brother is settling well into his new job?" Philip asked, returning the hug, but Will could feel him peering over his shoulder, trying to get a look inside. He was a younger version of Will, right down to the dark curls and even deeper brown eyes, but his build was like their father's while Will was taller and leaner.

Will studied him. His brown tweed suit must have come from Macy's. His raven hair fell over his forehead from under his hat. When had he turned into such a dandy? Will had tried to raise him right, but the lad's course was far from the one Will would have chosen for him. Becoming a private eye. Their father would roll over in his grave.

Philip started for the lighthouse. "I'm famished. Anything to eat in this place?"

Will pressed his lips together, and his arms dropped to his side. He fell into step with his brother. "I have a pot of soup on. It should be ready." He knew better than to ask again why Philip was here. The man never revealed anything until he was ready.

Philip's expression turned sulky, and he stared up at the lighthouse. "When you said you were taking this post, I thought you quite crazy. Now I'm sure of it. There's nothing out here."

"I like it that way."

Philip rolled his eyes. "You'll never make a decent living doing this. Join me in my business. You're observant and astute. You'd be an asset."

"No thanks. I'll be able to study the weather without distraction."

Two horses pulling the ambulance stopped in the road by the lighthouse. Philip stared as two orderlies ran toward the lighthouse. "You rescued the injured sailors?"

Will stopped and turned toward his brother. "You know about this already?"

Philip shrugged. "There was another boat taken about a month ago just north of here. The owner retained me two days ago. He received a tip from a woman here that another ship was in jeopardy. I was heading this way, but see I was too late. Did you watch it happen?"

Trust Philip to be in the right place at the right time. Will finally nodded. "Yes, but I've already told the constable all I know."

Philip's smile was ingratiating. "So, tell your brother too. Recognize anyone?"

"No. They were too far away. I managed to rescue two sailors they threw overboard, but that was all." He stopped as the orderlies came out with a stretcher. They slid the injured man into the back of the ambulance, then went back for the other one.

Philip started toward the ambulance, and Will grabbed his arm. "Where do you think you're going?"

"To question the witness."

Will restrained him. "You will not. Both those men are too befuddled to talk to you anyway. Let them be."

Philip tried to shake off Will's arm, but Will held fast. "You will not take advantage of my position."

"This has nothing to do with you," Philip said, raising his voice. His face reddened. "I'm just doing my job."

Will continued to block his brother. "You can do it tomorrow."

The orderlies appeared with the other man, and Will restrained Philip until the ambulance clattered away with the doctor's buggy trailing behind. "Come inside and eat."

"I want you to take me seriously," Philip said, his voice rising nearly to a shout. "This is my chance to launch my career in the right way. When I get enough money, I can buy my own boat, have a nice house."

"Philip, you have better talents than to spend your life this way. Digging into the lives of criminals. Consorting with unsavory people. It's time to grow up. You're twenty-two. There's still time to go back to school. Papa wanted more for you than this."

Philip waved his hand. "He wanted me to be an engineer. There's not enough money in that. This is the way to make something of myself. You're doing what you want. Why shouldn't I?" He cast a sly glance Will's way. "I suspect the idea of some solitude to study the coastal weather played a part in your decision to put in for this job."

There was no getting through to his brother. Will shrugged. "I might manage to put a balloon or two into the atmosphere in my spare time."

Philip turned to look at the whitecaps rolling in on the tops of the blue waves. "Pretty place to do it."

Will nodded toward the lighthouse. "You want to see inside?"

"What's to see? It's just a lighthouse."

Will bit his tongue. Philip reluctantly followed him to the sentinel on the cliff. The sound of the waves was a soothing murmur. Seagulls cawed overhead and dived toward the flotsam of seaweed the white foam left behind on the sand. In a few hours he would attempt to light the lens and get that foghorn going.

"I don't know anything about maintaining a lighthouse," Will said. He gestured to a wooden bench at the cliff's edge. "I've arranged for a day's instruction though. He'll be here tomorrow."

"I still can't believe you put in for this. What's even more miraculous is that you got it with no experience."

Will sat on the bench. "The man who interviewed me was intrigued with what I knew about weather and tides. I believe he thought the knowledge might help me here."

Philip joined him on the bench. "Indeed. So, Will, what did you see?"

He wouldn't rest until he heard Will's story. Might as well tell him now. Will pointed to the right of their position, out past a point that jutted into the bay. "The ship was taken right out there."

"It was for the gold onboard," Philip said.

Will glanced at him. "How much was it worth?"

"Two hundred thousand dollars."

He whistled. "It would be heavy then. They'd need buckboards to transport it when they're ready to take it off the ship."

Philip nodded. "Or a team of pack animals. So someone here probably had the conveyances ready and waiting to off-load it. Is there any way to a main road without going through town?"

Will shrugged. "I just got here myself. I have no idea of the lay of the land yet." He glanced at his brother. "What of this female informant?"

Philip hesitated. "I don't think she'll talk to me. I hoped you might speak with her."

Will frowned. "I don't understand. You *know* her personally?"

His brother turned his face toward the sea. "I've met her."

Will struggled to keep the exasperation from his voice. "When? How?"

His brother hunched his shoulders but didn't turn to face him. "We had a fling for a while, okay? It's none of your business."

Will's fingers curled into his palms, and he struggled to keep his voice even. "You're forcing me to make it my business." The lad was never going to grow up. And why should he when Will was always there?

Philip turned a pleading gaze on Will. "You surely want to see those butchers brought to justice."

Will's protest died on his lips. He *did* want to catch the barbarians who had done this. "What do you want me to do?"

"Just go see a woman by the name of Eliza Bulmer. Tell her you're investigating the taking of the ship and heard she might know something of it. See what she tells you. Ask her what she knows of Albert Russell. She mentioned the man's involvement."

"Very well. But that's as far as I'm prepared to go. I need to focus on learning how to run this lighthouse."

"Good luck, Will," Philip said, rising from the bench. His gaze was already on the boat down at the wharf. "Call me in a day or two and let me know how it's going."

"You're leaving?"

"I have some other avenues to investigate. I'll be in touch."

Will watched his brother jog down the hill then over to the beach. He stood there until Philip reached the distant quay and mingled with other figures. He turned and stared at the lighthouse, then back at his bicycle.

He'd ride to town and find this Eliza Bulmer.

THREE

BY THE TIME Nell arrived, it was already nearly time for Katie to get off work. Maybe she'd overreacted to what she'd heard. Eliza might have left the house—that's why there had been only silence on the telephone. Katie turned over her headset and exited the building into the last of the day's rays. Addie North was waiting outside for her. The two had been best friends since Addie moved to town a year ago. That friendship had continued even after Addie married John North. They had fallen in love when Addie took a post as governess to his son Edward.

"Something has happened," Katie told her. "Do you mind delaying our dinner for a few minutes?"

Addie's gleaming auburn hair was on her shoulders, though she wore a chapeau. Her green eyes glowed with enthusiasm. "I'm at your disposal for the evening. Is something wrong?"

As she strapped on her skates, Katie told her friend what she had overheard. "I'm sure she's fine, but I want to check on her to ease my mind."

Addie skated alongside Katie. "I would call John to accompany us, but he's outside with Edward. Since we leave tomorrow, he wanted to tire the boy so he's not a whirling dervish onboard the ship."

"I simply want to check on Eliza." She glanced up at her friend. "How is your mother?"

"Driving everyone crazy. Even a badly sprained arm isn't enough to keep her from wanting to putter in the garden."

"Perhaps I can stop in and keep her company for tea one day this week."

"She'd like that."

Out on the sidewalk, Katie paused to let pass the seamstresses hurrying home from the garment factory across the street. Church bells pealed out the time. The scent of bread wafted from the open door of the bakery. "I'm quite sure I'm overreacting." She smiled. "We'll check on Eliza, then go to dinner."

The quickest way to Eliza's house would be down the alley behind the drugstore and over to Ocean Boulevard. When the way cleared, they skated across the street. Lifting her skirts free of the mud puddles from the afternoon rain, she skated down the alley to exit on Redwood Boulevard with Addie on her heels. The houses here were more modest than Katie's home by the sea. Most were single story and the paint was peeling away from the corbels and gingerbread. Two women eyed them as they moved toward the Bulmer house. The kohl on the women's eyes and the smears of red on their lips proclaimed their occupation.

Katie slowed, admitting to herself why she normally avoided this part of town. No one, not even her best friend, knew this part of her history . . . but that wasn't why she was here. She was here to check on Eliza. *Eliza*, she said firmly to herself.

But as they skated on rough brick sidewalks toward Eliza's, Katie slowed. The house was on the corner, the last one before Cannery Row. The modest five-room home with only a covered stoop out front turned its curtained windows as a blank face toward the street. It was in better shape than most.

Katie eyed the seemingly empty building. No shadow of the woman who bore her lingered in the house next to Eliza's. If she walked inside, she wouldn't smell lily of the valley or catch a glimpse of her skirt swishing around the corner. Wherever Florence Muller had landed, she'd never be back here again.

Addie's breath came fast as she kneeled to remove her skates. "What's wrong?" She glanced from Katie to the house.

"Just assessing what to do." Despite her brave words, Katie's limbs still refused to carry her across the street. Florence had been gone from this place for many years. She drew in a breath. "Let's go." She walked briskly to the front door and rang the bell. The bell rang inside, but she heard no steps coming to the door.

"See if it's locked," Addie suggested.

Katie tried the knob, but the door wouldn't open. "Locked." She listened and thought she heard a faint cry from inside. "Did you hear something?"

Addie shook her head. "You're still concerned, aren't you?"

"I think we need to make sure Eliza's all right. Let's get the constable."

"We could call from a neighbor's," Addie suggested. She pointed to the house next door.

Florence's old house. "Not there," Katie said, turning the other direction. She hurried to the dilapidated house around the corner. There was no doorbell, so she rapped on the peeling paint of the door. When a man with a grizzled chin opened the door, she drew back.

"Whatcha want?" he demanded.

"Could you place a call to the constable and ask him to meet Katie Russell next door?" She pointed to the Bulmer residence.

"What's Eliza done now?" the man asked.

"I'm concerned for her safety," Katie said.

He shrugged. "She always lands on her feet."

"If you'd be so kind," Katie said. "Tell the constable we'll await his appearance at Eliza's front door."

"I don't have a telephone." He shut the door in her face.

"Let's go back," she told Addie. They traipsed back to the Bulmer house. Katie tried ringing the bell again and got the same response of silence.

"Maybe she had to go out," Addie said.

"Maybe."

"But you won't be content until you know for sure," Addie went on with a smile. "That's so like you, Katie. Always trying to fix things."

Katie smiled. "It's a curse." She knocked again. Nothing. She sighed. "Let's get the constable."

With the skates dangling from their hands, the women walked along the street back toward downtown. The constable was in his office, but he wore a harried expression. A strong odor of smoke filled the room. Constable Brown was a slender man. He wore a badge on the lapel of his tan suit.

He nodded at the women. "Miss Katie, Mrs. Addie. What brings you here at the dinner hour?"

Katie told him about the call she'd overheard. His brown eyes sharpened as he listened. "I tried ringing the bell but no one came to the door. I—I thought I heard something from inside. A cry."

Brown rose and reached for his bowler. "We'll check it out." He opened the door for the women, and they went to his buggy.

There was just barely room for the three of them. Though Katie prayed Eliza was all right, she realized she would look very foolish if the constable broke in and nothing was wrong. But what if she *was* right?

The buggy stopped in front of the Bulmer house. A bicycle leaned against the side of the house, and the door stood ajar.

"I thought you said the door was locked," the constable said.

"It was." Katie scrambled down from the buggy without waiting for the constable's assistance. She rushed toward the door, but he called her back.

"I will go first, if you please, Miss Katie." He strode past her and entered the house with the women on his heels. He tucked his nightstick under his arm and doffed his hat.

Katie peeked past his shoulder as they stepped into the entry. The stench of mothballs hung in the air. Maybe Eliza had been packing away clothing. She said she was trying on a wedding gown . . . Pausing, she listened. She and Addie exchanged a glance. A faint sound came to her ears. *There.* "Down the hall," she said. Lifting her skirts from the scarred floors, she darted past the constable. The pocket door to the parlor stood open by two feet. She peeked inside.

A man stood with his back to them, looking down at a baby girl lying on the sofa. Katie guessed the child to be about a year old. Brown locks curled around her pudgy cheeks. She was just waking up and was making the nonsense sounds Katie had heard.

The little girl sat up. "Ma-ma?" she asked, glancing around the room. The child didn't seem to be afraid of the man. Katie tore her gaze from the child and realized there was no sign of Eliza. There was also no phone in this room, so the scuffle she overheard did not happen here.

She backed out of the room and held her finger to her mouth. The constable scowled, then shrugged and said nothing to the man. She motioned to the constable and Addie, and they stepped past the open parlor door and across the hall. The hinges creaked as she pushed another door open and stepped into the kitchen.

She spied the telephone on the wall. "The scuffle had to have occurred here," she whispered. Addie nodded. Katie saw only a wood-burning cookstove and a dry sink filled with dirty dishes.

"Why did you not wish me to confront the man?" the constable asked, crossing his arms over his chest.

"I wanted to see if Eliza was all right before you questioned him," she said. "I saw there was no phone in the parlor. She was in this room when I spoke with her last." She stepped deeper into the room. It was empty. No Eliza, no body. A chair lay on its side though, an ominous witness to the struggle she'd overheard. "Eliza?" she whispered. "Are you here?"

"I shall check out back then speak with the man in the parlor." The constable brushed past her to the back door. He opened it and stepped onto the stoop. Katie heard a sound behind her and whirled to see the man standing in the doorway with the baby in his arms. A spreading stain on his shirtsleeve and the stench of urine told her the condition of the diaper resting on his forearm.

The baby rubbed her dark eyes and whined. "Dada," she said.

Katie stared at the man. He had dark eyes. Maybe he was this child's father. "Who are you?" she demanded.

He stepped closer. "I came in when you didn't answer the door. Your child needs attention." He clutched the baby around the waist and held her out to Katie.

She eyed him with suspicion. He had to know she wasn't the baby's mother. "Where's Eliza?"

His dark brows winged up. "Aren't *you* Eliza Bulmer?"

She tried to place his accent. Pennsylvania? The East Coast? She guessed his age to be early thirties. He wasn't the manner of man who normally drew her attention since she preferred blond hair and blue eyes, but she had to admit he was attractive. She was close enough to see the golden flecks in his dark eyes.

"I'm not Eliza, as you well know." She nodded to the baby. "She called you daddy."

His eyes widened. "I just found her in the parlor. I've never seen her before."

The baby clutched at him and chattered "dada, dada," as if to contradict him. He colored and frowned. Urine dripped from the diaper to the linoleum.

"Oh dear, she's quite soaked," Addie said.

"So is my shirt," he said.

Katie backed away from him. The kitchen seemed too small and close with his bulk filling it. "Give me the baby," she said, holding out her arms.

He handed over the child. "I was trying to do that, but you didn't seem to want her."

She wrinkled her nose at the strong odor. "Where are her diapers?"

He shrugged. "How would I know?"

So he was still going to lie. "I think we should fetch the constable. He's out back. Eliza seems to be missing."

"I agree. It's odd she left the child alone."

"I'll get him," Addie said. She stepped out the back door and spoke with the constable. He turned and glanced at the man standing in the kitchen then followed Addie inside.

Katie stared at the man, who returned the favor. His perusal caused her to shift from one foot to the other. "I shall seek a diaper for her while you explain your presence to the constable," she said, reaching for the baby then motioning for Addie to follow.

"I don't trust that man," Addie whispered on the way up the steps.

"Neither do I." Katie found the baby's room at the top of the steps on the right. The room smelled of stale urine. The diapers were in a battered dresser. She snatched a square cloth and a fresh gown then found the bathroom. The little girl popped her thumb in her mouth and regarded Katie with solemn dark brown eyes. As far as Katie was concerned, the eyes told the story. That and the "dada" the little girl had babbled. Katie removed the soggy clothes then washed the baby's red bottom.

"She really needs a full bath," she told Addie. Katie placed the fresh diaper under the wiggling baby then struggled with the pins.

"Here, let me help you," Addie said. She knelt beside them on the rug and managed to pin the diaper in place. It sagged a bit, but at least the little one was clean and dry once Katie slipped on the pink gown.

"I heard something," Addie said softly. "I think the men are outside."

Katie nodded and moved to the door. When she unlocked it and stepped back into the hall, she found the stranger leaning against the wall with his arms folded across his chest. She caught a glimpse of the constable's back as he disappeared into a room down the hall.

"The constable is searching the house," he told her.

She handed the baby to him. "Here's your daughter," she said.

His arms went around the child when she thrust her against his chest. "I told you she's not mine."

"And I don't believe you. Where is Eliza?"

"I just got here. I checked the other rooms but there's no one here."

Katie brushed past him and peered into the other two rooms. They were empty as he said. She found the constable in the third one. "Nothing?" she asked.

Brown shook his head. "Her belongings all seem to be here. I know Eliza. She was trying to break out of the barmaid profession so her daughter wouldn't be ashamed of her when she grew up. She'd been hired as a maid. But she'd never leave Jennie alone." He followed Katie to the hall where Addie stood with the man.

The baby whined and struggled to reach for Katie but she tried to ignore the plaintive sounds. "I think I could use a cup of tea. I'm sure the baby must be hungry."

The man's dark eyes looked her over. "Look, Miss . . ."

"Russell," she said. "Katie Russell. This is my friend, Addie North. You're new in town." He nodded. Since he wasn't offering any information, Katie glanced at the constable. The baby's wails intensified, so she finally took her. The little girl plunked her head on Katie's shoulder.

The dark-eyed man hesitated but didn't drop his gaze. "I'm Will Jesperson. I'm the new lightkeeper."

"It's been unmanned for two months," Brown told Katie. "It's about time we got a new keeper. I met Mr. Jesperson earlier. Which doesn't explain why you're here now, Mr. Jesperson."

The lightkeeper glanced away. "My brother asked me to call on Miss Bulmer."

"And you came in without an invitation?" Brown asked.

"I heard the baby crying."

Katie studied his neat vest and smart hat, tucked under his arm. Most lightkeepers she'd seen dressed more casually. His hair was a mass of closely cropped curls.

He glanced at Katie. "You mentioned tea. Perhaps we could all use a cup."

She led the way down the steps to the entry then back to the kitchen. The constable continued to ask the man questions, but she couldn't hear well enough to determine the words. Addie stepped past her and pumped water into a pan and put it on the stove. Mr. Jesperson glanced around the room then righted the toppled chair. He knew more than he was saying about Eliza's disappearance—she could see it in how he averted his eyes. She jiggled the restless baby in her arms and watched Addie wash some cups.

"I'll make some toast for the baby. I would imagine she's hungry," Addie said.

"I'll help you," Katie said. She passed the baby back to Mr. Jesperson and began to search through the cupboards. Addie had the tea and cut-up toast for the baby ready when the kettle whistled. When Katie carried the steaming cups of tea to the table, she found the tot situated on his knee.

The baby reached for the toast and stuffed a piece in her mouth.

The tea sloshed into the saucer when Katie plunked it in front of Will. "She's much too comfortable with you for you to be a stranger to her."

"I just laid eyes on her for the first time today."

"I agree with Katie," Brown said. "I would like to hear more of why your brother asked you to call on Eliza."

He dropped his gaze. "She's, ah, a friend of my brother's. He wanted me to meet her."

"I don't believe you," Katie said before Brown could answer. The constable frowned and shook his head.

"What are *you* doing here?" Jesperson asked.

She pulled out a chair and sank onto it. "Looking for Eliza." Addie sipped her tea beside her and watched with wide eyes.

"There is something more going on here. Exactly what do you suspect me of?"

"We find you with a baby you claim never to have seen and the mother is nowhere to be found. Anyone would be suspicious."

"You never answered me," he said, staring at Katie. "Why are you here? Are you a friend of Miss Bulmer's?"

She took a sip of tea to avoid answering. Her gaze fell on the telephone. "I came to check out the phone. There was a call I tried to make today that came here accidentally. I'm an operator at Central."

He sighed and rubbed his temple. "Right now, what I want most is to find out where Miss Bulmer is and give her back this baby."

Katie stared at Jesperson. He wasn't telling her the truth.

FOUR

WILL SHIFTED THE baby in his arms and studied the face of the young woman across from him. Though the brim of her wide hat shaded her face, there was no mistaking the suspicion in her eyes and in the face of her companion. The constable, too, though he hid it better than the women. One glance into the child's eyes had made him wonder if she could be his niece. Philip had admitted to a relationship with the child's mother. This was the last thing Will needed.

And what of the young operator's last name? Russell. Philip had mentioned an Albert Russell. Could there be a connection and that was why she was so interested in finding Miss Bulmer?

"Have you any notion of where we might find Miss Bulmer?" he asked. "And for what reason she might have left this child alone?"

Miss Russell picked up her cup of tea then put it back on the table without meeting his gaze. "I don't know."

There was more going on here than Miss Russell admitted.

Will glanced at the baby, who was playing with his watch chain. "Strangely enough, this child seems content to be cared for by strangers."

"Miss Eliza often leaves her in the care of neighbors or friends." The constable's voice was heavy with disapproval. He eyed Katie. "Let's go over what you overheard again."

Miss Russell clasped her hands in front of her, glanced at Will as if she was reluctant to share, and then plunged into her story. "I was on

337

the phone with Eliza and heard what sounded like a scuffle. A man came in and they argued. The man's voice was muffled but something about it was familiar."

"Familiar?" the constable asked.

She shook her head. "I just can't place it." She looked up at him. "Eliza never came back to the phone."

So that was why she'd come. He lifted an eyebrow in her direction. To her credit, at least she flushed, aware that she'd been less than forthcoming. But as he studied Miss Russell's face, he knew she still wasn't telling them everything.

Constable Brown glanced at Will. "And you, sir? What did you see when you arrived on the premises?"

"The door was locked," Miss Russell said.

Will's neck burned. "I, ah, picked the lock."

The constable looked him over, and Will heard Miss Russell gasp. "I heard the baby crying, and when no one answered, I managed to jiggle the lock. She was soaked and hungry. And very much alone."

"Very disquieting," Brown said, frowning at him and then out the window. "I'll see if Miss Eliza has gone back to her old haunts."

"Old haunts?" Will asked.

Brown shrugged. "She plied her trade at the taverns, but in the last couple of months she had been working in a respectable job."

Will gulped and glanced at the baby, who had fallen asleep with her round cheek against his shoulder. He suspected little Jennie might be his brother's child, and this new piece of information about Eliza's morals made him suspect it all the more. "What about this baby? What will you do with her?"

"I would have taken her to the orphanage but it caught fire this afternoon," Brown said. He sighed and lifted a brow. "It's been quite a day."

Will winced. "Was anyone injured?"

Brown shook his head. "The volunteer fire department reacted very quickly and everyone escaped injury."

"Thank the Lord," Miss Russell murmured. She glanced at the baby on Will's shoulder.

"I don't know what I'm going to do about the child," the constable said. "The director of the orphanage is out of town, and we are having difficulty placing the children in temporary homes."

Those eyes. So like Philip's. This baby was likely his responsibility. His grip tightened on the child. "I'll take her," Will said at the same time as Miss Russell.

He wished he could recall the words. What was he thinking? Since he was new to town, finding a woman to care for the baby might be difficult.

Miss Russell batted a strand of hair that had come loose from its pins. "What do you know about caring for a child?" Her tone held a challenge.

The baby smelled sour again. Miss Russell was right. What did he know? Still, he wasn't a man to back away from duty. "Not much. But I can learn."

"Why would you want to care for a baby?" the constable asked.

Will let out a sigh. "She might be my niece."

The constable squinted and took in Will's face. "Your niece, you say? And might your brother have something to do with Miss Bulmer's disappearance?"

"Of course not! Philip has been in the city." Will clamped his mouth shut short of revealing his brother had been in town today. Surely Philip had nothing to do with this situation.

"I don't think a man is the right person to care for a baby girl," Miss Russell said. "I doubt you have any idea how to change a diaper."

He lifted a brow. "How hard can it be?"

"Do you know anything at all about what a baby eats? When she'll need to nap?"

"Do you?" he shot back. They glared at one another, and he realized she wasn't backing down. She was a busybody. Will had seen them before. Spinster women who had nothing else to do but interfere in other folks' business. "Why do *you* want the baby?"

Color rushed to her cheeks. "She needs a place to stay until her mother comes back. You're a stranger to all of us. For all we know, you did away with Eliza then came back for the baby."

The constable took a toothpick from his pocket and stuck it in his mouth. He fixed Will with a stare. "That so, Mr. Jesperson? I must admit you seem to show up wherever there's trouble. You saw the problem with the ship earlier, then you show up here."

"I have never met Miss Bulmer. I came to see her at the request of my brother."

"For what purpose?" Brown asked.

Will suppressed a sigh. He was going to have to tell them everything. "My brother is a private eye. He has been retained to investigate the piracies that have occurred in the past couple of months. When the owner of the *Paradox* spoke with him, he said Miss Bulmer had called with information. My brother asked me to speak with her since she might not be inclined to discuss anything with him, given their past relationship."

The constable's lips tightened. "I won't have him interfering in my investigation. I'm in charge in Mercy Falls."

"He isn't even here. He's back in the city."

"Have him stop by my office when he comes to town," Brown said.

"What about the baby?" Miss Russell asked.

Brown took another chew on his toothpick. "Sorry, Miss Katie, but he seems to have a claim to Jennie. If he's a relative, it's his right to care for her."

Her cheeks turned even redder. "But you don't even know if he's telling the truth! For all we know, he could be a kidnapper. Or worse! We found him here with Eliza gone. Surely that is disquieting, to say the least."

"If it will calm your fears, I can prove I'm the lightkeeper." Will passed the baby over to her then dug his posting duties out of his pocket. He handed the paper to the constable, who skimmed it and handed it back.

"He's got all the right credentials, Miss Katie," Brown said.

"That still doesn't prove he's her uncle!"

"Look at her, Miss Katie." The constable gestured to the baby in her arms. "Don't you see a family resemblance?" He fixed a stare on the lightkeeper. "I'm assigning temporary guardianship to you, and if your brother cares to, he can apply for permanent custody as her father if Eliza doesn't turn up."

Shaking her head, Miss Russell pressed her lips together, then her head came up and she stepped toward the door. "If there's anything I can do to help with the baby, please do let me know. Just toggle the phone for Central and ask for me."

Will watched her and her friend move toward the door with the constable on their heels. He tried to quell the rising panic. She was right. He didn't have the foggiest notion of how to care for a baby. "Wait," he said. "If you could help me figure out what to take to the lighthouse for the baby, I'd be grateful."

She stared at him a moment and then turned toward the stairs. "Let's see what we can find, shall we?"

Will followed Miss Russell's swaying skirt up the steps and prayed he hadn't just made the biggest mistake of his life.

❦

Katie found a small bag in the closet and began to pack some of the tiny gowns she found in a chifforobe. Mr. Jesperson set the baby on the floor and moved to join her. "Let me make it clear I don't trust you," she told him. "Not one bit. Who is going to care for her? You'll have duties to attend to." When he didn't answer her but continued to layer the suitcase with clothing, she wanted to throw something.

The new lightkeeper glanced at the sleeping baby on the floor. "What did you hear on the telephone that made you rush here?"

The impersonal tone in his voice reminded her of the constable's. Dispassionate, analytical. "Who is going to care for that baby?" she asked, ignoring his question. "She needs a bath. The urine will irritate her skin. And she might still be nursing. What will you feed her? She can't live on toast."

To her relief, a touch of uncertainty twisted his mouth and he abandoned his persistent questions. "Perhaps you could give me some advice. I've never cared for a baby before."

"Then why did you insist on taking responsibility?" she asked.

He lifted a brow. "You want to believe it's because I did away with Miss Bulmer, but nothing could be further from the truth, Miss Russell. My brother admitted to a relationship with the woman just this afternoon. Then I arrived here and actually saw the child. She favors my brother a great deal."

"I want to believe you," she said. "Otherwise, I don't know how I can stand back and let you take this darling child."

"I don't see how it's your choice. The constable has already made his decision."

She bristled at the finality of his tone, even though what he said was quite true. "I shall draw a bath for Jennie in the kitchen sink. You can finish the packing."

"I thought we had everything."

"I'd suggest you poke through the kitchen and see if you can discover any pap feeders or a banana bottle. That will tell us what she's been eating. If you find none, you will need to purchase some. Some pap too."

The glance he cast toward the baby held doubt. "Pap feeder? Banana bottle? What do they look like?"

She sighed. "You really are a complete neophyte at this, are you not? Take the suitcase and come along. I shall look myself." She scooped up the little one and carried her down the steps. "Hello there, sweet girl," she said, smoothing the curls back from the baby's face.

Jennie struggled and Katie put her against her shoulder. "Ma-ma?" Jennie asked.

Katie patted the baby's back. "Mama isn't here right now. We're going to have a bath. Do you like your bath?" She reached the dry sink. Addie was on the telephone with her husband, John. Katie stopped the drain and pumped water into it. "Could you bring me some hot water from the stove?" she asked Will.

Mr. Jesperson grabbed the kettle of hot water and poured it into the sink. Katie tested the temp with her hand until it had cooled enough. "That's perfect," she said. She laid Jennie on the counter and stripped the clothes from her tiny body, then plunked her into the water. The child gasped then giggled and began to splash the water. "I shall need a towel and washcloth," she said.

"I'll check the bathroom upstairs." Mr. Jesperson left the kitchen and his footsteps pounded up the stairs.

"I need to head home for a bit to calm John," Addie said. "Edward had another seizure and is calling for me."

"Oh, of course!" Katie said. Addie's stepson had epilepsy, and he was especially clingy to his new mother after a seizure. She smiled good-bye at her friend and rinsed the baby. Already, the stench of urine was fading.

When she first heard the creak behind her, she assumed Mr. Jesperson had returned with the linen items. She flicked a glance behind her and saw a man in a brown tweed suit. A handkerchief covered his face like some kind of bank robber. It took a moment for her confused brain to recognize this man was smaller than Mr. Jesperson and his suit was a different color.

"Get the kid and come with me," the man said, his voice muffled by the cloth covering most of his face. His dark eyes glittered above the red handkerchief.

Katie gasped and stepped between him and the wet baby. She seized a frying pan and whirled to face him. "Get back!" She swiped the air with the frying pan and barely missed the man's head. His hand went to his pocket, and he withdrew a gun that appeared no bigger than a toy. Before she stopped to think, she swung the skillet again and it connected with the man's wrist. The pistol dropped from his fingers and skittered across the floor. The baby jabbered something unintelligible behind her, and Katie glanced back just long enough to assure herself that the baby was still sitting in the water.

The man dived toward the gun, but she threw the skillet at him. It hit him in the head and knocked him to the linoleum. "Mr. Jesperson!" she screamed.

The attacker sprang to his feet and ran for the back door as Mr. Jesperson's footsteps pounded down the stairs. The man left the kitchen door gaping open behind him, and Jesperson skidded into the room.

He glanced toward the baby splashing in the water. "What's wrong?"

"A man," Katie gasped. "That way." She pointed to the open door. "He tried to take Jennie."

Mr. Jesperson dashed through the door. Katie turned back to hang onto the side of the sink. Her knees were wobbly, and her hands shook now that the danger was past. The gun still lay on the linoleum. She normally tended to run rather than fight, and her reaction had surprised her.

Mr. Jesperson came back inside. "He's gone." He picked up the towel and washcloth he'd dropped and laid them on the counter. "What happened? Tell me everything."

Katie recounted everything from the moment she realized the house held an intruder. "There's the gun," she said, pointing it out to him. She dipped the washcloth in the cooling water and with a trembling hand, quickly finished rinsing the baby.

He stooped and picked it up. "A Derringer."

She shuddered and rinsed the soap from Jennie's tender skin. "It's an evil little thing."

He nodded. "It might be small, but it could have killed you. Are you sure he wanted the baby? What did he say?"

"He instructed me to pick up the baby and come with him."

"He might have wanted you."

"I'm quite certain his intent was to take her, and he wanted me to come along to care for her." She lifted the dripping child from the water. Jennie howled until Katie wrapped her in the towel. As she turned around, she spied a pap feeder. A nice one in blue and white. "That's what we were looking for," she said, pointing to it.

"Looks like a gravy bowl," he said.

"It's not." When the baby saw him pick it up, she began to cry and point to it. "I think she's still hungry. Check the cupboard and see if there is any pap formula."

"I have no idea what I'm looking for," he said, pushing aside the blue and white gingham over the shelves.

"Look for Nestlé. That would be the most likely formula," she said.

"I see nothing like that."

"Is there milk in the icebox? I can make it with flour and milk." She began to dress the baby in a white gown.

He peered into the icebox. "Yes, there's milk." He took it out and sniffed it. "Smells okay."

"Here, you take her." She thrust the baby into his arms then took the milk and measured out a pint into a pan. She added a pint of water and a tablespoon of flour and put it on the stove. When the bubbles began to roll, she stirred it and put it in the pap feeder. "I'll feed her as soon as it cools." She nodded toward the high chair by the table. "Make sure you take that with you."

Jennie continued to wail and reach for her, so she took the baby from Mr. Jesperson's awkward grip and tried to soothe her, but the baby refused to be consoled.

Her cries—the cries of a little girl, lost and abandoned—twisted Katie's heart, bringing forth memories she wasn't quite ready to face.

FIVE

THE WIND RUSHED past Katie's ears as she skated home in the twilight. She quite disliked being forced to leave little Jennie in the care of the lightkeeper, but Bart would be waiting for her by the time she got home. She crested Mercy Hill, and then her skates rolled faster down the slope toward the house. The sea foam hurtled toward the shore on the crest of the waves, dark blue in the dim light. The salty scent lifted her mood. She loved living by the ocean.

Gaslight glimmered through the windows and she smelled the pot roast their cook had put in the oven this morning. Katie sat on the bottom step, removed her skates, and then hurried to the front door. The first thing she noticed when she stepped inside the house was the scent of liquor. A pool of liquid ran between broken pieces of glass on the floor. Someone had dropped a bottle of whiskey. Or thrown it.

She dropped her skates in the corner by the bench. "Mama?" she called, her voice quivering. Something was very wrong. Her mother would never allow a liquid to mar her redwood floors. She rushed down the hall to the parlor and found her father bending over her mother, who reclined on the davenport. Bart, a grave expression on his face, stood off to one side with his hands behind his back.

"Mama?" Aware of the accusation in the glare she tossed at her father, she lowered her eyes. He adored Mama. He would never hurt her. "What's happened?"

Her father lifted a brow. "Don't raise your voice, Katie. You'll hurt her head. Someone struck her with a whiskey bottle."

She stepped to her mother's side. Her mother attempted a smile, then a moan issued from her mouth. Katie laid her hand on her mother's forehead. "Did you call the doctor?" she asked her father.

"I did," Bart said, stepping toward her. "He's already come and gone."

She didn't want Bart here. This was a family matter. When he tried to grasp her hand, she stepped away. "What did he say?"

"The doctor assured me Inez will be fine," her father said, his voice trembling. "It appears worse than it is." He stepped back so Katie could kneel at her mother's side.

The maid hurried in with a wet cloth. Katie took it and pressed it to the lump on her mother's forehead. "Who attacked her? A thief?"

Bart cleared his throat. "I came up the porch steps with your father as a man rushed out the door. He had a kerchief around his face and I didn't recognize him. Of course, I hurried inside to check on you and your mother."

Her father nodded. "I found your mother lying on the entry floor with the maid caterwauling over her."

A kerchief. Katie started to ask the color then shut her mouth. How silly to think it might be the same man who attacked her at Eliza's. Her father's voice shook as he went on, and Katie realized he was more upset than he was letting on. Whatever his faults when he was drinking, she knew he loved her mother.

She lifted the cloth from her mother's forehead. "The bleeding has stopped." The doorbell rang.

"That must be the constable. I called him." Her father strode out of the room. His voice floated back as he greeted the lawman at the door.

"Is there anything I can do, Katie?" Bart asked, his voice like velvet.

She shook her head. "You've done so much already."

"I've been waiting nearly forty-five minutes." His voice held reproach.

"I'm sorry. I was held up."

"I wanted to talk to you—"

She shook her head. "I can't think of anything but Mama right now. Please, go on home. We'll discuss this all another day."

He frowned and his eyes searched her face. "Very well," he said stiffly. "It's clear that you'd rather be alone. I'll leave you."

She reached toward him as he stalked toward the hall, then dropped her hand. Her emotions were in too much turmoil to deal with him now.

Her father led Constable Brown into the parlor, glancing back at Bart and then to Katie in dismay.

Katie ignored him and moved away from the davenport to allow the constable to kneel with her mother. She stood by her father with her hands clasped in front of her. Questions hovered on her tongue, but she couldn't ask them if there was a chance her mother would overhear.

"Well now, Mrs. Russell," the constable said. "What's happened here?"

He glanced at Katie. She shook her head, and he said nothing about having seen her earlier.

Katie's mother struggled to sit up then gave up the effort and lay back against the pillow. "Where's Katie?" she asked.

Katie moved back into her mother's line of vision. "I'm right here, Mama."

Fear lurked in her mother's eyes. "Don't go anywhere, darling. That man was looking for you."

Katie put her hand to her throat. "For me?" She shouldn't have ignored her misgivings earlier, but she hadn't wanted to worry her parents. The constable's eyes sharpened. She would have to tell him about the man as soon as possible. It was possibly the same intruder.

Her mother pressed her hand to her forehead and winced. "I heard something in your room and called out, thinking it was you. When you didn't answer, I went to investigate and found that man exiting your bedroom. He ran down the steps when he saw me, and I foolishly chased after him."

Katie's father shook his head. "Very foolhardy, my dear."

"I realize that, Albert," she said, her voice soft. "I didn't stop to think. I caught at his sleeve when we reached the front door. He grabbed the whiskey that had just been delivered and struck me in the head with it. That's all I remember until I found myself lying here. I assume you put me here, my dear?"

Her husband nodded. "You were frightfully pale and had blood all over your face. I feared you were dead." His voice broke.

Katie's mother patted his hand. "I'm fine. You mustn't fret."

"So you have no idea who this man was?" the constable asked.

"Not at all. He wore a brown tweed suit, and his face was hidden with a handkerchief."

Katie gasped and put her hand to her mouth. "It *is* the same man."

Brown looked at her. "Does that mean something to you?"

She nodded. "After you left, a man came in the back door and tried to make me and the baby go with him. He was dressed that way too. Mama, what time was this?"

Her mother raised up. "About an hour ago. What baby, Katie? You're not making any sense."

"Eliza Bulmer's baby." She saw her father jerk and his eyes widen. "Eliza is missing, and the baby was alone in the house."

"How did you happen to find the child?" her father asked. He picked at a piece of lint on his trousers.

There was no easy answer to that question. Not with her mother and the constable listening. "I think I'll fix some tea. Would you care for some, Constable?"

"No, thank you. My wife is keeping supper warm for me, so I'd best hurry home. But Miss Katie, why would someone be looking for you? What have you stuck your nose into now?"

"Perhaps he dislikes telephone operators," she said, forcing a smile. "Eliza is missing, Constable. Maybe she's reluctant to help them and they came back for the baby to . . . encourage her."

Brown pursed his lips. "The argument you overheard. Perhaps it was the same man, and he wants to know what you heard."

"I heard nothing that would tell me who he was."

"He might not know that," the constable said. "I have a man combing the waterfront for Eliza. Until we sort this out, please, Miss Russell, stay in public places, will you? I don't like how reckless this man has already been, trying to get to you." The constable clapped his bowler back onto his head and headed for the door.

Katie left the room before anyone could ask more questions. Even pouring hot water into the teakettle didn't settle her shaking hands. So the man was looking for *her*, not the baby. What could that mean? Her hands shook as she filled the tea caddy with loose tea. She poured hot water from the teakettle on the stove into the teapot then retrieved the cups from the cupboard. Her stomach growled and she felt a little sick. Perhaps a tea biscuit would settle her nerves.

"Katie?" Her father stood in the doorway with his tie askew and his vest unbuttoned. "Do you know more than what you told the constable?"

She turned back to the tea and poured it into her cup. "Do you want tea, Papa?"

He blew out a sigh. "Yes, please." She put sugar in his tea then handed it to him. His gaze probed her face. "Are you ready to tell me?"

She nodded. "I was on the phone with Eliza. A problem with the lines caused her phone to ring when I was calling another customer. She let the phone dangle, and I heard her speaking with a man."

"What man?" his voice trembled.

Something about his voice . . . She stopped and replayed in her head the conversation she'd heard. That's why the man sounded familiar. He sounded like her father. But it couldn't have been. Her father would never betray Mama.

"Katie, you're beginning to alarm me."

She lifted her eyes to his. "It sounded like you, Papa," she said. "Eliza told the man she needed money from him to raise the baby or she would go to his wife and daughter." She licked dry lips. "Is little Jennie your child?"

Tea sloshed over the edge of the cup and into the saucer as he put the cup on the counter. "This is not an appropriate subject to discuss with you, Katherine."

His use of her full name betrayed his agitation even more than his shaking hands. "I have to know, Papa," she whispered. "Another man took Jennie with him because he wondered if the child might be his brother's."

"What man?"

"The new lightkeeper. Will Jesperson."

"I don't know him."

"He arrived in town today."

He stroked his mustache. "He took the child?"

She nodded. "But if this baby belongs to you, we must tell Mama. She will want to do the right thing and bring her here."

He sighed. "Eliza Bulmer is a–a woman of loose morals."

It was true. All of it. She couldn't bear to think of it, but she had to know. "She told you Jennie was your child?"

"I'm not going to discuss it with you, Katie. It's most inappropriate."

She steeled her emotions against his stubborn gaze. "Because you don't want to admit what you've done to Mama? Or because you doubt Eliza's veracity?"

His brows drew together. "This doesn't involve you."

"I've been dragged into it, whether you like it or not. And what about Jennie?"

"If an upstanding man is willing to take responsibility for her parentage, I fail to see why you persist in sticking your nose into this affair. Leave it be." He set down his cup with a rattle and turned to walk out.

"Did you kill Eliza?" she blurted out then put her hand to her mouth.

He stopped and turned to face her. "Is that what you think?" His eyes were hurt. "You know me much too well to jump to such a conclusion. At least I hope you do."

Looking into his familiar face, she couldn't believe she'd actually harbored the notion her father could be a killer. She closed her eyes, thinking back. "I heard you leave. But then the door opened again. There was a frightful thump—what I assume was Eliza, hitting the floor."

Katie opened her eyes again. His face was white, and she knew that he had been there. "Did you tell this to the constable?" he asked.

She nodded. "But not about your voice. I didn't place it until a few moments ago."

"I did not go back," he said, his voice firm. "You must believe me, Katie. I couldn't bear it if you thought I might do something like that. There is no reason to implicate me in this. Please, Katie."

She gave a reluctant nod. "All right, Papa."

SIX

THE CHILD'S SOLEMN gaze never left Will's face. He'd already unloaded the buckboard, and he studied the baby sitting on the rug in front of the fireplace. The clock on the mantle chimed eight times, and twilight was giving into night. He'd need to wind the light soon. Philip had better arrive by then to take charge of this little girl.

"A-a, eh-ooh?" she asked. Her index finger pointed for emphasis.

Her expression indicated she was quite sure he knew exactly what she was saying. "Er, I see," he said, feeling like a fool. Was he supposed to understand the string of vowels? "Are you hungry?"

Her small fingers seized the edge of the chair beside her, and she pulled herself up until she stood beside the chair. She sidled around the cushion toward the end table that would support her weight. She glanced at him as if to ask if she was permitted to touch it.

"I think we'd better move you." He lifted her away from the chair and she squawked until he deposited her next to the davenport. Her eyes brightened, and she began to walk the length of it. What did he give a child to play with? And what had he been thinking to take responsibility for her? He'd thought he would insist Philip take charge and grow up, but he had no guarantees his brother would own up to his part in this child's life.

Carriage wheels crunched on gravel outside. Will scooped up Jennie and carried her to the front door in time to see his brother step onto the porch. He carried a glossy black bird on his arm.

"What the devil do you have?" Will demanded, eyeing the bird's yellow wattles.

"A present for you. His name is Paco. He's a mynah."

"I don't need a bird."

"Well, I have no place to put it." Philip eased the bird from his arm onto a nearby table. "And I understand he's quite valuable."

"You've been playing cards again, haven't you?" Will said.

Philip rolled his eyes and shrugged off his coat, hanging it on a peg by the door.

"I thought you intended to pursue this job like a man, Philip. You promised me."

"I am pursuing my job," Philip said, shooting him an aggravated look. "Sometimes that means I must pursue clues where my informants are most likely to be, regardless of whether or not you approve of it."

The mynah screeched and Philip dumped a handful of seeds from his pocket onto the table. The creature picked up one and cracked it. "Step away from the cake!" it screeched.

Will was in no mood for another responsibility. He glared at the bird.

Philip glanced from Will to the baby in his arms, seeming to see her for the very first time. A frown gathered his brows. "Who is *that*?" he asked. The baby wrapped her arm around Will's neck. "Your daughter," Will said, staring hard at him.

Philip took a step back. "I have no inclination to decipher your ramblings, Will. What are you talking about?"

Perhaps he'd been too abrupt. "When did you last see Eliza Bulmer?"

His brother straightened then brushed past Will into the foyer. "Do you have any coffee?"

"In the kitchen." Will followed him down the hall to the kitchen and watched as his brother poured a cup of coffee from the pot simmering on the wood range. "Are you going to answer my question?" The baby squirmed in his arms and he set her down on the rug by the back door. She began to clang together the pot lids he handed her.

"Why this sudden interest in Eliza?"

Will clenched his fists. "Examine this child's eyes and nose and guess what I'm thinking."

Philip set his cup on the table and stared down at the baby. "That child isn't mine—if that's the conclusion you've jumped to."

"Oh no? When did you have this relationship with Eliza?"

James shifted uneasily. "A couple of years ago, I guess. Maybe a little less." His gaze stayed on Jennie. "Lots of people have brown eyes."

Will swept his hand toward the little girl. "Look at the way her hair grows at her hairline. And that cowlick. I believe she's your daughter. Did Eliza ever tell you she was pregnant?"

"I haven't talked to her," Philip said, his tone sullen.

"When did you last speak with her?"

"I received a letter a year ago asking me to call on her, that she had something of importance to tell me."

"Jennie is about a year old."

Philip held his hands out in front of him. "That is very flimsy evidence to try to prove this child is mine, Will. I don't believe it. Why wouldn't she ask for money when she discovered she was pregnant?"

"Maybe she was waiting for you to show up so she could discuss it in person."

"Why don't you just ask Eliza? How did you get this child anyway?"

Will studied his brother's expression. No trace of guilt darkened his eyes or tugged at his mouth. If something had befallen Eliza, Will didn't think Philip was involved. "She's missing. I found the baby alone in the parlor when I stopped by to speak to Miss Bulmer."

"She left a child of this age alone?"

"A chair was overturned in the kitchen. I fear foul play."

Philip picked up his cup and took a sip. "And you thought I had something to do with that? For what purpose?"

"I don't suspect you of harming Miss Bulmer, but I do believe you need to be a man and take responsibility for your child."

"You are not going to foist this baby on me without proof I'm her father!"

Jennie's face crumpled. She dropped the pan lids and began to wail. Will lifted her from the rug and put her against his shoulder. "There, there." He patted her back awkwardly.

The baby wailed louder, and he smelled a distinctly unpleasant aroma wafting from the direction of the diaper that hung heavily from her bottom. "I think you'd better change her, Philip."

"Me? You brought her here. I have no idea how to change a baby and no desire to learn."

Will shifted the squalling child to the other arm. "Do you seriously expect me to believe you don't see the resemblance between this child and yourself?"

Philip thrust out his chin. "She's not mine."

"You don't think she could possibly be yours? That you didn't have relations with the woman?"

Philip's gaze wandered off. "I fail to see how this is any of your business, Will."

"Grow up, Philip. Be a man and take responsibility!" He tried to hand the baby to his brother, but Jennie clung to him and wailed all the more.

"You brought her here. She's your responsibility. Maybe her mother will turn up tomorrow." Philip wheeled and stalked out of the kitchen.

The front door banged a few moments later, and Will stared into the red face of the little girl. His shirtsleeve was soaked in a most unpleasant manner, and the stench from the diaper filled the kitchen. He would have to do this by himself. Cursing himself for failing to consider his brother's temperament, he rushed to the case of baby paraphernalia Miss Russell had packed and extracted a diaper. Holding the baby at arm's length, he went back to the kitchen and found a cloth, which he dampened with warm water from the teakettle sitting on the stove. He laid her on the counter and undid the pins. Flinching at the odor of feces, he cautiously peered inside the soggy scrap of cloth.

And cringed at the mess inside.

How did one go about cleaning up a child when she kept trying to roll over? Keeping one hand on the baby, he rolled up his sleeves and set to work. Fifteen minutes later Jennie was gurgling her nonsense words happily while he was drenched in perspiration and covered with flecks of dark matter he didn't want to think about further.

He had no idea how he was going to survive the contretemps he'd gotten himself into.

❧

The light flashed on the switchboard. Katie's eyes still felt gritty from lack of sleep. Nell would be here by six o'clock and she could go home. She'd hated to leave her mother this morning, but Papa had arranged for another clerk to come in to man the store. He would watch over Mama himself. Katie had called the constable the moment she got to her switchboard, but there had been no sign of Eliza and no clue to the identity of their attacker.

A light flashed on the board. She plugged in the toggle. "Operator."

"Katie Russell?"

The voice echoed strangely in her ear, and Katie glanced at the switchboard to see the location. The skating rink. "This is Katie Russell."

"What did you hear yesterday, Miss Russell?"

Her tongue dried. "Who is this?" She vaguely heard the door bang behind Nell as she came in and removed her hat in preparation for the evening shift.

"You'd better keep your mouth shut, miss. The boss don't take kindly to interference."

She wetted her lips. "What have you done with Eliza?"

Nell's head turned sharply, and she stepped toward Katie. "What's wrong?" she whispered.

Katie shushed her. "That baby needs her mother. Where is Eliza?"

"You don't want to go where she is. If you tell anyone what you heard, you'll join her."

"Why did you try to take Jennie?"

"That doesn't matter. Not now."

The headset clicked in her ear after the ominous words. She tore it from her head and handed it to Nell. "I have to go," she said. If she hurried, maybe whoever had called would still be at the rink.

"Katie, wait, who was that?" Nell called after her.

Katie jammed a pin through her hat and rushed out the door without answering. She didn't take time to strap on her skates but just grabbed them up and ran across the street and down to Hibiscus Street. The gaslight hissed a greeting as she reached the door to the skating rink. From inside she could hear the thump and rumble of skates on hardwood. Pushing inside the door, she glanced around for the telephone. Cigar smoke hung thick in the air. She spotted the telephone on the wall behind the counter.

She stepped to the wooden bar. "Is that the only telephone here?"

The woman behind the counter, a blonde who obviously had rouge on her cheeks, nodded. "Sorry, we don't allow anyone to use it." She popped her chewing gum.

The scent of the Tutti-Frutti gum wafted Katie's way. She'd never seen the woman before. "Did you just come on duty?"

"I've been here for two hours."

It was a man's voice she'd heard. Katie was sure of it. "Has anyone asked to make a call?"

"I told you. We don't allow no one to use it. I'd get in trouble if I let you."

Katie kept her voice low in spite of the noise from the skates. "I don't wish to use it. I want to know who used it fifteen minutes ago."

The young woman popped her gum again and her gaze shifted away. "Told you, no one."

"I'm the operator. A call came from here fifteen minutes ago. It was a man."

The woman picked up a pencil then put it down again. "No ma'am. No calls from here."

"I won't tell your boss, but I have to find out who it was. I know it was from this telephone unless there is another one in the building. Some fellow sweet-talk you into letting him make a call?"

The girl flushed. "It was a short call. There was no harm."

"Did you know him?"

The blonde shook her head. "He was quite the gent though. Dark brown hair and eyes. Tall with nice shoulders and a smile that, well, you understand."

"Of course," Katie said. It sounded like the lightkeeper. "Did you get his name?"

The woman shook her head. "I tried, but he didn't hear me when I asked."

"Is he still here?"

"No, miss. He left just before you arrived."

Katie knew many of the people skating. Perhaps one of her friends could recognize him. "Did anyone else see him behind the counter?"

"I don't think so. I was careful. I blocked him a bit. I didn't want anyone else to ask to use the telephone." The girl looked shamefaced.

"Did the man skate at all?"

The woman nodded her head vigorously. "Oh yes! I wouldn't allow just anyone to place a call."

"Is he still here?"

"Might be," the woman said with a shrug. "Didn't see him leave."

"Do you know what he was wearing?" Katie knelt and strapped on her skates.

"A brown tweed coat and white shirt. Very dapper."

"My thanks." Katie paid her money and skated out onto the floor, shoving aside her fear.

The thunder of the rolling skates was a welcome sound. She scanned the rink and the tables, but there was no tall man in a tweed suit. She rolled around the rink for a few minutes while she assessed who was here. Some were more observant than others. A woman would be most apt to have noticed a handsome man. Katie discounted most women in the rink until she saw Sally, a parlormaid at the North household. Katie lagged at the handrail circling the room until Sally drew parallel.

"Could I speak with you a moment, Sally?" she asked.

"Miss Katie, did I do something?" Sally asked.

"Of course not. I'm hoping you can help me," Katie said. The other woman's troubled face cleared, and they skated off the floor to a backless bench. Once they were seated, she nodded toward the skaters rolling around the floor. "There was a man here earlier. I wondered if you'd noticed him."

The young woman tucked a stray strand of hair back into place. "A man, miss? What did he look like?"

"Very handsome, I hear. Dark brown hair and eyes. A brown tweed coat."

"Oh, I couldn't have missed him! A real dresser, he was. Very dashing. He took me for a spin around the floor and asked me to go to his room. I gave him what for, I'll tell you that. What kind of girl does he think I am?" Sally's voice rose the longer she talked.

Katie paused. "Did you get his name?"

"No, miss."

"You say he asked you to his room. So he's not from Mercy Falls. Did he tell you where he was staying?"

"Oh yes. At the Redwood Inn."

Katie knew the proprietor. She'd have to see if he would tell her anything.

SEVEN

THE BABY SAT on a blanket with some pots and pans to bang on. The sunset cast orange bands onto the undersides of the clouds in a glorious display of God's majesty. Will watched it a few moments then went back to searching for his weather balloon.

Paco, the mynah, meowed from a perch Will had made near the door. The first time the bird had done that, he'd been sure a stray cat had wandered in. Now he was getting used to the bird's strange noises. He eyed the baby. He had to have help. His lightkeeper duties would entail working all night and sleeping during the day. The baby wouldn't sleep all night and all day too. Philip hadn't shown his face after he stormed out, and Will was certain his brother had gone back to the city. Will was too tired to be angry.

He jotted down the description of the sky in his notebook then scanned the horizon for the weather balloon. Was it still afloat? It would ascend to a high altitude, then burst and drop. He was eager to get the readings from the instruments. A flash of white caught his eye and he spotted the burst balloon over on the rocks two hundred yards down the beach. Scooping up the baby, he hurried to the location and set her down, then retrieved the balloon and his instruments. The lamp on the lighthouse would need to be lit shortly, and the night's work of tending the light would begin. He didn't know how he was going to get through it all.

Lanterns wavered along the quay down the beach. Boats were

docking or shoving off. This was a peaceful place, and he missed the city less than he'd imagined he would. Sighing, he picked up Jennie and turned to retrace his steps. When he crested the hill, he saw a shadow move in the twilight down by the road. Squinting, he realized a buggy had pulled up while he was occupied. The man, an older gentleman in his late forties or early fifties, strode toward where he stood. The fellow wore a dark three-piece suit and bowler. His attention was fixed on the glow of lamplight spilling from the front window of the lighthouse, and he hadn't noticed Will yet.

Will dropped his balloon and stepped out of the shadows. "Good evening. May I help you?"

The man jumped then collected himself. "Mr. Jesperson?"

"That's right." Will studied the fellow who hadn't taken his eyes off Jennie. "Something I can do for you?"

"Might we step inside?"

"We may, but I'd like to know who I'm speaking with first."

The man extended his hand. "Albert Russell."

Will barely choked back an exclamation. Albert Russell. The man Philip wanted him to ask Eliza about. "You're related to Miss Katie Russell?"

"My daughter."

"Come in." He led the way to the lighthouse and ushered his guest to the parlor. "Coffee? Tea?"

"Thank you, but no. I can't stay long." Mr. Russell glanced around the room, one of five inside. "Pleasant living quarters. Remote out here, but well appointed."

"Quite." Will was impatient to find out what was on the man's mind. He put a wriggling Jennie on the floor, and she toddled over to grasp at Mr. Russell's pant leg.

The man patted her head awkwardly. "Your daughter?"

"No." Will didn't elaborate. He was sure Miss Nosy Operator had filled her father in on the situation from last night. "How can I help you, sir?"

The man glanced at the baby then back to Will. "I'll be honest with you, Mr. Jesperson. I'm looking for one of my possessions that I'd left at Miss Bulmer's. It is no longer at her premises. I thought perhaps you picked it up with the belongings you brought here for the baby."

"I brought nothing but diapers and clothing." Will knew guilt when he saw it. "You had a relationship with Miss Bulmer?"

The man flushed. "That is hardly your concern."

Was this why his daughter had offered to take Jennie—because she was aware of the affair? Will glanced at the baby, who seemed quite comfortable in Mr. Russell's presence. Of course, Jennie didn't seem to fear strangers. The man's brown eyes were the same color too. But he didn't have the cowlick like Jennie's. That resemblance was to Philip instead.

It wouldn't hurt to ask though. "Is Jennie your child?"

"No, she is not," the man said, his voice rising. "Did my daughter tell you that?"

"No. How are you so certain Jennie is not your child?"

"The woman was hardly faithful to any one man. And the chit looks nothing like me." Mr. Russell waved his hand in a dismissive gesture. "I realize my eyes are brown, but hers are shaped differently. Nothing about her resembles me or Eliza, so she must look like her father."

"Dad-dad," Jennie chanted, banging on the man's knee with her small fist.

Will raised a brow. "She seems to know you."

Mr. Russell removed the child from his side and straightened. "Of course she does. However, that does not mean that I sired her."

She promptly began to wail. Will scooped her up. "So what item are you looking for?"

"It was a pocket watch. Engraved with my name on the back. My mother purchased it for me on my twenty-fifth birthday, and I'm quite loathe to part with it."

"I found nothing like that. You're sure it's not at her house?"

Mr. Russell shook his head. "I searched the house before I came out here. It's not there." He rose. "Thank you for your time. I'll be off now."

Will walked the man to the door and shut it behind him. "Now what was that all about?" he asked the baby.

❧❧❧

The Redwood Inn was in a part of town that had once been fashionable but now bore the marks of neglect. It was still respectable, but only just. The hotel was ornate and massive but its glory days were twenty years in the past. Time had taken its toll on the corbels and ginger-bread trim, which had lost much of their paint. Katie skated to the picket fence gate. Darkness had fallen but the glow of gaslight pushed back the shadows with a warm yellow light. She removed her skates and walked up the porch. The bell tinkled on the door when she pushed inside.

Mr. Wilson was polishing the wooden counter when she entered. "Miss Katie," he said. "What brings you here so late?" He glanced at the grandfather clock in the corner as it chimed the time, eight o'clock. He used to stop by to play pinochle with her father, and he never failed to bring her a stick of peppermint. But it had been some years since he had done that.

A high shelf circled the room. Birds and animals of every kind stared down on her. Mr. Wilson was a taxidermist as well and he took every opportunity to display his handiwork. She shuddered and averted her eyes. "I need some information, Mr. Wilson." She joined him at the counter. The registry lay right in front of her but she had trouble reading it upside down. Besides, she didn't know the man's name.

"What's that, Miss Katie?"

"Do you have any new guests here right now? A man, in particular. Dark hair and eyes. Youngish, maybe midtwenties. Snappy dresser."

The man bared his teeth in a grin that showed a silver-capped tooth. "You scouting for a beau, Miss Katie? I thought you and Mr. Bart were cozying up."

Heat flamed in Katie's cheeks. "Of course not, Mr. Wilson. This inquiry has nothing to do with any romantic feelings. Is the man here?"

"No ma'am, but I think I know who you mean. He picked up his things a few minutes ago and left to catch the packet to the city."

"What was his name?"

"Joe Smith." The proprietor smiled again. "A false name, I'm quite certain, but I don't pry into the business of my customers."

"Did he say why he was in town?"

"I didn't ask. That would be taken for nosiness." He gave her a pointed look.

"Thank you, Mr. Wilson. Have a good evening." She retraced her steps to the gate by the sidewalk and put her skates back on. It would be useless to go to the dock. The last packet for San Francisco would have departed by the time she could get there.

She skated slowly back toward her house. As she reached the edge of town, she stopped to adjust her right skate and saw her father's buggy turn from the road to the lighthouse. Why had he been out there? She was tempted to go find out. Pausing at the lane that led to her house, she decided she couldn't bear not knowing. She skated down the concrete road to the lighthouse. When the road turned to macadam, she removed her skates and walked the rest of the way.

She heard the foghorn before she saw the lighthouse. Her breath came fast by the time she saw the light blinking its warning. As she began the climb up the hillside to the edifice atop it, she heard the wail of the baby. "That man," she muttered. She quickened her step and reached the front door. The crying wasn't coming from inside the house but from around the other side, near the cliff. Was Mr. Jesperson harming the child? Her hands crept into fists, and she flew around the corner of the house to confront him.

Mr. Jesperson had Jennie against his chest and he was walking back and forth across the grass. The faint refrain of "The Old Rugged Cross" lifted on the wind, and Katie stopped short. He was *singing* to her? A lump formed in her throat. Maybe he wasn't such a bad sort. Her father had never sung to her, but he was kind and indulgent most of the time. She didn't know why she was allowing such dark suspicions to sway her emotions this way.

The baby's cries faded then stopped. The little girl's head stayed down on Mr. Jesperson's shoulder, but he continued to hum and pat the tiny back. Such a small baby on such a big shoulder. He was even more attractive when he was showing such tenderness to a child. Her earlier misgivings assaulted her. Could he really be the baby's father and not his brother as he'd claimed?

Before she could examine the thought further, he turned and spotted her in the moonlight. Wariness replaced his placid expression. She managed a smile. "Is she asleep?"

"Finally. Let me put her down."

He carried Jennie to the door. Katie followed him into the house, where he laid the baby in a crib in the parlor.

"There's no bedroom for her?"

He shot her a quick glance. "I'm supposed to stay in the light tower all night, but there is no way I can do that and watch her too. I moved her crib in here so I can nap on the sofa between trimming the wicks."

"You look tired," she said, observing the circles under his eyes.

"I was unable to sleep today after being up all night." He covered the baby with a blanket then patted her back when she stirred. "Why are you here?"

"I wanted to find out why my father was here."

He turned, and his brown eyes crinkled with his smile. "Just can't stand it, can you, Miss Nosy Operator?"

Heat rushed to her cheeks. "I shouldn't have come." She turned toward the door.

"At least now I know why you wanted to take charge of Jennie," he said.

She turned back to face him. His expression warned her of the meaning of his words. "He admitted his involvement with Eliza?"

"In so many words. He was looking for a pocket watch he left at her house. Did you see such an item?"

"No." She knew the watch of which he spoke.

"I assume he fears if it's found he'll be a suspect in Miss Bulmer's disappearance."

"He had nothing to do with it," she said quickly. She wished she was as convinced as she sounded. "I'm sorry to trouble you. I'll be on my way."

"I quite dislike you traveling back to town alone in the dark," he said. "Why don't you take my horse? You can bring it back tomorrow. After the attack on you in the kitchen yesterday, I'm unwilling to see you in harm's way."

She nodded. "I appreciate your thoughtfulness, Mr. Jesperson. I shall return your horse tomorrow."

"He's in the barn at the base of the hill. The saddle is in the shed. Do you need assistance?"

"No, I'm comfortable around horses."

He glanced at the baby. "I wish I could say the same about Jennie. Do you know of a reliable woman I could hire to help care for her?"

"I'll think on it," she said. "Thank you again for the loan of your horse." She was eager to get away from his probing, curious eyes. She escaped the lighthouse, saddled the horse, and galloped for town.

EIGHT

KATIE BOLTED UPRIGHT at the pounding on the front door. Her father hadn't been home when she arrived last night. He'd probably been out drinking. Or trying to cover his tracks with Eliza. After rubbing her mother's forehead with peppermint oil to help her migraine, Katie had fallen into bed after midnight. She glanced at the clock on the mantel. Only six a.m. Who could be rousing them so early?

The maid's soft voice murmured down the hall, then Constable Brown's voice echoed in the foyer. "I must speak with Mrs. Russell," he said.

Katie leaped from the bed and grabbed her dressing gown then shoved her feet into slippers. She fumbled for the doorknob and nearly fell over her kitten, Nubbins, who entangled himself around her ankles. After extricating herself from the cat, she stumbled into the hallway and rushed down the stairs to find the constable pacing the redwood floors.

"Ah, Miss Katie, I must speak with your mother."

Katie tightened the sash on her gown. "What's wrong, Constable? Mama went to bed with a migraine and I don't wish to disturb her if we can avoid it."

The constable was pale, and he had dark circles under his eyes as if he'd been up all night. "I'm afraid it can't be helped. Please call your mother."

Katie gulped at his serious expression. Was that compassion she glimpsed? "Very well. Get Mama," she told the maid.

Her mother's voice spoke from behind her. "I'm here, Katie. What is the commotion?"

"Come into the parlor, Mrs. Russell," the constable said, his voice grave.

Her mother took Katie's hand in a fierce grip. The women obeyed the constable's directive and sank onto the gray horsehair sofa at his gesture. Her mother leaned her head against the doily that covered the back of the sofa. Katie didn't let go of her hand. Whatever was coming was bad, very bad.

Brown cleared his throat. "Mrs. Russell, I regret to inform you that your husband was discovered in the pond at the base of Mercy Falls this morning at four o'clock."

She squeezed her mother's fingers. "No," Katie whispered. "Is he—dead?" Hysteria bubbled in her throat.

"No, but he's gravely ill. I had him transported to the hospital."

"Was it a—a suicide attempt?" The falls was notorious for attracting the despondent.

"It appears so."

Suicide. All the doubts crashed over her head again. It made him appear guilty of Eliza's disappearance. This was her fault. She should never have let him know she'd overheard.

Katie's mother had still not spoken. She sat motionless and without expression. "Mama?" Katie choked out.

"I believe I shall go back to bed," her mother said in a clear voice. "This migraine is quite unmanageable."

Katie fought to keep her tears at bay, to be calm for her mother. She and the constable exchanged a long look. She slipped her arm around her mother's shoulders. "Mama, did you hear what Constable Brown said? Papa tried to do away with himself."

Her mother clapped her hands to her ears. "I don't want to hear anything more from you, Katie," she said, her voice shrill. Hysteria was in the last note of Katie's name. Her mother's eyes went wild. "Your father would never do such a thing. Never! What would our friends say?"

"I think we should call the doctor," Katie mouthed to the constable.

He nodded. "In the hall or the kitchen?"

"The kitchen."

He slipped out of the room while she hugged her mother. "He'll be all right." But would he? The constable's manner had been most grave. What if her father died? Her mother would never survive the trauma. Her parents had always been so close . . . or at least that was what she'd thought until she learned of Eliza's involvement.

Her parents. Today had brought back too much of the past, before they'd taken her in. She preferred not to remember all that pain.

Brown stepped back into the room. "He's on his way."

"What happened? How was he found?"

He shrugged. "An early morning hunter discovered him half in the water and dragged him all the way out. He has a bad cut on his head."

"Will he live?"

His expression turned grimmer. "The doctor is examining him. He's unconscious. Does your father have any enemies? The break-in yesterday, Miss Eliza's disappearance, the attack on you. Might they be connected?"

She glanced at her mother. "I'd like to wait until my mother is under the doctor's care before we discuss this further."

"Of course." His keen gaze probed her face. "Do you fear his suicide attempt is connected with Miss Eliza's disappearance?"

"I–It's possible," she choked out. The doorbell rang. "That must be Dr. Lambertson. Could you get it? I don't wish to leave Mama alone."

"Certainly."

Katie's tongue was as dry as sand. Her eyes burned, and her throat convulsed with the effort to hold back the sobs building there. How much should she tell the constable? How could he find what had happened to Eliza if she wasn't honest with him? Of course, her father was not responsible for Eliza's disappearance, but if she kept anything from the constable, she wouldn't be doing the right thing. When the doctor turned to tend to her mother, she slipped down the hall and beckoned to the constable to follow her.

"Miss Katie, what are you hiding from me?" The constable's voice was gruff but kind.

She bit her lip. Her father had begged her to stay quiet, but what if he hadn't tried to kill himself? "I realized why the man's voice on the phone was so familiar," she told him. "It was my father who argued with Eliza."

He took out a cigar and struck a match. "I see," he said, drawing in a puff. "You feared I would assume your father was involved in her disappearance if you told me the truth?"

"I didn't realize it was his voice at first. I just knew it sounded familiar." She sent him a pleading glance. "Truly, Constable, I wasn't hiding it from you. I realized it after we talked."

"So you think your father came back and disposed of her?"

"No!" She wetted her lips. "I think someone else came in. In fact, what if Papa didn't try to do away with himself? What if that man attacked him?"

"What would be the motive? I suspect Miss Eliza was blackmailing him." His voice was heavy with disapproval.

"I asked my father if he was Jennie's father. He denied it and I believe him." She knew her tone lacked conviction and put more force into it. "Papa's a good man. He wouldn't hurt anyone."

"Not even when he's drinking?"

Heat raked her face. "Not even then."

"When did you see him last? Did he seem despondent?"

She hesitated. "I glimpsed him on his way back from the lighthouse last night."

"Why was he there?"

"Mr. Jesperson told me he was looking for a pocket watch he left at Eliza's. He thought perhaps Mr. Jesperson had picked it up with Jennie's things."

"Why would it matter?"

"His name was on it. I'm sure he didn't want his relationship to become common knowledge. There's something else you need to know, Constable. I received a threatening telephone call last night just before I left work."

"Did you recognize the voice?"

She shook her head. "But the call came from the skating rink. I rushed there to see if I could perhaps catch the perpetrator, but he'd left for the Redwood Inn. When I went there, I was informed he'd left town. According to Mr. Wilson, the man called himself Joe Smith. A fake name, of course."

Brown puffed on his cigar. "Miss Katie, you need to let me do the investigating here. You're going to get yourself in trouble. I told you—you need to watch yourself."

"I'm sorry, Constable. You're quite right."

He continued to study her. "So that is why you offered to take Miss Eliza's child. You suspected little Jennie was your sister."

She opened her mouth to say she didn't consciously know why she'd wanted the child, but before she got out the words, she saw a shadow move.

Her mother spoke from the doorway. "Child? What are you saying, Katie? That your father had another child?"

Katie didn't want to face her mother's accusing stare, but she forced herself to wheel and look at her mother's stricken face. "I'm not sure, Mama. We have no real way of knowing now."

"I'll leave you to deal with her for now," the constable said. "We will talk more tomorrow." His voice held a note of warning.

Her mother grabbed the door frame for support, and the doctor seized her arm to steady her. "I've administered laudanum," he said. "She needs to go to bed."

"I'll see she gets there." Katie took her mother's hand.

Her mother jerked her fingers away. "Not until you tell me what you're whispering about out here. I shall speak to your father about this. He'll be most distressed at your accusations." There was a wildness in her blue eyes, and her mouth pulled to one side.

Katie pitched her voice to a soothing tone. "Let's talk about it tomorrow. You're about to fall down."

"The laudanum will let her sleep," Dr. Lambertson said. "Let me help you get her to bed."

With Katie on one side of her mother and the doctor on the other, they managed to get her to the high bedstead before she collapsed. "Will she remember any of this when she awakens?" Katie asked.

"I hope her head is clear after resting a few hours," the doctor said. "But it's been a hard blow to her mind. I'll check in on her later in the morning. Stay with her until then."

He took his leave, and Katie arranged for the groom to take Mr. Jesperson's horse back to him. She dragged her pillow and quilt to the floor by her mother's bed. Nubbins followed Katie into the soft folds of the bedding. The kitten curled up on Katie's chest and closed his eyes, but Katie watched her mother's chest fall and rise. She prayed for a way to open out of this confusion.

⁓⁂⁓

The sugar failed to cover the bitterness of the tea. Katie took another sip, hoping the beverage would sharpen her mind. The grit in her eyes reminded her of the tears she'd cried most of the morning. And the reason for them. She watched the sun illuminate her sleeping mother's pale face on the pillow. If only she would awaken with the light of sanity in her eyes after sleeping for a few hours. Katie set her tea on the bedside table.

When the blue orbs focused on Katie's face, her silent prayer was answered. Her mother sat up and reached for Katie's hand. "Have you been here all along, darling? What time is it?"

Katie hung onto her mother's cold fingers. "I didn't want to leave you. It's ten. How are you feeling?"

Her mother's eyes filled. "Your father wanted to leave us, didn't he? I can't fathom it."

"We don't know that for sure, Mama. Someone broke in here and attacked you. What if that same person hurt Papa?" She'd rather believe that than that her accusations had driven her father over the edge of sanity.

Her mother clutched Katie's hand. "Don't think this is your fault, darling. I didn't want to worry you, but your father's business is in trouble. I fear that was why he jumped off the falls, regardless of what this business with Miss Bulmer might lead us to believe."

Katie shook her head. The haberdashery had always seemed indestructible, bustling with customers. They had a good life, one of comfort and respect. "You mean in danger of bankruptcy?" The very thought filled Katie with horror. The shame of it all would destroy Mama. She'd grown up with the best of everything.

Her mother twisted a lock of loose hair around her finger. "He told me two weeks ago. The bank had turned down his request for a loan on the business, and this house is mortgaged for the maximum amount."

Katie tried to absorb the dreadful meaning. "We shall have to move?"

"We may have no choice." Tears flooded her mother's eyes, and she glanced around the lavishly appointed bedroom.

Katie followed her gaze. Damask curtains hung at the windows. The fine blue rug had been imported from Persia. The bed linens were of the finest silk.

Her mother's lips trembled. "My father built this house, and I was born here. I don't know how I shall bear this."

"I–I have my job," Katie said. When her mother's face didn't change, Katie realized how ridiculous that sounded. Her meager earnings would never support this household. The servants, the upkeep. Not even with additional hours.

"We could sell the haberdashery, I suppose," her mother muttered. "Perhaps it is worth something. It is the only shop in town. Surely someone would like to own it."

"When Papa recovers, he'll know what to do." Her father always had a plan. And he *would* recover. "I shall go to the hospital and check on him this morning. Perhaps I can discuss the situation with our solicitor tomorrow," Katie said.

"The thought of it gives me a sour stomach," her mother said, leaning back against the pillow. She focused her gaze on Katie. "Bart Foster is still pressing his suit, is he not?"

Katie heard the hope in her mother's voice and could see where this was going. "Yes, he is. I . . . but I don't know him well yet, Mama. I have not thought of marriage."

Spots of color came to her mother's face, and her grip tightened. "I've groomed you for a respectable marriage, my dear. You're twenty-five, past time for marriage. You have no better prospects."

Katie nodded, but acid burned the back of her throat. Bart was handsome enough, but her pulse didn't flutter when he took her hand or paid her a compliment. But did that matter when she'd always been expected to make a suitable alliance? She couldn't bear to see her parents spending the rest of their days in a hot flat over the garment factory. Not if it was within Katie's power to attend to the matter.

Her mother glanced away. "Bart has approached your father about a partnership at the haberdashery. An infusion of new stock and new energy would save it."

Their maid, Lois, appeared in the doorway. "Miss Katie, Mr. Foster is here. He heard about your papa."

Katie tried to ignore the hope in her mother's face. "Bart is here? Show him into the parlor, please." Katie pushed her loose hair away from her face. Though she'd dressed, she hadn't taken time to put up her hair or wash her face.

Pink rushed to her mother's cheeks. "Put on your blue dress and pinch some color into your cheek. And leave your hair down. I know it's not proper, but your curls are very fetching. Men are quite fond of seeing a woman's hair down."

Heat ran up Katie's neck. "Under the circumstances, I thought this gray one most appropriate. I'm sure he's here to offer his assistance, Mama. Besides, I couldn't marry without a suitable engagement. A year at least."

"You *must*, Katie," her mother said, flinging back the covers. She staggered from the bed and gripped Katie's shoulders. Her eyes held a feverish glint. "It's the only answer. You're attracted to him anyway. He holds so much power and wealth."

Katie tried to twist away, but her mother held her firmly. "But what if he finds out who I really am?" If people knew she wasn't really Inez Russell's daughter, would her friends all desert her?

"How could he possibly find out? My dear sister knows better than to show her face here after all these years."

"She might hear of my marriage and come back to demand money." The idea had plagued Katie most of her life. She never wanted to see the woman who had abandoned her again.

"Just let her try!" Katie's mother stepped back and dropped her hands to her sides.

"I wouldn't want to humiliate Bart." Or to face such disgrace herself.

Her mother's face softened. "I've often wished we could wipe away the memories you have of your early years with Florence. I did the best I could to salve your wounds with love."

"You've been a wonderful mother," Katie choked out. She hated to talk about Florence. The memories still made her ache.

Her mother made a shooing motion. "Make yourself presentable, my dear. Your future husband awaits."

Katie made herself smile back into her mother's serene face. "Yes, Mama, the blue dress." She hurried to her room and changed into her new dress then raked her fingers through her curls so they lay on her shoulders in casual abandon. Tucking a hanky into the sleeve of her dress, she descended the stairs and stepped into the parlor where she found Bart Foster standing with his hands clasped behind him as he stared into the garden. Sunshine gleamed on his carefully combed blond hair.

His appearance never failed to remind her of his status in the community. His navy suit had been tailored in the city, and he stopped to have his shoes shined every morning. His grandfather had been a Mercy Falls's founder, and every unmarried woman in town cast longing gazes his direction. She should be thrilled he gave her more than a passing glance. And of course, she was. As his wife, the specters of her past couldn't harm her. She could hold her head high.

He turned and spied her standing in the doorway. "My dear Katie, I came as soon as I heard." He crossed the Persian rug and took Katie's hand in his.

She returned the strong pressure of his fingers. "I'm so glad for your help and strength, Bart," she said. Though they'd been on first names for two months now, she still relished the way the syllable rolled off her tongue. The admiration in his blue eyes never failed to lift her spirits, though today the warmth of his gaze only raised her mood slightly above the floor.

Keeping her hand in his possession, he led her to the sofa. "How is your mother?"

"She's . . . resting," Katie said. Her mother would be mortified if Bart became aware of how she'd fallen apart this morning at the news.

He squeezed her fingers. "What is your father's condition?"

"I don't know yet. I'm going to check on him shortly."

"I would be glad to accompany you."

"Thank you, Bart, but I have several errands to run as well. I wouldn't want to take up so much of your time. I'm sure your father expects you at the sawmill."

"I have some meetings later this morning." He pressed her hands far longer than was appropriate. "Telephone the office if there is anything I can do."

"I shall do that."

His gaze lingered in her hair. "You look quite lovely today."

The heat of his glance made her want to wind her hair into a French roll and cover it with a chapeau. "Thank you." Her mother's advice had been right. She only wished the touch of his hand would make her feel something beyond . . . invaded.

He gave her fingers a final squeeze. "I should go and let you get to your errands." He paused as though to give her time to object.

She knew she should offer Bart refreshment, but she wanted to find out about her father. To confront him and see if he'd really tried to do away with himself. It was so difficult to have to shoulder the burden to try to make sure everyone was taken care of. She knew she had to figure out a way to meet everyone else's expectations.

She rose and smiled down at him. "Thank you for stopping by, Bart. You're a good man." He smiled his pleasure, and she ushered him out then leaned against the door and closed her eyes. Mama would expect a full report.

NINE

THE BABY'S HOWL awakened Will. He'd been dreaming he was in a hot air balloon floating along the clouds with his barometer. He opened scratchy eyes and got up. The clock on the mantel struck ten thirty. He'd slept since dawn when he'd extinguished the lighthouse lamp, and most fortunately, so had Jennie.

"Are you hungry, honey?" he asked. "Want some bread and jam?"

She gave him a toothy smile and reached up. "Ree," she said.

Did she just try to say *hungry*? He scooped her up. She'd wormed her way into his heart so quickly. In the kitchen, he deposited her in the high chair Katie had suggested he bring from the Bulmer residence, then spread a slice of bread with butter and jam. He cut it into pieces and placed it in front of her.

She rammed a piece into her mouth. "Umm, umm," she mouthed around her food.

Cute the way she did that when she ate. He prepared some oatmeal for himself, and when she reached for it, he fed her a few spoonfuls. After breakfast he cleaned her up, changed her diaper, and carried her back to the parlor where he put her on the floor with some wooden blocks. Too bad Philip wasn't here to bond with his baby girl. She was quite charming. He glanced out the window and saw a horse and rider at the bottom of the hill. Constable Brown dismounted and trekked up the hillside toward the lighthouse.

Will sighed and went to open the door. "Good morning, Constable Brown. What brings you out here?"

"I wish to speak with you, Mr. Jesperson."

"You're looking a little tired. Busy night keeping the peace?" Will asked, stepping aside to allow the constable to enter.

"Bad night," the constable said.

Will led him to the parlor. "Have a seat."

Brown sank onto the sofa. "I don't suppose you have any coffee?"

"I do." Will went to get a cup for the man, and when he came back, he found the constable dangling his closed pocketknife in front of the baby's rapt face. "I don't think that's the best thing for her to play with," he said.

"She can't get it open. It's much too difficult."

Will retrieved it from Jennie anyway and distracted her with the pan lids before she could wail. "So what's the problem, Constable?"

"Albert Russell was found half-drowned at Mercy Falls last night."

Will put down his cup of coffee on the marble-topped table beside him. "What happened?"

"Attempted suicide, I suspect."

"He'll be all right?"

The constable hesitated. "He was still unconscious this morning when I checked at the hospital. The doctor isn't sure if he will recover."

"I'm sorry." He was too. He thought of Miss Katie and the pain she must be going through. Suicide. Did it have anything to do with Miss Bulmer and her call suggesting Philip investigate Russell? "How does that correspond to your visit here?"

"Miss Katie mentioned her father came to see you yesterday. Looking for a pocket watch."

Will nodded. "He was here just a few minutes."

"Did he seem upset? Distraught?"

"Not suicidal, by any means. He asked if I'd seen the watch, and I told him I had only taken baby items from Miss Bulmer's house."

Brown took out a cigar. "Did he seem upset that it was missing?"

"He did not seemed pleased. Look, Constable, I find it difficult to believe the man tried to kill himself. Especially in light of Miss Bulmer's disappearance and the attack on Miss Russell."

Brown rolled the cigar in his fingers and nodded. "There is that. I was about to mention it to you. I spoke with the owner of The Redwood Inn. He described the man as in his midtwenties with dark hair and brown eyes. A nice dresser."

An image of his brother flashed through Will's mind, but he pushed the thought away. Philip would never threaten Miss Russell. Besides, he'd gone back to the city. Hadn't he?

Brown took a gulp of his coffee then set it on the table beside him. "Where is your brother, Mr. Jesperson?"

The man was no fool. Will might have implicated Philip in this mess by admitting he suspected Jennie was Philip's daughter. Will kept his expression impassive. "He's in San Francisco. Investigating the missing ship, as I mentioned."

Brown took out a notebook. "What's the name of his agency and where can I find him?"

Will told him and watched while the constable wrote it down. "If you suspect Philip of involvement in this, you're mistaken, Constable."

"Of course, of course." Brown put his notebook away and rose. "I shall be in touch."

"Constable, while I have you here—" Will began.

The man turned with a questioning expression. "Is there another problem?"

"Not a problem, necessarily. I wondered if you'd heard anything else about that missing ship."

"We found some more bodies floating in the bay. Barbarians, that's what those pirates are."

"Any clues to solving that case?"

"It's as dead as the squid I saw on the beach. I've combed the roads and coastline for clues, but they've vanished." Brown raised his brows. "Now see here . . . why don't you leave the investigating to me?"

Philip had told him that local law enforcement tended to be proprietary about their investigations. "You're quite right. In the worry about Miss Bulmer, I forgot something my brother told me. I mentioned he'd asked me to speak with her. There was a man she thought might be involved in the taking of *Dalton's Fortune*."

"The ship that was taken a month ago," the constable said. "Who was the man?"

"Albert Russell."

Light dawned in Brown's eyes. "Perhaps his daughter is not as far off as I'd thought. She wondered if he might have been attacked."

"Or he was involved and would rather kill himself than go to jail."

"True." Brown put on his bowler. "Thank you for your time, Mr. Jesperson. Our discussion was most interesting."

Miss Bulmer had said to check out Albert Russell. Was it only revenge or had the man truly been involved?

Katie tiptoed into the room. She still trembled from seeing her father's still form, settled under a crisp, white sheet. His chest had barely moved up and down and he hadn't opened his eyes, though she'd called his name and held his hand until the nurses had shooed her out.

The light from the open curtains illuminated her mother's blotchy, aging skin. She was beautiful to Katie, though. What other woman would have taken her in and loved her so completely? Katie went to the window and struggled to release the heavy drapes from the tiebacks.

"I'm awake."

Katie turned at the sound of her mother's voice. "I was going to let you sleep."

Her mother plumped the pillows and sat up. "I can't hide in bed forever. How did it go, darling?"

"Very well. Bart was solicitous and offered to escort me to the hospital, but I declined his offer. I went to check on Papa and then to see about the state of his affairs."

Her mother sat up. "How was he?"

Better for her mother to realize how serious his injury was. "Unconscious. The doctor is doing what he can."

Her mother swallowed hard. "He's strong. I believe he will be fine. I must go to him." She struggled to sit up.

Katie pressed her back against the pillow. "Not yet. The nurses told me we must stay away and not tax his strength."

"They'll not keep me from my husband's side. You must help me to dress and go to him." Her mother gripped Katie's hand. "You're so competent, my dear. I don't know what I'd do without you. Now tell me about Bart."

The springs groaned as Katie sat on the edge of her mother's bed. "I–I don't really love Bart, Mama. Am I even ready for marriage?"

Her mother patted her hand. "Love will come in time, dear girl. This modern-day obsession with love is ridiculous. Respect is what you need for a marriage to flourish. You respect him, do you not?"

"Oh yes. He's a good man. Honorable."

"And wealthy. There will be no problems he can't handle with his family's money and influence behind him." She put her hand on her forehead. "My head aches quite dreadfully."

Katie positioned herself to massage her mother's head. The weight of responsibility pressed her down. What would it be like to choose a man who seemed somewhat . . . unsuitable? Mr. Jesperson's brown eyes flashed through her memory, but she told herself not to be ridiculous. He was the last man on earth her mother would accept. A lightkeeper earned a bare pittance. There would be no more pretty dresses and slippers, no more baubles and perfume, let alone a chance for her parents to keep their home and servants. Such things were only important to Katie because they ensured that the people she admired would never know the squalor from which she'd come. A woman had to think of future children and caring for her mother. That was how things were done. Inez had made that clear.

Her mother's smile faded. She seemed to gather herself. "Katie, did I dream it or did you say your father had a . . . another child?"

Katie paused in her ministrations. "Oh Mama, I'd hoped you wouldn't remember."

"Tell me what you know."

Unable to watch the pain in her mother's eyes, Katie plucked at the sheet. "I was at the switchboard. I overheard Papa talking to Eliza Bulmer. She said her child was his responsibility."

"Did you ask your father about it?"

"I did. He admitted to a relationship with Eliza but didn't believe Jennie was his child." She dared a peek at her mother and found the older woman stone-faced.

Her mother shrugged. "Please don't harbor any pity for me, dear girl. Men find it quite impossible to be faithful. This is something you shall discover one day."

"Never," Katie said under her breath.

Her mother smiled. "You're young and idealistic. I was quite happy to run the household and let your father take his pleasure elsewhere. It relieved me of the duty."

Duty? There was much about the love relationship Katie didn't understand. "The Bible says a man is to love his wife as his own flesh. Surely it's not too much to ask that my husband would want only me." She'd read the Song of Solomon and longed to find true love for herself.

"Sometimes you're such a child, Katie." Her mother closed her eyes and pressed her fingers to the bridge of her nose. "Where is this baby? I must see it for myself."

"She's with the new lightkeeper out at Mercy Point. Mr. Jesperson."

"How old is she? And why does he have her?"

"I think she is about a year old. He seems to think she might be his brother's child."

"But you're not convinced."

Katie shook her head. "No, Mama. Not after what I overheard on the phone."

"Does she look like your father?"

"She has dark eyes, but then, so does the new lightkeeper. I would assume his brother does as well."

"Oh dear. Such a conundrum. We must get to the bottom of it. But secretly. Tell no one your suspicions. Bring the child to me and let me have a look at her. I'm quite sure I shall be able to tell." Tears hung on her mother's lashes. "This is too much for me to bear. You must fix it somehow, Katie."

Katie bit back the question, *how?*, and nodded. "I'll go out and check on her. It's the least we should do."

"I want to see her."

"I can't do that. What if someone sees me bring her here?" That was assuming Mr. Jesperson even allowed her to take Jennie.

"You are well known for your acts of charity, my dear. Our neighbors will think you are doing one more good deed."

"And if you determine she is Papa's daughter?"

Her mother fell back against the pillow. "It's too much for me to think through. Let's take one step at a time, shall we?" She plucked at the covers. "Your priority must be to make a suitable marriage. How close is Bart to declaring himself?"

"I have so little experience with men, Mama."

"Has he held your hand with obvious reluctance to release it?"

Katie nodded. "He did that today."

"Has he kissed you?"

Katie's cheeks burned. "Of course not, Mama!"

Her mother's bark of laughter came. "My dear, there is nothing wrong with allowing the man you want to marry to kiss you. Once you're sure his intentions are honorable, of course. Bart has not hidden his open admiration for you. He's been pleased to show you around town, and I suspect he will invite you to come to dinner at his home with his parents very soon."

"He may slow down the relationship now," Katie said. "Now that . . . well, Papa."

Her mother's gaze narrowed. "Is that what you'd like?"

Katie forced a smile. "I'm just upset, Mama. So much has happened in the last twenty-four hours."

Katie saw the fear drain from her mother's eyes. "I like Bart very much. He'll be a good husband and a good father." She swung her legs out of bed. "Now help me dress. I must tend to your papa."

TEN

KATIE STOOD LOOKING at the man in the bed. The murmur of voices from nurses tending to others in the ward faded as she prayed for her father to live. His eyes were closed, and his skin was nearly the color of the sheets. What would they do if he died? She touched his hand. "Papa?" she whispered. "I've brought Mama to see you."

There was no response. Not even a flutter of his lids. She glanced at her mother seated on the other side of the bed then turned her attention back to her father. The bruise on his forehead was huge and mottled. There were a few cuts on his face, and she saw a lump on the back of his head poking up through his thin hair. Could someone have struck him and thrown him over the falls? She knew she was grasping at straws.

Her mother leaned closer. "Albert? You must wake up now." There was no response. "Leave us, Katie. I'll stay with him. Go see about that child."

Katie hesitated then pressed a kiss on his cold cheek and hurried out of the hospital. Out on the sidewalk she strapped on her skates and skated toward the bank. Before she reached it, she saw a familiar horse and buggy. *Addie.* Her friend was certainly on her way to Katie's house. Katie waved, and John guided the horse to the side of the street. He helped his wife alight, and the two young women flew into each other's arms.

Katie clung to Addie while John and his son, Edward, stood to the side of the road. Addie's dog, Gideon, pressed his nose against Katie's leg as if to comfort her. The dog was well known for being able to sense distress.

"Katie, I'm so sorry," Addie whispered. "How is your father? Did you just come from the hospital?"

Katie nodded. "He's still unconscious. I–I'm not sure he'll live, Addie."

Addie pressed her hand. "God is in control. When I pray, I feel he is telling me not to worry. That your father will be all right. Be strong."

"Let me buy you some lunch," John said. He stood in front of the café and opened the door, gesturing inside.

Katie followed him and his family into the café. A waitress seated them at a corner table. They ordered the special roast beef plate. Gideon lay at Katie's feet.

John sipped his coffee. "If there is anything we can do to help, you have only to tell us, Katie." Six-year-old Edward tugged at his sleeve and whispered in his father's ear. "Ah, we'll be right back. Edward needs to visit the men's room." He took the hand of his son, and the two went toward the back of the café. Gideon got up and followed them.

"How are you really doing?" Addie asked.

"I'm frightened. Something more than we realize is going on." Katie told her friend about her father's visit to the lighthouse in search of his pocket watch and about the threatening phone call she received.

"So you think your father might not have tried to kill himself?" Addie asked. "That whoever is responsible for Eliza's disappearance tried to harm him? I quite dislike bringing this up, Katie. But what if your father suspected? What if he was worried he would be accused and chose to end his life rather than face the dishonor?"

Katie sipped her tea. "I have considered that, and you could be right." But it still felt wrong to her. There was something more, something she was missing.

"How is your mother this morning?"

"Better. Bart's call lifted her spirits considerably."

"So Bart came to call already," Addie observed after a short silence. "I wondered if he would come immediately. He seems quite taken with you."

"Mama wants me to marry him," she said. "We–We are in financial straits. My father's business is on the verge of bankruptcy. A favorable marriage is our only hope of keeping this estate. It would destroy Mama to lose it. She was born here."

Addie leaned forward. "Oh Katie, don't let such a thing sway your decision. Real love is worth waiting on."

"Mama says the most important thing in a marriage is respect."

"Of course I respect John, but I love him too. More and more I have come to believe that the most important thing is to know that God has a plan for your life. We do well to listen and obey that plan."

"I know you're right, but how do you *know*?"

"Jehovah-Shalom," Addie said. "God, our peace. I see you're unsettled about Bart. That tells me right there that he isn't the right man. When we follow in the way God has laid out for us, we have peace."

"I'm not sure I've ever experienced true peace," Katie said.

"It's because it's hard for you to let go of control," her friend said. "You think you have to manage everything. Learn to turn loose of things, Katie. God really does know what he's doing."

"That's hard to see right now."

Addie reached over and patted her hand. "Does your mother know about Eliza?"

Katie nodded. "I tried to keep it from her, but she overheard me tell the constable."

"Have you heard how little Jennie is doing?"

"I saw her last night at the lighthouse. Mr. Jesperson seems to be very good with her. He was singing to her when I arrived." Katie smiled at the memory. It had so warmed her heart.

Addie stared at her. "Why are you smiling so strangely? Are you attracted to the lightkeeper?"

Katie wiped the smile from her face. "Of course not. I know nothing about him."

"I knew nothing about John either, but I was drawn to him from the moment we met. Sometimes it happens that way."

"Not in this case," Katie said with enough emphasis she hoped would convince her friend. She glanced at the dog trotting back toward them on Edward's heels. "I do believe Gideon exercises peace."

Addie laughed. "Nothing ruffles that dog. If we could all be so even tempered." She glanced back at Katie. "Don't change the subject, my dear. I saw Mr. Jesperson. He's quite handsome."

"I like blond men," Katie said. "The lightkeeper appears almost dangerous. Such dark eyes."

"I think he is a strong man. Protective. You saw the way he took charge of the baby. What woman wouldn't respond to that?"

"Me," Katie said. "You must put him out of your head. I know nothing about the man and what I do know, I rather dislike. He's much too overbearing."

She almost believed it until she remembered the way she'd heard him singing to the baby. It was most endearing.

❧

Katie sat in the third pew with her mother. The minister gave a final prayer, and the worshipers began to stand in their pews and greet one another. Several hurried over to ask about her father. She shook their hands as they assured her they were praying for him. He'd regained consciousness but was still incoherent. She looked past her mother to where Bart stood with his parents. Good people. Good friends.

But would they be so kind if they knew the truth?

She shook the unpleasant thought away. They would never find out. She escorted her mother outside toward their buggy. Live oaks shaded the green expanse of the yard. Buggies and a few automobiles lined the road. Mr. Jesperson held Jennie facing forward in his arms as he strode across the lawn toward her. Katie glanced toward her mother. Good, she was occupied with a group of ladies. Katie moved to intercept him. This was not the time to allow her mother to inspect the child. Not in front of all their friends.

"Mr. Jesperson," she said. "How surprising to see you."

He took the hand she offered. "I make a practice of being in God's house on Sunday."

Her heart gave an unwelcome flutter at the touch of his warm fingers. What was the matter with her? Bart was just across the yard with his parents. It was most unseemly for her to even notice the broad span of gray wool on Mr. Jesperson's chest or the curl in his dark brown hair. "I hope you will understand when I say, please don't make yourself known to my mother. She's in no condition to deal with Jennie's presence."

"I wouldn't dream of it," he said.

The baby reached for her. Katie took the child and kissed her soft curls. She'd always wanted a baby sister. The child smelled clean and fresh as though she'd just been bathed. "You seem to be having no trouble caring for her. She is quite content."

"I wish I could say the same for myself. I must find someone to help me." He scanned the crowd with a hopeful expression. "Is there anyone here you might recommend?"

Katie opened her mouth to tell him she had no idea who he might hire when Addie joined them. "You remember Mr. Jesperson, don't you, Addie?" Katie said.

Addie offered her hand. "Of course. And little Jennie too."

Katie ignored the sidelong glance her friend slid her way. She noticed the way Jespserson's sharp gaze scanned the crowd as though he were looking for someone. Probably still on the hunt for a nanny for the child.

He held out his arms for Jennie, who pointedly turned her head and clung to Katie's neck. "Na, na," she said, shaking her head for emphasis.

The child's small hands clutched at Katie's neck, and a warm sensation settled in the pit of Katie's stomach. It felt good to be so wanted. She kissed the soft cheek nestled so close and inhaled the scent of the toddler. What a blessing it would be to care for this little one every day.

"Katie, introduce me to your friend."

Katie turned to see her mother standing behind her. "Mama," she faltered. How did she get out of this? An awkward pause ensued.

Her mother extended her hand. "I'm Inez Russell. You must be Mr. Jesperson."

Katie should have known better than to try to hide anything from her mother. "This is Jennie, Mama." She turned the baby around to face her mother.

"Hello, sweet pea," her mother cooed to the baby. "Aren't you a little bright-eyed girl?" Jennie reached for the older woman and grabbed at a ribbon on her hat. "Will you let me hold you?" The baby held out her arms and Katie transferred her. Her mother's gaze roamed Jennie's face. "Her eyes are quite dark. Much like yours, Mr. Jesperson."

And Papa's. Katie didn't say it but she saw the fear in her mother's eyes. She wanted to point out the way the baby's hairline differed from her father's and how Jennie's eyes varied too. But she held her tongue. Her mother liked to come to her own conclusions without coercion.

Jennie reached for Mr. Jesperson and he took her. She laid her head on his shoulder and began to hum to herself. After a moment, she lifted her head and squawked at the man.

"She's tired and wants me to sing to her," he said, his voice apologetic. "I should take her home."

Katie found it impossible to hide her smile. The baby had the man wrapped around her little finger.

"I would welcome a call from you in a few days," Katie's mother said. "There is much to discuss."

Katie's smile faded. Her mother obviously thought she saw some resemblance between the baby and her ailing husband.

"I should be most pleased to speak with you," Will said, his eyes flicking between Katie and her mother, clearly understanding the direction of Inez's thoughts. "Do understand, though, that you have not yet met my brother. If you were to see him, you would know there is no doubt about this child's parentage." He nodded to Katie and Addie. "Good day, ladies. I'm sure I'll see you again quite soon. If you hear of a dependable woman looking for a live-in position as nanny, please send her to me."

Eleven

WILL OPENED ONE scratchy eye at about eleven o'clock in the morning. Jennie slept in the crook of his arm. She'd howled the whole night long, and he'd hauled her up and down the lighthouse steps as he tended to the light. They'd fallen into bed at dawn, but even then she'd been restless next to him and hot enough to make his forehead break out in a sweat.

Hot. Wait a moment. Was she ill? He touched her skin and found it dry and very warm. Holding her against him was like nestling up to the hot coals in a fireplace. She coughed and the harsh bark made him sit up and stare at her. Spots of red dotted her pudgy cheeks. He scooped her up and leaped from the bed. While he had no notion of where to find the doctor, someone in town could direct him. He rushed down the steps to the front door and yanked it open to come face-to-face with Miss Russell's fist poised to land on the door.

Her eyes matched the color of the sea foaming at the foot of the cliffs. What would you call the shape of her face—heart-shaped? The high cheekbones were pink. So were the full lips above her narrow chin. The lilac dress and wide-brimmed hat she wore were in the latest fashion, and she clutched her bag in her gloved hands as she stared up at him. She looked every bit as beautiful as she had at church yesterday.

She dropped her hand. "Mr. Jesperson. You were going out?"

Before he could answer, the baby let out a wail loud enough to call Poseidon from the depths of the ocean. He shifted Jennie to his other arm. "Could you direct me to the doctor?"

Miss Russell peered into the baby's face. "She's flushed."

"I think she has a fever." He handed the baby to the woman with a sense of relief, then stretched out the cramp in his arm muscle.

Miss Russell put her hand on Jennie's forehead. "A high fever. We must get it down right away. Run some tepid water in the sink."

He sprang to do her bidding. Had he done something wrong? Perhaps this was all his fault. Another person might have recognized the child's condition last night by her inability to settle. After pumping water from the hand pump into the dry sink, he poured in enough hot water from the kettle on the stove to bring the temperature to lukewarm.

Miss Russell crooned to the wailing baby then tested the water. "Perfect." She laid Jennie on top of the cabinet and quickly stripped her clothing off. The tiny girl screeched when Miss Russell eased her into the sink. "I know, sweetheart," she said.

She splashed water along the baby's skin for what seemed an eternity. Will wanted to clap his palms over his ears so he didn't have to listen to the child's cries. "I'll get a towel," he said. He rushed up the steps to the bathroom and found a stack of towels in the corner cupboard by the claw-foot tub. By the time he got back downstairs, the baby's wails had tapered off to an occasional hiccup.

He opened the towel between his hands, and Miss Russell lifted the dripping wet baby from the water and deposited her into the folds of the terry cloth. He wrapped the edges around Jennie, and Miss Russell cuddled her against her chest. The baby's eyes closed.

"She seems better," he said.

"For now. We should let the doctor examine her to ensure she doesn't have something like diphtheria." She quickly dressed the sleeping child and lifted her to her shoulder.

"I'll get the buggy ready. You'll have to direct me. I don't know where to find the doctor."

She followed him into the entry. He paused and glanced down at her. "How did you happen to come by this morning?"

"It can wait," she said.

He studied her face and noticed the dark circles under her eyes. "Is something wrong?"

She sighed. "My mother wants to see Jennie again. She's always one to do her duty."

"I'm certain she's my niece. When you meet my brother, you'll be convinced as well." He stepped onto the porch. A buggy was parked outside. "Could we take your buggy?"

"Certainly."

He took Jennie and noticed she wasn't as hot. Once he helped Miss Russell into the buggy, he handed the baby up to her then climbed in himself. "Why is your mother so willing to believe Jennie is your father's child?"

She glanced at the baby sleeping on her shoulder. "I think she knows I believe it."

"And why are you so sure?"

She bit her lip and looked away. "I overheard Eliza demand money from him. For what other reason could she have been black-mailing him?"

His pulse quickened. He could think of something else. Maybe Miss Bulmer wanted money to stay quiet about the taking of the ship. But perhaps he was wrong about Philip being the father. His gaze fell on Jennie's swirl of a cowlick. Just like his brother's. His doubt ebbed.

"My brother is investigating the taking of the *Paradox*."

"Yes, you called me about it," she said.

He raised a brow. "You were the operator I spoke to?"

She nodded. "I don't understand why you bring that up now. We are discussing Jennie's parentage."

He slapped the reins against the horse's back, and the buggy began to move. "You asked why else Miss Bulmer might be blackmailing your father."

Horror filled her eyes, and she whipped her head from side to side. "My father had nothing to do with the ship. Besides, Eliza disappeared only a short time later."

"Another ship was taken a month ago. My brother said Miss Bulmer had suggested a man in town was involved. Albert Russell. There is no other Albert Russell in town, is there?"

"No. But what you're suggesting is impossible. I know my father. He would never do such a thing."

He heard the quaver in her voice. "I'm sorry. I did not mean to upset you."

She arranged her skirt on the seat. "If your aspersions on my father's name are meant to deter me from my duty to Jennie, you have failed. You can't possibly want to care for a baby!"

He turned the horse's head from the county road to the main street to town. "It has most certainly complicated my life. But sometimes duty demands we do the inconvenient."

The woman gave him a severe glance. "A baby is more than a duty."

He urged the horse forward. "Indeed she has already crept into my heart. But isn't duty part of why you're here?"

Her bonnet hid her face. "I love children. I already care about her. She would not be hard for me to love."

"Nor for me. She's an engaging little mite." The sea air blew his hair over his eyes, and he realized he'd forgotten to grab his hat. "Can we agree we both want what is best for Jennie?"

"Of course."

He glanced at the wind blowing wisps of shiny hair across her cheeks. He didn't want to be enemies with this woman.

TWELVE

KATIE DIDN'T LIKE the child's lethargy. Her initial goal to let her mother get another peek at the baby had evaporated the moment she saw the child. "Can you go a little faster? We need to get her to the doctor," she said again.

The towering redwoods cast a shadow over the macadam road, and the damp odor of the ferns growing along the banks added to the sense of isolation. What did she know of this man? She still suspected he had something to do with Eliza's disappearance. The buckboard reached the edge of town. Church bells rang twelve times. The scent of fudge from the candy shop lingered on the breeze.

She glanced at the telephone office. Under normal circumstances she would be at work, but she'd taken a few days off since her father's . . . accident. She directed Will to the doctor's office, the downstairs rooms of a brownstone on the corner of Mercy and Main.

He parked the buggy then jumped down and took the baby from her before assisting her from the conveyance. She glanced toward the doctor's office. People jammed the waiting room and spilled out the front door. Katie stopped and put her hand on Mr. Jesperson's muscled arm.

"What's wrong?" he asked.

"I'm not sure," she said. The voices from the waiting patients held panic and fear. "I don't know if we should take the baby into that crowd."

"Let me see what's going on." He thrust the baby into her arms.

She rested her head on Jennie's soft hair. The child did seem to be better. Her little body didn't radiate heat, and her brown eyes were more alert. Her nose was running now. Perhaps Katie had overreacted. It might only be a cold.

The little one grasped a lock of her hair in her fingers. "Um?" the baby said, pointing to an oak on the tree lawn.

"Tree," Katie said. She patted down Jennie's cowlick. A woman whose back had been to the street turned, and when Katie caught a glimpse of her face, something kicked in her chest. It couldn't be Florence. Too many years had passed, and the woman's memory was too dim. Still, there was something about how she stood with one hand on her hip that sent a shock of recognition vibrating along Katie's spine.

She tried to sort through the vague memories in her head. This woman's dull hair and lackluster complexion didn't match the vibrant woman she still dreamed of. But it had been twenty years since she'd seen her. Was it possible? She rejected the thought, but her gaze still lingered on the woman who stood talking to a man in the doorway.

Mr. Jesperson walked back to where she stood jostling the baby, who squirmed to be put down. He stopped four feet from them and blocked her path to the door. "We're not going in there."

"What's wrong?"

"Smallpox." He stared down at the baby. His eyes opened a bit wider. "She looks better."

"I think her fever has broken." She noticed the panic spreading among the waiting crowd. "All those people fear they have smallpox?"

He nodded. "I don't want to run the risk of spreading it to you and Jennie. I'll take the buckboard home so I can bathe, and then I'll return for you. Is there somewhere you can take Jennie to avoid any contamination?"

"My father's haberdashery shop," she said, pointing to a brownstone down the street. "I'll wait for you there. His assistant would have closed it for lunch, but I have a key. I want to telephone home and check on my mother to see if she has any news of my father." She glanced at the baby. "Her nose is running a little so I think it's just a cold."

"Let's hope it stays that way," he said, his mouth grim. He stepped past her to the buckboard. "I'll be back as quickly as I can." He leaped into the buckboard, took the reins, and then urged the horse into a canter down the street the way they'd come.

She glanced toward the doctor's office again, but the woman who had caught her attention was gone. Maybe she'd made it inside. Quite silly to be so taken with a stranger. Katie shifted Jennie to the other arm then hurried down the brick sidewalk to Russell's Haberdashery. After she dug her key from her bag, she stepped into the empty shop. The smell of the store was a familiar one: wool, pipe and cigar tobacco, and the spicy scent of cologne combined in a very masculine aroma— one she'd always associated with her father. Her throat closed, and she breathed the odor of her childhood.

What would happen to the store? Her mother said it was nearly bankrupt, and the realization that her life might be changing forever swept over her. Though people were kind, she saw the questions in their eyes, the censure. They all wondered why her father would try to kill himself.

The baby had fallen asleep, so Katie balanced her in the crook of her arm and went to the telephone hanging on the wall. She rang through to Central and asked for her home. When the maid answered the phone, Katie asked for her mother.

"I'm sorry, Miss Katie, but your mama took sick right after you left," Lois said. "High fever, hurtin' all over, vomiting. Even breaking out in spots." Her voice quivered. "The doctor been by. He said i–it was smallpox. We're already quarantined."

Dear God, no! "Take every precaution. I'll be there as soon as I can."

"No, Miss Katie. Your mama would have my hide if I let you come into a sick house. You go stay with a friend. Maybe Mr. Foster would take you in. I'll take care of your mama."

"I want to care for her," Katie said. "I'll be fine."

"If your mama was to lose you, she would go crazy. You listen to what I say now, miss."

Rather than arguing with Lois, Katie rang off. The baby's nose was running freely now, and her skin was cool and dry. Katie prayed the baby hadn't been exposed to the pox. They'd have to stay at the shop. Her father had collected some old suits to give to the poor, and she found the box of them in the back and made a bed on the floor for Jennie by the front counter, then covered the suits with a clean sheet she found in a cupboard. The child rolled to her side when Katie laid her down.

Driven by a compulsion she couldn't explain, Katie wandered the shop. She remembered the days before the drink had gotten control of her father. The joy on his face when she skated in to see him after school. The Saturdays when she helped by stocking shelves and hanging jackets and pants. Little by little, everything changed. She could always tell when he'd had a shot of whiskey. His reddened eyes would narrow when he saw her. Instead of smiling, he would bark orders at her. She still didn't understand why she was made to pay for her mother's sins. The months when he didn't drink would gradually wipe away the pain, and she'd think it would never come again. It always did though. Always.

She stepped into the back room. Wooden counters and a sewing machine for alterations sat as though waiting for the tailor. If the store closed, what would happen to the people her father employed? It would be hard to find work with the depression. She touched the smooth, cool surface of the Singer sewing machine. Soon dust would gather on its surface. Wandering along the shelves and counters, she remembered the days when workers crammed the place. Those days would never come again. Now garment factories churned out ready-to-wear. Her gaze fell on the shelves that hid the safe. What if her father had more money than they knew of? It might help them weather the stormy days ahead. She knew the combination.

She dug her glasses out of her bag and perched them on her nose before shoving away the stacks of wool and cotton to reveal the safe. Her hand touched the dial. It had been years since she had opened it. The safe refused to unlock on the first try. She ran through the sequence again and it popped open. She pushed the door as far as it would go and peered inside. Stacks of paper lay inside along with a money pouch. Hope surged until she picked up the pouch and found it too light. Sure enough, it was empty. She dropped it onto a shelf and lifted out the papers in the back of the safe. She glanced through them. Contracts, invoices, and receipts were all she found.

She stopped at a note that read: *Ship will dock an hour early. Have men waiting.*

The second directly under it read: *Operation perfectly executed. Booty more than expected. Will transmit location tomorrow.*

Booty? Her throat closed. Mr. Jesperson thought her father was involved in the piracy of the ships. She couldn't bear to admit to herself that he might be right.

THIRTEEN

WITH HIS SKIN raw from scrubbing as hard as he could in the hot, soapy water of the bath, Will dressed then washed down everything he'd touched. With a twinge of regret, he tossed a match to the clothing he'd thrown into the fire pit outside and dashed back to the horse and buckboard. An hour had passed since he left Miss Russell in town with the baby and he wanted to get them as far away from the pestilence as possible. He urged the horse to a trot.

Bluebirds sang from the berry bushes along the side of the road, and he watched the clouds building in the west over the water as the buckboard bounced along the rough road. With Miss Bulmer missing, he wasn't sure where to look for the next link. But it wasn't his problem. His brother could handle his own case. He had enough to handle.

He scanned the hillside, blanketed with some kind of blue wildflowers. Pretty place, this northern coast, but a little more tame than he was used to. He normally strode city streets and dodged clanging streetcars and rearing horses. This was exactly what he had been longing for.

As he looked around, he noticed two men atop a hill in a cypress grove. One man wore dungarees and a floppy hat. The other appeared to be a businessman dressed in a suit and bowler. They hadn't seen him yet. He reined in the horse in the shadow of a large tree and watched them a moment. Taken at a casual glance, there was no real reason for his unease. A landowner might have been giving direction to one of his hands, but something about the way the men talked seemed furtive. That alone made Will's senses go to alert. He wished he were close enough to overhear. He watched the man in the bowler point out to sea, toward where the point jutted into the bay.

Where the pirates had overrun the ship.

He told himself not to jump to conclusions. There could be any number of reasons to gesture to the point. He watched the suited man count out paper money and hand it to the worker. The man in dungarees tipped his straw hat then walked off. The businessman saw Will and scowled before he turned and strode away.

When both men were out of sight, Will started back toward town. He took out a notepad and jotted down descriptions of the men and of the incident. It was probably nothing, but he wanted the criminals brought to justice after seeing what they had done to the sailors. If these men had anything to do with it, he didn't want to miss any details to report to his brother.

He reached Mercy Falls and saw that the streets were deserted. Blockades declaring quarantines closed several roads, and he saw more signs on doors. There was no problem finding a spot to park the buckboard outside Russell's Haberdashery. Most businesses were open but had few clients.

There was a CLOSED sign in the window of the haberdashery. He turned the knob and found the door unlocked. The bell jingled when he stepped into the shop. Jennie stirred from a makeshift bed on the floor then turned her head and went back to sleep. Rather than calling for Miss Russell, Will walked through the store to the back room where he found the woman peering into a safe.

"Are you all right, Miss Russell?" he asked.

She jumped and turned at the sound of his voice. He caught a glimpse of her blue eyes behind her glasses before she snatched off the spectacles. "You startled me." She shut the door to the safe and locked it. "I believe Jennie is still sleeping."

"She is. She barely stirred when I came in." He watched her thrust a paper into her bag along with her glasses. It was none of his business. He followed her toward the front of the store. "Do you know who lives out by the lighthouse? I saw a fellow in a tweed suit and bowler talking to another man in that cypress grove. The one atop the hill with all those wildflowers?"

She stopped and turned to face him with a puzzled frown on her face. "No one lives there. It's part of a conservatory area. The only people I've seen there are gardeners."

"One might have been a gardener. The other was clearly not."

Her expression sharpened to keen interest. "Can you describe him?"

He grinned. "You really *do* like to be kept up on everything, don't you?" When pink touched her cheeks, he held up his hand before she could answer. "Please don't think I'm being critical. I can see you're the one I should bring any questions to."

"What kinds of questions? And why would you care, Mr. Jesperson? It hardly concerns you. The constable won't take kindly to interference."

"He wouldn't care for your involvement either," he pointed out, hiding another smile when she blushed again. The current trend of simpering beauties who were only interested in parties and fripperies made her intelligence rather appealing. Though she barely reached his chest in height, he'd begun to admire the way she barreled through any problem in front of her.

Whimpering noises came through the doorway. "The baby is awake," she said, turning on her heel.

He followed her swishing skirt into the storefront. Jennie had crawled from her makeshift bed and sat in the middle of the floor, rubbing her eyes and working up to a wail. Miss Russell scooped her up and nestled her close. "There, there," she said.

The baby quieted, staring at Will with inquisitive eyes. She waved an index finger his way. "Eh, eh?" Jennie said with a question at the end of her nonsensical syllables.

"That's Mr. Jesperson," Miss Russell said.

"You think she's really asking who I am?" he asked.

"Of course. She's very smart. You can see it in her eyes."

Will let the baby grip his finger. "Uncle Will," he said, touching his chest with his other hand. "I'm Uncle Will. I think I am anyway."

"She needs her diaper changed." Miss Russell pressed her lips together then plopped the baby back on the bedding and dug in the satchel for a fresh square of flannel.

He watched while she removed the sodden diaper that hung loosely around the baby's waist. She finished changing the baby and allowed Jennie to stand then toddle over to explore the base of the coatrack. Miss Russell stepped to the window and peered into the empty street.

"No one is moving about much," he told her. "I saw quarantine signs on some houses as I passed. I should get Jennie out of the threat of contamination."

Her cheeks were pale when she turned back to face him. "Yes, indeed!"

"Did you reach your mother?"

"I talked to our maid. Mama was too ill to come to the phone."

"Ill?" he asked. "Not smallpox?"

She bit her lip and nodded. "So the doctor said. Our maid forbade me to come home and said she would care for my mother, but my place is with her. I only waited so you could take Jennie. I didn't want to expose her."

"If she's been quarantined already, you won't be allowed to enter the home."

"Oh dear. I hadn't thought of that," she said. Her gaze wandered to the baby, who had managed to pull herself up on the coat stand. "Perhaps I could sneak in."

"And then what? You'd be sick, too, unable to get out and wondering what was happening on the outside."

"My mother needs me."

"I have a feeling you'd be a most impatient nurse," he said.

Her black lashes lowered to her cheeks as if to mask her feelings. "You don't even know me."

But somehow he did. "I know more than you think. You like to know what's going on and that indicates you like control. You abhor the unexpected. You can't *make* your mother get well any sooner by hovering over her." Her lids raised to reveal eyes bluer than any he'd ever seen. Like a summer sky just before dusk. A frown crouched between her eyes, and she turned her gaze away. He could tell his assessment had been spot on. And she didn't like it.

"Addie and John left today for their trip to Europe. I should telephone Addie's mother and see if I can stay there. I'll do that now." She went to the telephone and rang Central, then asked for the Carrington residence.

He listened to her instruct the operator to call her friend's home. From what he gathered from the conversation on this end, the Norths, Lady Carrington's daughter and son-in-law, had left town just before the disease had broken out, and several servants had already fallen ill at their residence. Jennie crawled to him and pulled herself up on his pants leg. She studied him with alert eyes and lifted her arms.

"You want me to pick you up?" He lifted her as Miss Russell rang off. "I would assume staying at the Norths' is not an option?"

"There is illness at the big house," she said. "And Lady Carrington has no spare room in her tiny cottage. Besides, I'm still quite determined to sneak home and care for Mama."

The phone rang and she jumped. "No one knows I'm here but Lady Carrington." She picked up the earpiece and held it to her ear. "This is Katie," she said into the mouthpiece. "Oh, Mr. Daniels, Nell must have told you where I am." She listened a moment. "I see. I'll have to get back to you. I'm going to try to get home." She listened, and her expression fell. "Oh, I see. Very well. Once I arrange for lodging, I'll call you back." She rang off and turned toward him with a frown on her face.

"Is something wrong?" he asked.

"That was Mr. Daniels, owner of the Mercy Falls Telephone Company. With the illness raging through town, he doesn't want to run the risk of having no operators. He was going to arrange to have a switchboard brought to my house, but he's informed me that roadblocks are set up to enforce the quarantine. He doesn't believe I'll be able to get home. Once I find a place to stay, he'll make arrangements for a switchboard, and I can work from there instead of going into the telephone building."

"Any idea where you could stay?" Will had an idea that just might work.

"I have other friends. The Fosters would be happy to have me, but they would be most disapproving of having a switchboard set up in their home."

There was plenty of room at the lighthouse. He'd barely gotten any sleep this morning. Caring for the child while he worked every night hadn't been a good situation either. He could use some help with the baby, but he didn't like admitting he felt inadequate to the task ahead of him. He could hardly ask her to stay at the lighthouse without a chaperone, though. There did not seem to be a respectable answer to the dilemma here.

"You're frowning," she said. "Is something else wrong?"

"I'm quite exhausted," he admitted. "After being up all night, a lightkeeper must sleep for a few hours after dawn. Caring for a sick baby has made that difficult. An ideal solution would be for you to stay at the lighthouse, away from the pestilence, and help with Jennie. There is adequate room for the switchboard as well."

She blushed again. "Without a chaperone? That's hardly suitable, Mr. Jesperson."

"That's a problem," he agreed. "One I'm not sure how to solve."

She said nothing for a long moment. "I have an idea," she said finally. "Lady Carrington is alone at her cottage. Her nurse fell ill and has not come in to work, and Mr. Carrington left this morning on a business trip before he realized she would be left alone. The housekeeper was unsure what to do to help. I could ask Lady Carrington to chaperone. Then I could help her and care for the baby as well."

"What's wrong with Lady Carrington?"

"She is recovering from a fall she took on her horse two weeks ago. Her right arm was sprained, and she needs some assistance in dressing and preparing meals. Very light work."

"She has no family to help her?"

"Her sister Clara lives in town but she went with the Norths' to help care for Edward on the trip."

This young woman was a take-charge sort. He had to admire that. She didn't wait for his answer but went to the telephone and rang up Central again, repeating her request to be connected to the Carrington residence. He listened to her persuasive tones as she talked to the woman on the other end of the line. He had no doubt she could talk a seaman into buying a house in the desert.

She hung up the earpiece. "It's all settled. We shall stop to pick her up on our way out of town. Addie left a few things there I can borrow to wear. I do dislike not caring for my mother though."

"You have no choice," he said.

"There is always a choice," she said.

He smiled. "You can't control everything, Miss Russell."

She thrust out her small, pointed chin. "I can try. In fact, before I agree to this for sure, I want to try to get home."

FOURTEEN

THE BABY PLAYED with the buttons on Mr. Jesperson's jacket. Katie kept her gaze on the passing scenery of coastal redwoods and hillsides covered in wildflowers. What was going on at home? Not knowing how her mother was doing moment by moment was difficult to deal with. It grated at her, not to be where she was needed most. She'd tried to see her father but had been turned away from the hospital, and then they'd tried three different avenues to get home and she'd been turned back at every one.

She stole a glance at him from under her lashes. The way he'd put his finger on her need for control unsettled her. He looked down at Jennie and smiled. The love in his gaze left a warm sensation in the pit of her stomach. Not many men would take on a burden like little Jennie so readily. She stole a second glance. She didn't want to notice his wide shoulders or the unruly black hair that spilled from under his hat and curled at his collar. She needed the security of a stable future. Like she would have with Bart.

"Lady Carrington lives at the end of this lane," she said, pointing to a narrow opening between neatly trimmed rhododendrons.

"Not with the Norths?"

She shook her head. "The cottage is just a summer home for them. Lord Carrington has an estate in England."

He guided the horse into the drive. The Carrington cottage came into view. Framed by the overhanging limbs of redwood and hemlock, the quaint cottage had been freshly painted with a coat of cheery yellow with white trim. A small porch held two rocking chairs. It was only a one-bedroom, as different from Lord Carrington's castle in England as possible. Once the horse stopped in front of the home, Katie handed Jennie to Mr. Jesperson and clambered down without waiting for assistance. Being in Mr. Jesperson's company had her every nerve tingling with awareness. Holding her skirts in the blustery wind, she hurried up the steps to the front door.

The door opened and Addie's mother peeked out. "There you are, Katie. I'm so worried about your mother. Have you heard how she is?" She adjusted the sling on her arm then stepped out to give Katie a quick hug.

"She was too ill to come to the phone, but our maid seemed confident she would be all right."

"I'm sure you're most distressed. Come in, child. There are some things of Addie's in the chest that should keep you for a few days."

Lady Carrington turned a brilliant smile in the man's direction. "Your baby has your eyes."

The baby squirmed to be let down, but he shifted her to his other shoulder. "I found her abandoned at Miss Bulmer's residence," he said. "But I believe she is my niece."

Lady Carrington's smile faded. "Oh dear me, I hope I haven't offended."

"Certainly not," he said. "Thank you for agreeing to stay with us at the lighthouse. Quite frankly, I find myself out of my element."

His confession of misgivings endeared him a bit to Katie. She'd thought his confidence knew no bounds, and from what she'd witnessed, he was most competent. "I shall collect a few things."

She left them on the porch and stepped into the cottage. The trunk of clothing was in the bedroom, and she selected several items and layered them in a bag Lady Carrington had evidently left out for her use. Daily laundry might be necessary for a few days, but this situation would be resolved as soon as the epidemic passed. By then she might have figured out her father's involvement in the ship incident.

When she returned to the porch, she found Lady Carrington holding Jennie in her lap on the swing while the lightkeeper loaded the buggy with bags. Mr. Jesperson took her bag and his hand grazed hers. Her skin felt warm from the contact, and her cheeks responded with heat as well. He retrieved Jennie and strode back to the buggy with Lady Carrington on his heels. Though he offered a hand, Katie clambered into the buckboard by herself, then settled Jennie on her lap when he handed the baby to her. He helped Lady Carrington into the buggy. Katie was glad Lady Carrington was between them.

Once they were on the road, the baby relaxed against her in sleep and grew heavy, but Katie welcomed the child's warmth in the chilly wind that whistled through the redwoods. Fingers of fog crept out of the woods and along the ground and sank into the low spots along the road. The buckboard rounded the last curve, and the craggy coastline lay before them. Whitecaps raced to touch the land then ebbed away, leaving behind kelp and seaweed whose odor mingled with that of the salt. Katie filled her lungs with the salty scent. A dim light shone through the fog from the lighthouse perched on the hillside. There were no neighbors. Maybe this wasn't a grand idea when she knew so little about Mr. Jesperson. And Katie had dragged Lady Carrington in on it as well.

Mr. Jesperson stared at the lighthouse. "I didn't leave a gaslight on," he said. "I wonder if Philip is there?" He flicked the whip above the horse's ears, and the animal broke into a trot. "I must get to the lighthouse and start the foghorn. This fog rolling in will soon be as thick as gravy."

As the horse cantered up the lane to the lighthouse, a bundle of white on a black rock down by the water caught Katie's attention. "What's that?" she asked, pointing. She squinted to see through the fog.

"I'm not sure. Wait here and I'll check it out." He stopped the buggy and leaped to the ground.

Katie wasn't about to wait behind. She passed the sleeping baby to Lady Carrington, who cradled her awkwardly in one arm, then followed him. The wind whipped Katie's skirts and she had to grab them to stay modest. The slope was slick with moisture from the fog, but she managed to reach him when he was halfway down to the white rags. Rocks rattled down the slope and she called out to him.

"Just couldn't handle not knowing what was happening?" He grinned and held out his hand to help her down the hillside.

She hated to be laughed at but she reluctantly accepted his assistance. The loose rocks demanded she cling to his warm fingers, and together, they sidled down the slope. As they neared the pile of white cloth, she stopped but still clutched his hand. Her gaze traveled to the heap of fabric on the sand. Swaths of white from the wedding dress lay matted on the rocks. She gasped and clutched his hand more tightly.

"Miss Russell, what is it?"

"It's Eliza . . . she was wearing a wedding dress . . . the last time I spoke with her." She let out a strangled cry and turned to press her face against the comforting warmth of Mr. Jesperson's wool jacket.

⁘

Will cradled Katie against his chest. He wasn't used to holding a woman. Her hair smelled like some kind of flowers, and her bonnet brushed his chin. When she stepped away, he had to force himself to drop his arms. "Are you sure this dress belongs to Miss Bulmer?"

She brushed the tears from her face. "I–I don't know. Not for sure. But she's missing, and she was wearing a wedding dress the last time I spoke with her."

"Does the constable know this?"

She shook her head. "I didn't mention it to him. It didn't seem relevant."

He glanced up the hillside to the older woman standing at the front stoop. "I'll tend to this matter," he said. "If you would be so kind as to get our little group settled, I'll make sure there's no . . ."

"Body," she finished for him. The moisture in her blue eyes made them as luminous as the sea. "Poor Eliza." Her gaze went back to the dress on the rocks. "And poor Jennie."

He hadn't stopped to think of what Miss Bulmer's possible death would mean for the child. Now what did he do about her? His brother was going to have to bear some responsibility. "I'll help you up the slope. Could you call the constable? And if my brother is there, ask him to join me, if you would be so kind."

She nodded. He assisted her along the slick rocks to the top of the hill then retreated back to the yards of fabric. He studied the tides and the wind then noticed a small island offshore looming out of the wisps of fog. Gauging the distance and the force of the waves, he wondered if Eliza had been dumped on the island and the tide had carried her dress here. He didn't disturb the dress, but he squatted beside it and looked around in the dim light. The buttons up the back were broken or torn off. He walked quite a ways up the beach but saw nothing more.

He needed to poke around the island. After all, there was no assurance the constable himself wasn't involved in the piracy. It wasn't uncommon for a man sworn to uphold the law to be found breaking it. Footsteps crunched on the sand, and he turned to see his brother striding toward him.

"You found Eliza?" Philip's voice was hushed.

"We found a wedding dress," Will corrected. "Miss Russell said that when she spoke last with Miss Bulmer, the woman mentioned she was trying one on." His brother stepped closer, and Will noticed the way he blinked his eyes. "You cared about her."

"Of course I cared about her," Philip snapped. "I'm not a cad." He stared at the heap of bedraggled white on the sand then glanced out at the waves. "The tide is coming in."

Will pointed at the island. "I was thinking about looking out there for her body. She might have been dumped on the island."

"She was murdered, of course," Philip said. "She'd hardly go swimming in such attire."

"You think it was because of her involvement in the taking of *Dalton's Fortune*?" Will asked.

"I suspect so. Her tip to my client indicated she was involved. The company president sent me a telegram to let me know he'd received a ransom demand for the *Paradox*. He got back *Dalton's Fortune*."

"So they haven't sunk the ship."

"Unless it's a ruse to get more money." Philip nodded toward the island. "Let's go search."

"We should wait for the constable," Will said.

His brother snorted. "You know how inept local law enforcement is. Why do you think the shipping company hired me?" He set off down the beach, heading toward the pier. Will followed him. A skiff was tied up on a mooring at the end of the pier. They stepped over a smelly heap of kelp just before the pier and walked the length of the boards to the boat.

Will steadied the boat as Philip climbed into it then stepped in himself. The boat rocked in the waves and he nearly tipped, but he regained his balance and untied the rope. Philip settled onto the seat at the bow, so Will shrugged and took the seat with the oars. Putting his back into the work, he rowed out past the breakers and angled the skiff toward the small island teeming with gulls and frigate birds. Twilight was coming on fast in the low fog, and he realized he should have started the foghorn before he left. They would have to scout the island fast and get back to shore to tend to his duties.

Philip jumped out of the boat with a splash and dragged the

dinghy to the rocks. "It shouldn't take long to walk the perimeter. You go that way and I'll go this way," he said, gesturing to Will's left.

Will nodded and picked his way across the driftwood and flotsam. He found no sign of Miss Bulmer, but he did spy a large footprint that had been partially erased by the surf. The heel imprint was the only clear mark. A man who rolled over on his shoe. Not much to identify but it was enough to indicate someone might have dropped her here. He patted the sand and shoved back the vegetation in search of the missing body. Though he didn't truly expect to find Eliza so easily, he was still disappointed when he came up empty-handed.

He stood and brushed the sand from his hands. If he didn't get moving, the twilight and fog would make it impossible to see the shore. His foot struck something as continued around the island. The gleam of yellow caused a hitch in his lungs. A pocket watch lay partially buried in the sand. He picked it up and rolled it in his fingers. It was imprinted. He squinted to make out the letters: Albert Russell. His gut said it was too much of a coincidence to ignore.

With the watch safely in his pocket, he headed toward the dinghy. Something rustled in the thin, scrubby foliage nearby. Before he had time to consider if it was the wind or an animal, he was struck hard in the back. The heavy weight of his attacker bore him to the ground and pressed his face into wet mud and decaying vegetation.

Will fought back, driving his elbow into the gut of the man atop him. Air hissed through the attacker's mouth as the two fought silently in the fog that swirled along the shrubs and weeds. The man held a knife aloft, and Will got a glimpse of a skull on the shank of it. He managed to get his knee up then kicked out. The man rolled off him and Will leaped to his feet. His adversary did the same and Will stood poised to jump back into the battle. To his surprise, the thug turned and ran off. Will gave chase, but an exposed tree limb tripped him up and he hurtled back to the mud. He was unhurt except for a scrape on his cheek, but the man had disappeared.

Will bounded to his feet. "Philip!" he shouted. "Watch out!" He rushed back toward the dinghy. When his brother didn't answer, he picked up his pace and reached where the boat lay beached. There was no sign of Philip. Darkness had fully descended. Will shouted for him again, and this time he heard a groan. He moved toward it and nearly tripped over his brother's legs.

Philip groaned again. He muttered something unintelligible. Will touched his brother's face and his fingers came away sticky. Blood poured from a huge knot on Philip's head. "You're going to be all right, Philip."

Between the fog and the starless night, he couldn't see his hand in front of his face. Would they have to spend the night in the cold and damp? There'd be little opportunity for rest with the likelihood of an enemy lurking, and Philip needed to be warm, dry, and possibly under a doctor's care. Without being able to see the shore, he might as easily row for the open sea as for the lighthouse, her lamps still dark. A pang of guilt ran through him. Fine lightkeeper he was turning out to be.

Then he heard a wonderful sound: the foghorn brayed from off to his right. The deep tone was the sweetest sound he'd ever heard. He managed to get his brother into the dinghy, then shoved it into the water. He put his palms to the oars and rowed toward the sound, rolling through the dark.

FIFTEEN

THE FOGHORN TOLLED its warning in the dark. Tendrils of
mist snaked around Katie's ankles and distorted what little she could
see in the wash of the light from the lantern she held in her hand.
Will should have been back by now. She caught herself thinking of
him by his first name. When did that happen?

She swung the lamp back and forth, though she knew it was futile.
The lighthouse behind her now blessedly threw out more light, but
was it even penetrating the fog more than a few hundred feet? With
the constable's help she'd managed to wind the light. Lady Carrington
was keeping an eye on Jennie, but there was still no sound of oars in
the water or the slap of water on a dinghy. If she hadn't glanced at the
pier just before twilight, she would never even have known they'd
taken the boat out to sea. Irritating men.

The constable joined her. "I fear he's lost his bearings. Where did
you say they went?"

"I'm not sure. I went to call you, and when I came back out, I saw
them rowing a small skiff out to sea. There's a tiny island out there.
Perhaps he went there."

"Why would they head there?"

"He didn't reveal his plans to me," she said, unable to keep the
displeasure from her voice.

"It's getting quite late. I need to get back to town. When he arrives,
would you telephone me, please?"

She stared at him. "Aren't you going to search for them? They might be in distress." Her main concern was for the lightkeeper, but the thought of being alone in the dark frightened her as well. Someone might have killed Eliza, and that person could still be lurking about.

The constable took out a cigar. "Miss Katie, it's far too late to attempt a rescue. The fog will clear in the morning. If he hasn't returned by then, I'll commence a search." Brown turned to depart.

She extended her hand toward him. "That might be too late!" She shivered, wishing it didn't matter to her that Will had been foolish enough to go out on the sea in these conditions.

"They are grown men. They'll have to take their chances on their own foolishness," the constable called over his shoulder. "Butting into my investigation and all. Now see that you aren't foolish too. Get to the lighthouse and lock it up tight until morning."

His trim figure vanished in the fog. Katie strained to see out past the mist, but it swallowed up even the sound of the waves lapping at the shore. The eerie silence unnerved her. The foghorn bellowed again, and she jumped at the sudden blast of noise. Maybe she should go down to the shore and wave her light. She picked her way down the beach through the seaweed-strewn rocks. If they came to shore down that way, they might not see the lighthouse. Even now, it was dim behind her.

Katie's shoes slid on the slimy stuff, and she teetered on the edge of a steep drop-off. The lantern fell from her hand and shattered on the granite shards. What little light she'd had blinked out as she pinwheeled her arms and tried to maintain her balance. Her right hand caught the sharp edge of a rock and she steadied herself before managing to climb down to the sand.

When she stood on trembling knees by the water, she drew in a shaky breath and blew it out. The sound of the foghorn rolled through the mist again. When it ended, she cupped her hands to her mouth. "Will!" she shrieked. "Can you hear me?"

No voice answered her. She stepped closer to water, taking comfort in the rhythmic sound of it, lapping on the sand. She started to shout again then heard something odd. Was that a moan or the wind? A wave washed over her shoes, and she gasped as the frigid water touched her skin. A grinding sound came to her ears. Was it a boat scraping on the rocks? If only she could see. She strained to hear. There it came again. Something bumping on the rocks.

"Will!" she screamed again.

"Katie!" Will's voice held relief and something else. She moved in the direction of his voice. Shivers raced down her spine at the way the sound seemed to echo around her, out of nowhere. This fog was disorienting.

Waves soaked the hem of her dress, and she lifted it from the strands of kelp floating on the foam. The sound seemed close, about six feet away, though she could still see nothing and wished she had the lantern. "Will?"

"Here!" he called. "We're stuck on these rocks . . ."

She waded farther into the cold water. The sand fell away under her feet, and her head went under the water. Her wet skirts weighed her down and salty water filled her nose and mouth. Her toe touched something solid and she pushed off with all her might. Her head broke through the waves and she gasped in air. The salt burned her eyes and nose. Panic closed her throat as her sodden skirts threatened to drag her down again. She flayed about, trying to stay afloat.

Strong fingers closed over hers and the next moment she was lying on the bottom of the dinghy breathing in the oily scent of pitch. She coughed up salty water then gagged at the taste.

Big hands smoothed her hair back from her face. "You're all right. I've got you," Will said. "Cough it up."

She coughed again then sat up. "I thought you were dead."

"We might have been if you hadn't started the foghorn."

He hadn't let go of her hand yet, and she found herself wanting to cling to him. Which would never do.

⌒ᗩᔕ⌒

Will rolled the watch around in his pocket. The fireplace radiated warmth to his frozen limbs. The gray chair was quite comfortable, and he could go to sleep right here if he allowed himself.

"What did the fellow look like?" Philip asked, his voice weak but intent.

Will struggled to remember something about the man who had jumped them.

"He was heavy, and he had hard hands."

Philip touched the goose egg on his temple and winced. "That's not much to go on."

"Well, you were there too! What'd *you* see?" Will rubbed his head.

Katie came into the parlor with a box in her hand. She'd been remarkable. Fearless, as she'd leaped to his aid. If not for her clear thinking in starting the foghorn, things might have turned out very different.

She bit her lip as she approached his brother, who was lying on the sofa. "I found a first aid kit under the sink in the kitchen. I'm not very good at this."

She placed the box on the table beside Philip and lifted the lid. His brother was quiet as she tended to his cuts. Will read dislike in the rigidness of her shoulders as she dabbed antiseptic on Philip's skin. The glare she shot at him delighted Will, but he stuffed that happiness down deep until he had a chance to examine just why he didn't want Miss Russell to be impressed with his younger brother's good looks. She washed his wound then dabbed iodine on the cut and positioned a bandage around his head.

She turned toward Will. "Now you."

"I'm fine," he said.

"There's a small cut on your cheek and one on your hand. It's best to tend to them now."

She knelt beside him and dabbed iodine on the minor injuries. With her this close, he could smell the sea on her skin. Tendrils of wet hair had escaped her pins, and a long curl brushed his cheek. He resisted the urge to entwine it around his finger. She put a plaster on the cut and stepped back and turned. He watched her replace everything in the box.

"You look quite fetching in glasses," he said softly.

She colored and whipped them from her face, sticking them in the pocket of the apron she wore over her dress. "There is some acetylsalicylic acid powder in here. Does your head pain you?" she asked Philip.

"I don't want anything like that, but I wouldn't refuse coffee."

"There is some in the kitchen, in the cupboard by the sink," Will said. When she nodded and exited the room, he found himself watching her swaying skirts.

He glanced at the pocket watch. She needed to know about it. Philip was nodding off again, so Will rose and padded out to the kitchen. He found her measuring coffee into the pot on the stove. "There is something you should see."

One perfectly shaped brow arched. "Another problem?"

When he opened his extended hand, the watch lay in his palm, inscription up. The color drained from her face. She picked it up. "Papa's watch. Where did you find it?"

"On the island just before I was attacked." He watched the knowledge come into her face—the idea that her father might have had something to do with throwing Miss Bulmer into the sea.

Those blue eyes slammed shut then opened again, blazing with pain. "I don't believe my father would harm anyone."

"He did show up here looking for this watch," Will reminded her.

"That means nothing." She turned her back on him and went back to preparing the coffee.

He watched her stiff back and knew she wouldn't say another word. Retracing his steps, he found his brother sitting up again with his head in his hands. "How are you feeling?" Will asked.

Philip lifted his head. "Like I was just beat up."

"Did you see who attacked *you?*"

"No. One minute I was walking the shore, and the next second my face was in the sand." Philip cradled his head. "At least this will get me off the hook with the constable."

"I'm not so sure about that," Will said. "He was already suspicious of your whereabouts the night Eliza disappeared."

Color rushed to Philip's face. "If you hadn't offered to take the child, he wouldn't have known anything about me."

"A Jesperson doesn't run from his duty," Will said.

"I'm not that child's father, Will!"

"You can't be sure, can you?" Will was suddenly weary of his brother's constant excuses. "You refuse to take responsibility for anything, Philip. Nothing is ever your fault. You will take Jennie home with you and own up to your situation." The very thought of losing the baby made him cringe, but it was right that she should be with her father.

His brother bolted from the sofa. "I will do no such thing!"

Before Will answered, Miss Russell stepped back into the parlor with a tray of coffee in her hands. She glanced from Will to his brother with wide eyes.

She set the tray on a table. "I couldn't help but overhear. You don't believe Jennie is your daughter?"

"I do not," Philip said emphatically.

"There is the possibility that she is my sister," she said.

Philip shot Will an enraged glare. "I see. Does my brother know of your suspicion?"

"Of course. We argued over who should take charge of Jennie."

"I see." Philip's mouth grew more pinched. "You've been unable to convince my brother of that fact?"

Will barely suppressed the urge to roll his eyes. "Jennie's appearance convinced me, along with your admission of a relationship with the woman." Miss Russell's cheeks turned pink, and he realized how inappropriate their conversation was. "I apologize for the indelicacy of this discussion, Miss Russell. Please forgive me."

She handed over a cup of coffee without speaking. "I don't believe any of us know for sure who Jennie's father is," she said, narrowing her eyes at Philip. "But don't you feel some responsibility since you don't know for certain?"

He scowled. "She's not my child."

"You're quite positive?"

Philip hesitated, but that was all it took for Miss Russell to set her coffee on the table and cross her arms across her chest. "What about Eliza? Did you harm her?"

"Of course not!" Philip scowled at her. "I think your father did away with her." He rubbed his head. "For all I know, he's the one who attacked me on the island."

"Don't be ridiculous. He's in the hospital."

"Are you sure?" Philip's voice was taunting. "Why don't we place a call and see?"

"He's not even conscious," she said.

"Or he's playing possum," Philip shot back.

"I'm not going to stay here and listen to your hideous innuendoes." She marched off and the stomp of her footsteps on the stairs echoed back.

"She's quite the spitfire," Philip said. He took a sip of coffee and grimaced. "Too strong." He put it on the table.

Will took a cautious gulp and shuddered. "You were goading her."

"I suppose I'd best stay around," Philip said, with a sly glance at Will.

Will scowled, though he knew his brother was baiting him. "If you have plans to court Miss Russell, that's not acceptable."

"Don't tell me a woman has finally caught your eye." Philip's grin was cheeky.

"Don't try to change the subject. We were discussing your duty to Jennie," Will snapped.

Philip splayed out his hands. "I had nothing to do with the baby or Eliza's possible murder. I'm only here to find those ships and the missing money."

Will sighed. Philip's constant denials were beginning to sway him. "You had a relationship with the woman."

"So did a lot of men."

"I'd like to believe you. But Jennie looks a lot like you, Philip. Even has your cowlick. And those eyes are shaped like yours."

"Babies all look alike," Philip said. He took another gulp of coffee. "If I thought for a moment she was my child, I'd admit it and take responsibility for her."

Will stifled a scoff and decided not to remind his brother of the many times he'd left Will to smooth ruffled feathers, broken promises, and missed appointments. The boy was so unreliable. No, not a boy. Man. It was time Will recognized that his brother was a grown man. He needed to let Philip endure the consequences for his actions. Even if it was the hardest thing he'd ever had to do.

He walked toward the stairs. "You'll sleep on the sofa so you're near Jennie. If she wakes up in the night, you can care for her. I'll be tending the light."

"Lady Carrington already has her."

"I'll get her. She's our responsibility until we get this figured out."

"I know nothing about babies! Besides, I have a date tonight."

"Cancel it! I don't know anything about children either. But we're both going to have to learn. Jennie is not Miss Russell's charge. She is ours."

"Russell!" Philip said. "Is her father Albert Russell?"

"He is."

"He tried to kill himself. Maybe he knew I was on to him. He must know something about the two ships being taken. If only you'd been able to talk to Eliza before she went missing."

Did his brother ever think of other people? "Forgive me for not getting *your* job done the way *you* wished."

"Eliza's the one who knows what's happened here," Philip said. "I can feel it in my gut."

"The baby is what is important here, not your investigation. Jennie's *mother*—not your *informant*—is missing, probably dead. Doesn't that mean anything to you?"

"Of course it does," Philip said, his voice sulky. "But I must solve the case to get paid."

"There are more important things than your career. I hope you'll figure that out sooner rather than later." As Will led the way up the staircase, he despaired of ever seeing his brother grow into a man.

What made him think he could raise a little girl when he'd failed so miserably with his brother?

Sixteen

WHAT WAS THAT squawking? Katie opened a bleary eye. Lady Carrington slept beside her. The two women had shared a bed, and Katie had been so concerned about disturbing the older woman that she'd lain awake, struggling to not move. Their bed had been comfortable but hardly the luxury they were both used to. A simple yellow and green quilt covered the mattress on the iron bedstead, and a rag rug was the only thing to warm their feet. The curtains were frayed and worn but clean. They'd obviously been left here by the previous lightkeeper and his family.

The sound came again. She swung her legs out of bed. The other woman didn't move. Katie belted her robe around her and tiptoed to the door. She snatched her glasses from the dresser beside it. Light slanted through the curtains. She should have been up already, seeing to the baby. She opened the door and stepped into the hall in her bare feet.

A voice barked, "Step away from the cake!"

The harsh tone made her shiver. She was tempted to flee back to the safety of her bedroom—after all, a killer was still on the loose—but curiosity won out and she eased down the steps. It sounded like the man was in the kitchen. If he was talking about cake, that would make sense. She scurried along the painted wood floors to the door to the kitchen. It was closed. No more sound came from the other side of it. Her hand grasped the cold ceramic knob, and she gave it a twist and a shove until the door opened a crack. She peered inside as the grating voice repeated its command.

She saw no one in the small room. Pushing the door open further, she stepped past the icebox and glanced around, seeing it with fresh eyes in the bright wash of daylight. No one here. The simple wooden counter held a dry sink. Curtains covered the shelves under the counter. There was a wood range that took up most of one side of the kitchen. The floor was green-and-gray linoleum, in good condition, and everything was clean. Her gaze swept the room.

Something moved at the table. It took a moment for her to realize a giant bird stared back at her from its perch on the back of a chair. Newspaper lined the floor under the perch. The black avian stretched its neck then picked up a nut from the table and cracked it open.

"Step away from the cake!" The bird sidled a few steps toward her.

"It's a bird," she breathed. She moved nearer to the table and held out her hand.

"I wouldn't do that if I were you," Will said from the doorway. He was dressed in a white shirt, open at the collar and slightly wrinkled, over gray slacks. His hair was wind-tossed. He brushed past her and held out his hand. The bird stepped delicately onto his wrist. "He doesn't like strangers, and he's apt to nip you."

She snatched her hand back. "He's beautiful." The bird preened as if he heard her. The light glistened on his wings. Her fingers itched to stroke him. "What is he?"

"A mynah. He talks."

"I heard him. How long have you had him?"

"A few days. Ever since Philip got tired of taking care of him." Will carried the mynah to the back door and out onto the stoop where he put him on a perch.

She followed him. "Was he out here last night? I didn't see him. And won't he fly away?"

"He was in a covered cage in my bedroom last night. His wings are clipped. He's a homebody too. Likes being waited on hand and foot."

"A typical man."

He grinned. "A suffragette, are you? Marching in the Easter Day parade?"

She tipped up her chin. "And if I were?"

One dark brow lifted and his generous mouth twitched. "I'd say you've got courage. The vote for women is long overdue."

His stance surprised her, but she just nodded and kept her attention on the bird. "He keeps saying that about the cake. Whatever does it mean?"

"I haven't the least notion. It's rather annoying." He dusted the nuts from his hand and moved back to the kitchen.

Katie followed after a backward glance at the parrot. She wanted to just sit and watch the bird. "How is Jennie this morning?"

"Still sleeping."

"And your brother?"

"Doing the same. He refused to get up with her."

"You're sure she is his daughter?"

"I'm reasonably certain."

She wanted to turn from the way his dark eyes probed hers. He was much too intimate in his ways.

"We must decide what is to be done with Jennie," he said. "My brother appears unready to accept responsibility."

"My mother would like to spend a little more time with her."

"Do you think she might be your half sister?"

"It will be difficult to ascertain the truth," she admitted, stopping momentarily in the doorway to the parlor. "Unless my father regains consciousness." She bit her lip. "What I heard was very incriminatory."

"I took the liberty of calling to check on your father this morning. No change in his condition. He's still unconscious. I was informed again that no one could visit until the smallpox epidemic was past."

She winced at the news. "Thank you." A knock on the door sounded, and she realized she was in her nightgown and robe.

"I'll get it," Will said, exiting the kitchen.

Hardly respectable to be talking with the devilishly handsome Will Jesperson in her nightwear. She started to follow him but the telephone on the wall rang. She snatched the earpiece from the hook and spoke into the mouthpiece. "Mercy Falls Lighthouse."

"The constable hasn't been by to see me, so I think you've been a good girl," the man on the other end said. "See that you keep your mouth shut. I can get to your father in the hospital with no problem. You wouldn't like how I could hurt your mother."

The voice was the man who had called from the skating rink. "What do you want?" she whispered.

"Just to remind you to stay quiet about anything you heard Eliza say."

There was a click in her ear. "I don't know anything," she said, but there was no one on the other end. She toggled the switch to summon the operator.

"Operator," Nell's voice said.

"Nell, where did that call come from that you just put through?"

"How are you, Katie?" Nell asked. "I wish we could go back to the office. I don't like working from home."

"Things will be back to normal soon. About that call. Where did it come from?"

"The shipping office down at the dock. Is something wrong?"

It would be useless to go down there. "The man didn't identify himself. I just wondered. See you soon, Nell." Katie hung the earpiece on the hook then rushed from the kitchen and up the stairs to the bedroom.

Lady Carrington still slept as Katie dressed and poked hairpins into her coil of curls with shaking hands. The menace in the man's voice terrified her, but of course her parents were safe. Orderlies wouldn't let the man near her father, and her mother was protected by the servants. Though they'd been little help when that man attacked her with the whiskey bottle. She would just call and make sure everything was all right when she went back downstairs.

She removed her glasses and tucked them into her pocket. When she went back downstairs, she heard the low murmur of male voices in the parlor. She sidled past to the kitchen and had Nell ring her mother. After the maid assured her all was well, she checked in at the hospital. Her father's condition was unchanged. Relieved, she stepped out of the kitchen and entered the parlor. She found Bart seated by the fireplace with a cup of coffee in his hands. Why did her heart sink when she wanted so much to love him?

He put down the cup and bolted to his feet. Dressed in a light gray sack coat, he oozed wealth and status. "Katie, I apologize for such an early call. I phoned your house and your mother said you'd been forced to come here to avoid the sickness in town. My home is completely free of the disease. You should have called me." His voice held reproof, as did his stern expression.

She stepped into the room and forced a smile. "That's very kind of you, Bart. My boss asked me to arrange to set up the switchboard where I was lodging. I couldn't presume upon your mother in such a fashion."

His smile faltered. "I'm sure she wouldn't have minded," he said, but his tone lacked conviction.

"Mr. Jesperson was in need of a nanny for the child, and I was in need of a temporary home. After fetching dear Lady Carrington as a chaperone, it seemed an equitable arrangement."

"Mr. Foster tells me the two of you have an understanding," Will said, his tone frosty. His dark brows were drawn together. "I can well fathom his trepidation at your temporary residence here."

Bart nodded. "We have plenty of room, Katie. I'd be happy to take you back to the house."

Katie's spine stiffened. "Thank you, Bart, but as I said, Lady Carrington is here too. I wouldn't want to impose with extra guests. I've also already arranged for the switchboard to be delivered here and it should be arriving momentarily. You'll see—it will all be over soon and everything will be set back to rights."

Bart's mouth pulled downward, but he took her rejection with reasonable grace. "Yes, well, I also stopped by to bring you up-to-date on the status in the town. The constable and Dr. Lambertson moved quickly to quarantine any possible cases of smallpox. They feel the cases will drop off soon if everyone stays calm and remains at home as much as possible."

"Good news," she said. "Is there any idea where this disease came from?"

He nodded. "A ship brought it in. It's been quarantined at its mooring up in Oregon."

"Your family is all well? You know my mother has come down with the disease and everyone was at church. They could have been infected."

"The doctor says a patient is only contagious when they have a fever and the pustules break out. Your mother was perfectly fine at church, was she not?"

"Yes, she was fine until yesterday."

"So perhaps you will escape as well."

Katie hadn't stopped to think about the possibility of having contracted the disease—or of passing it on to the baby and everyone else in the house. She prayed none of them would get sick. And that her stay at the lighthouse might be God's leading—that she could discover what had happened to make her father want to kill himself.

Will kept busy for the next few days. After getting up around one o'clock every afternoon, he cleaned the windows on the lighthouse, touched up paint on the tower, organized his equipment, and avoided the pretty Miss Russell as best he could. It was easy enough—he took over the duty of watching Jennie about the time she needed to sit down at the switchboard or Mrs. Carrington needed a rest.

He saw little of his brother. Philip was presumably out looking for the missing ship, commandeered by the pirates, but seemed to spend more of his time talking to men at the quay every day.

As far as Will knew, Philip had found no real leads until the day he asked Will to accompany him along the coast. An informant had told Philip he'd seen a ship pass that way. Will had awakened at eleven and his duties were done, so he agreed. Katie was on the switchboard in a corner of the parlor. He doubted she would notice or question the fact he was gone. And Lady Carrington and Jennie seemed to have made for a special relationship, content to be together for hours at a time.

The temperature hovered near sixty-two degrees, and there wasn't a cloud in the sky as he guided the buckboard down a muddy lane that was more potholes than road. Philip had been told this narrow path led to the section of coastline where the ship had last been spotted.

Philip readjusted his grip so as to not get unseated. "This is complete wilderness."

"It will be difficult to find the ship if they went upriver some-where," Will said. He pulled the buckboard to a stop. The mare tossed her head and snorted then leaned down to munch a patch of grass. He tossed the reins around a shrub as he got down, then walked out to a spit of land that poked into the sea. The whitecaps foamed against the rocks and left the tang of salt in the air. Seagulls squawked overhead.

Philip joined him and the two stood staring out at the rugged coast lined with redwood and hemlock. The sea breeze nearly took Will's hat, and he grabbed at it before it careened off the cliff. "Looks like nothing has ever happened out here," he said. "Peaceful and serene."

Philip wrinkled his nose. "Rotting kelp." He pointed at the

steaming piles of tangled kelp on the rocks below them as the gulls pecked through the mess for bugs.

Will ignored the smell. He stared out past the breakers to where the shoreline curved in and out again, then he looked back to the woods again. No one lived out here but bears and hawks. If they intended to press further into this area, they'd have to do it on foot or horseback. He buttoned his jacket against the stiff wind. "You ready to go back? Nothing is out here."

Philip shook his head. "Not yet. As far as I know, no one has probed this area very well." They walked along the coast as far as they could but found nothing. "It's pure wilderness," he said. He turned and set off along the rocky beach.

Will shrugged, his attention on the interesting cloud formation overhead. "Because there's nothing to see."

"Perhaps." Philip turned and climbed up a small cliff that blocked the way.

Will followed, reaching for one handhold after another. As soon as he got home, he'd look for the weather balloons he'd released this morning. On the other side of the cliff, he settled in to watch the tides. They had walked for nearly an hour.

"Philip, are we going to walk all the way to Oregon?" He kicked a stone into the air. It pinged off the rocks as it fell toward the water. Instead of a splash, he heard it *clank* against something. He dropped to his knees and peered over the side. A ledge projected out from the face of the escarpment, ten feet below. Something glinted on it. From his position, it appeared to be the ring from an old harness.

"What is it?" Philip asked, backtracking to his brother.

"Perhaps nothing." Will couldn't let it go though. He grabbed a tree root sticking from the ground and slipped over the side.

"What are you doing?"

"Going to see what's down there." Will lowered himself until his feet dangled three feet from the ledge. He took a deep breath and let go, praying the ledge wouldn't collapse. He slid down the rock face, then fell to his knees on the ledge. It held. Dusting himself off, he got up and glanced around. Vegetation blocked the cliff wall but he thought he glimpsed a hole in the rocks. He shoved aside a hedge nettle to reveal a cave. The opening was about three feet in diameter.

"What's down there?" Philip called.

"A cave. Wish I had a lantern." Will tried to see further into the space, but the sun only illuminated the first two feet. He thought he saw something glitter inside. Maybe mica catching the sunlight. He knew he should grab his brother's hand and get out, but an inner compulsion made him press farther into the cave. He had to put his hands on dried gull dung to squeeze through, but they would wash.

He waited a moment for his eyes to adjust. The dank space smelled of dirt, mold, and sea salt. From what he could see, the walls opened out from the mouth of the cave another three feet on either side. The space was fairly good sized, and the ceiling rose overhead to about nine feet tall. He could crawl inside and stand up, but his efforts would be useless without a lantern.

"You coming up?"

"In a minute," he called to his brother. He peered toward where he'd seen a shimmer. Was that a chest? He crawled in a little farther until he could run his fingers over a leather chest bound in brass. The metal must have been what he saw gleaming in the sunlight. The thing was padlocked, so he couldn't open it. It was about one foot by two. Small, but when he tried to lift it, he found it heavy. Panting, he dragged it toward the opening and out into the open air.

"Everything okay?" Philip called down.

"I found something. A chest. We're going to need a rope to get it up. There's one back in the buckboard."

"A chest?" Philip's voice sharpened. "I'll come down."

"No! Then we'll both be stuck here. We need that rope."

"It will take me two hours to walk there and return!" Displeasure coated Philip's words.

Will craned his neck to stare up into his brother's face. "Hurry. Perhaps I can pick the lock while I'm waiting."

Philip glanced out to sea. "I don't like leaving you here alone. Why don't you come with me? The chest will be safe enough."

"Seems foolhardy to leave something that might be a valuable clue. Whoever stashed it here might come back."

Philip's brow creased. "And do you have a weapon if he does?"

"No."

"Here, catch." Philip brandished a pistol.

Will caught it and stuffed it in his waistband. "I'll be fine. Hurry!"

"Watch yourself. I shall be back as soon as possible."

Philip's face disappeared from above. It sounded as though Philip was moving fast. They'd meandered their way here, so perhaps his brother would return in less than two hours. Will glanced at the sun that was nearly overhead. His stomach growled, but there would be no lunch for him. That, too, was back at the buckboard.

He picked up a rock to try to knock off the padlock, but before he brought it down, he heard a rustling from the opposite direction of where they'd left the buckboard. The sounds of male voices drifted toward him.

He shoved the chest back into the cave then scrambled inside with it. Moments later a rope dangled in front of the opening. Someone was coming down.

SEVENTEEN

"OPERATOR," KATIE SAID. She chatted a moment with Mrs. Silvers and found out most people were beginning to recover from smallpox and there had been no new cases, though the existing cases would be contagious until the scabs dropped off. Another couple of weeks and the town would likely be totally clear of the scourge. She connected the woman's call to her daughter-in-law. Once she heard the other woman pick up, she saw the lamp light for another call. It was Mr. Gleason calling the bank. No chitchatting with him.

There was a lull when the switchboard remained dark, then Katie's shift was over. She checked in with Nell to make sure the other woman was ready to go at her remote location, then removed her headset and stretched. Working away from the office had proven to be rather enjoyable. There had been no problems so far.

Lady Carrington came in, chasing the toddler, and gave Katie a weary look. Jennie reached for her.

"You want to go outside?" Katie scooped her up and smiled at Lady Carrington. "I have her. You go and rest." Lady Carrington gave her no argument and they went out the back door, stepping past the bird.

Paco gave her a baleful look and shifted on his perch. "Step away from cake!" he screeched.

Jennie flinched and hid her face against Katie's shoulder. "There is no cake," Katie muttered. Though it sounded good, she wasn't in the mood for baking. Truth be told, she was an atrocious cook. Her mother had tried to teach her, but Katie's mind always drifted out the window to the city streets and what she was missing.

Jennie craned her neck to watch the birds soaring overhead as Katie strolled the beach. The sea breeze tugged at the tendrils of hair that had escaped her pins, and she pushed them back from her face with an impatient hand. The blue of the sea reflected the brilliant sky overhead. The whitecaps were like frosting on the tops of the waves. She shook her head at her constant thoughts of cake. Silly bird. She stopped to stand Jennie on the beach. The baby stooped and grabbed a fistful of sand and started to cram it into her mouth until Katie stopped her. The sun struck Katie's face and she realized she hadn't seized her hat.

Katie let Jennie hang onto her finger as the baby toddled along the shore of the water. Her giggles mingled with the sound of the surf and soothed Katie's jitters. All morning long she hadn't been able to raise anyone at her house. All was well, she told herself—her father was holding his own and surely her mother was fine. But then, why wouldn't Lois pick up?

A movement caught her eye, and she noticed a female figure approaching from the road. She wore a white lingerie dress that swayed around her slim figure. The broad brim of her hat shaded the woman's face. The parasol she carried blocked the view even more, but something about the way she walked seemed familiar to Katie. The buggy in which she'd arrived was at the steps to the lighthouse.

Katie smiled as the woman stopped a few feet away. "May I help you?"

The woman lifted her head, but her hand still shaded her face. "I'm looking for Katie Russell."

Katie stepped nearer. "I'm Katie. Have we met?"

The woman dropped her hand, and the sun pierced the shadows thrown by her hat. "Don't you know me, darling?"

Every muscle tensed. The seashell Katie had found fell from her hand. Her heart rebounded against her chest wall, and she struggled to breathe. No, it couldn't be. She wouldn't let it be true. She squeezed shut her eyes and drew in a deep breath. When she opened them again, the mirage was still before her. As solid as the ground under her feet. It was no ghost, no figment of her imagination. Was that powder on the woman's face? And blush. She concentrated on the shocking makeup rather than on what she longed to deny.

The woman in front of her was Florence. The woman who bore her.

The moisture dried on Katie's tongue. She continued to stare at the woman smiling back at her. The years had not been kind to Florence. Katie couldn't think of her as her mother. Inez Russell was her mother.

"Cat got your tongue?" Florence stepped nearer. She touched a gloved finger to Katie's cheek. "I would think you would be overjoyed to see your mama."

Katie flinched then attempted to harness her racing thoughts. "What are you doing here?" she managed past her closed throat. She scooped up the baby for comfort.

"You don't seem glad to see me." Florence's pert smile faded, and she tugged on one glove. Her blue eyes, so like Katie's own, narrowed, and she gave the parasol on her shoulder a spin.

"I–I'm shocked," Katie said. "I never thought I'd see you again." She glanced back at the house. All she could do was pray Lady Carrington didn't happen to look outside. Katie had to get rid of this woman. Quickly, before anyone saw them together. "Did you go by my parents' house?"

Florence's brows drew together even more. "When I reached town, I stopped to buy some headache powder but quickly left the doctor's office when I learned of the smallpox making its rounds. When I inquired about the Russells, I was told you were out here. You are the one I came to see anyway, not my treacherous sister."

"Did you go see Papa?"

"I was denied entrance until the smallpox is past, but the doctor said he was improving. I slipped down the hall when no one was looking and peeked into his room though. He's gotten quite old, hasn't he?"

Katie said nothing. Most likely the woman had no idea she'd aged as well. It was as though a giant hand squeezed Katie's soul. She wanted to wail and cry, but more than anything else, she wanted not to have to look into this woman's face. "I think you'd better go. There's nothing for you here."

"You're the only reason I'm here."

"We severed all ties years ago."

The way the woman pressed her lips together accentuated the lines around her mouth. "You mean Albert severed them. I want to weave them together again."

Weave them together again? There weren't even ruins left of that original foundation. "I have no interest in a relationship with you," Katie said. "You abandoned me to go off with your boyfriend. Is that supposed to be forgotten now?"

Florence grimaced. "I just went out for a little fun! I was coming back. You had to go running to Albert. Of all people." Her voice was thick with disgust and she rolled her eyes.

"I was five years old! Much too young to be left alone at night. I was frightened." Katie still remembered the terror of the night with a strange man knocking on the door in search of her mother. "That man you'd been with the night before. Harold something. He came by after you'd gone out. I—I didn't like the way he looked at me." She shuddered.

"He wouldn't have hurt you," Florence said with a hard smile. "But I know you were young. I forgive you."

Katie clutched the baby to her chest. *She forgives me?* Her stomach roiled with nausea. "Why are you here? You were always too busy dancing and going to parties to even notice me. I have a new life. If you care about me at all, you'll leave before anyone finds out."

"Finds out what?"

She bit her lip. "That you're my mother," Katie finally whispered.

Florence stared. "You mean people think the Russells are your real parents? How is that possible?"

Katie hunched her shoulders, wishing she didn't have to broach the subject at all. "You were only in town for a week in that boarding-house. You were going by a different name. My father had just moved here and Mama was still packing up in San Francisco. She arrived the morning after Papa took me in."

"So everyone assumed you were their daughter," Florence said slowly.

"I *am* their daughter. In every way that matters," Katie said, her voice fierce. "If you're here for money, Papa doesn't have any."

Florence laughed. "Do you truly expect me to believe that, Katie? I'm not stupid. The Russells are wealthy. My dear sister is rolling in money. There is no reason she shouldn't share with me since I gave her my own flesh and blood." She glanced toward the house. "Aren't you going to offer me some tea?"

"No. I want you to leave, forever. My life is fine without you. I have a mother. I don't need another." Katie raised her voice. "Please, can't you just leave me alone?"

Florence's mouth grew pinched. She stared at Katie with a specula-tive gleam in her eyes. "How much will you give me to go away?"

Katie took a step back. "I have no money."

"Then you'd better get some." Florence twirled her parasol again and turned back toward the buggy. "Move quickly, Katie. Or I will tell everyone your mother is a vaudeville dancer and a lady of the night."

The woman sauntered away and left Katie staring after her with her hand to her throat. This couldn't happen—not now.

Staring at the rope dangling in front of the cave opening, Will tried to decide what to do. It was dark in here. He could move to the back and try to hide. Observing what was going on might be more profitable. And prudent. But if the man climbing down here had a lantern, he might be discovered, and the idea of being caught, hiding out, grated at him.

He heard the men talking topside. The one with a gruffer voice said, "We need to get this stowed and ready. The next ship will be here in two days. Once we get the plunder from it, we can get out of here."

The pirates. They were planning another theft.

The rope in front of him swayed, and the tip of a boot appeared. Will didn't have long to make up his mind. He stood and stepped to the back of the cave. As soon as he moved away from the opening, it was too dark to see. He held his hands out in front of him and groped along the rough rock walls. Shuffling across the uneven floor, he walked about fifteen feet before he came to the back of the space. He crouched and swept his hands around to try to find something to shield him from view. There was nothing. He stood and faced the light at the front of the cave. He withdrew the pistol tucked into his waistband.

A figure blocked the light in the cave's opening. The man stooped and peered into the cave. Will knew him right away—the worker who'd been talking to the businessman on the hillside. When the fellow stepped into the cave, Will saw he had no lantern attached to his waist.

The man moved to Will's left, toward where the chest had been stashed. Will realized he hadn't gotten the chest back into the place where it had resided. It sat two feet further from the opening and was not shoved against the wall. The fellow crouched and moved his hands along the rock wall. Will heard a clatter and something scrape. Then a tiny light flared, and he saw a lantern and matches in the man's hand.

Will crouched down and pressed back against the rocks behind him. If he stood still, perhaps the man wouldn't examine the rest of the cave. The wick caught flame, and the lantern's warm yellow glow pushed back the shadows in the cave to two feet in front of Will. He remained just barely covered by the dark. As the light probed the other corners of the space, he saw the outline of the cave better. It widened to about eight feet and went back into the hillside fifteen feet or so.

The fellow set the lantern down and crouched in front of the chest. Will could only pray the pirate didn't remember exactly where he'd placed it last. A click echoed against the cave walls and the man lifted the lid on the box. Will sidled to the right so he could see better. His boot scraped a loose rock. He froze when the fellow stopped and lifted his head. The man reached toward his waist, and Will caught the gleam of a gun in the lamplight. His fingers tightened on his own gun, but before the fellow withdrew his weapon, another man called down from atop the cliff.

"Chesterson, are you about done? I need to get back." The accomplice's voice was cultured.

"Almost," the workman shouted. "Give me a minute." The man tipped his head and listened with his hand still on the butt of his gun. Will didn't move. "Lousy rats," the man muttered. He knelt in front of the chest again and withdrew a stack of ledgers. He laid a compass and other instruments on the rocky floor. A metal lockbox came out next.

Will couldn't let the evidence get away. He brought up his pistol. The man pulled out a burlap sack then put the lockbox into it before tightening the top and turning back to the rope dangling outside the opening. Will relaxed a bit when he realized the man intended only to take a small portion of the contents of the chest. Could he apprehend the perpetrators? If he let them leave, Will might not be able to discover their identity. But if he stopped them now, Philip might never find the ship itself. Uncertain how to proceed, Will took another step and a rock rattled.

The man whipped out his gun and turned toward him. "Don't move!" he barked.

Will had the advantage because he could see the man and the guy couldn't see him. "Drop it! I've got a gun on you," he said. Will's finger tightened on the trigger, but rather than dropping his gun, Chesterton fired. Something struck Will on the left side of his head, and his vision blurred. He struggled to stay conscious, to depress the trigger on his pistol, but he was dizzy. The next thing he knew, he was falling. His hand struck a rock and the gun clattered across the rock floor. Then a cold metal barrel dug into his forehead.

"If you move, I'll kill you," the man said. He dragged Will roughly to his feet.

Will's head throbbed, and a wave of nausea struck him. The man half-dragged him toward the front of the cave. Philip's pistol was somewhere behind them and of no help to him. He had no strength to fight the man's rough handling. In the shaft of sunlight streaming into the mouth of the cave, Will saw the hard glint in the fellow's eyes, the cruel twist of his mouth. This was no gardener but a thug dressed as one.

"We've got a problem," the man shouted up to his partner. "There's a snoop in here."

"What?" The accomplice's voice was faint, as though he'd moved away from the edge. When he spoke again, he was louder. "Did you shoot him?"

"Yeah, I nicked his head. What should I do with him?"

There was silence for a long moment. Will felt his strength beginning to return. If he could ward off action for a few more minutes, he might be able to get out of this.

"Kill him," the man above said. "We leave no witnesses."

"We should make it look like an accident," Chesterton said, "so no one comes looking for us. Maybe tie him up here and let him die on his own, then come back and take off the ropes?"

"He'll stink up the cave. Besides, that's too risky. He might get away," the voice said from above.

There was another pause. Then the man's hand tightened. He hauled Will out of the cave opening. Will's muscles tightened in preparation for a fight. He wasn't going down without a struggle. Before the other man from above spoke, the thug's grip on Will's arm turned painful. Will had no time to realize what was happening. He went sailing off the ledge where they stood. He plummeted toward the waves crashing on the rocks fifty feet below. His arms pinwheeled out, and he bit back a shout.

Time seemed to slow as he fell over the cliff face. If he struck the rocks, he was a dead man. He barely had time to pray before the water rose to meet him. A wave took him under and battered him against the rocks. Something struck his forehead. Saltwater filled his mouth. His lungs burned with the need to breathe. He couldn't see, couldn't tell where he was or how to escape the roiling ocean.

Pain shot up his arm when a wave rolled him into another rock. The waves tossed him until he lost all sense of time. He made it to the surface, took a lungful of air, but then was hit by another five-foot wave, which drove him down again. He was barely able to stay conscious.

His arms flailed as he grasped for something to cling to. His hands scraped a rock and a fingernail tore from his forefinger, but he barely felt it. His head came up and he drew in a breath before the sea took him under again. His backside scraped sand on the bottom, and then the current shot him to the surface again, suddenly twenty feet out. When his head next broke the surface, he found himself rolling out to sea in the grip of an undertow. He weakly tried to swim to shore, but the strong current carried him farther away. His arms came up but were puny weapons against the power of the sea.

He would never make it to shore.

EIGHTEEN

KATIE CHEWED HER scone but it was like choking down sand. The sun shone through the window into the parlor, but its cheery presence wasn't enough to lift her from the gloom that had encased her since Florence had confronted her hours ago. What was she going to do? If the good folks of Mercy Falls found out her real heritage, any respect she'd managed to earn for herself would be gone. No one would take kindly to being deceived for all these years.

Jennie played at her feet, and Katie didn't smile when the baby giggled at her. She felt like crying instead.

"Katie, dear, is something wrong?"

Katie glanced at Lady Carrington. Her green eyes were filled love and concern. Katie managed a smile. "I'm not hungry. I didn't sleep well last night." She took a sip of her tea.

"I saw you speaking with a woman earlier. You haven't been yourself since. Who was she, my dear?"

The tea scalded Katie's tongue and she choked. Setting down the cup, she searched for some way to avoid Lady Carrington's question. She smelled the stew on the stove. "Does the stew need to be stirred?"

Lady Carrington sniffed the air. "I think perhaps you're right. I shall be right back." She put her tea on the table and rose.

Katie leaned against the back of the sofa and let out the breath she'd been holding. Her head throbbed and she still felt sick. Of all the things she'd tried to control over the years, this was the one she'd always known would become a wildfire if any wind blew on the spark.

She longed to speak to Mama. First to be sure she was truly making a recovery and then to ask for advice. But no, she couldn't tell her of Florence's demand. Not now when she was so sick. Papa was no help either. He was still incoherent. It was Katie's duty to protect her mother, to smooth the rough road ahead. If she had the money, she'd gladly give it to Florence to make her disappear, but as far as she knew, there was little money for them to even live on.

She rubbed her forehead and got up. A shout came from outside, and she went to the front door to see what was causing the commotion. The buckboard was parked at the foot of the hill below the lighthouse. Philip ran up the slope toward the house.

He shouted again. "I need help!"

Her pulse picked up speed. She threw open the door and stepped out onto the porch. "What is it?"

He reached her. "Something's happened to Will!"

A brief vision of Will's dark smiling eyes flashed through her mind. He had to be all right. "He's been hurt?"

Philip stood panting and red-faced from his run up the slope. "We found a chest in a cave. He sent me to the buckboard to get a rope to haul it up. When I got back, he was gone. The gun I'd given him was lying on the cave floor, and I found blood by the opening to the cave. A piece of his shirt was caught on the ledge hanging out over the ocean. As if—as if he went over the side."

"And the chest?"

"It was still there."

She tried to place this cave of which he spoke. "Are you saying the cave was in a rock face overhanging the sea?"

He nodded. "Just south of here, down Hanging Rock Road. We walked about an hour beyond the end of the road down the beach.

He had to have a rope or someone to help in order to get up with the chest."

"Could he have climbed down?"

"No way. It's a fifty-foot drop."

"You fear he—he fell?" She covered her mouth in horror and wanted to close her eyes against the mental picture of Will's broken body on the rocks.

Philip went even whiter. "He wouldn't have left of his own free will. He was waiting for my return with the rope, and he would have been stranded on the ledge without help."

She didn't want to believe anything could harm that strong man. "I'll come with you. We must call the constable. Get a search party."

"I'll have Lady Carrington call the constable. You and I will go by boat to search for him. If he fell into the sea, perhaps he needs our assistance." She could only pray he was still alive. Anyone diving into the sea was more likely to hit rock than water.

She stepped back inside and told the older woman what had happened.

Lady Carrington promised to call the constable. "Take my yacht. It's moored down at the dock."

"Thank you so much!" Katie returned to find Philip gazing out to sea. "What is it?"

"I'm not sure," he said. "I thought I saw something out there."

"I saw binoculars in the well house," she said. "I'll fetch them." She rushed around the side of the house and threw open the wooden door to the building that housed the pump for the well. A pair of binoculars hung on the wall by the door. She grabbed them and stepped back outside. The currents could have carried Will close to the lighthouse from where Philip had told her they'd been. She handed the binoculars to Philip. He trained them on a spot just to the left of the lighthouse. She prayed for Will as his brother scanned the waves.

Philip lowered the binoculars. "It's just driftwood," he said, his voice sharp with disappointment.

"Let's take the binoculars with us. If you suspect he's adrift, we'll need them. The constable will be searching the land," she said. "Lady Carrington has a small yacht moored nearby."

He stared at her. "You can sail?"

"A bit."

"I'm an expert seaman," he said.

He led her down the stone steps to the road and down to the pier where the boat floated. Under less stressful circumstances, she would have delighted in exploring the hold and expansive deck. She stepped into the boat as he held it steady. He hopped in with her and grabbed the rigging on the small craft. The sails flapped then billowed with air. Once the rope was loosened from the piling, the wind caught the canvas and the boat picked up speed. She moved to the bow and brought the binoculars to her eyes. Finding a man in this vast sea would be as difficult as finding an unbroken seashell on the rocks.

She put down the binoculars. "So you believe the pirates who took the ship stashed that chest? And that they found Will, I mean Mr. Jesperson, at the cave, that they—disposed of him?"

Philip paled. "I hope not, but the evidence—" He broke off, his voice choked.

She shielded her eyes with her hand and stared out at the rippling waves, hoping to see Will's hailing wave. The thought that he had been harmed made her shudder.

Philip steered the boat with obvious expertise. "I think we should keep it about a hundred yards offshore," he called above the flapping of the canvas and the rush of the wind.

"There's a riptide that runs along here," she said. "I've heard it said that the current hugs the shoreline only about fifty yards out. Perhaps we should go in a little closer."

He nodded and moved the rudder. The boat veered toward shore.

Katie looked through the binoculars again. She saw an albatross floating atop the waves, several pieces of driftwood but no man in the whitecaps. "How far is this cave?" she asked.

"We're a ways out yet," Philip said.

"How long since you left him?"

"About three hours. If he'd gone over the side just before I got back, that would have been about two hours ago."

She prayed that God would buoy him up and keep him safe until they found him. Spending that kind of time in fifty-degree water would be deadly.

Philip pointed. "There is where we left the buckboard."

"Then we should be seeing him if he is in the water." She redoubled her efforts to find anything in the sea. "Will!" she screamed over the sound of the wind and waves.

Her eyes ached from the brilliance of the sun bouncing on the water. A gull flew up with a startled squawk. She moved the binoculars to that direction. At first she saw nothing but whitecaps and moved on.

A flutter of something made her return her gaze. "I see something!" A white face appeared then vanished in the water again. "It's a man!" She pointed in the direction, twenty feet closer to shore. Will clung to a piece of driftwood. One hand waved weakly, then the movement made him lose his grip on the log. He made a grab at it but it floated away.

His head went under the water and she screamed. "He's drowning!"

"Take the rudder!" Philip yelled to her when they were ten feet from Will.

She moved back to where Philip was shucking his shoes and jacket. She steadied the rudder as he tossed the anchor overboard. The boat slowed as the weight took hold.

"Haul down the sails!" He dove overboard and with swift strokes, aimed toward Will.

Praying frantically, Katie raced to the mast and yanked down the sails. By the time she returned to the railing, Philip had reached the spot where they'd last seen his brother. He floated and glanced around. Katie saw a dark head break through the waves behind him. "There! He's there!"

Philip turned around and grabbed him by the collar. Katie grabbed a life preserver and tossed it at the two men when she was sure Philip had seized hold of Will. Philip snatched at it with his other hand and missed. The preserver floated on past. She pulled it back to the boat and hefted it again as Philip fought to keep his brother's head above the water. This time it landed nearer the two, and she nearly shouted with victory when she saw Philip grab hold of it and slip it over Will's head. Philip towed his brother toward the craft.

She rushed to the stern and grabbed Will's arm as the back of the boat slewed in the water. Panting, she helped Philip get Will into the craft then held out her hand to assist Philip, but he shook his head.

He waved off her help and grabbed the side of the boat. "Tend to Will," he gasped. He treaded water, gasping for oxygen.

Katie turned to Will, who was lying on his stomach on the deck. She pressed her fingers to his neck. Nothing. Panicking, she slid her fingers to another spot and tried again. There. A slight pulse pumped against her fingertips. But he wasn't breathing. She pressed on his back until seawater spewed from his mouth and nose, but she still saw no signs of his lungs filling with air.

"Please, God, let him breathe," she whispered. She rolled him over and wiped his face with her skirt. A shadow loomed over her, and she realized Philip had managed to get aboard.

"He's not breathing," she said, trying to keep her voice calm. She tipped his head back and pinched his nose closed. She'd only watched a demonstration about this technique and had never tried it, but she couldn't stand by and let Will die.

Running over the steps she remembered, she checked to make sure his airways were clear then pressed her lips to his and began the kiss of life. His lips were cold and tasted of seawater. She tried not to believe she ministered to a dead man. When he didn't respond, she pushed on his chest and tried again. Nothing.

"Breathe, breathe," she begged. Her eyes burned, and her throat ached with holding in her emotion. She shook him and screamed into his face. "Don't you die, Will Jesperson!"

He had to live. She couldn't bear it if he died. She pushed his chest then filled her lungs again and blew oxygen into his mouth. Were his lips a bit warmer? She was nearly afraid to hope. She drew in another deep breath and leaned down.

He coughed, and she rolled him onto his side. Water ran from the corner of his mouth. His eyes opened and she nearly cried with relief.

"Where's your hat?" he asked through a strangled voice before he closed his eyes again.

Katie let out a laugh of surprise and then sank back on her heels and gave in to her tears.

NINETEEN

WILL WANTED TO feel those warm lips on his again. The ones that had called him from a deep, cold place. He shuddered as the cold sank further into his bones. He'd been sure he was dead. There was little he remembered other than an eternity of fighting the cold and the waves until he'd given up all hope of surviving. Then he'd felt warmth and passion, a call he couldn't resist. Katie. He opened his eyes and watched the beautiful woman who had saved his life weeping beside him.

Katie must have seen his involuntary movement because she glanced at his brother.

"Where do you think we could find a blanket?" she asked, wiping her face.

When she moved to follow his brother, Will grabbed her hand. She turned back toward him with her blue eyes wide.

"You kissed me," he said. "Somehow it made me want to come back."

Color rushed to her cheeks but she held his gaze. "It wasn't a kiss. I was putting air into your lungs."

He clutched her hand more tightly. "Your mouth was warm. I was cold—so cold." An explosion of shivers shook him. He wanted to pull her down to him and wrap his arms around her, bask in her warmth.

She put her hand on his forehead. "Your brother is looking for a blanket in the hold. We'll head for shore and the doctor shortly."

His eyes strayed to the strands of gleaming brown hair that the wind had released from its pins. He'd never seen a more beautiful sight. "You don't have your hat," he said.

Though she smiled, the anxiety still stayed in her blue eyes. "So you said. I rushed out with Philip to try to find you and quite forgot it."

A lady never went out without her hat. He could see a smattering of freckles across her nose and a pink tinge already on her forehead. Miss Katie Russell was no typical lady, only concerned with propriety and decorum. He'd never known a woman to put herself out in such a way for another. He struggled to sit up then bit back a groan. His chest burned when he tried to pull in a deeper breath. His head throbbed and his skin felt as though it had been stripped away.

She placed a warm hand on his chest. "Lie still. I don't want you to further harm yourself."

He put his cold hand atop hers. "What is the saying . . . when someone saves your life, it belongs to them?"

She flushed a deeper pink. "Anyone would have done the same."

When she tried to withdraw her hand, he kept it pressed to the place over his heart. "I don't think so. You're a remarkable woman, Miss Russell."

"It's Katie," she said. "You can call me Katie."

He nodded. "With something like this between us, I think first names are in order. In fact, I thought I heard you call me by name when I was in the water."

Sparks of awareness pulsed between them. Will told himself it was because she'd given him the kiss of life, but he suspected it was more than that.

His brother returned with a wool blanket in his hand. He tucked it around Will. It smelled musty but the warmth it offered was all Will cared about. "Thanks," he said. Shudders wracked him again.

Philip crouched beside him. "What happened?"

When her gaze sharpened with interest, Will struggled to sit up again, and this time, with Philip's help, he made it. He leaned against the side of the boat and Katie helped him wrap the blanket all around him.

"I was about to bust open the lock on the chest when a rope fell to the ledge. Our pirate friends."

"What makes you say it was them?" Philip asked.

"Before they knew I was in the cave, I saw one open the chest. Where else would ship equipment come from? I saw a logbook, compass, other instruments. I'd wager it's from the missing ship."

"Why hide that stuff? They could send it to the bottom of the sea with the ship."

Will rubbed his aching head. "It was one of several chests. I guess they took them all in case there were valuables. They'd want to know what they had in their possession before they ransom it back to the shipping company."

"Was it the men you saw on the hillside?" Katie asked. "The ones you questioned me about?"

He nodded. "And they are planning something else."

Philip winched up the anchor. "Why do you think they have something planned?"

"I heard them say something about a ship bound with money coming in two days."

"Did they name the ship?" Katie asked.

Will shook his head.

"Bet we can figure it out," Philip said.

She glanced at his brother. "What a thrilling life you must lead as a detective! I think I should like to help you find the pirates."

"The Pinkertons' reputation lately has made all detectives appear that they're accepting bribes and hobnobbing with criminals," Will said. "You'd lose your precious respectability."

She turned away and studied her hands. "What makes you think I care a fig about respectability?"

"You're quite eager to take on any and every responsibility that looks your way. That usually denotes a strong streak of respectability."

"I could say the same about you."

"That's true," Philip put in. "Case in point: taking charge of the little girl when she's not even mine."

"What is the truth about Jennie's heritage?" she asked. "We really must sort that out. Quite soon."

"See, there you go again. You can't help but take charge." Will moved his head and winced.

"Can we save this conversation until he's doing better?" Philip asked.

Will glanced at his brother. "I'll be all right."

Her sunburned skin turned even pinker as she glanced back and forth between the brothers. "We can't let this situation continue. That poor child deserves better. We need to get her settled."

"I thought once we found her mother we'd ferret out the truth," Philip said. "Finding her mother's killer is the goal now. That may be the only way we figure out Eliza's involvement in all of this and who fathered Jennie. But I can't do it alone." Philip shot a quick glance Will's way.

Will sighed and lifted a hand up to his head. It was aching. "I'll do what I can, but remember, I have another job as well. I must perform the duties I'm being paid for."

Katie glanced from Philip to Will and back again. "Surely you two don't still suspect my father."

Will opened his mouth to mention the pocket watch at home on his dresser then closed it again. No sense stirring up a painful subject. The truth would come out sooner or later.

"His suicide attempt indicates guilt," Philip said, jerking on the tack so hard the boat veered toward the shore. He righted course.

Will smothered a sigh. While he didn't believe Philip had anything to do with Miss Bulmer's death, he hated to think what Katie's father's potential guilt might do to her.

She turned to him. "I'm going to help you get to the bottom of this. My father had nothing to do with Eliza's murder, and I'm going to prove it!"

"You're not an investigator."

"Neither are you." Her eyes glowed. "And I know everyone in town. And nearly everything that has gone on in this community for years."

❧

Katie's face felt tight and dry. She stared at the apparition in the mirror. A red-faced horror stared back at her. If her mother could see her now, she'd be *tsking* and shaking her head as she exclaimed about the fact that Katie had gone out without a hat or parasol. Whatever had she been thinking yesterday? Bart was coming to take her to lunch at his home this morning. She could only imagine what his parents would think when they saw her.

She touched her red, roughened cheeks. There was no way to hide the damage. She finished her hair, but no adjusting of her hat covered the sunburn on her face. Sighing, she removed her glasses and tucked them away, then closed the bedroom door behind her and proceeded down the steps. Bart would be here any moment. She should have telephoned him this morning and canceled the plans. When she reached the foyer, Will was exiting the parlor with Jennie in his arms. He was still pale and his head was bandaged.

The baby smiled and reached for her. Her small teeth gleamed in her smile. Katie took the baby then had to rescue a feather the child grabbed from her hat. "Has she eaten lunch?"

"I fed her." His gaze probed under her hat at her sunburn. "Does it hurt?"

"A little." She nuzzled the baby's soft cheek. "How are you feeling?"

"I'll live." He paused and studied her face as she adjusted her hat to shade it better. "You could wear your glasses. They would hide part of your face." His voice was full of amusement.

"I think not," she said.

"You look quite fetching in them. Rather intelligent. I like intelligence in a woman."

Her hot face flamed still hotter. Was he mocking her? She couldn't tell if he was serious or not. She heard steps on the front porch then saw Bart's familiar bowler through the door window. "I must go."

She handed the baby to him and turned toward the door, but not so fast that she missed the frown that gathered in his forehead. There was a skip in her pulse. He couldn't be jealous, could he? A smile lit her face when she opened the door. The delight faded when she saw Bart's eyes widen at his first glimpse of her.

"Is that a sunburn?" he asked.

She opened the door and stepped out onto the porch to escape Will's amusement. "It is, indeed. I got a little too much sun yesterday."

He couldn't seem to look away from her face. "You lost your chapeau?"

She turned her face away and took his arm. "I went boating yesterday."

"Ah, the wind blew it off." He picked up her gloved hand and patted it. "Most unfortunate."

Some perverse impulse made her tell him the truth. "Not really. I quite forgot to take it."

He stumbled on the grass. "It is of no matter. You look lovely."

His gallant words made her wince. A woman never forgot her hat. It just wasn't done. He was bound to wonder what could have caused her to behave in such an unseemly way. And now to show up to his house with a sunburn. She blinked her eyes as they blurred. It was most uncharacteristic of her. Her mother would be appalled too.

She said nothing more as Bart helped her into the carriage then climbed in after her. The coachman urged the matched horses away from the sea toward town. She stayed on her side of the seat. If she'd been at home instead of the lighthouse, she might have dared to purchase a bit of powder to cover the evidence on her cheeks.

"Mother is delighted you're coming," Bart said. He reached over to take her hand again.

She checked the impulse to pull away, but she smiled at him and left her fingers clasped in his. With Florence demanding money, it was even more imperative that Katie marry. It was growing more difficult to fight her attraction to Will, but now she had Florence to contend with. She could not allow things to spin out of control.

The carriage stopped at the grand porch attached to the three-story stone manor. She'd skated past it many times and had longed to see inside. Now she would have the opportunity. Bart helped her down and escorted her up the wide steps. A doorman opened the double doors for her, and she stepped into a foyer so elegant she nearly gasped. The walls were papered in silk and the wood floors gleamed. Though her own home was beautiful, this was in the very latest style and lavish beyond comprehension. She needed to act as though she were used to this kind of luxury.

Holding her head high, she stepped onto a thick, plush runner. Bart led her into a grand drawing room with so many expensive items it was all she could do not to stare. Though the curtains were held back with ties, the room was a bit dark, which suited Katie fine. It would make it more difficult to see her sunburn.

Mrs. Foster smiled from her seat on a pink velvet sofa. "Katie, my dear, I'm so pleased you could join us. You sit right here by me." She patted the space beside her.

Katie dropped her hand from Bart's arm and went to join his mother. "I'm honored at your invitation, Mrs. Foster. You have a lovely home." Bart's mother was lovely too. Though she had to be in her fifties, her skin was still smooth and unlined. Long black lashes fringed her brown eyes.

Mrs. Foster beamed. "I picked out everything myself. Mr. Foster wanted me to hire a designer from the city, but I wanted our home to reflect my tastes, not someone else's. If you like, take off your chapeau, dear. Make yourself comfortable. We want to be like family."

Katie untied the strings of her bonnet. If she kept a bright smile on her face, perhaps the other woman wouldn't notice. She removed her hat and smoothed her hair a bit. "Luncheon smells delicious."

"Cook is preparing lamb," Mrs. Foster said. Her eyes widened when she glanced at Katie, but she quickly recovered. "Are you too warm?"

"No, I—I got a bit too much sun yesterday."

"She went boating," Bart said. He dropped into a chair across from them and crossed one leg over the other. "And the wind took her hat."

Katie started to frown at his lie but forced herself not to react. He had every right to be ashamed of her appearance.

"The sun can be quite brutal," his mother said, her gaze still lingering on Katie's cheeks. "I have something that might bleach those freckles out again. Let me fetch it for you." She rose and hurried from the room.

Katie kept her smile fixed in place though she wanted to burst into tears.

TWENTY

WHEN WILL SAW the constable dismount in front of the lighthouse, he knew what he'd come for. It was the last thing Will needed. He'd already been muttering under his breath and throwing things ever since Katie had gone off with her dandy.

When Will had gotten back last night, the constable had been there but Will hadn't been up to answering questions. He had hoped to have longer than overnight before the constable returned, demanding answers. The man was bound to order them to get out of his investigation.

He put down the polishing cloth and climbed down the ladder from his perch atop the lighthouse. His muscles screamed at the indignity after the beating they'd endured yesterday in the sea.

"Constable Brown," he said in greeting when the men met outside the front door of the lighthouse.

"Morning, Mr. Jesperson." The constable took out his cigar and struck a match. He puffed and a curl of smoke drifted Will's way. "You look a tad better than last night. I trust a good night's sleep has cleared your mind enough to answer some questions." He gestured to a bench overlooking the crashing waves.

Will nodded. The men settled on the bench. Gulls cawed overhead and swooped low to snatch crabs on the rocks below the lighthouse.

Brown gestured with his pipe at the bandage on Will's forehead. "Ready to tell me the full story now?"

"I fell off a cliff."

"I know there is more to it than that." Brown puffed on his pipe. "Care to explain why you were investigating instead of getting a message to me? I've found nothing to indicate that our pirates are still in the area. If there's evidence to the contrary, I should be the first to know of it."

"Sorry, Constable. I was hardly out for a leisurely sail," he said, gesturing toward his head. "One of our pirates threw me off that cliff." Will launched into what had happened the day before as the constable's cigar smoke curled around his head.

Brown lifted a brow. "Sounds like a tall tale to me. Are you pulling my leg? Pirates hiding a chest in a cave. Care to show me the spot?"

"Maybe in a day or two. A two-hour hike along the shore is a bit beyond me today. There's more though, Constable. I heard them mention they planned to take another ship due here in two days. That would be tomorrow."

Brown's gaze sharpened on Will's face. "Is this a ploy to distract me from my real questions?"

"And what would those questions be?"

Brown puffed on his cigar for a long moment. "Miss Eliza's disappearance. I find it an odd coincidence that her wedding gown was found right below this lighthouse." He pointed his cigar at the rocks below. "Don't you think it strange too?"

Will kept his expression impassive. "I arrived a few hours after her disappearance. I have never met the woman."

"Yet you were at her home when I arrived. And you took charge of her child. There is much more that you're not saying. Where might I find your brother?"

"He went for a walk on the beach." Will caught a movement down by the pier and tensed when he recognized Philip.

Brown turned his head and saw the figure as well. "Is that your brother?"

"Yes."

"Excellent. I shall wait and speak with him." He puffed content-edly on his cigar as Philip drew nearer.

Philip's confident stride soon had him within hailing distance. Brown rose and motioned for Philip to join them. The wary expression on his brother's face made Will tense again. Though he believed his brother had nothing to do with Eliza's disappearance, if Philip were cocky or his answers failed to satisfy, he could find himself behind bars.

"Constable Brown. I wasn't expecting to see you here," Philip said when he reached them.

Brown puffed on his cigar before answering. "Mr. Jesperson. What do you know about Miss Eliza Bulmer's disappearance? I suspect your involvement in solving the *Paradox's* disappearance is merely a ploy to dispose of your former mistress."

Will flinched. "That's ridiculous, Constable. Philip was legiti-mately hired by the shipping company. Telephone them and check for yourself."

The constable didn't look at Will. "Shall we let your brother answer for himself?"

"Look, I know nothing about Eliza's death," Philip said, splaying his hands outward. "Our relationship was over two years ago."

"You say she's dead. How would you know that when we've found no body?"

Philip flushed. "It certainly appears she's dead. Her dress was found right here, and Miss Russell said she was wearing it the day she disappeared."

"I would like to know the details of your relationship," the con-stable said. "How did you meet her?"

"Through a mutual friend."

"And that friend's name?"

"I'd rather not say."

Brown puffed his cigar again. "I'm afraid I must insist."

Will had to admire the constable's tenacity. Some would have done a perfunctory investigation and gone on. "You'd better tell him, Philip," he said.

Philip thrust his hands in his pockets. "Mr. Russell."

Will straightened. "Katie's father?" When his brother nodded, he wanted to strangle him. "Why have you said nothing about this?"

"It had nothing to do with me."

"You told me to talk to Miss Bulmer about Albert Russell, yet you already knew him."

"Shut up, Will," Philip said through gritted teeth.

Too late, Will realized how incriminating his words were. Was Philip trying to frame Albert for Eliza's disappearance? Nausea roiled in his belly. He wouldn't believe his brother might be capable of such a thing and yet it certainly looked suspicious.

"I only met Russell one time, at the gentlemen's club in San Francisco," Philip said. "Eliza was with him and another man. Russell introduced us and asked me to take her back to her hotel. He had a meeting he was late for. I never heard the name again until I was told she'd said he was involved in the disappearance of *Dalton's Fortune*."

"Who was the other man? Can he corroborate your story?" Brown asked.

"Mitchell is his last name. The club could tell you how to get hold of him." Philip glanced at Will.

Will thought of the watch on his dresser. It was his duty to tell the constable about it.

Brown frowned at Philip. "Why did you send your brother to speak with Miss Eliza? Did you intend to offer her money for the child?"

"Of course not! She had contacted my employer and indicated she had information that might help me find the pirates. But you know all this. Her correspondence with the owner of the ship indicated she could tell me who masterminded the theft. She asked for a fee in return."

Brown puffed on his cigar before answering. "So she wanted to be paid for the information."

"She did," Philip said.

It was a common demand. Philip probably was used to forking over money for the clues he needed to solve cases.

"Did my brother tell you about Russell's watch?" Philip asked.

Brown glanced at Will. "What watch?"

"I found a pocket watch on the island out there." Will gestured offshore. "Engraved with the name Albert Russell."

The constable's eyes widened, and he took another puff of his cigar. "You tell Miss Katie?"

"I did."

"Bet that went over big." He puffed in silence for a moment. "It appears Mr. Russell may be involved in this even deeper than I thought. He might have disposed of Miss Eliza then tried to kill himself rather than get caught. If he recovers consciousness, he can explain much of this."

"Unless the pirates took care of both of them. Miss Russell believes her father was attacked."

Brown shook his head. "I'm still not convinced the pirates are around here. Makes no sense to me. Why not take their loot and get out?"

"How? There is no way in or out of here without going through Mercy Falls or down the coast and risk a blockade. It makes sense to wait until the furor dies down then get the gold out."

"Maybe." He put out his cigar, then nodded at the men and headed back to his horse.

Will glanced at his brother and caught an expression of relief flitting across his face. He didn't want to believe Philip had anything to do with this mess, but he wasn't entirely certain.

❧

The luncheon had been an ordeal. It was clear by the quick, darting glances Mrs. Foster sent her way that the sunburn horrified her. By the time Bart escorted Katie outside, her eyes burned from holding back tears, and her throat was sore and tight. She longed to go to her own house.

"Are you all right?" Bart asked when the carriage pulled away from the manor. "You're very quiet."

"Were you ashamed of me, Bart?" She touched a gloved finger to her cheek. "About my face?"

"Of course not." He shifted on the seat, glanced at her, then looked away.

"But you lied to your mother. I told you I forgot it."

"There is nothing wrong with my attempt to help you put your best foot forward with my mother," he said, still staring out the window.

"There is if you feel you have to lie."

His gaze swung back to her. "I'm not sure I'm comfortable with you staying out at the lighthouse. This isn't like you. What kind of influences are you under that you'd go out unprotected? A lady just doesn't do that."

She bit back the hot words trembling on her tongue. If this man were to be her future husband, then of course he would be concerned about her reputation. "Lady Carrington is there," she reminded him. "There is no cause for worry."

His scowl turned darker. "I heard that the lightkeeper's brother is there too. It's not seemly, Katie. I think you should stay here, at the house. If we're to be married, no one would think anything about it."

"I didn't know we were to be married," she said. She chewed on her lip and wished she could recall the words. She was hardly ready to push him into a declaration when she was full of such indecision.

"I thought it was understood," he said. "Your father gave his blessing for me to court you. As soon as I'm in a position to marry, I intend to ask you to marry me."

In a position to marry? He was nearly thirty, the only son of a wealthy father. She kept a smile pinned to her face and said nothing to encourage him. If he waited a bit, she hoped to be able to summon more enthusiasm for a life shared with him. Though their future needed to be settled soon. Her parents were counting on her.

Still, perhaps he was feeling as much indecision as she. The thought did little to comfort her. If he wasn't totally enamored with her, and she had conflicted emotions too, what hope was there for a relationship? This indecision was so unlike her. All her life she'd been groomed to make a wise choice of husband. Bart would be the perfect spouse.

When she didn't answer, he rushed on. "I'll be in a position soon. I don't want to be dependent on my father when I take a wife. I intend to strike out on my own and start my own company."

His ambition encouraged her. "Doing what? Open another sawmill?"

He scowled. "Not in a million years. I hate the noise, the dirt. I want to open a Macy's."

She'd love to be part of that kind of enterprise. "Wouldn't that take an exorbitant sum?"

His earnest blue eyes sought her face. "I have some backers. It's figuring out how to tell my father I'm not following in his shoes—that'll be the tough part."

"I'm sure you'll explain it so he understands."

He pressed her hand. "You're so easy to talk to, Katie. When I'm with you, I think I can do anything."

She smiled and clung to his fingers. "I know you can do whatever you set your mind to, Bart." If only the touch of his hand moved her the way being with Will did. She was so confused. Addie's words had haunted her lately. God had a plan for her and she would feel peace when she found it. She longed for that peace but it seemed so nebulous and unattainable.

She saw a figure standing on the sidewalk, walking away from them down a side street. The men on the benches watched the woman saunter past, and Katie heard a low whistle. Even before the sun pierced the shadows under the woman's hat, she knew it was Florence.

She must have clutched Bart's hand because he studied her face. "Is something wrong?" he asked.

"N–not at all," she said. She asked him a question about the potential Macy's store to distract him, and he immediately launched into his plans, warming to the subject.

Katie had to find some way to get Florence out of town. Katie had no idea where she could find the kind of money the woman demanded. Not unless some of the papers she'd found in her father's safe were worth something. She should have examined them more closely.

"Would you mind if we stopped by my father's shop a moment? I need to get into the safe," she asked.

"As you wish." Bart leaned forward and gave the driver directions.

Minutes later the carriage stopped in front of Russell's Haberdashery. Bart exited the carriage and helped her alight. "Please, just wait here," she said when he acted like he was going to accompany her. "It won't take me but a moment." She smiled and brushed past him to the door, which she unlocked before stepping inside. The shop was closed for the day.

She stepped through to the back room, where she rotated through the safe's combination and unlocked it. The papers were on the bottom. She lifted them out and retrieved her glasses from her pocket. A brief scan showed her hope was in vain. These were all old contracts and nothing that showed any money due. She replaced them and spun the lock, and her heart was leaden as she retraced her steps.

Blinking in the bright sunlight outside the shop, she locked the door. Bart was chatting with two gentlemen, not looking her way, and the bank was just at the end of the block. She walked quickly to the bank and approached the teller.

"Good afternoon, Miss Russell," the young male teller said. His mustache twitched as he spoke. "You're quite brave to be out and about with the epidemic still raging."

Katie had been so preoccupied, she hadn't stopped to think about why the bank was practically deserted. "I'd best not stay out long. I wondered if you could give me the balance in all of my father's accounts?"

"I've heard of his condition. Me and the missus have been praying he'll awaken soon. It will just be a moment while I consult the ledger." The teller vanished down the hallway.

Katie clutched her gloved hands together. Though she knew it was a futile hope, she prayed there was more money than she'd been told. Perhaps Papa had another account where he'd saved money for their future. She turned and glanced through the plate glass window into the street. There were few passersby. She hadn't heard of any new smallpox outbreaks, but people still feared stepping outside their homes.

The teller returned and slid a piece of paper across the counter to her. "Here you are, Miss Russell."

"Thank you." She glanced at the slip of paper as she turned toward the door. When she saw the total, she stopped and glanced back. "You're sure this is all his accounts?"

"Yes, miss. I know it's not much." His brown eyes were apologetic.

Not much was an understatement. One account held only a thousand dollars and the other held two thousand. Perhaps her father would know more. She retraced her steps to the buggy and asked Bart to take her to the hospital.

"I can't allow you to go there, Katie," he said. "Not while it houses people with the pox. Surely you've been telephoning to check on your father's condition."

"Of course I have," she said. "I thought a visit from me might bring him around to a more lucid frame of mind."

"The nurse will tell you when you're allowed entry," Bart said.

"I should like to see my mother. I could speak to her through the window."

"The road to your house is blocked, and I'm quite unwilling to see you endanger yourself. I'll take you back to the lighthouse."

There was no arguing with him. Katie would have to come back by herself. She sat staring silently out the window until Bart's carriage drew up outside the lighthouse.

"I do hope you will think about moving to our house for the remainder of this smallpox outbreak," Bart said, helping her alight from the buggy.

"I shall take it under consideration," she said. When he might have bent to give her a kiss on the cheek, she stepped back. "Thank you for lunch," she said. "I must go."

She fled up the hillside before he could protest. When she reached the lighthouse, Lady Carrington met her at the door.

"Katie, my dear, the doctor called. Your father is beginning to regain consciousness. Dr. Lambertson says not to come until the smallpox is past, but he wanted you to know of Albert's improvement."

"I have to talk to him," Katie said.

"They won't let you in."

"Then I shall have to sneak in." She had to know the truth of the events swirling around her. She turned and retraced her steps. Will's bicycle was lying at the bottom of the slope, so she grabbed it and climbed onto the seat. She rode back to town and turned down the street to the hospital. The barricade ahead warned her she couldn't go through that way, so she dismounted, left the bicycle parked under a tree, then darted through several yards and down an alley to finally arrive at the hospital's back entrance.

She tugged on the heavy door but it was locked. If she went around to the front, she would be turned away. Before she could decide what to do, the door opened and a woman dressed in a maid uniform stepped out. Katie seized the handle and slipped inside, though the woman called after her.

Papa's ward was on the second floor. A back stairway opened off the hall, and she peeked into the stairwell. Empty. Lifting her skirts, she scampered up the steep steps to the second floor landing. The hallway held a lone nurse pushing a cart with bedpans. Katie lifted her head and sailed into the hall as though she had every right to be there. The nurse barely gave her a glance before disappearing through a doorway. Katie peeked in after her but the ward held only women. She hurried along until she found one inhabited by six men. Her father's bed was the last one on the right.

She approached him lying there. He bore little resemblance to the vital father she was used to. His thin hair was in disarray on the pillow. His normally florid complexion was pasty. His eyes were closed.

She touched his hand. "Papa?" she whispered. "It's Katie. Are you awake?" She noticed a curtain by the bed and pulled it closed to shield her presence from anyone passing by.

Her father's lids fluttered, and he opened his bleary eyes. He blinked then focused on her face. "Katie?" He returned the grip on her hand.

He knew her! Tears burned her eyes. She pulled up a nearby chair and put her head close to his. "How are you feeling, Papa?"

"Thirsty," he said, licking his lips.

She saw a glass of water on the table beside his bed and helped him sit up. He drank greedily then fell back against the pillow as if the effort had exhausted him.

"Papa, what happened?" she asked.

"When?"

"You were found in the pond at the base of Mercy Falls. Has the constable been over to talk to you?"

He rubbed his forehead. "I don't know, Katie."

"Did someone shove you into the falls?"

His pale blue eyes studied her face, then he nodded. "Don't ask me who pushed me. I don't know. I have my suspicions though."

"Were you involved with the theft of gold from the *Paradox*?" she asked. When he flinched, she had her answer. "You were, weren't you?" This would hurt her mother terribly.

"My business is in trouble," he said. "No one was supposed to get hurt. We were just going to take the money to survive the recession. When they killed those sailors . . ." He swallowed hard and shook his head. "I was going to turn them in."

"You can still do that."

"No, I can't. A man stopped by here last night. At least I think it was last night. It was dark and I was so confused. He said if I talked, he'd kill you and your mother."

"What about Eliza? Your watch was found on the island where her body was dumped."

He shook his head. "We argued and she slapped me. I grabbed her shoulders and pushed her away. Later I realized my watch was gone. She must have had it in her hand or pocket when she was killed. I had nothing to do with it."

"What did you argue about?"

"It's not your business."

She hadn't thought he would tell her. "Did you recognize the man's voice who called on you? If you can tell the constable . . ." She didn't want to tell him she'd received threatening phone calls.

"I can't tell anyone and neither can you. There are more people involved than this one man. If he's identified, they'll just hire someone else to take his place. I don't even know how many are a part of it. Too many."

"But the constable suspects you of killing Eliza! You'll go to jail."

"I have no choice."

She bit her lip. "There's more, Papa. Florence is in town."

His lip curled. "Your mother? So that's why you're here asking these questions? I knew the time would come when you'd revert to her ways. Like mother like daughter."

She'd heard it too many times. "She's not my mother!"

His eyes narrowed. "What does she want?"

"Money."

"I am nearly bankrupt."

Katie sat back in the chair. "I told her that, but she is threatening to tell Bart's family about my heritage."

Panic filled his eyes. "You must not allow that to happen! How much does she want?"

Katie told him and watched his eyes cloud over. "Is there any way to get that amount?"

"I don't know where. We are mortgaged to the hilt. Perhaps I can get a loan from Bart without telling him what I need it for."

"I'd rather not be beholden to him."

Her father frowned, but before he could speak, a hand swept the curtain back to reveal a scowling male orderly. He glanced from Katie to her father then jerked his thumb. "Out," he said. "No visitors allowed."

Katie rose. "Good-bye, Papa." She rose and swept past the orderly but his dark gaze followed her all the way to the door.

TWENTY-ONE

THE BABY GRABBED Will's ear and chattered something full of vowels and totally incomprehensible. He managed a smile though he'd been in a bad mood ever since Katie had left with that blond dandy.

"You are so cute," he said. He showed her the pap feeder and she grabbed it. He settled on the sofa with her and dribbled the pap into her mouth. He glanced up and met Lady Carrington's soft smile.

"You're wonderful with children, Will," she said.

He tugged on his tie and glanced out the window without replying.

"I don't expect her back for at least another hour," she said.

"Who?"

Her smile widened and her skirt swished as she walked into the room and settled in the armchair. "I'm not quite blind and doddering yet, young man. Anyone with eyes can see how you watch Katie."

"She's just a . . ." He searched for the right word. It wasn't *friend* and it wasn't *acquaintance.* His head felt a little funny when he remembered the way he'd awakened to the press of her warm lips on his frozen ones. Could he actually be harboring strong emotions for Katie?

Lady Carrington chuckled. "Love is like that, Will. It sneaks up on you." She sobered and took a sip of tea. "I've often wondered about the sadness I sometimes glimpse in Katie's face. I don't see it when she's with you. There is something special between the two of you. Nurture it and see how it grows."

Were his feelings so clear that even Lady Carrington could see? His chest tightened at the thought that he could be so transparent. "I think I'll go see if my balloon has descended, if you don't mind watching the baby. I need to run down to the harbor for a few minutes too."

Her eyes were wise and held amusement. "Run along, my dear. This will all catch up with you sooner or later."

He grabbed his hat and escaped into the sunshine with heat rising on his neck. The balloon had fallen on the beach, and he set off at a brisk jog. Once he wrote down the readings on the instruments, he glanced at the sky. Rain was coming, if his readings were correct. He dragged the remains of the balloon out of the way of the tide. He would dispose of it on his way back. The tide was coming in, and he veered away from the encroaching foam on the waves as he walked toward the harbor.

The quay teemed with activity. Stevedores hauled crates to waiting ships, and fishermen sat on the pier with their poles dangling into the water. One of the fishermen would be most likely to have the time to answer a few questions.

He walked to where an older man sat in dungarees. "Catching anything?"

With a glance from under gray brows, the man said, "Yup."

Will settled on the boards beside him. "You live around here all your life?"

The fellow jerked a bit on his line. "Born and raised."

"You hang out here a lot?"

"Look, young fellow, just spit out what you're looking for. I ain't got all day."

Will grinned. He liked the direct approach himself. "I heard there's an important shipment coming through tomorrow. You know anything about that?"

"Even if I did, what's it to you?" The man studied him from under his battered hat. "I ain't seen you around."

"I'm the lightkeeper."

The man's face changed and he actually smiled. "That's good work you do, son. The old lightkeeper saved my bacon back in '80. Storm tore my ship from stem to stern. I was clinging to a piece of the boat and he came rowing out to get me. Best sight I ever saw."

"About the ship? I want to be on my guard after the last instance of piracy."

"Can't be too careful," the man agreed. He spat a dark stream of tobacco into the clear blue water. "Way I hear it, the *Hanson Queen* is due in here late afternoon. She's carrying the pay for the navy. Don't reckon she'll be docked long, and I hear she'll have guns mounted just in case."

"That's good news. Perhaps the pirates will hear of it and stay away." Will watched the old man another moment. "You hear any scuttlebutt about the last ship? Any idea who did it and how?"

The man spat again. "Sometimes it don't pay to listen too close."

The guy knew something. Will could see it in his clouded eyes. "You think they're still around?"

"They ain't going nowhere."

"Residents?"

The man shrugged and jerked on his line. "Got a big one. Been nice talking to you, but I do believe we're done." He rose and reeled in his fish, a big rockfish.

⋅⋅⋅❦⋅⋅⋅

Will was out when Katie returned in the afternoon. Her spirits dragged along the ground with her skirts. She inhaled the salty scent of the sea a final time before stepping into the house.

When she walked into the parlor, Jennie squealed in delight. Katie scooped her up and kissed her soft cheek. "I thought you'd be napping," she said. Katie's smile faded. It would be most difficult to leave this place and not see the baby every day. "Where is Will?" she asked Lady Carrington, who was seated in the armchair with a book in her hand.

"Down at the harbor. Philip is in town."

She wished she could share with Will what she'd learned from her father. Katie put the baby back by the blocks. "I believe I'll change then go for a walk."

She went to her room and changed from her dress to a white shirt-waist. As she buttoned the skirt, she heard a rustle in the pocket. When she slipped her hand inside, she found a slip of paper. She pulled it out and glanced at it. It was the note she'd found in her father's safe. The one about the ship docking an hour earlier. Now she realized what this note had to be referring to. She'd forgotten all about it.

Her spirits lifted but she told herself it had nothing to do with the fact that she was going to find Will. The safest path to the beach led out to the road and back past the rocky hillside to the rocky sand. Billowing clouds carried the tang of rain to her nose. Orioles sang in the bushes along the hill.

She saw a figure striding away from the dock. The long stride and the wide shoulders brought a smile to her face. How odd that she could recognize Will from such a distance. As he neared, she realized he seemed to be gazing off into the horizon as though he was deep in thought. He didn't see her until he was five feet away. The faraway expression changed to sharp awareness that made her heartbeat race.

"You're back," he said, stopping when he reached her. "Have a splendid time?" His tone was wry.

"Very nice," she muttered, not wanting to think of Bart now. "I thought I'd take a walk and intercept you. There's something I want to show you."

A teasing smile came. "I'm crushed. I thought you came out to greet me because you missed me."

She couldn't help but return his smile, but she didn't know how to respond to his words. Was he actually *flirting* with her? Sometimes in the night she remembered the way his eyes had opened after his near drowning and he'd stared into her soul. She could taste again the salty flavor of his lips. How cold he'd been. Some connection had been forged in that moment and she didn't know what to make of it.

"What, no response?" he asked. "I guess that means you didn't miss me. So what did you want to show me?"

"This." She pulled the note from her pocket and handed it over. "I found it in my father's safe the day the smallpox epidemic broke out. At the time, I had no idea what it meant, and I quite forgot about it."

He took it from her fingers, unfolded it, and looked it over. "Your father's handwriting?"

"No. I don't recognize the handwriting."

"It sounds as though he was involved with the piracy."

She winced at the definitive tone in his voice. "I still can't quite believe it. There's more," she said slowly, the words pulled from her tongue. "I spoke with my father today. He admitted to me that he knows something of this matter." When Will's face darkened, she rushed on. "He's not a bad man. He thought no one would be harmed." Even as the words spilled out, she realized how utterly ridiculous her statement sounded. She rubbed her forehead. "He has his faults but this shocks me."

"What faults?"

Did she trust him enough to tell him the truth? Yes. "He is the kindest man on the face of the earth, as long as he isn't drinking. When he imbibes alcohol, he changes."

"Many men do." He took her hand and she allowed it, finding the warmth of his touch comforting. "He has struck you?"

"Not physically. Only with his words."

"That can be even more painful. He is kind to your mother?"

She nodded. "Always. She makes excuses for him. Often months, even a year or two, go by between bouts of drinking. He usually only drinks when things aren't going well for him in some arena of his life."

"Has he been drinking lately?"

She hesitated then nodded, still clinging to his hand. "I'd begun to hope he had tamed his demons."

"Do you know what has not gone well for him?"

"His business is struggling."

One brow rose. "Perhaps he became involved in the theft of the gold to dig his way out of a financial hole," Will said.

"He admitted as much to me today."

He appeared lost in thought for a moment. "I have to admit something, Katie. I had to tell the constable about finding your father's watch."

She flinched, and a sense of betrayal tightened her throat. "You know what he will assume. That Papa murdered Eliza and dropped his watch while he was disposing of the body."

"Perhaps that *is* what happened."

"I know my father. He would never do something like that."

He kept a tight grip on her fingers. "His involvement with Eliza may have spiraled him into something quite out of character. A beautiful woman can make a man quite lose his head."

His words were almost tender. Katie's gaze darted to his face and found him staring at her with such an intent expression that the moisture in her mouth dried instantly. His gaze dropped to her lips. His grip on her fingers tightened. He was going to kiss her.

She jerked her hand away and stepped back. "We must be getting back," she said, feeling out of breath, as if she'd just run down the beach.

The disappointment in his eyes matched an ache building in her chest.

TWENTY-TWO

WILL GLANCED AT Katie from across the table. She'd been quiet and withdrawn since they returned from the beach. Had she sensed he had nearly lost his head and kissed her, or was she still upset that he'd told the constable about the watch? The thought that she had run from him was quite discouraging. Maybe she had no feelings for him.

Jennie picked up a piece of jam and bread between her forefinger and thumb in the pincher movement he found so amusing. She looked at it then threw it to the bird, who was waiting for just such an opportunity. Paco gobbled up the tidbit. She giggled and threw down another piece. Strawberry jam smeared her face.

"It's your supper, not the bird's," he said.

She puckered at the rebuke in his voice, and he quickly gave her a sip of milk from her cup. Her milky smile as he put it back down was a reward in itself. He offered her a spoonful of potato and she accepted it, though her brown eyes studied his face. She was a most charming baby. He glanced at his brother, who was writing in a notebook. Not that Philip seemed to notice her. He shook his head. Surely there would be some sort of biological pull if the two were related . . .

"If you'll excuse me, I'm rather tired tonight," Lady Carrington said. "I think I shall retire and read for a while."

"I'll come help you," Katie said.

"I think I shall try to prepare for bed by myself tonight. My arm is getting much better. Did you see your mother when you were in town today, Katie? You never said."

"No, the quarantine is still in effect. I'm forbidden to enter the house for at least another week to ten days."

"I thought perhaps you stepped into the yard and conversed through the window."

"Bart was with me, and he was reluctant to let me endanger my health."

Lady Carrington nodded. "Wise, I'm sure, my dear." She rose. "Good night."

Will echoed the good nights. Even Jennie chattered something that sounded like "night." The tiny girl waved her chubby hands toward the older woman then tossed another piece of bread to the bird.

Philip stood and stretched. "I do believe I'll wander down to the quay and see what's going on. See if I can dig up any more information about tomorrow."

Will narrowed his eyes. He watched in tight-lipped silence as Philip gave them a casual wave, then strode out of the kitchen. He was probably on his way to play poker under the guise of doing detective work. Which was probably the best way to obtain information, but . . .

Katie seemed to sense his agitation. She stood and began to clear the table. "I'll do the dishes if you can mind Jennie for fifteen minutes."

"She's still eating. I'll help you."

That brought her out of her fog. Her eyes were clear as she glanced at him. "You want to help with dishes?"

"I'm good at washing if you want to dry."

She smiled. "I do believe I would pay to see such a thing."

"The only payment I would exact is a round of checkers after Jennie is down for the night."

"Seems cheap enough. We can discuss the case over the game."

He'd hoped to speak of his growing feelings but it was clear she wanted to avoid such a topic. "Very well."

After depositing the dishes into the sink, she took the kettle from the wood range and poured hot water into the sink. She added soap flakes and swished it. "Your turn," she said, her smile widening.

He grinned and plunged his hands into the hot, soapy water. As he washed the dishes, he handed them to her to rinse in a tub of clean water.

"How did you learn to wash dishes?" she asked.

"I often helped my mother."

She shot a quick glance his way. "Just you? Not Philip?"

He shook his head. "He was more likely to be out playing."

"Are your parents still alive?"

His smile faded. "They died in the Galveston hurricane."

She put down the dish she was drying. "Oh Will, I'm so sorry. That must have been terrible."

"The worst of it is that it could have been prevented if anyone had listened to the early weather warnings."

"Weather warnings? You mean specific to the day? Not the almanac?"

He shook his head. "There are many scientists who are working to forecast the weather. A warning was issued about the hurricane but no one paid any heed. There is still much skepticism about the accuracy of the forecasts. We are getting more accurate every day."

"*We?*" she asked. "Do you forecast the weather as well as care for the lighthouse?"

He grinned. "Sounds quite outlandish, doesn't it? Weather is my passion though."

"Is that why I saw you with a balloon?"

"Yes. It collects data from the upper atmosphere."

"How very fascinating," she said.

"I'd like to do it full time someday," he said, surprising himself with the admission.

She smiled and her eyes lit with amusement.

"What's so funny?" he asked.

"I thought you might join your brother in the investigation business. You are naturally curious. Just like me."

He grinned. "No one is that nosy. I'm only helping Philip because I saw that ship being seized."

The baby jabbered something with a lot of vowels as though in approval. He noticed her tray was empty. "Are you done, little one?" He handed the last dish to Katie.

"Done," she echoed, lifting her arms toward him.

Katie laughed. "Did you hear that? She actually said a word."

"She's smart," he said.

"I'll clean her up," Katie said. She put down the plate in her hand.

"I've got it." He grabbed a clean towel and wet it, then wiped the goo from Jennie's face. She squirmed and wailed at the indignity then gave him a smile when he removed the tray from her high chair and lifted her in his arms. She planted an open-mouthed kiss on his cheek.

He turned from the table to intercept a strange expression on Katie's face. Softness lurked in her eyes, and a half smile lifted her lips. Their gazes locked, and he saw that awareness flash into her eyes again. His pulse lurched. He wished he had the nerve to kiss her.

❧

The log in the fireplace glowed and danced with flames. The heat was welcome with the damp chill creeping into the room from the rain sluicing down the windows. Katie arranged the checker pieces on the board table then pulled an armchair close. Will carried in a kitchen chair and set it down across from her. She draped a shawl around her shoulders and settled on the cushion.

"I play a mean game of checkers," she said.

"I've got an hour before I have to wind the light again."

She smiled, though her heart ached. The last time she'd played had been with her father. They often had a game after dinner. Would those times ever come again? So much had changed.

"Is Jennie sleeping?" he asked.

She nodded. "It didn't take her long. Is Philip still gone?"

He glanced at the window. "I wound the light and started the foghorn. I'll have to check on things in a few hours. I doubt Phillip will be back until late."

At his remote tone, she lifted a curious glance to his face. "You're the oldest?" The Galveston hurricane had been in 1900—eight years ago. Philip would have been thirteen. "Is it just the two of you?"

"And my sister, Ellen."

"Where is she?"

"Following her dreams. She's been crazy about babies ever since she was a child. She's a midwife in Boston."

She smiled at his indulgent tone. "How old is she?"

He thought a moment. "Twenty-five, I think."

"And unmarried?" Philip and Will were both handsome and she imagined Ellen was a dark-haired beauty as well.

His smile was wry. "She'd be the first to march in a voting rights for women parade. The man who marries her will have to be the adventurous, strong sort."

Ellen sounded like someone Katie would like. "I hope I get a chance to meet her."

"I've invited her to spend the summer with me."

She stacked several of her checkers together and tried to ignore the way her pulse skittered when he looked at her. Strange that she'd known him such a short time and yet he was the first thing she thought of every morning when she awakened.

He pushed a checker forward to another square. "You know this area. Are there any inlets or hidden coves along the shore where we might look for that ship? If we had found it by now, we might've had a clue on how to stop what is to happen tomorrow." He rubbed his head. "But that's not my worry, as the constable is quick to tell me. And Philip is the private eye, not me."

She sat back in the chair and considered the question. "My father owned a sailboat for a time, and my family explored the coastline from here to Oregon over several summers. There are plenty of places to hide a ship. The trees grow thick, and unless someone enters the bays and inlets, one would never see it."

"Anything in particular come to mind?"

She started to shake her head then stopped. "There is a river that is navigable in the spring floods. A side stream leads off to a small lake, but part of the year you can't take a boat in or out of the lake. Anything still there in July is stuck until the following spring. There is also a small inlet about ten miles up the coast. My family and I stumbled on it accidentally during a storm. You can't see it from the ocean until you get close."

"Those are possible places to look. Anywhere else?"

She found it difficult to think with those midnight eyes on her. They'd been to so many locations in her father's boat. "There's one other place. It's a deserted island inside a cove. On the backside, nearer to the land, is an inlet into the center of the island. Those are the only possible areas I can remember."

He moved the checkers around on the board. "Thanks. Would you mind showing us where they are after tomorrow?"

"Of course. Weather permitting." She smiled. "You're so interested in weather, perhaps you can predict what tomorrow will bring. What did your balloon indicate?"

He rose and grabbed a small notebook on the desk under the window. Flipping it open, he stepped to a spot beside her and showed her rows of neatly printed numbers. "These are temperatures, barometric pressures, and humidity."

The numbers made no sense to her, but she enjoyed seeing the way his voice rose and the color came to his face. And he was close enough that her mouth went dry. "What do they tell you?"

He jabbed at the page. "Things are pretty stable right now except for this slight dip in barometric pressure. This light rain will intensify, and a real storm could be headed our way."

"How interesting." She had trouble marshaling her thoughts with him so close. Being with Bart didn't affect her pulse or her breathing. It was disconcerting. She liked the predictable. Bart was dependable and well respected. That was better than exciting. This pull she felt toward Will was something to be fought, not embraced.

She pushed a checker to the next square. "What do you do with all those numbers?"

The light in his eyes faded. "Whenever it's possible, I call my observations in to the Weather Bureau."

"And they compile it with other numbers?"

He nodded. "There are many amateur meteorologists around."

She liked seeing his eyes lighting with passion. "Only amateur? Is it possible to make a living at weather forecasting?"

"If I moved to one of the major centers and worked there, I could make enough to live on."

The glow in his face died and she wanted to see it come back. "I see you have much passion for it. You could try for a job and see where it led."

"I've thought about it. I like what I'm doing now, but mostly because it gives me the chance to study the weather and tides. Besides, this way I'm close to Philip and can help him stay focused on making a success of his business."

"It's not your responsibility to care for him," she said. "He's a grown man."

He gave her a wry smile. "That's the pot calling the kettle black. Someone else in this room feels responsible for other adults."

Her cheeks grew hot. "That's different. My parents need me."

"It's exactly the same. Your parents should feel responsible for you, not the other way around."

"My father has always been a good provider. I'm sure he's shattered by his failure." She looked down at her hands. "I don't know what we're going to do."

"No money to live on?" His voice held sympathy.

"Hardly anything. The house is too expensive to keep up. I expect we shall have to sell it and get a smaller place in town. Mama will be devastated. She was born in that house."

He frowned. "I'll make Philip split the finder's fee with you if your tips on the location of the ship earn out. The gold will be long gone but the ship itself is worth something."

She gasped. "Seriously?"

"Of course."

"How much would that be?" She began to calculate expenses. Maybe she could pay off Florence too.

"Your half would be ten thousand dollars."

A fortune. It would care for her mother for some time even after paying Florence. "Perhaps the boat isn't at any of the places I suggested," she said.

"We shall see." He grinned and then moved a checker piece. "You could always marry Bert."

"Bart," she corrected.

"He looks like a Bert. All proper and full of starch. He wouldn't contradict his mother if you paid him."

"You don't even know him."

"What's to know? He's had a silver spoon in his mouth all his life and has never had to work for a thing."

She couldn't deny it. "You can scarcely hold his birthright against him. Besides, he doesn't plan to take over his father's business. He wants to open a Macy's."

"Just as I said. Too proper to get his hands dirty."

"You're goading me now."

He grinned. "Maybe a little. He's not good enough for you."

"You don't even know him. Or me."

"I know you better than you think. I haven't shared this house with you for about a week now without realizing you long for adventure but you're too afraid to go after it."

She shifted on her chair and glanced away from his penetrating eyes. "I like things to stay calm and controlled," she said. "Adventure is too uncertain for me."

"Nice try." He chuckled.

"I don't like surprises," she said. "If I know what's going on, I can plan for every eventuality."

"You're not convincing me. It's more than that. You jumped in that boat without a hat and came running to find me. If you were as staid as you'd like people to believe, you would have waited to let the constable take care of it." His gaze dropped to her lips.

He was remembering that kiss of life. The same way she was. The moment stretched out between them until she gave an uncertain laugh and moved a checker piece. "Your turn," she said.

Surely it wasn't disappointment that lodged in her belly when he dragged his gaze from her to the board.

TWENTY-THREE

WILL SAW THE ship nearly to the dock. It might be the *Hanson Queen* but it was hard to tell from here. He noticed Katie struggling to keep up with him and slowed his stride to match hers.

"Is that the ship we're watching for?"

"I think so. It's one that size." He yawned.

"You haven't slept yet. Philip should be doing this."

"He's still sleeping off his liquor."

He offered his hand to assist her onto the pier, and after a moment's hesitation, she put her gloved fingers in his palm. Once they were on the rough boards, she started to pull away but he held fast. "The walking surface is uneven."

Her cheeks colored but she let him keep possession of her hand. Her gaze darted up and down the dock, and he wondered if she was assessing the occupants for anyone who might recognize her.

She tugged her hand free then placed it on his elbow. "It's a bit more proper," she whispered.

He grinned. "I dare you to take off your hat and let your hair down from its pins."

Her full lips curved in a smile. "I don't think so."

The docking of the ship broke his bantering mood. He read the name on the bow: *Hanson Queen.* "That's it," he said. "I'm going to talk to the captain. You wait here."

Her fingers tightened on his arm. "I think not. My presence here might be misconstrued if I'm alone."

"Of course. Forgive me, I would never put you in a compromising position. I'll wait until he disembarks then approach him." He stepped to the side of the dock as the sailors poured down the gangway. Several armed men in uniform stepped onto the dock and took up position on either side. At least the ship had protection, as reported.

The number of exiting sailors slowed to a crawl. When no one had disembarked for several minutes, he straightened. "Let's talk to an officer since the captain hasn't come out."

They approached the closest officer, who gave Will a sharp look then lifted a curious smile to Katie. Will tamped down the jealousy that surged in his gut. She didn't belong to him.

"Good morning," he said. "I'm glad to see you're guarding this ship. I have information that indicates pirates may have targeted it. Could you fetch the captain?"

"You questioning our ability to protect this ship, buster?" the sailor demanded.

"Of course not. I just wanted to pass along the warning."

"Duly noted. We're allowing no loitering around the ship. I suggest you be on your way."

He wasn't going to get far with the man. "Come along, Katie," he said. He led her away. "Touchy fellow."

"At least you told him. If anything happens, it's no fault of yours. And the sailor seemed competent." She glanced over her shoulder and smiled at the fellow who was staring after her.

"He was quite taken with you."

She glanced up at him from under the brim of her hat. "He was being polite."

"I think not."

"You sound angry."

"I'm not angry. Just . . . concerned." He nearly laughed at his defensive tone. What a fool he was. If she harbored no tender feelings for him, the best thing to do was squelch the emotion churning his gut.

She said nothing for several minutes until the noise of the dock was a dull hum behind them and they were walking along the sand back to the lighthouse. "You've been engaged in my personal life but have said little about your own beyond your parents' unfortunate deaths."

"I'm touched you care," he said, his grin widening.

"Forgive me," she said, her tone frosty, "I didn't intend to pry." Her gaze stayed down and didn't meet his. "I merely wondered if we should expect a fiancée to join you soon. This town has never had a bachelor for a lightkeeper. Most have families to keep them company."

"I've never been even close to marriage," he said. When her expression didn't change, he touched her chin with his fingers and tipped her face up. "Look at me, Katie."

"We should be getting back," she said, looking away. "My shift on the switchboard is about to start."

No more games. "I care about you much more than I should," he said.

Her lids opened wide and she met his gaze. Her shocked expression delighted him. He bent his head, and his lips brushed hers. Their warmth coaxed him to kiss her again.

She jerked away and stepped back. "Mr. Jesperson!"

His grin widened. "And here I thought we were on a first-name basis."

"You're being quite forward." She swallowed but didn't look away.

"I should apologize but I'm not one bit sorry."

Her cheeks flamed with color and she put her gloved fingers to her mouth. Her eyes were sparkling and he didn't think it was with outrage. She hadn't slapped him either. He was going to make an attempt to woo her, he decided. While he might not succeed, he couldn't just give in and let that dandy from town have her without a fight.

The service was poorly attended but Katie hadn't expected the church to be full with the sickness around. She sat in the third pew on the right with Will, who held Jennie, and Lady Carrington. Philip had made an excuse and disappeared down to the docks. She was very conscious of the bulk of Will's arm when it occasionally brushed hers. She had barely slept the last few nights. All she could think about was his kiss on the beach.

She could almost feel Bart's eyes drilling into the back of her head. He sat two rows back with his mother and father. She'd had to refuse his insistence on her sitting with them, since there was no room in their pew for all of them. But she admitted to herself that even if there had been room, she would have preferred to sit elsewhere. It made no sense. Every time Bart made an attempt to draw her closer into his family circle, she resisted. What was the matter with her? Bart could give her the respectability she craved, but all she could think about was Will, just inches away.

When the service ended, she spoke with friends and acquaintances. Most reported improving conditions of those afflicted with smallpox. She trailed out the front door and down the steps behind Will and the rest of her little family. *Family.* That was how she was coming to think of the group staying at the lighthouse. Such notions needed to be stamped out.

A flicker of movement by a live oak tree caught her attention. A woman stepped out from the shelter of the tree. The large chapeau obscured her face, but Katie didn't have to see the rouge on her cheeks and lips or the pompadour to know it was Florence. Her hands clenched the handle of her bag as Will turned to look at her.

He frowned and glanced back as though to see what had so alarmed her. "Is there someone you need to see?"

The woman edged behind the tree, obviously having accomplished her mission. "No, no one." Even if she was not intended for Bart, even if she fell for another, it would be devastating if her birth mother's identity came out now.

Katie reached for the baby, who gurgled her vowels at her. The soft warmth of little Jennie's body comforted her. She pressed a kiss on the baby's curls and turned her back on the woman. *Go away, please go away.* The women wouldn't be so bold as to approach her in front of everyone.

The Fosters joined them. "Is there anything I can do for your dear mother, Katie?" Mrs. Foster asked. The smile she directed to the baby appeared strained. "And how is your father?" She uttered the last word in a hushed tone, disapproval tugging at her mouth.

"I so appreciate your willingness to help," Katie said, shuffling Jennie to the other arm. "I've spoken with Mama every day of late, and she's quite improved. The servants have been taking good care of her. Papa is also growing stronger."

"Would you care to join us for dinner?" Bart put in.

His mother shot him a quick glance, which Katie interpreted as a rebuke. A few drops of rain plopped onto the sidewalk. "Thank you, but I must get the baby out of the weather. It's beginning to rain."

Bart nodded. "Things will be back to normal soon. This quarantine will end and you'll be back home. I'll be able to take you to dinner and the nickelodeon." His voice held deep satisfaction.

His mother's smile was stiff. "And we'll have a dinner party to announce your engagement."

Katie saw Will tense. She clutched the baby to her chest a little too tightly, and Jennie squirmed. "We—we're not engaged, Mrs. Foster."

The woman's brow lifted, and she glanced at her son. "After you're engaged, of course," she said.

Had Bart told his parents they were engaged? Maybe even purchased a ring? Katie's throat closed at the thought. She wasn't ready.

It was one thing to think about marrying him, but another thing altogether to actually take that step.

The woman under the tree moved again, and Katie realized that even if she were ready to marry Bart, she might not have the option if the woman told anyone the truth. Everyone, even Will, would think she had withheld the truth of her heritage. And she had. She needed to get Florence out of town before the Fosters and everyone else in town found out about her. But Katie had no idea how to accomplish it.

Jennie reached for Will. He took her, and Katie turned away. "I'm going inside the church a moment." She desperately needed the release of tears and to seek God's succor right now. There was no one to talk to, no one to share her problems with except God.

"We'll be in the carriage. Take your time," Will said.

Through a rapidly building blur of tears, she directed a pleading glance at Bart, and he nodded stiffly. If she'd offended him, she was most sorry, but she couldn't stand here making small talk another moment. She lifted her skirts and hurried across the wet grass to the church door.

The scent of old wood and wax greeted her when she stepped inside and approached the altar. The solitude of the holy place descended on her. She sat on the front row in the wash of light from the stained glass window above the pulpit and clasped her hands in her lap. With her head bowed, she pleaded for strength to do whatever was necessary to care for her parents and for Florence to leave town before the truth came out.

Was that even something she could pray for? Wasn't God all about truth? She'd been living a lie for twenty years. No, not a lie. Her true parents *were* the Russells. The woman who had birthed her was no more than a brood mare. Katie's allegiance was to the mother who had soothed her hurts and braided her hair. Calm washed over her. What gain would Florence receive from revealing Katie's heritage? All leverage would be gone. The woman had as much to lose as Katie.

The door creaked behind her, and she turned to see a figure slip through the door. The wide chapeau betrayed her identity. "You shouldn't have come. Someone might see you."

"They'll just think I was a fancy woman who is finally repenting," she said with a saucy laugh.

Katie winced at such crude talk. "Why are you following me?"

Her satin skirts swishing, Florence drew nearer. "I thought about what you said when we spoke before. I think you need to know the truth now. My dear sister probably never told you the whole story, has she?"

Katie stared at the woman, willing her to tell what had happened so long ago. "Truth?"

"Albert was mine first. My sister was his second choice. I wanted to be an actress and Albert couldn't deal with it." Her beautiful face scowled. "No one tells me what to do. I was determined to show him I could succeed, so when I had the opportunity to join a vaudeville show, I took it. It was only after I left that I discovered you were on your way, but I wasn't about to go back to Albert and hear his 'I told you so.'"

Katie passed her hand over her forehead. "Y–you mean he's my real father?" She'd always believed her parents were really her aunt and uncle. It explained so much. Why her father constantly said what trash Florence was. Every thought of her brought up memories of his own indiscretions.

Florence's eyes flashed with triumph. "I knew you were an innocent to my sister's scheming ways."

Florence was close enough now for Katie to smell the perfume she wore. It was something spicy and overpowering. Strong enough to make Katie's eyes water. Florence had left the gentle fragrance of lily of the valley behind.

Katie stood and faced the woman. "Yet they raised me and you didn't."

Florence's eyes flashed. "Come now, you appear to have fared just fine."

She reached out and touched a curl of Katie's hair. It took

everything in her not to shy away from her touch. "If you're smart, my darling, you'll run far away from that uptight man in the tweed jacket. I've seen his type before. He'll expect perfection. What will he do when he finds out your real mother is a woman of the world?"

There was so much more to it than Florence was saying. Katie had to know all of it. "Why were we even in Mercy Falls? To ask for money?" Florence winced and Katie realized she'd guessed right. "That's it? You wanted money?"

"Raising a kid isn't cheap! It was time he paid his share. But he paid up. Oh yes, indeed. My dear sister was determined to have you since she couldn't have any of her own. It was the perfect time for them since only your father had arrived in town." Florence fumbled with a sequined bag and withdrew an embroidered hanky. She dabbed at her eyes. "It wasn't easy for me, Katie. Not easy at all. I love you. I always have."

For a moment Katie almost believed it until Florence put down the hanky and Katie saw a hard shine in her eyes. "If you loved me, you wouldn't want to cause trouble for me. You'd leave and never come back rather than try to ruin my life."

"I wish I could, but I'm broke, darling. I don't like putting the squeeze on you, but I have no choice." Her voice took on a wheedling tone. "Surely your loving father has put the money I need at your disposal."

Katie shook her head. "He has not. I'm not even sure how we will survive on the little left in the bank. It will be a while before Papa is back to work. His business is failing. We may have to sell everything."

Florence's placating manner vanished. "I know a lie when I hear it, Katie. I'll give you a few more days. If you won't give me the money, I'll see if your intended can spare some for the mother of his wife-to-be."

Katie watched Florence saunter toward the door and knew the woman would do exactly as she threatened, if only for revenge against Mama.

TWENTY-FOUR

THE RAIN SETTLED into a drizzle. Will peered through the curtain of gray toward the church. Still no sign of Katie. Jennie slept on Lady Carrington's lap. The horses stamped their hooves impatiently. "I'll be right back," he told her. He shoved open the carriage door and stepped out into the rain.

The cold drops bounced off his hat. He skirted mud puddles and hurried to the door of the church. In the vestibule he shook the moisture from his clothes and glanced toward the sanctuary door, where he heard the low murmur of voices. He recognized Katie's voice but not the other woman's. Interrupting them might not be a good idea.

The woman drew closer to the door and said, "I know a lie when I hear it, Katie. I'll give you a few more days. If you won't give me the money, I'll see if your intended can spare some for the mother of his wife-to-be."

He stepped around a pillar and caught a glimpse of a gaudily dressed woman as she moved through the vestibule and exited the church. The smirk on her face raised his ire. He puzzled over the words he'd heard. It sounded as though she had demanded money from Katie. What had she meant about being Katie's mother? She resembled Katie, but the woman didn't seem to have any pox on her face, and she'd been out in public when she was supposed to be quarantined. But why would she attempt to blackmail Katie?

He moved back through the vestibule then opened the door to the sanctuary. The sound of soft weeping made him pause in the door-way. He saw Katie kneeling at the altar under the stained glass window. Sobs shook her shoulders and she fumbled for a hanky in the sleeve of her dress. She dabbed at her eyes then rose and turned toward the door.

She stopped when she saw him. "How long have you been there?" The skin around her eyes was reddened.

"Long enough," he said gently. "That woman was your mother?"

"She's not my mother!" Katie clasped her gloved hands together.

"But I overheard her say—"

She walked toward him. "Whatever you heard, it's no business of yours."

"Fair enough, but if you're in some kind of trouble, I'd like to help you."

She reached him and paused. "Why would you think I'm in trouble?"

"I overheard her try to blackmail you."

Color stained her cheeks. "You listened?"

"I came looking for you and was in the vestibule. I didn't intend to eavesdrop."

Her shoulders slumped and she grabbed the back of a pew. "Oh what am I going to do?" she whispered.

"Let me help you, Katie. Who is that woman?"

She bit her lip and raised moist eyes to his. "The woman who bore me. *Not* my mother."

"I don't understand."

"She abandoned me when I was five. She's Mama's sister. A–and it appears Papa is my real father. I'd always thought it was one of Florence's men friends." She bit her lip. "I'm sorry. I didn't mean to tell you all of that."

"I know how to keep a secret. But why is it a secret? If you were five, surely people know you are not Mrs. Russell's daughter."

She shook her head. "We couldn't bear for people to know I was born to a woman who danced and entertained men. No suitable man would want anything to do with me. My reputation would be gone. I'd have to leave Mercy Falls in disgrace."

He wanted to object to her conclusion but she was right. "You moved here after the Russells took you in?"

She nodded. "Papa had just moved to Mercy Falls. I assumed it was coincidence that Florence brought me here. Now I know it was because she wanted money from him. Mama wasn't here yet, and we went to visit my father. I liked him right away. Perhaps I always knew . . ." She paused, lost in reveries, then shook her head and continued, "A few nights later Florence left me alone, something frightened me, and I found my way back to the Russell house. My father took me in, and when Mama showed up the next morning, everyone in town assumed I was their child. I never knew what happened to Florence."

"Perhaps your father paid her off."

She nodded. "I think that must be what happened."

"And now she's back, wanting more money."

She tucked her hanky back into her sleeve. "She didn't believe me when I told her Papa's business was in trouble."

"So she is threatening to ask Mr. Foster for money."

She paled. "Yes, and she mustn't. Mama . . . I would be ruined."

He studied her panicked expression. "The truth usually comes out sooner or later. If Mr. Foster loves you, it won't matter." The thought of her marrying that fellow made him thrust his hands in his pockets.

"It matters to me."

He offered his arm and she took it. He guided her toward the door. "So now I understand a little more about you."

Her fingers tightened on his arm. "Whatever do you mean?"

A wave of tenderness surprised him. "Your intense desire never to be faced with a surprise. I understand now."

Her smile was weak. "Would you care to translate?"

"You feel the need to control things so you're never faced with a situation like that again. But you should remember that your real friends will stick by you. If others don't, they never really cared about you."

She thrust out her chin. "It must not come out."

"Truth always comes out, Katie. Who you are has nothing to do with who bore you. God rejoices over you and who you are as a person. That's where your worth comes from. Not from fickle men. Or women."

"I know that."

They reached the door and he opened it for her. "Then put it into practice."

She glanced up at him. "You don't understand how important this is to me."

He didn't answer as she preceded him out the door. With her real mother in town, she hadn't a hope of keeping this quiet. He'd seen the resemblance. It wouldn't be long before someone else did too.

❦

The rain pattered on the carriage top and the scent of wet ground filled the air. Katie pointed out the road to Will, who nodded and turned the horses. He sat hunched on the driver's seat in a rain slicker. Rain sluiced off the brim of his hat. She thought she could trust him with her secret. What did it say about their relationship that she was so comfortable with his knowledge of her background? And moreover, that she so feared Bart and his mother finding out?

"Katie, dear, are you sure this is wise?" Lady Carrington asked. The baby slept in the crook of her arm.

Katie craned her neck to see through the downpour. The house would be visible any moment. "I must see how Mama is doing."

"But the quarantine," the older woman protested. "Your mother is still contagious."

"I'll stay well away from the window." Ever since Mrs. Foster had mentioned it, she couldn't get it out of her mind. The carriage had barely come to a halt when the rain slowed then stopped. Katie flung open the door and stepped down before Will could assist her. "I won't be long," she said.

His dark eyes held sympathy and concern. "Would you like me to come with you?"

"That's not necessary," she said before he could jump down from the seat. "I need to do this alone." Though he knew much of the story, there was more he didn't know. She told herself it was best to keep it that way.

The wet grass soaked her feet before she reached the house. She stopped about five feet from the window, which was open a crack. "Mama," she called. "Are you awake?"

"Katie? Is that you?" her mother's voice was weak but clear.

Katie whispered thanks to God at the sound of her voice. She didn't dare move closer. "It's me, Mama. Can you come to the window?" Though they'd spoken by phone, she needed to *see* her mother. And she needed to tell her of Florence in person, not over a buzzing line.

A few moments later the window rose higher and her mother's face appeared. "Katie, darling, I've missed you." Red pox marred the creamy complexion of the older woman. She appeared thinner and her hair lay in disarray on her shoulders, but she was smiling.

Katie didn't know where to even begin. Her mother's frail appearance gave her pause. Perhaps it should wait. Nubbins came running from the backyard. The kitten was drenched and mewing. Katie scooped him up and held her against her chest. "Poor kitty, I think I'll take you home with me. I've missed you." There was that word *home* again. How peculiar when she was standing in front of her home and felt no real inclination to move back into her room.

She studied her mother's face. "You're healing, Mama."

Her mother smiled. "I'm getting stronger by the day. How are you, Katie? You look pale. Are you well?"

"I'm fine." She wetted her lips. There was no way to navigate this story in a delicate manner. "We have a–a problem though." She hated to burden her mother when she was so sick but what else could she do? "I need some guidance, Mama."

Her mother's smile faded. "What is it? Your father has died, hasn't he? You must tell me. Oh dear, I spoke to him on the telephone today and he seemed to be getting stronger."

"Wh–what? No, of course not, Mama. He's fine. I saw him." Her mother's question drove thoughts of Florence from Katie's head. "Why would you say that?"

"Your father would never try to kill himself." Her mother leaned her head out the window. "I've thought this over. Someone had to have tried to hurt him. You know he's a good man, Katie. It was only when he's drinking that things are . . . difficult."

"I know, Mama. He's doing fine though." She couldn't tell her mother what Papa had revealed.

"He would never deliberately leave me to face the problems ahead without him. Your father isn't a coward. He's a fighter."

"Mama, please listen," Katie said, trying to keep a desperate edge from her voice and failing. "Florence is in town. Demanding money."

Her mother's eyes widened. She grew even paler and her mouth hung open. She disappeared from the window. Katie heard something scrape on the floor, and then her mother's face appeared again, a bit lower. "I had to sit down," she said, her voice quivering. "My sister came to see you?"

"Yes. She's after more money, Mama."

"She deserves nothing from us," her mother said in a trembling voice. "In twenty years she has not even so much as sent any of us a Christmas greeting. We didn't know if she was dead or alive. She simply vanished."

"I know."

"What makes her think we would give her money?"

"To keep her quiet. Otherwise, she will go to Bart and ask for money. She'll tell him she's my mother." Katie could barely even say the words *my mother*. Florence had no concept of what being a real mother entailed.

Her mother put her hand to her throat. "She can't do that! Bart's parents would put a stop to his courtship if they knew."

"I know." She blinked back the moisture in her eyes.

"How much money does she want?"

"Five thousand dollars."

Her mother gasped. "Katie, whatever shall we do? There isn't that kind of money."

"I could offer her what we have, but if I give it to Florence, there won't be anything left to live on."

"She doesn't deserve one penny!" her mother cried. "Oh if only Albert were here. He would soon put a stop to her shenanigans."

The rain picked up and Katie felt the dampness to her bones. It added to her weariness and despair. "But he's not. And you need to guard your health. It's up to me, and I don't know what to do."

Her mother leaned farther out the window. "You simply *must* get Bart to propose. Soon."

A lump formed in Katie's throat. "Is it fair to him, Mama? I mean, what happens if he finds out the truth after we're married?" She couldn't believe she was arguing for telling him the truth. But Will was right. The truth always came out. And when it did, she didn't want her husband to think she betrayed him.

"Don't you dare whisper a word of it!"

"All right, Mama," she said, trying to soothe her mother's agitation.

"Get rid of that woman, Katie. Somehow!" Her mother's voice rose nearly to a shriek. She broke off and began to cough.

Katie checked her impulse to spring forward. "Mama, are you all right?"

The fit of coughing stopped. Her mother wiped her mouth with a hanky and seemed to gather herself again. "I don't know what we shall do if it becomes known in town. It's not only Bart and your chance to become a Foster, you know. All of society will shun us. Because we passed you off as my own child. No one likes to be hoodwinked. I couldn't bear the pity either. We would have to leave Mercy Falls."

Katie nodded, though the thought made her cringe. "We have a total of three thousand dollars, Mama. We can't give her all our money."

"Perhaps we could get a loan from the bank."

"We have no assets to put up."

"The haberdashery," her mother suggested. "I don't think there is a mortgage on it."

"Papa told me it was all mortgaged," Katie said. She glanced back at the carriage. "I must go, Mama."

Her mother reached out a hand through the open window, as if she longed to touch her. "Are you getting along all right? How curious that you're staying at the lighthouse."

"I'm enjoying caring for the baby."

"Oh yes, the child. Might I see her again? From a distance?"

It was one thing to risk her own health, but Katie wasn't willing to risk Jennie's. "I think that we should wait until you are well. Will has taken responsibility for now and we really have no money to raise her."

Her mother's brows rose. "Will? You are on a first name basis with the man?"

"It seemed sensible."

Her mother shook her head. "Oh Katie, my dear. Watch yourself. Your future is planned out already. There is no room in it for a poor lightkeeper."

"I know, Mama. I know my duty."

Her mother frowned. "Duty? But surely you want to marry Bart, do you not?"

The dark clouds seemed lower than they'd ever been. The rain drenched her, and the wet grass chilled her toes. "Of course I do," Katie said before the fear grew in her mother's eyes. "I am praying for your rapid recovery, Mama. I'll talk to you soon." She turned and fled back to the carriage with the kitten in her arms for comfort.

TWENTY-FIVE

KATIE HADN'T BEEN able to stop shivering since they'd arrived back from town. Will had built a roaring fire and she sat as close as she dared in dry clothing. A now-dry Nubbins lay sleeping on her lap. She'd towel-dried her hair and it lay still damp on her shoulders. The rain continued to come down outside, sometimes in a drenching downpour and sometimes in a gentle patter. The scent of oatmeal cookies drifted from the kitchen and she heard Lady Carrington banging pots.

Will kept staring at Katie from the sofa then looking away when she glanced in his direction, and Katie wished she was the one who had insisted on making dinner.

Jennie had fallen asleep on the rug. "I'll go put her in her crib," Katie said.

"Let her sleep," Will said. "If you move her, she'll awaken in a grumpy mood."

"I don't want to move anyway," she said. "This chair is just now warming up."

He rose and grabbed the knitted afghan that was draped over the back of the sofa. His eyes were soft as he laid it over her. "Better?" he asked.

She nodded, her mouth drying at his nearness. Pulling her hands from under the wrap, she willed him to head to the lighthouse and not confuse her even more. "Nubbins will like it too."

He rolled his eyes. "A cat. We have quite the menagerie here." As if in answer to his remark, the bird meowed in the kitchen. Nubbins sprang to full alert, his ears flicking. He jumped from the sofa and crept toward the kitchen. "Good thing the bird is in his cage," Will said.

Her gaze drifted to the window, where raindrops still sluiced down the glass. "You were right about the weather," she said.

He smiled. "I like being right."

To her relief, he moved over to the window, giving her room again to think straight. "Do you want to talk about what happened today?"

Katie strained to hear what was going on in the kitchen. It sounded as though Lady Carrington was chopping vegetables. "There isn't much to say about it. I can't pay what she's demanding."

"I wouldn't pay her anyway."

She pressed her lips together. Did he want her to be humiliated? "I must help you and Philip find the ship and the missing gold."

"And then what? Pay her off and worry about the next time she wants money?"

He was right. This situation could be never ending. "I'm not sure I have the courage to just let it be known."

"You're the bravest woman I know. People who care about you will stand by you. I'll be one of them."

She swallowed hard and didn't look away from the intensity of emotion in his face.

"The woman's appearance changes nothing, Katie. You are still your own dear self. Courageous and beautiful. Fiercely loyal. Why is respectability so important to you?"

He thought she was dear? Courageous? And . . . beautiful? No one but her mama had ever told her that. "My father, he–he often intimated I would turn out poorly. I want to make him proud of me."

He scowled. "Did he throw this Florence in your face?"

The penetrating knowledge in his eyes made her glance away. "You are most astute," she said, her throat tight.

"Your desire for respectability is really a desire for peace, I think. That comes from being comfortable in your skin—with who God made you to be. Not trying to be something you're not. Being willing to be transparent, without airs."

Her pulse raced even thinking about such transparency. "What if people reject who I really am?"

He leaned forward. "They won't, Katie. You're beautiful, inside and out. And if some do, so what? We answer to God. We belong to him. We are his children. His bride. His brothers and sisters. You can rest in that. Peace is a beautiful thing."

His eyes held a mysterious tenderness that drew her. She wanted to be able to rest in the peace he and Addie talked about. To turn over control. Would marrying Bart bring that or just make her more fearful of letting anyone see the real Katie Russell? "How do you learn to rest in that? To make that enough?"

He glanced at the baby. "Do you think Jennie thinks she must hide who she is? She knows she has our total love and acceptance. We have God's in that same way. That can give us confidence to put down the masks and be who we were created to be."

She shuddered and tried to tell herself it was from the cold and not from sheer terror. "Sometimes I dream that the whole town knows who I am. I see people point and turn their backs on me. Whisper about me when I'm not looking. I can't bear pity."

He knelt in front of her then clasped her hands in his. "So don't accept it. Hold your head high. You are not Florence. You are your own self."

His hands were warm. Steady and strong. Just like the man himself. "I'll try to remember that."

He lifted her hand to his mouth and turned it over, then kissed her palm. His intense gaze stayed locked with hers. With his lips pressed against her skin, she couldn't think, couldn't breathe. Bart never affected her this way. What did it all mean?

All she would have to do was lean forward just a bit, show her attraction to him, and he would take the lead. He would draw her into his arms and kiss her again. She knew from the experience on the beach that all thought left her when he kissed her. Was that the place to find peace?

But no, it had to be more than sheer attraction, didn't it? Addie said God had a plan for her life and that finding it would bring the peace Katie sought. Peace wasn't in a man, but in God.

Mrs. Carrington appeared in the kitchen doorway. "I need a day off, children. When this atrocious weather breaks, I suggest we go for a sail up the coast. We can take Jennie out for some fresh air."

Will moved away from Katie and stood near the fireplace.

"It sounds like a lovely idea," Katie said. "I can point out some coves Will and Philip might want to investigate. Any idea when this storm will end?" she asked him.

"By my readings, I think it will break tomorrow and turn beautiful."

"We can make a picnic. It should be quite pleasant to take my boat along the coast," Lady Carrington said.

"Can I do anything to help you tonight? You've been quite mysterious about what we're having for dinner."

"The stew is my specialty secret. I haven't even shown Addie how to make it yet, though I will do so when she comes home. Enjoy the fire a few more minutes. I'll call you when it's ready." She stepped away with a satisfied smile.

Katie glanced up to see Will watching her intently. A sail with him sounded quite lovely.

❦

The foghorn tolled its warning into the night. Katie rolled over and stared at the dim light shining in the window, wondering why she was awake. As Will predicted, the storm had passed and the moon was out, but the storm surge still crashed against the rocks. She sat up and pushed her heavy hair from her face.

Katie wasn't sure what had roused her, but the skin on the back of her neck prickled. The cat leaped from the bed to the floor, but Nubbins was silent in his movement. She held her breath and listened to the night sounds: the surf crashing on the rocks, the owl that roosted in the light tower hooting, and the blare of the foghorn.

Was that a shout? She leaped from the bed and ran to the window. She stared out to sea. The sliver of moon outside illuminated a boat riding the waves toward the rocks. It listed to one side, and she realized it was damaged. A man pulled a dinghy toward the water. Will was going to attempt a rescue. He needed help.

She grabbed her robe and thrust her arms into it. With her robe belted, she ran for the stairs. Should she rouse Philip? She peered through the open door of his bedroom and saw the covers still smooth. He wasn't home from his night at the quay yet. She rushed down the steps and made her way outside. When she reached the porch, she paused and saw Will was already out on the rolling sea. He was rowing with all his might toward the ship that was breaking apart on the rocks.

It took a lot of courage to do what he was doing. She wished she'd been able to get out there in time to help him. While she couldn't put her back to the oar, she could pray. She gripped the porch post and prayed that he would rescue the three sailors, that all of them would return safely to shore. Will had reached the boat and was pulling a man from the waves. Another man leaped into the dinghy and nearly capsized it. A few minutes later there was nothing much left of the boat, and Will was rowing back to the beach.

Katie leaned against the post and whispered a thank you. She thought of the medical kit, and as she turned back to the house to fetch it, she saw a shadow flit by the end of the porch. She froze.

"Philip?" she asked, her voice quavering. When no one answered, her sense of unease grew. "Who's there?"

An inner warning bell rang. She should get inside. Turning, she stepped toward the door, but before she got more than two feet, hands grabbed her and she was pulled back against a hard chest.

The man's hand went over her mouth. "Did you tell the constable?" he hissed in her ear.

She couldn't speak with his hand smelling of horse over her mouth. All she could do was shake her head. If only she had her shoes on, she'd try stomping on his instep. He dragged her toward the edge of the porch, out of the beam flashing from the lighthouse lens.

She couldn't breathe, couldn't think. If she could get her mouth free, she'd scream, though she doubted anyone would hear her over the sound of the surf. She seized the man's wrist with both hands and yanked downward. She opened her mouth until she saw the glitter of a knife blade.

"Scream and you're dead," he said in a hoarse whisper.

She was good at recognizing voices because of her job, but she'd never heard this one before: guttural with an East Coast accent.

"What did you tell the constable?" he demanded.

"N–nothing," she choked out.

"He showed up to talk to my boss. You must have told him something." His fingers tightened on her throat. "I want to know what you said."

"I told you—nothing."

The man's grip tightened, and he swore. "You tell your father that if he talks, you're dead. You and your mother both."

Several men came stumbling up the path from the beach. The man's hand fell away and Katie reeled at her sudden release. She could only see the broad back of a man melt into the darkness. She thought he might be dressed in overalls but she couldn't be sure. The survivors of the shipwreck moved past her as she stood in the shadows.

"There are dry clothes in the well house," Will called to them.

"Thanks," one of the men said. They all went around the corner of the house, and the door to the shed creaked open.

At least the men were unhurt. When at last she saw Will's broad shoulders crest the top of the hill, her feet seemed to move of their own volition.

A trace of whiskers darkened his chin. His tired eyes sharpened when he saw her. "What's wrong?" He reached out and grasped her shoulders.

She nestled against him. All she wanted was to inhale his musky scent and rest in his strength. "There was a man with a knife," she said, her voice barely above a whisper.

His fingers tightened. "Where?"

"On the porch, but he's gone now."

"He threatened you?" His voice was a low growl.

"Yes. He wanted to know what I overheard. And what I told the constable." She didn't repeat the threat against her and her mother.

"Did you tell him you didn't know anything?"

She nodded. "I don't think he believed me." Her fists grasped the cotton of his shirt and she buried her nose into it even more.

"I'll look for him."

"No!" she said as he started to pull away. "Just hold me a minute." Shudders wracked her shoulders as she remembered the knife. Will embraced her more tightly and she rested there a few more moments before she lifted her head. "I'm okay now. I don't think I've ever been so frightened."

His rough hands smoothed her hair. "I wouldn't let anything happen to you."

"You weren't there," she reminded him.

"God was, though."

She heard the smile in his voice and smiled too. "Of course."

Waves lapped at the sides of the boat. The sails billowed with air above Will's head. He smiled as he saw Katie sitting on the deck with Lady Carrington. Jennie played with blocks at their feet. The seas were calm today, blue and beautiful. They had a picnic lunch aboard. He'd invited Philip to come, but after the attack on Katie the night before, his brother decided to speak with the constable and see who he'd interrogated.

The mynah rode the waves on one of the crossbeams as if he were scouting for land. "Six steps, matie," he squawked. Nubbins hissed from under Katie's seat when the bird meowed. Will grinned. They were like a family out for a pleasure ride. The thought made him turn his gaze from where it wanted to linger . . . Katie's face.

"Ahoy," Katie called. She joined him at the helm and pointed. "Just past that thickly forested finger of land, there is a tiny inlet that looks as though it goes nowhere. It does. Veer into it and angle the boat around to the left. Don't worry how tight it is. The passage is deep and will widen soon enough."

He nodded and concentrated on guiding the boat. Katie grabbed the railing with one hand as the sailboat, leaning with its sails full of wind, veered toward the passage she'd indicated. He would have missed it if it hadn't been for her. In fact, it appeared so narrow he would have guessed the boat couldn't fit. The trees on either side nearly brushed the side of the boat, but he could see the water was as deep as Katie promised. A few more feet and they were through the narrowest part. The shores on both sides receded and the passage grew wider and wider. A small bay opened in front of him. The few feet of rocky sand soon gave way to heavy forest.

"Isn't it charming?" she asked. "We used to come here every Sunday when I was small."

"Lovely," he said, looking at her. The pink in her cheeks was most becoming. Her blue dress deepened the color of her eyes. He forced his attention back to the inlet ahead of him. It was clear and empty. There was a nice beach to his right. "How about we have lunch there?"

"Looks good to me. I'm hungry," she said.

He steered the boat toward the shore until just before he would scrape bottom, then dropped the anchor overboard. They had no dinghy attached, so he leaped over the side into the cold water. He held out his arms for Lady Carrington then carried the older woman to the beach, where he set her on her feet, before returning for Jennie. The baby wound her fingers in his hair and smiled, showing her small teeth. He grinned back and carried her to Lady Carrington.

His pulse was running away in his chest when he returned to the yacht for Katie, and he told himself it was the exertion of slogging through the water from the boat to the shore. Katie's smile was a bit uncertain, but she slipped over the side and he caught her. The top of her bonnet brushed his chin and she weighed hardly anything in his arms. He caught the scent of lavender. It made him want to hold her closer. Her arms came around his neck and she slanted a glance into his face. The little point of her chin and the way her eyes tipped up at the corners intrigued him.

"I'm sorry you have to carry me," she said.

"I'm not." The words were out before he could stop them. He grinned at the way the color washed up her neck. He liked the feel of her in his arms, the way her breath stirred the hair at his sideburns, the smell of her. They reached the shore, but he didn't put her down right away. Instead, he carried her onto the sand to where Lady Carrington stood with Jennie at her feet, scooping up sand.

He set Katie down and waded back to the boat where he climbed aboard and grabbed the wicker basket of food. As he jumped back into the water, he saw movement off to his right. Narrowing his gaze, he saw a flutter of red. A shirt? He rushed the rest of the way to shore, dropped the basket at Katie's feet, then took off at a run to where he'd seen the flash of color. He heard a noise behind him and realized Katie was on his heels. It would do no good to tell her to go back.

He reached the black sage clumps and glanced around. The vegetation here was matted down with footprints. Large ones. A man, maybe two, had milled about in this area. A chill ran down his back. He stooped and picked up something glinting in the sun, nestled among the matted weeds. A knife. It had a snake's head on it. Just like the one from the night they discovered Miss Bulmer's wedding gown . . . and were attacked.

He wheeled to face Katie. "Get out of here!"

Twenty-six

"What's wrong?"

He turned her toward the beach. "It's dangerous. I'll take care of it."

She turned back around and folded her arms. "I'm coming with you."

A forest mist curled around Katie's feet. The dankness of the vegetation filled her nose. This place felt sinister, but she pushed away her sense of foreboding and tried to see what Will was trying to hide.

His arm came out and blocked her forward movement. "You are the most inquisitive, bullheaded woman I've ever met," he said.

Katie managed not to smile at his peeved tone. She peered around him at the flash of silver in his hand. "Is that a knife?"

He thrust it in his belt then took her arm and turned her back toward the beach. "I shouldn't have brought you out here." He glanced over his shoulder toward the thick forest. Tension etched the line of his shoulders.

She tried to see where he was looking but all she noticed were tall redwoods that blocked out the light and ferns waving in the breeze. That sensation of being watched intensified. "What's wrong?"

"Let's get out of here." He propelled her away from the coolness of the woods toward the beach.

She tried to look around him. "I think those footprints were fresh. Whoever left that knife might still be around."

"The very reason that I should get you to safety."

They stepped out into sunshine. Gulls cawed overhead and her earlier sensation of danger seemed overblown.

He stopped and pulled out the knife he'd found. "This knife. The guy who attacked me on the island the night we found Miss Bulmer's wedding dress had it."

She shuddered and stared into the coolness of the tall trees. "You mean he's been here?"

"He had to have been there just a few moments ago. I saw his shirt. That's what made me go look."

She quit trying to resist. "We should get Lady Carrington and Jennie out of here."

"You too. I'll have you take the boat out a safe distance."

"Now wait a minute." She dug her heels into the sand. "You're going to investigate it, aren't you? Yes, we'll get them to safety, but when you go to check it out, I want to help."

"I don't want you hurt."

The concern on his face warmed her. "That fellow nearly killed you. You need me." His lips twitched then stilled, but she saw the amusement in his eyes. "Really. You need assistance. You don't even have a weapon, do you?"

He moved her closer to Lady Carrington. "I have his knife."

"What if he has a gun?" They were nearly within earshot of Lady Carrington, and Katie didn't want to worry her. "Please, let me help you. I led you here in the first place. You can't take my help one minute then shut me out the next."

The frown remained crouched between his eyes. "I won't have you in harm's way, Katie. I–I care too much about you."

Before she had time to respond, something whizzed over her head.

"Run!" He grabbed her arm.

She picked up her skirts with her other hand and dashed across the sand with her feet barely touching the ground.

Bullets spit at their feet and Katie nearly stumbled, but Will's hand on hers kept her moving until she regained her balance. The sharp retort of the gun stopped.

"What's happening?" Lady Carrington asked as Will scooped up Jennie and grabbed the older woman's good arm.

"Danger! Run!" Katie splashed through the water toward the sailboat. The water dragged at her skirts and she nearly lost her balance. She glanced back to see Will coming with Jennie in his arms and Lady Carrington at his side. There was no sign of the shooter and she thought they were far enough away from the woods that bullets couldn't reach them unless the man was ready to be seen.

She finally reached the boat but had no strength to climb the rope ladder, so she stood panting in chest-high water until Will reached her. He boosted Lady Carrington onto the ladder and the older woman clambered slowly up the rope then took the wailing baby he handed up to her.

"Your turn," he told Katie. His big hands spanned her waist and lifted her.

She forced herself up the ladder. Lady Carrington was sitting at the top and reached out to her with her good hand. "I can make it," Katie said. She hauled herself up until she stood on the deck, Will right behind her. The bird fluttered and squawked above her head. Will cranked the anchor up and hurried to set sail.

"I don't see anyone," Katie said, taking Jennie, who was reaching for her. The little one lay with her head on Katie's shoulder and one fist clutched at her neck.

"I think they just wanted to scare us off. They could have hit us. We were close enough."

She peered toward the woods. "Maybe you're right." She hoped so. It was one thing to investigate with Will herself, but she didn't want Lady Carrington in any danger.

"Step away from the cake!" the bird squawked. "Six feet back."

She jumped at the loud noise. "Stupid bird," she muttered. The wind blew a salty breath into her face as the boat got underway. She moved to the bow and watched the blend of redwood bark and deep green leaves recede as Will took it through the inlet. A hundred yards offshore, he trimmed the sails and threw out the anchor. He shucked his shoes and removed his belt and shirt.

"Why are we stopping? Where are you going?" She had a sinking feeling she knew.

"I'm going to swim back and investigate."

She grabbed his arm. "You can't go by yourself. It's too dangerous."

"I'll be fine, Katie. If there's a chance to end it now, I want to take it. You were accosted last night. He could have killed you."

Before she could respond, he leaned forward and brushed his mouth across hers. The sensation of his lips on hers was intoxicating. Of their own volition, her fists grabbed his shirt and she returned his kiss.

His hand cupped her cheek and he smiled into her face. "If I'm not back in an hour, take the boat back to Mercy Falls and contact the constable."

"But—" Before she could finish her protest, he was gone over the side. She heard a splash then saw his head, dark and sleek as an otter, moving through the water. She ran to the rail and prayed for his safety. He had to come back safe and sound. She couldn't bear it if anything happened to him.

With the realization that she loved him, she put her fingers to her lips where the taste of his mouth still lingered.

❧

The fifty-degree water chilled Will's skin through and through by the time he rose dripping from the sea. A brisk wind rustled the treetops and left him shivering. He skirted the rocks and headed for the forest where he'd found the knife. Not a twig snapped under his carefully placed bare feet, and he flitted from trunk to trunk, stopping often to listen. He heard nothing other than birdsong and the rustle of leaves in the breeze.

A smile lingered on his face from the way Katie had kissed him back. He sobered and reminded himself to focus on his objective so he could return to kiss her again. Pausing, he inhaled the dank loam of the forest and focused his senses on the task at hand. He reached a small clearing and paused behind a rock. The remains of a campfire lay scattered in the center of the space, and a few logs had been pulled up for seating. He stepped from behind the shelter of the rock and approached the ashes. The scent of campfire still lingered. Kneeling, he put his hand over them. Warm.

He rose and scanned the area. He saw two different sized shoe prints. Whoever they were, they'd taken their belongings and departed. He followed the beaten path to the other side of the meadow. The faint trail continued through a stand of redwoods. As he walked through the forest, he heard the sound of surf. The woods gave way to beach and he saw waves lapping onto a rocky shore. It was another bay, different from the one they'd entered. A small rocky island jutted out of the water in the distance.

And a large sailing vessel was anchored in the water offshore. His pulse jumped. The *Paradox* floated just before him. He'd found it.

He hung back in the shelter of a redwood and let his gaze roam the ship. The pirated boat looked intact. The sails were tied down and he could see no breaches in the wooden sides. No one stood on the abandoned deck either. He glanced around the rocky shore. There was no sign of the men whose trail he had followed here. A flicker of movement caught his eye and he saw a smaller boat in a narrow channel leading away from the *Paradox*. Squinting, he realized one of the figures aboard wore a red shirt.

He cautiously exited the shelter of the forest and picked his way across the sharp rocks. The men hadn't seen him. Wading out into the cold water, he walked as far as he could toward the ship then plunged in and swam toward the boat rocking in the waves. He edged to the starboard side and climbed the rope ladder. When he reached eye level of the deck, he glanced around and listened.

The ship was a silent, floating tomb. Not a sound except the flitter of the hanging sails came to his ears, so he heaved himself aboard. He shuddered with the chill. It wasn't just the swim and the wind but the knowledge of what had happened to the crew aboard this boat. Bloodstains marred the deck as a testament to the brutality of the pirates. There had to be more of them than the two he'd seen. Two men couldn't have dispatched the entire crew by themselves. He listened again before he made another step but the ship was silent. Whoever had assisted the men was no longer aboard. He was certain he was alone.

His bare feet slapped along the planking and left an echo hanging in the air that was a bit unnerving. The flapping of the loose sails added to his sense of unease. He found the door to the hold and descended a few steps until the light gave out. There was no lantern around, so he retraced his steps. His best option was to summon the constable and bring him to this location. But first Will needed to inform Philip that the ship had been found.

He shielded his gaze and stared out across the water. There was no sign of the two men in the boat. His heart paused then pounded painfully at a sudden thought. What if this inlet fed into the same area as the other one? The men would come out by the boat where Katie, Jennie, and Lady Carrington waited for him.

Will ran to the edge then paused, forcing himself to think. It would take longer to swim to shore then traipse back through the forest. If there was a vessel anywhere near the *Paradox*, he'd make better time by sea. He did a quick scan and found a lifeboat with oars. A few moments later he was on the water and rowing with all his might. With every flex of his arms, he prayed he would reach them in time.

TWENTY-SEVEN

KATIE GLANCED AT the watch pinned to her blouse. Will had been gone nearly forty-five minutes. She was not going to leave him behind. If he didn't come in a few minutes, she was going to go looking for him. Her fingers strayed to her lips again. Every time she thought of that kiss her pulse raced. She wanted to see if the love she'd felt in his arms would swell again at the sight of him.

"I don't care for your expression," Lady Carrington said. "You're planning something."

"I'm going after Will," Katie said, making her decision. She put Jennie on the other woman's lap. "It's been nearly an hour. I'm not leaving him behind."

Lady Carrington pulled the sleeping child to her. "Katie, you're no match for men with guns. We would help Will much more if we garner help for him. Do you know how to sail well enough to get us back to Mercy Falls?"

"We can't just sail away and leave him behind!"

The mynah squawked. "Step away from the cake! Six feet!" He fluttered his wings as Nubbins stalked him.

Katie scooped up the kitten. "Oh do be quiet," she muttered to the bird. They had thought this would be a pleasant day for a sail. How distressing that it had turned into a dangerous foray into enemy territory. "Don't you know any other words?" She glanced around for any weapon she might take with her. There was nothing here. She was going anyway.

Starting toward the rope ladder, a movement caught her attention. Squinting, she stared at the boat that had appeared from around the spit of land ahead. At first she thought it might be Will and he'd found someone to help him return by sea, but as the dinghy neared, she realized one man wore a red shirt. A flash of red was what had attracted Will to the place where he'd found the knife. Her unease deepened when she realized the men seemed to be rowing straight at them.

"Lady Carrington, I think the men who shot at us are coming our way."

"Oh my," Lady Carrington said. She rose and stepped beside Katie. "What shall we do?"

"I'm going to try to get us out of here." Katie reached for the anchor winch and cranked it, keeping an eye on the approaching vessel. She rushed to the sails and began to raise them, but one pulley got hung up. She yanked on it, it swung free, and then caught again. In terror, she looked back to the boat. Her pulse raced when she saw how close they were. "We're not going to make it," she said. "Get below!" She rushed Lady Carrington and Jennie into the hold and followed them down.

She glanced around for anything she might use as a weapon. There was a bed and some cupboards. She threw open the cabinet doors and flinched at the strong odor of mildew. Nothing but enameled tin plates and cups. A glint caught her eye, and her gaze landed on a knife back in the corner. She grabbed it then rushed up the ladder to the deck. The boat was eight feet away when she reached the railing at the bow.

Keeping the knife in her right hand hidden in the folds of her skirt, she raised her left hand. "Are you in need of assistance?" she asked with a smile.

"Ahoy! Yes, we need help."

At the sound of the man's voice, Paco squawked and fluttered his feathers. "Eight feet down!"

The man in the bow was dressed in trousers and a vest. His mustache was neatly trimmed and waxed. His dark good looks with the gray wings at his temple would turn the head of most women. Her memory flashed back to the description of the man at the skating rink who had called her. Could it be the same man? Her attention veered to the second man in the boat. He wore a red gingham shirt and dungarees held up with suspenders. Maybe the man who had attacked her the night before? They were clearly from very different social standings. And they also matched Will's description of the two men he'd seen talking and pointing to the sea. Her fingers tightened around the knife when she saw the sun glint on the rifle in the bottom of the boat.

The fellow in red kicked an oilcloth over it and smiled. "Ahoy there. We're about worn out and could use a ride back to Mercy Falls. Can we board?"

"I'm sorry, but no," she said. "We're not heading to Mercy Falls." At least not until she had Will safely aboard.

"Could you take us to the nearest town then?"

Again she shook her head, softening it with a smile. "I'm sorry, but we're not going to town anytime soon."

"We can wait," the man in the vest said. He clutched his stomach. "I'm not feeling well and I would appreciate some assistance."

"In that case, I must insist you keep your distance," she said. "I cannot run the risk of exposing myself or my friend to the smallpox that has been spreading."

The man in red reached under the oilcloth and brought up the rifle. "You'll do as you're told, miss."

The small dark hole of the gun barrel focused on her. Her chest squeezed, but she shook her head. "You're not coming aboard," she said, diving to the deck.

She crawled to the rope ladder. It clanged against the side of the boat as though one of the men had grabbed hold of it. Working furiously, she sawed the knife against the rough hemp. When the knife cut through the last strands, the ladder splashed into the water. One of the men shouted an oath. It wouldn't slow them down for long, but if she could untangle the sail, they might be able to get away.

Scooting along the deck, she reached the mast and began to work on the tangled sail. She heard a *thump* and knew the dinghy had touched her sailboat again. The angle would be wrong for them to fire on her until they got to the deck. Stepping up her efforts, she jiggled the ropes, and the sail finally rose into the air. The wind billowed into the white canvas and the vessel began to move.

But not soon enough. Katie saw a hand slap the top of the boat, then another one. She ran to the bow of the boat intending to slash the hand with the knife, but she couldn't bring herself to do it. Instead she stomped on his fingers with her boot. "Go *away!*" she screamed.

"Yeow!" The man dropped back into the boat.

Before she had time to rejoice, hard hands seized her from behind. She felt hot breath on her neck and she twisted in the brutal grip. The man in the red shirt sneered at her, then dragged her back away from the rail.

"Come on up, boss," he called. "I've got this little she-cat corralled." The bird squawked again. "Shut up, Paco," the fellow snapped.

Katie twisted in his grip without hope. She had to save Lady Carrington and Jennie.

❦

His palms ached and so did his back. Will put all his strength into fighting the waves. He reached the thickly forested point and rounded it, straining to see the sailboat in the distance. There it was, but the boat had moved from its original location. Frowning, he lifted the oars from the water and stared. Katie's dress was clear but two other figures moved on deck. Neither of them was Lady Carrington, and with a sinking sensation in his belly he recognized the red shirt.

He'd been right. The men had gone straight for the sailboat. The women were at their mercy. The dinghy bobbed in the waves as he considered his options. If he rowed right up to the sailboat, he'd be seen. His best option was to swim. The distance appeared daunting but God would be with him.

Leaving the boat behind him, he slipped into the sea. As soon as the cold slammed into his bones, he realized how weakened he was from his previous swim. The frigid water sapped his energy and slowed his movements. The sailboat seemed to recede in the distance as he put himself into stroke after stroke toward it. It seemed an impossible task at first, but as his body cut through the waves, a bit of warmth crept into his limbs from the exertion.

A seagull dove toward him then veered at the last minute. He wished he could swim as effortlessly as the three sea lions whose sleek heads passed him in a blur. He paused and treaded water a few moments. The boat still seemed impossibly far away. Voices carried over the water, but he was breathing too hard to be able to make out the words. Katie's defiance was clear in the tone, though, and he feared for her.

Once he caught his breath, he struck out for the boat again. *Stroke, kick, stroke, kick.* His methodical movements finally began to draw him near enough to the boat that he thought he was going to make it. As he neared, he switched to a breaststroke to create the least amount of noise. He was now close enough to make out the conversation.

The sound of the men's raised voices carried over the water. "Tell her to open the door!" The man's anger nearly vibrated the air.

"Don't you unlock that door!" Katie yelled.

Was that a slap he heard? Will reached the aft side of the sailboat.

"You want more of that, you little witch?" the man demanded. "Get that door open or I'll use my fist next time instead of my palm."

Rage coiled in Will's belly. The man had struck Katie. He would pay. Will grabbed the line on the anchor and rested a moment to gather his strength to board. He needed to explode over the side with enough force to overpower the man with the gun he'd seen glinting in the sun.

"You're just as independent as your mother," another male voice said.

"Florence is not my mother!" Katie spat.

Will heard a tussle, and under the cover of the commotion, he began to climb up the rope that held the anchor to the boat. His arms ached dully and so did his back. He gained the railing and peered over the deck. The men had their backs to him. He hoisted himself onto the boards and crawled behind the bulkhead.

Katie's eyes flickered and he knew she'd seen him, but the men noticed nothing amiss. Her right cheek was bright red from being struck and his anger reared again. The only weapon he possessed was the knife tucked into his belt. The man in the red shirt still held a rifle loosely in his right hand. If Will could figure out a way to gain possession of the gun, he'd have the upper hand. He stepped out from his hidden place and mimicked jabbing a fist in someone's stomach.

Katie didn't respond but he knew she'd seen him. He waited until she raised her voice.

She shook her finger in the businessman's face. "You imbeciles! If you think for one minute I'm going to allow you to lay a finger on Lady Carrington, you are sadly mistaken." She turned as if to walk away. The man in the vest caught her by the arm and she whirled. Her right fist came up and arced into his midsection. He collapsed to his knees and gasped for air.

Will leaped onto the back of the man with the gun. One hand got caught in the fellow's suspenders, but Will succeeded in getting it free. The man bucked him off then dived on top of Will. Will grabbed the fellow's throat and squeezed then brought up his knee and kicked out. The man went flying, without the rifle in his hand.

Will leaped up and seized the gun. He was breathing hard as he stood over the man in the red shirt.

Katie ran to him, and he put one arm around her waist. An emotion he didn't want to name clutched at his chest at the sight of her. "Lady Carrington and Jennie are below deck?" he asked. When she nodded, he held her tighter in relief.

The mynah squawked and ruffled his feathers. "Six steps," he croaked.

Both men rose and faced him. "Who are you?" Will demanded.

The businessman's eyes flickered but he said nothing. He shot a warning glance at his accomplice, who abruptly shut his mouth.

"You're going to jail," Will said.

The businessman smiled. Perspiration dotted his handsome face, and he mopped his brow with the sleeve of his tweed jacket. "Look, we can cut a deal. Let us go and I'll see you get a share of the money."

"That's not how it works. You killed the crew. That kind of barbarism has to be punished."

"We had nothing to do with that. The men I hired took things into their own hands."

Will saw the flicker of falsehood in his eyes. "I don't believe you."

The bird sidled to the edge of his post. His feathers fluttered as one leg slipped over the edge of the railing where he perched. He squawked and fluttered his wings but didn't catch his balance. The mynah's weight landed on Will's shoulder, and the bird's wings fluttered in his face.

Will tried to catch himself, but he was weak and standing off-kilter. He fell onto one knee. Before he could react, both men were over the railing. Two splashes sounded. He ran to the bow and saw them swimming toward shore.

"Stop!" he shouted. Raising the gun, he sighted down the barrel then lowered it. He couldn't shoot any man in the back, not even murderers like these two.

Katie joined him at the railing. Her fingers crept into the crook of his arm. "I was so glad to see you. I couldn't have held them off much longer."

"I heard you face them down. You were very brave."

"I couldn't let them harm Lady Carrington or the baby."

He stared into her eyes. The emotion in them caused his throat to close. He didn't know much about women, but even he could recognize love when he saw it. Did he dare to do something about what he felt?

TWENTY-EIGHT

THE WARM PRESS of Will's fingers on her waist was a sensation she wanted to savor—as was the intense look in his eyes. Katie allowed herself to lean against him for a moment and remember the kiss they'd shared. But it was best not to think about that.

She pulled away. "I'd better get Lady Carrington." She went to the hatch and called through the closed door. "You can unlock it now."

When she heard the older woman throw back the lock, Katie lifted the door open. Lady Carrington's eyes were wide with alarm.

"Where are those men?" Lady Carrington asked.

"Overboard," Will said, helping her up to the deck.

"Y–You made them walk the plank?" the woman quavered.

He grinned. "No, they went of their own volition." His smile faded. "We have to fetch my brother and the constable. They will try to move the *Paradox* and I can't stop them."

Katie gasped and shuffled the baby to her other shoulder. "You found it?" She couldn't keep her eyes off Will. He seemed taller, broader, more handsome than she'd ever seen him. Like a knight in shining armor, he'd come barreling over the railing to save the day.

His gaze lingered on hers. "Sure did. In a second hidden bay. Hard to find, but it's there."

The finder's fee. He'd promised half to her. She could pay off Florence. "They mentioned my mother," she said slowly. "Florence must be involved in this somehow."

"Maybe that's another reason she's here," he said.

Katie's throat felt tight. For some reason, she felt near tears. Florence's visit to Mercy Falls had nothing to do with her. She was an afterthought. A convenient way to get more money. Well, she didn't care.

Will's charcoal eyes studied her face. "She's not worthy of causing you a moment's pain, sweetheart."

The endearment was pleasant to her ears. The tenderness in his eyes made her eyes well, and she turned her gaze before he could see. "We'd better get to Mercy Falls and summon help." She nearly winced at her frosty tone. Did she want to push him away? Maybe so. If she let him get close, she might be forced into a decision she wasn't ready to make.

"Of course." His tone lost its warmth.

Retreating to the stern, she found a deck chair and settled in. Her feelings for Will changed nothing even though she wished it would. For just a moment she imagined life as Will's bride. There would be no placid days where life moved in expected patterns.

Lady Carrington joined her. "You care about that young man, Katie Russell," she said. "I saw him kiss you before he dived over the side."

"I don't want to," Katie forced herself to say. "I plan to marry Bart Foster."

"Somehow I doubt that will happen. Love comes when it's least expected." The older woman had a faraway look in her eyes.

Katie shot her a quick glance. "I want to please my parents, to take my place in society as they expect. I don't want to upset anyone."

The older woman's smile was sad. "I made the wrong choice for the very reasons you mentioned, Katie. I wanted to stay close to my parents, and I wanted my pleasant life to continue to run like a placid stream."

"You had a second chance with Lord Carrington," Katie pointed out.

"God blessed me with that, but it's rare we get a second chance." Lady Carrington's expression was kind. "The ups and downs in life are good, my dear. They keep us from boredom."

Katie captured a stray lock of hair and pinned it back into place. "I don't like surprises."

"Do you think God wants you to never grow? Surprises can be both good and bad. You can't control everything. That's God's job."

"Surprises can hurt. They come out of nowhere and slam into you like a Pacific storm. Sometimes you never recover."

"God is our husbandman. Sometimes he makes a snip there, a cut here. It's all designed for our good, though it can be painful at the time."

Katie tapped her forehead. "My intellect knows you're quite correct, but I like things to be controlled and expected."

Lady Carrington smiled. "Controlled can be quite stifling. Think of how your handsome lightkeeper makes you feel. More alive in his presence than you ever felt?"

Katie couldn't deny it so she said nothing at first. Then she said quietly, "What if he drowns saving someone? What if he leaves me?" She wanted to add, "Just like my mother left me," but she clamped her teeth against the admission.

Lady Carrington's eyes filled with compassion. "Darling, what if that fear keeps you from really living? Surely ten years or even one year experiencing life to its fullest is better than never knowing what real love is like at all."

Katie shook her head. "I'd rather avoid pain."

The older woman chuckled. "Life can be quite untidy, can it not? You think you have it all mapped out, then God plants a vine next to you, and the next thing you know, everything has changed. Embrace what God has for you. Somehow I don't think it's Mr. Foster." She closed her eyes and sighed. "I shall take a nap. The circumstances have exhausted me. But I wouldn't have missed it for the world, would you?"

With the woman's eyes closed, Katie knew no response was necessary but one welled in her throat anyway. "No," she said. "I wouldn't have wanted to miss it. It was quite . . . exciting."

Lady Carrington smiled but didn't answer, and Katie was left to ponder the admission she'd made. A lack of surprises also meant a lack of excitement. Her fingers crept to her lips again. Though he'd never kissed her, somehow she doubted that Bart's kiss would affect her the way Will's had. Suppose she found the courage to change her life's course. Nothing was set in stone yet. That option dangled in front of her dazzled eyes, but she very much feared the love for the handsome lightkeeper that swelled in her bosom.

❧❀☙

Will tied up the boat and helped the women alight onto the dock. "I'll telephone the constable," he said. "I fear the men will be long gone, though," he told Katie.

She nodded and said nothing as she walked up the beach to the lighthouse. She'd been distant on the way back. Their earlier closeness seemed as transient as the fog beginning to waft down from the wooded hillsides. As he'd steered the sailboat back to harbor, he'd decided he was going to pursue Miss Katie Russell. He'd convince her he was a far better choice than that dandy from town.

The roar of the sea was the only sound as they traipsed to the lighthouse. He glanced at his pocket watch. It was only four o'clock, though it felt much later. His job was the lighthouse. Philip would have to pursue the criminals. He stepped into hall. "Now to telephone the constable."

"I'll just call on the switchboard," Katie said. "It will be faster." She settled in front of the switchboard and connected the proper jack.

Will watched her as she told the constable what had happened. Her beautiful face was animated and alive. How did she think she would ever be happy burying herself in a mediocre life with a man she didn't really love? It wasn't what she wanted, not deep down.

Convincing her of that fact would be his goal over the next few weeks. He was a patient man. She couldn't tell him she had no feelings for him. Her response to his kiss had proven that.

Katie spun around on the stool. "He'll meet Philip at the dock. He's quite excited."

"He should be. This is a huge break." He frowned. "You're sure you've never seen those two men before? They seem to be from the area."

"I don't know them. The businessman matches the description of the man who used the telephone at the skating rink to threaten me."

"I never would have guessed our pirates would be businessmen."

"Nor I. Perhaps the depression has them searching for a way to stay afloat."

He nodded. "I need to find Philip before the constable arrives. Will you be all right?"

She tipped up the pointed chin he found so adorable. "We'll be fine," she said.

There was a distance in her gaze he found disconcerting. "What are you planning?"

She didn't meet his eyes. "Nothing."

Nothing he could do about her mood now. He went in search of Philip. He only found his brother down at the dock after asking around. Philip was aboard a beautiful sailing yacht that looked as though it had fewer than ten hours on it. Pristine condition with white sails and an immaculate deck. Will motioned to his brother. Philip frowned but joined him on the dock.

"I found the *Paradox*," Will said. He told his brother what they'd discovered. "Katie called the constable. You're to meet him in an hour to go out looking."

Philip shook his head. "Can't do it tonight, Will. I have a chance for something big." He hooked a thumb toward the man in the dapper suit aboard the yacht. "Hudson Masters sent his man to hire me.

He wants me to track his missing wife. We've got a lead on her. We're about to talk it over on the yacht."

"B–but what about this job? You're so close to wrapping it up and collecting the finder's fee." Katie would get her share too. He had to make sure that happened.

"It's a minor detail to take the constable out to the ship. Surely you can handle that. This is a huge opportunity for me, Will. If I come through on this, he'll funnel enough work to me that I'll be able to afford anything I want."

Will struggled to keep the disappointment out of his voice. "This is your job, Philip. Not mine."

Philip's gaze was pleading. "If this comes through, we're sailing to Hawaii. I've always wanted to go."

"Fine. I'll take care of it." Like always.

Philip's smile faltered then he shrugged. "I'll make it up to you, Will. I'll have to shove off right away though."

"I just don't understand. Why not see this through first?"

"Hey, you should be happy! I'm handing off a payday to you. Just be sure to cut me in, all right?" He paused, looked down at the floor, then back to Will. "I'm not like you. I'd rather have some fun and take my pay as it comes. And *this* job is bound to make the missing *Paradox* pale in comparison." He tipped his hat. "I'll see you tomorrow."

TWENTY-NINE

THE FOGHORN SOUNDED in the night, and the glow from the light tower added to the last of the sunset. Katie had lit the light early because she had to run to town and Will wasn't back yet. She pinned on her hat and told Lady Carrington she would return as soon as she could. She wound the light to allow herself a little more time, just in case, then hitched the buggy and went to town.

It was only seven o'clock, but Mercy Falls was quiet, still in the grip of the smallpox scare though the danger was mostly past. Katie disembarked the buggy outside The Redwood Inn. The gaslights lining the street hissed as they illuminated the decaying neighborhood. Katie's chest was tight as she squared her shoulders and walked up the front steps. The smell of cooking cabbage wafted out the open windows of the café next door and her stomach clenched uneasily. She'd barely managed to get down a mouthful or two of food at supper with this facing her.

Holding her head high, she marched up the steps to the large building. It was only as the bell tinkled over the door that she realized people might wonder what her business was with Florence. And she had no idea what name the woman was going by this time. She nearly retreated to the buggy but the man behind the reception counter looked up from the ledger.

"Miss Katie, what brings you to the neighborhood again?" he asked.

She forced a smile at the grizzled proprietor. "Good afternoon, Mr. Wilson. Is the hotel full these days?"

He shook his gray head. "Most folks skedaddled at the first sign of the smallpox."

She advanced to the desk across the worn red carpet. "Has your household escaped it?"

"We have indeed. Even the missus has stayed well, though she's been working at the hospital. I heard your mama was not so lucky. She is doing better?"

She glanced at his open registry book. "Recovering nicely. Papa too." When he lifted an expectant expression to her and said nothing more, she cleared her throat. "Um, I'm looking for a woman, but I'm unsure of her name. In her early fifties. Dresses rather indiscreetly."

His mouth tugged downward. "Ah, you mean Mrs. Muller."

So she still used the same name. "Is she here?"

"Far as I know. She came in just after lunch, and to my knowledge, hasn't left. Room ten. Up the stairs and clear to the back on the right."

"Thanks, Mr. Wilson. Give your wife my regards." Ignoring the curiosity in his eyes, she lifted her skirts and went up the wide staircase to the second floor. The red carpet was even more worn on the treads, though clean.

She marched down the hall. The rose wallpaper was faded but still tightly adhered to the wall. The wide woodwork was battered. She paused outside room ten. Listening, she heard no sound from behind the wooden door. Confronting the woman wasn't something Katie really wanted to do. She squared her shoulders, took a deep breath, and then rapped on the door.

Moments later the door opened, and Florence peered out. "Oh, it's you."

She stepped out of the way to allow Katie to enter. Her green dress showed too much bosom, and her hair was a bit disheveled and loose on her shoulders. Katie stepped into the room. A sweetish odor hung in the air and she couldn't quite place it. She glanced around. The bed was unmade and discarded clothing lay in a tumbled heap at the foot of it. Toiletries covered the dressing table. A tray of partially eaten food was on the floor by the door.

Florence shut the door behind her. "Did you bring my money?"

Katie winced at the rapacious excitement in the woman's voice. "I told you I have no money to give you."

Florence flounced away to sit in a chair by the window. She picked up the hairbrush and tugged it through her unbound hair. "Then why are you here?"

The deeper she penetrated into the room, the heavier the scent became. It nearly sickened Katie. "What is that odor?"

Florence smiled and put down the brush. "My happy smoke."

Opium. Katie took a step back when she saw the pipe on the table beside Florence. "I know why you're really in Mercy Falls," she said.

"Oh?" Florence picked up the pipe and then put it down again.

"You helped with the piracy. We found the ship. And some men who know you."

Florence coiled her hair around her head. "I have no idea what you're talking about."

"I don't believe you."

Florence shrugged. "You may believe what you wish. Piracy? This isn't the 1700s, daughter."

"I'm not your daughter!"

"You even look like me." Florence finished pinning her hair. She rose and touched Katie's chin. "From your heart-shaped face to the way your eyes tip up. Albert used to call them 'cat eyes.'"

Katie loathed the thought of her father whispering to anyone but Mama, yet studying the woman's face, she knew it was true. "I didn't come here to speak of my appearance."

"Then get on with it and let me get back to what I was doing." Florence glanced at the pipe again with longing in her eyes.

"I know you have plenty of money. You were surely paid handsomely for your part in stealing the gold from the ship."

"A woman can never have too much money, my dear."

Katie grew tired of the dance around the truth. "I'm giving you no money so you might as well leave town with what you've gained from your piracy. I won't be blackmailed."

Florence smiled. "So it's quite acceptable for me to pay a visit to Mr. Foster?"

Katie decided to call her bluff. "Do whatever you like. He won't pay you anything either." She retreated to the door. In spite of her bravado, her pulse kicked up. What if the woman did just that—went straight to Bart?

She twisted the knob on the door. If she ever saw the woman again, it would be too soon.

"Wait!"

Katie turned to face Florence again. "We have nothing more to say to each other."

The woman rose and approached her. "I regret many things, Katie, but nothing more than the fact I wasn't allowed to raise you. I quite dislike seeing how much you despise me."

Katie's throat closed. "You always cared more about yourself than you did about me. I remember many nights going to bed to the sound of you laughing with a male visitor. You seldom noticed I was in the room."

The softness in Florence's eyes vanished. "Did you think I didn't deserve a life too—a little fun?"

"All I knew was that you never noticed me unless you wanted me to fetch your shoes or something. No child deserves to be cold and lonely."

"You were so young. I doubt you can remember much of those days. You always had a vivid imagination."

Faced with Florence's emphatic statement, Katie paused. Was it possible her memories were faulty? But no. The night she ran to the Russells was seared into her mind. No coal for the fire that night. No food in the room. Her mother had promised to bring her back something, but it had been hours. That dreadful man's appearance had been the final straw.

"Good-bye, Florence." She stepped through the door and shut it behind her.

A crash sounded in the room as though Florence had thrown something at the door. The words Katie heard from the woman would have made a sailor blush. With that much rage, she feared Florence would go straight to Bart. For a moment, Katie almost hoped for such an outcome.

It would make her path much clearer if marrying into the Foster family was no longer an option.

❧

The mynah squawked a greeting as Will walked up the hillside to the lighthouse. His steps dragged with fatigue but he was smiling. He'd heard the foghorn while still in the bay and the light had pierced through the haze as well. Since Philip was gone, Katie must have done it. Dear girl. The ship had still been there when he led the constable to the location, but the men were long gone. He'd also placed a call to the owners to let them know it had been recovered. The finder's fee would be deposited in his account. But his smile faded when he remembered the lives lost could never be recovered.

He heard the sound of horse hooves and turned to see Katie arriving in the buggy. The sight of her lifted his fatigue. Reversing his direction, he headed to the road to greet her. When he reached the buggy, he realized she'd been crying. Her reddened eyes and stained cheeks made him wince.

He reached up to help her down and she hurtled into his arms. He embraced her and held her close, resting his chin on top of her head. "What's happened, love?"

She retreated and pulled her hanky from her sleeve then dabbed her eyes with it. "I went to see Florence. She is such a liar. Of course, she claimed to know nothing about the piracy."

"I think it would take more than that to make you cry," he said. He stuffed his hands in his pockets to keep from pulling her close again.

She nodded. "She tried to make me think I didn't remember my childhood clearly. I thought I'd dealt so well with her neglect, but I realized it still hurts to know the woman who bore me cared for me so little."

A declaration of his love trembled on his tongue, but he reminded himself she seemed set on staying in Mercy Falls. If he followed his dream of a career in weather, there would be no soaring edifice of a house or servants. Still, there would be enough to care for her. He opened his mouth then shut it again. Maybe she would be better off with Foster.

"Did you find the ship?"

"We did. You'll be getting a nice finder's fee. You can pay off Florence and keep your secret intact." He wanted to add *for now* but clamped his teeth against the words. She already knew his opinion.

"I'm giving her nothing," Katie said.

His pulse leaped. "You've broken it off with Foster?"

She shook her head. "I don't think Florence will do anything. I called her bluff."

He swallowed his disappointment. "She might do it to spite you. Then what?"

"Then it was meant to be."

He offered his arm. "You sound very philosophical about it. I fear your attitude will change if she goes to see Foster."

"I shall deal with it if I have to."

Their gazes locked. The glow in her eyes held Will. Her lips parted and he took it as an invitation. His left hand went around her waist and his right drew her close. She closed her eyes and he bent his head.

The taste of her was intoxicating. Sweet and pure. She fit into his arms perfectly, as though made only for him. He chose to believe that was true, despite her seeming reluctance to put Foster aside. They belonged together. Her arms crept up to his neck and he deepened the kiss, savoring her response. Whether she wanted to admit it or not, she cared about him.

When she finally pulled away, he was loath to release her. Her right hand stayed on his chest and he covered it with his. "I don't think you should marry Foster," he whispered. "Not when there is this emotion between us."

Pain darted into her eyes. "I have to care for my parents. I fear Papa will go to prison."

He knew there was a good possibility that would happen. The constable knew Russell had something to do with the piracy. "I'll take care of your mother," he said.

"A lightkeeper's salary wouldn't pay for the upkeep on the house." Her voice rang with sadness.

He could tell her of the money in the bank, but he wanted more than her gratitude. "I love you, Katie. I believe you love me. You wouldn't kiss me like that if you didn't." He willed her to hold his gaze, but her lids shuttered her eyes. She started to withdraw her hand, but he held it place. "Look at me, Katie."

"I can't," she said in a choked voice. "You make me weak. I must be strong."

"Be strong enough to do what's right for you. For us. I never thought I'd want to marry, but I can't see my life without you in it." Her lids flickered, and he caught a glimpse of their blue depths before she lowered them again. "I know you love me," he said.

Her eyes opened then, blazing with color and passion. "What

difference does it make, Will? It would kill my mother to take her from her home. She's done everything for me. How can I not sacrifice for her?"

"I understand about duty, darling. It's driven me my entire life. But duty is a cold companion. You haven't even talked to your mother about your true feelings. I can't believe she wouldn't want to see you happy. I might not have a fortune, but I'm respectable too."

She bit her lip. "She loves me," she admitted. "But she thinks she knows what is best for me."

"I'd like to see her myself."

"I–I don't know. I wouldn't want her to suffer a relapse."

"I promise not to upset her."

"Very well." She tried to withdraw her hand again.

He lifted her fingers and kissed her gloved palm. "I want to hear you say you love me, Katie."

Her eyes widened. "I–I cannot say it yet, Will. Not until I know if our situation can be resolved. Once words like that are spoken, I can never go back."

"We can't go back now."

"If it's necessary, I can try," she said in a barely audible voice.

She tugged again and he let go of her hand. He watched her lift her skirts and run for the lighthouse. She might not have admitted it yet, but he knew love when he saw it. And he wasn't willing to give it up. He'd woo her with kisses and an outpouring of love that she couldn't resist.

THIRTY

THE FIRE FLICKERED in the fireplace. The scent of popcorn still lingered in the air. The house felt empty to Katie with Will up in the tower. Jennie played at Katie's feet with the kitten. The little one grabbed Katie's skirt and pulled herself up then toddled across the floor to where Lady Carrington sat on the sofa. The baby plopped on the floor and grabbed at the ball of yarn at the older woman's feet. As her wrist healed, she'd gotten back to knitting a bit.

Lady Carrington glanced at Katie. "You're very pensive this evening, my dear. Is there anything you'd like to talk about?"

Katie put down the copy of *McCall's Magazine* she'd been reading— or not reading—and forced a smile. "Life can be so confusing."

"Your color was high when you came in this evening. I saw you speaking with Will when you arrived."

"He wants to speak to my mother. About . . . us."

Lady Carrington put down her needles. "He's declared himself?"

Katie nodded. It had been all she could think about since he'd told her he loved her.

"And how did you respond?"

Katie laced her fingers together. "I–I'm not sure what I think."

"How did you feel when he told you of his intentions?"

"Terrified of making the wrong decision," Katie admitted.

"You love him, my dear. It's written all over you."

THE LIGHTKEEPER'S BRIDE   547

Katie lowered her gaze to the floor. If she didn't admit it, she wouldn't have to deal with it just yet. "It's so very difficult to think about disappointing my mother."

"You are so bound up in meeting your mother's expectations. And that young Mr. Foster's, too, I fear." The older woman glanced at the baby on the floor. "If you were this child's mother, would you withhold love from her if she didn't do exactly as you said?"

"Of course not. I adore her."

"How much more should you become the bride of a man who loves you for yourself and not for some preconceived idea of what a wife should be. A husband is to love his wife as Christ loves the church. With a sacrificial love. Can you say that is what Mr. Foster feels for you?"

"No." Bart liked her looks and thought she would be a good adornment on his arm. When he looked at her, she never felt as though he saw inside to her soul. Not like Will did.

"Will sees the real me," she said. The baby tugged on Katie's skirt and she picked her up. Staring at the beloved round cheeks and brown eyes, she prayed this baby would only know total love and acceptance. How had Katie gotten so far off track?

"I'm not sure I've ever experienced that kind of love," she said slowly. "Even Mama has high expectations."

"God loves you that way."

Katie nodded. "Of course. I meant human love." Will loved her that way. No wonder her soul responded to him with such passion. A love like that was most difficult to resist.

"Will you let him speak to your mother?"

Katie nodded. "Would you pray with me that Mama accepts him and sees the goodness in him?"

"You know I will, my dear." Lady Carrington rose and picked up her yarn. "I believe I shall retire. It's been a most grueling day."

"I think that's an understatement." Katie smiled as the older woman dropped a kiss on Jennie's head then exited the room. "It's about time for bed for you, too, little one," she told the baby.

"Ah-ah, do-ee," Jennie said. Using her index finger and thumb like pinchers, Jennie picked up a piece of lint from the floor and started to put it in her mouth before Katie took it away from her. She puckered up her face to howl and Katie picked her up. "How about a bath, sweetheart?" The baby gave a jerky nod and smiled. Katie carried her into the kitchen past Paco, who squawked at them.

"Step away from the cake!" he screeched. "Six feet back."

She scowled at the bird. Why on earth would someone teach a bird such a ridiculous thing to say? She shook her head and lifted the teakettle from the stove. As she poured the hot water into the sink then pumped in cold water, she thought back over the day. They'd found the ship but the gold was still out there somewhere. The pirates too. She paused. She'd recognize them again, though, and they had to know that. Would they come after her? They knew who she was because they mentioned her mother. One of them might even have been the one who dared to attack her here, before.

The bay by Wedding Cake Peak should have been one of the places she'd thought of. When Will described the cove where he'd found the boat, she'd remembered it. The passage to it was difficult to find and wasn't always open this time of year. At least she'd have the money to let her mother keep the house. And what if she turned that money all over to her mother? Then she could marry Will and not fear that her parents would lose their home. But her mother was a spendthrift. What if the money ran out? Her way would be clearer if she could help Will find the missing gold as well. Then there would be plenty of money to do both. Care for her mother and marry Will. But where could the pirates be hiding with it?

She didn't have long to find out. Hope stirred in her heart. If she could get the money to care for her mother, she would feel freer to follow her heart.

❦

Will watched Katie stir the porridge and lift it from the stove before ladling a bowlful for him. Her hair was still down on her shoulders and the sun lifted the brown to honeyed highlights. He needed to get some sleep this morning after tending the light last night, but he'd rather stay up and watch her. Lady Carrington had fed Jennie then taken the child into the parlor to rock her for a bit, though pieces of bread and jam still littered the linoleum floor. He meant to use these few moments alone to discover if Katie would allow him to speak with her mother today.

He'd never expected it to consume his every thought. As he'd tended to the light last night, he'd spent most of the time thinking about her and how he could convince her to marry him.

Their eyes caught and held when she turned toward the kitchen table. Color rushed to her cheeks. "Don't look at me like that," she said.

"Like what?" he asked, enjoying the sparkle in her eyes.

"Like you might . . ." Her blush deepened.

"Do something like this?" He rose and took the bowl of oatmeal from her hands and placed it on the stove. She entered his arms with no resistance. When he broke the kiss, he inhaled the sweet aroma of her breath. "Let's talk to your mother today."

"If you wish," she said softly. She stepped back and picked up the bowl of oatmeal.

He took the bowl from her, then carried it to the table. He'd rather kiss her again. The bird squawked on his perch by the door. "I wish Philip had never gotten that bird," he muttered.

"Where did he get it? I assumed he'd had it a long time."

"Did I hear someone mention my name?" Philip walked into the kitchen with his hair uncombed and his tie still askew. He yawned and dished up some oatmeal on the stove then joined them at the table.

"We were talking about your mynah," Will said.

"Good old Paco. He's something, isn't he?"

Will regarded the bird with disfavor. "If you like him so much, why am I stuck with him?" He watched his brother, who flopped into a chair in cocky fashion. "So did your big deal come through?"

Philip flashed a smile his way. "Sure did."

"Then you can take your bird with you. He loves being on a boat. We took him out yesterday."

Philip shoveled a spoonful of porridge into his mouth. "He came from this area, or so I'm told."

Will frowned. "What are you talking about?"

"I told you this," he said, glancing at Katie as if he didn't want to go into it in front of her.

"No you didn't."

"Those men yesterday," Katie said slowly, her eyes widening. "The bird got all excited when they came aboard. He was squawking and fluttering his wings. I just remembered the man in dungarees called him Paco. I assumed he'd been watching us. I didn't consider Paco might know him."

"What difference does it make?" Philip's head was down as he took another spoonful of food.

"Philip, tell me everything you know about this bird."

Philip shrugged and finally met Will's gaze. "I won him in a game in San Francisco. The guy was a businessman from this area, or so he said."

"What did he look like?" Katie put in.

"Description of the man? Do you know his name?"

"Just his first name. Ethan. Dark hair with wings of gray on the side. A mustache he kept waxed. Wore a bowler. Very distinguished and quite a hit with the ladies at the party."

Will exchanged a glance with Katie. "Sounds like the man, doesn't it?" She nodded and he stared back at his brother. "Anything else? Why did he put the bird up?"

"He was losing. His man had the bird on his arm and I admired it. He threw it in rather than end the game to go after more money. He lost anyway." Philip's voice was pleased.

"What did his partner look like?" Will asked.

"Older than Ethan, maybe in his fifties. Bald. Wore dungarees with suspenders."

It had to be the same two men. Will sensed Katie's excitement too. "They said they were from Mercy Falls?'"

Philip frowned. "Now that you mention it, they said they were heading home. I heard one say something about Mercy Falls, so I assumed that's where home was."

Katie shook her head. "I know most of the people in town and neither of these men were familiar."

"Did you get a sense for this Ethan's profession?" Will asked.

"I thought maybe he was a banker," Philip said.

Will had been expecting a railroad tycoon or some other kind of high roller. "What made you think that?"

"He said something about 'my bank' as though he owned one."

Will waved his hand in a dismissal. "I've said that myself."

"It was something in his tone. I could be mistaken though."

"Anything else you can think of?"

Philip shook his head. "Not really. He seemed cut up about losing old Paco here. Asked if he could buy him back. I told him I'd consider it."

"Did he ever show up again?"

"I left town a little early."

"Why was that?"

Philip rose and carried his bowl to the sink. "I didn't like the looks of this man. Something told me he might try to do me harm."

"And you didn't say a word about this to me."

"It's my investigation, as you've been quick to point out," Philip said.

"I think this bird belongs to the men who took the gold," Will said. His brother seemed unconcerned with what Will had just told him. "Where are you going?" he asked as Philip headed toward the door.

"I have to pack. The boat is pulling out tonight."

"Tonight? That's crazy, Philip. I need some help with this case. You're the one who dragged me into it and it's about to get wrapped up."

His brother gave a heavy sigh. "You can finish up the details and collect our money. I'm leaving tonight, Will. If there's anything I can do in a few hours, I can help out, but that's it."

Will pressed his lips together. "I was up all night tending to the light. I need some rest. You could poke around in town. See what the constable found out after he took custody of the ship."

Philip wrinkled his nose. "I'll pack, then go to town and ask around."

Will was tired, cranky, and fed up. "Never mind. Do what you want. That's all you've ever done."

Philip folded his hands across his chest. "You have no idea who that guy is who hired me for this new job, do you?"

"Does it matter?"

"Of course it matters! If I solve this, I'll have enough work to keep me solvent for ten years. He's Hudson Masters, who owns the biggest newspaper conglomerate in the country. He's always digging into dirt. If I come through for him, I'm set."

Wide-eyed, Katie glanced from Will to his brother. "So you're leaving, Philip? Just like that? When your brother needs you?"

Philip laughed. "You two are just alike. All bound up with what others expect of you. Life is too short to live it for duty. Sometimes you have to follow your own dream, not someone else's."

"When have you ever followed anyone else's?" Will demanded. "You don't know what *duty* means."

Philip spread his hands. "I'm grateful you knew your duty, Will. But I'm not like you. I'm never going to fit into the mold you want. I'm not a younger version of you. I'm just not." Philip threw up his hands. "Oh what's the use? You never listen." He stomped out of the room.

Will opened his mouth to call after his brother, then clamped it shut. His brother looked so much like their father that Will had often caught himself expecting him to act the same way Dad did. What did Will himself want from his life? He'd never asked that question. It hadn't seemed important with his duty before him.

He glanced at Katie. "Do you see the resemblance, Katie?"

She met his gaze. "I've tried to see either Philip or my father in her, but I've never been sure."

"You think Philip is right?"

Her gaze went soft. "You're a caretaker, Will. It's quite admirable."

"You're not answering my question."

"He might be."

"Then who does Jennie belong with?"

"I'm not quite sure," she said softly. "I don't think either one of us wants to give her up."

THIRTY-ONE

MAYBE SHE WAS wrong. Katie stood outside Will's bedroom door and studied the hallway wallpaper with flowers and birds on it. Her hand was still raised to knock. She should let him sleep. He'd only come up here three hours ago. But this was important. Surely she was right.

Excitement curled in her belly and she couldn't wait any longer. Her fist fell on the door. "Will?" There was no answer so she knocked again. "Will, I'm sorry but I need to talk with you." She thought she heard a muffled groan, then the pad of bare feet.

The door opened and Will stood in the doorway with his hair askew. He wore a robe and slippers. A stubble of whiskers darkened his chin, and the muskiness of his skin nearly enticed her to step closer, but she held her ground. "I'm sorry to awaken you, but I think I know where we can find the gold!"

He rubbed this roughened chin. "Honey, what are you talking about?"

The endearment in his voice caused pleasure to curl up her spine. She was hopelessly in love with him. So much so that tears filled her eyes. She couldn't speak to even tell him why she'd come. It didn't even seem important with the emotion flooding her right now. She couldn't marry Bart.

"Hey, hey, what's wrong?" He drew her into his arms.

She allowed herself the luxury of leaning into the sanctuary of his strength. "I–I'm fine. I'm just overwrought."

His rough hand smoothed her hair and he kissed her forehead. How had she endured life without him in it? His warmth enticed her to burrow deeper against him, but she must be strong. She closed her eyes and composed herself, then drew away and lifted a smile into his face. "I know you're exhausted but I believe I know where we should look for the gold!"

He raised a black eyebrow. "What have you discovered?"

She clasped her hands. "The bird had the clue all along."

"Paco?" He frowned. "What are you talking about? That dumb bird only knows two things to say."

"Exactly. It's the cake." She knew it sounded quite ridiculous so she rushed on. "Wedding Cake Rock. The rock out in the bay where we found the ship."

"I remember seeing it."

"The bird says, 'Step away from the cake.' And 'six feet back.'"

"Over and over," he agreed, his smile coming quickly.

"What if it's a clue to where the gold is hidden?"

"You mean the cake refers to that rock?"

She nodded. "Indeed. I think we should check it out."

He crossed his arms over his chest. "Katie, that's hardly likely, is it? That thing is all rock and gets lashed with storms. I can't see where they could hide anything there."

She hadn't thought of the storms. Her certainty faltered. "Still, there could be something there."

"It's possible, I suppose." He yawned again. "Let me get some rest and we'll run out there this afternoon."

His tone indicated he was only humoring her. "All right. You get some sleep." She stepped away and his arms fell to his sides.

"A good night kiss?" he asked, reaching for her.

She went back into his arms willingly and lifted her face for his kiss. He bent his head, but she heard footsteps coming up the steps and drew back.

He dropped his arms. "Later," he whispered and shut the door.

She stepped briskly forward toward the stairway and met Lady Carrington at the top. The older woman had Jennie in her arms. The baby reached for Katie and she took her. Jennie grabbed at the comb in Katie's hair. "I think I'll go see my mother," she told Lady Carrington.

"I thought Will wanted to speak with her."

"I'd like to warn her so it isn't such a shock. Will and I have something else to do when he gets up anyway."

"Splendid idea," the other woman said. "I was about to put this little one down for a nap."

Katie kissed the baby's pudgy cheek then handed her to Lady Carrington. "I shall return in a couple of hours. Do you need anything from town while I'm out?"

"I believe we're fine, my dear. Give my regards to your dear mama."

"I will." Katie went down the stairs and out the door where she hitched the buggy and started to town.

When she'd talked to her mother last night, she'd discovered the doctor said she no was longer contagious. Katie was eager to see her well. As the buggy rolled through town, she noticed more people out and about. People waved and called to her. She stopped to speak with Nell a moment and discovered the other telephone operator was eager to get back to the office. The infection truly seemed over.

Which meant she could move home within days.

The very thought filled her with dread. Her mother would expect her to come home. She *should* go home. But the thought of leaving Will and Jennie . . . It was no use. Lady Carrington was bound to want to return to her own home, tomorrow or the next day at the latest. And Katie couldn't stay at the lighthouse without her.

Smiling stiffly at passersby, she turned the horse onto her road. Moments later, she pulled up outside her house and clambered down. Adjusting her hat, she put on a happy expression and went up the steps to the front door.

The house was quiet when she entered the foyer. "Mama? Where are you?" She crossed the polished wood floor to the parlor and found her mother seated in the chair by the front window. Her head dipped to one side and she snored lightly. The pox on her face had faded, though some were still an angry red against the pale skin. A wave of love washed over Katie as she watched her mother. She crossed the few steps to the chair and knelt by it.

When she touched her mother's hand, the older woman's lids fluttered up. "Hello, Mama," Katie said softly.

Her mother straightened and clutched at Katie's hand. "Darling, I'm so glad to see you!"

Katie embraced her. "I've missed you so much."

Her mother fingered the fading marks on her cheeks. "I still can't believe they're gone." Her eyes brightened as her gaze roamed her daughter. "You look quite well, my dear. Blooming, in fact. Has your young man declared himself?"

Katie had intended to tiptoe into the subject, but the words spilled out before she could help herself. "Mama, I love Will Jesperson."

A frown crouched between her mother's eyes. "The lightkeeper? Oh no, no, Katie, that's ridiculous. You're much too precious for me to allow you to marry a man with no prospects."

Katie managed to keep her smile in place. Her mama just didn't know Will. "Wait until you meet him. He's quite wonderful."

Her mother took her arm in a firm grasp. "You haven't broken it off with Bart, have you?"

"Well no, not yet. There's been so much going—"

"Oh, good. And what about my sister? Is she still in town?"

"She is. But Mama, I didn't come to talk to you about them. It's about Will. He wants to speak with you himself."

She heard a footfall in the hall and turned as her father entered the room. "Papa, you're home too?" She embraced him and found him thinner and much more frail. "How are you feeling?"

He dropped heavily into a chair. A livid scar still marred his forehead. "What are you saying about the lightkeeper, Katie? I've already promised your hand to Bart. He asked for my permission. Of course, I was delighted."

"Without even discussing it with me?"

"I thought you had feelings for Bart," Albert said, frowning. He shook his head. "You've always been a good girl, Katie. Your mother and I have done so much for you." He passed his hand over the beads of perspiration on his forehead. "Don't fail us now over some silly romantic notion."

"It's not a silly notion, Papa."

"You must talk her out of this, Albert," her mother said.

He patted her hand. "Katie has always done her duty. I'm sure she will do so this time as well."

"What about Florence?" Katie's mother asked.

"I'll handle Florence," he said, his voice grim.

"I love Will," Katie whispered.

"It's out of the question." Her mother smiled. "Let's not continue to speak of such unpleasant things. Let's celebrate being a family again." She smiled at Katie and Albert, her eyes bright. "I'll ring for tea."

⟶✦⟵

The sun refused to be restrained behind the curtains, which meant the bright rays kept coaxing Will from any kind of restful sleep. He groaned, rolled over, and glanced at the clock on the fireplace mantel in his bedroom. Only a little after twelve. He hadn't shut his eyes for more than fifteen minutes at a stretch. Every time his lids closed, he saw Katie's face. So earnest and excited about her so-called "clue" and he'd disregarded her conclusion.

He swung his legs out of bed, quickly washed and dressed, and then went in search of Katie. He saw Lady Carrington in the yard with Jennie. Lady Carrington was rolling a ball and Jennie was trying to toddle after it. The kitten pounced after her.

A family man. That's what he'd become in this past month. And it felt good. His brother and sister had been teenagers when he took over their care. This was different. Jennie was as much his child as anyone's, and he couldn't imagine giving her up now. But what court would grant custody to a bachelor?

He grabbed his hat and stepped into the yard. The baby squealed when she saw him and lifted her hands. He scooped her up and she planted an open-mouthed kiss on his face. He grinned, quite ridiculously pleased at her obvious affection.

"Katie isn't here?" he asked Lady Carrington.

She shook her head. "She went to town to see her mother."

She hadn't waited for him. What did that mean? "I believe I'll join her if you're all right with the baby?"

"I'm doing splendidly. We just had lunch, and we're enjoying the sunshine. Run along, dear boy."

He handed Jennie off to her and went to the barn at the foot of the hillside. Katie had taken the horse, so his only option to get to town was to ride the bicycle. He set off on it. It was hard going in the gravel at the side of the road, but he reached the edge of town and found it thronging with people, all eager to get out now that most had been let off quarantine. By the time he reached the main street, he was hot and thirsty. Hungry too. He parked the bike at the café beside the roller rink and went inside. He ordered ham and potato salad. Halfway through eating his lunch, he noticed Katie's beau two tables over by the window.

Bart saw him at the same time. He rose and walked to join Will. "Mr. Jesperson," he said. "It's not often we see you in town. Is Katie with you?"

"No," Will said. He could have told the smiling young man where she was, but he had no intention of allowing the man to interfere in the coming interview with Katie's mother.

"A shame," Bart said. "I'm quite eager to speak with her." His smile beamed out. "I picked this up a few days ago and it's burning a hole in my pocket. I'm quite eager to see how she likes it." He pulled a small box from his pocket and opened it to reveal a glistening diamond ring nestled in velvet. "I've been waiting on some backers for my new business. The groundwork has all been laid and I can finally see my way clear to supporting a wife."

Will recognized when he was being warned off, but he didn't have to like it. "Congratulations," he said, his tone sharp.

Bart seemed not to notice Will's curt manner. "This union of our families was something both of us have wanted for several years."

"An arranged marriage? How archaic."

Bart flushed then. "Hardly just an arranged marriage. I quite adore her. Any man would be most fortunate to have Katie as a wife. I received her father's consent yesterday."

"Congratulations," Will said shortly. "I must go."

"If you see Katie, don't tell her," Bart called after him. "I want to surprise her."

Will didn't answer as he strode out the door. Did Katie know her father had made these arrangements? She'd never mentioned it. He mounted the bicycle and rode out to her mother's house. The buggy was still parked in front of the stately manor by the ocean. The roar of the sea soothed his agitation. He laid his bicycle in the grass and went up the walk to the front steps. The windows were open, and he heard the low murmur of female voices, though they were too soft to make out any words. Then a man spoke. Her father? His gut tightened at the coming confrontation.

He rang the bell. A maid in a white apron over her gray dress opened the door to him. He gave her his card and she had him wait in the entry while she went to announce his presence. A few moments later he heard Katie's light step.

She rushed into the hall. "Will, what are you doing here?"

"I understood you to say we were going to speak to your mother together," he said.

She practically wrung her hands. "I'm not sure today is the right time," she whispered. "Papa just returned home and—"

As if to contradict her, her mother's voice floated from the parlor. "Katie, bring that young man in here."

Katie pressed her lips together and she looked near tears. "I don't think this is a good idea."

He took her arm. "Let's just see, shall we?"

"Very well," Katie said.

She led him down the hall with its richly flocked wallpaper to a large parlor papered in green silk. The woman seated in the damask armchair wore a stern expression. Her back was straight and her chin high. He recognized the challenge in her gaze and knew this interview was not going to go well. Her husband was in an armchair. He seemed to look Will over and dismiss him.

Katie glanced from her mother to Will. "Mama, Papa, this is Will Jesperson." She stepped into the room and settled on the sofa.

When Will started to sit beside her, her mother gestured for him to take the other armchair closer to her. Will glanced at Katie then did as he was bid. "It's good to meet you, Mr. and Mrs. Russell. We've prayed for you both every night during family prayers."

"Family prayers?" Mr. Russell blustered. "Hardly, Mr. Jesperson. Katie is not part of your family, and neither is Lady Carrington."

Will glanced at Katie. When he saw the appeal in her face, he bit back his initial heated response. "I meant nothing by the comment, sir. Just that we prayed for you and your wife. We've been very concerned."

"Thank you," Mrs. Russell said, her tone frosty.

Will leaned forward and concentrated on the woman. Surely she could be swayed by how much he loved Katie. "Mrs. Russell, I love your daughter very much."

Her father interrupted with his hand held up. "Enough, Mr. Jesperson. You're hardly of the same social standing as Katie."

"My grandfather was Thomas Jesperson, founder of Jesperson, Texas, Mr. Russell. He came from very old money. I assure you that I can provide for a family."

His smile was condescending. "It's all been arranged, Mr. Jesperson."

Katie visibly swallowed. Will didn't like the way she wilted in her chair. He understood duty, but this was something more.

THIRTY-TWO

KATIE AND HER parents stood on the front porch as Katie took her good-byes. There was no room in the buggy, so Katie had to let Will ride his bike back to the lighthouse. She'd read the disappointment in his face as he said his farewell.

"He's a nice enough young man, but he's not for you, Katie," her mother said when Will was out of earshot. She patted her daughter's arm. "I must lie down for a bit. Go collect your things and I'll arrange for the groom to pick you up."

"I can't leave Jennie," Katie said.

Her mother looked at her father. "You deal with this, Albert. I'm exhausted." Her mother went inside.

"You need to stop this nonsense. Your mother is quite right," her father said. "Bart will make a much better husband. He's going to take over the haberdashery and turn it into a Macy's. You own a quarter of the block, and it's the perfect location."

"*I* own it? Whatever do you mean?"

"I put it in your name some time ago."

"Why?"

He shrugged. "Tax reasons, my dear. It was expedient."

"Does Bart know this?"

"Of course."

"So he is courting me for the property?"

His brows drew together. "For such a smart girl, Katie, sometimes you're a silly child with your head full of dreams and fluff. Just like your mother."

She stuffed her hurt and focused on her father's words. "I thought it would be a while before he got the money to build his Macy's. He hadn't mentioned it to his father."

Her father cut his gaze away. "He's found the money."

She studied his expression and the way he wouldn't meet her gaze. Businessmen. The pirates had been businessmen. "Was Bart in on your scheme as well?"

He laughed. "Daughter, you have a vivid imagination."

"I don't understand something, Papa. If you received your portion of the gold, why are you in such desperate straits financially?"

His mouth grew pinched. "My partner has withheld my portion of the money. I can hardly complain to the constable, can I? And he knows it."

"Has the constable been to see you?"

Her father nodded. "I told him nothing."

"Papa, you must!"

He shook his head. "I'll not risk you and your mother. I know these men, Katie. They would seek revenge. There are too many for the constable to get them all before they carry out their threat."

She shuddered, remembering the harsh tones of the man who had grabbed her on the porch. She'd believed him too. "God will take care of us, Papa. But you must do the right thing." His jaw flexed and she knew he wouldn't tell the constable. "Does the constable suspect you in Eliza's death?"

He shrugged. "He was pleasant enough. I assured him I had nothing to do with it. I think he believed me."

Katie hadn't been sure what to think, but staring at her father, she believed him incapable of murder. "Who killed her, Papa?"

He held her gaze. "I don't know for sure, but I suspect one of my partners found out she was selling her information."

"How was she involved in this?"

"She was hired to get close to the ship captain when the boat docked here a few months ago. She was to find out when *Dalton's Fortune* was making its money run. She transmitted the information and the heist was successful."

"So successful you all decided to do it again with the *Paradox*."

"Unfortunately, yes."

"Why was she selling the information?"

"Because she was greedy." He swayed where he stood. "I must rest."

He had a lot of room to talk. She wished she had the courage to say it to him. "I'm not coming home, Papa. Not yet. I must think about this." Ignoring his angry blustering, she went to her buggy. She had a lot of thinking and praying to do. Will had said little as they'd left, and she was thankful he was not pressing her. This was a decision she had to make on her own.

The clopping of the horse's hooves melded with the chirps of the birds in the shrubs as the buggy rolled along the road. Mercy Falls was just ahead. If only Addie were here to talk things over with. Katie missed her dreadfully. When she thought of marrying Bart, she felt no peace. Only disquiet in her soul.

She rounded the curve into town and slowed the horse. The buggy's wheels rolled along the cobblestone surface and the thumping drowned out her thoughts. On a whim, she parked the buggy outside her father's shop and went inside. The scent of pipe tobacco and men's clothing surrounded her when she stepped inside. The two men shopping nodded at her, as did the clerk who worked for her father. She wandered the front display room, pausing occasionally to touch a hanging jacket or adjust a hat display. What would this place be worth? There was still a good amount of stock here and the shop was the only haberdashery in town. Surely someone other than Bart might want to buy it. The town needed the shop to stay open.

The bell tinkled on the door and she whirled to see Bart step into the store. "Bart, what a surprise," she said, forcing a smile.

"I saw you come in. I was across the street at the bank." He crossed the few feet separating them and took her hands. "I've missed you, Katie. I was going to call to take you to dinner and the nickelodeon. You've been cooped up with that baby for too long."

"How sweet of you," she said. When he frowned, she realized he'd expected her to say she missed him too. But she had barely given him a thought all week.

I can't marry him.

Katie knew it with every fiber of her being. He was pleasant enough. Handsome, rich, respected. But she loved Will Jesperson. And she couldn't live a lie anymore.

"I talked with your father. He seems to be doing quite well," Bart said, drawing her to a quiet corner of the store.

"Yes, he is," she managed to get out.

"Has he said—what happened?" His mouth twisted.

"It wasn't a suicide attempt," she said, reading the distaste on his face.

Doubt still lurked in his eyes. "I certainly hope not."

"He didn't try to kill himself," she insisted. What would he say if he knew what her father had done was so much worse than an attempted suicide? Her father somehow hoped to keep it all quiet, but truth had a way of coming out. Especially something this big.

Bart's face cleared. He released her hands then reached into his pocket and withdrew a small velvet box. When he withdrew his hand, a piece of paper fluttered out. He didn't notice it as he glanced toward the door as one of the customers exited.

She scooped it up. "Wait, Bart, this fell from your pocket." She glanced at the paper and saw the handwriting. She'd seen the writing before and she struggled to remember. She gasped when it became clear.

He turned at the sound of her distress. "What's wrong?" he asked.

Her fingers clutched the note and she pulled it away from his outstretched hand. "Is this your handwriting?"

"Yes." He reached for it again but she stepped back. He frowned. "Whatever is the matter?"

"My father had a note in his safe," she said. "It was from you."

He shrugged. "Perhaps, but what of it? We often did business. I bought all my wardrobe from him, and surely you know by now that I hope to buy the haberdashery."

She clamped her teeth against the accusations cascading through her mind. Bart was in on the piracy. Maybe the mastermind. Katie nearly took another step back. She frantically searched for something to say that would make him put that velvet box away but her words dried on her tongue. In a daze she noticed the showroom was empty now. The clerk had put the CLOSED sign out and had left with the last customer, as if he had figured out that Bart was about to propose. They were alone.

When she didn't answer him, Bart opened the box to reveal a marquis engagement ring. He went to one knee and took her left hand in his. "I'd intended to do this over dinner and candlelight, but I can't wait. Katie Russell, would you do me the honor of becoming my wife?" His blue eyes were earnest and warm. He released her hand long enough to pluck the ring from its case, and then he took her hand again and slipped the ring on her finger.

The touch of his hand sent shivers through her. He was evil. She pulled her hand from his and shook her head. "I'm sorry, Bart. I can't marry you." She tugged the diamond from her finger and pressed it back into his hand.

Bart shot to his feet. "I should have waited," he said. "Any woman wants to be romanced a bit. We've been apart too long, with the quarantine and all. I was too eager."

She had to get out of here, away from him. "It's not that at all. I'm honored you would ask me. I've just realized I can't marry a man I don't love."

His face clouded. "I care very much about you, Katie. I thought you felt the same way about me. But no matter. We have a much better basis for marriage than mere love: respect, equal social standing, the same goals for our lives. Our marriage would be steady and quite happy. I'm quite certain you will come to care for me in time as I care for you."

"I think I want more than that," she choked out past a tight throat.

"Your father promised . . ." He broke off and cleared his throat.

"My father promised what?"

"That I could marry you."

This square city block was perfect for his Macy's. Her father had lied to her about Bart's involvement. No, that wasn't right. He'd never answered.

Staring into his face, she searched for the truth. "It's clear you don't love me either, not really. You said you *care* for me. That's not love. We get along. Our union is suitable. That might be enough for you to agree to marriage, but I've discovered it's not enough for me. There is no spark between us."

His brows drew together. "Of course there is. You're overwrought. I love you, Katie. I'm sorry if I wasn't clear."

Katie heard no ring of truth in his voice though. His eyes were evasive, crafty. As she stared, his face changed. His eyes grew shuttered and his mouth twisted. He put the ring back into his pocket.

"Something has changed you. It's that lightkeeper, isn't it? You must marry me, Katie. It's been decided." He took a step toward her.

The hard light in his eyes made her stomach plunge. "You aided the pirates. You and Papa took the gold," she said, backing away.

❧

Will rode the bicycle back toward the lighthouse. His spirits dragged at how it had gone with Katie's parents. Katie had been impossible to read, but he knew how she treasured her mother. It would be difficult for her to go against her parents' wishes. Could he even ask her to? It would cause a break in their relationship.

He pedaled out of town toward the coast. The going got harder and harder until he realized he had a flat tire. He dismounted and kicked the tire. A team of horses pulling a heavily laden wagon lumbered toward him. As it drew near, the driver reined in the horses and stopped beside him. He was a portly man in his forties with a grizzled beard.

"You from around here?" the driver asked. "I'm looking for the old Houston place. I hear it's hard to find."

"I'm new here," Will said, straddling his bicycle. "I've never heard of it. As you can see, I have a flat tire. Could I get a ride back to town?"

The fellow looked him over then shrugged. "If you don't mind waiting while I make this delivery."

"Not a problem. I'll just throw my bike in the back of your wagon." Will tossed his bike on top of some boxes covered with a tarp then climbed up next to the driver. "I appreciate it. Where is the property you're looking for?"

The driver consulted his notebook. "The driveway is off Oak Road."

"This is Lighthouse Road," Will said. "Oak Road is back to the highway then four miles down." He'd seen the road but had never been on it. "What is this fellow's name?"

"Hudson Masters."

The name was familiar. It was the fellow who had hired Philip.

The driver continued to talk. "I hear he owns a bunch of newspapers. He's opening a new one over at Ferndale."

"It sounds like his place is about halfway between Mercy Falls and Ferndale. Where are you based?"

"Ferndale," the man said.

Will directed the driver to the road and the lorry lumbered around the corner and down the highway that traced the coastline. The driver spotted the turnoff to the estate. He turned the big wagon into the narrow lane. The house was a three-story brick mansion with peeling paint and a few broken windows. If Will had seen it from the road, he would have assumed it was uninhabited.

"Looks vacant," he told the driver.

"It's been empty for years. The renovations are going to take a year. A businessman from the city bought it a couple of months ago and has been renovating it."

"He's living in this shack?"

"I heard he's living in two rooms when he's there. He conducts much of his delivery by telephone and telegram. He's there today to take delivery of the floor tile himself."

Will studied the derelict building. It could be magnificent. When the wagon came to a stop, he leaped down. "I see no buggy or horse," he said. His senses tingled the way they always did when something didn't feel right. A businessman from the city. Could it possibly be the man who had taken the ship?

The driver jumped down and tugged the tarp off the boxes of tile. "He might not be here yet. I'm an hour early."

"I'll give you a hand." Will helped the driver haul boxes of tile to the front porch. It was still sound structurally, but the paint had peeled from the redwood boards. The men stacked the tile to the right of the door.

"I have to wait around," the driver said when they were done. "He's paying me for this load when he arrives."

"I think I'll look around," Will said, his senses on full alert. He brushed his hands off on his pants and went around the side of the house.

There were two barns, a chicken coop, a well house, and another shed in the weedy expanse behind the home. This place had been quite the estate back in the day. He shoved open the first barn door.

Dust motes danced in the air as he stepped inside. Rusty tack hung on the walls. The stalls were empty except for old hay. He poked around until he was satisfied that the structure held no secrets. Shutting the door behind him, he went to the second barn. It appeared to have been in more recent use. The tack on the walls was new and a gleaming buggy sat in one stall. There was a horse in one enclosure and droppings in another so the man must own two horses.

He examined the barn but found no gold or other clues. When he stepped back into the sunshine, he heard voices. The owner must have returned. Taking care not to be seen, he sidled around the side of the house. Two men stood talking by the porch. Though the businessman had his back to him, Will recognized the dark-haired man immediately.

He'd found his pirate.

THIRTY-THREE

SHE'D THOUGHT HE was so mild-mannered and kind. Katie stared at Bart and wondered how she'd been so deceived. "You killed all those sailors."

He held out his hands. "I had nothing to do with that. No one was supposed to be harmed. The men we hired took it into their own heads to deal with witnesses."

More than ten men had died that day.

She doubled over and breathed through her nose. She tasted bile in the back of her throat and willed herself not to throw up. When her nausea passed, she slowly straightened and stared at Bart. "Why did you kill Eliza?"

He reached out to her. His face darkened when she flinched. "It wasn't me. I cared about her. My partner got wind that she was going to sing about who was involved in taking the gold. He had her killed."

She put her hand to her head and thought it through. The baby. "You cared about Eliza? Then Jennie—"

"Is my daughter," he said, finishing her thought. "But it means nothing. You're the one I love." His voice rose.

She stared at him. "She looks nothing like you."

"She looks exactly like my mother," he said.

Katie nodded, remembering his mother's flashing dark eyes. "But I heard Eliza try to blackmail my father. Why would she—" Katie took a step back. It was all clear when she thought about it. "I understand. He wanted a marriage between you and me. Eliza was going to tell me about the baby and ruin everything if he didn't give her money."

"She wouldn't have done it," he muttered. "She wanted us to leave, start over somewhere else. Nothing I told her could make her understand I wasn't marrying her."

"No, you wanted this property to build your Macy's," she said.

"It's more than that, Katie. Things can still work out. No one has to know about this. I have plenty of money to help your parents."

"I'm not marrying you!"

"Then your parents will be destitute."

She stared at him. "You refused to pay Papa unless I married you," she said. "That's why he's still pushing me toward this."

He reached for her and she stepped back again. He dropped his hands to his sides. "I care about you, Katie, but make no mistake. I mean to have this property."

"No. You can't have it. Or me." She lifted her chin in defiance but the menacing look in his eye made her take a faltering step backward. "I'll scream," she tossed out. "The constable will come running."

"You won't tell him," he said, his voice calm, still advancing. "You have no proof and I will testify that I saw your father kill Eliza. That would destroy your mother."

Her back touched the glass display case. "You're despicable. You allowed your own daughter to be abandoned."

Pain darkened his eyes. "My, uh, associate didn't realize she was there. When I heard about her disappearance, it was nearly midnight. I arrived to look for the baby and found the house empty."

"I'm sure you were quite happy you were spared your duty."

"This is getting us nowhere," he said through gritted teeth. "You'll sign that deed. Now."

"I don't have it," she said.

"It's in the safe. Your father told me that much." He took her arm in a punishing grip and pulled her toward the back room. "You're going to open the safe and get it for me."

No amount of twisting lessened the tight grip on her arm. She finally gave up and allowed him to propel her forward. "My signature would need to be witnessed."

"Then we'll go to the county recorder and get that done and the deed transferred at the same time." He shoved her, and she fell to her knees in front of the safe. "Open it."

She rose and faced him. "No."

"You'll be an orphan by nightfall if you don't do what I say," he said through gritted teeth. "Open the safe!"

How could she have been so deceived? This man was a monster. "What's to prevent you from killing us the moment you have the deed in your possession?"

"Because you'll know that if you say anything, you'll all be dead." He touched her chin. "I don't want to hurt you. Don't you see? This didn't have to come down this way. You could still marry me. I'd make you a good husband, I swear."

"Don't you touch me." She slapped his hand away. "Don't you ever touch me again."

His eyes grew cold again. "Open the safe, Katie."

"Very well," she said. She twirled the dial until the safe clicked open.

Bart pushed her aside when she threw the lever and opened the door to the safe. "I'll get it," he said.

She watched as he riffled through the documents inside and then emerged, a small grin of triumph on his face. "Now we'll get it transferred."

She smiled, glancing at the clock. "It's too late," she said. "The county office is closed. Today is Wednesday."

His face reddened and he swore. He raised his hand as if to strike her but she refused to cower and lifted her chin to stare him down.

He dropped his hand and grabbed her arm. "Then we'll have to get your signature witnessed elsewhere."

She still didn't trust him not to dispose of her once he had control of the property. As he shoved her out the back door, she prayed for a miracle.

⌒✿⌒

Will froze when he realized who the property owner was. He started to shrink back behind the corner of the house when he felt a hard metal object in his back.

"Hands up," a hard voice said in his ear. It was a dauntingly familiar voice. Will raised his hands. The fellow shoved him forward. "Move."

Masters turned as they approached. His eyes flickered but he said nothing when he saw Will. Will glanced at the driver and saw he was unaffected. Apparently, his boss was paying too much for him to notice Will's compromised situation.

"Mr. Jesperson, you've caused me untold misery lately," Masters said. "But your interference has come to an end today."

The man behind Will grabbed a rope. Will flexed his wrists as best he could as the man bound his hands behind him and shoved him toward the lorry. "Take him to the mine and shoot him. You can dump his body down a shaft."

The driver nodded toward the lane. "Wait a second, boss. Someone's coming."

A horse pulling a buggy came cantering up the drive. The sun was in Will's face so he couldn't see who was in it until the conveyance stopped and the occupants stepped out. His gut clenched when he saw Katie's white face. Bart had hold of her arm and she winced as he marched her toward the group. Will clenched his fists.

Bart shoved her and she fell to her knees in the dust. Will started to leap forward but the man behind him grabbed his arm and pushed him the other direction. He stumbled and went down on one knee then struggled upright. "Katie, are you all right?"

"I'm fine." She rose and brushed the dirt from her skirt. "That was unnecessary, Bart," she said.

Will had never seen the urbane young man so agitated. His face was flushed and he was breathing hard. Bart clenched and unclenched his fists. Katie started toward Will but Bart grabbed her arm again, the muscles in his jaw flexing.

"What's all this?" Masters demanded. "Why is she here?"

"She turned me down!" Bart said, his voice aggrieved.

Masters snickered. "You weren't as charming as you thought. What about the deed?"

Bart held up a paper. "Right here. But her signature needs to be witnessed. Then I can get it recorded."

Masters sighed heavily and pinched the bridge of his nose. "Foster, once again, you've brought me into something that you should have handled yourself."

Bart faltered. "I'm sorry. I wasn't thinking. I only—"

"You have two witnesses right here," the businessman interrupted, flinging his hands in agitation. "Just get your foolishness resolved so we can move on. Do you have a pen?"

Bart felt in his pocket. "No."

Will had no idea what they were talking about but his pulse leaped when he heard Katie had refused Bart's marriage proposal. His gaze locked with hers but his elation faded when he saw the despair in her eyes. They were both in mortal danger and his hands were bound behind his back. She was free though. And Katie was a fighter.

Masters motioned to the driver. "Get a pen from my desk." The big man nodded and headed for the house.

That left three against two. If only Will had his hands free. "What deed are we talking about?"

"Shut up," Masters said, his voice bored. "If he says anything else, shoot him."

If Will could free his hands, he'd disarm this guy in a second. He twisted his wrists. Did they give just a bit? He thought so. The other guy was watching his boss, and Will flexed his arms again. Nothing.

The driver returned. "Here's the pen." He handed it to Bart.

Bart grabbed Katie's arm and thrust the pen into it. "Sign."

"No."

He struck her and she fell to the ground. Will leaped forward, driving his chest into the other man. "Big man," Will yelled in Bart's face before the man in overalls could drag him off. "Hitting a woman. Does that make you feel strong? You're scum!"

Katie was back on her feet. Her cheek was red but her head was high. She put her hands behind her back.

"Don't sign it," Will said. "It's the only way for you to stay alive."

"A lot you know," Bart said. "If I have to, I'll get her signature forged. But I'll make sure she sees her parents are killed in front of her. She'll go to her grave knowing what she caused."

Tears leaked from Katie's eyes. "I can't believe you'd do something so horrible," she said, her voice low.

"I will," he hissed. He grabbed her arm and took a few steps toward the buggy. "Come on. We'll go fetch them right now. They're expecting the happy couple anyway."

"No," she said, wrenching her arm from his grasp. "No. I'll sign it."

"Don't do it, Katie!" Will burst out. "He'll kill you the minute you've signed."

She looked at him with regret and resignation in her eyes, then took the pen Bart handed her and signed the document.

Bart grabbed it from her hands. "Get rid of both of them," he told Masters. "I'll get this recorded tomorrow."

"What about Jennie?" Katie asked. "What will happen to her?"

Will glanced from her to Bart. "Why would he determine what happens to her?"

"She's his daughter," Katie whispered. "What about Jennie, Bart? Don't hurt her."

Bart shrugged. "Maybe your friend Addie will adopt her. If not, I suspect she'll end up in an orphanage. Or perhaps I can convince your mother she is Albert's daughter." He laughed. "I have no interest in her."

THIRTY-FOUR

THE SEA BREEZE ruffled Katie's hair and tugged at her bonnet. The sky showcased hues of magenta and indigo as sunset approached. The boat rounded a finger of land and she saw Wedding Cake Rock looming in the distance. Terror replaced her elation from earlier in the day when she thought the rock might be a clue. But now the only thing ahead of them was certain death.

She sought solace in Will's gaze. If she had to die, at least they would die together. He smiled but his eyes were dark pools of regret. The sailboat dropped anchor in the bay and Bart lowered the dinghy.

"You first, my dear," he said, smiling. He grabbed Katie's arm and helped her down into the boat. "Now your poor knight." He practically shoved Will into the boat, and he fell heavily onto the bottom. "Chesterton, get down there and make sure they don't jump overboard." The man in overalls nodded and jumped into the boat.

Katie knelt beside Will. She helped him to a seat as Bart and Masters descended to the dinghy. The men guided the boat past Wedding Cake Rock to the wild shoreline.

"Try to loosen my ropes," Will whispered.

She sat closely beside him and slid one hand around to his wrists. Her fingers tore at the rough rope, but if she'd managed to loosen them at all, she couldn't tell it.

"Get away from him," Bart ordered.

Katie moved to the center seat. It was only moments until the boat scraped bottom at the shore. The men piled out and Bart helped her into the water. The waves soaked her skirt to her knees as she slogged to land.

"That way," Masters said, pointing to a barely perceptible trail through the ferns and weeds.

Their captors marched them through the vegetation that crowded in on every side. Birds were beginning to find their night perches in the trees and the forest was silent except for the snap of breaking twigs and the tromp of feet. In a clearing up ahead, Katie could just make out the remains of the old gold mine. How long before the men shot them? Surely they would wait until they were close to the shaft that they intended to hide their bodies.

She prayed to meet death with courage. Now that it faced her, she found the peace she'd been looking for. It had been here all along. All she'd had to do was trust in God and remember that her future wasn't here in this place but in heaven. She'd looked at this temporary world too much and at eternity too little. Such a revelation, and it came too late to change her actions with other people. The control she sought had all been an illusion.

Fred stepped past them to what appeared to be a cellar door. He heaved it open to reveal a yawning darkness. When he turned back around, his pistol was up and pointed at Will's chest.

"No!" she screamed, throwing herself in front of Will. Her movement was mistimed and she barreled into Will. They both went down in a heap as the revolver discharged. She felt the wind of the bullet as it passed.

"Imbecile!" Masters snapped. "Get them in front of the shaft. I don't want blood on the ground."

He moved toward them but Will erupted in a flurry. He leaped onto Chesterton and both men fell into the shaft. One of the men shouted as they fell and Katie's throat closed. She scrambled to her feet and ran to the open shaft.

"Perhaps we can let the mine itself do the job," Bart said. He moved toward her.

Katie knew he intended to throw her into the shaft as well. She could do nothing for Will now, so she dodged Bart and ran for the forest. The darkness was falling fast. Perhaps she could escape Bart and Masters then circle back to the boat and get help. She found a thick swath of ferns and dived into them, burrowing into their covering.

Holding her breath, she listened for footsteps. She was about to think they'd taken another path when she heard the stealthy snap of a twig three feet from where she lay. Barely daring to breathe, she strained to see through the deep shadows. There, was that a boot? Yes. The man moved on past her then came back. It wasn't until he spoke that she realized it was Bart.

"I know you're here somewhere, Katie. I can smell your cologne water." His boot came up and he brushed his foot across the vegetation four feet away. "Come out now and I'll make sure you don't suffer. It will be fast, I promise. I wish you'd said yes. I care about you, I really do. This saddens me that it has to end this way."

His footsteps slowed and he turned toward where she hid. He was coming straight for her. He would find her. She refused to be run to the ground like a quaking rabbit. Her muscles coiled to rise from her hiding place, but before she could move, she heard a shot then the sound of two shots in rapid succession. Bart whirled and ran back toward the camp.

Nearly sobbing with relief, Katie rose from her hiding place. Maybe Will wasn't dead after all. He needed her help. She grabbed up a stick nearly as thick as her wrist and ran for the clearing herself.

The shots echoed in Will's ears but the bullets had missed him, praise God. He crouched in the darkness. The fetid air of the mine shaft made him want to cough but he suppressed the urge. His adversary would find him if he did. He strained to hear where Chesterton might be crouching, waiting to shoot at him again.

A stone rolled to his right. Then a sliding, scraping sound. It was now or never. Will rose from a crouch and launched himself at the sound. His body collided with another one and he realized he was at Chesterton's back. He reached out and grabbed at the man's right arm. His fingers grazed the gun and it fired again. The flash left spots dancing in his vision in the darkness, but he managed to wrest it from the man's hand.

He stuck the barrel against Chesterton. "Don't move."

The man stilled. "You won't shoot me."

"In a heartbeat," Will promised even though he wasn't sure he could really do it. He climbed off Chesterton but kept a hand on his arm and the gun in his neck. "Move."

The way up was past fallen timbers and loose boulders. They'd fallen a good twenty feet, and Will's body stiffened in a hundred places. The men shuffled toward the dim glow, and fresh air began to replace the fetid stench of the mine as they climbed. The last vestiges of twilight illuminated the tunnel as they neared the shaft's opening. "Not a word or I shoot," he whispered to Chesterton. He shoved him up the final few feet until his head was out of the shaft.

Whack! Chesterton slumped to the side of the shaft and Will shot through the opening and tackled the figure waiting at the top. It was Masters. The two men wrestled until Will got the older man pinned beneath him. He jammed the pistol under Masters' chin. "One more move and I'll pull the trigger."

He heard something behind him and turned to see Katie with a thick stick in her hands. She'd hit Bart over the head as he was about to bring a rock down on Will's head. He leaped to his feet and dragged Masters up.

"Where's Chesterton?" Katie asked, her voice breathless as she joined him.

"Masters beaned him. He probably thought it was me, coming out. Good job on Bart." He couldn't keep the satisfaction from his voice.

Katie grabbed a rope and brought it to Will.

"We can make a deal," Masters said as Will bound his wrists behind him. "We'll cut you in for a portion of the profits. The gold we took from the ship will get this mine up and going again. It's a sure thing. We'll all be millionaires."

"You're like a snake," Will said. "You'd bite me the minute my back was turned." He took out his pocketknife and cut part of the loose rope off. There should be enough to tie up Bart too.

"No, no, I wouldn't," Masters said quickly. "We can make this work."

"You can make it work in jail." Will shoved him toward Bart's inert form. "Here," he told Katie, handing her the remaining rope. "See if you can truss him up."

She tied the unconscious man's arms behind him. "He's out cold," she said. "I don't think we can get him to the boat."

"We'll send the constable back for him. Chesterton too."

"I hate to leave him here. What if there are bears or other wild animals?"

"They'd spit him out the minute they tasted him." He shoved Masters toward the path to the bay.

Will had so much he wanted to say to Katie but not while he had an audience. They reached the beach, climbed into the dinghy, and headed out. "You were so brave, Katie," Will said. "I am proud of you."

"Save the hearts and flowers for later," Masters said, his voice thick with disgust. "This isn't over yet."

"I think we shall have no trouble proving our case," Katie said. "Where is the gold you pirated? If you give that back, maybe it will go easier on you."

They reached the sailboat and Masters leaned back and shook his head. "I'm not getting on that boat."

"You'd rather drown?" Will asked. He grabbed the man and yanked him forward.

"You aren't like Bart, Mr. Jesperson. You have too much integrity to kill an unarmed man. Just let me go. I'll disappear and you'll never hear from me again."

"I can't do that. I think you know it too," Will said.

"I'll not bring disgrace upon my family," Masters said, his voice tinged with desperation.

Before Will could react to the intent in the man's voice, Masters dived over the side of the dinghy and disappeared in the dark water. Will leaned over the side of the boat. "Masters!" The man would never be able to swim in the dark, rough seas bobbing the boat. A storm was moving in and the waves would only get worse. "Do you see him?" he said to Katie, above him in the sailboat.

"No, not a sign of him!" She rushed to the other side. "Not over here, either!"

Will climbed into the sailboat and walked the perimeter. When he returned to her side, he said, "He's gone. Just like that."

THIRTY-FIVE

STANDING BESIDE WILL in the bow of the boat with the sea breeze in her face, Katie could forget the terror of the night before. Jennie played with blocks on the deck as the boat rode the crest of the waves toward the bay. She squealed with delight every time a block was knocked over. Lady Carrington sat in a deck chair knitting while Nubbins pounced on her ball of yarn.

"Still no sign of the gold," Will said. "Constable Brown says Bart isn't talking."

"What about Masters?"

"They recovered his body."

Even though he hadn't lived to see it, the news was splashed all over this morning's paper. "So much for sparing his family the pain."

The mynah squawked on his perch. "I still think the bird is giving us a clue," Katie said. "We're going to find the gold today."

His smile lingered on her face. "I hope you're right."

Would his smile always make her heart sing? Since they'd come back from the bay, he hadn't spoken of his love. Maybe her parents had discouraged him too much. Or maybe he'd realized he didn't love her after all. She'd been too shy to bring up the subject. He raised her hand to his lips. Katie's heart caught in her throat.

"We need to talk. Very soon, Katie," he said.

She nodded then looked toward the black rock formation thrusting its head from the sea. Wedding Cake Rock. Waves foamed and receded on its sides. Gulls swooped and dove after the crabs clinging to its rocks. It appeared so inhospitable, she wondered if she'd brought them out on a wild goose chase. "I'm not sure where we can anchor."

Will peered over the side. "Looks shallow here. I'll drop anchor." He threw the anchor over the side. The boat slowed then rocked on the waves. He lowered the dinghy.

Lady Carrington put down her knitting and rose. "I shall get lunch out while you're gone so we can eat when you get back. I can feed the baby to keep her busy."

"It shouldn't take long," Katie said.

Will tossed the shovel and a lantern into the dinghy. He helped her onto the boat and clambered down to join her. She sat in the bow as he rowed them toward the forbidding rock. The boat scraped bottom and he leaped into the water and dragged the dinghy ashore on a flat spot of rock. Katie scrambled out and stood looking at the sea-lashed landscape while he retrieved his tools.

"Well, Miss Detective, where do you suggest we look first?" Will's smile lit his eyes.

Katie shielded her eyes from the sun that pierced beneath the brim of her bonnet. "That's what we call the wedding cake," she said, pointing to the rock that appeared to be a three-tiered cake. "Let's go there and see if we can figure out what the bird is saying." Will's warm clasp kept her from stumbling over the slick rocks. They picked their way through the loose boulders and slick deposits of seaweed to the base of the rock.

"This appears to be the only place where the wedding cake is accessible," she said. "The other avenues are straight up." She no longer cared about her finder's fee but the joy of solving the case and returning the stolen property.

"Paco always says, 'Step away from the cake,' and 'six feet down,'" Will said. He thrust the shovel into the shallow, rocky soil. "I doubt we can even dig in this stuff."

Katie stared at the various boulders and ledges. She'd hoped to find a cave or something similar that would house the gold. The space would need to be large enough to hold stacks and stacks. She stepped forward and scrambled a few feet up onto the side of the lopsided wedding cake. When she looked back toward Will she saw it. A jutting rock prevented spying the opening from below. "Will, a cave," she called. It was to her right and down three feet.

"Wait for me." Will scrambled up the sliding rocks to join her. "You can't see it from below," he said when he saw the slit of the opening. "Wait here."

"Oh no, I insisted we come out. I wish to see it with my own eyes." She slid down after him until they stood at the opening to the cave. The only way in was on her hands and knees.

Will lit the lantern and thrust it into the cave. A golden gleam bounced back at them. Stacks of gold lay in front of Katie's dazzled eyes. "So much gold," she breathed.

"It would have stayed here forever if you hadn't been so sure the bird knew about it," Will said. "Let's get to town and tell the constable to come retrieve it."

"We did it, Will," she said, turning to him. "We found the gold and the ship. Everything."

He touched his fingertips to her chin and stared into her eyes. "It's amazing. And it's largely due to you."

Katie wished he would kiss her, declare himself, but he just rubbed his thumb along her chin, dropped his hand, and turned back toward the boat. Maybe her indecisiveness had cost her his love.

The buggy rolled through Mercy Falls. The town looked different to Katie now. She'd wanted so desperately to *be* someone, to be a person who was looked up to. Now she knew who she really was. Her worth was not in an earthly husband but in her heavenly one. Even if she never married, she would be who God created her to be. She vowed never to forget that.

Will stopped the buggy in front of the constable's office. "I'll be right back. Do you want to come?"

She spied Florence across the street. "There's something else I need to do first," she said. When he disappeared into the building, she climbed down from the buggy and stepped across the street to where the older woman stood examining a dress display in the department store window. She paused. They were all dignified, respectable dresses, nothing like what she was wearing. Could her mother be yearning for something . . . different?

Florence turned and saw her. "Well, you certainly fell on your feet," she said. "I wish I could say the same for myself. I expect the law to arrest me any time. It's a good thing you didn't marry that man."

"God was looking out for me," Katie agreed.

Florence studied her face. "Something has changed about you. You don't seem as angry."

"I wanted to tell you that I forgive you," Katie said. Her hand went to her mouth when she realized what she'd said and that she actually meant the words.

Florence's smooth face didn't change but her eyes did. First there was a slow blink then a gathering of moisture in their blue depths. Her mouth trembled a little. "That's very good of you, Katie," she said, her voice husky. "I did the best I could."

"I know that now. Things could have been much worse." Katie reached out and embraced the woman who bore her. "Thank you for that." The familiar scent of the older woman's lilac sachet brought a wave of nostalgia.

Florence clutched at her and a sob burst from her throat. "I'm sorry for everything. Sorry I tried to get money out of you. I'll do just fine on my own. I always have."

She saw Dora Curry approaching. The woman owned the soda

shop and was the biggest gossip in town. Dora's brows rose when she saw Katie speaking with a woman dressed like Florence, and Katie smiled. "Good afternoon, Dora. I'd like you to meet my real mother, Florence Muller. She is Mama's sister and has been gone from town a long time." She felt rather than saw Florence start with surprise.

Dora's steps faltered a moment but she stopped and extended her hand. "Delighted to meet you, Mrs. Muller. Katie is a wonderful girl. We love her very much."

Katie saw how much Dora meant her kind words and her throat tightened. She'd been so worried about impressing people that she'd failed to see genuine love and respect when it was right in front of her face. "Thank you, Dora," she said, her voice choked. "I realize more and more how very blessed I am to have grown up in this town."

Dora pressed her hand. "I must get back to the shop." She glanced at Florence again. "You have a very special daughter."

"I think so too," Florence said.

Katie saw Will step out of the constable's office. She waved to him, and he started across the street, dodging a fast-moving horse and wagon. "I want you to meet my young man, M–Mother," she said. "He's the handsome one across the street."

Florence's eyes brightened at the term. "I'd be most honored."

Will reached them. His dark eyes went from Katie to Florence. "I do believe this must be your mother, Katie. You look very much like her."

Katie didn't even wince. "Yes, Will. Florence, I'd like you to meet Will Jesperson. He found the pirates and the ship."

Will took Florence's gloved hand. "I'm delighted to meet you, but I don't deserve all the credit. Thanks to Katie, the gold was recovered today as well."

Florence's expression turned flirtatious. She glanced at Katie. "You said your young man was handsome, but I do believe he looks like a pirate himself. No wonder you're quite smitten."

Will grinned. "She said I was handsome? I like the sound of that. I like *smitten* even more."

Heat rushed to Katie's cheeks and she avoided the light dancing in his eyes. "We must go. It's nearly time for tea and I don't want to interrupt Mama in the middle of it."

"Do you think I might come as well?" Florence asked tentatively. "I should like to see my sister."

"I–I'm not sure she would be ready for that without preparation," Katie said. She could only imagine the explosion when the two sisters reunited.

"I think she should come," Will said. "It's time the old feud was laid to rest. They are sisters."

Katie clutched her hands together. "Very well. As long as we are all prepared to face a situation that might not be what we'd hoped."

"I'm ready," Florence said, adjusting her hat. "Thank you for making it possible. Perhaps Inez can forgive me as well."

As they walked back to the buggy, Katie prayed they would find her mother in a forgiving frame of mind. She cast a sidelong glance at Will. If only he would declare himself so she could broach that subject with her parents as well.

THIRTY-SIX

THE SCENT OF chocolate wafers wafted on the breeze when Will helped the ladies down from the buggy. He longed to have Katie to himself, to discuss their future, but there hadn't been the right moment.

Katie led the way to the front door. "Wait here a moment," she told Florence. "I want to prepare them."

Will nodded and escorted the older woman to a rocker on the porch. "We'll be right back," he said. "Enjoy the birdsong and the sound of the sea." He took Katie's hand and they stepped inside and found her mother in the parlor. The tea had not yet been brought out from the kitchen.

Her mother saw her and held out her hand. "Katie, my dear girl. Did you just arrive?"

Katie crossed the plush carpet and took her mother's hand. "Just in time for tea, I hope. I smelled the chocolate wafers."

"You're always in time. I suspected you might come by and instructed Agnes prepare for guests."

"Where is Papa?"

Her mother's eyes filled with tears. "He went to see the constable. To confess."

Katie gasped and turned to Will, groping for him. He stepped to her side and put his hand on her back. He wanted to embrace her but feared offending her mother.

"He'll go to jail," she whispered.

Her mother nodded. "After you were nearly killed, he couldn't stand by and say nothing." Her eyes welled. "I shall never be able to hold my head up here again."

"Your friends know and love you, Mama. I've discovered what God thinks of us is more important than admiration from mere acquaintances."

Her mother dabbed at her eyes with a hanky then glanced at Will. "I thought you might come with her."

Katie sank onto the sofa beside her mother. "I wanted to make sure it was all right to bring him in. You're still not quite well and I didn't wish to overtax you."

Mrs. Russell reached up and took Will's hand. "I want to thank you for saving Katie's life. After she called last night, I lay awake for hours wishing I'd been kinder to you." She shook her head. "I can't believe Bart would behave in such an uncivilized manner. I quite misjudged him. And you, too, young man."

It was a start. When she released his hand, Will shoved them in his pockets. "It's quite all right, Mrs. Russell. Katie is very precious to everyone."

Katie leaned forward and took her mother's hands. "There's another visitor, Mama."

Her mother's smile faded. "You sound so serious, Katie. Who is it?"

"Your sister."

Her mother paled. "Florence is here?"

"On the porch."

Her mother rose and wrung her hands. "How could you bring that woman here?"

"I realized she made mistakes, but she did the best she could, Mama. I think it's time for all of us to sit down and talk. To forgive and forget. I'm thankful she didn't stand in the way of letting me grow up with you and Papa."

"I can't see her," Mrs. Russell said, her voice rising.

"You can and you will," Florence said from the doorway. "You stole my daughter from me, Inez. That's the real problem you don't want to admit."

Bright spots of color appeared on Mrs. Russell's pale cheeks. "I have no idea what you're talking about." She glared at her sister again. "I'd like you to leave, Florence. I told you I never wanted to see you again, and I meant it."

Tears glistened in Florence's eyes. "You stole her, Inez. You had Albert pay me to disappear."

"You took the money," Katie's mother said. "You could have come here and demanded her back but you didn't."

"You'd been waiting for a chance to get your hands on her from the day she was born."

"You didn't deserve her! Always gone with your men friends. Never a thought for what Katie needed. She was better off with us."

"I don't deny that," Florence said. "But you can at least be grateful. Thanks to me you had a daughter you were never able to bear yourself."

Will stepped between the two women. "Let's all sit down and have some tea," he said. "I think we can all agree that Katie turned into a remarkable young woman. The past is over. Let's all move forward." To his relief, the women moved stiffly to separate sides of the room like boxers squaring off. At least the verbal sparring had ended. Katie sat with her mother on the sofa while Florence took the armchair by the fireplace. He decided to play it safe and sit on Katie's other side.

The maid entered with a tray of chocolate wafers and a teapot with teacups. She served them all through a silence as thick as the fog on a cold night. Will balanced the ridiculously tiny teacup on his knee and wondered how he might help mend the breach dividing them.

Florence put down her cup. "No one can ever say I lacked courage, so I'll say it, Inez. I'm sorry. I've made some poor choices in my life, but it was my life to ruin. Not yours."

Mrs. Russell said nothing at first. She sipped her tea. "Mama?" Katie said, her voice encouraging. "I forgive her. I want you to do the same."

"Leave us, Katie," Mrs. Russell said finally. "I wish to speak to my sister in private. Take your young man for a walk. Show him the azalea garden."

Katie put down her tea. "Very well." She glanced at Will.

He rose and extended his hand. She took it and rose from the sofa. "Call us when you are ready." She led him down the hall to the back porch and out into the garden. The azaleas were in bloom. Her destination was a stone bench in the middle of the garden. "I hope they don't come to blows," she said when they reached the bucolic spot.

He kept hold of her hand. "I think they'll work it out. They both care about you." How did he bring up the subject of their future? Just launch into it or ease up to it gradually? He decided to take his cue from her. If she didn't care for him, he'd fade into the background and do whatever made her happy.

❧

Hummingbirds darted from red blossoms. Katie plucked a white azalea bloom and caressed the silken petals. She couldn't look at Will. He'd said nothing and there had been ample opportunity.

She plucked the blossoms. *He loves me. He loves me not. He loves me. He loves me not. He loves me.*

"Katie, are we going to talk about us?"

She hardly dared to raise her gaze to meet his. He looked so handsome in his white shirt and black pants. His dark hair gleamed in the sunlight. "Is there an 'us,' Will?" she asked.

"I've told you how I feel. Several times. You've skirted the subject. Is it that you don't think I have the means to provide for you?"

She smiled. "Since last night, I've realized that only God can provide for me in the end. Anything we have is from his hand. This life is temporary, and I was too focused on the here and now."

"I see peace in your eyes," he said, taking her hand. He tossed the remains of the flower to the grass.

"It's about time, don't you think?" She clutched his fingers. "I love you, Will. I didn't want to say it because I was afraid, but I've loved you for a long time."

His black eyes lit with joy. He raised her hand to his lips and pressed them to her palm. "What if I tell you that we're moving to Texas to take a lighthouse there?"

"I'll go wherever you go," she said, keeping her voice steady even though her heart sank within her.

"What if I want to move to Chicago to work with the Weather Bureau?"

"I think you'll have to buy me some new clothes to deal with the cold," she said.

His grin widened. "What if I tell you I'm staying in Mercy Falls?"

She just barely managed not to squeal when she saw the assurance in his eyes. "Really?" she whispered.

He nodded. "The new Weather Bureau has asked me to provide them with data from the coast. It doesn't pay much, but it's a nice supplement to my salary as lightkeeper." He leaned over and kissed her nose. "Your parents will be able to live on our reward money."

"You wouldn't mind? By rights, it is ours."

"I'll provide for my own wife," he said. "I rather like the sound of the word *wife*."

Her pulse stammered at the smoldering passion in his eyes. She leaned forward and brushed her lips across his. He slipped his arm around her, and in the next moment, she found herself on his lap. His kiss intensified and she wound her arms around his neck and kissed him back with every bit of love she'd longed to express. His hands took the hat from her head and removed the pins from her hair until it all lay on her shoulders. She knew she should object. Her mother would be quite horrified when she went inside in obvious disarray, but she didn't care as she kissed him back.

He suddenly jerked his mouth from hers and stared into her eyes. "We need to slow down or I fear I might lose my head," he said.

She leaned her head against his chest and heard its wild pounding that matched the beat in her own. Gulping in air, she finally lifted her chin and stared into his tender eyes. "So do I get to help you tend the lamps and rescue people?"

"I don't think I can keep you safely in the parlor now that you've learned to let your adventurous side go," he said. "Jennie will learn early to explore her world."

Katie's elation faded. "What about Jennie? What if Bart's parents want her?"

He shook his head. "I saw them in the constable's office and they were quick to take me up on my offer to keep her. They promised to have the papers drawn up quickly if I would keep quiet about her real parentage."

"So she is ours?"

"She is indeed. We shall see about adding some brothers and sisters for her."

Heat ran up her neck at the expression in his eyes. Though things were a bit uncertain right now, she realized she rather liked the unknown. One thing was quite sure, life with her lightkeeper would shine as bright as his Fresnel lens. "I think I should have another kiss," she said, pulling his head down to hers. "A budding bride needs the practice."

ACKNOWLEDGMENTS

IT IS SUCH a privilege to do another project with my wonderful Thomas Nelson family. Publisher Allen Arnold (I call him Superman) is so passionate about fiction and he lights up a room when he enters it. Senior Acquisitions Editor Ami McConnell (my friend and cheerleader) has an eye for character and theme like no one I know. I crave her analytical eye! It was her influence that encouraged me to write a historical romantic mystery, and I'm glad she pushed me a bit! Marketing Manager Jennifer Deshler brings both friendship and fabulous marketing ideas to the table. Publicist Katie Bond is always willing to listen to my harebrained ideas. Fabulous cover guru Kristen Vasgaard (you *so* rock!) works hard to create the perfect cover—and does it. And of course I can't forget my other friends who are all part of my amazing fiction family: Natalie Hanemann, Amanda Bostic, Becky Monds, Ashley Schneider, Andrea Lucado, Heather McCoullough, Chris Long, and Kathy Carabajal. I wish I could name all the great folks who work on selling my books through different venues at Thomas Nelson. You are my dream team! Hearing "well done" from you all is my motivation every day.

My agent, Karen Solem, has helped shaped my career in many ways, and that includes kicking an idea to the curb when necessary. Thanks, Karen, you're the best!

This was my first opportunity to work with Lisa Tawn Bergren, and it was a wonderful experience. I was initially a little intimidated because Lisa is such an accomplished novelist in her own right. Her expertise with historical settings (her latest books are *Breathe, Sing,* and *Claim*) was a great asset. Thanks so much, Lisa!

Writing can be a lonely business, but God has blessed me with great writing friends and critique partners. Hannah Alexander (Cheryl Hodde), Kristin Billerbeck, Diann Hunt, and Denise Hunter make up the Girls Write Out squad (*www.GirlsWriteOut.blogspot.com*). I couldn't make it through a day without my peeps! Thanks to all of you for the work you do on my behalf, and for your friendship.

I'm so grateful for my husband, Dave, who carts me around from city to city, washes towels, and chases down dinner without complaint. Thanks, honey! I couldn't do anything without you. My kids—Dave, Kara (and now Donna and Mark)—and my grandsons, James and Jorden Packer, love and support me in every way possible. Love you guys! Donna and Dave brought me the delight of my life—our little granddaughter, Alexa! Though I tried my best to emulate her cuteness in the scenes with Jennie, I'm sure I failed!

Most importantly, I give my thanks to God, who has opened such amazing doors for me and makes the journey a golden one.

Reading Group Guide

1. Have you ever discovered something about a loved one that had been so hidden you didn't believe it at first? How did this make you feel?

2. Will believed in taking responsibility for our actions. If his brother wouldn't do it, Will would. What did you think about that? Was he right?

3. Katie didn't want anyone to know of her real background. What are the advantages and disadvantages of letting out the truth in our lives?

4. Katie's feelings for Will were revealed when she forgot her hat. Actions speak loudly. What is the most loving thing someone can do for you?

5. Stepping into criminal activity can happen in small steps. What steps led to Katie's father getting involved in something criminal? What should he have done to stop?

6. Katie didn't like surprises. Do you like them or do they frighten you the way they did Katie? Why do you feel this way?

7. Have you ever been torn between duty and love? How do you decide the right course of action?

8. Katie had a plan for her life. How can you tell if your plans parallel God's plans?

9. Do you crave adventure or for the days to flow by evenly? What can you do to step outside of your comfort zone?

10. Katie realized that God was the one who was her ultimate Provider and this life is temporary. Do you hold to things here too tightly? What can you do to begin to have an eternal perspective?

THE
LIGHTKEEPER'S
BALL

For Ami

ONE

THE NEW YORK brownstone was just half a block down from the Astor mansion on Fifth Avenue, the most prestigious address in the country. The carriage, monogrammed with the Stewart emblem, rattled through the iron gates and came to a halt in front of the ornate doors. Assisted by the doorman, Olivia Stewart descended and rushed for the steps of her home. She was late for tea, and her mother would be furious. Mrs. Astor herself had agreed to join them today.

Olivia handed her hat to the maid, who opened the door. "They're in the drawing room, Miss Olivia," Goldia whispered. "Your mama is ready to pace the floor."

Olivia patted at her hair, straightened her shoulders, and pinned a smile in place as she forced her stride to a ladylike stroll to join the other women. Two women turned to face her as she entered: her mother and Mrs. Astor. They wore identical expressions of disapproval.

"Olivia, there you are," her mother said. "Sit down before your tea gets cold."

Olivia pulled off her gloves as she settled into the Queen Anne chair beside Mrs. Astor. "I apologize for my tardiness," she said. "A lorry filled with tomatoes overturned in the street, and my driver couldn't get around it."

Mrs. Astor's face cleared. "Of course, my dear." She sipped her tea from the delicate blue-and-white china. "Your dear mother and I were just discussing your prospects. It's time you married."

Oh dear. She'd hoped to engage in light conversation that had nothing to do with the fact that she was twenty-five and still unmarried. Her unmarried state distressed her if she let it, but every man her father brought to her wanted only her status. She doubted any of them had ever looked into her soul. "I'm honored you would care about my marital status, Mrs. Astor," Olivia said.

"Mrs. Astor wants to hold a ball in your honor, Olivia," her mother gushed. "She has a distant cousin coming to town whom she wants you to meet."

Mrs. Astor nodded. "I believe you and Matthew would suit. He owns property just down the street."

Olivia didn't mistake the reference to the man's money. Wealth would be sure to impact her mother. She opened her mouth to ask if the man was her age, then closed it at the warning glint in her mother's eyes.

"He's been widowed for fifteen years and is long overdue for a suitable wife," Mrs. Astor said.

Olivia barely suppressed a sigh. So he was another of the decrepit gentlemen who showed up from time to time. "You're very kind," she said.

"He's most suitable," her mother said. "*Most* suitable."

Olivia caught the implication. They spent the next half hour discussing the date and the location. She tried to enter into the conversation with interest, but all she could do was imagine some gray-whiskered blue blood dancing her around the ballroom. She stifled a sigh of relief when Mrs. Astor took her leave and called for her carriage.

"I'll be happy when you're settled, Olivia," her mother said when they returned to the drawing room. "Mrs. Astor is most kind."

"She is indeed." Olivia pleated her skirt with her fingers. "Do you ever wish you could go somewhere incognito, Mother? Where no one has expectations of you because you are a Stewart?"

Her mother put down her saucer with a clatter. "Whatever are you babbling about, my dear?"

"Haven't you noticed that people look at us differently because we're Stewarts? How is a man ever to love me for myself when all he sees is what my name can gain him? Men never see inside to the real me. They notice only that I'm a Stewart."

"Have you been reading those novels again?" Her mother sniffed and narrowed her gaze on Olivia. "Marriage is about making suitable connections. You owe it to your future children to consider the life you give them. Love comes from respect. I would find it quite difficult to respect someone who didn't have the gumption to make his way in the world. Besides, we *need* you to marry well. You're twenty-five years old and I've indulged your romantic notions long enough. Heaven knows your sister's marriage isn't what I had in mind, essential though it may be. Someone has to keep the family name in good standing."

Olivia knew what her duty demanded, but she didn't have to like it. "Do all the suitable men have to be in their dotage?"

Her mother's eyes sparked fire, but before she spoke, Goldia appeared in the doorway. "Mr. Bennett is here, Mrs. Stewart."

Olivia straightened in her chair. "Show him in. He'll have news of Eleanor."

Bennett appeared in the doorway moments later. He shouldn't have been imposing. He stood only five foot three in his shoes, which were always freshly polished. He was slim, nearly gaunt, with a patrician nose and obsidian eyes. He'd always reminded Olivia of a snake about to strike. His expression never betrayed any emotion, and today was no exception. She'd never understood why her father entertained an acquaintance with the man, let alone desired their families to be joined.

"Mr. Bennett." She rose and extended her hand and tried not to flinch as he brushed his lips across it.

"Miss Olivia," he said, releasing her hand. He moved to her mother's chair and bowed over her extended hand.

Olivia sank back into her chair. "What do you hear of my sister? I have received no answer to any of my letters."

He took a seat, steepled his fingers, and leaned forward. "That's the reason for our meeting today. I fear I have bad news to impart."

Her pulse thumped erratically against her rib cage. She wet her lips and drew in a deep breath. "What news of Eleanor?" How bad could it be? Eleanor had gone to marry Harrison, a man she hardly knew. But she was in love with the idea of the Wild West, and therefore more than happy to marry the son of her father's business partner.

He never blinked. "I shall just have to blurt it out then. I'm sorry to inform you that Eleanor is dead."

Her mother moaned. Olivia stared at him. "I don't believe it," she said.

"I know, it's a shock."

There must have been some mistake. She searched his face for some clue that this was a jest. "What happened?"

He didn't hold her gaze. "She drowned."

"How?"

"No one knows. I'm sorry."

Her mother stood and swayed. "What are you saying?" Her voice rose in a shriek. "Eleanor can't be dead! Are you quite mad?"

He stood and took her arm. "I suggest you lie down, Mrs. Stewart. You're quite pale."

Her mother put her hands to her cheeks. "Tell me it isn't true," she begged. Then she keeled over in a dead faint.

⚜

Harrison Bennett tugged on his tie, glanced at his shoes to make sure no speck of dirt marred their perfection, then disembarked from his motorcar in front of the mansion. The vehicle had rolled up Nob Hill much too quickly for him to gather his courage to face the party. Electric lights pushed back the darkness from the curving brick driveway to the porch with its impressive white pillars. Doormen flanked the double doors at the entry. Through the large windows, he saw the ballroom. Ladies in luxurious gowns and gentlemen in tuxedos danced under glittering chandeliers, and their laughter tinkled on the wind.

His valet, Eugene, exited behind him. "I'll wait in the kitchen, sir."

Harrison adjusted his hat and strode with all the confidence he could muster to the front door. "Mr. Harrison Bennett," he said to the doorman.

The man scanned the paper in his hand. "Welcome, Mr. Bennett. Mr. Rothschild is in the ballroom."

Harrison thanked him and stepped into the opulent hall papered in gold foil. He went in the direction of the voices with a sense of purpose. This night could change his future. He glanced around the enormous ballroom, and he recognized no one among the glittering gowns and expensive suits. In subtle ways, these nobs would try to keep him in his place. It would take all his gumption not to let them. It was a miracle he'd received an invitation. Only the very wealthy or titled were invited to the Rothschilds' annual ball in San Francisco. Harrison was determined to do whatever was necessary to secure the contract inside his coat pocket.

A young woman in an evening gown fluttered her lashes at him over the top of her fan. When she lowered it, she approached with a coaxing smile on her lips. "Mr. Bennett, I'd hoped to see you here tonight."

He struggled to remember her name. Miss Kessler. She'd made her interest in him known at Eleanor's funeral. Hardly a suitable time. He took her gloved hand and bowed over it. "Miss Kessler. I wasn't expecting to see you here."

"I came when I heard you were on the guest list."

He ignored her brazen remark. "It's good to see you again. I have some business to attend to. Perhaps later?"

Her eyes darkened and she withdrew her hand. "I shall watch for you," she said.

And he'd do the same, with the intent to avoid her. "If you'll excuse me." He didn't wait for an answer but strolled through the crowd. He finally spied his host standing in front of a marble fireplace. A flame danced in the eight-foot hearth. Harrison stepped through the crowd to join the four men clustered around the wealthy Rothschild.

The man closest to Harrison was in his fifties and had a curling mustache. "They'll never get that amendment ratified," he said. "An income tax! It's quite ridiculous to expect us to pay something so outrageous."

A younger man in a gray suit shook his head. "If it means better roads, I'll gladly write them a check. The potholes outside of town ruined my front axles."

"We can take care of our own roads," Rothschild said. "I have no need of the government in my affairs. At least until we're all using flying machines." He snickered, then glanced at Harrison. "You look familiar, young man. Have we met?"

Flying machines. Maybe this meeting was something God had arranged. Harrison thrust out his hand. "Harrison Bennett."

"Claude's son?"

Was that distaste in the twist of Rothschild's mouth? Harrison put confidence into his grip. "Yes, sir."

"How is your father?"

"Quite well. He's back in New York by now."

"I heard about your fiancée's death. I'm sorry for your loss."

Harrison managed not to wince. "Thank you." He pushed away his memories of that terrible day, the day he'd seen Eleanor Stewart for what she really was.

"Your father was most insistent I meet you. He seems to think you have a business proposition I might be interested in."

Harrison smiled and began to tell the men of the new diamond mines that Bennett and Bennett had found in Africa. A mere week after Mr. Stewart's passing, Mr. Bennett had renamed the venture to include Harrison. An hour later, he had appointments set up with three of the men as possible investors. His father would be pleased.

Harrison smiled and retraced his steps to the front door but was waylaid by four women in brightly colored silk. They swooped around him, and Miss Kessler took him by the hand and led him to a quiet corner.

"Let's not talk about anything boring like work," she said, her blue eyes sparkling. "Tell me what you love to do most."

He glanced at the other women clustered around. "I'm building an aeroplane. I'd like to have it in the air by the time earth passes through the tail of Halley's Comet."

She gasped. "Do you have a death wish, Mr. Bennett? You would be breathing the poisonous fumes directly. No one even knows if the earth will survive this."

He'd heard this before. "The scientists I've discussed this with believe we shall be just fine," Harrison said.

"I assume you've purchased comet pills?" the blonde closest to him said.

"I have no fear."

The brunette in red silk smiled. "If man were meant to fly, God would have given him wings. Or so I've heard the minister say."

He finally placed the brunette. Her uncle was Rothschild. No wonder she had such contempt for Harrison's tone. All the nobs cared for were trains and ships. "It's just a matter of perfecting the machine," Harrison said. "Someday aeroplanes will be the main mode of transcontinental transportation."

The brunette laughed. "Transcontinental? My uncle would call it balderdash."

He glanced at his pocket watch without replying. "I fear I must leave you lovely ladies. Thank you for the conversation."

He found Eugene in the kitchen and beckoned to his valet.

Eugene put down his coffee cup and followed. "You didn't stay long, sir," he said. "Is everything all right?"

Harrison stalked out the door and toward the car. "Are there no visionaries left in the country?"

Eugene followed a step behind. "You spoke of your flying machine?"

"The world is changing, Eugene, right under their noses—and they don't see it."

Eugene opened the door for Harrison. "You will show them the future, sir."

He set his jaw. "I shall indeed."

"I have a small savings set aside, Mr. Bennett. I'd like to invest in your company. With your permission, of course."

Eugene's trust bolstered Harrison's determination. "I'd be honored to partner with you, Eugene. We are going to change the world."

TWO

BIRDS SANG IN the shrubs that surrounded the tiny courtyard. Olivia hadn't thought her mother would be up to eating dinner, but once the matron was revived, she had taken charge again. Mr. Bennett joined them for the meal on the terrace, but there was little conversation after the servants dished up the soup.

Olivia fingered the locket with her sister's picture in it and wished she would awaken and find this all a bad dream. *I don't believe it.* She must have spoken, because Mr. Bennett's dark eyes were on her face when she put down her soupspoon.

"Eleanor was buried in Mercy Falls, California, yesterday. Those are the facts, Miss Olivia."

Did he not even care? His dark eyes held no emotion. "With none of her family there to mourn her?" she choked out. "Why were we not informed of her death before now?" She clutched her skirt in her fists.

"I asked Harrison to leave the conveyance of the news to me. In any event, you could not have arrived before her interment. I didn't wish you to receive this news via a telephone call or a telegram."

"What were the circumstances of her drowning? Did a boat capsize?"

He shrugged. "It appears she went swimming alone."

"That's impossible! Eleanor hated the water. She has never gone swimming in her life."

"Olivia, stop your interrogation at once," her mother said. "Nothing will bring your sister back to us." Her mother took a dainty spoonful of soup. "It is through no fault of ours that the marriage will not take place, Mr. Bennett. I expect you to uphold your part of the arrangement and sign the papers transferring fifty percent of the new mine to us."

Her mother's audacity dried Olivia's welling tears. She waited to see how Mr. Bennett would respond.

Mr. Bennett stirred sugar into his tea, then put his spoon back on the saucer. "I'm afraid that's impossible, Mrs. Stewart. It's too bad your husband's dearest wish is unable to be fulfilled." He pursed his thin lips. "There will be no property transferred without a wedding."

Her mother's smile was ingratiating. She glanced from Mr. Bennett to Olivia. "Well then, I still have a marriageable daughter. Without a blue-blooded wife, Harrison will always be merely nouveau riche and outside the best society."

The man nodded. "The agreement between your husband and I was that the two families be joined. I do not care how that is achieved. One daughter is as good as the next."

"Your son can't possibly change his affections so hastily," Olivia said.

The man shrugged his slim shoulders. His mustache twitched. "He'd barely met Eleanor before her death. He is amenable to doing what is best for his family. He will still be agreeable."

Olivia hardly knew what to say, how to stop this insane proposal. She knew her mother was stressed. Six months ago her father had died when the tunnels of a newly acquired African diamond mine collapsed on him. His body was never recovered, nor were his financial investments, which had been exhausted along with the old mines. Time since then had seemed an eternity of watching pennies and struggling to pay the servants while keeping whispers of their change in fortune secret from the society in which they moved. A well-made marriage would give Olivia the power to change their circumstances. But the cost was so high.

Mr. Bennett's gaze flickered back to her mother. A cold smile lifted his lips. "You are willing to send Olivia to marry Harrison?"

"It is what my husband wished. I assume you will draw up the papers to give me a share of the mine?" She dabbed her lips again. "I still don't quite understand what happened to the first mine. My husband had such high hopes for it."

Mr. Bennett shrugged. "Mines play out, as this one did. The new black-diamond mine has many years of production ahead of it. An inheritance from my late grandfather is what enabled me to purchase it. As I've mentioned, Mr. Stewart's agreement to join the families was his contribution to the investment. You'll never want for anything."

She was being sold off like a piece of jewelry at an auction. Olivia leaped to her feet. "No one has asked me if I am willing." She rushed across the flagstone and jerked open the door that led into the house. Her mother called after her, but Olivia ignored the summons and raced up the steps to her room, where she collapsed onto her bed.

Tears scalded her cheeks, and she punched her pillow. "I *won't* marry him! I won't!" she said fiercely to the china doll in the middle of the bed. She sat up and rubbed her wet face with the back of her hand. How would she get out of this?

She noticed the mail on her bed table, and the slanted writing on the top envelope made her breath catch in her throat. It almost looked like Eleanor's bold cursive. She picked it up, her pulse hammering. It *was* Eleanor's handwriting. Olivia ripped open the envelope and glanced at the date. A week ago. She must have written it just before she died.

The letter was short and to the point.

My dearest sister, Olivia,

    I am in dire straits and I need you to come to me at once. I don't know where else to turn. Please don't think it my usual exaggeration when I say I fear for my future, and it will be Harrison's fault. Come at once. Tell no one.

Your loving sister,
Eleanor

Harrison's fault? What could she mean? Olivia remembered the last time she'd seen her sister. Eleanor had been dancing around her bedroom in a new blue gown. She'd been so delighted in the adventure of moving clear across the country. Eleanor had been a shooting star in Olivia's life. How could she ignore this plea, even from the grave?

Could Eleanor have been murdered?

"I shall find out," she said to the doll staring at her. "If Harrison is responsible for her death, I shall have him brought to justice."

She rose and went downstairs to make a proposal to her mother. Bennett had left, and her mother was still on the terrace.

"Mr. Bennett is gone?" Olivia asked.

"He left after your most childish outburst." Her mother rubbed her forehead.

"A migraine?" When her mother nodded, Olivia took a deep breath. "I'll go to Mercy Falls." She held up her hand when her mother opened her mouth. "But only on one condition. Don't tell Mr. Bennett just yet. I want to see if Harrison and I will suit first."

Her mother's smile faded. "And if you don't?"

"Then I'll come home. I want until summer to decide. Surely you can get by for that long. Go stay with Mrs. Astor. She would be glad to welcome you for the season."

Her mother shifted in her chair. "I imagine she would. I could close the house and save that expense." She studied Olivia's face. "But I suspect there is something you are not telling me, my dear."

It was better for her mother not to know of Eleanor's plea. If Mother knew of the danger, she would forbid Olivia to go. "I'll be fine."

Her mother sighed. "If only I'd borne your father a son, I would not be in this situation. We would have a man to lean on, but I have only you now. I fear I have no choice but to agree to this harebrained scheme. Otherwise you will reject the marriage outright, correct?"

Olivia folded her hands in her lap and nodded. Her mother leaned back in her chair. "Very well. I hope you know what you're doing," her mother said. "If you refuse Harrison, we'll be unable to keep our change of fortune secret any longer. You'll be forced to accept the first swell who offers for you."

Olivia could only pray for divine providence.

⌁⌁⌁

Olivia leaned on the ship's railing and watched the dark landscape slide past. She had traveled across the country in Mrs. Astor's private train car. When Olivia and Goldia reached San Francisco, they caught the packet to Mercy Falls, though what she really wanted was to reboard the train and go home. Everything in this faraway land was alien to her, from the wild Pacific Ocean foaming on the rocks to the rough stevedores working at the wharf.

They were nearly to Mercy Falls, and she wanted nothing more than to see the buildings of New York instead of the towering trees of this thickly forested coastline. The fog curling from the base of the trees and over the whitecaps made her shudder.

She sighed and toyed with the strings of her hat. She already missed home, though there would be much to see and do here. For the first time she would see the manor house her father had built in this town four years ago. It was a way of being closer to him.

"Are you frightened, Miss Olivia?" Goldia asked, joining her at the rail.

She shook her head. "I've an idea though, Goldia. I'm going to be known here as Lady Devonworth."

"I thought you hated using your title."

"I do. But I'd rather not be known as Olivia Stewart. Harrison will be on his guard if he knows I'm in town. With a different name, I can observe him unhindered. I boarded this ship as Lady Devonworth, so please remember not to call me Miss Olivia."

Goldia's lips pursed. "I don't like it, miss. If someone really harmed Miss Eleanor, you could be in danger."

To Olivia, the plan seemed straightforward. Her maid's vapors were quite silly. "Not if I'm able to keep my identity a secret. I'll find out what happened and bring the culprit to justice."

"Well, I'm scared," the girl said. Olivia turned away from the waters to face her.

Was that a man in the shadows? Olivia squinted into the darkness. "Who's there?" she called. No answer came, but a cat strolled into the wash of light, and she relaxed. "It's so damp here. Could you fetch my shawl?" she asked her maid.

Goldia nodded and hurried away. The fog quickly muffled the sound of her footsteps. Olivia stared at the lighthouse twinkling in the distance. Everything would change soon, and she would have to assume a role.

A sound came behind her, and she assumed it was Goldia until she smelled a man's cologne. She half turned at the furtive, sliding noise, but before she could see who was joining her, hard hands seized her from behind. The man's breath smelled of mint. She flailed at the assailant, but her fists struck only air. Her slippers slid along the polished deck, and the next moment she found herself bent over the railing, facing the turbulent water. The hard rail dug into her stomach and stole her breath. She tried to scream, but panic closed her throat as her balance tipped toward the water and away from the boat. With a last push from her assailant, she was plunging into the waves with her arms pinwheeling.

Cold water closed over her head. She fought the pull of the sea on her soaked skirt. A current took her deeper. Panicked, she kicked toward where she thought the surface was, though there was no light to guide her. Her head broke through, and she drew in the sweetest breath she'd ever known before the waves grabbed her. Before she went under again, she saw a light winking to her right. With her lungs full of air, she groped at her laces. Before she managed to get her boots off, her chest began to burn with the need to breathe. With that weight removed, she was able to rocket back to the surface. Gasping, she dog-paddled in the waves. She gulped in air, gathered her strength, then struck out toward the blinking light.

Her arms and legs ached as she fought the current. A cramp struck her calf and she cried out. Her head went under the waves and she gulped salty water. She was going to drown, just like her sister. She struggled for the surface.

A hand grabbed her arm and yanked her up, pulling her out of the depths. Hands flipped her onto her back, then a rough palm cupped her chin. The next thing she knew she was being towed toward shore.

Her bottom hit sand. She smelled kelp and felt seaweed around her waist. Then arms dragged her forward until she lay across hard thighs. She gagged up seawater.

"Are you all right?" a deep voice asked. The man sat her up.

She blinked water out of her eyes and realized she was still sitting on his lap. His hands gripped her forearms.

Water dripped from his dark hair down his face, and his breathing was as ragged as hers. "Were you trying to kill yourself?" he demanded.

"Someone pushed me," she said. "A man. You were on the ship?"

"I didn't see anyone push you." His tone indicated he doubted her words. "I heard you scream and I ran to the railing."

"You jumped in to save me?"

He shrugged. "I could hardly do anything else. It was clear you were not going to make it to shore by yourself."

Something about him was familiar, but it was too dark to make out much more than the tilt of his head and his dark hair and eyes. She struggled to stand. "Thank you," she said. "You can let me up now."

He moved her off his lap onto the shore, then stood and offered her a hand. She allowed him to help her up. "Is that the lighthouse?" she asked, pointing toward the beacon on the hill.

"Yes, I'll get help. Stay here." He jogged off into the darkness.

She wasn't about to sit and wait when someone had just tried to kill her, but he didn't answer when she called out after him. He was quick, and her voice was too raw and thin from the salt water to be heard over the waves. She walked on wobbly legs toward the lighthouse.

❧

Harrison pounded on the door to the lighthouse and Will Jesperson answered the summons. Harrison had been friends with the light-keeper ever since Will moved to town, and the keeper was quick to grab a lantern and a blanket.

"The woman says she was deliberately thrown overboard?" Will asked as they picked their way back down the rocky slope.

"That's what she said."

"You believe her?"

Harrison paused to catch his breath as Will swept the light around the area. "I saw her in the water and thought she might have jumped, but she seemed panicked. She's lucky I was there."

"Her skirts might have dragged her down," Will agreed.

Harrison frowned and stared at the landscape. "I know this is where I left her. I told her to wait here."

"Maybe she went to the dock to try to rendezvous with her family. Let's look there."

Harrison went in the direction of the stevedores' shouts as they carried crates from the ship that had just docked. "Why would she run off?"

"She didn't know you. Not likely to obey the orders of a stranger." Will held the lantern aloft, but the yellow glow revealed nothing but a few crabs scuttling out of the way.

What might have made her leave? He didn't like the direction his thoughts led. What if she really had been attacked? "You suppose whoever attacked her came back?" Harrison asked.

"The thought crossed my mind too. It's worrisome," Will said.

They reached the quay. Harrison stopped several men alighting from the ferry and explained what had happened. Two men pushed a dinghy into the waves and shoved off. Harrison prayed they didn't find the pretty lady's body.

It took Olivia much longer than she anticipated to make it to the brick residence attached to the light tower. She was shaking and winded by the time she reached the top, probably because she had been unable to find a path and climbed awkwardly over rocks instead. She heard a shout in the distance and realized the man had gone back another way to find her. He and someone else were shouting for her, but she didn't have the strength to answer them.

Her arm shook as she raised her fist and pounded on the door. Inside, a child squealed, and the happy sound put her at ease.

The door opened, and a pretty brunette stood wiping floury hands on an apron. A little girl of about three stood by her feet. The woman's smile faded as she registered Olivia's condition. "You're soaking wet! Come in." She stepped aside.

Olivia stepped into the welcoming warmth of the hall. Some kind of beef dish was on the stove for dinner, and her stomach gave a rumble at the aroma of onions and tomatoes. She shivered as the young woman led her to the fire in the parlor. The little girl scampered after them.

The woman draped a throw around Olivia's shoulders. "Was there a shipwreck? Will was called out to help a victim."

"No, no, there was a man." Olivia clutched the warmth of the wool to her. "H-He threw me overboard." It had really happened, hadn't it? Some man had tried to kill her and nearly succeeded.

The other woman gasped. "Oh my dear! We need to get you out of those wet clothes. We're of a similar build. Let me get you a towel. You stay by the fire." She rushed from the room and her feet pounded up the stairs.

Olivia's eyes burned, and she fought the sting of tears, aware it was a reaction to her near drowning. She managed to smile down at the little girl who regarded her with big, dark eyes. "Might I ask your name, little one? You're very cute."

"I'm Jennie," the little one said, reaching a chubby hand to Olivia's wet skirt.

The other woman's footsteps came back down the stairs, and she entered the parlor with a cotton dress and a towel slung across her arm. "I took the liberty of bringing you a change of clothing. Here you are. I'll take Jennie into the kitchen with me. No one will disturb you while you change."

The strength ran out of Olivia's legs and she nearly fell. "I-I think I shall need your assistance," she said.

"Of course." The young woman stepped behind Olivia and released the laces on the back. "What's your name?"

"I'm Olivia Stewart." Too late she realized she'd revealed her true identity.

"I'm Katie Jesperson. My husband is the lightkeeper here." She helped Olivia step out of her ruined clothes, then dropped a clean dress over her head.

The warmth of the fabric enveloped her, and Olivia let out a sigh. "I'm so cold," she said.

"Sit by the fire." Katie pushed her gently into the folds of an overstuffed chair. "Let me dry your hair." She took out what pins hadn't been removed by the sea until the heavy dark locks hung on Olivia's shoulders. Katie toweled it briskly. "Your hair is so lovely."

"Thank you." Shuddering, Olivia sank back into the warmth of the chair. Katie put down the towel, then tucked a quilt around Olivia. "I shall call the constable as soon as we get you settled. What was the name of your ship? Do you have companions who will be worried about you?"

"It's the *Atlantis*. My maid will be quite upset when she can't find me."

"I'll make sure she is informed of your whereabouts when Will gets back."

Who would have thrown her overboard? She hadn't spoken to anyone but Goldia. When the cat at her feet meowed, she remembered the cat on the ship and the shadowy figure of a man she thought she'd seen. What if someone had overheard her talking to Goldia and realized she was really Olivia Stewart? Could the man have had something to do with Eleanor's death? Maybe it was even Harrison. And the man who had rescued her. He'd come from the ship. Had he seen something in spite of his statement to the contrary?

Olivia reached toward Katie as she started for the door. "I'm registered as Lady Devonworth. May I ask you not to mention the name Olivia Stewart to anyone?"

Katie stopped and stared. "I don't understand."

Olivia hardly knew where to begin. "I'd rather people know me by my formal title," she said. "My father was a duke who came to New York in his twenties."

Katie frowned. "Stewart. Are you related to Eleanor Stewart?"

Olivia couldn't lie. Not when the woman had been so kind. "She was my sister. But no one must know that. Not yet."

Katie bit her lip. "I don't like deception."

"Please, only for a little while," Olivia begged. "I need to find out who wants me dead. I want to find out what happened to Eleanor. What did you hear of her death?"

"I know only that she drowned while swimming."

Olivia shook her head. "Eleanor was terrified of the water. She would never have put one toe in the ocean."

Katie's eyes widened. "You fear she was murdered?"

Murder. Such an ugly word. Olivia nodded. "I know of no other explanation."

"She was not herself the week before she died. Somber and unhappy. Could she have done away with herself?"

"Not Eleanor! And even if I could be persuaded of such a fate for her, she would not have drowned herself. Not with her overwhelming fear of water."

"Someone tried to harm you. I must admit that bolsters your suspicions. You must tell the constable."

"Not yet," Olivia said. "I don't want to run the risk of anyone finding out I'm investigating. We can tell him of the attack, but he only needs to know my formal title. I intend to keep it that way for now."

"Very well. But may I tell my husband?"

Olivia wanted to ask her to keep it to herself, but she could hardly come between a man and his wife. "He will keep it to himself?"

"Of course. Will is a man of honor."

"Very well." At least she'd found a friend and ally her first day in Mercy Falls.

THREE

HARRISON STRODE ALONG the quay under the glow from the street lamps. The *Atlantis* bobbed offshore. Several dinghies plied the waters with lanterns, but he heard no shouts of discovery. The wind freshened and brought the scent of rain to his nose. The first drops fell moments later.

Will glanced at him. "It's been more than an hour."

Rain began to patter harder, and Harrison adjusted his hat to keep the moisture off his face. "Now that she's missing, I'm beginning to rethink her account. Maybe someone really did toss her into the sea."

"You told the constable her story?"

"Yes. He seemed to give it as little credence as I first did."

Will shrugged. "She'll turn up sooner or later. Nothing we can do with the storm coming in. Come to the house for coffee. Katie made cookies this afternoon. And fresh bread."

Going back to the empty manor house didn't appeal. Since Eleanor's death, Harrison found himself seeking out friends. Being with Will and Katie held more allure than he could resist. "My thanks. If you're sure I wouldn't be intruding."

"You're one of Katie's favorite people. And Jennie's. My daughter will be in your lap before you can take your first bite of cookie."

Harrison's spirits lifted at the thought of the little girl. She'd taken a liking to him last summer. Will and Katie had thrown a party on their anniversary and the whole town had come out for it. Jennie had attached herself to his leg all evening.

He'd thought he might have a little one of his own in the next year. Until he saw Eleanor's true nature.

He noticed a captain approaching along the shore with another sailor and hailed them. "Are you in charge of this ship?" he asked, gesturing to the floating hulk in the waves.

"Yes," the man said.

"I pulled the woman out of the sea. What have you heard?"

The captain tipped his hat back on his forehead. "I didn't see her go overboard, but First Officer Nettles here did. Nettles, tell this man what you saw."

The other man was about forty. Slim, with a weathered face and a hooked nose. "Wasn't much. I heard a shout and rushed to the railing. I saw Lady Devonworth in the water. A few minutes later a man dived overboard."

"That was me. She screamed?"

Nettles shrugged. "A scream or a shout. Not sure what it was."

The same shout he'd heard. "Was the sea rough enough to cause her fall?" He hadn't thought it that rough, but perhaps a woman leaning on the railing could have been pitched overboard.

The captain shook his head. "This was before the storm moved in. Mild seas and just a little wind. Not even any rain."

"Then how did she get into the water?" When the men glanced at one another uneasily, Harrison stared at Nettles. "Did you see anyone else at the railing?"

"No, sir."

"No footsteps, nothing?"

The man hesitated. "There's often folks on deck, sir. There's always footsteps."

Lady Devonworth. She was titled, so maybe she had money. A kidnapping might have netted a blackguard some money, but she was worthless dead. Unless it was a kidnapping gone wrong?

"Thank you for your time," he told the men. When they walked away, he turned back to Will. "That coffee is sounding better and better."

⌒⧏⧐⌒

Flames danced in the fireplace. Dry now, Olivia's hair lay on her shoulders and she'd finally stopped shivering. Katie's simple blue dress fit Olivia's slim figure perfectly. What was she going to do? It was clear someone wanted her dead. If the man discovered he'd failed, he would try again. She was tempted to get on a boat and head back up the coast, then take the first train home. But no. She was here to find out what had happened to Eleanor.

Katie bustled back into the room with more tea on a tray. "Now that Jennie is down for the night, we can chat. You have color in your cheeks now," she said, putting the tray on a table. "My, you're quite beautiful. Your hair is lovely. And such dark eyes. Like a Spanish dancer."

Heat rose in Olivia's cheeks, and she began to wind her hair back up on her head. "I can't thank you enough for your hospitality. I'm so sorry to impose in this way."

Katie poured tea into a cup and handed it to her. "It's not an imposition at all! I shall quite enjoy feminine company."

Olivia glanced at the clock on the mantel. "It's only eight? It feels like much later."

"You nearly drowned. That would wear anyone out. There are fresh linens on the bed in the guest room. Whenever you are ready for sleep, I'll show you to your room."

"You're too kind." Olivia was ready to lay her head on the pillow and forget a murderer stalked her. She added sugar to her tea, then heard steps and male voices outside on the porch.

Katie rose. "That's probably Will. Let me tell him what's happened."

"Who is with him?"

"Let me check." She went to the window and pulled back the lace curtain. "Will has Harrison Bennett with him."

Olivia held back a gasp. "You can't tell him I'm here!"

"Will he recognize you?"

The front door opened and footsteps came down the hall. "I don't think so. I was only ten the last time I saw him, and he barely noticed me."

Katie stepped toward the door. "Stay calm. You have to meet him sooner or later."

Olivia rose and nodded as two men stepped into the room. She studied the face of the man who had caused her so much heartache. Harrison's shoulders were broad under the cotton shirt he wore. She'd expected him to be in a suit and exuding wealth and power. His dark hair curled above his ears and along the nape of his neck. He reminded her of a sleek panther that hid its power and true danger until one least expected it.

He stopped when he saw her. "There you are," he said.

She recognized the voice at once. Harrison Bennett was the man who had rescued her from certain death. Her words left her and all she could do was stare.

"We've been scouring the sand and the dock for you, Lady Devonworth," he said, glowering. "I told you to stay put. Do you have any idea how much worry you've caused?"

She found her tongue. "I could hardly stay alone on a dark beach when someone had just tried to kill me. And I must say I resent your tone, sir. You hardly have the right to order me to do anything."

His scowl deepened. Then his dark gaze lightened and he laughed. "You've got a temper, Lady Devonworth."

Katie stepped between her and the men. "It's good to see you, Harrison. I'm sorry to say Jennie is in bed. She'll be so disappointed to have missed you."

Olivia didn't care for the amusement on Harrison's face. And she did *not* have a temper.

The other man chuckled feebly at the obvious tension in the air. "You must be the mermaid Harrison pulled from the sea. I'm Will Jesperson."

Olivia smiled and held out her hand. "Your wife has befriended me when I needed it most, Mr. Jesperson. Thank you for your hospitality."

"We're honored to have you in our home," he said. "How did you end up here?"

Katie helped him out of his anorak. "You can interrogate her by the fire. I'll get some cookies and coffee."

Olivia watched Harrison. Surely women flocked to him. Confidence oozed from his broad shoulders. His square jaw was clean shaven, and his black hair curled a bit on his collar. He returned her perusal, and she averted her gaze.

His brown eyes held no recognition, just curiosity. She extended her hand and glanced at Katie. "You know my name, but you have not introduced yourself."

He took her hand. "Harrison Bennett."

Olivia managed not to snatch her fingers away as he bent. When his lips brushed her skin, she nearly yelped. As soon as it was seemly, she put her hand behind her back. "Are you a businessman, Mr. Bennett?"

"My father and I own some diamond mines in Africa," he said. "We also have a silver mine or two and a few lumber tracts. Our newest acquisition is a black-diamond mine."

With his deep voice and smooth manners, she had no doubt he managed to sell investors on anything he wanted. "I've never seen a black diamond. How interesting. I should like to see one."

"The local jewelry designer recently purchased some. I should be delighted to show them to you."

Jewelry wasn't something she was able to buy right now, but the ruse would allow her to spend time around him. "I need to let the servants at the Stewart manor know I've arrived and am unharmed. If you wouldn't mind escorting me to the residence tomorrow, perhaps we could stop by the jewelry store on the way."

His brows rose. "There is no one in residence there."

"No indeed," she said. "Mrs. Stewart is still mourning the death of her daughter, but she urged me to stay as long as I like. I'm quite tired of the season's parties. The idea of spending time in the country is most alluring."

His smile faded. "If you are close friends of the Stewarts, why did you not immediately indicate you recognized my name?"

"You're right. I should have done so at once. I'm sorry for your loss." The words of condolence nearly choked her, but she managed to keep her smile fixed in place. She settled into the chair by the fire.

"Thank you."

His curt reply made her curl her fingers into her palms. Didn't he care at all about Eleanor's death? "What were you doing on the ship?" she asked.

His brows rose. "The same as you. Coming here. I was returning from business in San Francisco."

Her cheeks heated. "Of course." Could he have been the man who threw her overboard? How convenient he was on the same boat. What better way to gain her trust than to rescue her?

FOUR

THE MOTORCAR HIT a muddy pothole, and if not for Harrison's quick grasp of her arm, Olivia would have gone flying. They sat in the backseat as the driver, Thurman, navigated the rough road, and she was conscious of his elbow brushing hers.

The glowering clouds had temporarily stopped spitting rain, and she could only hope they reached shelter before the storm hit. The rain would ruin her new gown. The canvas top would block little of the elements. At least Will had retrieved her belongings from the ship.

She grabbed the side and hung on for dear life as the open-body Cadillac bounced along the rough streets. She craned her neck to take in the town of Mercy Falls. It was quite attractive to her dazzled eyes. She'd expected nothing more than wooden storefronts in what she considered a backwater, but it was a bustling town with well-dressed men and women strolling the brick sidewalks.

Being with Harrison Bennett set her on edge, but the only way to find out what happened to Eleanor was to spend time in his presence. He would make a slipup that would lead her to the truth.

Thurman parked the automobile in front of a stately stone storefront that boasted a large display of jewelry in its picture window. Harrison leaped over the side of the car and came around to assist her. "The pieces in the window are of paste," he said. "The real items are in the safe."

She lifted her silk skirt free of the mud puddle outside the motorcar and stepped onto the sidewalk with his assistance. "What a pretty town," she said, staring at a charming white church with a tower.

"I like it." The bell tinkled as he opened the door for her.

She stepped onto marble floors. Gold foil papered the walls. The tin ceiling was painted gold as well.

A woman behind the counter discreetly poured tea into delicate china. "Would you care for sugar, Lady Devonworth?"

He must have alerted the staff to her visit. "Two sugars, please." She accepted the tea and sipped it as she moved toward the glass counters. Sparkling jewels captured the light from the chandeliers overhead. She caught her breath at one necklace. "That almost looks like lace," she said, pausing over the display.

The woman beamed. "The platinum adds to that illusion. The weight of diamonds in this piece is five carats total, though they are small to grab the light in a lacelike display."

What was she doing here? She couldn't afford any of this jewelry, not until Bennett made good on his promise. All she had was the small sum she'd brought with her, and that had to last for the summer.

The woman lifted the necklace onto the glass. Harrison lifted it from its black velvet home and draped it around Olivia's neck. It was cold at first but quickly warmed on her skin. She touched the delicate filigree and fingered the glittering diamonds. They were of top quality and picked up facets of light from every direction.

"I quite adore it," she said.

He clipped dangling diamond earrings to her ears. The brush of his warm fingers against her neck made her shiver. She forced herself to stand her ground. He turned her toward the light from the windows and motioned to a full-length mirror. She was not a covetous woman, but seeing her reflection made her long to keep the necklace. "I've never seen anything so lovely."

His gaze never left hers in the mirror. "Nor have I."

Her cheeks burned at the intent in his gaze. What a rogue he was. "And the price?"

"Five thousand dollars."

"I'll think about it," she said, turning away from the mirror. "If you don't mind, we could stop at the manor and let the servants know where to pick up my things."

"Of course."

"If you would be so kind as to undo the clasp." His warm fingers grazed the back of her neck again. She didn't like the way her pulse leaped. The cad knew how to make a woman respond to his touch. No wonder Eleanor had been so enamored. Olivia vowed not to be as weak as her sister. She could see through this man's mask.

He handed the necklace to the sales clerk, and Olivia stepped away before he could remove the earrings. "I can get these." She quickly took them off and handed them to the other woman.

When his fingers touched her elbow, she didn't move toward the door. Not when she had so many questions. She hovered over the display case. "Where are those black diamonds you praised?"

"Right here." He pointed to a bracelet studded with black and white stones.

The black diamonds glittered against the white ones. "Did you buy any of these lovely pieces for your fiancée?" She glanced at him from under her lashes and saw him flinch.

"Unfortunately, I saw Eleanor very little," he said, his tone frosty. "When she arrived, I was on a trip to Africa. She died four days after I returned."

"It was an arranged marriage?"

His brows lowered and his lips thinned. "I'm sure you know it was, Lady Devonworth. If you're such a close friend of the family, you would be quite aware of these things."

"I beg your pardon. I didn't mean to offend you," she said. When his glower didn't diminish, she turned up the wattage on her smile until his lips twitched. She moved toward the door with him.

So, Eleanor had seen little of him, yet she died four days after his arrival from Africa. What did it all mean? And how could Olivia get the truth out of him?

⚜

Harrison guided the young woman past the manicured lawns to the sweeping portico of Stewart Hall. The high surf from the approaching storm pounded on the rocks below. The woman's pointed questions about Eleanor left him on edge. He quite detested high-society women who were only interested in gossip.

"The front door is open," Lady Devonworth said.

A man carrying rugs emerged from the open door. Harrison recognized him as footman Jerry Bagley. The young man didn't see them and carried the rugs to the line at the side of the house. A rug beater lay on the ground. He draped the rugs over the line and picked up the beater.

"Jerry, if you have a moment," Harrison called.

Jerry whirled with the beater held up like a weapon. His pug-nosed face relaxed in a smile when he saw them. He struck a pose and dropped the tool. "A woman drove me to drink and I never had the courtesy to thank her for it," he said in a snide drawl.

"W. C. Fields," Harrison said. "Good job."

The young man grinned and picked up the beater again. "He's easy to do. I've got a part in a vaudeville that debuts in two weeks. I hope you can come."

"I wouldn't miss it."

Jerry glanced at Lady Devonworth and his eyes widened. Harrison knew he was taking in the luxury of her silk gown. "This is Lady Devonworth. I assume the house has been prepared for her visit."

"Yes, sir. Mrs. Stewart called several days ago. Mama has been cracking the whip over all of us." He glanced at Lady Devonworth. "She told us to expect—"

"I'm so glad she called to let you know to expect me," Lady Devonworth said. "I'm at the lighthouse right now, but I wanted to make sure you were ready for my arrival."

Harrison stepped past Jerry. "I'll introduce Lady Devonworth to your mother." He guided Lady Devonworth toward the door. "This is your first visit, correct?"

"Yes. Mr. Stewart had the place built four years ago. Or so I was told," she said. "Mrs. Stewart has not seen the manor." Ever since she'd stepped from the car, she'd been aloof. She also hadn't looked at him.

"It's quite large," he said, mounting the steps. He noticed her eyes widen as they stepped into the grand hall. Silk papered the walls. The redwood floors gleamed. A sweeping staircase six feet wide rose to their left. The ceiling in the foyer was fifteen feet high. "The parlor is this way," he said, touching his fingers to her elbow again. She flinched at his touch, and he frowned. He guided her to the large parlor on the right, where they found the housekeeper furiously dusting the items in the china cupboard.

"Mrs. Bagley," he said. She whirled to face him. Her face hardened when she saw him. He pretended not to notice. "This is Lady Devonworth. She had a bit of an adventure yesterday, but she's quite all right."

The older woman wiped her hands on her apron and studied the young lady. Thora's faded blue eyes brightened, and she gave a slight nod as if she approved. "As soon as that lazy son of mine brings in the rugs, the house is ready. Your room has been prepared, Lady Devonworth." She didn't look at Harrison again and did not address him.

Her dislike was nothing new to Harrison. "I'll be pleased to fetch your belongings, Lady Devonworth. You can rest in the parlor and I'll be back with them."

She flushed and shook her head. "That won't be necessary. I can hardly vacate the lighthouse without thanking Will and Katie for their hospitality. If you'll run me back to their home, I'll spend a final evening with them and come tomorrow. If that's all right," she said, directing her question to Thora.

"Of course, your ladyship," Thora said. "If you'd like, I can show you around before you go."

"I should like that." The young woman fell into step beside the housekeeper. Neither looked back at him.

Harrison started to go after them, then decided against it. He didn't care to force his presence on them. "I'll wait here," he said.

He stepped to the window and watched Jerry beat the dirt from the rugs with vigor. The last time he'd been here was the day Eleanor disappeared. He'd come to take her to lunch, and she was pale and quiet. She said hardly anything to him over the meal and had been quick to ask to return home. Now he knew she had to have been planning her suicide.

He was lost in thought for so long he barely registered the women's return. When Lady Devonworth stepped back into the parlor, he was struck with her beauty. Her hair was so dark it was almost black. Her eyes were large and brown, shining with curiosity and a zest for life he found quite appealing. The warm tones of her skin paired with her eyes gave her a stunning beauty that was accentuated by her high cheekbones.

She must have noticed him staring, because faint color tinged her cheeks. "Is everything all right?" she asked.

He liked her voice too, husky and vibrant. It was too bad she made little pretense of hiding her distaste of him. He was unsure what he'd done to displease her. "Is everything to your liking?"

"It's an exquisite home. The ballroom on the third floor is the largest I've ever seen. It would hold nearly the whole town. I don't believe Mrs. Stewart realizes how lovely this place is."

He had no interest in the ballroom. "I'll take you back to the lighthouse if you're ready."

"Of course. I'll return tomorrow," she told Thora. Lady Devonworth put her hand on his arm and allowed him to escort her to the motorcar.

The driver started the Cadillac. Harrison climbed into the backseat with her. "Are you angry about something, Lady Devonworth? Your eyes have been spitting fire at me."

She turned those magnificent eyes on him. "I've been wondering why your fiancée would choose to drown herself," she said.

He stiffened at the rudeness of her comment. "You're very outspoken," he said. "And you don't know me, certainly not well enough to ask such pointed questions about something that is none of your concern. Your set may enjoy gossiping about such a horrific tragedy, but I do not. I'll take you home now and I'll thank you to keep your questions about my personal life to yourself."

FIVE

OLIVIA'S CHEEKS WERE still burning when Harrison stopped the motorcar on the road at the bottom of the hill to the lighthouse. He couldn't let her out fast enough. The surf roared off to their left. Her questions must seem to be extremely rude to him, but she refused to let his opinion matter to her. Not until she was sure of his innocence or guilt. An apology was necessary to smooth things over, but it would pain her to make it.

"Thank you for the day," she said when he opened the door for her. "I beg your pardon for my rudeness. It was quite unconscionable. I can only plead fatigue has addled my brain."

A muscle in his jaw twitched, and pain twisted his mouth. "I accept your apology, Lady Devonworth." He escorted her up the steep steps to the lighthouse. "I'll leave you here, if I may?"

"Of course," she said. She watched him retreat to his auto. He got in front with Thurman. Something like remorse stirred in her, but she ignored it. He deserved every bit of discomfort she might bring him. She would *not* regret anything she said. She pushed open the door.

She met Will in the yard. He wore a distracted expression. "Is there something wrong?" she asked.

"I fear we have a major gale heading our way."

She glanced at the sky, clearing now. "How can you tell? It looks fine."

"The calm before the storm. The barometric pressure is very

low. I must prepare. You'll find Katie inside." He hurried toward the foghorn.

Olivia stepped into the foyer. "Hello?" she called.

"In here, Olivia." Katie's voice floated down the hall. She stepped into view through the doorway and met Olivia before she reached it. "My best friend, Addie, is here."

"You told her about me?"

Katie shook her head. "I've told her nothing, though it pained me to be secretive with her. I assure you anything you wish to discuss is safe with her though. She is most trustworthy."

"Thank you for keeping my secret." Olivia followed Katie into the parlor, where she saw another young woman seated on the sofa. The woman's dark auburn hair was on top of her head, and she wore the latest style of hobble skirt. Olivia hated the style. It was difficult to walk with the hem so tight around the ankles.

"Lady Devonworth, this is Addie North, my best friend," Katie said. "Addie, L-Lady Devonworth from New York." Her bright smile faded as she stumbled over Olivia's title.

Olivia exchanged a glance with Katie. She didn't want her to feel constrained by the lack of candor. "I appreciate the way Katie has helped me, Addie. If I may call you Addie?"

"Of course," the young woman said, glancing at Katie with a question in her eyes. Katie looked away.

Olivia liked the looks of this young woman, and she needed friends right now. She felt so alone. And frightened. She glanced at Katie and gave a slight nod before seating herself in the armchair by the fireplace. "Katie has quickly become a friend when I was in dire need of one," she said. "She assures me you are trustworthy."

"Any friend of Katie's is someone I would defend with my last breath," Addie said. "I hope you will rest in the care we can give you. Katie told me of your near drowning. I hope you're feeling quite recovered."

"I am, thank you." Olivia studied the woman's earnest expression. "My name is Olivia Stewart," she said. "Lady Devonworth is a title I seldom use, but I would plead for your discretion. Let me tell you what has happened." She plunged into the fearful circumstances that had ended with her arrival at the lighthouse. "Someone did his best to ensure I never reached these shores, so I must keep my survival quiet for now."

The color had leached from Addie's cheeks. She smoothed her silk skirt. "My lips are sealed," she said. "This is horrible."

"I gave Katie permission to tell Will. I would not want to come between you and your husband, so you may tell him. I need some allies."

"You can trust my Will and Addie's John," Katie said. She handed Jennie her dolly.

"Do you have any idea who might have done this?" Addie asked. "Did your sister have any enemies?"

Olivia exhaled. "I suspect Mr. Bennett."

Katie's worn boots hit the ground and she stood. "I must disagree most vehemently, Olivia. We have often had Harrison in our home. I don't believe he has one evil bone in his body. Will thinks most highly of him, and Jennie quite adores him."

"Don't you find it most peculiar that someone threw me overboard, and Harrison was on the ship with ample motive and opportunity?"

"But he saved you!"

"It might have been a ruse. Some men are good at hiding their true character. Something happened to my sister, and I mean to find out the truth."

Addie's hand went to her throat. "You fear foul play?"

"She was terrified of water."

Addie's eyes widened. "Ah. So she wouldn't have been out swimming. The attack on your own person bolsters your belief as well," Addie said. "But I agree with Katie. Harrison is an honorable man. He would never have hurt Eleanor. Nor you."

"Harrison was in Africa when she arrived," Katie said. "She came to tea with us a few times at Addie's house. I liked her very much."

"What about . . . suicide?" Addie asked.

Olivia swallowed hard. "She was full of laughter. Marrying Mr. Bennett was all she talked about before she left. I've never seen Eleanor despondent. Never once in her twenty-three years."

Katie took a bite of her cookie. "Perhaps she heard lies about him. I believe you're quite wrong about Harrison. We'll help you get to the bottom of it though. Harrison is one of the most eligible bachelors in town. The unmarried girls were downcast when Eleanor showed up."

Olivia could well believe it. His dark good looks drew attention. "Did Eleanor say anything to either of you about him?" she asked.

Addie paused. "We last saw her two days before she died. She was more quiet than usual. She said something about a letter she'd received from her father."

Olivia's jaw dropped. "From our *father*? He died six months ago."

"That's what she said, from her father."

The blood rushed from Olivia's head and she felt faint. "I don't understand. That was all my sister said?"

Katie bit her lip and glanced at Addie. "Didn't she say something about asking Harrison to explain?" She rubbed her head. "I can't quite remember."

"That's right!" Addie said. "I'd forgotten too. She said Harrison would be able to explain it all, and that she couldn't wait for him to get home."

"I must find that letter," Olivia said slowly.

The lighthouse accommodations were more rustic than Olivia was used to. A handmade quilt covered the mattress on the iron bedstead in her room. Matching curtains hung in the windows. There was no closet, only a chifforobe against one wall. A bowl and pitcher of water rested atop the dresser.

But the room held a warmth she'd never experienced in the elegant mansion on Fifth Avenue. These people were different too. Accepting of who she was. They didn't know she knew the Astors or that she hailed from one of New York's most prominent families. Olivia suspected they wouldn't care if they did know.

She jotted down in her journal her impressions of Mercy Falls, then put down her pen when a knock came at the door. "Come in," she called, knowing it had to be Katie.

But it was little Jennie who popped through the door. "I came for a good-night kiss," she said. She ran to Olivia and tried to climb into her lap.

Olivia lifted the little girl onto her knees. Jennie wrapped her arms around Olivia's neck and turned her cheek up for a kiss. The feel of the warm little body in her arms was quite delightful. She hadn't been around children much, and hugging Jennie, she wished it had been different. The child's trusting expression and round cheeks touched her heart in a way she'd never experienced.

Olivia brushed her lips over the soft cheek smelling of talcum. "Good night, darling." She glanced up to see Katie in the door.

"I hope she didn't disturb you." Katie stepped into the room and held out her arms to her daughter.

Olivia handed Jennie up to Katie. "I loved it."

The wind picked up outside and rattled the windowpanes. Katie frowned when the first spatters of rain struck the glass. "Will says we're in for a bad gale, not just a rainstorm."

"How does he know?"

"He's a weatherman. Always playing with his weather balloons and instruments. He calls in his findings to the weather bureau." She smiled. "Good night."

"Good night." Olivia turned out the light when the other woman shut the door. She tried to settle in for sleep, but her thoughts churned. Could she be wrong about Harrison, or was he just very good at charming his way into women's graces?

She realized the wind had increased in velocity. The gale howled, and she sat up and watched the rain sheeting down the glass. The window rattled, then the glass broke. Rain came in a straight line through the opening. She leaped from the bed and called for the Jespersons. She wrenched open the door and in the hall met Katie, who had Jennie in her arms.

Katie thrust her daughter to Olivia. "Get downstairs! I'll try to cover this hole."

Thunder rumbled and the wind howled again. Jennie clutched Olivia and whimpered. "It's okay," Olivia said, patting the little girl's back awkwardly. The child's sobs ratcheted up with the storm.

She rushed down the steps with the child. When she reached the parlor, sparks were flying onto the floor from the wind churning down the chimney. Olivia set the little girl on a chair and grabbed a rug. She beat out the embers, then took the poker and separated the logs so the fire could die down. Sparks flew out and burned her dress, but she quickly extinguished them. The windows all over the house rattled, and the howling of the wind made her want to cover her ears.

She scooped up the sobbing child. "It's okay, Jennie. The fire is out." Olivia ran to the steps. "Katie, are you all right?"

Katie rushed down the steps. "I couldn't get it covered. I've never seen a storm like this. I wish Will were inside." She plucked her daughter from Olivia's arms.

"Where is he?" Olivia asked.

"In the light tower. I'd insist he come down, but it would do no good. He'll stay up there until the ship that crosses this time of night has passed safely." She paced the floor, humming to Jennie as the wind intensified.

Olivia grabbed an afghan from the back of the sofa as the chill seeped into the room. The storm continued to beat against the building. In spite of the storm's fury, the little girl put her head on her mother's shoulder and slept.

A horrendous crash came from somewhere above them. Katie turned wide eyes on Olivia, then thrust her wailing daughter at her. "I have to check on Will!"

Before she ran up the stairs, more crashes came, then a door banged. Footsteps ran toward them and Will took the final three steps in a leap.

"Get out! The whole thing is coming down." He grabbed Jennie from Olivia, then herded them all to the door.

Olivia paused, not wanting to go out into the storm. How bad could it be?

Katie plucked at her sleeve. "We must get out, Olivia. Come now."

Olivia allowed her friend to lead her out of the lighthouse.

Glass shattered and timbers creaked. They exited into driving rain. The wind nearly knocked Olivia over as she struggled to see through the downpour that instantly drenched her. A huge crash sounded behind them, and she whirled to see the lighthouse collapsing. Every window in the house had been blown out. The tower toppled to the ground.

SIX

WIND AND RAIN lashed Harrison's motorcar as his driver navigated the flooded road from Ferndale to Mercy Falls. It was a wonder the driver could see, though this Cadillac model had a windshield. Still, sheets of rain came in all around the canvas top. Harrison couldn't even see the beacon from the lighthouse in the storm. They were on the outskirts of town. He had responded to a call to help transport a family driven from their home by a flash flood to a relative in Ferndale.

Thurman braked abruptly, and Harrison leaned forward. "What's wrong?"

"Look, sir." The driver indicated a bedraggled column of people out in the storm.

"Good heavens, it's the Jespersons," Harrison said when he saw the man's face. He got out into the drenching rain. "Get in!" he shouted above the din of the storm.

He ushered them into the backseat, then realized there were three adults plus Jennie. Lady Devonworth was with them. He climbed into the front beside his driver. He put his arm on the seat back and turned around to stare at his passengers. Lady Devonworth wore only a nightgown. She shivered in the soaked garment.

"This isn't any drier, but it might warm you," he said as he shrugged off his wet jacket. He handed it back to her, and she murmured her thanks as she slid her arms into it.

Even with dripping hair, she was the most beautiful woman he'd ever seen. Those gypsy black eyes were exotic and compelling, even with her lashes dripping wet and water running down her cheeks.

"What's happened?" he asked.

"The storm blew down the lighthouse," Will said. "I knew it had some weak areas, but I hadn't been able to get money from the Bureau of Lighthouses for repairs."

"Totally gone?" Harrison asked. Will nodded. "No wonder I couldn't see the beacon. I thought it was because the storm was so bad."

"I just pray no ships were grounded out there without it. I think the *Lucy* had already gone past."

"Thank God you were all uninjured. You were in the building when it came down?"

Will nodded. "I was in the tower and barely escaped. I got the women out, and the next gust caved in the roof. It's totally destroyed."

"You're all unhurt. That's the important thing." Harrison glanced at Thurman. "Let's get everyone to my house."

His driver nodded. "We'll be home in five minutes."

"Turn up the heat," Harrison told Will. "The gas burner is by your feet."

Will complied, and the burner sputtered. The rain blew in on everyone in the backseat. He tucked his coat around his daughter, then slipped his arm around his wife. "I've never seen a storm like this. The wind speeds topped a hundred miles an hour."

"You're welcome to spend the night at my house," Harrison said. "You too, Lady Devonworth. Unless you'd rather I have my driver take you to the Stewart manor?"

She hesitated. A wary expression crossed her face, then she shook her head. "I don't want to rouse the household at this hour. Thank you for your kind offer. I shall take you up on it."

The car reached his home, and Thurman braked at the sidewalk. "I have an umbrella, sir," he said.

"I think we're all too wet for it to matter," Harrison said. "Don't trouble yourself. The rain is slowing. Ready to make a run for it?" he asked his guests.

When they nodded, he got out, then helped Lady Devonworth out while Will lifted Katie and Jennie from the motorcar. They all ran for the front door. Harrison held on to Lady Devonworth's elbow and hurried her toward the haven inside. They burst into the warmth of the foyer and shook water all over the floor.

He saw Lady Devonworth take in the opulent hall and the curving staircase to the second floor. "It's more grand than I need," he said. "But my father insists on the best of everything."

Mrs. Lindrum rushed toward them with towels. "Oh goodness, Mr. Harrison, you're all going to catch your death of cold. Come in by the fire." His housekeeper motioned to the ladies to follow her.

His collie, Nealy, bounded to meet him. He rubbed his dog's head, and Nealy whined, then went to greet the women. Lady Devonworth jumped back when she saw the dog. Her eyes went wide.

She darted behind Will. "Get him away!"

"Nealy won't hurt you," Harrison assured her.

Her face went even more pale. "I was bitten when I was a child," she said softly. "Dogs terrify me."

He clucked his tongue. "Nealy, come." The dog came to his side and lay down by his feet.

Katie and Lady Devonworth left the wet towels on the floor and disappeared through the parlor door. Harrison toweled off his hair, then followed with Will, who still had Jennie in his arms. She lay quietly with her head on his shoulder and her eyes wide as the thunder roared outside.

"Want some cookies and milk, honey?" Harrison asked her. She nodded and reached for him. He took her and held her close. "You're cold. I'll get you a blanket." He carried her into the parlor with the women and asked Mrs. Lindrum to fetch refreshments. An afghan was on the sofa, and he wrapped it around the little girl.

When she snuggled her head against him, he saw Lady Devonworth's attention fixed on them. "She likes me," he said.

"Obviously," she said.

There was a note in her voice he didn't quite understand. Surprise or disquiet? She seemed wary around him too, and he'd given her no reason to distrust him. He couldn't figure her out.

⚬❈⚬

The hot chocolate warmed Olivia's insides and her teeth finally quit chattering. Mrs. Lindrum had found clothing for the ladies to change into. The dressing gowns could have covered her and Katie twice over. They were darned and worn, obviously the housekeeper's, but at least they were dry and clean.

Olivia pushed aside one of the blankets Mrs. Lindrum had wrapped around her, then glanced around the guest room. It had been newly redecorated. Had Eleanor ever stayed here? Olivia could have gone to Stewart Hall, but she couldn't resist this opportunity to learn more about Harrison, to explore his house for clues.

She put down her mug and went to the door. Putting her ear to the wood, she listened. Nothing. Hopefully everyone was in bed. It was after ten. She eased open the door and stepped into the hall. Darkness cloaked the space. She didn't know the house so it was going to be hard to find her way to the staircase. Inching along with her hand on the wall, she felt her way to the end of the hallway. The wall under her fingers ended, and the staircase opened in front of her. Pale light shone from below. Her feet made no sound as she tiptoed down the runner covering the polished wood steps.

Once she reached the foyer, she paused and looked both directions. She'd already been to the left, so this time she turned right and found a doorway opening into a library. Not even knowing what she was looking for, she stepped in and shut the door behind her.

The room was dark, but she'd seen electric lights in the parlor, so she ran her hand beside the door and twisted the knob she found. The room flooded with light. She glanced at the shelves. It was not the typical library for a man. The glass shelves held a mishmash of popular titles. Dog-eared and worn, they weren't the leather-bound copies that were only for show. The desk wasn't the ornate object so often chosen for its imposing size. It was austere, but more of the Arts and Crafts movement. Papers littered the battered top. Harrison actually used this desk. He didn't bring people in here to impress them with his furnishings.

She moved deeper into the room and glanced at the titles. A complete collection of Mark Twain filled a shelf, and Jack London novels crowded another. The next shelf held Doyle novels. She raised her brows at the collection of Austen novels, and a smile lifted her lips. The man had a romantic side? He seemed all business.

The door creaked behind her, and she whirled to see Harrison standing in the doorway. He was in his dressing gown, and his hair stood on end like a boy's.

He stopped and stared. "Lady Devonworth? Is something wrong?"

She stepped away from the shelves. "Not at all. I . . . I couldn't sleep."

"Ah, I am in the same predicament. I see your solution is the same as mine." He gestured to the shelves. "Find a good book to read."

"I'm sorry if I am intruding."

"Feel free to choose what you like."

"You have read all these books?"

"Most of them." He moved to the shelves and pulled down *The Call of the Wild.*

She couldn't help the smile that curved her lips. "Even Jane Austen?" She touched the spine of *Pride and Prejudice.* "This looks well read." He chuckled, and she found her smile widening. The man was much too charming. She pulled the book down. "Afraid to answer me?"

He nodded. "I can see it now—you'll announce it at a party some time. My reputation will be ruined."

She laughed. "Seriously, you've read Austen?"

"Of course. I undertook a study of your fair sex some years ago. Women are most bewildering."

"Did the books help?"

He shook his head. "I still find women indecipherable."

Her smile stilled, but the question on her lips sprang out. "Do you agree that a man with a fortune is in need of a wife?"

His smile vanished. "So might say women who are only interested in a man's wallet." He stepped to the door. "I'll bid you good night and leave you to choose your own reading material."

She warned herself not to be taken in by him, as her sister had been. He was not the man he presented to the world. She just had to prove it.

SEVEN

THE BREEZE LIFTED the hair on the back of Harrison's neck as he bent over the aeroplane's engine. He tightened a bolt, then closed the hatch. Perfect afternoon for flying. And it would wash away the last of the bad taste left in his mouth from that woman's nosiness. What was she doing in his library last night? He doubted it had been to look for a book.

"Let's get in the air!" Jerry Bagley yelled from the open-air cockpit of the biplane. "Sundown will be here too soon. And Mama will be after your hide if I'm late."

Harrison nodded and cranked the propeller over. Mrs. Bagley thought he was going to get her son killed, and she worried whenever Jerry was away from the house. Harrison cranked the propeller again until it caught and began to whirl.

He ducked under the wing and climbed in front of the young footman. He waved at his mother, who sat in her wheelchair at the edge of the field. She waved back, and he prayed he'd make her proud today. Her attendant, Mary Grace, maneuvered the chair into a better position and adjusted the black blanket around his mother's knees. The ribbons on his mother's straw hat fluttered in the breeze, and she wore a bright smile.

Jerry slapped him on the back and gave him a thumbs-up. Harrison opened the throttle as far as he dared, and the aeroplane began to roll over the uneven ground of the meadow. It picked up momentum as it went. The wind nearly snatched his leather hat from his head, and he hunkered down and watched the trees coming much too fast. He'd have to brake if he didn't get lift soon.

He leaned forward. "Come on, come on," he whispered. The wheels on the flying machine bounced, then didn't touch ground. He guided the nose up. Just like that, they were in the air. Five feet above the ground, then ten, then twenty. Moments later the machine was soaring over the tops of the trees. His grin nearly split his face, and he shrieked his elation into the howling wind as he pumped his fist in the air. He grinned back at Jerry, whose eyes were huge in his freckled face.

He waggled the biplane's wings at the speck far below that was his mother. His chest was near to bursting. It was the highest he'd ever successfully lifted a flying machine into the air. He guided the plane over the ocean's whitecaps, then down to land on the field. The wheels bumped and the plane went aloft again before settling down. Once the machine slowed and stopped, he leaped from the seat and clambered down.

His mother's face shone with pride and she waved to him. Mary Grace rolled her chair toward the plane.

Harrison rushed to meet them. "We made it over the trees, Mother!"

Esther Bennett had been in the wheelchair for ten years—ever since she was struck by a carriage—but Harrison had never heard her complain once. Though she didn't understand his passion for flight, to her credit, she'd given up trying to talk him out of working with the plane.

"You're a real birdman, Harrison," she said when he reached her. "I'm so proud of you. I'll telephone your father tonight."

His grin faded. "I'd rather you didn't. When he comes to visit, I'll have to endure one of his lectures about not wasting my time."

She gripped his hands. "He only wants what's best for you, Harrison. He's very proud."

"He has a strange way of showing it," he said. "All I ever hear is how much time and money I waste on my 'little hobby,' as he calls it."

"Everything your father has, he fought for. He wants you to have all the advantages he never had. I'm sure he will be quite proud of you when he hears this news."

Harrison nodded but said nothing more. This was a topic they would never come to agreement on. "Did you hear the lighthouse blew down last night?" he asked. "The Jespersons and their guest spent the night with me."

His mother gasped. "Are they all right?"

"Yes. They escaped the structure before it fell, and I found them standing in the downpour. They were all having breakfast when I left this morning."

His mother adjusted her hat. "A guest was with them, you say? Who is it?"

"A Lady Devonworth from New York."

She pursed her lips. "I thought I knew all the peerage who resided in the city. I've never heard of her."

"She was staying with the Jespersons temporarily but is going to reside at Stewart Hall. I believe she plans to take up residence today. She appears to be a close friend of theirs."

"It's quite odd she would be staying there with none of the Stewarts in town. Especially considering the circumstances. Was she a friend of Eleanor's?"

"I don't believe so." Now that he thought about it, he wasn't sure of that at all. She'd offered her condolences but said nothing about her relationship to the young woman. Lady Devonworth said very little about herself, in fact.

"What is she like?"

He shrugged. "Typical for that set. Interested in balls and parties." He stared back at the aeroplane. The comet was coming soon, and he planned to make history. He'd be soaring above the treetops when that star grew bright, and if the colors of the tail flashed in the sky as he hoped, flying into it would be the ultimate test for him, proof that he was more than his father's mouthpiece. He'd be proud of himself even if his father rolled his eyes at his accomplishments.

Debris littered the sand and rocks. Olivia grabbed a tattered dress that the wind had draped across a tree limb. Tears rolled down Katie's cheeks as she stared at the wreckage. Jennie didn't seem to notice her mother's distress. She scampered through the mess, retrieving toys.

Will shouted and waved his arms. "Farther out!" he shrieked at the ship offshore. The boat veered closer to the dangerous rocks. He ran to the edge of the cliff, but the vessel seemed to pay no attention.

A grinding noise split the air. Will groaned. "They're grounded. I'd better get help." He jogged down the slope and off toward the pier.

Katie stooped to pick up a battered pot. "What are we going to do?" she asked. "Will called the Bureau of Lighthouses. There is no money to rebuild right now. We have to wait until they can ask Congress for money."

"B-But where will you live? Do they know it's completely uninhabitable?"

She nodded. "They know. We could stay with Addie and John, but they have guests right now. I suppose we'll have to find a place to rent."

"You can stay with me," Olivia said. "There's plenty of room at Stewart Hall, and I'd like the company." When she saw she had Katie's attention, she smiled. "I need protection too, remember? You'd be doing me a favor. With Will in the house, an attacker would be less likely to strike again."

"You're sure?" Katie asked. "It might be several months."

"You can stay until the lighthouse is rebuilt, even if it's a year or two." Her gaze swept the destruction. "The whole thing is gone."

Katie's gaze was on the grounded ship. "Men will die while we wait."

Olivia had come close to dying in that water. Shuddering, she stared at the waves rolling to shore. "What about raising the money yourself?"

Katie scooped up her daughter. "An ice-cream social isn't going to raise the kind of funds we need."

Olivia stared at the Fresnel lens shattered on the ground. "I have an idea," she said slowly. "I'll host a ball at the manor house! A masquerade. We'll call it the Lightkeeper's Ball. I'll invite all my friends from New York. It will be a huge event and a way for them to see the Wild West. My friends will *love* it!"

"Why would your friends travel three thousand miles to attend a ball?" Katie asked, her brow furrowed.

"You don't know how bored my set gets. The summer season is coming, and they are always looking for something new to do or try. Anything that is remotely different or adventurous will have them rushing to join in."

The more she thought about the idea, the more she knew it would work. The bored New York set was always up for the unexpected. Instead of going to Newport for the summer, she would talk them into coming here for a May ball, then a summer on the Pacific shore.

"How much money would it take to rebuild?" Olivia asked.

"At least fifteen thousand, according to Will. The lens will have to be replaced."

She waved her hand. "That's nothing to my friends. Just one of them could pay that."

Katie's tears had dried and a smile made its way to her face. "Seriously, Olivia? You'd really be able to do this?"

"I've planned dozens of parties. This will be no problem."

Katie hugged her. "Thank God he brought you here when he did!"

Olivia wasn't used to physical displays, but there was something about her friend's fierce embrace that warmed her. People in her set tried not to show emotion. It felt good to know she could do something for these friends who had helped her when she needed it most.

They spent the morning picking through their things to see what was salvageable. Addie and John North arrived to help as well. Olivia wished she'd had her trunk delivered to Stewart Hall instead of to the lighthouse. Nearly everything was ruined. Most of Katie's things were torn and ripped as well, and she sniffled occasionally as the extreme damage became apparent.

Olivia heard a man's voice hail them and turned to see Harrison loping up the slope in their direction. He stopped when he reached her, his mouth gaping as he took in the destruction.

He stooped to pick up a broken doll.

"There isn't much left," Olivia said.

He turned the doll over in his hands. "I bought this for Jennie. I must buy her another."

He had bought the doll for Jennie? She studied his crestfallen expression. How much of his concern was real? Could she be wrong about him?

EIGHT

STEWART HALL SEEMED cold and lonely. The Jespersons were purchasing necessary items in town. Olivia arranged the skirt of her dress, one of Eleanor's she'd found upstairs, on the velvet sofa in the parlor and sipped her tea. Scones lay untouched on the silver tray.

Servants hurried past in the hallway, and the scent of dinner being prepared wafted into the room. The aroma of roast beef was no more appetizing than the scones to her. She closed her eyes and imagined herself back home. At this time of the afternoon, her mother would be attending to correspondence and going over household bills with her secretary. The birds would be chirping on the cherry trees out back, and her cat would be lying in wait on the patio in hopes one of them would lose all caution. Before her departure, Eleanor would have been chattering about the latest party or the new dress she'd ordered.

Olivia almost thought she could feel her sister's presence here. She'd sensed it yesterday too. Closing her eyes, she imagined Eleanor running through these halls. She would have livened the stuffy rooms and brought excitement into every corner. Putting down the cup of tea, she rose and moved to the window. The housekeeper would know where Eleanor had been buried. Olivia intended to visit the grave this afternoon. It was something she'd been dreading. She'd much rather remember her sister with her blue eyes alight with life and laughter.

She went to find Mrs. Bagley. The woman was supervising the

polishing of silver in the butler's pantry. Footmen rubbed at the forks and barely glanced up when Olivia stepped into the doorway.

Mrs. Bagley turned with an armload of linens in her hands. "Lady Devonworth. I didn't see you there. Is there something I can do for you?" The doorbell rang. "Jerry, would you get that? You'll have to sign my name for the delivery." She put down the linens. "How can I help you?"

"I'd like a moment of your time, please." Olivia walked back into the dining room with the housekeeper following her. The rest of the servants didn't need to overhear their conversation.

"Is something wrong, miss? Your room is not to your satisfaction?" the woman asked. "I put you in the room we'd prepared for Miss Olivia. Is she coming at all now?"

"I'll be the only one in residence for now," Olivia said, skirting an outright lie. "The room is lovely, thank you. You've been here a long time, Mrs. Bagley?"

Thora bobbed her head. "Ever since Mr. Stewart built the manor four years ago."

"Then you were present when Eleanor Stewart resided here?"

"Of course. Much too good for the likes of Mr. Bennett."

"You don't like Mr. Bennett?"

"It's not my place to say anything."

Olivia didn't point out that the woman had just said that very thing in so many words. "Did he not treat Miss Eleanor well?"

Mrs. Bagley sniffed. "He's an adventurer, that one. He'll never settle down. I fear he's going to get my son killed one of these days."

"Killed? How?"

"Him and his flying machine. He's turned Jerry's head with it."

"Harrison has a flying machine? He seems all businessman and not at all an adventurer."

"He's not what you think."

"What is he like, then?" At some point Olivia knew the woman would clam up, but at least she was talking for now.

"Full of notions and big plans. All the ladies cluster when he's around."

Olivia could well believe that. "Did he get along with Eleanor?"

"Miss Eleanor didn't see much of him. He was gone when she first arrived. Quite unforgivable for him to be off gallivanting when his bride was coming."

"Did you see her the day she died?"

The woman glanced up, then back to the rug on the floor. "Yes, miss." Her tone was sullen. Though she didn't have the nerve to question Olivia's interest, her tense shoulders and reticent manner told the story.

Olivia said, "I told her mother I would see what I could find out about the circumstances leading up to Eleanor's death."

"As you wish, miss."

"So how did she seem?" Olivia asked, letting her impatience show in her voice.

"Perfectly normal. She ate her breakfast, then called for the open motorcar to be brought around. She had a luncheon engagement."

"With whom?"

"She didn't say."

"She was home for dinner?"

Mrs. Bagley shook her head. "When I heard the front door, it was after midnight. I had the maid take her breakfast up, but the bed was empty. It didn't appear to have been slept in."

"I want to visit Miss Eleanor's grave. Where might I find it?"

"There's a graveyard beside the Mercy Falls Community Church. She's along the iron fence at the back. Near the biggest tree."

"One more question. I heard Eleanor received a letter from her father. Can you confirm that?"

"I don't snoop in the mail, Lady Devonworth," Mrs. Bagley said, her tone offended.

"Of course not. I didn't mean to imply you did. Thank you, Mrs. Bagley." Olivia rushed away, not wanting the housekeeper to see her impending tears.

She reached the entry and started for the parlor. The sound of carriage wheels rattled through the window. She glanced toward the circular drive and saw Goldia alight from a cab. It would be just like her to blurt out Olivia's real name in the excitement of being reunited. It would be best for their first meeting here to be in private so the servants wouldn't be made aware.

"I'm going to my room for a few minutes," she told the footman. When confusion clouded his eyes, she brushed past him and rushed up the steps. He would wonder why she was explaining her movements to him.

In the sanctuary of her chamber, she sat in the upholstered chair by the window and listened for her maid's footsteps. Olivia had chosen this room the moment she saw it. The colors of palest blue with touches of yellow were her favorite.

Goldia's quarters would be on the third floor at the back of the house. Perhaps Olivia could creep up the back stairway and find her. She waited for ten minutes, then opened her door and slipped into the hall. No one was about. The rooms and halls were confusing, and she got turned around twice before she found the door to the third floor. The steps creaked under her feet, and she winced, then reminded herself it would be perfectly natural for her to be exploring the manor.

The third floor was well lit. She went from door to door and realized the entire floor was a ballroom with the exception of a bathroom and enormous butler's pantry. She'd seen the ballroom when Harrison first brought her here, but she'd thought the servants' rooms would be up here too. She found another set of stairs and ascended them to the attic. As soon as she stepped onto the wide, unpainted boards, she heard voices. The servants' quarters had to be here. She ducked down a hall as the door ahead opened and the chambermaid stepped out. Once the woman went down the steps, Olivia tiptoed to the room the woman had vacated.

Goldia stood by the window. A white cap covered her blond hair, and her normally pink cheeks were pale. Olivia gave a curious glance around the room. She'd never been in a servant's room before. Her mother had always taken care of the staff. The starkness surprised her. No rug on the floor, minimal furnishings, and an iron bed with peeling paint were the only furnishings.

She shut the door behind her. "Goldia," she whispered, holding a finger to her lips as her maid whirled to face her with wide eyes.

"M-Miss Olivia?" the girl stammered. "Oh my dear Miss Olivia! I thought you were dead until that nice lightkeeper told me different!" She flew across the room to throw her arms around Olivia in an extravagant gesture. "I was so relieved when I got the message."

Olivia hugged her back, relishing the relief in the tight embrace. "Shh, Goldia, remember that you can't tell anyone who I am."

Goldia rubbed her forehead. "I don't see how you can fool anyone for long, Miss Olivia. Someone is bound to figure it out."

Olivia bit her lip. "I fear the news getting out after that man tried to drown me."

"Hire a bodyguard," the maid suggested.

Olivia shook her head. "It's more than the danger. I am quite determined to find out who killed Eleanor."

"Mr. Harrison would help you," Goldia said. "He cared about her."

"I suspect he had something to do with her death," Olivia said, her voice hardening. "He is the last person I would ask for help."

"What can I do, miss?"

Olivia stared at her maid. Goldia had been a stalwart champion and constant companion for three years. "Some friends of Eleanor's told me she received a letter from our father that distressed her. I need to find that correspondence. It must be here in this house."

Goldia put her hand to her mouth. "That's impossible, Miss Olivia. Mr. Stewart is dead."

"I know it seems unlikely, but I believe the woman who told me about it. Perhaps it was sent before Father's death and was delayed somehow. You must help me find it."

❦

Harrison knocked on the door of the mansion with a doll for Jennie in his hand. His eyes burned from the late-night work the past two days. The doorman showed him to the parlor, where he found Lady Devonworth on the sofa. The deep garnet in her dress made her dark eyes look even more magnificent. She was a most annoying woman, but he couldn't deny she was one of the most beautiful ones he'd ever seen.

"Good afternoon, Mr. Bennett," she said.

"Lady Devonworth." He brushed his lips across the back of the hand she extended to him.

"You look a bit tired, sir. Are you well?"

"Quite well. I've been working late."

She motioned to the space beside her. "Please join me for tea and dessert. The cook here is very talented. The cranberry trifles are delightful."

He sat gingerly on the edge of the sofa. The delicate perfume she wore wafted to his nose. He would never fit in with her kind of high society. Why did his father even wish it? Harrison would much rather be soaring on the wind.

"Where are Katie and Will? I brought a new doll for Jennie." He showed it to Olivia.

She took the bisque doll and traced the cheeks and nose. "Is this a Kestner doll?"

"It is. Don't you think she looks like Jennie?" The eyes and tiny teeth had caught his attention the moment he walked past its department-store shelf.

"She does, yes. Jennie will be thrilled." She handed it back to him. "Katie took her to buy some shoes. Will is meeting with someone from the Bureau of Lighthouses. I don't expect either of them home for several hours."

He took a treat when she offered the plate. The cranberry trifle flooded his tongue with flavor as he searched for some kind of light conversation. He was used to talking with men where the topics ranged from politics to the approaching comet.

"Are you settling into the house?" he asked, desperate to break the silence.

"Oh yes. It's quite lovely. Not exactly my taste," she said, glancing around the parlor. "I'd love to get rid of the velvet and replace it with damask or silk. It's a little heavy and stiff. But redecorating is hardly worth the cost when so many people are out of work and struggling to put food on the table."

He raised his brows but said nothing.

"You look surprised, Mr. Bennett. I do have thoughts in my head beyond fashion and parties. For example, I've been watching the comet's approach. Do you think we shall all die if the earth passes through the tail? There was a peddler here yesterday trying to sell us comet pills. The silly housekeeper actually bought some."

"So you doubt our danger?" Harrison asked.

"Don't you?" Her full lips tilted in a smile. "I see nothing in the Bible to indicate the earth's demise will be from poisonous gas."

She was more intelligent than he'd given her credit for. "I've talked to several scientists. Some believe our destruction is imminent and others laugh it off."

"What about you?"

He shrugged. "I intend to be in the air if we are lucky enough to pass through the tail."

Her hand holding the cup of tea paused on its way to her mouth. "The air? In your flying machine?"

"That's right. I'm a birdman," he said. "I got it to four thousand feet this week."

She glanced down and said nothing for a long moment. "I've longed to experience a flying machine ever since I saw one three years ago."

"You're not afraid?"

She leaned forward. "No. I should like to go up sometime."

He eyed her. "I'm looking for investors. Would you be interested in being part of the venture?"

She sipped her tea. "I'm interested, Mr. Bennett. I had a small stake in a flying machine in San Francisco, but it crashed and the pilot decided he had no more interest in it."

To Harrison's shock, he discovered he was enjoying talking to the woman. She was interesting and articulate. "I'd be honored to show you my plane. I envision someday there will be air travel between here and New York." When she didn't laugh, he went on. "Even between New York and Paris."

She nodded, her dark eyes grave. "I have no doubt you're right. We're on the cusp of great discoveries. Our nation is full of inventive, intelligent people. The changes we shall see in the next twenty years will be amazing." She took up her tea again. "Did Eleanor go up in your plane?"

"She did not." Until she'd brought up Eleanor's name, he'd actually begun to like her.

NINE

OLIVIA SIPPED HER tea and watched him with Jennie on his lap. The little girl was exclaiming over her new doll. Who was he under that businessman's attire? Had his dangerous streak frightened off Eleanor?

"You're looking quite pensive," Katie said, taking off her gloves. A whiff of fresh air clung to her clothing. She handed over her purchases to a maid before joining Olivia on the sofa.

Olivia forced a smile. "It's been a tiring few days. Have you heard how Will's meeting went?"

Katie selected a trifle, then shook her head. "I didn't see him in town." She smiled at Harrison. "You are a hero in Jennie's eyes. All she's talked about today is how sad she was about her broken dolly."

"Mommy, she has eyes that move!" Jennie rocked the doll back and forth.

Katie got up to examine the doll. "She looks a little like you, sweetheart."

Olivia worried about Katie's pale cheeks and the circles under her eyes. "Are you all right? Perhaps you need to rest."

She nodded. "I shall do that in a little while. I'm quite hungry." She nibbled on the cranberry trifle.

Olivia looked back at Harrison. Could a man who was so tender with a child actually be a murderer? It seemed so out of character. She hadn't expected to find anything that challenged her views of the man. Especially within days of setting foot in Mercy Falls.

"How is your mother?" Katie asked him.

"Quite well. She came out to watch me fly the other day."

"What does your aeroplane look like?" Olivia asked.

"Why are you so interested in flight, Lady Devonworth?" he asked. "I must say, it's a bit peculiar."

There was more than curiosity in his face. It sounded like admiration in his tone too. "There's something so—free—about not being tethered to the earth," she said. "It appears to me that you would have an entirely different perspective on the earth from up there too. I peruse any pictures taken from an aeroplane. I'd love to see the ground from high up like that myself."

"It's a rather dangerous pastime."

She sipped her tea. "There have been accidents but few fatalities. Have any women learned to fly yet?"

"Not to my knowledge."

Though she wanted to proclaim her intention to be the first, she knew it was impossible. Her friends would be scandalized if she learned to fly. Something so outrageous wasn't done. "Jennie is asleep," she observed.

"I don't mind."

"Perhaps you should put her in her bed," Katie said.

He glanced down at the child with the doll still clutched in her arms. "If you would be so kind as to show me to her room?"

"I'll do it," she told Katie when she stared to rise. "Rest."

Olivia led the way up the staircase to the small room that held Jennie's things. It was outfitted in pink and white. The white bedstead was small and low to the ground, perfect for a three-year-old. She pulled back the covers. He laid the little girl on the sheet, then unlaced her shoes and gently tugged them from her feet.

A lump formed in her throat as she watched him exercise such love and tenderness toward the child. She reminded herself that even murderers were sometimes fathers. Loving a child had nothing to do with his true character.

He tucked the doll into her arms, then pulled the covers up around Jennie. When he turned to exit the room, his dark eyes were gentle. The gentleness vanished when he looked at Olivia. "What do you have against me, Lady Devonworth? We've only just met, yet you bait me at every turn. Do you enjoy seeing me squirm when Eleanor's name is mentioned? I know what people say—that she would rather die than marry me. It's all gossip. I would have thought an intelligent woman like yourself would look deeper."

"People think she killed herself?" Though Katie and Addie had mentioned the possibility, Olivia hadn't realized it was the speculation of the public.

"The topic has been mentioned."

"Why do you care what I think?"

He pressed his lips together. "I have no idea why I care," he said. "For some reason it grates that you would be so quick to believe the worst."

Her pulse jumped in her throat. She examined his expression. Was that genuine hurt in his eyes? Surely he wouldn't really care what she thought. Was he attempting to use his charm on her?

"I don't really know you, Mr. Bennett. I apologize if you thought I was being judgmental. I told Eleanor's mother I would try to discover more about what happened to her."

His lips pressed together. He brushed past her. "Good night, Lady Devonworth."

She followed as he stalked down the stairs. The front door slammed. That had been awkward. She feared the coldness between them would thwart her investigation. She had to take more care to hide her disdain.

Katie met her at the doorway when she entered the parlor. "It sounded as though Harrison slammed the door on his way out."

"I fear I angered him with too many questions about Eleanor."

"Oh dear. He's really a wonderful man, Olivia. Why are you so sure he murdered Eleanor?"

"Don't you find it odd that she died within days of his return to town? It was an arranged marriage. Perhaps he objected."

"That doesn't mean he murdered her."

"Harrison said others in town have speculated she killed herself rather than marry him. Is this true?"

Katie nodded. "No one really knows what happened, so they talk."

"I don't believe it. Something happened to her. I intend to find out what." She realized her friend was even more pale. "Are you all right?"

"I . . . I need the bathroom." Katie rushed down the hall to the room on the left.

Olivia heard her retching and followed. "You're ill."

Katie was white as she turned from rinsing her mouth in the sink. "I'm increasing."

"How lovely!" Olivia hugged her and led her back to the parlor. "Does Will know?"

Katie shook her head. "I didn't want to tell him until I was sure. I saw Dr. Lambertson today, and he confirmed it."

Olivia guided her to the sofa and lifted her feet onto the cushions. "All the more reason for the ball to be a success, so we can get to planning the nursery."

Stewart Hall was quiet. The Jespersons weren't up yet, though Olivia supposed the servants were busy below on the first floor. She crept down the hall to her sister's room. It still held the essence of Eleanor's perfume. Olivia stood by the bed and closed her eyes. She could nearly hear her sister's laughter.

Goldia touched her hand and broke the spell. "Are you all right, Miss Olivia?"

Olivia opened her eyes. "I miss her, Goldia."

The maid's eyes were moist. "She's in a better place."

"I hope so." The prospect of heaven always confused Olivia. How could a person know when she was good enough to get there? She'd gone to church all her life but never had a sense of knowing who God was, or that he really knew her soul. Eleanor's death made Olivia think more about her own life.

She went to the closet and opened the door. The space was nearly as big as a room. Pink and blue silk dresses festooned with lace hung inside. Hatboxes were stacked nearly to the ceiling. Slippers lined the floors. Eleanor's perfume wafted into the air, even stronger now. She'd culled the dresses suitable for her own figure the day she arrived, but it was time to search for clues.

Olivia caught the sleeve of the closest dress, a royal-blue satin with a white lace overlay. "I remember when she wore this to the Astors' ball last season," she said.

"I'm surprised she brought it with her," Goldia said.

"I think she wanted to recapture that night. I expect she found an occasion to wear it here. No one would have seen her in it before."

Goldia nodded. "What are we looking for? Just an envelope?"

Olivia began to rummage through the clothing. "I assume she left it in the envelope, but she might not have. If it was truly important, she would have hidden it somewhere."

"Maybe with her jewels," Goldia suggested.

Olivia shook her head. "It's the first place someone would look." She stepped deeper into the closet, allowed the aromas to envelop her. The dresses rustled as she brushed past them. She ran her fingers along the luxurious fabrics. Eleanor was so much more equipped for this life than she was. Most of the time she felt she was living someone else's life. Wasn't there more to her existence than the next party and the latest fashion? Though she was ashamed to admit it to herself, she felt a real purpose in tracking down who had harmed Eleanor. She found her mind and spirit quite engaged with the puzzle. Though of course it was so much more than a puzzle. She wanted whoever had killed her sister brought to justice.

Pushing aside several dresses, she studied the back of the closet. Plain plaster walls painted pink were all she saw. She studied the floor and baseboard. Nothing.

"I'd like you to go through all the hatboxes," she told Goldia. "Perhaps she hid something there."

Goldia cast a dubious glance at the shelves. "That will take a fair amount of time, Miss Olivia."

"Lady Devonworth," Olivia reminded her. "You must get into the habit. Oh, and let's be quick about it. I intend to visit Eleanor's grave later this morning. You will accompany me?"

"Yes, miss."

"You start on the boxes. I shall examine the bureau drawers." Olivia was only too glad to leave the closet behind with its lingering essence of Eleanor. She glanced around the lavish bedroom. Had Eleanor redone this herself? The decor appeared newer, more feminine, than any other room except Olivia's own chamber. The paper on the walls was a delicate basket pattern in pale pink and ivory. The bedspread was pink silk with a lace skirt. The Persian rug under the bed appeared new, as did the furniture, the newest Arts and Crafts style.

She eyed the bed, then lifted the skirt and thrust her hand under the mattress as far as she could get it. Her fingers touched nothing but the springs. She knelt and peered under the bed. Not even dust. She rose and went to the dresser. The mirror bounced her reflection back at her. She quite loathed her olive coloring. Her mother had called her a little gypsy when she was a child. She'd wanted hair like sunshine, just like her mother's and Eleanor's. Instead, she'd taken after her father's mother, who was of French descent.

Olivia picked up the picture on the dresser. It was of the two sisters on Olivia's last birthday. They'd been told not to smile, and the somber expressions on their faces contrasted with the merriment in their eyes. Had it been only three months ago? She felt so much older now than twenty-five. Grief would do that. In quick succession she'd lost her father and her sister.

"Lady Devonworth," Goldia said. "I found this in the crown of a hat." She held out a vellum dance card.

Olivia stepped to the closet and took the card. "She appears to have danced more than once with Mr. Frederick Fosberg," she said. "I don't recognize the name. Mr. Bennett's name is not on here."

"Maybe the dance took place before he returned from Africa. Miss Eleanor was here for nearly three months. She came right after your birthday."

Olivia studied the scrawled names on the card. "She danced with the gentleman four times. That's hardly proper when she was engaged to be married."

Could she have been wrong? Maybe Eleanor had fallen in love with another man in Harrison's absence. And why hide this dance card? A memento of a forbidden romance, perhaps?

"I'm surprised Katie or Addie didn't mention it to me. Surely the whole town noticed. I need to find this man and see what he meant to Eleanor." She rubbed her head. "Maybe I'm wrong and Eleanor did throw herself in the sea rather than be married to a man she did not love."

"I don't believe it," Goldia said.

Olivia heard noises in the hall. "Let's go." She pulled the door shut behind them.

Jennie ran toward her, and Olivia scooped her up. The child still had her new doll clutched under her arm. She planted a kiss on Olivia's cheek. "Are you hungry? I think breakfast should be ready." When the little girl nodded, Olivia set her down. Jennie took off for the staircase.

Katie joined Olivia at the top of the stairs. She smiled a good-morning. "You look like you're feeling better."

"I'm actually hungry."

"How did Will take the good news?"

"He's over the moon!"

Before she went downstairs, Olivia laid her hand on her friend's arm. "I found this." She showed Katie the dance card. "Do you know this man?"

"Mr. Fosberg. I met him at this same party. I saw Eleanor with him, but I thought they were discussing business."

"So she did not seem overly friendly with him?"

Katie bit her lip. "Well, there was some talk at Addie's party," she admitted. "I did my best to squelch it, but you know how gossip can spread."

"Did Eleanor say anything to you about seeing him again?"

Katie shook her head. "She was soon caught up in a whirlwind of social engagements. I didn't see her nearly so often after the party."

Olivia thanked her and the two women went down to the dining room for breakfast. She saw the morning post and snatched the new edition of *Woman's Home Companion*.

"I love that magazine," Katie said. "I like the Kewpie pages."

"That's what I wanted to read," Olivia said. She motioned to the servants to begin serving as she seated herself at the long table. Toying with her water glass, she glanced at her friend. "Sometimes I think I'm just like one of the Kewpies. Expected to be cute and accomplished on the outside and perfect in every action. Posed for the most advantage without a thought in my head."

Katie leaned over and patted her hand. "You're more than a Kewpie. You have wit and insight. You challenge the status quo. You're quite remarkable."

"I should have been born a man," Olivia said. "My insight does me no good when I'm stuck in a box."

"God expects you to use those gifts. You just have to be brave enough to do it. Ask God how he wants you to use your gifts."

She'd never considered asking God something so personal. He was, well, God. He couldn't be bothered with mundane problems. Did Katie really talk to him on such an intimate level? It was much too personal a question to ask.

TEN

BIRDS SANG IN the oleander bushes lining the graveyard. Some sweet flower left its presence on the wind. Olivia had dreaded yet longed to come today. The grave would be fresh, still uncovered by grass.

Goldia walked beside her with a basket of flowers. Neither of them spoke in the somber moment. The minister had said Eleanor rested under a live oak tree overlooking the ocean. She scanned the cemetery and walked in the direction of the waves' murmur. There was the iron fence Mrs. Bagley had mentioned.

Goldia pointed to a huge tree. "There it is, Lady Devonworth."

Olivia spotted it at the same time. The mound of dirt appeared so stark and lonely. Tears came to Olivia's eyes, and she quickened her steps though she longed to run away. She reached the grave and sank onto her knees. The scent of raw dirt stung her nose. "Oh, Eleanor," she whispered. "I can't bear it."

"Miss Olivia," Goldia whispered.

Olivia lifted her head and started to correct the maid when she saw the reason for Goldia's alarm. Harrison Bennett was striding toward them with his collie in tow.

She hastily rose and brushed the dirt from her skirt. How dare he intrude on this moment? And with a *dog*?

"Mr. Bennett," she said when he reached them. "I didn't expect to see you here."

She didn't care for the way he studied her expression. She was much too vulnerable right now to hide her agitation. And tears hung dangerously close.

He grabbed the dog as it started toward her. "I could say the same, Lady Devonworth," he said. "Though I suppose propriety demanded you bring flowers. Did you know Eleanor personally or are you just interested because you are using their home?"

"I knew her very well," she said, not caring if she revealed too much. "I've known her since she was a child. She was a lovely girl."

"So she was," he said. "You've never said how you know the Stewarts. Are you neighbors?"

She bit her lip, wishing she were more prepared for the questions. She should have thought of how to explain her connection.

"I'm surprised Eleanor never mentioned you," he said.

"You hardly spent much time with her," she said. "You yourself told me you'd only come back to Mercy Falls four days before she died."

"True enough."

"So what are you doing here?" she countered.

He glanced away as if he didn't know how to answer her. "I saw the Stewart crest on your carriage," he mumbled. "My mother asked me to issue an invitation."

If he only knew how they would have to sell everything, even the manor and the carriage, if she didn't make an advantageous marriage. "Invitation?"

He proffered a card. "She'd like to have you to tea."

"I didn't realize your mother was still alive," she said, then when his brows rose she wished she could call back the words. "I mean, your father is often in New York but he makes no mention of a wife. I'd heard of the accident and assumed . . ."

Lines of pain creased the skin around his mouth. "I believe he's rather ashamed of her since she's been in the wheelchair."

"I'm sorry," she said. "I meant no harm."

"I'm sure there are even more rumors than I know about," he said, his voice harsh.

"I should be honored to have tea with your mother," she said, wanting to ease the darkness in his eyes. "This afternoon?"

"If you please."

"Where does she live?"

"In the house across the street from mine. I've tried to convince her there is plenty of room in my home for her, but she abhors the idea of being a burden. Besides, Father comes every few months, and he and I . . ." He shrugged.

"You don't get along with your father?"

"You could say that." He grinned. "I see what you're doing, Lady Devonworth. We had been talking about you and you so adroitly changed the subject."

Her cheeks warmed. "Not at all. I'm an open book, Mr. Bennett."

"More like murky water," he said, grinning. He glanced at Goldia. "I don't believe we've met."

It was uncommon for someone to want to be introduced to a servant. Was his concern all a show? "This is Goldia. She was employed by Miss Olivia Stewart, a-and was looking for a new position. I was happy to give her one as I was in need of a good lady's maid. Olivia spoke very highly of her."

"So you know Olivia as well. You never said."

Why had she mentioned the name Olivia? It was a disastrous mistake. He was focusing too much attention on her relationship with the Stewarts. Surely he couldn't suspect her real identity, could he? "I know the Stewart family quite well, all of them. Why else would they give me free access to their home?"

"Why indeed," he said. The glint in his eyes vanished. "I'd be pleased to escort you to tea at Mother's. Shall I call for you at twelve thirty?"

"Yes," she said. His mother might reveal something. And surely she'd met Eleanor.

He bowed. "I'll leave you now until this afternoon." His long legs quickly carried him away.

"He knows something, miss," Goldia said. "That one is too smart for his own good."

Olivia waved away the concern. "I'm more interested in finding out what his mother knows about Eleanor's death."

⌘

"I'm sure we shall find Mother in the parlor," Harrison said as he led Lady Devonworth down the hall. Had he ever been so aware of a woman's presence before? The slightest movement of her hand on his arm made him uncomfortable. "I am most grateful you agreed to my mother's request. She doesn't have many friends."

"Because of being crippled?" she asked. She paused to take in the portraits of his ancestors in the foyer.

He nodded. "It's difficult for her to meet for lunch or tea, and the sidewalks are not always easy for her attendant to navigate with the wheelchair."

She turned back toward him. "You are her only child?"

"I had a younger brother who fell from a tree when he was ten. He died of a broken neck."

"I'm so sorry."

The odd thing was she seemed to mean it. Her husky voice was soft, and the dark eyes she turned on him were liquid with warmth. There was so much about her that he didn't understand. Her presence in the graveyard raised so many questions. Her reddened eyes and obvious distress were out of place. She herself had said the Stewarts were friends, not relatives, so why such obvious grief? And every time he tried to dig into her background, she turned the conversation away from herself.

Piano music tinkled out from the parlor. "Your mother?" Lady Devonworth asked.

He nodded. "She's very accomplished."

He led her to the parlor, where he found his mother seated at the grand piano. Her fingers danced over the keys in Liszt's "Dante Symphony," and her eyes were dreamy. She wore her hair up and even had a hint of rouge on her face.

His mother stopped playing when she saw them in the door. A smile brightened her eyes. "Hello! I lost track of time, my dear."

The dog rose when he saw them. Lady Devonworth flinched, and he ordered the dog to lie down. "He won't hurt you," he said. "Collies are great dogs."

"It was a collie that bit me."

"That's quite unusual. Were you teasing it?"

She frowned. "I don't remember. I was a child. But it should have been trained not to attack."

"True enough," he said.

"Give me a moment to get settled on the sofa," his mother said.

"Of course." Harrison raised a brow in Lady Devonworth's direction, then led her back to the hall. "She doesn't like others to see her struggle," he said. "Shall I show you around the house until her attendant helps her to the sofa?"

"I should like to see it."

With her fingers on his forearm, he felt tongue-tied and awkward, but he escorted her toward the morning room. The house was so large and grand, he often felt lost in it, but Lady Devonworth would be quite at home with its silk-covered walls and plush carpets.

"Did your mother get along with Eleanor?" Lady Devonworth asked.

Her preoccupation with Eleanor truly annoyed him. "This is where Mother does her morning correspondence," he said, indicating the white desk by the window. Her questions were entirely inappropriate. A lady of her caliber should have realized by now that her persistent questions were the definition of rudeness.

"It's quite lovely," she said, glancing around the blue room.

Mary Grace appeared behind them. "Mrs. Bennett is ready to receive you," the nurse said.

At least he didn't have to hear any more of Lady Devonworth's questions. He escorted her back to the parlor. His mother was pouring out the tea. Blueberry scones were arranged on a silver tray. "Mother, this is Lady Devonworth. Lady Devonworth, I'd like you to meet my mother, Mrs. Esther Bennett."

"I've been longing to meet you, Lady Devonworth," his mother said. "Come sit beside me and tell me all about yourself."

He suppressed a smile. This had been a grand idea. His mother could pry the slightest secret from the most reticent person. Once Lady Devonworth was seated beside his mother, he dropped into the leather chair by the fireplace and settled back to watch his mother do her magic.

Wariness flickered in Lady Devonworth's eyes as she sipped her tea and studied the older woman. "You have a lovely home, Mrs. Bennett."

"I'm sure you're used to much grander surroundings," his mother said. "My son tells me you are a longtime friend of the Stewarts. What does your father do, my dear?"

Lady Devonworth took a sip of tea. Harrison was sure it was a delay to gather her thoughts. And he was certain her cheeks paled. His tense muscles relaxed. Watching this unfold would provide much entertainment. He'd been no match for the lady's questioning, but his mother was a master.

"Might I have a scone?" Lady Devonworth asked.

"Of course." His mother lifted the silver tray to the young woman, then put it back on the table after Lady Devonworth had selected a pastry. "About your father?"

Harrison's lips twitched. His mother was not about to let the young woman slip out of the net.

"Business is so boring, don't you think? My father has often spoken of his various interests, but it goes right over my head." She laughed daintily. "I'd much rather talk about this charming town. I quite adore Mercy Falls already. I'm sure Eleanor Stewart loved it the moment she saw it. I'm surprised she didn't stay here with you, though. To help you in any way she could."

Spots of color appeared on his mother's cheeks at the implied condemnation. "Of course I invited her! But the girl loved parties and wanted to plan several luncheons and evening soirees. It was too much for a lady in my condition. We both agreed it was best for her to have her own space."

Harrison gaped, then shut his mouth. Lady Devonworth had slipped through the snare with no effort.

"Oh, Eleanor loved parties. I can see how such merriment day and night would be quite wearing for you," Lady Devonworth said. "She was quite the chatterbox."

"The girl talked incessantly," his mother said. "In quite an entertaining way, of course," she added hastily.

"Of course. Eleanor was a most charming girl," the younger woman said.

Harrison had no idea that his mother hadn't liked Eleanor. He stared at Lady Devonworth and saw the frown crouching between her eyes. The silence was beginning to be awkward.

Lady Devonworth sipped her tea. "Do you know Frederick Fosberg?" she asked him.

"The attorney from the city who owns a house up the mountain?"

"Yes, the attorney," she said.

He shook his head. "Not personally. How did you hear of him?"

She nibbled on her scone. A delaying tactic, of course. She was quick to ask questions but less apt to answer them. "I may need his services, and I wondered if you would recommend him."

"I've met Fred a few times," his mother said. "He has done some business with your father on occasion, Harrison. A fine young man.

In fact, he's due to come to town in a few days. If you'd like to meet him, Lady Devonworth, he'll be our dinner guest on Friday night. Do come."

"I'd be delighted," she said quickly.

"My husband thinks the world of him. He's a hit with the ladies in town. A most eligible bachelor."

Lady Devonworth smiled. "I'm only interested in his business acumen."

Harrison resolved to find out what he could about this Fosberg. The lady had a purpose in her questions.

ELEVEN

OLIVIA HAD LIKED Harrison's mother, but the stress of navigating dangerous questions had drained her. She rubbed her aching head. She'd been prowling the second floor since the servants retired for the night. She should seek some rest herself, but she needed to find the letter. Eleanor was a pack rat, and Olivia knew she wouldn't have destroyed it. It had to be in this house somewhere.

She glanced around the last bedroom on this floor. Goldia had made subtle inquiries of the other servants, and this room had never been occupied. It was at the end of the hall. The hissing gaslight cast a yellow glow over the burgundy wallpaper. She'd poked through the empty closet and pulled out every drawer in the dresser but found nothing.

"Olivia."

She flinched and her head came up. The whispered voice came from nowhere. She strained to see through the shadows in the room. "Who's there?" The man had called her by name, a name she'd taken great care to conceal.

"It's me, Olivia."

Her heart leaped against her ribs. Her throat went tight. The voice sounded vaguely familiar, almost like her father. Was it a ghost? She backed toward the door. She needed to get to safety. She grasped the doorknob and yanked on it. The door refused to open. She tugged on it again, the muscles in her throat still blocking any sound.

"Olivia," the voice whispered again. Something clanged.

It was no ghost. That's when she realized whoever it was had to be using the mansion's speaking tube. She yanked on the door again, but it refused to budge. Had he locked her in? She knelt on the redwood floor and peered through the keyhole. No light. Something blocked it from the other side. Her breath came fast. Could someone be hanging on to the doorknob, laughing at her puny efforts to escape?

The mental image washed away her fear and released the tightness of her throat. She pounded on the door. "Let me out!" She twisted the knob again but the door held fast. The window. She rushed to the window and threw up the sash. Salt air tugged loose strands of her hair.

Leaning out the window, she searched the dark yard below her. There was nothing to enable her to climb down from this height. She would find no purchase on the smooth stone of the facade. When she pulled her head back inside and went back to the door, she thought she heard a slight click. She twisted the knob again, and this time it turned easily. Her initial impulse was to yank the door open, but what if the man waited on the other side?

She snatched her hand back and stared at the closed door. She couldn't stay here all night. Forcing herself to turn the knob again and pull, she peeked into the shadowed hall. Empty. She twisted the knob to extinguish the lamp, then rushed down the deserted hall toward her bedroom. The hallway was better lit here, and the tightness in her chest eased as the shadows fled. Outside her door, she paused. What if he was waiting inside? She needed assistance.

The servants were already abed, but there was a speaking tube in all the bedrooms. She could summon Jerry or one of the other footmen. Will was nearby also. She could call for him, but the thought of rousing the entire family deterred her. She went past her door to Eleanor's bedroom. She felt along the dark wall. *The knob for the lights should be here somewhere.* Her fingers encountered the round switch and she twisted it. Light illuminated the room. It was empty. She went to the speaking tube by the bed.

"Thora, we have an intruder in the house. Please send Jerry or one of the men to my room immediately." She didn't like the way her voice shook.

There was silence, then her housekeeper's sleepy voice answered her. "Right away, Lady Devonworth."

Olivia went back to the hall and waited under the wash of light. She was safer out of the shadows. Moments later footsteps pounded down the steps from the third floor.

Still buttoning his shirt, Jerry burst out of the enclosed stairway. He was barefoot. "Lady Devonworth, you said there is an intruder?"

Her limbs had begun to tremble. Olivia nodded and fought the burning in her eyes. It was just a reaction, but she couldn't give in to it. "He spoke into the speaking tube."

"What did he say?"

She bit her lip. "He just whispered my name."

He herded her to her room and opened the door. "Wait here until I check the house."

"What if he's in my room? I . . . I was elsewhere."

He glanced at her with a question in his eyes but didn't ask where she'd been. Flipping on the light, he left her standing in the doorway while he examined her bedroom, including the closet. When he found nothing, she entered and sank onto the chair by the dresser.

"Thank you," she said. "I shall lock the door after you."

"I'll report back after examining the rest of the house. The other footmen are scouring the grounds."

When he left, she rose and threw the lock on the knob. It couldn't have been her father's voice. He had been dead for six months.

❧

The tree would provide the perfect frame for his new aeroplane. Harrison pointed out the specimen he wanted, and the lumberjacks set to work. He would never admit it to his father, but he enjoyed getting out of the office and seeing how men worked with their hands. When he was a teenager working here to learn the ropes of his father's latest acquisition, he'd liked exercising his muscles hauling timber and running his end of a saw. It gave him a chance to clear his head and be one with God. Even now, he liked doing more than pushing papers.

His valet, Eugene, worked alongside him as he loaded some boards for the wings onto a trailer. "You've been quiet today, sir," Eugene said.

"Just thinking about the new flying machine. I've come up with a new idea. What would you think about something on the bottom? Like skis. Something that allowed it to land on water?"

"On water? You mean the ocean?"

He shook his head. "Probably not the ocean. The waves would upend it. I was thinking about a lake. The weather would have to be calm."

Eugene paused and wiped his brow with a red kerchief. "It might work. Are you going to attempt to build it on this machine?"

"I believe so." Eugene's calm gaze lingered on Harrison's face. "What is it?" Harrison asked.

"You're a true visionary, sir. I never realized until now."

Harrison stopped and tugged on his collar. "Hardly a visionary, Eugene. It's interesting though, no?"

"The world is changing, as you've said," his valet said. "Men like you will help shape it, if you have the courage to lead."

Harrison thought of his father's hard face. "Some expectations are hard to break."

"They are. Even your father's expectation for you to marry a Stewart lady. What will you do now, sir?"

"I know one thing. I'm not going to marry some highbrow just to satisfy my father's desire to be part of the nobs."

"What will become of Mrs. Stewart?"

"I wouldn't want Mrs. Stewart to be deprived of her fortune."

"Perhaps your father will give her a fair part of the mine anyway."

"I don't see him ever being willing to do that."

"Did Mr. Stewart ever discuss this matter with you personally? The marriage, I mean."

"No." That fact had always bothered Harrison. Arrangements had been made while his father and Mr. Stewart were in Africa. His father had come home from that trip with the agreement in his pocket. And Mr. Stewart was dead.

"I'm going to tell Father to pay her anyway," he said.

Eugene nodded.

Harrison pressed his lips together. In the past five years he'd seen the desire for more and more money consume his father. They were comfortable. There was no need for more. But his father wanted to be accepted as one of the premier families in America. He lusted after that power to an unhealthy degree.

TWELVE

THERE WAS A brook around here somewhere. Olivia could hear it gurgling and churning over the rocks. Redwoods towered overhead, their leaves so high she nearly couldn't see them. Addie held little Edward's hand, guiding her son as the women picked their way along the path through the forest. His German shepherd, Gideon, nosed after a ground squirrel, and Olivia kept an eye on the dog.

"Are we almost there?" Olivia asked. Something about the mist curling around her boots and the lack of city noise had her glancing over her shoulder.

"Nearly there," Katie called. She was the vanguard of the little group.

Olivia heard it then—the roar she'd mistaken for the wind in the trees became more prominent. The falls came into view. Clear water tumbled from the black rocks to the pool of water at the base. The dog barked and raced to leap into the clear lake.

"The perfect spot to plan the ball," Addie said. She set down the basket she carried and withdrew a red-and-white checkered table-cloth from it. Once she spread it on the ground, she began to lift sandwiches wrapped in waxed paper from the basket.

Olivia settled beside her and watched the little boy and his dog frolic in the water. She glanced into the shadows of the trees. Their location was exposed and dangerous. She needed to tell her friends about last night's intruder. At least Jerry had come with them. She felt safer with a man in attendance. He hovered a discreet distance from their little picnic.

"Have you had any success in finding the letter?" Katie asked.

Olivia shook her head. "I've poked through every corner of Eleanor's room, and most of the other bedrooms. I can't imagine where she hid it. I'm beginning to consider the possibility that it might not be in the house," she admitted. "If I don't find it, I'm not sure how I shall find out what so disturbed her. But there's more."

She told Addie about finding the dance card. "I thought you might offer insight, Addie, since you attend more parties. Katie doesn't really know Mr. Fosberg. Do you know the man?"

"Oh yes. Every matchmaking mama in town has her claws out. I'm surprised he hasn't gained twenty pounds from all the dinners he's been invited to."

"He has accepted all the invitations?"

Addie handed her a sandwich. "Indeed he has, though I haven't heard he's paid any particular attention to one young woman over another. He's opening a branch of his law office in town, and he's happy to make the acquaintance of anyone who might need his services."

"You've met him personally?"

Addie nodded. "I spoke with Eleanor in the garden the night he came to that dance you mentioned. I asked her about him when we spoke. She said they were discussing business."

"That was Katie's impression too," Olivia said. Katie nodded. "What kind of business could she possibly have? Our attorney handles everything. Even Mother has no head for business."

"She didn't elaborate," Addie said.

Olivia bit her lip. "There was an intruder in the house last night," she said. She told her friends about the whispers from the speaking tube.

Katie shuddered. "I'm most fearful for you, Olivia. You should have roused Will."

"I should have done just that." She tipped her head to the side. "Do you hear something?"

"What did it sound like?" Katie asked. "I hear only the wind."

"Almost like a child crying." The noise came again, a plaintive wail that lifted the hair on the back of her neck. "It sounds like it's coming from that tree." She rose and went to the base of a giant redwood. The trunk's diameter was so wide that if she stood with her arms outstretched, her fingers would not reach the outer edges.

She peered up the rough red bark. The pungent odor of the crushed needles under her feet filled the air. Something moved in the high branches. Squinting, she tried to make out what it was.

Katie stared up into the treetops too. "I do believe it's a kitten," she said.

"How could a kitten get so high?" Olivia asked. Another wail floated down from the treetops.

"It probably climbed."

"How can we get it down?"

"We would need a lumberjack," Addie said, joining them. "He could shimmy up with no problem."

"There is some activity going on at the lumber camp," Katie said. "I'll run over there and fetch help."

"Not by yourself," Olivia said.

"I'm quite used to hiking in the forest."

"I shall go with you," Olivia said. "Addie can stay with Edward so his enjoyment of the lake isn't cut short."

"As you wish." Katie pointed toward a trail through the redwoods. "It's that way."

The women set off. At first the trail followed the river, cutting a swath through the valley far below them. Then it began to climb out of the gully until they walked a track barely wide enough for their boots. One misstep and Olivia knew she could plunge to her death. She soon felt a blister on her right foot. Insects buzzed in her ears, and a light mist hung in the air that made it seem she breathed liquid.

"Are you managing all right?" Katie asked. She didn't even appear to be out of breath.

"I'm perfectly fine," Olivia said, biting back a request to stop a moment. She forced one foot in front of the other. This was no stroll on well-tended sidewalks.

They reached a break in the trees overhead, and Olivia looked down at the mass of the lumber site. It hurt her heart to see the majestic trees lying broken on the forest floor.

Her attention was caught by a familiar set of broad shoulders. Instead of a blue morning coat, Harrison wore a red-and-black checkered shirt and trousers held up with suspenders.

She pointed. "What's he doing here?"

"His father owns this camp. I suspect he's here overseeing." Katie started down the trail.

Olivia followed. She told herself the only reason her pulse had leaped when she saw Harrison was from fear.

❧

A movement caught Harrison's eye on the trail and he realized two women were picking their way along the narrow track to the camp. Alone. Squinting against the sun in his eyes, he frowned when he realized it was Lady Devonworth and Katie.

He moved to intercept them with Nealy on his heels. Lady Devonworth stepped into a shaft of sunlight. Her hair gleamed like a raven's wing. Her skin held a blush of color from her hike through the forest. He couldn't take his eyes from her. Since when did a lady hike through a redwood forest? Since when did she visit a lumber camp full of loud men?

He joined them. "Good afternoon, ladies. What drives you to such a rough place?"

Lady Devonworth eyed his dog and stayed back. "We found a kitten up a very tall tree. Only a lumberjack could get it down."

He could only stare at her. She'd come all this way for . . . for a cat? The moment stretched out. She held his attention until he recovered himself.

"I can get it down," he said before he could help himself. He wouldn't miss seeing what this was all about. "Let me get climbing hooks and a rope."

"You can climb a tree that high?"

"I worked every summer of my youth here at the camp. My father thought it important I learned to work. I was a tree topper." He liked the shock on her face. There was more to him than met the eye as well.

After he fetched the equipment and rejoined them, he pointed to the path. "Lead on, ladies."

Olivia's color was still high when she turned and walked back the way she'd come. Katie shot him a quick glance and smiled. There was sympathy in her eyes and he wasn't quite sure where it had come from. Or why.

Lifting her skirts, Olivia kept her head down and her gaze on the ground. She stumbled over a tree root. Her foot slipped toward the ravine. She screamed and threw out her hands but missed the branch that hung low.

Harrison leaped toward her, but Nealy dived past him. The dog latched onto her skirt. Harrison heard the cloth rip, but it held until he could seize her hand and pull her back to the path.

Her chest heaved as she fought for breath. She glanced past him to Nealy. "The dog saved me."

"He's trained to save," he said, putting his arm around her. He led her to a tree trunk. "Rest here a minute."

Katie rushed back to where he stood over Lady Devonworth. "Is she all right?"

"I nearly went over the edge." The lady swatted at a fly with a shaking hand. "Nealy grabbed me."

"Good boy," Katie crooned, rubbing the dog's ears. "See, a dog isn't so bad. Not all dogs are like the one that bit you, my dear. Pat him. He won't hurt you."

Nealy turned his dark eyes on the lady, and Harrison saw her shudder. He didn't think she would touch the dog, but she reached out her hand. Nealy took a step closer and pushed his long nose against her hand. She snatched her hand back, then moved it to his ears. She gave him a perfunctory pat. He wagged his tail.

She smiled. "I think that means he likes me."

"He likes everybody," Harrison said. "Are you strong enough to proceed?"

She nodded, and he helped her up. "Let me go first," he said when they reached a narrow path that led down. "I can assist you both." When she stood aside, he brushed past her and clambered down the incline, then turned and extended his hand. Her gloves were looking a bit worse for the wear. "I hope this creature is worth the loss of your gloves," he said. "I doubt your maid can remove the stains."

"I have others," she said, clutching his hand as she half slid, half stepped down the path.

They stood toe to toe, and he saw gold flecks in her dark eyes. Her breath was as sweet as the scent of the camellia blooming along the path. He should step away, but he stood frozen with her hand in his.

She pulled her hand free. "You need to help Katie."

"Of course." His face burned as she moved past him. He assisted Katie down the slope. "We are heading to the falls?" he asked her.

"We are. Addie stayed behind so Edward and Gideon could swim."

"We're not far now."

He let the women go ahead of him while he tried to figure out why he was acting such a fool. Was he so discomfited because she had a title? He'd never been one to take note of such inconsequential things. There was something different about Lady Devonworth.

He quickened his step to catch up with the ladies. The roar of the falls sifted through the trees, and he heard the dog bark and a child giggle. Nearly there. He reached the ladies and together they entered the clearing where Addie sat beside the lake. Edward splashed and swam with Gideon while she looked on. Nealy barked and ran past them to join the fun.

"We're back," Katie called.

Addie scrambled to her feet and hurried toward them with a smile. "That kitten is nearly hoarse from crying."

Harrison heard it then—the wail was faint and scratchy but frantic. "Which tree?"

"Here." Lady Devonworth stepped to the other side of the path and laid her hand on a giant redwood. "Up there." She pointed and he looked up. A tiny face was visible through the leaves. Three hundred feet up.

He whistled. "How'd that cat get up that high?"

Lady Devonworth raised a brow. "Climbed, I presume."

"Brilliant deduction, Sherlock," he said, grinning. She blushed and glanced away.

He dropped the rope from his shoulder, then strapped on the leather belt. After connecting all the hooks, he handed her the strap. "Circle the tree and bring it back to me on the other side."

He expected her to hold the grimy thing like she might a snake, but she gripped it firmly in her hands and hurried to do his bidding. Moments later she was on his other side.

"Is it big enough?"

He nodded and snapped the ring into his belt. Placing his feet against the rough bark, he began to shimmy up the tree. Though he wasn't about to admit it to her, it had been a good five years since he'd climbed a tree. And it was a long way up. Inch by inch, he traversed the big tree. The kitten cried all the more as he got closer.

His chest burned and his breath came hard by the time he reached the feline. "You're fine, cat," he said when the kitten backed away.

Grabbing it by the scruff of its neck to avoid being bitten or scratched, he tucked it inside his shirt. Its claws dug through his undershirt into his skin and he nearly howled himself. "Stupid cat, I'm trying to help you," he muttered.

The kitten loosened its claws, then snuggled under his armpit. Nothing like making it even more difficult to get down. He tried to reposition it, but it complained and grabbed him again, so he gave up and began to climb down. The muscles in his thighs cramped, and his hands were developing blisters, but he pressed on. The more he hurried, the sooner he could get rid of this cat. He was perspiring by the time he reached the ground. With a last shove, he dropped his booted feet to the soil and stood gasping at the foot of the tree.

"Great fun," he said, masking his rough breathing.

"Is the cat all right?"

He reached inside his shirt and grabbed the feline. "Youch! You little tiger, let go of me," he said. He succeeded in unhooking the kitten's sharp claws from his skin and pulled it out to view.

"Oh you poor darling," Lady Devonworth said, her voice soft.

The gentle sound of her voice went straight to his gut. He'd like to hear her use that tone with him.

THIRTEEN

JUST WATCHING HARRISON'S gentleness with the kitten did something to Olivia's midsection. In his common garb, she noticed the way his biceps bulged under his shirt and the mass of muscle in his thighs as he'd climbed the tree. Averting her eyes as he approached, she reminded herself that it was quite unseemly to notice such things.

"How about some sympathy for me?" he asked. "The wretched beast clawed me all the way down. I risked my life for it with no gratitude."

"I'm most grateful," she said. "Do your scratches need attention?" She made sure her tone dripped with impudence.

He grinned. "You're offering to tend to my wounds? I might take you up on that."

Her cheeks flamed at the flirtation in his voice. He was smooth, very smooth. "I'm sure you shall live," she said. "And thanks to you, so will Tiger here."

"I wouldn't name the monster if I were you. It's hard to let go once you name them."

"I have every intention of keeping Tiger," she said. "Such an adventurous animal deserves a home."

"He might not be happy cooped up after he's been allowed to roam free."

"You say that as though you have experienced it," she said. "Do you not enjoy your work?"

He lifted a brow. "A man can be good at something and still long for more."

"Are your planes what you long for?"

His expression sharpened. "I see the flash of interest every time the subject is brought up, yet you seem perfectly happy in your gilded cage."

She glanced away, unable to hold the intensity in his eyes. "I'm quite content with my place."

"What is your place? To be the fashion expert? To arrange flowers so beautifully your friends are astonished? Somehow you seem more ambitious than that. And much more intelligent."

She tried to hide her shock. "Ambition is more fitting for a man than a woman."

His grin widened. "A rather old-fashioned view. Your father's or your own? The times are changing."

"My father was a disciplinarian who felt women were pretty baubles for a man's arm. Somehow I think you share that view."

His lips tightened. "If you knew me at all, you would know how absurd that statement is."

She smiled, trying to defuse his anger. "My spies tell me every woman in town has her cap set for you."

His dark eyes flashed. "It's my money they are interested in."

She found that hard to believe. He had a magnetism that would draw any woman. Except her, of course. "Then you could have your pick of women to marry."

"I may never marry. I want a woman who will see me and not my bankroll." He raised a brow. "I think you are trying to deflect the conversation away from my question. What would you like to do if you could be more than that pretty bauble?"

What if she could be more than a debutante pursued for her title? What would she do with her life? For a long moment she allowed herself to dream of actually flying a plane herself, not just riding in one. But it was quite impossible. Her mother would be scandalized. Not that this man would understand.

"I can see you're thinking of something you'd like to do. What is it?"

"We have extra sandwiches if you'd like to share our lunch," she said.

"Coward," he said softly as she turned away.

She kept her gaze straight ahead and marched away with the kitten in her arms. The man was entirely too attractive. If she were the kind to notice something like that. Which she was most decidedly *not*.

Tiger began to knead her forearm where he lay nestled. She rubbed the kitten's head and he settled down on her chest.

Harrison fell into step beside her. "What are you ladies doing here in the first place?"

"Taking some fresh air while we plan the Lightkeeper's Ball."

"I'm sure you're most adept at planning such things. I suspect you could plan a ball or organize a suffragette march with equal accomplishment."

"I'm sure you have little experience with suffragette marches."

"More than you, I would wager. I'm on the board of the Mercy Falls group. I've marched in more events than you can count."

She stopped and stared. His expression was grave as if daring her to question his statement. "You support the woman's right to vote?"

"My mother is the smartest person I know. She knows more about the issues than my father does. Why shouldn't she have the vote? It's ludicrous it's not allowed yet."

He was serious. She closed her open mouth. What did she say to that? She could hardly express how much she admired him for that simple thing.

She stepped toward the pool of water. The clear stream gurgled over the rocks most charmingly. Her leather-bound journal lay on a rock where she'd dropped it. It was open to the list of things she planned for the ball. She stepped forward to grab it, and her foot slipped into an unseen hole and she toppled forward. Sharp pain seized her left wrist as she went down hard. The cat's claws dug into her arm. Her wrist throbbed in unison with the kitten's wails.

He knelt beside her with his hand slipping around her waist. "Are you injured?"

"My wrist," she managed to gasp out as she gripped it with her good hand.

He touched her forearm. "May I?"

Gritting her teeth, she nodded. His fingers probed the flesh of her wrist, already swelling. "I don't think it's broken, but it's a bad sprain. We should have it looked at."

"There's a doctor at Eaton Manor," Addie said. "It's not far."

Olivia had forgotten the consumption hospital was so close. "Perhaps we should go there. It's quite painful," she said.

The pain encasing her wrist spread up her arm. Eaton Manor would have something to help with the pain. Harrison pulled out a handkerchief and tied the ends together, then slipped it over her neck and under her elbow to support her arm. The pain began to ease. She was close enough to see the way his thick dark hair curled over his collar. Close enough to smell his bay rum pomade. She averted her eyes and prayed for this journey to soon be over.

Olivia's wrist throbbed in time with every step she took. Harrison led them over the uneven ground toward the large stone house looming in the distance. Nealy bounded ahead, then turned back occasionally as if to ask if they were coming.

"It's quite lovely," she said when the three-story manor home came into view. The kitten purred against her chest.

Addie and Katie walked on either side of Harrison. "It used to belong to Addie," Katie said. "She sold it to a group who turned it into a home for consumptives."

"How admirable," Olivia murmured. Perhaps John hadn't wanted to maintain such a palatial home. It was the most elaborate structure she'd seen in Mercy Falls since she arrived, rivaling the finest New York residences. Harrison helped her mount the wide steps to the double doors.

"Stay," he told the dogs.

"Let me warn them that we need assistance," Addie said, brushing past them. "Nann," she called out as she stepped into the hall.

A smiling woman hurried to greet them. In her forties, her merry blue eyes radiated welcome and interest. Her hair was still mostly light brown and coiled into a bun at the nape of her neck. She wore a high-collared gray gown with a cameo at the neck.

"Mrs. North, how lovely to see you."

"My friend is injured, Mrs. Whittaker," Katie said, gesturing to Olivia. "This is Lady Devonworth from Stewart Hall. We could use some assistance."

Nann's smile turned to an expression of concern. "Bring her into the waiting room," she said. "Dr. Lambertson is here right now. He's with one of our residents, but I'll fetch him at once. This way." She turned a bright smile Olivia's direction. "My daughter Brigitte is in service at the Stewart home. She's one of the chambermaids."

Olivia managed to smile past the pain. "I shall have to seek her out and say hello."

Harrison steered her forward to the doorway where Nann stood waiting.

"The waiting room is here," Nann said. "I'll have an empty exam room ready shortly. I need to disinfect it first."

Olivia could see the table in the examination room. "What is this place?" she whispered to her friends.

"It's a healing place for consumptives. They've done wonderful work here," Addie said. "Nann was a consumptive herself. She's in such good health now that she wanted to help others in her situation and was quick to accept this position when it was offered."

"She seems very nice, but you can smell the sickness here."

Katie nodded and put her handkerchief to her nose. Her face was pale. "I shall have to wait on the porch. I'm feeling a bit poorly."

"Oh my dear, do you want me to come with you?" Addie asked.

"I just need some fresh air."

"Edward can play. I'll come with you." Addie patted Olivia's hand. "You'll be fine. Harrison will take good care of you."

Her lungs squeezed. "I want to go home," she begged. "Please. I'm fine."

Addie glanced from her to the doorway where Katie had gone. "Let me check on Katie. I'll arrange for a car to get us. You can go home very soon."

Nann Whittaker stepped out of the exam room. "We're ready for you, Lady Devonworth."

"Really, I don't want to trouble the doctor," she protested as the woman led her to the examining room and helped her sit. "It's merely a sprain. Rest and ice are all I need." She started to slide from the table, but Harrison seized her arm.

"You'll be home soon enough. The doctor will be here in a moment," he said. His hand touched her back, and he cradled her head to his chest.

She could hear the *thump-thump* of his heart against her ear. Something about his touch drained the pain from her wrist.

"It won't hurt to have the doctor take a look," he said.

Her teeth began to chatter. Was it from the pain? "I'm cold," she said.

Harrison released her a moment. He shucked his flannel shirt, revealing a white undershirt beneath it. He placed the warm flannel around Olivia's shoulders. "Better?"

The flannel encased Olivia and the warmth that lingered from his body seeped into her skin. She nodded as the shaking began to subside. "Thank you," she whispered, clutching the edges of the shirt to her throat. His manly scent lingered in the cloth and calmed her.

"Here's the doctor now," he said, stepping back after a final embrace.

Olivia glanced up to see a gray-haired gentleman with erect shoulders step into the room. He had a stethoscope around his neck, and his necktie was askew. But his kindly expression did much to calm the last of her jitters. A woman in her fifties with a kind face and graying hair in a bun was on his heels.

"A slight accident, I see?" He stepped to the examination table and took Olivia's arm in his warm hands.

She winced when his fingers probed the swollen flesh of her wrist. "I fell."

He nodded and continued to press on her wrist and arm. "No real harm done. It's a severe sprain though, and you need to rest it for at least three days. I'm going to send some powder home with you for the pain. Keep ice on it and keep it elevated on a pillow. I'll stop and check on you tomorrow. Where might I find you?"

"This is Lady Devonworth," Harrison put in. "She's staying at Stewart Hall."

The doctor turned to his nurse. "Mrs. Fosberg, would you fetch some pain powder? I'll write out instructions on its use."

As the woman hurried from the room, Olivia stared after her. Fosberg? Could she be related to the Frederick Fosberg who had danced so often with Eleanor? Surely Fosberg was a very common name, especially in this area so settled with those of Scandinavian descent.

It seemed an eternity before the older woman came back with a bag of white powder in her hand. Olivia accepted it with a smile. "Mrs. Fosberg, I've heard your last name before in connection with a young man by the name of Frederick. Is he any relation?"

The woman's smile broadened and she stood taller. "That would be my boy. I'm so proud of him. He worked his way through college to become a well-respected barrister in the city. How did you hear of him?"

"I mentioned that I was in need of an attorney, and he was recommended."

"You couldn't go wrong with hiring my boy. He has his own office in San Francisco. After the Great Earthquake, he kept right on working when the other barristers abandoned the city. He's brave, that one. Handsome too. He's due to town in two days. Shall I have him call on you?"

"Please do. I have much to discuss with him." It would be a better way to find out about him than at Mrs. Bennett's dinner party. And she'd start by finding out what the young man's relationship had been with her sister.

FOURTEEN

HARRISON TOOK THE bumps as lightly as possible, but the woman beside him still winced when they hit the unavoidable potholes. He breathed a sigh of relief when Stewart Hall came into sight. He let the dog out on his side and told him to stay.

He parked the automobile by the front door. "Don't forget your blasted cat." He deposited the kitten in her good arm.

"I very much appreciate your kindness in making sure I got home," Lady Devonworth said. The cat meowed and she gasped, holding it out from her. "It's got sharp claws. It's going to ruin my dress."

"Give it to me." He grabbed the kitten and stuck it inside his undershirt. "Stupid cat," he muttered.

A young woman with a white apron over her black dress opened the door. "Poor Lady Devonworth," she said. "I have your bed turned down and ready."

"I really don't want to take to my bed. It's barely three," she protested. "Goldia, show us to parlor."

Harrison shook his head. "The doctor said to keep your arm elevated on a pillow. Besides, you've had a shock and need to rest. Show me her room, Goldia."

The maid glanced at her mistress, then scurried up the stairs. He ignored Lady Devonworth's objections and propelled her up the sweeping staircase. The maid gestured to him from a door halfway down the wide hall decorated with gold foil. "This is Miss Olivia's bedroom," he said.

Lady Devonworth stopped and stared up at him. "How would you know such a thing?" she whispered.

Her face paled, and he realized how his remark had sounded. "Please don't misunderstand. At Eleanor's last party, she showed her guests around the mansion and remarked that no one was allowed to stay in this room except her sister. Eleanor said she'd had it decorated to Olivia's tastes and was eager to see how her sister liked it."

"I see." The woman's voice seemed choked.

Were those tears in Lady Devonworth's eyes? He led her to the bed and stepped back. She was most decidedly pale and shaken. "Are you in pain?"

She glanced away and straightened her skirt. "A bit, yes. I shall have Goldia prepare me a pain draught."

She started to remove his flannel shirt, but he put his hand on her arm and shook his head. "Keep it until your maid helps you change into something warmer. I'll get it later."

She stopped and hugged the shirt close again. "Thank you for your kindness, Mr. Bennett."

He bowed. "I'm happy to be of assistance, Lady Devonworth. If you are in need of me at any time, ring me and I will be here in minutes."

"You're too kind," she said, not looking at him.

He studied her a moment before backing out of the room and taking his leave. Her manner had changed most abruptly when he mentioned she was in Olivia's room. Perhaps it was the pain in her wrist. What else could it be? He strode down the hall to the stairs. At the top of the steps, he hesitated when he heard Goldia call his name.

She was huffing by the time she reached him. "Mr. Bennett, sir."

"Is she all right, Goldia?"

Her hazel eyes narrowed. "She wants that kitten."

He'd forgotten he still had the blasted cat tucked into his shirt. He yanked the cat out into the light of day. It yowled its misery to the world and tried to claw its way back inside his shirt. He hastily handed it to the maid.

Goldia curtsied. "Thank you, sir. Miss, uh, Lady Devonworth was most upset at the thought that she wouldn't have the kitten in her possession."

He watched her scurry back down the hall with the cat nestled against her. He found to his dismay that he really didn't want to leave.

⟡

Cradling the kitten, Olivia fell back against the pillow. Her eyes burned, and she gulped back the sob building in her throat. Eleanor had decorated this room for her and she hadn't known it. She glanced around the lavishly appointed bedroom. The silk, blue and white with touches of palest yellow, had spoken to her the moment she'd taken stock of her surroundings. No wonder. Eleanor had known exactly what Olivia would like.

Goldia touched her hand. "Miss Olivia?"

Olivia didn't have the heart to remind her to call her Lady Devonworth. "I'm all right, Goldia. Just shaken up. Could you fetch me some tea?"

"Yes, ma'am, but I wanted to tell you I found this while you were out." Her hand went to her pocket and she held up a letter addressed to Eleanor. "I recognized your daddy's handwriting. I think this is what we've been searching for."

Olivia stared at the thin envelope in her maid's hand. Even from here, the familiar loop of the letter *J* made her pulse leap. Her hand shook as she reached for it. The paper felt fragile in her fingers. She slipped the letter from the envelope. It wasn't her father's usual thick vellum but a cheap, coarse paper. No monogram, just plain paper. She unfolded it and began to read.

Dear Eleanor,

I know this letter will come as a distinct shock to your sensibilities, as you have believed me dead for six months. Through no fault of Bennett's, I'm very much alive. Take every precaution against him. Avoid him at all costs. His son as well. You must break off the engagement immediately and return home. But take care, daughter! Surround yourself with those you can trust. Make sure you are on guard every moment. I fear for your life. I am nearby and I shall be in touch. In the meantime, depart from Mercy Falls immediately!

Your Loving Father

Olivia stared at the date at the top of the letter. A mere month before Eleanor died. Eleanor hadn't run from town soon enough. She must have been reeling from the shock of realizing her father was alive. *Or had been, a month ago.* Where was he? According to the letter, he was nearby. But where?

"Miss Olivia?" Goldia said. "You're scaring me. What's the letter say?"

"You didn't read it?"

"Of course not, miss. Weren't my place to read it. Besides, it's hard for me."

Olivia studied her maid's face. Did she dare tell Goldia the contents of the letter? Goldia had been with her since Olivia was twelve. If she wasn't trustworthy, who was? "It's from my father," she said.

"I was right!" Goldia smiled and clapped her hands.

"He's alive. He warned Eleanor to leave town. He said that Mr. Bennett had something to do with the circumstances and is dangerous."

Goldia's smile faded. "What about Mr. Harrison?"

Olivia hadn't wanted to think about Harrison. "Father says he's dangerous as well."

Goldia shuddered. "Handsome men sometime are."

"Father told Eleanor to avoid him and to break off her engagement. He must have had a good reason for such a drastic order."

An inner warning sounded at her father's lack of clear explanation, and she realized she didn't *want* to believe Harrison could be guilty of any devious behavior. Something in her rebelled at her father's autocratic orders as well. She'd spent her whole life trying to make up for the fact that she wasn't the son he wanted, and she realized she was tired of being treated as a lesser human being.

Goldia clasped her hands together. "Maybe he was mistaken. Did the letter say why he hasn't let your mama and you know that he was alive?"

Olivia inhaled as if that would stop the pain that swept over her. "He didn't mention me or my mother." What possible reason could he have for cutting them off so completely? Hadn't he realized how devastated they were by the news of his death? Her memories of her father were conflicted. She adored him, but he seldom noticed her.

She had to notify her mother at once. "I need to place a telephone call," she said.

"The only telephone on this floor is in the big bedroom at the end of the hall. Where your sister stayed."

Olivia swung her legs to the side of the bed, dislodging the kitten, who gave a protesting yowl. Her wrist throbbed at the movement, and she held it in the air with her other hand as she followed Goldia to their destination. She collapsed into a chair by the bed next to the stand that held the telephone.

"I could use that tea now, Goldia," she said. In truth, she wanted to be alone for this conversation. Once her maid nodded and scurried down the hall, Olivia lifted the receiver and rang for central. She gave the number to the friendly-sounding woman on the other end and waited. A transcontinental call took longer than local connections.

"Ringing now, Lady Devonworth," the operator said.

Olivia's fingers tightened on the earpiece, and she pressed it tightly against her head. Her mother was bound to be overcome by the news. And what if the operator listened in? "Hello?" she asked cautiously. When the operator didn't answer, she relaxed.

"Stewart residence," the housekeeper said.

"Iola, it's Olivia. I'd like to speak to my mother, please."

"Oh, Miss Olivia! I'm so relieved to hear your voice. I will fetch your mother straightaway."

Olivia waited through a clunk and much fumbling on the other end of the line. Even after several years of answering the phone, Iola was still uncomfortable with the instrument.

Her mother came on the line. "Olivia, is that you?"

"Yes, it's me."

"I expected you to call before now. Have you met with Harrison?"

Olivia suppressed a sigh. All her mother cared about was marrying Olivia off to money. "Yes, but he doesn't know I'm Olivia Stewart."

"What?"

"I'm using my proper title of Lady Devonworth. I wanted time to get to know him with no expectations."

Her mother tut-tutted. "You're behaving in a ridiculous manner. How will he know if you suit if he's not thinking of a future alliance?"

"I'm trying to find out what happened to Eleanor."

"She drowned, Olivia. That's it. You can't bring her back. I miss her too, but we must look to the future. I suspected you would need my assistance. I'm making arrangements for a train now. I should be there by week's end."

"I thought you were going to spend the season with Mrs. Astor."

"So did I, but in spite of my hints, I never received an invitation. I suspect she's heard whispers of our financial situation. Which is why it is all the more imperative that you make a suitable marriage. I suspect she is no longer willing to introduce you to her friend either. This may be your last chance, Olivia."

"Have you seen Mr. Bennett? Is he still in town?"

"I have neither seen nor heard from him. I assume he's not in New York at the present time."

"If you see him, remember not to tell him that I'm in Mercy Falls."

Her mother let out a sigh of exasperation. "It's a good thing I'm coming out. You need a firm hand and guidance."

"I shall be happy to see you." As long as she could convince her mother not to divulge her identity. "I could use your help in planning a charity ball as well."

"Ah, I should love that. What's it for?"

Olivia told her about the destroyed lighthouse. "But there is much happening here you don't know, Mother. I'm not quite sure how to tell you this."

"What is it?"

Olivia drew in a breath. "I have most astounding news, Mother. Father is still alive."

FIFTEEN

THE NEXT DAY Harrison made a courtesy call to Lady Devonworth to inquire about her wrist. Her maid told him she was resting and couldn't be disturbed, but he couldn't help but wonder if the lady was avoiding him. He set to work on his aeroplane.

On Friday he finished reviewing a signed contract for a new acquisition for Bennett and Bennett. He knew the contract was fair, but his father would say he should have been harder on the buyout. Harrison knew God had given him the talent to work with numbers and money. Why then did he yearn for something more than creating this? Why did his spirit long to be in his machine soaring above the clouds? His mother said he was throwing away God's gift by not tending to his talent in the boardroom. Did God always expect a man to use a gift? What about his own desires?

Frowning, he pushed away the ledger. A movement caught his eye and he looked up to see his father standing in the doorway.

Harrison pasted on a welcoming smile and rose with his hand outstretched. "Father, when did you arrive?"

"An hour ago." The elder Bennett shook Harrison's hand. "What are you working on, son?"

"Just filing the purchase papers of Riley Hardware."

"Excellent! May I see them?" He settled in the chair on the other side of the desk and pulled the papers toward him. His smile faded as he looked them over. "You paid them more than I specified."

"I wanted to be fair."

His father sighed. "They agreed to the price."

"Only because they were in financial straits with a sick child. We can afford it."

"That's not the point! The sale affects our bottom line. I want you to redo this."

"No. I've already spoken with Mr. Riley, and he's most appreciative. The papers are signed. This deal will allow him to take his daughter to New York for treatment. And I've already authorized the money to be transferred to his account."

His father's face reddened and his lips tightened. "We've spoken about this before, Harrison. You have got to quit this kind of behavior or you will pauper us."

"Not much chance of that. Do you even *know* how much we have in the bank? It's astronomical. Almost obscene."

His father smiled thinly. "There is no such thing as too much money. Even with all our wealth, we still are not accepted in the highest echelon of society. *That* is my goal. With Eleanor dead, we have to find another woman in that set. Mrs. Stewart is trying to convince Olivia to take Eleanor's place."

Harrison folded his arms across his chest. "I'm not agreeing to anything like that again, Father. I'm tired of being auctioned off like a cow. I'll find my own wife, thank you. And I can assure you it will *not* be a Stewart. I'd rather be single than marry Olivia."

His father studied his face. "What has gotten into you, boy? This is important for your future."

"Eleanor betrayed me. I wouldn't trust a Stewart woman again."

"I'm sure your mother will be distressed to hear this."

Harrison wasn't about to let his father leverage the usual excuse of upsetting his mother, not when the older man cared not a whit about her feelings. He had all but abandoned her. "Mother wants me to be happy."

"She tells me you've been keeping company with a woman from New York. A Lady Devonworth."

"I'd hardly call it 'keeping company.' She's merely an acquaintance."

"Your mother says she believes her family is one of the Four Hundred."

The Four Hundred were the most elite families in America. They were the ones invited to the upper echelon of society balls, the ones who were invited to the best homes and the most elite clubs.

"Why do you do this, Father?" he asked. "Why do you care what a bunch of nobs think? To them we'll always be swells who are getting too big for our britches. We're doing all right. Making money, gaining a reputation. We don't need to be part of that set."

His father's jaw hardened. "Let me explain something to you, boy. General Marshall invited me to attend a luncheon at the Vanderbilt's. I arrived to find the invitation had been rescinded. I will not tolerate a humiliation such as that again. I *will* be accepted!"

There was no more to be said. It would do no good to point out how prideful it was to insist on being accepted by the nobs.

"What of this Lady Devonworth? She is unmarried, is she not?" his father asked.

"She is unmarried and I like her."

His father scowled. "I've never heard of the Devonworths. I doubt the woman carries the social clout of a Stewart, and I'm determined for you to marry a woman of quality who will allow you to walk in the highest levels of society. Most couples live separate lives anyway. Look at your mother and me."

"I'd like more from my marriage than what you two have." He knew it was the wrong thing to say the second the words left his lips.

His father drew himself up and huffed. "I don't know where you've gotten these romantic notions, boy. From that riffraff you hang out with, I presume. A lightkeeper and his wife. What kind of example is that for you to follow?"

"The best kind," Harrison said. "And what of that agreement with the Stewarts about the mine?"

His father's eyes glittered. "I shall continue to own controlling interest in the diamond mine. That was the agreement."

"But that would leave Mrs. Stewart and her daughter in desperate straits."

His father shrugged. "That's hardly my problem."

"You sound as though you hate her."

"She could champion me, introduce me to her set."

"She has tried that. She's had you to their dinners. It's hardly her fault the others don't include you on their guest lists."

"Whose side are you on, boy? You just told me you wouldn't marry Olivia if she were the last woman on Earth."

"That doesn't mean I want them punished for Eleanor's failures. Besides, I didn't know there was a side."

"There is, and you'd better stand with me."

"I don't think so, Father. I want nothing to do with something this dastardly. The marriage arrangement should stand. You shame me. I want you to give her the share of the mine that you promised. Then we'll be done with the Stewarts for good. We'll owe them nothing."

His father's mouth gaped and he stared. "I'll do no such thing."

Claude Bennett had never in his life done anything out of the goodness of his heart. When he came back from Africa with an agreement to turn over controlling shares in the diamond mine to Mrs. Stewart only if the two families were joined, Harrison was flummoxed. He had agreed to the engagement because he suspected his father had seized on Stewart's death as a means to gain complete possession of the mine. Harrison hadn't wanted the Stewart women left with no source of income. And the fact that the match would have benefited him too played a part. That engagement had been such a disaster that the mere suggestion of marrying Olivia in Eleanor's place was loathsome. He'd find another way to help the women if need be. Or manage to talk his father into it.

"We'll speak of this later." He turned toward the door. "I must call on Lady Devonworth. She suffered a sprained wrist a few days ago, and I wish to check on her."

"Tell her that I'd like to be introduced," his father called after him.

"Over my dead body," Harrison muttered under his breath. He stalked to the motorcar and climbed in. He started the engine and pulled away before he said anything more his father would try to make him regret. Having the man show up was going to be difficult. He'd push to be invited to the ball Lady Devonworth was planning. He'd play matchmaker at every turn and probably get Mother in on the efforts as well.

Harrison wished he could climb into his plane and fly off into the sunset. Never come back. See the world and see what else God had for him. Vistas beyond this small town and the climb to the top that his father wanted for him. When would he get to pursue his own dreams?

❧

Olivia's eyes were blurry from the hours of correspondence she'd done all morning. Her invitations to the Lightkeeper's Ball had gone out in the afternoon's mail. All that was left were the local people Addie had suggested. The florist had just left with an order for flowers, and Olivia had several people to interview for employment for the week leading up to the event.

Goldia stepped into the doorway. "Miss Olivia, Mr. Harrison is here."

Olivia put down her pen. "Very well, Goldia. Show him in."

"But, miss," Goldia hissed. "Your father's letter said to avoid him."

"I can hardly refuse to see him. He aided me when I was injured."

Her pulse pounded in her throat. She'd thought of nothing but Harrison in the days since she'd seen him. She hadn't wanted to remember the strength of his arms or the scent of his skin, but the sensations had plagued her sleep. In spite of her father's warning, she wanted to see him.

The dinner party at his mother's had been postponed due to Mrs. Bennett's illness. Olivia sat on the love seat and arranged her skirts around her. Pinching her cheeks, she wished for a mirror to check her hair. She had no reason to feel so nervous. He wouldn't harm her with all the servants here. Besides, he didn't know who she was. She told herself her jitters were only because of the danger and had nothing to do with the way she'd thought about him.

She heard his steps on the redwood floors and lifted her head to paste a welcoming smile on her face. When he appeared in the doorway, she swallowed hard. "Good afternoon, Mr. Bennett."

He bowed. "Lady Devonworth. How is your wrist? I trust you are recovered?"

"Completely, yes. The doctor called this morning and gave me free rein to do what I'd like."

"Any chance I could talk you into a flying lesson?"

Flying? Aware her mouth was agape, Olivia shut it. "You're serious?" His grin told her he knew how difficult she would find a refusal.

"Completely. I'm taking the plane up when I leave here."

She shouldn't be alone with him, but she was so tempted. The thought of soaring in the clouds mesmerized her. Perhaps she could find out more about his relationship with Eleanor. And hadn't she promised her mother that she would be open-minded to the thought of a match with Harrison? Without marrying money, the Stewarts' lives would change drastically. It was all riding on her. Besides, so far she'd found no evidence to link him to Eleanor's death.

But was that only because she no longer wanted him to be guilty? Her internal rationale fell flat when she remembered her father's warning. "Perhaps not just yet," she said, throwing away every contrary argument. "But might I watch?"

His white teeth flashed in his tanned face. "Of course. But I suspect you'll be sitting in the cockpit within fifteen minutes." He flicked a finger at the magazine that showed a Kewpie doll in a car. "I believe you're capable of more than mere wheels."

What was she made of? Sometimes she felt her only worth was in the prestige she could bring to a marriage. She didn't even know if she had any true gifts. She'd been trained to manage a household, be a complement to her husband, raise children, and be a wonderful hostess. The perfect Kewpie doll. Did life consist of more than that? Did anyone ever look below the surface? She was almost afraid to find out. It might make her discontented with her life. But with her mother's future riding on her choices, she was even more trapped.

"What time should I be ready for you to call?" she asked.

"As soon as you've changed."

She rose from her seat. "You mean *now*?"

His smile came and he nodded. "My mother was most disappointed to have to cancel tonight's dinner. She'd hoped to introduce you to my father." His tone turned ironic as she moved toward the stairs. "He wishes you to introduce us to your friends in New York. Expect a call from him. I tried to ward him off when he arrived today, but I'm not sure I was successful."

She froze with her hand on the banister. "Y-Your father is home?"

"He is indeed. He arrived this afternoon." He turned away from her. "You change, and I'll borrow some gear from Jerry."

No, no! Mr. Bennett would spoil everything. He would reveal that she was really Olivia Stewart. She fled up the stairs without a word.

SIXTEEN

THE STREETS OF Mercy Falls teemed with people. Men and women milled around the town square. Harrison frowned at the aura of unrest.

A red scarf around her hair and throat, Lady Devonworth leaned forward beside him in the motorcar. "Is something wrong?"

"I'm not sure." He guided the Cadillac to the sidewalk and hailed Mrs. Silvers, who worked at Oscar's Mercantile. "Mrs. Silvers, is there a problem?"

The woman wrung her hands. "Haven't you heard, Mr. Bennett? The news says we are definitely going to pass through the tail of Halley's Comet. We're all going to die in its poisonous gasses!"

The tail. Harrison's dream was about to come true. There had been some doubt about how close the tail would actually come. "I'm certain we'll all be fine," he said.

"We're all gathering at our churches to pray for God's mercy," she said, her voice rising. "You should join us."

"I'm sure God has this all under control," he said.

"It's just like the Revelation," she said. "This is the end of the world." She turned away and rushed down the street toward the brick church whose bell was tolling.

Lady Devonworth's eyes were wide. "Do you fear there is any truth to this rumor?" she asked.

He accelerated away from the sidewalk. "Most scientists believe we shall be fine," he said. "But I do know nothing about it will surprise God at all. That's enough."

She twisted her blue-and-white hanky in her hand. "You say that almost as though you know his thoughts."

"Isn't that what the Bible is for? So we know his thoughts and plans for us?"

Several blocks of tree-lined street went by before she answered. "In New York, church is the place where we meet our friends and show off our newest gowns. I have little experience with a God who cares what we do."

"He sees everything we do. And cares about it." He saw her eyes shutter. Did she not want God to see her?

"I try to do good to others," she said. "It makes me happy."

The society she moved in was foreign to him. An alien place where people thought their power and money would buy happiness. "Glad you can do what you like," he said, uncertain of how to respond.

Her large dark eyes caught his with their intensity. "What makes you think I can do what I like?"

"You just said . . ."

Her gloved hand waved in the air as though to brush off a fly. "I've been brought up to set the perfect table, to organize a party that's talked about for years, to take one look at a gown and know its worth."

He didn't glance away from the sorrow he saw in her eyes. "And this isn't what you want?"

"Would you be content with that?"

"There is more opportunity available to women now. Do something you long to try. You're going flying today. That's a start. God sees the woman inside. You can become that woman if you dare."

She laughed. "I hardly think my friends would understand. Their sole aim is pleasure and amusement. It didn't used to be that way. Mrs. Caroline Astor and others like her wanted to elevate art and American life for the good of the nation. The current set who have come behind her wish to use all the money at their disposal to impress others. They have no thought beyond the latest Newport party."

"Yet they are your friends."

She inclined her head. "They are. And Mrs. Alva Astor has been very kind to me, so it smacks of disrespect to speak like this. But there is a greed for power and status now in New York that is quite distressing. So many are self-serving in our culture."

"Are you seeing it only now that you're out of it?"

She turned toward him, her expression open. "Why yes, now that you mention it, I am. I'd like more from life."

"What would you do if you could?"

One dark brow lifted. He could watch her expressions forever. She was as complex as his aeroplane. More, really. He doubted he could ever fathom what went on behind that beautiful face.

Fiddling with her scarf, she stared out the windshield. "I would like to do something—worthy," she said, her voice a whisper. "My life seems so pointless. No one is my friend just because they like me."

Now was the time to ask her for money to back his dream of a seaplane. He could name it after her, and she'd leave a legacy of something worthwhile. But hearing the pathos in her final statement, he couldn't force the words past his lips. He liked her for who she was. He could almost wish she were penniless so he could woo her for herself alone.

He opened his mouth, then shut it again. The airfield came into sight. "We're here," he said.

Her shoulders straightened and she leaned forward. "It hardly looks able to fly. It's all cables and wires. Is it safe?"

He stared at it with fresh eyes. The thing looked like it was made of balsa wood and string. But it was strong, a good machine. "I've had it up several times."

She frowned. "What are those skis for?" She pointed at a pair of skis leaning against the building.

"They're for landing on the water. I'm going to attach them to the flying machine and try to land on a lake once I get the plane perfected."

"Planes can barely land on the ground. I must see it!" She was out of the car the moment it stopped. Her ribbons and lace fluttered in the air as she rushed to the skis. "These will allow it to land on water?" She glanced at the aeroplane.

The contraption had to appear strange to her. He ran a hand along a wire on the wing. "They will."

"But not today?" she asked, her voice tentative.

"The plane isn't ready for that yet. I haven't figured out how to attach the skis. I'll just take it up for a few minutes. I have to be back for dinner with my father."

Lady Devonworth's eyes lowered at his statement. She seemed to have little to say as Harrison pointed out the instruments and how the plane worked. Though she watched his every move, something changed. She became pale and withdrawn. Maybe her wrist still pained her. If so, this wasn't a good idea.

He got into the cockpit and started the engine. In minutes, the wind was rushing through his hair and he could see her waving her handkerchief far below. He kept it up for a few minutes, then made a flawless landing.

She rushed to the plane when it stopped rolling. Her cheeks were pink. "That was splendid!"

He grinned. "Ready to go up yourself?"

Her eyes sparkled and she nodded. "You're sure it's safe?"

"I wouldn't go up in it myself if it wasn't." He assisted her into the backseat of the aeroplane. "I think you'd better take off that scarf and put on this one." He held up a birdman's leather hat.

Her eyes widened and a genuine smile lifted her lips. "Oh, may I?" She reached for it.

"I don't think you can get it on with your hair up."

She nodded. Her slender fingers plucked the scarf from her head. When she pulled the pins from her hair, the dark tresses tumbled to her waist, and he had to shut his gaping mouth. He'd never seen such beautiful hair. Shot through with red and gold, it shone in the sun and held him mesmerized. Even when she jammed the leather hat over her head and down over her ears, her hair kept his attention.

He cleared his throat. "Your hair is going to tangle in the wind. Let's pull it back with this." Holding aloft a handkerchief, he approached her. "Allow me." Once he touched the softness of her hair, he wanted to plunge his fingers into those tresses. He wound the kerchief around as much of her hair as he could and tied it in a knot.

She'd fallen still the moment he approached. It was too much to hope that she felt the same attraction he did. She was difficult to read. He stepped back. "I think we're ready now."

The sunlight lit her face, revealing the curve of her cheeks and lips. He looked away and reminded himself to keep his attention on flying.

❧

The flimsy contraption that seemed more wires than anything substantial began to move. Olivia's stomach did a cartwheel, but she wasn't sure if it was the fact she was about to leave terra firma or if it was because she was still digesting the news that Mr. Bennett was in town. The outing today only delayed the inevitable chore of facing the man—and revealing her identity to Harrison.

The aeroplane shuddered, and she bounced with it over the rough ground. The crashing ocean was just ahead. They had to lift above the meadow soon or they would land in the whitecaps. Ocean spray left a salty taste on her lips, and the wind tore at the leather cap pinning her hair in place. Her lips stretched in an inane grin as the wheels bumped one last time and the machine began to glide on the unseen air currents she'd read about.

She was flying! Her gown billowed in the air, and she had to keep grabbing at it and wrapping it around her legs in a most unseemly manner to keep it under control. Her gaze raked the countryside below as the contraption rose higher and higher. In moments they were skipping over the tops of the redwoods. Far below she could see boats rolling on the sea. She and Harrison were higher than the seagulls swooping down to grab crabs from the rocks.

Was that an eagle's nest on the rocky crest ahead of them? She squinted and saw a baby bird with its open beak poking from the nest. A rush of exhilaration left her light-headed. She twisted to look back at the meadow, but it was gone. All that was below them were trees and more trees. The landscape appeared unfamiliar now, and she had no idea where they were. She didn't even see any roads.

She leaned forward to speak in Harrison's ear. "Where are we?"

Though he was shouting, the wind nearly stole his words. "It's wilderness below us. We're a good twenty miles from Ferndale."

She sat back. So far so fast? It seemed impossible. Tipping back her head, she stared in fascination at the clouds in the sky. She didn't ever want to go down.

The plane banked and began to turn. She touched his shoulder "We're not going back, are we?" she shouted in his ear.

He nodded. "Have to! Only enough fuel for a short flight."

Before she could show her displeasure, the machine shuddered. Her heartbeat faltered with the engine's sputter. She tightened her grip on his shoulder. "What's happening?" she screamed as the plane sank toward the ground.

"Hang on!" He fought with the controls.

Olivia quivered as the wings almost seemed to flap with every shudder of the machine. She clenched her hands together and watched the trees draw nearer and nearer. They were going to die.

"Oh God, save us," she moaned. She pressed both palms flat against her cheeks and closed her eyes, unable to watch their doom draw closer. There was no break in that line of massive redwoods.

When Harrison yelled, "Watch out!" her eyes flew open and she saw the trees part slightly to reveal a tiny meadow. The plane began to hurtle toward the space.

Though she longed to close her eyes, her lids refused to shut. Her brain cataloged everything about the scene in front of her: the stream on the far side of the flat space, the size of the redwoods, the rocks jutting up through the grass in places, the lupines growing at the edge of the woods, and the sparrows that squawked and flew out of the way of the giant bird about to crash on their turf. The scene stamped itself into her memory.

Down, down they went. The moss was incredibly green, the rocks so glossy. It would be the last thing she saw in this life. The wheels touched down with a *thump* that jarred her spine. The machine bounced skyward again. She gripped the seat and held her breath as the plane shot toward the stream at the other end of the meadow. The wheels touched down again, and this time they stayed down. All around her the wires and plane parts groaned and screamed. She saw a wing fly off followed by a part she didn't recognize.

Something knocked hard by her feet. Harrison shouted out something unintelligible before he was catapulted from his seat. The next thing she knew she was flying through the air. She saw blue sky through the trees, then her attention turned to the mossy ground rising to meet her. She inhaled the feculent scent of decaying leaves and dirt, then hit the ground and went end over end.

Seventeen

Plane parts littered the rocky ground. Harrison groaned and put his hand to his throbbing head. His fingers came away bloody. Lady Devonworth. Where was she? His head swimming, he staggered to his feet and looked around the clearing but didn't see her.

"Lady Devonworth," he called. Chirping birds answered him. He heard the sound of trickling water and realized how thirsty he was. There was no time for a drink though. She might be dying somewhere without help. The thought was unbearable. He called her name again and stepped past the strewn wreckage of his dream. There would be time to grieve the loss of his plane, but not now. He didn't dare allow himself to dwell on what this accident meant.

Stumbling over the rough ground, he stopped and peered under pieces of the plane. She had to be here somewhere. He double-checked what was left of the cockpit, then turned toward the trees. A flash of blue caught his attention. She was wearing blue. He ran toward the redwoods and found her half covered by a piece of the wing.

He dropped to his knees beside her. Twigs and moss were entwined in the long locks of hair unfettered by her cap.

"Lady Devonworth!" He touched her and nearly cringed at how cold she was. Was she dead? "Lady Devonworth?" He touched her cheek. When there was no response, he pressed his fingers to her neck and felt the strong pump of her pulse. "Thank you, God," he said.

Her legs were exposed. He averted his eyes and yanked her dress down over her limbs. When she didn't stir, he removed her leather cap and probed her head for cuts or lumps. All clear there. He didn't see any blood. Next he ran his hands down her arms. No broken bones. He needed to check her legs, but that felt much too intrusive with her unconscious and unable to give permission.

He rose and carried her leather cap to the stream, where he filled it with water. Back at her side, he dipped his fingers into the water and dribbled moisture onto her lips. Birds cawed overhead, and he heard the sounds of total isolation all around him in the absence of anything but nature. How far were they from help? In which direction did the closest town lie?

If Lady Devonworth couldn't walk, it might be days before they could get out. No one knew where they were, either. He'd told Eugene he was going up in the plane, but he hadn't mentioned which direction he was flying. At the time Harrison hadn't known himself. Eugene wouldn't know where to direct searchers when he failed to return. Goldia would be in the same predicament.

He dribbled water onto her lips again. "Lady Devonworth," he said softly. Her long lashes rested on her cheeks, but he thought he saw a flicker behind her eyelids. Touching her shoulder, he called her name again. Her eyes opened, and he was never so glad to see a glimmer of awareness as he was in the moment that he locked gazes with her.

"Harrison?" she said.

His name on her lips was so intimate he couldn't help but tighten his grip on her shoulder. "Does anything hurt?" he asked.

She shook her head, then winced. "My neck."

"Can you show me?"

She reached up to touch the base of her skull. "Here."

"May I?" he asked. She nodded and pressed his fingers on her neck at the hairline. "There's no cut. Perhaps you bumped it. Can you move your neck?"

"Yes." She rotated her neck. "Help me up."

"I . . . I didn't check your limbs. I fear you may have broken a bone."

She raised her head and reached toward him with her right hand. "I don't think so. I'm just bruised and sore."

He helped her sit. "Are you thirsty?"

"Very."

He held the leather cap to her mouth and she drank what water was left. "Let me get you more," he said.

"I'll come with you. I want to wash the mud off."

He helped her to her feet, but when she stepped onto her right foot, she cried out and fell against him. Cradling her against his chest, he supported her weight while she attempted to catch her balance. "Your ankle?"

"Yes," she said, her voice muffled against his shirt. "I fear I've sprained it."

"May I check it?"

She leaned away from him and nodded. "I suppose we'd better know how severely it's injured."

He helped her to a fallen tree at the edge of the woods. She extended her leg and he unlaced her boot. "I'm not going to take it off unless I have to. We might not be able to get it back on, and you'll need it if we expect to walk out of here."

"Very well." She bit her lip as he pressed on the flesh under the boot.

He detected no protrusion or dent that might be a broken bone, but he was no expert. If only a doctor were within walking distance. How was he going to get her out of here with a badly sprained ankle? Leaving her wasn't an option either. Not when a mountain lion or bear could happen along at any time. Or a wolf pack. The shadows were already lengthening. The redwoods would accelerate how quickly darkness fell.

"Is it broken?" she asked.

He realized the silence had gone on too long. "I don't believe so." He laced her shoe again. "Let's elevate your foot to alleviate the swelling."

She bit her lip and maneuvered to the moss, and he lifted her leg to the tree. "Wait here," he said. "I'll fetch you some water." He jogged back to the stream and filled the cap again. What about food? He had a small pack filled with sandwiches, but the food would be gone in one meal. There was no use in trying to keep some for tomorrow either. It was egg salad and would be spoiled without being kept cool. The ice block his cook had packed with it was bound to have melted by now.

They had no tent, no sleeping bags, no supplies. The moment they moved away from the stream they would have no water either. Searchers wouldn't have a trail to follow to this location. Their only hope was to walk out of here on their own two feet. When he returned with the water, he realized their situation was beginning to impress itself on her too. Her face was pale and her dark brows were drawn together.

"What happened? You said your plane was safe."

"It almost seemed as though we were out of gas, but there should have been plenty for our trip. I don't know for sure what happened. I shall investigate, though."

"You don't believe someone meant us harm, do you? After all, someone threw me off the boat."

He frowned. "I hadn't considered such a scheme."

"Did anyone know you meant to take me up in the plane?"

He thought back to his day. His father was aware of his plans. And Eugene was too. "A few people. I suppose someone might have mentioned it in town. But I'm sure our accident had nothing to do with you." He offered her another drink.

"We're stranded here, are we not?" she asked after taking a gulp of water.

She was too smart to swallow a rationalization, but he shrugged and forced a smile. "Just until your ankle heals a bit. With some rest, we should be able to make our way out."

"How far to the nearest town?"

"I haven't calculated that yet. I have a rough idea where we are, but I need to get my maps out and decide on the best course of action."

Her eyes widened enough for him to see the gold flecks in her dark brown eyes. She twisted a length of hair around her finger. "That means we shall be here overnight. Alone."

"Indeed. But I promise to be a perfect gentleman."

She glanced away, and a flush stained her cheeks. "I didn't doubt that for a moment. But people in town will talk."

"They may not even realize we're missing. I don't expect Eugene to raise a hue and cry."

"Goldia will," Lady Devonworth said, her voice trembling. "It will be all over the national news. My mother will see it. My friends."

"You can assure them nothing happened."

"It's not that easy," she said. "My reputation shall be ruined."

"Surely not!" Even as he protested, he knew how straitlaced New York society was. She would never again assume her previous social status so long as this hung over her head. "We can pray we are not newsworthy enough for the New York papers to pick this up."

She nodded but her eyes were shadowed, and he knew he'd failed to convince her. And with good reason. One whisper of this in the San Francisco paper and it would be all over the nation. The honorable thing to do would be to offer to marry her. He opened his mouth, then shut it again. Doing something so mad would only play into his father's plans at a time when Harrison was determined to forge his own path.

He rose and went toward the woods. "I'm going to gather some evergreen branches. We need bedding. Tomorrow I'll look for berries and anything else edible for breakfast. I have sandwiches for dinner.

Then we'll walk out of here first thing in the morning. With God's blessing, we'll reach a town by noon."

"Let's go tonight," she said. "If you fetch me a stick, I believe I can walk."

"I doubt you're able," he said. He stooped and grabbed a stout branch with a forked spot that he thought should hit her about right. Taking out his pocketknife, he whittled away the smaller branches on it and hacked it down to the right length. "Try that."

After he helped her to her feet, she fitted the forked spot under her arm and tried to step forward. Her awkward limp only lasted two steps before she collapsed. "I can't do it," she said.

"You'll be fine by morning," he said, helping her back to her spot by the fallen tree. But as he walked into the woods to look for supplies, he sensed everything was about to change.

Birds chirped around her as though they hadn't a care in the world. The throbbing in Olivia's ankle hadn't lessened, though it had been elevated for fifteen minutes. The forest seemed sinister, forbidding now that she was alone. The cool breeze through the redwoods made her shiver, and the mist that had begun to curl around the rough tree trunks and through the shrubs looked ominous. The picnic by the falls the other day marked the first time she'd ever been to the woods. Then, civilization was only a short walk away. Now, the wilderness pressed in on every side.

She strained to hear Harrison's return. *Harrison.* Heat blossomed in her cheeks as she suddenly remembered calling out his name when she awakened from the crash. Such familiarity must have shocked him. And made him wonder why she would think of him that way. He might read more into it than she was ready to deal with.

A rustle came to her ears and she sat up. "Mr. Bennett, is that you?" Aware her voice quivered, she tipped her chin up and pressed her lips together. She would *not* be afraid. If there was one thing she detested, it was a shrieking woman.

Harrison emerged from the shadows with boughs of evergreens in his arms. "It's just me. Were you frightened?"

The scent of pine enveloped her as he neared. "Not at all," she said, putting frost into her tone.

"What happened to 'Harrison'?" he asked, dropping the branches beside her.

"I beg your pardon?"

"You called me Harrison when you woke up. Why so formal now? If we're going to be spending all this time together, we might as well be friends enough to progress to first names."

She brushed a leaf from her skirt. "I hardly think we are friends, Mr. Bennett. Business acquaintances only."

"I've rescued a kitten on your behalf, seen you weeping at my fiancée's grave, and survived an aeroplane crash with you. We're about to spend the night alone in the forest together. I think that elevates us above acquaintances. What *is* your first name anyway?"

Tell him. She clamped her teeth against the words. With his inquisitive stare on her, she couldn't think how to deny his request without appearing rude. "I prefer you call me Lady Devonworth," she said.

The amused light in his eyes grew stronger. "Very well, Lady Devonworth, if you won't tell me, I shall have to make up one." He tipped his head to one side and regarded her. "With that dark hair and flashing brown eyes, you are a bit of a gypsy. I shall call you Esmeralda."

She had to laugh. "You've read *The Hunchback of Notre Dame*?"

"Several times."

"My mother thought it quite scandalous. She hates to catch me reading a novel."

He grinned. "It's going to be dark soon. I'll arrange the branches, then fetch our dinner."

His back was straight as the redwood beside her as he walked away. She hadn't wanted to offend him, but she couldn't bring herself to tell him. At least he'd made a joke of it.

The more the mist crept into their small camp, the more uneasy she became. It took him only a few minutes to arrange two beds of evergreen boughs and build a fire. There would be nothing to soften the prickle of the needles, and she planned to delay crawling into her bed for as long as possible. He left to scavenge the wreckage.

He returned with a wicker hamper. "Took me awhile to find it." He placed it beside her.

She opened the lid and found some sandwiches, pickles, and carrots. "This looks like a feast even if it is all squashed," she said to cover the way her tummy rumbled in a most unladylike way. She handed him some food and unwrapped her own sandwich from its covering of waxed paper. "It's still cold."

He settled beside her on the tree. "My cook knows how to pack a meal. I think there is cake in there too."

She nibbled on her sandwich and eyed him. When had she begun to like him, even trust him a little? "Maybe we should save it for breakfast. I didn't see any berries." Breakfast. The word reminded her she'd be spending the night with this man. Shivers made their way up her spine. It wasn't exactly *fear* she felt, but almost exhilaration.

When they got back to town, there would be repercussions. Her mother would ask what she thought she was doing to go off on a flight with this man. The society women would titter and talk behind their gloved hands. She could expect the invitations to balls and teas to dry up. The thought should fill her with horror, but she found she didn't care in this moment with the dying light slanting across the strong planes of Harrison's face. She watched his hands, so strong and capable, as he tossed his waxed paper into the hamper.

"I often have the oddest sensation that we've met before," he said.

"I've been to New York a time or two. My father has a house on Fifth Avenue. Have you met him? Claude Bennett?"

"Really, Mr. Bennett, we hardly run in the same circles," she said.

"True," he agreed, his tone mild. "There's something about the way you laugh." He gestured to the sky. "It's getting dark. I suggest we turn in before we are unable to find our way. It's cloudy. I suspect we'll have very little moonlight."

"Of course." She glanced at the woods. How on earth could she tell him she needed to make a trip into the trees alone?

He rose. "I think I'll take a little walk before bed. That way." He indicated the woods on the other side of the clearing. "Feel free to go the opposite direction if you like. Just don't get lost."

She watched him disappear into the mist, then struggled to her feet and grabbed her stick. He'd be back soon, so she'd better hurry.

EIGHTEEN

WHEN HARRISON RETURNED, he found the lady sitting on a log by the fire. The flicker of the flames threw shadows and light across her face. He stood under the concealing sweep of an evergreen and watched her for a moment.

The name Esmeralda suited her. Her dark brown hair cascaded down, obscuring her face. He couldn't decipher her. One minute he was sure she felt the attraction between them, and the next she was refusing to tell him her first name, as though he was beneath her.

He stepped into the clearing. "You should try to prop your ankle during the night."

"I will."

Darkness closed in fast, obscuring her features and the clearing. "Let me help you." He found her hand in the shadows. Her fingers closed around his, and he pulled her up, close enough for the scent of lilac to waft to his nose. He could have leaned down and pressed his lips against hers. For a crazy moment, he was tempted to do just that. What would she do if he did? Slap him? Scream? Probably. She considered him little more than a servant, and he didn't dare find out her response for fear of frightening her.

"This way," he said softly, leading her to the bed of boughs. The smell of crushed pine was sweet and pungent as he helped her onto the soft heap. "I'm sorry I haven't a covering for it."

"I shall be fine."

The branches rustled, but he couldn't see her expression. He dragged a log close. "Prop your ankle on this."

More rustling. "I can't find it," she said.

"Allow me." He patted the bed of pine until he found her foot, then guided it to the log. "Rest well. Things will appear much brighter in the morning." He moved to his own bed and lay down. The fragrance of pine enveloped him. Though he hadn't thought he could sleep, his eyelids grew heavy.

When he awakened, he wasn't sure at first where he was or what had alerted him. Sitting up, he strained to see in the darkness. The moon had come out from behind the clouds and made the mist curling through the clearing glow with an almost unearthly light. He glanced over at Lady Devonworth and saw her sitting up on her bed. Then the sound that must have awakened him came again. A snuffle and a scrape.

He scrambled from the branches. If only he had a gun or some kind of weapon. The noise was surely from an animal. Seizing the branch she had used for support, he whacked it onto the bed of pine so it made a crackling sound. "Get out of here!"

The animal roared. He realized he was facing a bear. With a stick. Lady Devonworth screamed, and he leaped between her and the beast. "Get out of here!" he shouted again, waving the stick in the air.

A hulking giant of an animal moved into a shaft of moonlight. A black bear. Harrison stood as tall as he could and waved his arms, shouting all the while. He debated about whacking the beast across the nose with the stick, but before he decided to escalate the encounter, the bear dropped to all fours and loped into the woods.

The arm holding the stick went weak, and he dropped it to his side. "It's gone," he said.

The next moment Lady Devonworth was in his arms with her face burrowed against his chest. "I was so frightened," she whispered. "I tried to call out to you but I couldn't speak."

Her hair was so soft under his hands as he smoothed her unruly locks. "We're going to be all right," he said, pitching his tone to a soothing murmur. He rested his chin on the top of her head as she trembled in his arms.

They stood entwined together for several long minutes. Harrison strained to hear any sound of the animal's return but heard only crickets and the hoot of an owl. When she finally drew away, he wanted to protest, but he let his arms drop instead.

He thrust his hands in his pockets to keep from reaching for her. "You should get some rest."

"What if it comes back?"

"I'll stand guard."

"You need sleep too."

"I'm wide-awake after hearing that bear roar." He forced a laugh, then grinned when her laughter tinkered out.

"Yelling at a bear." Her voice was amused. "I don't know what you thought that stick would do."

"I hoped it would make me look bigger than I was," he said.

"It appears you were successful." Her voice took on a husky quality. "I . . . I don't think I can sleep unless you are close."

"I'll be right here." He stepped past her and dragged the bundle of pine branches next to hers. "I'm not going to sleep though."

"You can at least rest. With the branch in your hand, of course." Her tone held a smile.

The boughs rustled as she settled back onto them. There was enough moonlight to see her face turned toward his. He sank onto his bed with the stick clutched in his hand.

She stretched out her arm, groping for his hand in the dark.

He grasped her cold fingers in a comforting clasp. "Are you chilled?"

"Yes. The mist is damp."

"Would you allow me to hold you, little Esmeralda? I promise to be a gentleman."

She laughed but didn't answer for a long moment, so he assumed the answer would be no, but she sighed and her fingers tightened on his. "Just a little while until I'm warmer. I'm so cold."

He crawled over closer to her and slipped his arm under her head. She rolled onto her side and snuggled against him as though she'd done it a thousand times. The tugging in the region of his heart was so strange. And unwelcome. She'd made it clear she had no romantic interest in him. Why then did he allow himself to hope they might have a future?

⌇⌇⌇⌇⌇

For a moment, Olivia thought she was snug in her own bed. Then she felt the stick of pine needles and the sound of birdsong. The stream gurgled off to her right.

"Good morning, Essie."

She turned toward the voice. Harrison was sitting at the stream with a makeshift fishing rig. "Essie?"

"Short for Esmeralda."

She had to smile. "Good morning," she said, sitting up. "What time is it?"

He pulled his pocket watch out and opened it. "Nearly eight."

He was staring, and she pushed her hair out of her face. She must look a sight. She undoubtedly had pine twigs and dirt in her hair. "How long have you been up?"

"About an hour." He gestured to the fish on the bank. "I'm about to cook our breakfast. Hungry?"

Her stomach rumbled in answer. "Starving. Can I help?"

"Know how to clean fish?"

She grimaced. "No, and I'm not particularly keen on learning."

His laughter boomed out and echoed in the treetops. She smiled back at him, then stretched. He was charming, even with twigs in his hair. "Was there really a bear here last night?"

He sobered and stood with the fish in his hand. "I saw the tracks this morning. He was big. But there's no sign of him now."

A fire crackled in the center of the clearing. Stones surrounded it. Olivia tried to stand, but hot pain gripped her ankle. She grabbed for the branch beside her bed. Even propping herself on it only allowed her to hobble a few steps before she had to rest.

Harrison watched her with a grim expression. "I don't think we're going anywhere today."

She struggled to hold back the tears. "We can't spend another night here. People really *will* talk. And what if the bear comes back?"

"Don't borrow trouble. We'll get you well and get out of here." He stooped and lifted her in his arms.

As he carried her toward the fire, she remembered last night. His compassion and gentleness. His courage against the bear. It wouldn't do to dwell on that too much.

He set her on the log. "After breakfast I'm going to put your ankle in the cold running water. We need to get that swelling down."

How was she going to get through another day alone with him? She watched him prepare the fish. Before long, the aroma of sizzling food mingled with the scent of wildflowers and pine.

He handed her some fish on a shaved spit. "Sorry there isn't a better way to serve it. I had to make do with what we had."

She took the stick. "I'm impressed you know how to do this. Haven't you always lived in a city?"

He nodded. "But my uncle used to take me on wilderness treks. We lived off the land. You never forget that stuff."

She bit into the juicy fish. The smoky flavor filled her mouth. She chewed and swallowed. "That's the best fish I've ever eaten."

He grinned. "You were just hungry."

She devoured her portion of the trout, then licked the juice from her fingers in a most unladylike way. Out here under trees that touched the sky, she was a different person from the woman who walked the streets of New York. She became aware that Harrison was watching her. Her hair was on her shoulders, and she had no idea what had become of her combs and pins. It would have to stay unbound. There was an intimacy in that, making her throat dry when she met his gaze.

He stood. "Let's soak your ankle awhile." He lifted her again.

She curled an arm around his neck. Being so close to him was nearly unbearable, but she couldn't quite figure out why. He was just a man. She'd met many men. Though her head told her this was so, her heart seemed to be telling her something else. When he set her beside the stream, she leaned down to unlace her boot and hide the heat in her face. Her fingers fumbled over the laces, but she managed to get the boot off. She wasn't about to raise her skirt in his presence though.

"I'll leave you to soak it," he said. "I'm going to gather firewood for the night. Let me get your crutch in case you need it." He retreated to the fire, then returned with the stick. "I'll be back in about an hour."

When his steps faded, she eased up the hem of her skirt, took off her stocking, then put her throbbing foot into the stream and gasped as the icy water encased her ankle. If she could just get the swelling down enough to get out of here, she could endure anything. The cold soon numbed her skin. The sun was warm on her face as it came out from behind storm clouds. She leaned back and let herself feel the sensations. When had she last relaxed to this degree? In the city she was always rushing to the next appointment or concerned with answering the mail.

She was always trying to live up to expectations. Now her reputation was about to be in ruins. How would she ever get past that?

When she could stand the cold water no longer, she pulled her foot out, let it air dry, then put her stocking and boot back on. The swelling seemed to be better, but when she tried to stand again, the pain was just as intense. She'd never be able to walk out of here today.

With the help of her makeshift crutch, she hobbled back to the bed and eased onto it so she could elevate her foot. If she did everything right today, maybe they could get out of here tomorrow.

Leaves crackled to her left, and she saw Harrison emerge with his arms full of logs. He dropped his load by the embers of the morning's fire. "Any better?"

She shook her head. "Not really. I managed to get here, though."

"I thought about making a litter that I could drag. I'm just not sure how far we're going to have to trek to find people."

She shook her head. "I'm not convinced I could endure the bouncing. It throbs whenever it's not elevated."

He squatted beside her. "I think we need to move our camping spot. We are right by the stream, which is convenient, but there are bear tracks and mountain-lion tracks all around that stream. They'll be back."

Her chest tightened and she glanced at the dark forest. "But where can we go to be safe?"

"I found a dry cave a few yards that way." He pointed to their right. "It's still close enough that we can fetch water, but it's out of the animals' path to the stream. I've already tossed some pine boughs together for bedding. All I have to do is move us and our things over there."

"But what if it's a den for a mountain lion or bear?"

He shook his head. "I checked it out thoroughly. No spoor around, just some bat droppings."

Her skin prickled. *"Bat droppings?"*

He grinned. "No bats sleeping in there now. We'll be fine."

"Can we stay here for now?"

He glanced around. "Bears are active in the daytime too. I think we'd better move over. You wait here while I move our few things. I'm going to leave the food hamper here though. There's nothing of value left, and the smell might attract animals. That was probably what drew the bear last night."

She watched him rummage through the strewn debris. He took a piece of seat, some wire and metal, then disappeared into the trees. Every rustle in the trees made her tense. Every noise from a squirrel left her wary. When he finally returned to help her to their new lair, she was ready to feel safe.

As he leaned down to help her to her feet, she heard a whine in the air. Harrison shouted something and jumped on top of her. His breath was ragged in her ear. Her face pressed into pine needles as his body covered hers. The sun had left, and a few drops of rain fell. Then it came harder. Hard enough to obscure the landscape and blur her vision. The drone of it pattering onto leaves and vegetation grew louder.

"Are you hit?" he asked, his voice frantic.

She pulled her mouth free of the suffocating vegetation. "No, no, I'm fine. What happened?"

"Someone shot at us," he said.

"A hunter?" Her thoughts raced. Had it been another attempt on her life? But why here? No one knew where they were.

"Maybe. I'd stand up and shout, but the rain will muffle anything I might say." Harrison helped her up and they set off through the trees. Clinging to his arm, she hobbled as fast as she could. Rain sluiced over her face and plastered her hair. The cave wasn't far, but they were soaked by the time they reached it.

He glanced around the space. "I'll start a fire in the mouth of the cave. And fetch a club."

He sat on guard at the fire the rest of the day. It was only late in the night when she felt the branches shift as she lay dozing. She lifted an eyelid to see the fire blazing away, protecting them from intruders.

"Just going to take a catnap, Essie," he said, his voice slurred.

He slipped his arm around her, and she curled up next to his warmth without a thought to how inappropriate it was.

NINETEEN

WARMTH PERVADED EVERY pore. Olivia snuggled closer to the comfort of the body against hers. The heat made her feel protected. Until the male scent made her eyes fly open. She was entwined in Harrison's arms, inhaling the aroma of pine and masculinity. At the same time she heard male voices. Turning her head, she saw four men peering into the cave.

Rolling away, she sat up and frantically swiped at her hair. "You've found us," she said.

The men didn't look at her. They ranged in age from twenty to forty, and all of them had twigs on their clothing and mud on their boots.

The constable shifted from one foot to the other. "Your valet convinced Mr. Peers to take us up in his balloon. I saw the smoke from your fire, so I knew where to head."

Harrison rose from behind her. He brushed pine needles from his shirt. "Smart thinking, Constable. We thought we'd have to try to walk out of here today. Lady Devonworth has a sprained ankle, and we've been unable to make the trek."

Could Harrison not see these men had tried them both and found them guilty of fornication? Olivia saw it in the quick glances they shot between her and Harrison. In the way they shuffled, and in the unease on their faces. She curled her hands into fists.

Harrison fixed the man next to the constable with a stare. "Quinn,

I'll thank you to keep this out of the paper. There was nothing unsavory happening here."

A reporter. Olivia wanted to hide behind a giant redwood. This would be all over the country.

The man took off his bowler and wiped his forehead. Though clearly only in his twenties, he was already balding. "It's already in the morning paper, Harrison." His mouth turned down and he shrugged. "It's news, my friend."

Her face blossomed with heat. From the Mercy Falls news, it would hit the San Francisco papers. Then on to New York, Chicago, Boston. She was ruined. But maybe it would be a small article and missed by the bigger papers. Unless he ran a follow-up story. She would try to talk him out of it.

She opened her mouth, then shut it again. It was impossible to miss the gleam of avarice in Mr. Quinn's eyes. He had every intention of writing about what he saw when he stepped into the clearing. Nothing she could say would sway him. Could he be paid off? She meant to try at the first opportunity.

She managed a smile. "I'm glad you're here, gentlemen. I fear I shall still need some assistance, even after two days' rest."

"We had a bear appear our first night, so we took to this place, which I could defend with a fire," Harrison said, grabbing the walking stick. "I fear neither of us got much sleep."

Olivia caught the double meaning in his words and saw the men's faces change as well. The constable was the only one who didn't smirk. She grabbed the stick from Harrison's hand and thrust it into the ground to keep from whacking him with it.

"Shall we depart?" All she wanted was to get home and shut the door and fall onto her bed.

Harrison helped her from the cave. The men began to gather strewn belongings and put the items in bags they'd brought. They all went back to the clearing. Harrison directed them to the most important plane parts. The silence was as thick as last night's mist. By the time they headed into the woods, she wanted nothing more than never to see any of these men again—including Harrison Bennett.

The stick did little to alleviate the throbbing in her ankle. The constable strode ahead, forcing branches out of the way and tamping down weeds to allow her easier access. Bugs swarmed her damp skin, and every step was a misery. It was going to take hours of this torture to get to civilization.

She blinked against the stinging in her eyes. She would not cry. It would take every ounce of fortitude she possessed to get through the next few days. The physical pain of walking out of here was nothing compared to the emotional anguish that awaited her. Surely there was a way to salvage this.

I could marry him.

The stray thought made her stumble, and only the stick prevented her from tumbling into the bushes. What of her initial suspicion of him? The only clue she had indicating his guilt was her father's letter telling Eleanor that the Bennetts were dangerous. But Harrison had rescued her from the sea, and he could have disposed of her out here in the wilderness. He'd been so gentlemanly, so concerned for her. He'd withstood a bear for her.

She didn't believe he was capable of murder, but that didn't mean she was ready to marry him.

⋖⋗

Olivia had never been so glad to see a truck in her life. Harrison assisted her onto the black leather seat next to Mr. Quinn, who would drive them out of here, then went around to climb in the back with the rest of the men.

Mr. Quinn glanced at her from the corner of his eye. The smirk in his eyes made her want to squirm, but she held her chin up and looked straight ahead. The interior of the truck smelled like oil or grease, but getting her dress stained was the least of her worries.

"I'm glad you appear to be unharmed, Miss Stewart," Mr. Quinn said, his voice smooth.

She started to thank him, then froze when she realized he'd used her real name. When she turned her head to look at him, he glanced back and his smirk widened.

"How do you know my name?" she managed to ask without her voice trembling.

"I know quite a lot about you. But I have to wonder why you are using some title instead of your given name of Olivia Stewart."

She had to convince him to stay quiet until she had a chance to reveal the truth herself. "It's very simple. I wanted to find out what happened to my sister."

One eyebrow rose, and the truck jerked to the right as he glanced at her. "You doubt that she drowned?"

"If I promise to give you the full story when I get to the bottom of the situation, would you promise not to print my name until my investigation is concluded?"

He pursed his lips. "I'd get your full cooperation to run the full story?"

She felt no qualms about promising that. The murderer would be behind bars. "Yes."

"It's a deal. So what makes you doubt she drowned?"

"I don't doubt she drowned. I just don't believe she willingly went swimming."

"Suicide?"

"She feared the water. If she were going t-to do away with herself, she wouldn't choose drowning."

His eyes gleamed. "So that leaves foul play."

She clutched the seat as the truck careened around a corner. "I fear so."

"Do you suspect anyone?"

A few days ago she would have been forced to admit she suspected Harrison. But that was no longer true. She shook her head. "I'm looking into some acquaintances she made while she was here."

"Like Frederick Fosberg?"

"How do you know about him?"

"She seemed to be making a fool of herself over him at a party I attended."

"Do you know the man?"

"Not well. I'm planning on doing a piece on him and the new business he's opening. Say, how about the two of us work together? I'll help you get to the bottom of this."

The last thing she wanted was this man poking into her business, but what choice did she have? "Thank you," she said, resigning herself to the inevitable.

❧

Harrison bounced on the wheel well when the truck hit a pothole. The constable sat beside him on the floorboards.

"How much talk in town?" Harrison asked Brown once they were underway.

"The town is abuzz with it. It's the only thing discussed at the soda shop and the mercantile. There is much speculation that perhaps the two of you ran off together instead of crashed."

As he'd suspected. "So the lady's reputation is ruined, is it not? Even if you tell of the wreckage you saw, people love a juicy rumor instead of truth."

Brown inclined his head. "I fear so."

Harrison turned to look at the steeples and rooftops of Mercy Falls in the distance. The lady had a high position to maintain. The only way to salvage her good name was for them to be married. This was his fault. He'd taken her up in the flying machine without a thought for her reputation. At the first opportunity, he would ask for her hand.

His mouth went dry at the thought. It was too much to even hope that she would say yes. He had money but no title. Her family would forbid such a marriage. And she'd been open about her friendship with Eleanor. He'd have to tell her the truth.

The truck rumbled into town. People turned to stare. He saw the women begin to talk at once. Some even turned their backs on the vehicle. All but one rubbernecker frowned. Addie's bright smile was like sunlight breaking through the trees. He waved and she hurried toward the truck with Edward and the dog Gideon in tow. When the truck stopped, she rushed to greet them.

"Thank God you're all right!" She peered past him. "But where is Lady Devonworth?"

He leaped to the pavement. "Her ankle was sprained in the crash. She's in the cab."

"Oh that poor girl." She went around the back of the truck and up to the door of the cab where Lady Devonworth sat.

Harrison followed her. When Addie opened the door, he reached past her with his hand extended. "Allow me, Es—I mean, Lady Devonworth."

She took his hand. When she emerged into the sunlight, he noticed she appeared pale and tired. "My house is just down the block. May I offer you rest there first? I'll take you home after tea."

"I'll come along," Addie added, glancing at the group of women staring at them.

"I'm so weary," Lady Devonworth said.

He slipped his fingers under her elbow and turned her toward his house. "A pain powder would help, I'm sure. I'll have my father summon the doctor."

She stopped. "Your father is at your house?"

"He's across the street in his own house, but I'll call him."

She smoothed her windblown hair. "I-I think I'd rather go home. We can summon the doctor from there, can we not?"

She was likely uncertain about meeting his parents in her present state. Besides, her departure would give him the opportunity to explain the situation to them without an audience. "As you wish."

He backtracked to the truck where the men still milled around. "Could I trouble you to take the lady to Stewart Hall, Quinn?"

"I'd be happy to." He tossed a cigarette to the ground and went to the cab.

Harrison assisted Lady Devonworth inside. "There's room for you, Addie. I can have Edward and Gideon ride in the back with me."

She took Edward's hand. "We'll just walk. It's only a few blocks. I'll stop along the way and fetch the doctor."

"Thanks." He leaped into the back of the bed, and the truck started off with a jerk.

With every bump along the street, his stomach tightened. How could he go about making this right without offending her? Surely she must be sick with worry about what this situation was going to do to her life. At least she could sort out the trouble here. Mercy Falls residents would be quicker to forgive this transgression than her friends in New York.

The truck turned into the tree-lined driveway of the Stewart home. A few gardeners lifted their heads when the truck pulled to a stop, then they went back to their work. A maid beat rugs over a line in the side yard. The running of the house had continued even though Lady Devonworth had gone missing. Did none of the servants realize the danger she'd been in?

As soon as the truck stopped, he leaped out. When he opened the vehicle's door, he found her drooping with exhaustion. Dark circles bruised the skin under her eyes. Without asking permission, he put his arm around her waist and helped her up the steps. She didn't even protest.

"Open the door!" He banged the front door with his foot.

Moments later Goldia opened the door. "Mr. Bennett! Oh no, is she hurt?"

He brushed past her with Lady Devonworth stumbling beside him. "The doctor is on his way." He went down the hall to the parlor and sat her on the sofa, then raised her boots onto the cushions.

"We must get your boot off," he told her. He glanced back at the maid, who stood behind him wringing her hands. "Would you help me?" He stepped away and allowed her to kneel by her mistress. "Careful of her ankle."

She unlaced Lady Devonworth's boots, then wiggled the right one. "It's not coming off."

He grabbed the boot heel and gave a tug. Lady Devonworth winced. "I think it's severely swollen," he said. "If you'd hold her calf, I'll try to get it off." Lady Devonworth gritted her teeth and gripped the cushions.

Goldia nodded and grasped the lady's leg under the skirt. He began to work the boot off her foot. When it popped free, he stepped back again. "Roll her stocking down."

Goldia nodded and worked the sock off Lady Devonworth's foot. She gasped. "Oh, sir, it looks terrible."

He winced when he saw the purple bulging flesh at the ankle and down the foot. When he glanced back at Lady Devonworth, she lay with her eyes closed. She'd probably fainted from pain. "Fetch some tea. She hasn't eaten much today either. Some toast perhaps?"

Goldia nodded and rushed from the room. Harrison pulled a chair close to the sofa and sat on it to wait for Addie and the doctor. He took her hand and studied the face of the woman he intended to make his bride. If only there was time to properly woo her, he believed he could actually love her.

TWENTY

OLIVIA GRITTED HER teeth against the pain in her leg. It radiated from her foot all the way to her knee. She groaned and flung out her arm. It hit something soft. She opened her eyes and became aware that she was lying on the sofa. In her house. A pillow cushioned her head, and light slanted through the curtains at the window.

Opening her eyes fully, she realized someone held her hand captive. She turned her head and stared into Harrison's face. Her heart thumped against her ribs at his intense expression.

"How did I get in here?" she asked. "I don't remember."

"I half dragged you." His smile was gentle. "How do you feel?"

"Like an elephant stepped on my foot."

He had flecks of mud and debris on his trousers. He continued to stare at her. "It's badly sprained. Maybe even broken. Addie should be here shortly with the doctor."

She became aware that he wasn't just holding her hand, he was rubbing his thumb across her palm in a most distracting way. If it wasn't so pleasant, she would snatch her hand away. His touch reached a place inside and made her feel warm and cherished in a most delicious way. Which was quite ridiculous, of course.

She struggled to sit up, but he shook his head. "Lie still. You need to keep that foot elevated. Besides, I need to talk to you."

His tone and expression were so grave that her pulse increased to a rapid pounding in her chest. "I-Is it my father? He's been found?"

When he frowned, she realized he knew nothing of her search for her father. Or who she was. Her secret was still safe. "Never mind. What is it you wish to say?"

His eyes grew more somber. "You saw the reaction in town to our return." When she nodded, he reached to the coffee table with his free hand and grabbed a newspaper. "This is the morning paper." He turned the front page around to face her.

She read the headline: HARRISON BENNETT AND LADY DEVONWORTH MISSING FOR TWO DAYS. She squinted at the print below it. "What does it say in the article?"

"It suggests we might have had a tryst and faked a plane crash to cover it up."

Her head swam. Exactly what she'd feared would happen. "We can refute it. Take a photographer to the site of the crash. And Mr. Quinn will print no more stories."

"Four men saw us there. Sleeping side by side."

Heat rushed to her cheeks and she flashed back to that moment. Had she ever felt as content as these past two mornings when she'd awakened in his arms? "There's no way to prove our innocence?" she asked.

He shook his head. "None. And there's more. Goldia told me she has fielded several calls from the papers. The San Francisco news ran the story in the evening paper." He pressed her hand harder. "I'm sorry, Essie. This is my fault."

By the utmost exercise of her will, she managed to keep down the bile that rose in her throat. This couldn't be happening. Her life and reputation couldn't be swept away so quickly. Her mother would hear this news and fear the worst. "I must call home," she murmured. She could only hope the New York papers missed it.

"There's time for that later," he said. "We must decide some things before the doctor arrives."

"What things?" She jerked her hand from his grasp and struggled to a seated position. He gently took her ankles and lifted her feet to the coffee table. Even that gentle motion made her ankle throb.

"Tell me," she said when he sat back in his chair.

"There is only one way to save your reputation," he said.

Though she wanted to shake her head at what she knew was coming, she couldn't move. He was right. Marriage was the only thing that could save her reputation now.

He took her hand again. "If we marry, no one will say anything. I will arrange for a private ceremony at once. We can announce that we were privately wed, and the kinder members of society will allow our prevarication to stand."

She shook her head. "I don't know what to say."

"If you prefer a more elaborate ceremony, I can arrange that too. We would suffer a bit more gossip, but it would be forgotten soon enough." His eyes became veiled and his mouth hardened. "Unless you fear it is more scandalous to marry beneath you."

Tell him the truth. She opened her mouth to tell him everything, but the doorbell rang and he rose. "There's the doctor." He moved his chair back from the sofa. "We'll discuss this later."

Addie rushed into the room with Dr. Lambertson on her heels. "How are you feeling, my dear?"

"I shall be fine," Olivia assured her.

The doctor moved to her side and began to press on her ankle. "It's quite a bad sprain, Lady Devonworth. It's going to take some time for you to recover." He nodded to Goldia, who stood hovering in the doorway with a tray of tea and cookies in her hands. "Fetch me some hot water and soap. I shall wash and wrap it."

Goldia handed the tray to Addie, then hurried from the room. When her eyes fell on the food, Olivia was suddenly ravenous and thirsty. "I'll take some tea," she said.

"Let me help you," Addie said.

While her friend poured out the tea, Olivia glanced at Harrison and found him staring at her. Her nerves fluttered at his expression. Her head began to ache. If only she hadn't gotten into that plane! This labyrinth was too complicated for her to find the way out.

Society would crucify her.

❧❀❧

Once the doctor finished wrapping Lady Devonworth's ankle and departed, Harrison walked with him to the door. "You don't believe the bone is broken?" he asked.

Dr. Lambertson shook his head. "She will need to stay off it for at least a week though. It's badly sprained. She should not have been allowed to walk on it for as long as she did."

Harrison nodded. "It's my fault. I crashed the aeroplane and we had no choice but to walk out of the forest."

"You should have made a litter for her and carried her out once help arrived."

"She was quite adamant about walking," Harrison said. "Thank you, doctor." He followed Dr. Lambertson out to the porch, where he saw a car roll to a stop in the driveway.

"Your father is back in town," the doctor remarked as he went down the steps.

Harrison watched the two men speak, then his father strode up the driveway. His bowler was perched perfectly on his head, and he swirled his gold-tipped cane as he came. His smile was full of confidence.

Harrison shook his hand. "Father, what are you doing here?"

"I had to see if my son had survived, of course," he said loudly. He leaned forward and whispered in Harrison's ear, "I forbid you to marry that woman. I did some checking. No one I spoke to has heard of the Devonworths. She's certainly not on par with Olivia Stewart."

"The crash was an accident."

His father grimaced. "Of course it was. I'd like to meet this scheming woman."

Harrison took a step back and crossed his arms over his chest. "She's indisposed."

"I'll only stay a moment. Your mother says the lady has a mind of her own but is quite beautiful. She must be to have you so enthralled."

Harrison barred the hall. "Please leave for now, Father. This is not the appropriate time."

The older man huffed, then stepped away. "Very well. Convey my regards." He jammed his bowler onto his head and stalked off the porch.

"Who was that?" Lady Devonworth asked when he returned to the parlor.

"My father. I must warn you that he will be most opposed to our marriage. He has his heart set on Olivia Stewart as my wife. I told him this was not the best time to make your acquaintance."

She paled and bit her lip. "Thank you. I should like to be at my best when I meet him."

"I suspect that will be at least a week."

She nodded and sat up straighter on the cushions. "Someone shot at us in the clearing," she said. "I can't help but wonder if the man could be the same one who threw me from the boat."

He frowned, realizing he hadn't even thought of the attempt on her life the day they met. "We've never really talked about that incident. Do you have enemies?"

"I didn't think so. But after our escapade in the wilderness, I began to wonder. Do you know why the plane went down? Could it have been sabotaged?"

"I never considered the possibility. I'll make a trek out to the site and check it out." He studied her downcast eyes and pale cheeks. "If what you say is true, perhaps the shooter meant to harm me." He shrugged. "Or it might still have been just a hunter."

Her eyes widened. "I hadn't thought it might be connected to you. Eleanor's death. Might she have been killed by someone who hated you?"

"Whoa, where did that come from? Eleanor has nothing to do with this."

"You must admit it was most strange. She feared the water. So why would she have gone swimming?"

The information made him flinch. "Eleanor feared the water? Did anyone mention this to the constable?"

"I don't know."

"You told me Eleanor's mother asked you to look into the circumstances of her death. So is that the real reason you're here?"

She looked down and didn't meet his gaze.

His lips twisted. "So now you think I'm safe? Because I let you walk out of the forest alive?"

"Yes."

"A more pressing matter is in front of you," he said. "Or do you want to ignore what happened today?"

"I can only tell the truth and say the plane went down."

There was still only one choice that he could see. "I believe you know better, Lady Devonworth. At least let us announce our engagement and explain why you accompanied me without a chaperone. We can break the engagement at a later date after everyone has forgotten this incident."

"I must speak with my mother. Perhaps the gossip hasn't reached New York. If so, this will soon die down."

"Don't wait too long. We don't have long to salvage your reputation." He found the thought of her reluctance quite unbearable.

TWENTY-ONE

PAPERS COVERED THE rosewood desk's polished surface. Tiger sat in Olivia's lap kneading her leg. The invitations to the Lightkeeper's Ball had all been sent out before the aeroplane accident, but Olivia was beginning to wish she'd never offered to hold the ball. Would anyone even come now?

She pulled a vellum sheet toward her, dipped her pen into ink, and began to list pieces of this strange puzzle that now preoccupied her.

> *Father's death*
> *Eleanor's death*
> *Eleanor's fearful letter to me*
> *The attack on the boat*
> *The mysterious voice in the speaking tube*
> *The letter from Father*
> *The shot in the forest*
> *The plane crash*

How did they all tie together? Was it possible these events were related to Harrison's family and not her own? She didn't see how it was likely. The kitten mewed when she quit petting him and jumped down. Olivia opened the drawer in the desk and lifted her father's letter from it. The cheap paper's creases were already becoming thin from the number of times she'd reread it. Her father's warning against

Mr. Bennett *and* Harrison couldn't be plainer. *If only Father would show himself and explain.* She didn't understand why he continued to allow the world to believe him dead.

She heard the doorbell ring and lifted her head. Was that a man's voice?

Goldia appeared in the doorway. "Mr. Frederick Fosberg is here, miss. With his mother, Mrs. Martha Fosberg."

"Show them in." She swept everything into the drawer, then shut and locked it. By the time she'd thrust the key into her pocket and maneuvered to the sofa on her crutches, Goldia was leading them into the room.

Mrs. Fosberg rushed toward her. "My dear Lady Devonworth, I'm so sorry to hear of your misfortune."

Olivia smiled. "Thank you, Mrs. Fosberg. Have a seat. Goldia, will you tell the cook to prepare some refreshments?"

No one else in town had called this morning. Well, hadn't she expected the cold shoulders? "Thank you for coming." These two were to be commended for braving the town's censure.

"I'd like to introduce you to my son, Frederick," Mrs. Fosberg said.

"I'm honored, Lady Devonworth," he said.

She studied the man who had seemingly mesmerized her sister. He had blond hair slicked back with pomade and a pencil-thin mustache. His sack coat was the height of fashion. It had narrow lapels and was fitted at the waist. The slight flare at the bottom gave him an athletic appearance. His trousers had an impeccable line. This was a man who took fashion very seriously. His blue eyes looked her over as well, and she didn't know if she cared for the amused glint in his eyes.

She inclined her head and repeated her planned story. "Mr. Fosberg, it's good of you to come. I'm in need of some advice on a sum of money left to me by my father. I'd like to invest it." He didn't have to know it was a paltry amount.

"I'm happy to assist you. My office is well known for guiding clients to good investments. May I ask how you heard of my services?"

"From Eleanor Stewart," she said, watching him closely. When wariness replaced the amusement in his eyes, she knew he was hiding something.

"You knew Miss Stewart?" he asked.

"Quite well. We grew up together. I heard she was quite taken with you."

The last of his smile evaporated. "I am happy to assist anyone in need of my services."

She would have to switch tactics. "I'm holding a ball to raise money for the lighthouse. I'll make sure you get an invitation."

His smile came almost too quickly. "Thank you for that, Lady Devonworth. I'm most honored you would think of me."

His set might be the only ones who would attend her ball after her fall from grace. "I shall save you a spot on my dance card," she said, putting on her best smile.

His eyes crinkled at the corners as he smiled back. "I should like that very much," he said, his voice soft.

"Did you meet Eleanor before she came here? I found a dance card for an event and noticed you danced with her quite often."

He sat back in the chair. "Lady Devonworth, is there something you are trying to ask me?"

What would he say if she told him the truth? "Her mother asked me to look into her death. When did you see her last?"

"The day before she died." He crossed his arms over his chest.

She didn't care if he didn't like being questioned. "How did she seem to you? Distraught?"

"She was fine. A little edgy. She kept looking out the windows."

His mother had been fidgeting. "Lady Devonworth, I don't understand why your questions are so pointed. The poor girl drowned. Are you suggesting she had a liaison with Frederick?"

Olivia's ankle throbbed, her head hurt, and she desperately wanted to talk to a friendly face about her troubles. "I don't know, Mrs. Fosberg. Eleanor's family is not convinced the drowning was accidental. I am trying to bring some closure to the situation."

The older woman smiled. "I understand, my dear. But Frederick hardly knew the woman."

"That's not exactly true, Mother," he said. "I will admit to my own doubts about how she died. She feared water. I don't understand how she came to be drowned in that manner."

Aware her mouth was open, Olivia snapped it shut. Goldia brought in refreshments and placed them on the table. She passed around blue-and-white teacups, then backed out of the room. When her maid was out of the room, Olivia took a sip of her tea and asked, "What can you tell me, Mr. Fosberg?"

He stared into the teacup balanced on his pinstriped pants. "I loved her," he said.

His mother gasped. So did Olivia. "How did she feel about you?" she asked.

"She was going to break her engagement to Bennett. I suspect he killed her when she did."

TWENTY-TWO

HARRISON TOOK AN appreciative sniff of the cool forest air. Pine, decaying bark, and leaf mold hung in the air. He'd needed to stretch his legs this morning after fielding questions all evening from his parents, so he took Eugene with him to collect the dismembered plane parts. The blue bowl of sky played hide-and-seek with them behind the towering redwoods as they hiked back to the site of the crash. He inhaled again and exhaled his worries.

Eugene paused to wipe perspiration from his brow. The normally immaculate valet had flecks of mud on his trousers and wide rings of moisture under his arms. "Are you sure this is wise, sir?"

"I need to see those plane parts. I want to check for sabotage."

Eugene lifted a brow. "Sabotage? How would you ever know? And for what purpose?"

Harrison couldn't explain his obsession. Everything had changed when he discovered Lady Devonworth believed Eleanor had been murdered. There was too much to explain away: the attempt on her life, the crash, the man shooting at them. He had no idea how they all fit together, but he wanted to find out.

"The clearing is just ahead," he said, pointing to where the path veered to the right. Ferns the size of trees grew in the shadow of the redwoods. A glint caught his eye, and he paused to stare at a crushed patch of weeds.

"What is it, sir?"

"I'm not sure." He knelt and picked away twigs and moss to reveal several shell casings. "I believe our shooter stood here." The shells were cool and hard in his palm. He pocketed all four of them. "I shall show them to the constable."

The men continued on toward the sound of rushing water. Harrison's spirits plunged when he saw the debris of his beloved aeroplane strewn around the open field. There was no putting it back together. He would have to start anew. At least he had some modifications in mind. There should have been plenty of gas in the tank, yet the plane had faltered as though it had no fuel.

Eugene stood beside him with his hands in his pockets. "Do we seek anything in particular?"

"The engine and fuel system," Harrison said.

"Righto, sir." His valet wandered off in the direction of the stream.

Harrison picked up pieces of plane and discarded them as he went. Finding what he sought would be difficult. Flies buzzed around his head, and his boots sank into the boggy ground. It was best not to dwell on his time here with Essie. Tossing and turning on his bed last night, he'd remembered the scent of her hair and the way she fit into his arms.

He tore his attention from the evergreen boughs. There was one last patch of scattered debris to examine. He lifted a wing and found the prize. The fuel tank. The damp ground soaked the knees of his trousers as he knelt and uncapped the tank. The interior was too dark to make out the level of liquid inside. He grabbed a nearby stick and stuck it into the tank. When it clanged against the bottom, he withdrew it. The end of the stick was dry. Empty.

"Did you find something?" Eugene's voice came from behind him.

"An empty tank." Harrison rolled the container over and followed the lines out. "I'm looking for a leak. See what you can find."

Eugene knelt beside him and dug through parts as well. "There's this, sir," he said, holding out a long end of fuel line.

Harrison almost didn't want to see it. If he found clear evidence of tampering, then what? He ran his fingers over the length of line. His forefinger snagged on a rough edge on the side away from him. When he turned it over, he found a hole. The edges went inside. Sabotage.

"It appears someone put a nail through this," he said, showing it to Eugene.

"Perhaps it happened when the plane crashed."

He shook his head. "There were no nails. This was deliberate."

His valet raised stricken eyes to his. "You think someone wanted you dead?"

"It appears so. No one knew I was taking Lady Devonworth up in the machine. It was a spontaneous decision."

Had someone killed Eleanor to get to him? And how did the attack on Lady Devonworth play into the killer's plan? Had someone gotten wind of her intention to investigate? Perhaps the attempt on her life was to deter her from being too nosy. He rubbed his head. None of this made sense. He needed to tell Lady Devonworth, though, warn her to be on guard.

"Let's go," he told Eugene.

"What about these parts?"

"I'll show the fuel line to the constable and ask him to investigate Eleanor's death as well."

"Sir? Miss Eleanor drowned."

"I discovered she was afraid of the water, Eugene. Lady Devonworth is a friend of the Stewart family, and they believe she would never have gone swimming."

The men left the gurgling brook behind and tromped out of the forest.

Olivia didn't want to believe Frederick Fosberg, but his blue eyes were full of truth. If only she had spoken with Eleanor before her death.

There were too many contradictions to know what to do. Whom to believe.

Eleanor had been happy to marry Harrison. She liked nice things and pretty dresses, and Mr. Bennett's promise that she would be the star of Mercy Falls had certainly had an impact on her. While Mr. Fosberg was attractive, Olivia doubted he had the money that Harrison had. Could Eleanor have actually fallen in love with Fosberg? Even if she had, that didn't explain her death. It was clear to Olivia that Harrison hadn't been consumed with a passion for Eleanor. He had merely been dutiful in a sensible arrangement. He would have bowed to her request to break the engagement, if in fact she'd made one.

Olivia prided herself on her ability to see past appearances and discover truth, but her abilities had failed her ever since she came here. "Do you know if she broke her engagement?" she asked Fosberg.

"When we last spoke, she was expecting him to call on her. She intended to tell him then that the two of us planned to wed."

Mrs. Fosberg sat wringing her hands. "You never breathed a word of this to me, Frederick!" She turned to Olivia. "My dear, I'm so sorry."

"I needed to know the truth." Olivia barely managed to speak past the constriction in her throat.

She didn't want to believe Harrison had harmed Eleanor. Maybe there was another explanation. Pain throbbed behind her eyes. Only decorum kept her from asking the pair to leave. She needed time to think this through, to analyze all the ramifications of what this new information meant.

Silence fell with the lengthening shadows. The Fosbergs drank their tea in a hurried manner as though they sensed Olivia's desire for solitude.

"Thank you for your candor," she said as the mother and son took their leave. "Do call again." When she heard the front door shut, she slumped onto the sofa and put her foot on the pillow.

She had reached for her tea when the doorbell rang again. Who would be calling when she was an outcast?

"Olivia!" a woman's voice called out from the hall.

Olivia bolted upright. "Mother?"

The sound of running feet came down the hall, and her mother burst into the parlor. Olivia had never seen her mother rush or show any indecorum. The older woman's cheeks were flushed, but her attire was impeccable, as though she had just left her house on Fifth Avenue.

"My dear girl," she cried, holding out her arms. She rushed to the sofa and embraced Olivia.

Olivia inhaled her mother's delicate rosewater scent and relished the tight squeeze of the maternal embrace. "I didn't expect you for another week," she murmured against her silk dress.

"I told you I would come at once."

Olivia pulled away and smiled up at her mother. "'At once' usually means after days of packing."

Her mother unpinned her hat and placed it on the table. "Not when you call with such momentous news. And when I arrived, I found you had been in an aeroplane accident! Really, Olivia, what were you thinking to go off with a man unchaperoned in such a hoydenish way?" She draped herself elegantly on the Queen Anne chair by the fireplace.

Olivia sat up and smoothed her hair. Though her ankle throbbed, she didn't raise it to the coffee table, an act her mother would find most uncomely. "I am trying to discover what happened to Eleanor," she said. "I've been spending as much time with Harrison as possible so that I can question him."

"Well, this is going too far!" Her mother nodded to the teapot on the silver tray. "Is that fresh?" When Olivia shook her head, her mother rang for the maid. When the girl appeared in the doorway, she requested fresh tea and cake before turning to Olivia with more questions. "I saw the newspaper, Olivia. You were alone with that man for two nights."

"Nothing happened, Mother."

"Of course nothing happened. I've raised you to know better than that." Her mother smoothed her dress.

Olivia clutched her hands together. "I'm told the news was in the San Francisco papers."

Her mother gasped and put her hand to her mouth. "Olivia, no!" She moaned and put her hands on her cheeks. "You're ruined." She fanned herself. "And I shudder to think what my friends will say if word of this reaches New York."

"I know, Mother."

Olivia had spent her life trying to be the perfect daughter, to make her parents proud of her. In one careless act of thoughtlessness, she'd thrown it all away. Harrison had said she could be the woman God saw inside if she had the courage. What if she used this opportunity to be herself?

"He offered to announce our engagement," she blurted out. "Should I allow it?"

Her mother's expression went from stricken to calculating. "Harrison offered to marry you?"

"He did. He said we could break the engagement after the furor died down."

The maid arrived with fresh tea and white cake squares. Silver clinked against china as she served them then slipped back out of the room. Even when they were again alone, her mother said nothing.

"Mother? What should I do?" Olivia asked.

Her mother sipped her tea and stared at her with thoughtful eyes. She put her cup and saucer on the table beside her. "It's tempting. But you realize we would be playing into Mr. Bennett's hands if we allow this? If your father's letter is to be believed, both men are dangerous. Perhaps they have been working all along to force you into this position. Whose idea was it to go in that plane?"

Olivia bit her lip. "Harrison's," she admitted. "But he knew I'd been longing to experience it."

"Ah." Her mother pressed her lips together. "Just as I expected." She sighed and took up her tea again. "'Harrison,' is it? I must say it would solve our financial pressures. I would insist Mr. Bennett make the financial arrangements at the announcement. I'll not wait until a wedding that may never happen."

"He would delay until the marriage, I'm sure."

Her mother smiled. "I could tell him I know his son planned to ruin you to force this engagement. He would not want that leaked. Then when we have the money, you could break the engagement. I'll take you to Europe to find you a man with money *and* a title."

Olivia stared at the smug expression on her mother's face. Had she always been so manipulative? "Mother, that's not honorable!"

Her mother sipped her tea before answering. "The pair killed your sister."

"I no longer believe Harrison guilty of anything like that."

The cup rattled on the other woman's saucer. "Your father believed otherwise."

"Besides, Harrison doesn't know I'm Olivia Stewart. You must say nothing to his father until I tell him."

"When do you plan to inform him?"

"As soon as possible." She dreaded it though. He didn't seem the type to tolerate deceit.

"Very well. Let's not speak of unpleasant things. What of this ball you are planning?"

"The lighthouse was destroyed in a storm, and there have been several ships lost already without its light. It must be rebuilt. The invitations have been sent."

Her mother sniffed. "I would imagine you'll be receiving refusals after the news of your disgrace gets out."

Olivia caught her breath. Katie and Will were depending on the success of this ball. If her naivety had destroyed it, she couldn't face Katie with the news. "It must be a success! What can I do?"

"Announce your engagement, I suppose. Your friends in New York will be curious to meet him. The ball could be an engagement ball as well. And a masquerade, you said?"

Harrison in a costume. She wanted to see that. "True. I would have to call them all, since the invitations have already gone. I never gave Harrison an answer to his proposal other than that I would speak with you about it."

"I don't see that you have much choice at the moment. Agree for now. You don't have to go through with it."

"But if I give him my word . . ."

"Don't be tiresome, Olivia. Now ring for the maid. My head is beginning to pound and I want Goldia to rub it with rosewater."

"Yes, Mother." The respite would give her a chance to consider all her options. She needed to sort through her emotions after learning from Fosberg that Eleanor was in love with him and planned to break her engagement to Harrison.

TWENTY-THREE

W ITH HER MOTHER upstairs resting, Olivia finished a letter to her cousin back in New York, then hopped on her crutches out to the garden with a journal. She always thought better when surrounded by nature. Her list of ominous events was tucked into the front cover.

She sank onto a stone bench by the topiary and dropped her crutches to the ground. The breeze brought her favorite aroma of freesia to her nose. This area of the garden held only white flowers, which lifted her spirits. A pond full of koi added the only touch of color to the area.

Opening her journal, she perused the list she'd started, then added Mr. Fosberg's accusation about Harrison, much as it pained her. Bees droned a sleepy song in her ears, but she was much too energized to think about a nap. She was missing an important piece of the puzzle, something that tied all these things together, but what?

A car door shut and she lifted her head from her journal. Peeking over the shrubs, she saw Frederick Fosberg striding toward the pillared porch. What was he doing back so quickly?

Hanging on to one crutch, she rose and hailed him. "Mr. Fosberg, I'm here."

His confident stride faltered, and he changed direction to join her in the side yard. "I'm sorry to disturb you again, Lady Devonworth. There were some things I wished to inform you of that I didn't want to mention in front of my mother. They are of a most confidential nature."

She settled back onto the bench, and he joined her. "Confidential?"

He swatted away a bee. "Indeed. This matter involves Eleanor's mother. It was for this reason I first met Eleanor. I wished to get a message to Mrs. Stewart."

She studied his earnest blue eyes, the determined jut of his jaw. "What message?"

He leaned forward. "As you know, I work for a large law firm based in San Francisco. Our headquarters building was demolished in the Great Fire that followed the earthquake. Fortunes were lost in that fire."

She knew it well. Her own family had suffered some financial setbacks, but her father had quickly recouped with wise investments. Or so they'd thought. "The news was full of it."

"We sold the lot recently. The new owner began excavation and discovered our vault, still untouched, under the ruins."

She had no idea where this was going, but she nodded. "Go on."

"I was sent to examine the contents. One of the safety-deposit boxes belonged to Eleanor's father."

She sat up straighter. "You found money? Stocks?"

He shook his head. "A will."

She waved her hand. "The way I understand it from the family, Mr. Stewart's will was on file with his attorney in New York. Odd that he had a copy with a San Francisco lawyer."

"When was it written?"

"Ten years ago."

"I have another will in my possession, Lady Devonworth. Newer than that. Written in 1906."

Four years ago. She couldn't contain a gasp. "And you told Eleanor this? Why did you not contact Mrs. Stewart directly?"

"I tried but was unable to get her address. I contacted Mr. Stewart's business partner, Mr. Bennett, but he told me it was of no matter. He claimed there was an even newer will on file."

"He lied to you?" It hardly surprised her. She didn't trust Mr.

Bennett. "But that still doesn't explain why you took this matter to Eleanor."

"When Bennett refused to let me talk to Mrs. Stewart, let's just say I became suspicious. The man has a reputation in the city that is less than savory. When I learned that a member of the Stewart family was in residence, I decided it would be too good an opportunity to pass up. I showed the will to Eleanor."

"I fail to see where you are going with this, Mr. Fosberg. What difference does the will's date make? Mr. Stewart is hardly likely to leave his estate to anyone but his wife and daughters."

He held her gaze. "It seems there was an heir that the family knew nothing about." He hesitated and cast his gaze to the brick path, then stared at her again. "This heir made a difference to the execution of the will."

She didn't care for the somber expression in his eyes. "An heir?"

"A son."

"Mr. Stewart had no son."

He glanced away. "It's a delicate matter to discuss with you, Lady Devonworth."

She realized her hands were clenching her skirt, and she forced herself to loosen her fists. "You mean an illegitimate son?" Her voice trembled. Her father had always wanted a son.

"Indeed."

"Did Eleanor discuss this discovery with Mrs. Stewart?" She knew there had been no such discussion. Her mother would have been prostrate with the news. It would have been impossible to keep from Olivia.

"She did not. She asked my help in investigating the matter further."

"What is this son's name?"

"Richard Pixton. But I suspect he's changed his name." He reached into his pocket and pulled out a sheaf of papers. "We managed to track him to San Francisco, where he boarded a steamer bound for Eureka four years ago. That ship reached port, but no one by that name has emerged in this area."

She studied the passenger list in his hand and found the man's name. "So you think he's here—in Mercy Falls—but under an assumed name?"

"I do."

"For what reason?"

He shrugged. "I have no idea."

"Do you think he came here to confront Mr. Stewart? I believe Mr. Stewart first began his trips to Mercy Falls about that time."

"I thought of that. I even wondered if Mr. Pixton killed him."

"What would that gain him?"

"A fine inheritance."

"Which he has never claimed," she pointed out.

"True enough. Eleanor wondered if he wanted more of the money. The will states that if Mr. Stewart's other heirs are dead, Mr. Pixton would inherit all of it."

The attempt on my life. "He must be here then. He must be the one who has been stalking me since I arrived. It was only by luck that I survived the murderous attempts."

He frowned. "Why would anyone wish to harm you?" He stared at her. "*You* are Miss Olivia, are you not? There is somewhat of a resemblance to Eleanor in the tilt of your eyes. It makes sense now why you would be investigating Eleanor's death."

Mr. Fosberg's stare was still drilling into Olivia. His question hung in the air between them. There was no way to get out of this without a flat-out lie, something she wasn't willing to do.

"I am Olivia Stewart," she said. "Please don't reveal it to anyone else. I need anonymity to find out who killed my sister."

His lips twisted and he opened his mouth.

She held up her hand. "However, I'm not ready to believe it was

Harrison Bennett who did it." She bit her lip. A week ago she was just as convinced he'd murdered Eleanor. *But that was before I spent so much time with him.*

Mr. Fosberg scowled, then stood and paced across the grass. "I'm sure he murdered her," he said, his voice hard.

She thought through her own misgivings. "Just because she broke their engagement is no reason to assume he is a murderer."

"He could have hired it done."

"Harrison doesn't know my identity even now. If he'd hired someone, he would have needed to obtain a recent picture of me to pass on to his henchman. So he would have recognized me immediately." Her arguments against Harrison being the killer gained strength the more she puzzled it out. Mr. Fosberg's dislike of Harrison added fuel to her determination to defend him. "I think it has to be someone else. Who else did Eleanor see when she was here?"

His jaw jutted and his eyes narrowed. "No one. You're as taken with the man as she was when she first came here."

She could see the complete dislike on his face. "Did you convince her he was untrustworthy? What do you have against him?"

He shrugged. "I can see you'll have to discover his true character for yourself. I'll take my leave now, Miss Olivia."

"Lady Devonworth," she corrected.

"As you wish." He put his bowler back on his head and headed to his car.

Would he keep her secret? It was all going to come out very soon. The moment Mr. Bennett saw her, he would reveal her identity. She had to tell Harrison, but it was going to take the right moment.

Mr. Fosberg brushed past a young maid carrying rugs and a rug beater toward the line. The maid sent him a smile that quickly faded when he didn't speak. Olivia watched him slam the car door. The automobile rattled back down the drive.

Something about the young woman's reaction intrigued her as the girl stood looking forlornly after the departing automobile. Olivia beckoned to the maid. "I'd like to speak with you a moment."

The girl dropped her burden and wiped her hands on her white apron as she approached Olivia's bench. "Yes, ma'am? Can I fetch you some tea or lemonade?"

Olivia shook her head. "Do you know Mr. Fosberg?"

The young woman was about nineteen with a fresh complexion, blond hair, and vivid green eyes. She took a step back, and her eyes grew wide. "I didn't do nothing wrong, miss. I just smiled at him."

"I'm not accusing you of anything," Olivia soothed. "What's your name?"

"Molly Chambers."

Olivia sent her a reassuring smile. "I'm told he spent quite a lot of time with Miss Eleanor. I'm wondering if his influence on her was of the highest nature."

The alarm in Molly's face ebbed and she glanced behind her, then took a step closer. "Mr. Fosberg is said to have a way with the ladies, miss."

Olivia remembered the way the girl had smiled. "Has he paid you undue attention, Molly?"

Quick color rushed to the girl's cheeks, and she didn't hold Olivia's gaze. "I'd rather not say, miss."

The girl had probably entered service by age fifteen. Had she been here the whole time or perhaps worked for the Fosbergs? "How long have you been employed by the Stewarts?" Olivia asked.

The girl's eyes went wide again. "You wouldn't let me go, miss!"

"No, no," Olivia said. "But I think you know more about Mr. Fosberg than you are willing to admit. Where did you work before you came here?"

Molly looked away and her lips turned sullen. "I was at Eaton Hall," she said.

"The consumption hospital Mrs. Fosberg runs."

"Yes, miss."

"You saw Mr. Fosberg there quite frequently."

Molly nodded but didn't look up from her perusal of the flowers.

Olivia pressed her lips together. How could she get the girl to tell what she knew? "Did Miss Eleanor know you had a relationship with Mr. Fosberg?"

Molly's gaze came up then, wide-eyed. "Oh no, miss!" She clapped her hand over her mouth.

"So you did have a relationship."

"Please don't make me leave," Molly said, tears in her eyes. "I love working here."

"I wouldn't do that," Olivia assured her. "How long did the liaison go on?"

Molly wrung her hands. "Until he decided he had a chance to marry Miss Eleanor. He warned me to say nothing to her."

"Are you still seeing him?"

Molly shook her head with vigor. "No, miss."

"Would you say his words are trustworthy?"

The maid twisted her hands again. "Oh, miss, don't make me talk anymore," she whispered. "I still love him."

The poor girl. Olivia could read between the lines. She'd best verify anything Mr. Fosberg told her. And also take anything this girl said with a grain of salt. It was possible she wanted Mr. Fosberg for herself and was seeing things through that filter.

TWENTY-FOUR

THERE WAS NO mistaking Fosberg's flashy automobile as it whizzed past Harrison's Cadillac. Or the fact that the man had been at Stewart Hall. It was the only residence out this way. Harrison slowed the vehicle and puttered out the macadam road to the Stewarts' house by the sea. As he parked and got out of his car, a swell rolled in with the sharp tang of kelp on the wind.

He rang the bell, but the butler told him Lady Devonworth was out back in the garden. He went around the side of the mansion to the labyrinth of garden paths. The scent of honeysuckle and the drone of bees hovered in the air.

A sound floated on the wind and he paused to listen. A sweet voice sang, "Come, Josephine, in My Flying Machine." He listened a moment and smiled when he heard, "Up, up, a little bit higher. Oh! My! The moon is on fire." The moon had seemed ablaze the night he'd lain in the clearing with her head cradled on his shoulder. Or maybe his emotions had affected his eyes. Right now the attraction he felt toward her was tangled up.

He squared his shoulders and walked toward her voice.

"'I'm a sky kid,'" she sang. Her voice faltered when he stepped into her view from behind the arbor. Color flooded her cheeks and her dark eyes flashed gypsy fire at him. "What are you doing skulking around?" she demanded.

His lips twitched. "One trip in an aeroplane and you're a sky kid, Essie?"

Her cheeks grew rosier and she tipped her chin up. "That's a ridiculous name! Did you just come to mock me?"

"No." He indicated the bench. "Mind if I join you?"

"Of course not." She scooted over, but her expression stayed remote.

He had no idea how she really felt about him. The iron bench was hard under his thighs. Nearly as hard as the line of her mouth. She hadn't been so cold when he last saw her. What had changed? Eyeing her expression, he doubted she would tell him.

With her fingers laced in her lap, she appeared to be a demure young woman who never did the unexpected, but he knew better. Something was brewing behind that beautiful face, but he suspected she'd only share what it was if he made her angry enough.

He cleared his throat. "Do you want to tell me why you're so angry with me?"

Her eyes narrowed. "When were you going to tell me that Eleanor broke off her engagement to you?"

He grabbed the tail of his temper as it attempted to escape. "Where did you hear that?"

"Does it matter?" she asked, a note of challenge in her voice. "It's true, isn't it?"

How much should he tell her? All of it or only enough to distract her? He thought he caught a glimpse of something in her eyes, a longing to be wrong. Or was it his foolish hope instead? "Do you really want to know the truth?" he asked in a quiet voice.

"I do," she said. Her voice trembled a little, but she put her hand over his.

He took heart from her impulsive gesture and placed his other hand over hers, then regretted it when she quickly pulled back. "I'll hold nothing back. But listen quietly and don't ask any questions until I'm finished. Agreed?"

"Agreed."

"She didn't break her engagement to me. I broke it." When she gasped and opened her mouth, he held up his hand. "Remember your promise. I'm not done." She shut her lips and he stared at her, willing her to believe him. "I know this isn't pleasant to hear, but I caught her and Fosberg in a . . . a compromising position."

She opened her mouth, then shut it again at his warning glance. She shuddered, and he realized how hard this was for her. She'd loved Eleanor. But he didn't think she knew her friend very well.

A toad hopped across the grass by his feet. He watched it go and tried to think of an easier way to tell her the story. There was nothing easy about such an unsavory tale. "I'll just say it," he said, his voice harsh. "She spent the night at his cottage two miles up the coast. I received a tip that I'd find them there. I didn't care enough about Eleanor to be upset, but I refused to be made a cuckold. His valet tried to dissuade me from entering, but I forced my way in and found the two of them in bed together."

She gasped. Or was it a moan? He wished he could take her hand but forced himself not to touch her. Her head was down and her shoulders drooped. "I'm sorry. I wish I could spare you this, but there's more. When they saw me, Fosberg leaped from the bed in his nightdress. Eleanor clutched the covers to her neck and screamed at me to get out. I told her I was leaving and that our engagement was at an end. By the end of the next day she was dead. So, yes, I do feel some guilt about her death. Perhaps she feared I would tell what I'd seen, but I had no intention of humiliating her."

"I-I can hardly believe it of Eleanor."

"I've told no one. Not even my father, though I'm going to have to tell him. He has a crazy idea to marry me off to Olivia Stewart. I wouldn't marry a Stewart if she were the last woman on Earth." He spat the name Stewart from his mouth.

Lady Devonworth went white and still. "So is that why you wish to marry me? To foil your father's plans?"

"No." He wasn't ready to tell her his feelings. "Have you spoken with your mother about my proposal?"

"I have. She believes it the proper thing to do."

"Is that a yes then?"

She nodded her head without looking at him. "I fear I have no choice." She raised teary eyes to his. "So she really did kill herself?"

He hesitated. "I don't know," he said. "She didn't seem the type to do harm to herself. I believe Fosberg would have been willing to marry her. He seemed quite besotted."

She nodded. "He said they were going to be married," she said, looking away.

He saw the guilt in her eyes before it was hidden from him. "What else did he say?"

"That she broke her engagement to you and that you killed her."

"I didn't kill her!" he said. When she didn't answer, his chest constricted. "Do you believe him?" *Please say no.* He held his breath and waited for her answer. Her hand crept across the metal to grasp his. He squeezed her fingers.

Her head came up and her eyes met his. "No," she said. "I don't think you're capable of murder."

He wanted to sweep her into his arms and press his lips to hers, but he restrained himself. There was time to win her. And he would.

❧

Gaslight chandeliers cast shadows in the cavernous dining room as Olivia pulled a chair out to sit by her mother, who was at the head of the table. Delicious aromas filled the air: barley soup, roast duck with cranberry sauce, and chateau potatoes.

Her stomach objected to the thought of food, but she took up her napkin and smiled at her mother. "Dinner smells heavenly."

Her mother gave her a sharp glance. "Whatever is the matter, Olivia? You look like you've lost your best friend. And where are your friends, by the way?" She leaned back so the footman could lay the napkin in her lap. "And I thought I saw your young man out there."

"I saw Katie in the upstairs hall. She and Will will be down shortly." She put her napkin in her lap. "Harrison was here, Mother, and I agreed to marry him. But there is a wrinkle in that plan. He is quite opposed to marrying Olivia Stewart."

Her mother shot her a startled glance. "What do you mean?"

"There were some problems between him and Eleanor. He said Olivia Stewart would be the last person he would ever marry." She bit her lip. "I could hardly tell him my name then."

Her mother shrugged. "An engagement will suffice for now to restore your reputation. You can break it in your own time and tell him the truth." She glanced at the mantel clock. "I like to dine precisely at eight. It's five after."

"Katie said to extend her apologies. Jennie was crying and upset, and they read her a bedtime story. She's been having nightmares since the storm destroyed the lighthouse."

Her mother's expression softened. "Poor child." She motioned to the other footmen hovering in the doorways. "You may serve the hors d'oeuvres." The men jumped to do her bidding and went to the serving tables, where canapés were arranged with caviar, cheese, foie gras, and liver pâté. Her mother selected the caviar only, took a bite, then dabbed at her lips with the linen napkin. "So you still haven't told me what is wrong."

Olivia glanced at the clock. She likely had ten minutes before their guests joined them. The subject was hardly dinner conversation, but her mother would never let it go until she pried out the information.

She sipped her water, then put down the crystal goblet. "Mr. Fosberg returned this afternoon. He told me a most distressing tale."

Her mother paused with a canapé halfway to her mouth. She put it down on her saucer. "About Eleanor?"

"It's about Father."

Her mother smiled. "He's located your father?" Her voice was as animated as a girl's, and a flush lit her skin.

A pang struck in Olivia's midsection. Her mother genuinely loved the man. Olivia wasn't sure how she herself felt. Her father had been like a king or nobility to her. She'd worshipped him and tried everything in her power to make him proud of her, to make him utter one word of praise. The discovery that he had feet of clay was a blow she wasn't sure she could recover from.

"No, Mother. H-He says he has a valid will that Father executed. It was discovered in a safe that was buried in debris during the Great Fire. It was written in 1906."

Her mother's eager smile faded. "Your somber expression tells me this is somehow bad news. You know how I detest it when you dance around information, Olivia. Out with it."

Olivia toyed with her spoon and stirred sugar into tea. "According to the will, Father has another heir. A son." She glanced up to see how her mother received the surprise.

The words seemed to echo in the high-ceilinged room. It was her mother's greatest shame that she'd never given her husband a son. If only she hadn't had to tell her mother this news.

Her mother's eyes grew wider as the words sank in. Her high color faded to a sallow yellow. Her throat clicked as she swallowed. "I don't understand, Olivia."

The facts. Stick to the facts in a neutral tone of voice that might calm Mother. Olivia somehow managed to speak in an even tone. "Father had an illegitimate son, Mother. The son was traced here to Mercy Falls but evidently changed his name, and Mr. Fosberg was unable to track him down."

"What is his name?"

"Richard Pixton."

Her mother's hands curled into fists, and she banged them onto the table so hard that Olivia's water glass toppled. "Pixton!" She swallowed again, and a single tear ran down her cheek.

"You know the name?" Olivia asked.

"Lulu Pixton was my personal maid. She threw herself at your father, and I dismissed her at once. I thought she went to live with her sister in San Francisco."

"That's where Richard was born." The older woman moaned at Olivia's words, an eerie sound that raised the hair on the back of Olivia's neck. Olivia reached over and took her mother's hand. "I'm sure Father didn't love her, Mother. I'm sure he was just trying to do the right thing. He was always careful to attend to his responsibilities."

"His responsibility was to me, his wife! And to his own children." Her mother rose so quickly that her chair tipped over. "I'm going to my room. I have a most dreadful headache. Give my regards to our guests." She rushed from the room.

Olivia dabbed the spilled water with her napkin. She motioned for the footmen to remove her mother's utensils and to repair the table. Her chest was tight, and she ached for her mother's pain. And where was Father? They needed him now.

TWENTY-FIVE

HARRISON SLID HIS arms into the vest Eugene held out. "I don't feel like eating dinner tonight, Eugene." Nealy looked up at Harrison's words as if to check that his master was all right.

Tonight he was to attend a celebratory dinner hosted by the owner of the business Harrison had just acquired. He was surprised his father had agreed to attend, given his displeasure over the price Harrison had paid.

"Yes, sir. Would you like me to make your apologies?"

"No, I have to go. Who knows what my father would say to Mr. Riley if I'm not there." He buttoned the vest, then grabbed the jacket from the form by the window. "I hope I'm not seated next to Fosberg. It's going to be all I can do not to throttle him."

He didn't expect an answer from his valet, and sure enough, Eugene simply took the clothes brush and went over Harrison's suit one last time. The valet was a great sounding board but seldom offered advice. He knew his place, though Harrison thought of him more as a peer than a personal servant.

"I think I love her," Harrison said. "How did that happen?"

Eugene knelt and gave the toes of his shoes one last buff. "I imagine it's the usual way, sir. She's very beautiful."

"Yes, she is. And I like her spirit. The way she analyzes everything. She takes something you say and hears what you're really saying underneath. How does she do that?"

"Women are most incomprehensible," his valet said. Eugene stood and stepped back. "I believe you'll pass muster and not put me to shame."

Harrison grinned. "I'll try to do you proud." He clapped a hand on Eugene's shoulder. "Have you ever been in love, Eugene?"

"No, sir. When would I have time?"

"We've had some attractive chambermaids. There was that pretty lady's maid my mother had a couple of years ago. What was her name?"

"Lucy."

Harrison tugged on his cravat. "Ah, yes, Lucy. Whatever happened to her?"

"She married the butler."

"That's right." He dropped his arm when Eugene gently pushed it out of the way to fix the blasted tie. "But I'm sure you've had ample opportunity to find a wife."

"A wife would demand more time than I can give her."

Harrison had already turned toward the door but veered back at Eugene's words. "Are you happy here?"

He studied his valet. Eugene was what, about twenty-five? Average height and slim build. Pleasant enough features. Brown eyes and a trim mustache. Harrison paid him well too, so Eugene should have been appealing to the opposite sex.

Eugene smiled. "I've been with you for four years, sir. I hope I may be so bold as to say I look up to you. You have been very good to me. My life is full."

"I realize that every important decision I've ever made, I've discussed with you. Though you never tell me what to do, talking it out has always helped. So what should I do about Lady Devonworth?"

"There isn't a woman alive who could resist you when you put your mind to wooing her, sir."

"Spoken like a true friend. So I just woo her? I've already proposed, but I'm sure she has no idea of my true feelings. She just thinks I merely want to do the right thing. I'm not sure how to go about letting her know how I feel."

"She's quite taken with your aeroplane," Eugene pointed out.

Harrison scowled. "Which is now strewn across half of California."

"You have the new model nearly completed. Ask her to go up in it again."

"I intend to have it finished by the time the comet's tail arrives in two weeks. But I need to be assured there will be no more sabotage." He glanced at Nealy. "Perhaps I will put Nealy to watching it."

Eugene stepped past Harrison and opened the door, then stood aside. "Has the constable discovered who was behind your accident?"

Harrison went past him into the hall. "I doubt he will. There are no clues. He's asked at the pubs and cafes, but there has been nothing for him to follow up on. I need to be especially vigilant before taking up the new plane."

He paused partway down the hall, then turned to see Eugene following five paces behind. "Take the night off, Eugene. Take a girl to dinner."

His valet's teeth gleamed as he grinned. "I'll see what I can do, sir. Though it would never do for both of us to be in love. Someone around here needs to have his brain engaged."

Harrison laughed. "You might have a point. Good night."

"Thanks."

Harrison jogged down the hall to the stairs and out the door to his car. He had instructed his driver to bring it around, but the Riley home was only a few blocks away and it was a beautiful night, so he decided to walk and waved the driver back to the carriage house. It took only five minutes to stroll to the Rileys'. When he stepped into the foyer, he could hear the tinkle of glassware and the murmur of laughter and conversation. The last thing he wanted to do was to make small talk when he could be working on his aeroplane.

He found the guests milling through the massive dining room.

Everyone was talking about the Lightkeeper's Ball, and the level of excitement about it was high, though the chatter stilled when he entered and he intercepted a few sly glances. Nothing like this had ever been done in Mercy Falls, and people would be unlikely to refuse to attend in spite of the scandal that had just erupted. Lady Devonworth's New York friends were another matter, however.

After chatting with the host and his wife, he found his way to the food. Tall linen-covered tables held hors d'oeuvres of every type. Footmen served glasses of champagne and wine. He greeted neighbors and customers as he made his way through the crowd to where his mother was talking to Addie and John North.

"There you are, Harrison," his mother said when he brushed his lips across her powdered cheek. "I was beginning to think I'd have to come drag you from your house."

"Just running a little late." He shook hands with John.

"We're celebrating," John said, his grin widening. Addie blushed and glanced away. John's grin told the story.

Harrison's mother rapped her fan on Harrison's arm. "They're going to be adding to their family."

"Congratulations." Harrison meant it. The Norths had been childless since their marriage two years ago and had hoped to give a sibling to Edward, John's son by a previous marriage.

A warm sensation enveloped him when he saw the way the Norths looked at one another. If only Lady Devonworth would look on him with that kind of love in her eyes.

Still smiling, he turned toward the door and froze. Fosberg had arrived.

❧

Firelight flickered in the huge stone fireplace. Olivia sipped her after-dinner tea and stared at the crackling flames. Her father's letter to

Eleanor lay in her lap. Will and Katie were playing checkers at the game table, and their banter flowed around her, but she paid little attention to what they said.

The Jespersons' game ended. "I'm going to peek in on Jennie," Will said.

Katie joined Olivia on the sofa. "You're very pensive," she said. "This news about a missing half brother has rocked you, has it not?"

"Very much," Olivia admitted. "I thought my father an honorable man. Aloof, but a good man."

"You seem nearly to idolize him. Was he home much?"

Olivia shook her head. "His businesses took him away quite often. Africa, California, Europe. When he was home, the world revolved around him. He often hurt me with his comments about how disappointed he was that I wasn't the son he wanted."

Katie wrinkled her nose. "I hate to hear that. I'm sure he loved you very much."

"I always felt I had to earn his attention. You know what I thought of first when I'd heard he died in that cave-in? That I would never hear him say, 'I love you.'"

Her friend squeezed her hand. "I'm sorry, my dear."

"So am I. But now there is another chance. I don't understand why there has been no communication from him since this." She lifted his letter off her lap. "Why hasn't he shown himself?"

Katie hesitated. "Are you sure it's not your wishful thinking? How can he be alive and here in town without being seen?"

"I've wondered the same thing. But I have to find him if he's alive," she said. "He's the only one who can straighten all this out."

"Are you sure that's his handwriting?" Katie asked.

"It certainly appears to be his."

"Will's brother is a private investigator. You could try to have him track your father."

Olivia shuddered. "I hate to involve someone like that in our private affairs."

"He wouldn't have to know the reason. You could simply say you suspect your father is still alive. And he'd be very discreet."

"Perhaps." Olivia stared at the letter. "I need to see the will that's in Mr. Fosberg's possession."

"He didn't show it to you?"

Olivia shook her head. "At the time I didn't think much about it. But after speaking with Molly, I wonder why he did not reveal it. I suspect his motives."

A smile tugged at Katie's lips. "You really don't want to believe anything bad of Harrison, do you?"

"I believe Harrison is honorable."

"Your attitude about him has turned around completely. When we first met, you suspected he murdered Eleanor. Now you are his staunch defender."

Olivia heard the amusement in her friend's voice and had to smile herself. "I know him better now. Or do you think I'm deceiving myself?"

Katie selected a trifle from the dessert tray. "I've never believed him capable of murder. He's been a friend to Will and me for years. I don't care much for his father, but Mr. Bennett's actions are hardly Harrison's fault." She nibbled on a chocolate éclair, then eyed Olivia. "You said Harrison offered to announce your engagement. What are you going to do?"

Olivia had thought of little else. "I agreed to the engagement. The ball will be an engagement ball as well."

Katie clasped her hands together. "Olivia, that's wonderful!"

"Don't rejoice too much just yet. He'll break the engagement when I tell him I'm Olivia Stewart."

Katie's smile faded. "What do you mean?"

Olivia held her gaze. "Eleanor was not . . . true to him. He is rather bitter about the Stewart family and told me that his father is insistent that he marry Olivia. But he said he would never do such a thing."

"I believe he cares for you, Olivia."

She wished she could hold such a happy view of the situation. "Mother sees nothing wrong with stringing him along until the scandal dies down."

"What does she have planned for you if you do break your engagement?"

"She intends to haul me to Europe. She has it in her head that Bennett and Harrison are responsible for Eleanor's death." She held up her hand when Katie smiled. "I know, I believed the same thing a few days ago. I'll convince her when I get to the truth."

"So what happens when you get to Europe?"

"Mother hopes to marry me to someone more suitable." Her spirits dipped just repeating her mother's plans. She didn't want to be married for status. Not to Harrison or to anyone else. "Sometimes I wish I were a common person, just a milliner or a dressmaker. It's dreadful to be sought after for what you possess."

"You should be careful what you wish for," Katie said.

"Oh, I realize how fortunate I am. And I'm grateful." She realized she sounded anything but grateful.

"God has you right where he wants you," Katie said. "He provides for our needs no matter how much money we have. Any money you have is from his hand."

Olivia had never really considered that God had given her family their money. Her father had been quick to take credit for their family's astute business sense. "I think I shall call on Mr. Fosberg tomorrow and ask to see the will."

"Do you want Will or me to go with you?"

Olivia shook her head. "I can handle Mr. Fosberg. I shall take Mother with me. He can't deny our right to see the document." She yawned. "I'm exhausted. It's been a grueling day. I think I shall ring for Jerry to carry me upstairs."

"I'm going up too. Jennie must be awake, or Will would have joined us."

Katie rang for Jerry, and the footman carried her up to her bedroom. "I can make it from here, Jerry. Thank you," she told him at the bedroom door. He put her down on the end of the bed and laid the crutches beside her, then left her alone.

If only she could shut her thoughts off. And her feelings. She wanted to talk to Harrison. Tonight. Right now. She rang the bell for Goldia.

Goldia stepped into the room. "There you are, miss. I have your nightdress laid out."

Olivia stood and balanced herself on the bedpost, turning her back to her maid. She allowed Goldia to undo the buttons and help her step out of the dress. She stood shivering as Goldia dropped the nightdress over her head, then sat in front of the dresser as the maid released her hair from its pins and began to brush it. The rhythmic touch of the bristles through her hair eased the tension in her shoulders.

"I thought I saw your father today," Goldia said.

Olivia tensed and turned to face the girl. "Father? Where?"

"At the general store. I was buying some ribbons for your new hat and saw him through the window. I ran out, but he was gone."

"Do you think it was really him? In broad daylight where he might be recognized?"

Goldia resumed brushing. "I only caught a glimpse so I can't be sure. But the walk was so familiar."

Olivia's heart lightened. "Perhaps he will be in touch with us soon." Maybe she would do as Katie suggested if he didn't show himself. A detective would track him down in no time. She thanked Goldia, then hobbled to bed and crawled under the covers after her maid pulled them back. Goldia extinguished the gaslight at the door, then exited, plunging the room into darkness.

Olivia snuggled under the sheet and her eyelids drooped. It seemed only moments later when her eyes popped open, but the moonless night told her at least an hour had passed. It was likely about eleven. She bolted upright in bed as a voice came from the speaking tube beside her again.

"Olivia. I need to talk to you. Come to the kitchen."

She grabbed the speaking tube. "Who is this?"

"Don't you recognize your own father, Olivia? Come to the kitchen. Now."

The imperious voice was clearly her father's. Without another thought, she reached for her dressing gown, belted it around her, then hobbled to the door on her crutches.

TWENTY-SIX

HARRISON MANAGED TO avoid Fosberg until the party began to disperse about eleven. It was difficult to keep smiling and talking to guests when he wanted to take the man by the collar and toss him into the street. He chatted with the Norths until he thought Fosberg was gone, then walked them to the door and said good night. When he turned to go back to the parlor, however, he spotted the man still inside. Fosberg stood talking to Harrison's parents by the fireplace.

Harrison stopped in the doorway and turned to exit, but his mother called to him. He turned back and approached the three. "I believe I'll say good night now."

His father clapped his hand on Fosberg's shoulder. "Good news, Harrison. Mr. Fosberg is leasing the building on Main and Sunset."

Their premier leasehold. Harrison looked at Fosberg's smug face. "I'm not leasing anything to him."

His father's smile faded. "Well, I am."

"Then you'll do it without me. I'm not signing any paperwork for it. The man has publicly accused me of murder."

His father stared from Fosberg to Harrison. "What are you babbling about?" he snapped.

"Ask him."

Fosberg was stone-faced. "You're speaking nonsense."

"Lady Devonworth told me of your belief that I killed Eleanor."

"I don't have to stay and listen to such nonsense." Fosberg brushed past Harrison.

Harrison followed him. "Do you deny your accusation? And you didn't even tell her the full story."

His father was on their heels. "Harrison, that's enough. I've already accepted Mr. Fosberg's offer. I have his check in my pocket."

"Then you have my resignation. I'll have nothing to do with helping him get established in this town." Harrison strode past Fosberg and slammed the door behind him. He heard his father bellow his name, but he ignored it and stalked down the driveway and down the street to his own house.

Now what? He had some money in the bank, but it would only pay his expenses for a few months. Though finances would be tight, he could devote all his energy now to researching flight. He could look for investors without being hampered by his father's expectations and the responsibility he felt toward the family business.

Now was his chance to follow his dream. Fosberg had just done him a favor.

When Harrison stepped into the hall, Eugene met him at the door. "Your mother is on the telephone," he said, taking Harrison's jacket.

Harrison's gut tightened. He went to the hall where the telephone was and picked up the earpiece. "Hello, Mother."

"Your father is quite upset, Harrison. Come over and talk this out."

Her tearful voice got past his defenses. "I can't. There is nothing to talk out. I'm not going to lease Frederick Fosberg anything."

"Your father says he's paying a good sum. It's just business, after all."

"And I've found such business practices aren't for me." He inhaled and hoped to gather courage. "This has been coming a long time. You know where my heart lies. I want to spend time on my aeroplane."

"Son, you have a God-given gift for numbers and business. How can you throw that away?"

Her reminder made him sag against the wall. It was the one thing he hadn't thought through. The gift. Was he throwing away something God intended him to use? He thought of the way he felt when he was working on a new acquisition. Getting the new business on a solid financial footing, finding its strengths and bolstering its weaknesses. He was usually able to focus and be involved, yes, but his mind often wandered to the design of his machine. So which was God-given?

"Harrison, are you there?" his mother asked.

"I'm here." He rubbed his forehead. "I don't know what to tell you, Mother. I'm not signing any lease with that man."

"What did you mean about his accusation?"

"He suggested to Lady Devonworth that Eleanor broke our engagement and I killed her in a rage." He'd told no one about what he'd seen at the cottage. No one but Lady Devonworth.

His mother gasped. "Surely the woman misunderstood him."

"She did not," he said.

"*Did* Eleanor break the engagement?" his mother asked.

"No. I did. But I don't wish to discuss the reasons." He exhaled heavily. "It's late, Mother. We're all tired. I'm going to bed."

"At least pray about this," his mother pleaded.

"I shall do that. But I think God has been leading me in this direction for a long time."

"Mr. Fosberg might have been upset about something. I'm sure his words were not as serious as you are making out."

"And I'm sure they were. Good night, Mother." He hung up the phone and went upstairs where Eugene waited.

His valet helped him off with his vest, then hung it up with his coat. "I quit Bennett and Bennett tonight."

Eugene paused in his brushing lint off the jacket and vest on the form. "Totally quit? For good, sir?"

"Yes. And it feels great. Tomorrow I'm going to go to the club and see about finding some investors to rebuild the aeroplane."

"I'm not sure it will be easy. Not after crashing the last machine."

"I have a great new design that I want to work on. I want to land it on water and prove it can be done."

"Should I look for another position, sir?"

Harrison stared at his valet. "Of course not, Eugene. I'm going to make a go of this. And I have enough savings to see us through for a while. You're indispensable to me."

But the reminder that others depended on his decisions tempered his elation. His entire staff looked to him for their support. He had to make this work. He looked at the bed, then grabbed casual clothes.

"I'm going for a walk," he told Eugene. He called to Nealy and stepped into the night air.

❧

Olivia nearly slipped on the slick surface of the stairs. Little moonlight came through the windows, and the servants had extinguished all the lamps. Holding on to the banister, she made her way down to the first floor by scooting on her bottom with her crutches in one hand. In the hall, she got the crutches under her arms, then lit the gaslight in the hall. Its hiss was nearly as comforting as the warm yellow glow it cast.

She moved through the labyrinth of rooms to the kitchen, a room she wasn't sure she'd ever been in. The cook was usually jealous of his domain, and she tended to leave him to his territory. She thought it was through this hallway, but she found herself in a place that dead-ended at a servants' bathroom.

Retracing her steps, she went down another hall. This time she saw a sliver of light under a closed door. She pushed the heavy door, and it opened into a large kitchen lined with cupboards, a mammoth stove, and a large chopping table. A small lamp only barely illuminated the space, but there were lots of shadowy corners that left her uneasy.

The room was empty. It held a lingering scent of garlic and cinnamon. "Hello?"

She stepped into the room, and the door swung shut behind her. She jumped and whirled when the latch clicked. Stepping back, she turned the knob and it opened easily. When she peered into the hall, there was no one there. The window in the back door drew her. She peered out into the sprawling yard, but it was too dark to see past the first two feet.

She turned back to the seemingly empty room. "Father?" she called softly. No one answered.

Where was the speaking tube he'd used? She glanced around the room and saw it by the door. There was a similar apparatus in most rooms in the house. Could he have used one in the parlor and intended to get here before she did? Pulling out a chair by the battered table against the wall, she sat down to wait.

Though it was late, all thoughts of sleep had fled. Where was he? She didn't know how long she waited. At least fifteen minutes. Toying with a fork, she listened for any sounds in the quiet house.

"I might as well go back to bed," she said aloud. She rose and pushed the chair back in. As it scraped against the floor, she heard something.

"Olivia," the voice called from outside. It was right outside the back door. Or so it seemed.

She limped toward the door, then paused with her hand on the doorknob. Why would her father want to talk outside in the dark? Was it even him?

"Olivia, come here," the man said again.

She listened closely to the voice. It *was* her father. She unlocked the door and hobbled with her crutches onto the back stoop. The ocean waves crashed in the distance, and she smelled the tang of salt in the air. "Father?" The dew drenched her cloth slippers as soon as she stepped onto the grass.

She moved farther into the yard. "Father?" The darkness was complete, and she couldn't see more than a foot in front of her face. If only she had a lamp. A bench should be to her right, so she moved in that direction.

A sound came from behind her. Before she could turn, a cloth covered her nose and mouth, and a sickeningly sweet smell made her cough and gag. She fought the strong arms that held her tight as the man dragged her backward. She was dizzy, so dizzy. She fought to stay conscious. She was dimly aware he was dragging her toward the cliff. Was this how Eleanor had died? Drugged and thrown into the sea right outside the house?

With renewed vigor, she dug her nails into her attacker's skin and heard him swear under his breath. Even now he sounded a bit like her father, but she knew he couldn't possibly be. Whipping her head back and forth, she managed to catch a fresh breath of clean air that cleared her mind. She tore into his skin with her nails again and wished she could sink her teeth into his wrist, but the cloth still partially covered her mouth.

His grip loosened, and she ripped free of his hands. The cloth fell away from her mouth. She screamed but all that came out was a choked cry. The chemical he'd used on the cloth had tightened her throat and dried her lips. She stumbled toward the house, but he was on her again before she'd gone two steps.

"You little hellion," he muttered in her ear.

That voice wasn't her father's. The cloth came toward her mouth again and she screamed. This time the sound was a little louder, but she didn't think anyone in the house would hear her.

"Harrison!" The suffocating smell enveloped her again, and the strength drained out of her legs. She sagged, and the man dragged her back toward the drop-off again.

She wasn't ready to die. It was her last thought before he pitched her over the edge.

TWENTY-SEVEN

THE MOON WAS out, illuminating the shrubs and flowers along Pacific Way. Harrison hadn't intended to walk this far. And he especially had no intention of walking past the mansion where Lady Devonworth slept behind the stone walls. He paused at the driveway to the Stewart estate. No lights winked in the windows. The only movement was the wind through the live oak tree branches.

What was he doing here? He'd thought a walk would clear his head, but it only made him more confused about what the future held. The night was silent, broken only by the distant sound of the surf on the rocks and the click of Nealy's nails on the sidewalk beside him. There was no voice from God telling him what he should do now. He didn't have much to offer a lady. No security, only his dream of building a flying machine that would make a difference.

It was only when he turned to retrace his steps that a troubling sound broke the night air. He paused, listening. A cat in distress? Had her dratted kitten gotten into trouble again? Shrugging, he took another step toward home, but Nealy whined and went a few feet closer to the house.

"Come on, Nealy," Harrison said, continuing to walk away.

He'd gone only three feet when he heard a woman cry out. The utterance sounded like *his* name. Nealy barked and ran toward the manor. Harrison whirled and looked toward the house to see if Lady Devonworth had spotted him and wanted to talk. The house was still dark and motionless. Now that he thought about it, the cry had been distant, apart from the house.

Though aware he was trespassing, he jogged around the side of the mansion to the backyard. The gardens were extensive. Shrubs and trees blocked his vision as he stared. "Lady Devonworth?" His voice seemed loud in the dark. "Are you back here?"

Nealy barked, a ferocious sound. The dog raced off into the night. He heard a man yell, "Let go of me!"

Harrison raced toward the sound. A dark figure bowled him over, then darted away, leaving a whiff of chloroform in his wake. Harrison jumped back to his feet. His inclination was to give chase, but what if Lady Devonworth was hurt? His chest tightened.

He turned back toward the sea and rushed on. "Lady Devonworth!" he yelled. The scent of chloroform increased his anxiety.

He followed Nealy's barking and found the dog at the edge of the cliff. The dog peered over the edge and howled. Harrison stared down into the water. The whitecaps caught the gleam of moonlight as they rolled to the rocks. He scoured the water, praying not to see a person in that treacherous riptide.

Nealy continued to whine even though Harrison commanded him to be quiet several times. His eyes narrowed. Was that an arm thrown above the waves? He dropped to one knee and leaned over the edge. His gut clenched when it came again. A person struggled in the rough seas below.

"Essie!"

Leaping to his feet, he kicked off his boots and tore the coat from his back, then dived over the cliff. He attempted to miss the rocks by timing his headlong entrance into the water to match the breaking waves. The wind rushed by his face and nearly took his breath away as he plummeted toward the salty spray. Seconds later the cold water closed over his head. His knee struck a rock, and pain encased his leg.

He kicked out with his good leg. His face broke the surface of the water and he drew a breath into his burning lungs. "Essie!" He jerked around wildly for any sight of her. Striking off in the direction where he'd last seen her, he swam several feet, then treaded water while he searched the waves for her.

Had he been mistaken? Maybe he had seen a piece of flotsam. The undertow pulled at him, trying to drag him out to sea. He let it carry him awhile, praying it would take him to her. The current turned and rolled him parallel to the coast.

"Where are you?" he screamed over the sound of the waves. If she'd been drugged, how could she fight the heavy surf? A splash sounded beside him, and he saw his dog swimming with determination to his right. A surge lifted Harrison high. As he crested the top and began to fall into the trough, he spotted a white face in the water. "Dear God, help me."

He began to swim toward her, but Nealy reached her first. The dog seized the collar on her dress in his teeth and began to paddle toward the shore. Harrison kicked closer to them, then dived to prevent a wave from washing him past her. Reaching out, he managed to grab hold of something. As his head broke the surface, he realized he had hold of her hair. With his other hand he grabbed hold of her arm and pulled her closer. Her eyes were closed and he couldn't tell if she was breathing.

"Good dog, Nealy," he crooned. "I've got her now."

The dog released her and swam alongside Harrison. Harrison pulled her close but still couldn't tell if she lived. He had to get her to land. The undertow took a tighter hold and tried to take him under, but he kicked out and managed to break its grip. Swimming at an angle to the shore, he fought the waves to keep her head out of the water. Inch by inch he drew closer to the rocks. At first he saw no place for a suitable landing. His strength was fading fast. His clothes dragged him down. His kicks were taking more and more energy, especially with his knee screaming with pain.

His head went under and he came up sputtering. Somehow he

managed to keep her nose out of the water. He willed her chest to move, for him to see some sign of life. Another wave lifted them and carried them toward the rocks. Just as he thought they were both about to be crushed against the teeth of the shore, he heard Nealy barking. The dog had reached a flat spot and pulled himself onto a smooth stone. Harrison thought they might be able to land. He struck out for it. The surge ended just shy of the cliffs, and his feet touched the bottom.

Half carrying and half dragging her, he staggered ashore and collapsed onto the sand. Panting, he rolled her onto her stomach across his legs and pushed on her back. Seawater came from her mouth. He pushed again, but she lay inert. He laid her face up on the rocks and patted her cheek.

"Get help, Nealy," he told the panting collie. The dog barked and ran away.

Harrison touched her again. "Don't die," he whispered. "I love you."

She was cold, so cold. Olivia coughed at the burning in her lungs and tasted salt and kelp. She gradually became aware of hard rock under her cheek and the warmth of a hand on her back.

"Esmeralda, you're alive."

Even half-drowned, she recognized the relief in Harrison's voice as he called her that ridiculous name. What was he doing here?

I love you.

The words in Harrison's voice reverberated in her head. What a strange dream she was having. She coughed and the harsh sound brought her fully to her senses. This was no dream. The Pacific roared off to her right, and its foam struck her in the face when she struggled to sit up. The black rocks cut into her palms, and salt stung her cut lips.

She coughed again. "What happened?"

Harrison supported her back. "Easy now. How much do you remember?"

She tensed. "A man. He put a cloth over my nose and it choked me. I think he threw me over the cliff."

He pulled her closer against his chest when she shivered. "He nearly knocked me down running away."

She managed to get her eyes to focus. "You're wet too. You saved me?"

"Nealy helped. God made sure we were in the right place at the right time."

He brushed his lips over her forehead, and she turned her face into his wet shirt. His arms held her close. The moment seared her with its intimacy. And those words continued to reverberate in her heart.

I love you.

Why did she hear them in her head? Her teeth began to chatter. "I'm so cold," she muttered.

"I've got to get you to the house and fetch the doctor."

He helped her up and turned her toward the black cliffs that glistened with moisture in the moonlight. There appeared to be no clear path to the top. She had little strength to climb, and her ankle throbbed. They walked a few feet, and she realized he was limping as well.

She paused and looked up at him. "Are you injured?"

"Just a bruised knee." His face was tipped up as he studied the formidable barrier in front of them. "I think there's a path around the point, but it's a little distance. Can you make it?"

"I don't have a choice."

They set off on the rocks slippery with kelp and seaweed. Her breath came hard through her burning chest. She realized she'd nearly drowned in the same manner as Eleanor. "I-I have to rest," she gasped. She sank onto a boulder.

He sat beside her, and his breathing was as labored as hers. "I'd go on to get help, but I'm not sure it's safe to leave you. Do you know who tried to kill you?"

She remembered the hard hands, the overpowering odor of the chemical-laden cloth. "I don't know. It was too dark to see." Staring up the rock face, she shuddered. "I think this is how Eleanor died. Was she found here?"

"Yes."

She shivered and clasped her arms around her. "I would have drowned if you hadn't saved me."

When her hand touched his, he grasped it and raised it to his lips. "I'm thankful God brought me out for a walk."

She remembered her panicked flailing when she struck the water. The way she'd prayed for God to save her. Had he seen her struggles in the water? Had he really provided a hero for her tonight, or had it all been coincidence? In the cold blackness of the sea, she'd felt alone and abandoned. Addie said God saw everything. Maybe she was right.

"Are you ready to try again?" he asked when she shivered once more.

"Yes." She hoisted herself up and clung to his arm along the slippery rocks. The wet nightdress hampered her every move and was heavy enough to slow her progress.

I love you.

Was that God talking to her? The voice had sounded like Harrison to her. Or maybe it was all a dream. Glancing at him out of the corner of her eye, she wished she had the courage to ask him.

"You're looking at me in a most odd way," he said. "Is there something wrong?"

"D-Did you speak to me before I awakened?" He glanced away, and she wished she hadn't said anything.

"I feared you were dead."

He wasn't going to tell her what he'd said. Were words of love on his tongue only her wishful thinking?

TWENTY-EIGHT

HAD SHE HEARD him? Harrison's lungs burned as he labored up the slope with his arm around Lady Devonworth's waist. Her ankle was still swollen, but she moved along better than he'd imagined she could. There was something in her manner that made him think she'd heard his declaration. He tried to tell himself he hadn't meant it—that only the extreme stress of the moment had prompted those words.

The truth was that she had entangled herself in his heart in a mysterious way. But then he'd never been in love before, so it was all new and amazing. He thanked God that she was alive. But the attacker was bold. He'd come right into her own yard and taken her from the presence of several people.

They crested the hill and limped toward the house. Lights glared from the windows, and servants ran to and fro in the yard. Nealy was barking frantically as if to try to get someone to listen to him. An older woman stood on the back stoop wringing her hands and weeping. She glanced up and squinted in the dark toward Harrison. Lady Devonworth was sagging with fatigue, so he swept her into his arms and started toward the manor. His knee felt like a spike was rammed into it, but he ignored the pain.

The woman started down the steps toward them. "Is she alive?"

"She's fine," he called. Nealy ran to greet them, his tired tail wagging.

"She's soaking wet. What happened?" She narrowed a glare at Harrison as if this were all his fault.

"He saved me," Essie murmured, reaching toward her. "I nearly drowned." Her hand drifted down to the dog. "Nealy too. Good dog." Nealy wiggled all over with pleasure as her hand grazed his ears.

"And what were you doing out in the middle of the night?"

"She'll explain later," he said. "She needs dry clothes. And a doctor." He brushed past the agitated older woman and onto the stoop. "Someone get the door and call the constable."

The butler sprang to yank open the door. "Stay, Nealy," Harrison told the dog on the porch. Goldia met him in the kitchen. "Show me to her room," he told her.

She opened the door to the hall. "This way."

The back stairs took them to the second floor. Her bedroom was four doors down. Goldia flung back the covers, and he deposited Lady Devonworth on the bed.

"Get her dry and warm," he said. "I'll get the doctor."

He backed out of the room and rushed down the staircase. He met the older lady in the hall. The woman probably wouldn't stoop so low as to use the servants' stairs. The icy glare she sent his way pained him as much as his knee.

"Have you phoned for the doctor?" he asked.

"He's on his way. And who are you?"

"I'm Harrison Bennett. Who are you?"

"Harrison." Her smile was weak. "I didn't recognize you, dear boy." She drew herself up. "I'm Mrs. Stewart, owner of this house. I should like to know what you were doing w-with Lady Devonworth in the middle of the night."

Eleanor's mother. He studied her cold expression. No wonder she'd raised a daughter who had little use for faithfulness.

"Saving her from a murderer," he said. When she gasped and put her hand to her mouth, he wished he hadn't been so blunt. "Someone chloroformed her and threw her over the cliff."

"Oh, that dear girl," Mrs. Stewart said, tears springing to her eyes. "Is she going to be all right?"

"I think so. She's cold and fatigued, but she was coherent and able to hobble up the hill." Or at least partway up.

Her smile faded and she looked him over. "How did you happen by, Mr. Bennett?"

"I was out for a walk. I heard her call my name. I ran to the backyard, and the man nearly trampled me as he rushed away. I got to the cliff and saw her in the water. If you look at the back of the lot, you'll see my boots and jacket."

"Indeed, the servants discovered your garments," she said. "A thank-you is in order."

"It was only by God's grace that I was able to get us both to shore. Your daughter wasn't the first person to die on those rocks."

She blanched and fell silent. His words were brutal, but he needed to be blunt to make her realize the gravity of the situation.

The doorbell rang, and the butler rushed to usher in the doctor. In the hubbub of the moment, he slipped out to the portico. Lady Devonworth wasn't going to want to see him again tonight.

❧

Harrison paused long enough to let Mrs. Lindrum know he would be in the carriage house until lunch. His knee still ached but he ignored it as he set out across the backyard to the building that housed his aeroplane. Nealy was on his heels. A voice hailed him and he turned to see Constable Brown waving to him. He paused under a live oak tree outside the carriage house.

"Saw you as I rounded the corner," Brown said. "I wanted to get your version of last night's events." He patted the dog's ears.

The man's brown eyes were friendly enough, but Harrison thought he saw a glint of suspicion. "I was in the right place at the right time." He explained what he'd heard and done.

Brown jotted in his notebook. "Can you describe this man who knocked you down?"

"It was too dark to see him. I smelled chloroform."

"Lady Devonworth said he drugged her. She thinks she scratched him."

"She didn't mention the scratches to me. That's surely a clue to look for. Did she say where the scratches were?"

"His arms. Which may not help us much unless the man rolls up his sleeves." Brown raised a graying brow. "Might I see *your* arms, Harrison?"

Harrison stared at him, then took off his jacket and rolled up his shirtsleeves to reveal unmarked skin. "Satisfied?"

"I had to check. Can you explain why you were there?"

He studied Brown's expression. The lawman had always been fair. "Do you remember when you first realized you loved your wife, Constable?"

The man grinned and took out a cigar. "Quite well, Harrison. I think I'm beginning to understand."

"I went for a walk with no intention of going past the manor. It was most fortuitous that I did, but there is no good explanation for it other than that I subconsciously hoped to catch a glimpse of Lady Devonworth."

"So the rumors of an impending announcement are true?"

"Yes," Harrison said. There was no reason to mention that his only ammunition was that the engagement would save her reputation.

"Miss Eleanor drowned in circumstances very similar to what Lady Devonworth faced last night. Only she was not so fortunate."

Harrison clenched his fists. "As I told you after the plane crash, I fear her death was no suicide. And someone fired on the lady and me in the clearing after the accident. After last night, Lady Devonworth's fears that she was the intended target don't seem so far-fetched."

"I shall continue to discuss this matter with Lady Devonworth."

He knew he should tell Brown about Eleanor's affair with Fosberg, but it felt very unsportsmanlike. Still, the man could help them find Eleanor's killer. He needed to know. "I would suggest you speak to Fosberg. He and Eleanor were . . . close."

"How close?"

"I'll leave him to tell you. Suffice it to say that I broke off our engagement."

"I will investigate the matter." Brown turned back toward the house.

"One moment, Constable." Brown turned around to face him. Harrison gestured to the carriage house. "I'm working on a new aeroplane, but I'm reluctant to try it out until I find out about the sabotage on my other machine. Have you uncovered anything about that?"

The constable shook his head. "A hole in a fuel line is too vague to trace. I questioned your neighbors and those who might have seen anything out at the airfield. I've turned up nothing."

It was as Harrison suspected. His new machine would have to stay under guard constantly. At least until his enemy revealed himself. And he would eventually. If Harrison had arrived at Stewart Hall a little earlier last night, the man would have been exposed and caught. He thanked the constable and headed out to his machine.

When he reached the door, he dug out his key and started to fit it into the lock. It took a moment for him to realize the lock dangled open. Strange that Nealy hadn't alerted him. Harrison clearly remembered locking the building two nights ago before going to bed. He nearly went to try to catch Brown, but if he left now, any intruder would escape. He pushed open the door and stepped into the space. Dust motes danced in a shaft of sunlight. The building was empty. His flying machine was gone.

Not a muscle could move. He stood gawking at the empty space. A thousand thoughts fought for supremacy, but uppermost was how the thief had managed to snatch the machine out from under Harrison's nose.

Something shuffled behind him. With his fists at the ready, he whirled only to see his father step from the shadows. Harrison's arms sagged to his side. "My flying machine. It's gone."

His father nodded. "I disposed of it. It was taking up too much of your time. I had it taken away yesterday afternoon."

His father's effrontery took his breath away. Harrison reminded himself that he was to honor his father even when the man did something this unfathomable. "I want it back. Where is it?"

His father advanced toward him. "Be reasonable, son. Let loose of this ridiculous dream. You have a bright future ahead of you in business. Don't let this hobby distract you. My father was like you. I went hungry many nights because he cared more about playing pool than about feeding his children."

Harrison had never heard the pleading note in his father's voice. Nor had he shared this information about his growing-up years. It explained a lot—why his father was so driven to succeed, why recognition mattered to him.

He fought the pity that might have excused his father's incredible behavior. "I'm not changing my mind. I'm done at Bennett and Bennett. Where is my machine?"

His father's coaxing smile faded. "In the scrap heap."

A crushing weight came down on Harrison's chest. He nearly couldn't breathe past the pressure. "I'll just rebuild it." He turned to the door before he could say something he might regret. John North had several carriage houses. He'd see if his friend would allow him the use of one.

TWENTY-NINE

THE SUNLIGHT WARMED Olivia. She stretched, then groaned as every muscle protested. She'd lain abed all day yesterday, but she was not going to stay down today. Even her ankle felt better. She sat up and rang the bell for Goldia. Breakfast would fortify her for the day ahead.

Harrison had left the other night without a word. She tried not to let his departure bother her. He knew she was going to be all right, so why should she have expected him to dance attendance on her until dawn?

Katie poked her head through the doorway. "I heard the bell so I thought you must be awake. How are you feeling this morning?"

"Nearly human again." She smiled to dispel the dark reminder of what had happened. "Has Harrison called this morning?"

Katie stepped into the room. "I haven't heard the telephone ring."

Her mother came through the door in time to hear Katie's last words. "I met that young man, Olivia. He's quite a handsome devil." Her mother handed her the dressing gown from the foot of the bed. "We've received an invitation to a ball at Buckingham Palace. There will be no shortage of wealthy nobility looking for brides. Once your engagement to Harrison is at an end, we shall find you a husband who deserves to marry into the Stewart family."

Olivia winced as she got out of bed and shrugged into the dressing gown. "I want more from life than that."

"Your father and I were married because it was the wise thing to do. And our life together was quite lovely," her mother said, her voice firm.

She'd thought her parents doted on each other, though her father was often off on his adventures to Africa while her mother made frequent excursions to Europe. But that matter of her father's infidelity changed all her perceptions. Her mother seemed to have forgotten that. Olivia wanted a marriage like Katie's. It was clear her husband wanted to be with her more than he wanted to be gone.

"I'm going to wear the blue silk today," she told Goldia.

"Are you going out?" her mother asked.

"I'm going to go see that will." Olivia sat in front of the dressing table and began to undo the plaits in her hair. Goldia picked up the silver brush and began to brush out the strands before styling it atop Olivia's head.

"Should I accompany you?"

Olivia could tell by her mother's tone that she'd rather step in dog dung. "I believe you need to come with me. You have more right to see it than anyone. But I will do the speaking."

"What if Mr. Fosberg refuses to let us read it?"

"Then I shall call our attorney and he can handle it."

"In that case, perhaps we should let Mr. Grayson take care of it all. No need to sully our hands."

Olivia turned to face her mother. "Don't you want to know what is going on, Mother? I know I do. If we have to involve our attorney, it could take weeks, months."

"There is that," her mother agreed. "Very well. I shall be in the parlor."

Freed of her mother's nervous energy, Olivia quickly finished her toilette. With her hat firmly pinned in place and the new dress swathing her slim figure, she sailed forth to do battle. Or as well as she could manage with every muscle aching from her adventure. Her mother had already called for the limo. The chauffeur drove them to town.

Olivia planned out her strategy as the automobile navigated the narrow streets. As the motorcar passed Harrison's house, she strained for a glimpse of him. How was his knee faring?

She had the driver stop for a moment at Oscar's Mercantile while she ran inside for some stationery. Mrs. Silvers's face lit when she saw Olivia.

"My dear Lady Devonworth, how are you? I was quite distressed to hear of your accident the other night."

"I'm fine, thank you. A little sore, but that is all."

"Thanks to Mr. Harrison." Mrs. Silvers pressed her hand to her bosom. "So romantic, the way he saved you."

She suppressed a smile. "Indeed."

"The whole town is buzzing about the ball! How good of you to invite all of us. I've always wanted to see inside Stewart Hall."

"I'll be honored to show you around," Olivia said, smiling. Though the ball was turning into even more work than she'd anticipated, for once she was planning something that was of greater value than showing off the newest dress.

The car pulled up in front of the Fosberg residence. "Wait here and I'll see if they'll receive us," she told her mother when the chauffeur opened the back door of the limo and helped her out.

With her card in hand, as well as her mother's, she rang the doorbell of the modest two-story home. On a tree-lined street in a nice neighborhood, it wasn't as grand as Olivia had expected. A middle-aged woman opened the door, and Olivia stated her business and dropped her cards into the silver tray.

"One moment, Lady Devonworth." The maid ushered her into the narrow foyer, then went down the hall.

A few moments later Mrs. Fosberg rushed out of the door on the right with her arms outstretched. "My dear Lady Devonworth, how kind of you to call! And your mother too?"

"She's in the car. Let me summon her. Is your son at home?"

His mother beamed. "He is indeed! I'll call him while you fetch your mother."

For an instant, Olivia had hoped he might be gone. She hated confrontation. But this was a discussion that had to be held.

Olivia sipped her tea and waited for a lull in Mrs. Fosberg's stream of conversation. Mr. Fosberg leaned against the wall by the window as he listened, but she sensed a watchfulness in the set of his shoulders and the reserved smile in his eyes. He knew they were here for a purpose.

When Mrs. Fosberg paused to draw a breath, Olivia jumped in. "Mr. Fosberg, I wonder if I might have a word with you in private?"

He straightened. "Of course."

"Mother, I'll be right back." She saw the relief in her mother's face as she followed Mr. Fosberg to the library. Her mother could be the backup if he refused to hand over the will.

He sat behind the polished desk and indicated the chair on the opposite side. "Please, make yourself comfortable."

She settled onto the creaking leather and clasped her gloved hands together. "I've come to take a look at my father's will."

He regarded her over the top of his steepled fingers. "I suspected as much."

"I admit I'm surprised you didn't show it to me right away."

"I thought it best to have your mother present. In fact, I think she should be here for this now." He rose. "Let me escort her in, and I'll read the will."

Olivia nodded, and he left the room. Perhaps she should have called their attorney and waited for him to come from New York so he could be present for this. She glanced around the room and took in the leather-bound books and certificate from Harvard. Several moving boxes were strewn about as well.

He entered the room with her mother in tow. Shutting the door behind them, he seated Mrs. Stewart beside Olivia, then went to the desk and opened the top drawer. He removed an envelope and slid a sheaf of papers from it. "This is the will."

Olivia nearly asked to read it herself, then decided against it. She could always ask to peruse it when he was done. She glanced at her mother, who was biting her lip. There was no real reason for them both to be so nervous, but she couldn't still the shiver that ran up her back.

Fosberg cleared his throat. "This is the last will and testament of Marshall Stewart. I'm not going to read every provision. You can read it for yourself shortly. However, I want to bring your attention to the part that will be the most contentious." He trailed a finger down the page, then laid it aside and went on to the next. "Here it is. You and your daughters have been designated a yearly stipend of ten thousand dollars. He goes on to say, 'To my son, Richard Pixton, I leave the rest of my estate and ask that he take care of my wife and daughters with any additional needs as long as they are living.'"

Olivia sat with her hands together. Her father had stripped them of nearly everything. Ten thousand dollars a year wouldn't begin to cover her mother's normal expenses.

Mrs. Stewart wetted her lips. "You can't be serious."

"I'm afraid so. You can see why I've been torn over how to proceed."

Torn? Olivia saw no remorse on his face. Would he be happy to see them impoverished? Did he have some personal stake in this?

"And where is this mysterious Mr. Pixton?" her mother demanded.

"I have been unable to locate him."

Her mother waved a dismissive hand in the air. "Then this changes nothing."

"I'm afraid it does. The estate will have to be transferred to his name. My firm has been designated to oversee the funds, which we will do until he can be found. I'll need you to submit a list of your living expenses so we can draw up a suitable budget."

Her mother rose. "You're telling me that we are now beggars? That our money will have to be funneled through your office?"

"Not beggars, ma'am. But, yes, any monies will need to be approved. We are trustees until Mr. Pixton is found. Then he will take over that duty."

Olivia found her voice. "We shall contest this, of course. Our attorney will be in touch. The money is still in our bank, and it will stay there. I fear you are only involved to earn the executor fees."

Fosberg's expression turned grim. "You would fight your father's wishes?"

"I am not convinced it is even his will."

He held out the paper. "Do you wish to see it?"

"I do." She snatched the will and scanned to the signature. It appeared to be her father's handwriting, but she didn't trust this smooth man. How much her opinion had changed in a few days.

"There are three copies in my possession," he said. "You are welcome to keep that one and show it to your attorney. I'm sure he will tell you that it is perfectly in order."

She tucked it into her handbag. "We shall see. Come along, Mother. I want to call our solicitor immediately."

Her mother rose as though her bones hurt. Her eyes were wide and frightened. Olivia refused to allow herself to believe the situation might come to pass. Her father couldn't possibly have wanted this to happen.

THIRTY

THE JUNKYARD HAD not yet disposed of his flying machine. Harrison arranged for it to be taken to the Norths' carriage house this morning, and he stopped to tell John it was coming. The Norths were outside. Addie wore gardening gloves and was puttering in the flower bed by the porch. John was playing baseball with Edward while Gideon ran barking between them. Nealy leaped out of the motorcar and ran to join Gideon.

Addie stood with a smile. A smear of dirt smudged one cheek. "Harrison, how good to see you! Have you time for refreshments? Lunch will be ready in fifteen minutes."

"I wouldn't turn it down," he said, returning her smile. "If you're sure I'm not too much trouble."

"Never! I'll tell the cook to lay a place for one more." She hurried to the door and went inside.

John tossed the baseball to Edward. "Play with Gideon and Nealy for a while, son." He joined Harrison at the porch.

"My aeroplane will be here this afternoon," Harrison told him. "I can't thank you enough for allowing me to store it here."

"My pleasure. I talked it over with Addie, and we want to invest in your new company too," John said. "We both believe the flying machines are going to be our future mode of transportation. I'd like to be a full partner if you're willing."

His friends' faith in him made a lump form in Harrison's throat. If only his own family had that kind of trust. "I could use a partner with your kind of business savvy," he said.

John clapped him on the shoulder. "We can talk about it after lunch. I have several other possible investors I would like to discuss with you. And a location for a factory to build our aeroplanes. We have much to do before the air show in a couple of months."

A factory. He hadn't dared dream that big. "Thank you," he said, his voice hoarse.

The rumble of an engine came from behind him, and he turned to see the Stewart limo stop in the driveway. He saw Lady Devonworth and Katie Jesperson in the backseat. Essie's smile was tentative, and he stepped off the porch to open the door for her.

She took his hand. "I didn't know you were invited for lunch. Perhaps Addie is matchmaking."

"I just stopped by. Addie didn't tell me she was having a party." He released her hand and helped Katie out as well.

"It's just us, not a party," Katie said, smiling up at him. She moved past, leaving him alone with Lady Devonworth.

She seemed tongue-tied and didn't look at him. He offered her his arm and she took it. They moved toward the house. "All recovered today?"

"A little sore. I see you are still limping a bit." Her tone indicated she was asking only as a courtesy.

Had her mother convinced her he'd played some part in the attack on her? Her eyes were shadowed and her mouth was strained. "You look as though you're still in shock," he said.

Her gaze met his then, and her eyes were filled with anguish. "I'm quite recovered from the other night. Th-The Stewarts received distressing news this morning."

They reached the foot of the steps. Katie and the others had already gone inside. He pressed her hand. "Can I help?"

She rubbed her head. "Mrs. Stewart doesn't know what to do. She discovered her husband has left his entire fortune to an illegitimate child. At least according to Mr. Fosberg."

"Fosberg told her this?" He shook his head. "I don't trust that man."

"I don't either, but I saw the will that he produced. It is supposedly a newer will than the one in the possession of the Stewarts' solicitor." She hesitated, and her fingers tightened on his arm. "There's more, Harrison. I'm not even sure Mr. Stewart is dead. I found a note sent to Eleanor just before her death. Mrs. Stewart is sure it's his handwriting."

He liked hearing his name on her lips. "This is almost too much to take in. I would do nothing about the money yet. It's still in Mrs. Stewart's possession, is it not?"

"Yes, but Mr. Fosberg is planning to take control of it."

"This seems entirely too convenient. Could Fosberg have forged the will? And the note to Eleanor from her father? What did it say?"

She glanced away from him, and he could tell she didn't want him to know the note's contents. "Tell me, Essie."

She sighed. "It warned her to run from you and your father. That you meant the Stewarts harm."

He pressed his lips together. "And you believed it?"

"At first," she admitted. "I know you better now."

Why would Mr. Stewart be hiding somewhere and allowing this to go on? "We need to find the man if he's alive. Unless this is all a forgery. Does Fosberg know you found the note to Eleanor?"

"No, I don't believe so."

"It's possible he warned her away from us Bennetts because he wanted her for himself."

The tightness in her mouth eased as they talked. "Katie is going to have Will's brother look into it." She glanced at the door. "I have to tell Katie and Addie that we might as well call off the ball. My friends won't come under the present circumstances, and I doubt we can raise enough money with only the townspeople in attendance."

He pressed her hand again. "What if we announce our engagement today? Would they come then?"

Her eyes filled with hope. "Maybe. Unless they hear that the Stewarts have lost all their money."

"I don't like your friends. They are fair-weather ones only."

"I never realized that until now." Her dark eyes studied him. "You're still willing to do this?"

Words of love hovered on his tongue, but he reminded himself this was an arrangement to save her reputation. She'd shown no indication she thought of him warmly.

He nodded. "Shall we tell our friends first? Then we can call the newspaper and put in an announcement. I'll call the New York and San Francisco papers as well. That will put an end to the gossip and, hopefully, your friends will be happy to attend the ball."

"We can call it an engagement ball as well. They will have even more motivation to attend." Her eyes sparkled. "It's a masquerade ball. I find I'm most interested in what you will wear."

"I'll have to give that some thought. And what about you? How shall you be dressed?"

"Perhaps Juliet. You can come as Romeo. It seems suitable for an engagement ball, does it not?"

She would need suitable jewelry for that, and he knew just where to buy it. And the exact piece.

❧

Still warm from the congratulations of her friends, Olivia rode with Harrison in his motorcar to tell her mother what they had done. Though the dog was in the backseat, she was no longer afraid of him. Nealy had saved her twice now.

Before they left the Norths' home, Harrison had telephoned Mr.

Quinn to arrange an interview. They'd scheduled a photography session as well. Everything was about to change.

She glanced at the handsome man beside her. What would it be like if he'd actually said the words she'd dreamed as she was gaining consciousness? How would it feel to be loved for herself and not for her pedigree? She had to tell him the truth. Now.

He parked at the manor. "Ready?" His eyes were warm and kind. Kindness was important to her. She'd seen too many dictator-type husbands.

He turned off the engine. "Before we go in, there is something I need to say."

She held her breath. Was he going to declare his love? Something squeezed in her chest, and she recalled the words she once dreamed he spoke to her. *I love you.* She should interrupt him and tell him who she was first, but she lacked the courage to do so.

"Go on," she said when he paused.

"The news will be out soon. I broke ties with my father and the family business. He is going to lease our premier property to Fosberg. We had words and I quit."

"Y-You quit? But you have such a good head for business. What are you going to do?"

"Build flying machines. John and I."

Her pulse jumped. "Oh, how grand, Harrison! Truly. You'll be part of a new era."

He raised a brow. "You're not asking how I intend to support a wife. Mrs. Stewart will ask, I'm sure. I have to tell her the truth and say I have some savings, but this venture is a gamble. I believe in it though."

She put her hand on his. "I believe in *you*, Harrison. Anything you put your hand to will be a success." The warmth in his eyes intensified. She knew she should snatch her hand away, but she left it in his, forward though the action was.

He squeezed her fingers, then raised them to his lips. When he turned it over and kissed her palm, her skin burned even through the glove she wore. What did her response to him mean? She'd never experienced this kind of reaction.

Tell him. No, she couldn't. Not now, with his eyes so tender. The moment he found out she was Olivia Stewart, those warm eyes would go cold.

"We should go in," she whispered.

"I suppose we should," he agreed, though he made no move to release her hand. "But first I—"

Someone touched her shoulder, and Olivia turned to see Goldia outside.

"Mrs. Stewart wants to see you, miss," she said.

Olivia pulled her hand out of Harrison's grip. "We'll be right in." What had he been about to say? She was afraid to imagine.

He climbed out of the car and came around to escort her inside. She liked being on his arm, fancied the way her head came only to his shoulder, admired the feel of his muscles flexing under her fingers where they lay on his arm.

"Take courage," he said under his breath when they stepped inside the parlor where her mother waited. "She's not your family. You don't have to answer to her, not really."

What would he do when he found out? She feared her deception would prove he should never trust a Stewart.

"There you are, my dear," her mother said. "You've been gone quite a long time." Her curious gaze touched Harrison's face.

Harrison stiffened beside Olivia. It was a stark reminder of how he felt about her family. How was she ever going to tell him the truth?

She clasped her hands together. "We have something to tell you, Mrs. Stewart. I've accepted Harrison's kind offer of marriage. It will be in tomorrow's paper." *Act surprised,* she mentally begged her mother.

Her mother stared, then nodded. "Quite fitting. Though you are not in her social standing, of course, Mr. Bennett. I applaud you for doing the right thing."

He gave a stiff bow. "I understand I'm not worthy of Lady Devonworth. But I can tell you that I will treasure her."

Treasure her. The words filled Olivia's heart. If only Harrison meant them. If only this wasn't a role he'd chosen to play to protect her honor. His restraint when dealing with her mother was admirable, especially considering the contempt he felt.

Olivia glanced at her mother's writing desk and saw the morning's post on it. A pile of letters was neatly stacked. From her mother's New York friends, no doubt. They would all be asking questions about the scandal. An engagement would polish her mother's tarnished crown as well.

"We have an appointment with the newspaper in a few minutes," Olivia said, brushing her lips across her mother's powdered cheek. "Mr. Bennett insisted we tell you first."

"Come back as soon as you can," her mother said as they moved toward the door. "We have much to discuss, my dear."

"We should be back by dinner. Mr. Bennett wants to talk to his mother. His father has departed until next month." Olivia took Harrison's arm again and they stepped out into the hall. "That went smoothly," she whispered.

He opened the door for her. "I managed to hold my tongue. It was clear she thought I was far beneath her family and yours."

The censure in his voice made her chest squeeze. How would she ever tell him she was a Stewart?

Harrison had little more to say on the way to the newspaper office. She tried not to care that he didn't bring up what he'd started to say before Goldia had interrupted. She wanted to ask him if he meant what he'd said about treasuring her. Maybe they could forget about canceling the engagement after the gossip died down.

She wasn't ready to show her heart to him. Not until she knew more about his feelings.

The small newspaper office smelled of ink and dust. Olivia wanted to jiggle her foot, but she forced herself to be composed and calm. If Quinn leaked a hint of who she was . . . She pasted on a smile when he stepped into the room.

"Ah, right on time," he said, going around to his chair behind the desk. "Where is your fiancé?"

"In the men's room. I must ask you to remember your promise to me."

His eyebrows rose. "You haven't told him you are Olivia Stewart?"

She held his gaze. "That's my business only."

He looked away. "I've done some digging into Eleanor's death. And into Fosberg." He pulled a file toward him and opened it. "Fosberg and she had a tryst two days before she died."

"I know about that," she said.

His lips tightened. "I thought we were working together."

"I was trying to protect my sister's reputation. I don't want that in any article."

"You promised me the full story."

She should have known better than to think she could evade him. "I meant the full story about who murdered her. I don't want her besmirched."

"She did that all by herself." He thumbed through his file. "Her body was found by a fisherman. Fully clothed right down to her shoes. She didn't go out for a pleasant swim."

Olivia shook her head. "Of course not. She was terrified of the water."

He nodded. "Makes sense. The constable was never satisfied that it was a simple drowning, by the way. He suspected your lover boy."

She sagged against the wooden back of the chair. "Why would he suspect Harrison?"

"Don't be a dunce. He had to have figured out his fiancée was playing footsie with Fosberg."

"He didn't harm her," Olivia said, her lips trembling. "I'm sure of it. What about Fosberg?"

"He's got a reputation with the ladies, but it appears he deserted his normal lady friends after he met Eleanor. The two seemed very close. One of his friends called him 'besotted.'"

"With Eleanor or the name Stewart?"

The reporter shrugged. "Who knows? Maybe both. He told his partner he was going to marry her out from under Bennett's nose. Almost like he had a personal vendetta against Harrison."

That was a new wrinkle. Olivia tried to recall if Harrison had acted like he knew Fosberg, but she thought he'd claimed not to before returning from Africa. "I shall have to ask Harrison about his relationship with the Fosbergs."

He leaned forward. "And that brings up something else. Fosberg's mother seems to have had a relationship with your father."

"What?" She restrained herself from leaping from the chair. "What kind of relationship?"

"I've been told it was romantic. She often invited him to dinner at her home whenever he was in town. He sent her flowers on two occasions."

Olivia shouldn't have been so rocked by the news now that she knew about the illegitimate son. Still, the revelation left her gasping. Had he been unfaithful his entire marriage?

THIRTY-ONE

THE COUPLE STOOD on the Bennetts' front porch. "News of our engagement should be in tomorrow morning's papers," Harrison said. "I need to tell my mother tonight."

Lady Devonworth hung back. "Do you think your mother will be displeased? Your tone suggests it. I assumed she would be happy."

She was probably picking up on his reluctance to open the front door. "My parents will be entirely *too* pleased," he said. "Especially my father. His desire was always for me to marry one of the Four Hundred. At least I won't have to see his smug face just yet." He forced himself to open the door. "Hello?"

"Harrison?" His mother's voice floated from the library. "I'm in here."

He took Olivia's hand and led her to the last door on the left. The library was his mother's favorite room. She had read every one of the eighteen hundred volumes in the cavernous room, many of them more than once. His mother sat in her wheelchair by the window with a book in her hand.

"My dear Lady Devonworth! I didn't realize you were with Harrison." She held out her hand. "Forgive me for greeting you in such a disheveled state."

"You look lovely, Mrs. Bennett," Lady Devonworth said, her voice shy.

The women clasped hands, and his mother pulled her down for a hug.

"We wanted to tell you some good news," Harrison said. "Lady Devonworth has agreed to become my wife. Our engagement will be announced in the newspaper tomorrow."

His mother squealed. "Oh, my dear boy, what tremendous news!" She held out her arms and he leaned down for her to embrace him. "We shall be most delighted to welcome you to the family, Lady Devonworth."

"That's most kind."

"This calls for a celebration!" his mother said, releasing her. "We must plan a party."

"The Lightkeeper's Ball is coming up," his fiancée said. "We thought we'd make it an engagement party too."

His mother beamed. "Of course, of course. I'm proud to tell the world." She sent a questioning glance at Harrison. "I suspect you and your father need to talk. You could call him in San Francisco."

"My plans have not changed, Mother," Harrison said. "John North is joining me in my new business."

His mother sat back in her chair. "It's much too risky for you to try this now. Not with a family to care for."

"I'm fully in support of this venture," Lady Devonworth said. "I want to learn to fly myself."

"You're just trying to find your way," his mother said to Harrison. "Your father did the same thing at your age. I don't believe you'll throw away a gift God has given you."

"I believe God has been leading me this direction all along, Mother. Passion shows the heart. I love aeroplanes. I'm better at designing them than I am at pushing pencils. Anyone can tally a row of numbers. God has given me a passion for my new work, and I'm going to follow it."

"You'll have a family to support, son. Please think about this."

"We must be going," he said instead of answering her. "Mrs. Stewart expects us for dinner shortly."

His mother motioned for him to roll her to the door with them. "How are plans for the ball coming, my dear?" she asked. "Is there anything I can do to help?"

They reached the door. Lady Devonworth smiled down at his mother. "Thank you, Mrs. Bennett. I'm sure I shall need your assistance as the day gets closer."

"Oh, do call me Mother, my dear." His mother's eyes were misty. "I've always wanted a daughter. This is a happy, happy day for me."

Harrison's gaze met Lady Devonworth's over his mother's head. Did she feel as much guilt at their deception as he did? He wished with all his heart that their engagement was real and that a wedding ceremony loomed in their future. He would do all he could to see that it happened.

The night air cooled Olivia's cheeks. They walked toward Harrison's motorcar in the moonlight, and she glanced up at the strong lines of his face.

He stopped. "Is something wrong?"

"I'm just thinking about the Stewarts' troubles. I realize we can believe little Fosberg says, but he told me that when he tried to contact your father about the newer will, Mr. Bennett brushed him off. Wouldn't your father have wanted to see it?"

"I would think so." His sigh came, heavy and full of frustration. "He's so driven about forcing his way into society. I could see him fighting to maintain his power, his chance to be one of the accepted set."

She stared at his dear face. How could she even tell him her other fears? She wetted her lips. "Harrison, what if your father arranged for Mr. Stewart to be in that cave-in?"

He stiffened. "My father is many things, but he's no murderer."

"It is so convenient that he would announce Mr. Stewart's death and at the same time present an agreement between the two families that no one knew about."

He shook his head. "What of your belief that Mr. Stewart may still be alive?"

She took his hand, needing human contact. Needing his comfort. "I don't know what to think about that. Why wouldn't he show himself? It's cruel to leave his family in this limbo."

He slipped his other hand around her and pulled her to his chest. His chin rested on her hair. "My dear, I fear someone is playing a vicious joke on you. Whoever it is knew you would come outside if you thought Mr. Stewart was there. And you did just that."

"Why would anyone want to harm me?"

He sighed. "I don't know. It makes no sense. If you were a Stewart, I could understand it. It could be this Pixton wants to eliminate the Stewart family so he can inherit the entire estate. Or maybe it's whoever killed Eleanor. He thinks you know more than you do."

She wetted her lips. Now was the time to tell him, but once she did, he would be too angry to listen to her concerns. "About your father and that agreement. Our attorney, Mr. Grayson, has managed the Stewart money for years. After your father came back, he said the old diamond mine was played out, but that he and Mr. Stewart had agreed to a partnership of the new black-diamond mine if the two families were joined. Mr. Grayson wondered if your father was hiding some shady dealings and trying to force the merger."

"Did Grayson get a chance to look at any of the diamond-mine books?"

At least he wasn't taking offense. She shook her head.

"Father had the agreement in his possession?" he asked. "I thought your attorney had it."

She tried to remember exactly how it had been revealed. "I'm sure Mr. Grayson said he had never seen the agreement before your father came home. The solicitor urged Mrs. Stewart to ask for an audit of the books, but she didn't want to upset you or your father when the two families were about to be joined."

"I wouldn't have been angry."

His words soothed her, but not as much as his touch. She leaned into his embrace and felt the pump of his heart under her ear. "Mr. Stewart lost a great deal of his money. The Stewarts no longer have the wealth of a generation ago. They have only their pedigree. Your father has a great deal of money. I'm sure that affected Mrs. Stewart's decision." She slumped against him. "It is quite dreadful to be auctioned off to the highest bidder. That's what was happening to me in New York. Before I met you."

Did his lips brush her brow? The touch was so light she couldn't tell. She closed her eyes and heard his voice again in her head. *I love you.* Why did that linger so when it had to have been the result of the trauma she'd suffered?

"God sees who you are inside, Essie. So do I. Your worth has nothing to do with your pedigree."

She raised her head and stared into his face. "The same could be said for you, Harrison. God sees how much imagination and passion you have for your aeroplanes. I heard the way your mother tried to manipulate you."

His lips twisted in a rueful grin. "Both of my parents are good at it. I usually find myself doing what my father wants. My mother's question affected me today more than his manipulation."

"When she asked if you were throwing away God's gift?" When he nodded, she patted his cheek. "If we have a passion for something and the ability to do it, surely that comes from him."

"I'm becoming more and more sure of that. God sees my ability. My ideas don't come from sheer human imagination."

His words tugged at her heart. God surely gave her the wit and intelligence she possessed. She knew she was more than a Kewpie doll to be posed for the most advantage. If she dared, she could make a difference in the world, just as a man could.

This would take some thought. "We should go."

"Of course." He released her.

Her name was all she had. Did she dare risk it by stepping outside what was expected of her? She thought she'd have the courage if Harrison were by her side.

THIRTY-TWO

THE HIGH-CEILINGED DINING room felt warmer and happier than usual to Olivia. It had nothing to do with the heat from the fireplace spilling into the damp evening. It was all about Harrison's presence at the head of the table over dinner. She barely noticed her mother and her friends at the table, only Harrison. Their hands touched when they both reached into the basket of dinner rolls at the same time. His eyes warmed her more than the fire. She liked having him here.

After dinner he walked Olivia to the library door. "I'll be happy to make the call to your attorney if you wish," he said.

His presence gave her strength and courage. How was that even possible when she'd disliked him so intensely in the past? "I need to do it myself, but thank you," she said. She left him outside the library and closed the door before she picked up the earpiece and told the operator she needed to make a long-distance call to New York. She gave the woman the number, then hung up to wait to be called back after the connection was completed.

She could almost feel Harrison's presence outside, and she remembered that word *treasure* again. Was there any hope at all that he might come to feel that way, or would all hope be lost the moment he discovered she was a Stewart? She turned to the bookshelves so she wouldn't run to the door and rush into his arms. She perused the titles but didn't really see them.

The telephone rang and she answered it. "I have your party on the line," the operator said in a nasal voice. "His wife gave me the number where he could be reached in San Francisco. Go ahead."

"Mr. Grayson," Olivia said. "I'm sorry to disturb you at night, but we have an emergency out here. It's quite fortuitous that you are in San Francisco."

"Miss Stewart, I'm always at your disposal," he said. "How can I assist you?"

His gruff voice had calmed her fears all of her life. Mr. Grayson had been their solicitor since before Olivia's birth. She could trust him implicitly. She launched into the latest claim on her father's estate. "What is our next step?" she asked.

"I need to see this so-called will," he said.

She glanced at the safe. "I have a copy in my possession."

"I'll be on the next packet ship to Mercy Falls in the morning. I'll be there by early afternoon. Will that be suitable?"

"We'll be here." All of her questions couldn't wait until then. "What if it's legitimate?"

"I find it difficult to believe your father would leave your future completely in the hands of an unknown man. He was most meticulous about his desire to assure himself of your future. I suspect a forgery."

"How would we find out if the document is forged?"

"There are experts who can determine that."

She hated all the *ifs* the situation left dangling. "And if it's real? Can we contest it?"

"We will indeed contest it if that is the ruling."

"One disturbing detail is that this unknown half brother of mine has not come forward. Until he does, our money would be in the control of Mr. Fosberg. Do you know him?"

"I do." It was clear Mr. Grayson was picking his words carefully. "Let me simply say I would not willingly allow him to oversee my money. What of Miss Eleanor's fate? Have you been able to discover anything?"

"I believe someone killed her, but I don't know who. However, I just became engaged to Harrison Bennett. So Mother's future will be secure when she receives part ownership of the black-diamond mine."

"Your father had great hopes for the first diamond mine, but the income from it has been less than stellar of late."

"Less than stellar?" Harrison was estranged from his father. Would he be disinherited? She shook her head. Mrs. Bennett had been delighted by the engagement. At least a marriage would give Mr. Bennett what he wanted. Perhaps she could negotiate a settlement for her mother.

If anything came of her feelings for Harrison. The stray thought hit hard. She'd tried to deny she felt anything for him, but she did. She always had.

"Miss Stewart, are you there?"

"I'm here, Mr. Grayson," she said, collecting her composure.

"I have not seen the will yet, and it has not yet been submitted to a probate judge, so right now you and your mother can do as you wish."

"There's another matter. It's possible my father isn't even dead." She told him about the note to Eleanor.

"I will want to see that note as well and have it evaluated for forgery."

"So you don't think it likely Father is still alive?"

"I knew your father for thirty years, Miss Olivia. He could be somewhat self-absorbed, but I don't believe he would cause you this kind of pain. Nor would he leave you to face danger alone. I'm quite certain if he were alive, he would show himself."

The more she'd turned the situation around and looked at it, the more she'd come to that conclusion as well, but the confirmation from her father's longtime friend flooded her eyes with tears. It was almost like receiving the news of her father's death again. She'd clung to that thin sliver of hope, ridiculous as it was.

"Thank you for your candor," she said, her voice choked.

"I wish it were otherwise."

"So do I."

"Good night."

"Good night," she echoed. She replaced the earpiece and opened the door to Harrison. He stepped inside with his hands in his pockets. "You reached him?"

"I did. It appears he too thinks the will might be a forgery. He claims to have experts who can determine that."

He withdrew his hands and stepped closer. He thumbed away the moisture from her cheek. "Why are you crying, darling?"

Darling. She loved hearing that word in his deep tones. His voice was so tender, so filled with what seemed to be genuine caring. She was afraid to trust it now that she was facing her own feelings.

"He thinks the note from Mr. Stewart is a forgery too. I hate to tell Mrs. Stewart."

Her mother's voice spoke from the doorway. "Come to the fire. I have the maid bringing in mulled cider. You can tell me what Mr. Grayson had to say."

Harrison's hand squeezed hers, then dropped away. Olivia sighed and followed her mother.

❧❀❧

The manor was quiet once Harrison left and the Jespersons went to bed. With Goldia following, Olivia tiptoed to the attic stairs and glanced into the yard before going up them. The guard Harrison had insisted on patrolled the property below. Not that Olivia would be unwise enough to obey a message sent through the speaking tube again.

She reached the attic floor. The lights were dim but cast enough illumination for her to make out the trunks pushed against the walls and the shelves stacked with wooden crates. She sneezed at the dust in the air and moved toward the trunk by the small attic window. Through the glass she could see the moon on the water—the sea that had nearly claimed her life twice. She shuddered and turned back to the task at hand.

Goldia clutched herself and rubbed her palms on her arms. "Miss Olivia, it's cold up here. Can we go?"

"We just got here, Goldia. I haven't even looked for them yet."

"Your mama will be mad if she knows you're snooping through her stuff."

"She doesn't have to know. If she'd just tell me what I need to know, I wouldn't have to snoop." Olivia opened the nearest trunk and sneezed again at the musty scent of old clothes.

"How do you know it's even here? Your mama has never been here."

"She was looking for her journals last summer and realized Father had taken the wrong trunk when he shipped out some books."

Though she raked her hands through the soft pile, she found nothing more than dresses from the 1850s. No journals. For as long as she could remember, her mother had kept a household journal where she listed daily events and jotted personal notes as well. Olivia wanted to find out more about Lulu Pixton. It wasn't a subject her mother was willing to discuss.

Closing the trunk, she moved to the next. Every trunk she checked had clothing. She glanced at Goldia. "Anything?"

"There are a bunch of books in this crate," her maid said.

Olivia joined her. "Recipe books. But we must be getting close." She replaced the lid and dusted off her hands before prying open the lid on the next one. "Here they are!" She lifted the journal on top and flipped it open.

"What are you doing up here?"

Olivia turned to see her mother at the top of the stairs. She was in her nightdress and dressing gown, and her mouth was tight.

Her mother glanced at the journal in Olivia's hand. "Those are private, Olivia." She approached with her hand held out.

Olivia passed it over. "I need to know about Lulu, Mother."

"That's in the past. I don't like to think about it."

"The past just caught us. We have to think about it. I need to be prepared for what's coming. Did the woman teach her son to hate us? Will he make our lives miserable when he shows up?"

Her mother turned the book over in her hands, then glanced inside. "This isn't even the right journal."

"Talk to me," Olivia begged. "This affects all of us."

"Come down to the parlor. I won't have this discussion in such an unsavory place."

Her mother retreated to the steps, and Olivia followed after dismissing Goldia. At last she might find some answers. She was possessed of a deep curiosity about her half brother. And what if *he* was the voice on the speaking tube? It wasn't unheard of for a son to resemble his father in voice and stature.

When they reached the bottom of the stairs, Tiger entwined himself around Olivia's ankles, and she picked him up. His gentle purr would help her endure what she had to hear. On her way to the parlor, she heard the doorbell. It was after ten, hardly the time for a social call. The butler went to the door, and she heard Harrison's deep voice. When he stepped through the door, his tie was cocked and he was hatless.

"What's wrong?" he asked as soon as he saw her. "I saw the light in the attic."

"Were you watching the house?"

He shrugged and his grin was shamefaced. "I know you have a guard, but I just wanted to make sure there was no other attack."

Warmth spread through her. "It's quite good of you to care."

"Oh, I care," he said in a quiet voice as her mother joined them. He reached over and brushed at her hair. "A cobweb," he said, a teasing light in his eyes.

"Mr. Bennett, do you realize the time?" her mother demanded.

"I'm sorry, Mrs. Stewart. When I saw the lights, I feared an intruder was afoot."

Her mother's expression softened. "Very well. Since you're helping my dear Lady Devonworth with this mystery, join us in the parlor for a discussion. I'll ring for cocoa." She sailed down the hall to the parlor.

Olivia exchanged a glance with Harrison. He raised a brow and she shrugged as they followed her mother. "Were you planning on watching the house all night?" she whispered before they entered the room.

"Just until I was sure you wouldn't be answering any summons by speaking tube."

His grin enveloped her with its easy intimacy. When his hand touched her back at the door, she wanted to lean into him and brush her lips across the faint stubble on his chin. Shocking. She moved quickly to sit by her mother on the sofa while he took the chair.

"This is most distasteful," her mother said after the maid left cocoa for them on the table. "I quite dislike remembering this time, my dear."

"I know." She waited to see if her mother would continue or if she would go to her room with another headache.

Her mother rubbed her head. "I have the most dreadful headache coming on." She sighed and stirred her cocoa. "I thought I could trust that girl. She'd been with me for so long."

"When was this? I don't even know how old Richard would be," Olivia asked.

Mrs. Stewart cast a wary eye upon Harrison. "It was right after my daughter was born. I nearly died after her birth. The woman took advantage of my infirmity to entice my husband into a relationship."

Olivia had heard the stories of how her mother hadn't left her bed for several months following her birth. "How did you discover it?"

"My mother told me about it, of all things. She caught them in the kitchen." The older woman shuddered and sipped her tea.

"Did you confront Lulu and . . . your husband?"

"I said nothing to him. He went away on business and I dismissed her at once. Actually, my mother handled it for me." She put down her cup. "It was quite distasteful. Lulu came crying to me, asking for me to reconsider my decision."

"Did you?" Harrison asked, his voice gentle.

"Of course not! I couldn't have a viper in my bosom. I had the servants remove her."

Olivia winced at the mental image of a pregnant young woman alone and friendless. "Did she have family in the area?"

"She sometimes visited a sister. I don't remember her name. It will come to me though."

"At least she had someone then."

Her mother frowned. "You sound sympathetic to her."

"I was just imagining myself in her situation."

Her mother fixed her with a stare. "You would never be so unwise."

"Of course not."

"Do you think she would be vindictive now?" Harrison asked.

"She wasn't that kind. She would have taken in every stray cat in the neighborhood if I would have let her."

Harrison leaned forward. "So Richard would be a few months younger than your daughter. Which one? Olivia?"

Olivia's mother nodded. "That's right. How do we even know if he's still alive? He hasn't come forward to claim anything."

Something about the situation had bothered Olivia, and she finally figured out what it was. "Mr. Stewart knew his name. He mentioned him by name in the will. So he had to have been in contact with Lulu after she went to San Francisco. Can we check bank records and see if he supported her in any way?"

Her mother blanched. "You're right. I hadn't thought it through." She rubbed her head and moaned. "That woman. I can't believe she would have been bold enough to contact him. And knowing my husband, he probably *did* give her money."

"We might be able to trace Richard that way," Harrison said, leaning forward in his chair. "With your permission, I'll get on it."

"Our solicitor will be here tomorrow. He can handle it," her mother said.

Olivia saw Harrison sit back in his chair. "I'd like you to be here when we talk to our attorney, Harrison," she said. "If you don't mind."

He straightened. "I would welcome the chance to help."

"M-Mrs. Stewart, you seem to blame Lulu for the entire situation. What of your husband's role?"

The older woman gave her a cold glance. "Men will always be men, my dear. You'll learn that soon enough." She rose. "We must get to bed. Lady Devonworth, you can see Mr. Bennett out." Her tone made it clear her daughter was not to dawdle.

Thirty-three

OLIVIA WALKED WITH Harrison to the front door and stepped out onto the porch with him. She wished she dared ask him what he had started to say several times. The gaslight by her head hissed and danced in the faint breeze off the ocean.

She took his hand. "Thank you for looking out for me tonight, Harrison. I want you to go home now. I'm going to bed and I promise I won't answer any summons."

He raised her fingers to his lips. "I'd rather stay awhile. Want to take a walk in the moonlight?"

She hesitated. Maybe she could get up the courage to tell him her name. "Is it safe?"

"I'll protect you," he said, smiling. "I'll have the guard walk a few feet behind us."

"I'd love to," she said.

"Need a wrap?"

"I'm fine." Just being around him warmed her more than any shawl. She took his arm and they strolled down the drive.

"I think we'd better stick to the sidewalk," he said, guiding her toward the street. "The gardens could hide an intruder."

They passed the guard, and Harrison told him to keep an eye on them. She liked the way he slowed his steps to match hers and the tender way he helped her down the curb. It seemed so much more than mere courtesy. Was it? The path was dark except for the occasional open arc lamp. Every time they stepped into the shadows, she wished he would stop, take her in his arms, and kiss her until she was breathless—which wouldn't take much, because she already had to force herself to drag in air whenever she was in his presence.

Was this love?

They walked in silence to the end of the block, then turned to go back the way they'd come. Olivia saw a movement near the shrubbery and paused. The glow from the arc light illuminated the figure of a man hiding in the bushes. Her fingers clamped onto Harrison's arm.

"There's a man watching us," she said.

"I see him. Wait here." He walked toward the shrubbery. "You there! Show yourself."

The leaves erupted and the figure raced off the other way. Olivia stared. There was something about the shape of his head, the way he held his shoulders. She started to shout, "Father," then choked back the word. Harrison gave chase to the fellow and she ran after them. The guard rushed past her and pursued the men as well.

The men vanished around the corner, and she paused to catch her breath. Her chest burned with the exertion, but she forced herself to break into a jog again. She turned the corner and saw Harrison coming back toward her.

"I lost him," he said when he reached her.

She seized his arm. "Oh, Harrison, I think it was Mr. Stewart."

He frowned. "Honey, are you sure? You thought the man who called you to the backyard was Stewart too. The lighting is poor. How could you tell? I couldn't make out anything but a dark shape."

She liked hearing the word *honey* on his lips. His doubt rattled her, though, made her question what she'd seen. "I can't explain it, but I think it was him. Something about the shape of his head. But why wouldn't he reveal himself to us?"

"We keep going round and round about that. Was he in any kind of trouble when he disappeared?"

She shook her head.

"Did he gamble?"

She stared down the street, willing the man to reappear. "He hates gambling. He says gamblers are fools."

She remembered the tilt of his head. "Could it be Richard? Maybe he looks like Mr. Stewart."

"I don't know. I suppose it's possible." He turned her back toward the house. "I want to get you safely inside. I should never have brought you out in the night."

The guard joined them and hustled them back to the manor. She kept glancing back for another glimpse of the man, but all she saw were shadows and shrubs.

❧

Silver chinked at the luncheon table on the terrace and mingled with the birdsong in the background. Lady Devonworth had insisted Harrison stay the night at Stewart Hall, and he'd been happy to oblige to ensure there were no more attacks. Though he hadn't done much to prevent last night's stalker. Harrison had tried to push the events from his mind by talking about aeroplanes with Will during the meal, but his thoughts kept going back to what had happened.

Mrs. Stewart's mouth was pursed and her eyes went distant every time she looked at him. He knew she blamed him for last night's near miss. And rightly so. He should never have taken his fiancée from the premises. He still shuddered when he thought about what might have happened. The man might have had a gun.

"Did you see this man Lady Devonworth claimed was Marshall?" Mrs. Stewart asked. She stared out the window.

"Only from the back. I thought he looked too slim to be Mr. Stewart." He raised an apologetic glance Lady Devonworth's way.

"I was probably mistaken," Lady Devonworth said.

How much of what Lady Devonworth saw was wishful thinking? If that man last night had been Mr. Stewart, he would have spoken to her. It was dark. No one was around. There was no reason for him to hide.

"What I don't understand is that if it really *is* Mr. Stewart, why would he want to harm you, honey?" he asked her.

She blanched. "Harm me?"

"He threw you over a cliff into the sea," he reminded her.

"That wasn't him. That man's voice was huskier than Mr. Stewart's, younger somehow too. I believe Mr. Stewart had left, and the attacker took advantage of the opportunity."

"You heard him call your name just before you went outside."

She bit her lip. "True. That lends more credence to the possibility that it's Richard Pixton." She stared at him, then at Mrs. Stewart. "But I'd thought he was trying to protect me," she said.

"Who, dear?" Mrs. Stewart speared a section of orange.

"Mr. Stewart. He saw us leave the premises and was watching to protect me. When we saw him, he had to run."

Harrison stared at her, not sure how her mind worked. "How do you reason that out?" Not that he totally disbelieved it, but it seemed a leap in logic.

"I keep seeing him just before danger strikes. I think he's doing the best he can for me."

Mrs. Stewart banged down her fork. "Oh, for heaven's sake! If my husband is out there, he would let us know. He's not a cruel man, and letting me mourn him if he's not dead is the height of cruelty."

Lady Devonworth's lips flattened. "I didn't mean to offend, Mrs. Stewart."

The doorbell rang. Who would call right at lunchtime?

"I imagine it's my brother Philip," Will said, scooting back his chair. "That lad pays no attention to time." He darted through the door to the dining room, leaving the door open behind him.

Harrison heard backslapping and boisterous greetings between the brothers. It appeared they had been separated for several months. Will returned to the terrace with two men in tow. Harrison appraised the younger of the two, Philip. Very young and a snappy dresser. But Will had said he was good at his job. The older, portly gentleman must be the attorney, Mr. Grayson. His hunch was confirmed when Lady Devonworth and Mrs. Stewart leaped up to greet him.

"Have you had luncheon, gentlemen?" Mrs. Stewart asked.

To his credit, Philip flushed. "No, ma'am, I came straight here from my boat."

"Nor I," Grayson said. "But don't trouble yourself. I can eat in town."

"Nonsense," Mrs. Stewart said. "I'll have two more plates brought. Sit here by me, Mr. Grayson." She indicated the chair to her right.

A hummingbird sat on the back of the chair, and it darted away when Philip approached. When he sat down beside Lady Devonworth, he eyed Mrs. Stewart as though he wasn't sure whether she would snarl or smile.

"Will tells me you have some experience in tracing missing men," Lady Devonworth said.

"It's my passion," Philip said. "How can I help you? Will was very vague."

Under the table, Harrison took her hand. She squeezed his fingers and a smile lifted her lips. Did she sense his feelings? Every time he tried to tell her, something interrupted. He was unsure if God was warning him off or if it was coincidence.

Mrs. Stewart dabbed her lips with the napkin. "My husband was reported dead after a diamond mine he was examining caved in."

Philip took a notebook from the inside pocket of his jacket and began to write. "Where did this occur?"

"At a black-diamond mine in Africa."

Will whistled. "I hadn't heard that. Black diamonds. I've never seen one."

"Marshall was most excited about the acquisition of that mine," Mrs. Stewart said. "The explosion buried fifty men. Their bodies were never recovered."

"Who informed you of this accident?"

"I received a telegram from Mr. Bennett. He'd been on the scene and was able to give us the details of what happened. Apparently, Marshall was there when a new lode was discovered. In the excitement, he wanted to see it for himself. Mr. Bennett was ill and stayed behind." She shot a narrowed glare at Harrison.

Lady Devonworth's grip on Harrison's hand had made his fingers numb.

"Do you suspect foul play?" Philip asked.

Mrs. Stewart played with her fork. "I didn't. Now I don't know." Her voice faltered. "Lady Devonworth here found a letter he sent to Eleanor. According to this letter—in Marshall's handwriting—he isn't dead. And he warns her against the Bennetts."

"Have you found any evidence this is true?"

Mrs. Stewart glanced at Lady Devonworth, who stared down at the table and said, "I heard a voice in the speaking tube that claimed to be Mr. Stewart. After I went down to meet him, I was attacked and thrown into the sea after being rendered unconscious by chloroform. And last night Harrison and I saw a man who resembled Mr. Stewart."

"Last night, you say? Where?" Philip put down his pencil.

"Just down the block." She described the man they'd seen. "I don't believe it could possibly be Mr. Stewart, though. He would never harm me."

"If he's here in town, someone has seen him."

"And no one has," Mrs. Stewart said.

"That's not exactly true," Lady Devonworth said. "Goldia thought she saw him in town."

"That girl is a flibbertigibbet. You can't believe anything she says."

Mrs. Stewart glanced at the attorney. "You need to find out if these documents are forged."

"I'll take them back to San Francisco with me. I have plenty of genuine examples of your husband's handwriting," Grayson said. "We shall soon root out the truth of the matter."

Glancing at Lady Devonworth's hopeful face, Harrison hoped she wasn't about to be hurt.

❧

The next two weeks passed in a whirlwind. Harrison had to go to San Francisco to talk to investors about his aeroplane. Olivia made personal long-distance calls to her friends but was not able to coax anyone to come to her Lightkeeper's Ball. All of them were distant and aloof. They'd seen the article about her being in the wilderness with Harrison, though none would have said so to her. Olivia ended the calls with a sense of disquiet.

Did she have any true friends? People who cared about her for herself and not her name or her money? Now what? She called Katie and Addie, and they helped her make calls to local people. Harrison's mother and some of the women from the church helped too, and by the end of the week, the butler was bringing in a flood of acceptances every afternoon.

Mr. Grayson had called with news that the signature on the will appeared genuine, and the news put her mother into a funk for two days, even though Olivia encouraged her with the reminder that Richard Pixton had not been found, and Mr. Grayson was filing to contest the will. Not even Will's brother had succeeded in locating her half brother. Nothing was going right.

Thursday morning she put on her hat and called for the car. She had to find out if what Mr. Quinn had mentioned about her father and Mrs. Fosberg could possibly be true. The driver took her by the Fosberg house first, and a gardener told her Mrs. Fosberg was inside.

Olivia instructed the driver to wait and went to the door, where she was escorted to the parlor.

"My dear Lady Devonworth," Mrs. Fosberg said, standing to greet her. "I just ordered tea."

Olivia smiled and settled onto the sofa by the woman. "Thank you for seeing me, Mrs. Fosberg."

"You seem quite grave, my dear. Is everything all right?"

Olivia smiled and accepted a cup of tea from the woman. "I'm fine. I hope you're looking forward to the ball as much as I am."

Mrs. Fosberg clasped her hands together. "Oh, I cannot wait! I am coming as Queen Victoria."

Olivia hid her amusement behind her cup. The sweet woman was short and rather dumpy. The fussy clothing Queen Victoria would wear would overpower her.

"The entire town is talking about it. Frederick's partner from San Francisco is coming, and several of his friends. I think you shall raise all the money needed to rebuild the lighthouse."

"I hope so. People have been very generous." She sipped her tea and tried to decide how to broach the subject. "Have you met Mrs. Stewart?" she asked finally.

The woman's smile vanished. "I have."

"How about her husband? He was in town on occasion."

The tea sloshed onto the saucer under Mrs. Fosberg's cup. "Oh dear," she said as it spilled onto her dress. She rang for a servant and asked for a damp cloth.

Olivia bit her lip. Had it been a ploy to avoid the subject? "I heard you and Mr. Stewart were friends," she said.

Mrs. Fosberg's lips trembled. "Where did you hear that? That nosy newspaper reporter, I presume? My son told me he's been asking questions about our family."

"I did not mean to offend you," Olivia said. "I merely wished to ensure you are comfortable meeting Mrs. Stewart at the ball."

Mrs. Fosberg's lips tightened. "I'm perfectly comfortable. Marshall and I were friends. He was a lonely man, and I was lonely as well. Our relationship is hardly your concern, Lady Devonworth, if I may be so bold."

"D-Did he speak of his wife and daughters?"

The older woman put the saucer down with a clatter. "His wife is a cold, heartless woman."

Olivia gasped at the characterization of her mother, then sat back in her chair. Perhaps the truth was not far off. Her mother had always been driven. She knew what she wanted and was determined to have it. "That's what he told you?"

"I heard it from other sources as well. But I'm not at liberty to repeat their names." Her smile came then, but it was strained. "Please, shall we move on to another, more pleasant topic?"

"Of course." Olivia knew when she'd passed the bounds of good manners.

⌀⌀⌀

Two days before the ball, Olivia started watching the clock. Harrison was due back. She *had* to tell him the truth when he arrived, even if it meant he broke their engagement. And she very much feared he would. The servants were busy hanging decorations and moving in extra seating and tables. The bedrooms would be ready for the guests to arrive.

When the doorbell rang, she was engrossed in the Kewpie pages of the newest *Woman's Home Companion*. She set the magazine aside and listened for one of the servants to answer the summons. When she heard Harrison's deep voice, she pinched her cheeks and smoothed her hair. Taking care to arrange her skirt becomingly around her, she looked toward the door with an expectant smile.

When he entered the parlor, she took in his attire. Leather jacket and hat, casual clothing. "You're going flying?" She couldn't keep the excitement from her voice. "The plane is ready for testing?"

"Past ready. I've been up in it three times. It performs better than any other flying machine I've ever seen. Today the comet is supposed to be as close as it is going to get. Want to come along?"

She sprang to her feet. "May I?"

He nodded. "I have something for you though. I didn't like the way your skirt was nearly caught in the aeroplane on our last adventure. I bought you an aviator's outfit." He held up a white-bagged garment. Unzipping it, he revealed a bloomers outfit.

Her mother would be scandalized. Olivia eyed it. The bloomers ended under the knee and had matching argyle stockings. A leather aviator's hat dangled from the hanger as well. Oh the freedom of such an outfit!

She reached for it. "I love it!"

"Get changed and I'll take you up for a lesson. We'll refuel, then go up again tonight when the comet passes."

She paused in her rush toward the door. "Aren't you afraid at all?"

He shook his head. "Scientists continue to say we're in no danger. But if they're wrong, being up there or down here won't matter much. And if we're about to step through eternity's door, I can't think of anywhere I'd rather be than with you."

She drank in his expression. The quirk in his brow, the daring tilt to his lips, the tenderness in his eyes. This day held more promise than she could take in.

"I'll be right back," she said, suddenly breathless.

Carrying the scandalous attire, she rushed to her bedroom. Goldia turned from putting clothing in the closet. She gasped when she saw what Olivia held. Shaking her head, she approached her mistress. "Oh no, Miss Olivia. Your mama would have my hide if I let you wear them bloomers."

"I'm wearing them." Olivia turned her back to her maid. "Unbutton me."

Muttering under her breath, Goldia did as she was ordered. "You go down the back stairs. Don't let your mama see you."

"I'm a grown woman. This outfit is perfectly modest." She pulled on the stockings, then stepped into the bloomers. Turning, she surveyed herself in the full-length mirror and nearly gasped. She was quite the modern woman. No longer a society miss but a daring adventuress. She rather liked the thought.

Twirling, she struck a pose. "What do you think?"

"It's scandalous, miss." Goldia turned away and shuddered. "What if your gentleman sees you like this?"

"He bought it for me."

Goldia put her hand to her mouth and muttered something indecipherable under her breath. Olivia smiled and hurried down to meet Harrison in the entry. When he saw her, his expression warmed. She held out her hand and he took it and raised it to his lips. He lingered overly long in the kiss he placed against the back of her hand.

"Are we ready?" she asked when he continued to stare at her.

He released her hand. "I've got something else for you in the auto."

Jewelry? Shoes? She wondered what might go with this outfit. When they reached his Cadillac, he grabbed a bag from behind his seat and pulled out a pair of coveralls.

She raised a brow. "You expect me to wear these? I hate covering up my new outfit."

"You don't want it to be stained, do you? The engine throws out castor oil."

"Oh, very well. But I'm not putting it on until I have to." She smiled and went around to the other side of the motorcar. She was a free woman. Harrison didn't have expectations of her other than that she be herself. Had that ever happened before? Not in her memory.

THIRTY-FOUR

THE WHITECAPS ROLLED along the blue ribbon of coast below them. The sun had begun its final plunge into the sea, and cliffs threw shadows onto the sand. Harrison steered the plane along the rocky cliffs rising to their right. The engine was performing beautifully, and the new wings handled the winds without a problem.

He glanced behind at Lady Devonworth. Her pink cheeks and wide smile telegraphed her enjoyment. Earlier in the afternoon he'd let her take the controls for a few minutes, and she'd handled them like she was born to fly. He gave her a thumbs-up, and she motioned it back to him with an even wider grin.

The sky began to darken overhead as the sun sank, throwing off pink and orange rays. He wanted to shout, to raise his fists in the air and exult in the experience. Halley's Comet was a bright star overhead. He saw no evidence of the tail. Smelled nothing of poisonous gas. Just the salt-laden breeze.

He was going to tell her how he felt about her tonight over dinner on the beach.

She touched his shoulder and pointed. He looked down at the battered lighthouse she was trying so hard to save. The perfect place. Though she was only pointing out their location, he lowered the flaps and prepared to land. The aeroplane glided on the gentle breeze. Lower and lower. The sunlight gleamed on the water, illuminating the way. He held his breath and set the plane down on the sand. The bumps were gentle. A perfect landing. A good omen for a perfect evening, he hoped.

After leaping from the plane, he secured it with ties, then helped her out. Gulls squawked overhead as they dived for their last attempt at fishing before nightfall. The tide was coming in, bringing flotsam and driftwood.

"Would you get out the basket in the back of the plane?" he asked Lady Davenworth. When she nodded, he rounded up an armful of dried-out driftwood and began to build a fire. He fetched the kerosene lantern and lit it. When he turned around, she had shucked the hated overalls. Her hair had come loose from its pins without the leather cap. He could only stare.

"Hungry?" he asked.

"Not really. It's all too exciting." She raised her arms over her head and lifted her face to the sky. "We're still alive, Harrison."

He grinned. "Are you ever going to tell me your name? I can't call you Lady Devonworth forever."

She paled, then smiled. "I rather like hearing you call me Essie."

It was a grand opening to tell her how he felt, but he didn't have the nerve. Not yet. "I don't smell anything, do you?" he asked. "No poisonous gasses."

She shook her head. "Just the sea."

"Let's take a walk and eat later then." He held out his hand and she took it. The way she wrapped her fingers around his in such a trusting way made him smile.

"Are you laughing at me?" she asked. Her other hand went to her hair.

"No," he said. "I'm just enjoying your company."

She squeezed his fingers. "It's been a lovely day."

They reached the hillside by the remains of the lighthouse. "Shall we sit?" he asked, indicating a flat rock barely visible in the quickly falling darkness. The lump in his pocket seemed bigger, more important.

When should he pull out the box? Before he told her how he felt or after?

She settled on the rock, and he sat down beside her. "I like being with you," he said. He wasn't good with smooth words. He cleared his throat. "I'm not saying this very well." Maybe his gift would say it better than he could. He slipped his hand into his pocket and brought out the ring box. "I have something for you."

Her attention went to the velvet box, and she went very still. She shifted on the rock, and he couldn't tell if she moved a bit closer or farther away. She offered no cues on how to proceed. His fingers were all thumbs as he fumbled to open the box. Now that his proposal was in front of him, he realized daylight might have been a wiser choice. Lamplight wouldn't reveal how lovely the ring was.

He succeeded in prying open the top. The ring sparkled against its black velvet backdrop. Tiny black and white diamonds circled the most magnificent white diamond he'd been able to find. When she gasped, he took heart. "I wanted to give you something no one else would have. Do you like it?"

"I-It's beautiful," she said. She reached for the ring.

"Allow me." He lifted it from the slit in the box and took her left hand. Her fingers were cold. Maybe this had been a mistake. She was likely to laugh in his face.

But she didn't. Her eyes were wide, and her mouth trembled as she stretched out her fingers. He took that as an invitation to slip on the engagement ring. The light from the lantern sparkled on it as she turned it to and fro.

"I'm not good with words, my love, so let me just get this out." He swallowed hard. "I want our engagement to be real. I know I don't deserve you, but no one will cherish you like I will. I'm asking you to trust me. To believe in me. To be by my side as we make a life together."

Her lips parted and he waited to hear the words of rejection he feared were coming.

❦

The engagement ring took her breath away. So did Harrison's words. Olivia stared at the glittering diamonds, then into his face. His eyes were brighter than the diamonds, more compelling than the comet she'd come out here to see. The pain of knowing that his love would fade when he discovered she was one of the hated Stewarts dimmed her joy. Was it possible his love could withstand the reality of her heritage? When they left this magical place, she had to tell him. It would either all end or he would find it in his heart to look past the Stewart name.

She wetted her lips. "Are you saying you love me?" she whispered. The wind whipped a strand of hair across her face, and she pushed it away so she could study his expression. Surely that was love in his eyes?

He rubbed his forehead. "Didn't I just say that?"

"Not exactly," she said, smiling. "I'd like to hear those words though. I've been waiting days on them."

He lifted a brow and a grin broke the worried set of his mouth. "I love you. I love the way you have to figure everything out. I love your optimism and how smart you are. You make me want to be better than I am."

"I thought you said you didn't have a way with words," she said, her voice husky. She cupped his face in her palms. "I love you, Harrison. I'd be honored to be your wife forever and ever."

A flash of light caught her attention and she looked up, dropping her hands. "Oh look, it's a meteor shower!"

The heavens were a display of fireworks like she'd never seen. Falling stars arced across the sky as they plummeted toward the ground. When she glanced back at Harrison, his face was tilted to the sky. His profile was strong and her soul filled as she looked at him.

He turned toward her, and she knew her whole heart was in her eyes. He palmed her cheek and rubbed his thumb over her lips. Her eyes closed when he leaned forward. His lips pressed against hers, and she exploded with feelings she'd never experienced. Heat swept over her skin, and she pressed closer to him, winding her arms around his neck. She wanted to be closer to him, closer than to anyone.

She couldn't think beyond this moment. Nestled against him with passion arcing between them, she had no concept of time or place. Just the feel of his lips on hers, the taste of his mouth, his arms holding her close. When he broke away, she made a sound of protest and tried to pull him close again.

He sprang to his feet and raked his hand through his hair. "We should be getting back." His voice shook.

As her cheeks cooled, she realized she'd lost her head. She'd totally forgotten propriety. A lesser man would have taken advantage of her innocence. Her trembling legs barely supported her as she slipped off the rock and put her hand in his.

"Can we see the comet?" she asked.

She focused on the heavens and tried to calm her ragged breathing. The sky was filled with stars, some brighter than others. The meteorite shower had ended. She saw the Big Dipper and Orion. The bright northern star was rising. She gulped and dragged in oxygen. What had just happened between them?

He looked up into the sky. "We were supposed to be able to see it, but all I see is Venus."

She'd seen stars when he kissed her. She'd like to experience that again, but the heat in her cheeks still surged when she touched his hand. "We haven't talked about when the marriage will take place."

He tucked her hand into his arm. "I think as soon as possible, don't you?"

Her cheeks flared again once she understood his meaning. What must he think of the way she'd clung to him? Did he think her a wanton woman? Maybe she was. Surely the feelings she'd had weren't normal. Her mother had never warned her of the way her flesh could respond to a man's touch. She'd thought the bedroom side of marriage was something to be endured, something that only delivered the children she wanted, not something to be longed for.

An awkward silence fell between them. She wished she knew whether her behavior had frightened him off.

His fingertip touched the moisture on her cheeks. "Are you crying? I didn't mean to frighten you. I just love you so much. I'm afraid I lost my head a bit."

He was apologizing when it should be her? "Did you think me overly amorous?" she asked. "I shall try to behave better the next time you kiss me."

His choked laugh was cut off as he gripped her shoulders in his hands. "Please don't change a thing."

His mouth came down on hers again and the same passion swept her up in its wake like the tail of the comet they'd heard so much about. Standing on her tiptoes, she pressed against him.

He pulled his mouth away but hugged her close. Her ear was over his heart and she could hear it going crazy. His reaction to her was just as strong as hers was to him. Her hand crept up to touch his face, and his heartbeat marched double time. She nearly laughed. He wanted her too. What a relief to realize she hadn't made him want to run from her.

By the time they flew back, her hair had come loose from its covering. Harrison landed the plane on the field, and Jerry rushed to help her down. She pushed her hair out of her face and steeled herself to tell Harrison the truth on the way back to the manor.

"You need to get home," Jerry said. "Your mother took a spill from her chair."

Harrison stilled. "Is she hurt?"

"A lump on her head, but she's been fretting for you since your father is still away and will be gone at least another week."

He'd be gone for the ball. Olivia managed not to smile.

"I'll go right there if you can take Lady Devonworth home."

"I'm going that way," Jerry said, flashing his grin.

Harrison brushed his lips across Olivia's forehead. "Sorry, honey."

She watched him walk away. She could savor his love for another night.

Harrison found his mother abed when he stopped by her house. He assured himself she was all right, brushed a kiss across her brow, then left her to rest. He paused in the hall and glanced at his father's office.

Since Lady Devonworth had mentioned her doubts about his father's dealings with the Stewart fortune, Harrison had determined to find out the truth.

His mother's butler motioned to him. "Sir, your fiancée called. She was checking on your mother and also asked you to call on her if it's not too late tonight. She said she needed to speak with you."

"Thank you." He waited until the butler went through the door to the kitchen, then Harrison went down the hall to the office and shut the door behind him.

His father's office was sacrosanct. No one came in without an invitation. No one sat in his father's chair, and it was all Harrison could to do to circle the desk and settle onto the leather cushion. No papers marred the surface of the polished desk. He tugged on the lap drawer and it slid open. Nothing there but pens and ink.

He methodically went through every drawer and examined every paper. Nothing was out of place until he picked up a notebook. He flipped through it and saw that the sheets were empty. As he closed it, he noticed impressions on the blank pages. Looking more closely, he realized some pages had been cut out.

He grabbed a pencil and put the notebook under a light. Using a light stroke, he smudged the paper with the impression. A signature began to appear.

Marshall Stewart.

Over and over, all down the page. The signature was the same. It varied in small ways, but the bold handwriting showed up as though someone had practiced writing the name. The only reason for that would be . . . forgery.

He closed his eyes briefly. His fiancée's fears were true. Harrison's father had orchestrated all of this. She had to know about this, but he didn't want to tell her. Not after this evening. Not after the acceptance and love he'd found in her arms. What if she didn't believe he had nothing to do with it?

But if she loved him, wouldn't she believe him? He cut out the incriminating page, folded it, then tucked it into his pocket. He'd put it in his office and tell her about it when he saw her. Honesty was best.

If his father had forged the will, what else had he done? Harrison opened the drawer that held the business books. The men had owned a diamond mine in Africa, and his father had just purchased a second one. Upon his marriage to Eleanor, the Stewarts were to receive half the income from the second mine. He studied the rows of numbers. Both mines appeared to be incredibly profitable, but hadn't Lady Devonworth said Mrs. Stewart's money was gone? With her share from the one mine alone, she should have been extremely well off.

Harrison rubbed his forehead. Could his father have been cheating the Stewarts? Had he misled them as to their financial condition to force them into agreeing to a marriage between him and Eleanor?

He flipped through the remaining pages of the ledger, but they were empty. He lifted the receiver on the telephone and instructed the operator to place a call to Mr. Grayson. When the phone rang and he was connected, he told the attorney what he'd found.

"Are the Stewarts paid anywhere near this amount per month?" he asked, quoting half of the current month's income from the original mine.

"That was the amount transferred last month, Mr. Bennett. Your father oversees what comes in and specifies what goes out to them as well."

"Do you think he's cheating them?"

"The only way to know that is to see how much the mine is actually making, not what he is transferring."

"How can we do that?"

"You'd need to talk to the banker who handles the account."

His father did business with the bank here in town. John North could put him in touch with the right person. "I can do that. I'll let you know what I find out." He hung up and took a deep breath.

If he discovered his father was a swindler, what would he do about it? Lady Devonworth wanted to talk to him, but he was going to put her off until tomorrow. He wanted to get to the truth first.

THIRTY-FIVE

OLIVIA SAT SIPPING lemonade on the terrace with Katie and Addie. This morning she had hustled around the house making sure the bedrooms were readied for overnight guests from San Francisco. Her first load of guests would arrive shortly on the packet, and the real work of hosting the ball would begin.

Bees buzzed a pleasant drone in the background, but she was out of sorts. She'd asked Harrison to come by last night, but he'd made his apologies. Now here it was the day of the ball—their engagement ball!—and she hadn't told him she was Olivia Stewart. How could she tell him today when the tension between them might explode and ruin the festivities?

Hummingbirds flitted from flower to flower in the espaliered planting that shielded the terrace from anyone in the yard. Even the fragrance of hibiscus failed to soothe her.

Katie leaned back in her chair. "I can't thank you enough for all you've done, my dear Olivia. The ballroom should be full tonight."

Olivia rubbed Tiger's ears, and he rewarded her with a loud purr. "And you and Will shall soon be back home. I expect the funds to pour in from the benefit."

"Is your costume ready?" Katie asked.

"Oh yes."

"You shall be the loveliest Juliet of all time," Addie said. She smiled and picked up Olivia's left hand. "You've said nothing about this, though

I've been waiting in agony for you to tell me. When did Harrison give it to you?"

Olivia turned it to catch the light. "Last night, the night the tail of the comet was supposed to show itself, but this was much more brilliant than the comet."

"You've said hardly anything about it to me either, and I've been dying to ask," Katie said. "Why did he give you a ring if you're going to break the engagement after the ball is over?"

Olivia put the cat down. He growled and stalked away with his tail in the air. "We aren't going to break it. I'm going to marry him."

She'd hugged the information close. It was a most delicious secret. Olivia wanted to take out the memories of last night and examine them with no doubts, no familial objections.

Addie leaped to her feet and grabbed Olivia in a hug. "I *knew* you two were meant for one another! I saw the way he looked at you."

"And you at him," Katie added, smiling widely. "I'm so delighted for you both." She sobered. "Have you told him you're Olivia Stewart yet?"

Olivia's elation collapsed. "No. Every time I think I have the courage to do it, something happens and I can't bear to spoil the mood."

Katie put her hand to her head. "But his father knows you! The minute you meet him, the truth is out."

"I know! Thankfully, he's out of town for the ball. Once the craziness of the party is over, I'll pick a quiet moment and tell Harrison."

"He's going to be upset that you waited so long," Addie said.

Olivia bit her lip. "Time just seemed to slip away."

Addie gave her a long look, then shrugged. "When is the wedding?"

Heat scorched Olivia's cheeks. "Soon."

Both of the other women stared at her hot cheeks. Katie glanced down at her plate of cake with a smile. Addie bit her lip but it failed to stop the curve of her mouth.

Olivia stirred sugar into her tea. "I've never been in love before. Is it—normal—to feel, um, flustered when he kisses me? T-To not want him to stop?"

Addie choked on the bite of cookie she'd just taken. Katie spilled tea on her dress. Olivia knew her face must be as red as the strawberries on the plate of refreshments. She was totally abnormal. A hussy. Harrison deserved better than a woman who threw herself at him.

Addie swallowed and the pink in her cheeks intensified. "It's normal when you love someone to, um, want to be with him. Passion between a man and woman is how it's supposed to be. It's how God designed it."

"You mean you feel that way too? I'm not a fallen woman?"

The other women laughed. They all looked down at their tea. Olivia's eyes burned when they didn't answer. Perhaps they would cast her off now that they knew of her base nature.

Finally Addie glanced up. "I've been married the longest, so I suppose I should answer this. Be thankful you have those feelings, Olivia. Too many women go into marriage only for convenience or arrangement. They endure the marriage bed with little emotion or feeling. God designed you to respond to your husband. He looked at the union of man and woman and said, 'It is good.' And it is."

Katie patted her hand. "And your love for Harrison will only grow if you let it." She smiled and her dimple flashed. "I'd suggest you plan that wedding very soon."

"Have you told your mother?" Addie asked.

Olivia shook her head. "She saw the ring, but I think she imagines it's part of the show. I'll tell her soon."

"He's a wonderful man," Katie said. "There should be no impediment."

"She's uncertain of Mr. Bennett's role in Father's disappearance. As am I. But Harrison had nothing to do with his father's schemes."

"What of Eleanor's death?" Addie's voice was gentle. "Have you abandoned any belief that Harrison had something to do with it?"

"Of course. He's saved my life several times." Even as she spoke, she was aware his appearance at the right times proved nothing. He could have hired someone to harm her and then intervened. But she knew him better now. He was not that kind of man.

"Who could be behind these attempts on your life?" Katie asked.

Olivia lifted her cup to her lips. "I suspect Richard Pixton."

"As do I," Katie said. "But I haven't been able to decipher a motive. He gets the money even if you live."

"Not if I'm successfully able to contest the will."

Addie nodded. "And with you and your mother out of the way, he wouldn't have to care for you." She tipped her head in a listening posture. "I think I hear a car arriving. I do believe the ball is about to commence!"

The bank was nearly empty. It would close for the day in fifteen minutes. Harrison shook hands with John. "Thank you for meeting me here on such short notice."

"My pleasure. I'm on the board of directors—so not an integral part of the day-to-day operations—but I hope to be able to answer any questions you might have."

His father's account included Harrison as a joint signer, but he'd never had the need to do more than arrange deposits and tally outlays. His father managed everything else. He followed John to a back office.

John shut the door behind them and led Harrison to a long table that held a stack of leather-bound books. "I've pulled the account books for you. They are always available for your perusal. I'll leave you to look through them while I tend to another matter. I'll be back to see if you have any questions."

"Thank you." Harrison pulled out a chair and opened the first book.

It didn't take long for his worst fears to be confirmed. The diamond mine was raking in a staggering amount of money, but his father was only transferring a thousand dollars a month to the Stewarts. Not only that, but Harrison saw an even more awful truth: Mr. Stewart had owned 80 percent of that mine. His father had lied to everyone in saying he'd paid for it alone.

So his father had been swindling the Stewarts out of money. The door opened behind him, but he didn't turn until he heard his father's voice.

"Harrison, what are you doing here?" his father demanded.

Harrison stood to face his father. "When did you get back in town?"

"I decided my son's engagement party was more important than business, so I turned around and came back. What are you doing?"

"I wanted to see the books. I have every right."

"I give you a detailed report every month, and you give those a cursory glance. If you wanted more information, all you had to do was ask. Instead you've gone behind my back?" His father closed the door behind them. Perspiration dotted his upper lip. His smile was more of a grimace as he crossed the room to the table where Harrison stood. He glanced at the open book. "What are you looking for?"

"Less than I've actually discovered," Harrison said, suddenly weary. "You've been cheating the Stewarts."

"I've done no such thing," his father sputtered. "Marshall left me in charge."

"Did he really? Or did you forge his name so you could swindle his family?"

His father paled and sank heavily onto a chair. "How do you know that?"

"I found the notebook. There were imprints on the blank pages."

His father's eyes pleaded for understanding. "Marshall's dead. This is my chance to be like the Vanderbilts. I had to take it. It was just going to be temporary until you were married to one of the Stewart girls. The families would be joined and I would give them everything they needed."

"But keep the bulk for yourself." When his father dropped his gaze, Harrison knew he was right. He felt sick. "You cut Mrs. Stewart's money so she would be forced to agree to your demand to marry Eleanor off to me."

His father took a handkerchief from his pocket and mopped his brow. "No one was hurt by this."

"What about Mrs. Stewart and her surviving daughter? You've been raking in the money and forcing them to live on a shoestring."

"Only for a few months," his father protested. "It was to ensure Mrs. Stewart went through with the wedding."

Harrison shut the account book. The thud echoed in the room. "You must make it right, Father."

His father's lips thinned. "I'll not have our name besmirched, Harrison. Keep quiet about this. I'll just start putting more money into their account. I'll tell Mrs. Stewart the mine began producing. Mrs. Stewart will never have to worry about money again. I'll settle a large amount on you and Lady Devonworth as well. You can tinker with your planes the rest of your life in comfort."

Did his father think he could *buy* him? "I don't want your blood money, Father."

"Blood money? I had nothing to do with Marshall's death."

"Rather convenient he died in that mine, wasn't it?"

"Surely you don't think your own father would stoop to murder?"

Harrison tapped a pencil against the financial records. "This much money can corrupt a man."

"His death was an accident, I swear it!"

Harrison studied his father's earnest face. "I hope you're telling me the truth, Father."

His father blotted his forehead again. "What are you going to do?"

"I'm going to tell Mrs. Stewart and her lawyer. They can ask for an audit of the books if they choose."

"If you do, all the money will go to Marshall's illegitimate son."

Harrison stopped on his way to the door. He hadn't thought of that. Perhaps it would be best to keep his mouth shut and ensure Mrs. Stewart and not the shadowy Richard Pixton got the money.

⤚❦⤙

Olivia stood in Stewart Hall's third-floor ballroom and surveyed the decorations. The space oozed glamour with its floor-to-ceiling mirrors festooned with garlands of lilies and orchids. A grand piano was in one corner with a stage for the band, and an enormous vase of roses and orchids sat atop it. The windows sparkled and would let starlight in tonight. The servants had scrubbed the floor, then poured milk onto the wood. The wood now gleamed after the milk had been washed off. There were so many orange trees and evergreen boughs that the space looked like a garden.

"It looks wonderful," Katie whispered. "Olivia, I can't thank you enough for what you've done."

"God brought you when we needed you," Addie said. "Just as he always does."

Olivia turned to smile at them. "I believe we shall raise all the necessary funds tonight. The town has rallied around us. All the ladies are still talking about their tour of the lighthouse grounds and the need for rebuilding. They thought it quite romantic."

"They don't have to stay up all night like Will does," Katie said, smiling. She whirled around the ballroom floor. "I'm going to dance until my feet hurt. I can't remember the last time I went dancing."

"Just don't overdo it, both of you," Olivia scolded. "I shall be watching out to make sure you rest."

Addie smiled. "Our men will be doing the same, I'm certain."

Olivia had never had friends like these two, ones who always pointed to Jesus in all circumstances. Her faith had been strengthened so much since coming here. She was beginning to believe she could be who she was inside.

She left her friends arranging flowers and went down to greet her guests. Mr. and Mrs. Broderick, a prominent family from San Francisco, arrived first. Mr. Broderick pressed a check for a thousand dollars into her hand, and she was nearly overcome with his generosity. She escorted them to the parlor to take refreshments. The Fremonts arrived next. Olivia admired Mrs. Fremont's elaborate Marie Antoinette gown and hairstyle and took them to join the other guests.

Her smile faded as she went back to the foyer. A familiar set of shoulders was getting out of a car. Mr. Bennett. What was she going to do? She had to avoid him until she could talk to Harrison. She hiked her skirts and raced for the ballroom.

THIRTY-SIX

CHAMPAGNE FLOWED WITH the conversation. Harrison stood still in a swirling kaleidoscope of brightly colored costumes and masks. The participants in the polka swept by him, and he stood out of the way, laughing as he saw the townspeople dressed in costumes ranging from peasant dress to Queen Victoria. The ballroom was packed, and heat shimmered in the air from all the bodies. The party spilled from the ballroom to the first floor and out to the lawn. He couldn't guess how many were in attendance. Hundreds? The whole town and the neighboring towns of Ferndale and Eureka, as well as the nobs from San Francisco.

He still hadn't seen Lady Devonworth and wasn't sure he would recognize her in her costume. Then he heard her laugh. He turned to see a beautiful woman with dark hair cascading to her waist. She wore an elaborate gown. Her dance card, a vellum paper with a tiny gold pencil, was attached to her wrist by a pale green ribbon. It looked empty, and he hoped she'd saved all her dances for him. She wore a white mask, but he recognized her pointed chin and full lips.

He bowed in front of her. "Romeo at your disposal, miss. Can I talk you into dallying in the moonlight with me?"

She fluttered her fan at him, and a smile curved her lips. "You're most outrageous, Romeo." She put her gloved hand on his arm. "I need to talk to you anyway. You've been avoiding me."

He led her to the center of the ballroom. "Ladies and gentlemen, can I have your attention?"

"What are you doing?" she whispered, glancing around. "Is your father here?"

"He's outside, I believe." He realized he hadn't introduced her to his father, but he'd gone too far to stop now when hundreds of eyes were fixed on them. "Folks, I'm the luckiest man alive. You all know the beautiful Lady Devonworth has consented to be my bride. As a token of my love, I have something special for her, and I want you all to share our joy."

He lifted the lid of the box that he had been carrying under his arm. The necklace she'd tried on at the jeweler's her first day in Mercy Falls glowed in the shimmer of candlelight. The ladies around him gasped, but he was waiting to see his Essie's reaction.

She put her hand to her mouth. "You remembered! It's exquisite!" Her fingers touched it, then she pulled her hand away.

"Let me." He took the intricate platinum chains from their resting place and stepped close enough to lay the piece onto her skin. The necklace was heavier than it appeared.

"I hope I don't break it," she said.

"It's not as fragile as it appears." He fiddled with the clasp on the back of her neck and inhaled the aroma of her perfume, something sweet like honeysuckle. He stepped back. "There. Take a look."

She went to stand before one of the ornate mirrors. "It's beautiful," she said, touching the lacy filigree.

"You look quite lovely," he said, his voice husky. He'd never seen her look more beautiful.

"I want one," a woman dressed as Cleopatra said to her right.

Other women agreed, and Harrison grinned as he realized he'd just likely sold more diamonds for his father. Where was the man anyway? Last time he'd seen him, his father had been talking to some nobs outside. He watched Lady Devonworth in the mirror.

She glanced at his face in the mirror and their gazes locked.

"I shall wear it with pride," she said, her fingers touching it.

He saw doubt and love in her eyes. "Is something wrong? You said you needed to speak with me."

She bit her lip. "There are several things I need to speak with you about. But in private."

He gestured at the smiling guests promenading around the floor. "The ball is a success. Let's pass the plate for the Jespersons while they are all in a spending mood."

He motioned to the footmen and instructed them to pass around silver platters. Lady Devonworth's smile grew as a mound of checks and cash grew on the plates being handed around. After the servants carried off the booty, he swept his fiancée into a dance. Holding her in his arms was the one thing he'd longed to do all evening. Her head barely came to his chin as he whirled her around the floor. Others joined them after the first pass around the floor.

He paused when a familiar form came to the doorway to the ball-room. "My father is here. I need to introduce you."

"Later, in private," she said, her smile fading. "I need to tend to a few things. I'll be back." She squeezed his forearm, then disappeared into the flutter of color and movement around him.

After half an hour, he went in pursuit but couldn't find her, so he wandered back downstairs where men were in the smoking parlor. They were discussing the disappointing appearance of Halley's Comet. He leaned against the wall by the fireplace and listened to their conversation.

A footman offered him a glass of champagne but he refused. Another footman announced a buffet supper was ready in the dining hall. He peeked inside to see if his fiancée was there. She stood talking to Mrs. Stewart at the damask-covered table. Even the heady aromas of creamed oysters, turkey, lobster salad, and salmon mousse failed to tempt his appetite when he was so concerned about what she needed to discuss.

A smatter of laughter echoed in the night, and he saw Jerry and his vaudeville friends performing their play on the wide porch. Harrison took his drink with him and went to watch. It was a comedy about four men from different walks of life. Jerry played a coal miner's son, and his passionate speeches about social equality made Harrison stop and think about how his father treated his employees. Maybe he'd been too hasty to disengage himself from the businesses. He could make changes that could bring a better life to their workers.

When the play ended, he went out to the lawn, where he found Eugene talking with a young maid, Brigitte, under a small alcove. Harrison plopped onto a chair beside them, glad to be out of the crush of people. Before he could say anything to Eugene, he saw Lady Devonworth making her way through the crowd to him.

She stopped when she saw him. Her attention went from him to Eugene. Her eyes widened. "Do you know this man, Harrison?"

He glanced at Eugene and saw his valet lift a brow. Harrison shrugged. "He's my valet, Eugene."

She rubbed her forehead. "I'd hoped you didn't know him." Her voice was a stricken whisper.

"Essie, what is this all about?" he asked. He rose and took her hand, but she pulled back. "What's wrong?"

She glanced from Eugene to Harrison. "Which of you is going to explain this to me?"

Harrison spread out his hands. "I don't know what you are talking about, darling." He pitched his voice low and gentle, aware people were glancing their way.

"Why were you hiding him without telling me?" She broke off on a sob and took a step nearer. "Please tell me there was a good reason for this. I didn't believe you would hide this from me."

"I don't understand what you're saying." He put his hands on her shoulders, but she shook them off.

"Do you think I'm blind, Harrison? That I couldn't see the resemblance to my father?"

Her father? He was totally confused.

"What's going on here?" Mr. Bennett's voice boomed from behind him. "Your voices are carrying." He glanced at Lady Devonworth and his eyes widened. "Miss Olivia?"

Olivia? "Father, this is my fiancée, Lady Devonworth."

"I suggest you have a talk with your fiancée, son." He reached over and ripped the mask from Olivia's face. "This is Olivia Stewart."

Harrison rocked back on his heels, and his gaze went to her as she stood with her head up and her eyes blazing. "Olivia? You're a *Stewart?* Is that why you refused to tell me your first name?"

A crowd had gathered around them, and he heard the name Olivia Stewart whispered from mouth to mouth. Her mother was white and motionless at the table, speechless for once.

"I tried several times to tell you," Olivia said. "That hardly matters now. What about Eugene?"

"Eugene?" He turned to his valet. "Do you have any idea what she's talking about? Who is it you resemble?"

His valet was grave. "I'm afraid I know exactly what she is saying, sir. She is speaking of my resemblance to my father. And her father."

The words fell like boulders, hitting him hard, stealing his thoughts. "Y-Your father?" He stared at Eugene, then to Olivia. "Wait, are you saying . . ."

"I'm saying I'm Richard Pixton." His steady gaze bored into Harrison. He turned and plunged off into the dark.

❦

"Come back!" Olivia sprang after the man, as much to avoid Harrison's stricken expression as to catch Richard. She raced through the crowd, but he disappeared in the throng and she lost sight of him.

Harrison reached her. She stared into his face, desperately wishing he would be able to explain away his part in this. "He's gone," she said.

"He won't have gone far. I'll find him." Pain contorted his features. "Let's go to the library."

Every eye watched them exit. Olivia held her head high but nearly lost her composure when her gaze met Addie's. Her friend's eyes were brimming with sympathy. Olivia stepped into the library, and Harrison shut the door behind them.

He swept the mask from his face and stared at it in his hands. "I didn't know he was Pixton."

"I believe you," she said. She steeled herself for his questions and accusations. "I wanted to tell you who I was, but you'd made it perfectly clear you could never love Olivia Stewart. I couldn't find the words to tell you."

He opened his mouth, then closed it again. "It appears my distrust of the Stewart family was well-founded. You're as deceitful as your sister. I hate lies."

Olivia clasped her hands together. "It wasn't exactly a lie. I do possess the title of Lady Devonworth."

He turned the mask over in his fingers. "Why did you hide your identity?"

"I wanted to find out what happened to Eleanor and thought I might accomplish that better if no one knew I was Olivia Stewart." The explanation felt weak, even to her. "After someone tried to throw me off the boat, I also feared to reveal my identity, in case the murderer made another attempt."

"I would have protected you," he said.

Olivia shriveled under the contempt in Harrison's eyes. They'd had a measure of trust between them, and it was gone now. Scattered and destroyed like his plane. She'd gotten used to seeing admiration in those brown orbs. Now they were cold, so cold.

"I *had* to find out what happened to her," she said. "My mother wanted me to marry you in Eleanor's place, but I told her I wanted to see if we would suit first. Once the masquerade was in place, I felt trapped. I planned to tell you, then you informed me that you wouldn't marry Olivia Stewart if she were the last woman on Earth. I wasn't sure what to say after that."

"You thought I killed her."

She hung her head at his accusation, unable to deny it. "I didn't know you then."

"So you went into this deception to try to prove I murdered her." His voice was shaky. "I honestly thought you loved me."

The pain in his voice stopped her heart. "I-I'm sorry, Harrison. I didn't think you killed her once I got to know you better."

"Yet when you saw Eugene, you assumed I knew he was your brother."

She bit her lip. "I was overwhelmed. I'm sorry. I should have trusted you more."

"Yes, you should have." He tossed his mask onto a chair. "Our entire relationship has been a masquerade. How appropriate." He turned and exited the library, leaving the door gaping behind him.

"Harrison!" she called after him. When he didn't turn, she slumped onto the desk chair and struggled not to give in to tears. This was her fault.

After a few moments, she rose on stiff legs and went to the parlor with a smile pasted onto her face. Her guests turned curious faces her way, but she moved through the crowd reassuring them that all problems had been smoothed over. If only it were true. By the time the grandfather clock chimed four in the morning, she was limp with the effort of keeping the smile in place.

"We want to tally the donations," Addie said. "Are you okay?"

Olivia managed a smile. "We'll talk about it later. Let's find out if the ball was a success, at least as a benefit."

"Want to do the honors?" Katie asked.

"Go ahead." Olivia didn't have the brain for figures tonight. She watched as the other women counted.

Katie glanced up, her eyes shining. "It's nearly twenty thousand dollars, Olivia!" She choked up and tears filled her blue eyes. "I can't believe it."

"Believe it," Addie said. "God always sees our needs."

"I was beginning to believe that until tonight," Olivia said. Her vision blurred and she grabbed her hanky to mop her eyes.

Addie embraced her. "What did Harrison say? Was he terribly angry and hurt?"

Olivia clung to her, inhaling her friend's comforting perfume. "He was. I feel terrible. But there's more. His valet is Richard Pixton."

Addie stiffened. "Pixton? The man we've been looking for?"

Olivia nodded against Addie's shoulder. "So all this time that we've been looking for the man, he was right under our noses." Fresh tears poured down her face. "Richard is the one who has been terrorizing me. Calling on the speaking tube. He's the one behind Eleanor's murder. He tried to kill me too."

Addie hugged her. "Oh my dear, I'm so sorry. But this isn't Harrison's fault. I can't believe he would have known this."

"He said he didn't. I believe him." She mopped her eyes again. "But he's hurt and angry I didn't tell him I'm Olivia Stewart, and he has every right to be."

Addie bit her lip. "I was afraid of that."

Olivia sniffled. "I know I should have told him."

"Have you gone to the constable yet?" Katie asked, putting her hand on Olivia's back.

Olivia pulled away from Addie. "Not yet."

Addie squeezed Olivia's fingers. "Olivia, trust God with this. He is there for you."

"Thank you, Addie. Pray for me." Olivia swallowed hard and pulled away. "I'm going to go see Harrison."

"Ask God to open your heart and eyes," Addie called after her.

Olivia rushed from the room. She grabbed a shawl from the foyer and stepped out into the night air. She could call for a car but she'd rather walk. Stars glittered in the black bowl of sky. Cicadas sang around her as she walked up the driveway. Walking through the silent town, she felt a presence. Were her friends praying for her? She was sure they were.

"Where is the truth in all this?" she asked God. "What is my purpose? Surely you have more plans for me than to live a vain existence of spending money and trying to impress people."

God could see into her heart. Better than she could see herself. If he had stirred some kind of desire for more in her soul, shouldn't she listen? Shouldn't she explore the parts of herself that God brought to light? She'd been doing that, but now she wasn't sure. Maybe it was selfish to want more than she had. To want a noble purpose.

"I'm going to do better, God," she said. "I'm going to listen more. Be thankful for everything you give me and hold it with an open hand. Even if you want me to be poor. Even if I have to give everything to this unknown brother of mine. I want to become the person you see. Even if it means letting go of Harrison too."

There was no lightning overhead, no dove flying up from the shrubs. But she could have sworn she felt God smile. Smiling herself, she quickened her step. Harrison's house loomed in front of her. There was a light on. She'd thought she would have to rouse him and Richard from bed.

Please, God, let him listen. Let him still love me. Squaring her shoulders, she stepped onto the porch and pressed her finger on the buzzer.

THIRTY-SEVEN

HARRISON PACED THE floor of his billiards room. Nealy followed him. He hadn't wanted to notify the constable, but it had to be done. If someone had asked who his best friend was, he would have named Eugene. To discover he'd been lying all this time—and was almost certainly the man who murdered Eleanor—made Harrison doubt everything in his life. His eyes burned and he rubbed them.

Olivia hadn't cared enough to trust him with her identity. That could only mean she had never trusted him at all. And she was a Stewart. Now he marveled that he hadn't seen it for himself. No wonder she knew all their business.

When the doorbell sounded, he stopped and glanced at the mantel clock. Nearly five in the morning. Only the constable would come at this hour. He strode down the hall and threw open the door.

Olivia stood on the porch. She still wore her Juliet costume and the necklace he'd given her. "May I come in?" she asked.

He stepped aside and turned his back on her as he retreated to his office, the closest room. The sooner she stated her purpose and left, the better. He heard her shut the door and greet Nealy, who had stayed behind. Traitor dog.

He flicked on the light in the office and went to stand by his desk as she appeared in the doorway. "What are you doing here at this hour?"

"I needed to talk to you."

He narrowed his eyes at her. He saw she still wore the ring as well. Why hadn't she taken it off?

She didn't look away from his glare. She glanced around. "Is Richard here?"

"I have no idea where he is. I haven't seen him since he ran off."

She twisted a long lock of hair around her finger. "He left town?"

"I'm not privy to his secrets. Nor yours."

A breeze fluttered through the window behind him and ruffled the papers on the desk. A storm was blowing in, but it was nothing compared to the storm in his soul.

Her attention never left him. "You totally trusted him?"

"I didn't suspect *you* weren't Lady Devonworth," he pointed out.

She had the grace to flush. "How long has he worked for you?"

"Four years. I counted him as a friend. My *best* friend. I hate to see him behind bars."

"Don't you even care that he killed my sister—that he tried to kill me?" Her voice broke.

He nearly moved to comfort her but stopped himself. "Of course I care. I told the constable to arrest him."

"Has he?"

He shrugged. "I haven't heard. When you rang the doorbell, I thought it was Brown."

The wariness in her eyes faded, and she gave a tentative smile. "I believe you, Harrison. I was just shocked at first when I realized he was your valet. I'm sorry."

"Why were you so quick to jump to the wrong conclusion?"

Her eyes pleaded for understanding. "I've been dressed up and posed just like the Kewpie dolls. Perfect hostess, obedient daughter, scion of society. It's hard to believe anyone would love me for myself and not for what I can do for them. I allowed my doubts about myself to carry over to you. I was wrong."

His anger began to ebb. "I only wanted you, Olivia. Not your name or your status."

Tears filled her eyes. She took a step toward him. The wind picked up again. The gentle breeze changed to a sudden gust that caught the papers on the desk and blew them across the room. She stooped and began to pick them up.

"I'll get them," he said.

She reached for a paper and froze. She snatched it up and stared at it, then up at him. His gut clenched when he remembered one of the papers on the desk. The forged signatures.

"Would you care to explain this?" she asked, holding out a paper. Her voice sounded thick.

He knew what it was without looking. "I was going to tell you about it."

"You forged my father's handwriting. You let me hope he was alive." Her voice was disbelieving.

He shook his head and took a step toward her.

She backed up, tears spilling down her cheeks. "I wanted to give you the benefit of the doubt. I wanted to believe that there was a good reason for Richard Pixton to be under your roof. You had me convinced I was wrong."

He reached a hand toward her, then dropped it when she flinched. "No, Olivia. It's not what you think. I found that at my father's house. See the pencil rubbing? I did that trying to figure it out. When I saw what he'd done, I confronted him about it. There's more I need to tell you about all of this, but not until you calm down."

"I'm perfectly calm, thank you." Her gaze searched his. "I want to believe you, Harrison." Her voice broke off in a sob.

"I had nothing to do with any of this, Olivia."

She passed her hand over her forehead. "I'm so tired I can't even think. I'm going home now. We'll talk about it later." She lifted her gaze and studied his face. "Can we get past this, Harrison? I want to. If you could understand how devastated I was by Eleanor's death, perhaps you could understand my determination to know the truth."

He thought about telling her he loved her, but he still couldn't wrap his mind around the fact that she was a Stewart. He let her turn and rush from the room. Moments later the door slammed.

❧

Tears poured down Olivia's cheeks as she rushed back to the manor. Harrison had shown no willingness to forgive her for hiding her identity. And heaven help her, she still loved him. What a pathetic fool she was.

The manor was dark as she made her way to her room. She closed the door behind her and fell onto her bed before she let out the sobs crowding her throat. Her life was in ruins.

She lay on her back and watched the stars through the window. Her fingers crept to her lips and she remembered the night he'd kissed her for the first time while stars fell from the sky. Burying her face in her pillow, she wished that day back again.

"Olivia." The words echoed from the speaking tube. "I need to talk to you."

She bolted upright. Her father's voice. She grabbed the speaking tube. "I'm on to you, Richard. I won't be taken in again."

Ghostly laughter floated up the tube, then the voice faded away. How dare he come here and taunt her? He knew she wouldn't fall for his ruse now. He'd done it to torment her. How had Harrison let such a viper into his household?

Tiger curled up against her and she caressed his soft fur. He was a comfort tonight. His ears flickered and he looked toward the door. Her skin prickled when he tensed. Was someone listening outside her door? She bolted upright.

A board creaked and she struggled to see her door in the moonlight. Was the knob turning, or was it a trick of the light? Before she could decide, the door eased open and a figure stepped inside. A woman's figure.

Olivia relaxed. "Goldia, what are you doing up at this hour?"

The light came on, half blinding her. She put up her hand to shield her eyes and realized it was her housekeeper. The door shut behind Mrs. Bagley. Swiping at the moisture on her cheeks, Olivia sat up.

"Is something wrong?"

"Yes, miss, we have a crisis. Could you come with me?"

Olivia swung her legs to the floor. "Of course. What's wrong?"

The housekeeper put her fingers to her lips. "It's your mother. Quietly, Miss Olivia. Your mother was most adamant that I didn't rouse the Jespersons."

Just like her mother to want to smother any gossip. "Is she ill?" Olivia rushed toward the door and followed the housekeeper into the hall. Instead of turning toward her mother's room, Mrs. Bagley turned left toward the stairs. Olivia followed Mrs. Bagley down the staircase to the first floor. She started past her to the parlor, but the older woman grabbed her arm.

"She's not there, Miss Olivia. This way." She beckoned for Olivia to come with her to the back of the house toward the kitchen.

What was her mother doing in the kitchen? But when they reached it, the woman continued out the back door toward the carriage house. Were they leaving the premises?

"Mrs. Bagley, where are we going?"

"She's in the carriage house, miss. She's had an accident."

An accident? What would her mother be doing wandering around the carriage house? Olivia darted past Mrs. Bagley and ran across the backyard. The carriage house was across the driveway and at the back of the property. What could her mother have been doing all the way out here where only servants went?

She reached the structure and stepped into the dusty space smelling of gasoline and oil. "Mother?" Straining to see in the dark, she could only make out the shrouded shapes of the automobiles.

The door slammed behind her, and a man's hard hands grabbed her. A rag was thrust into her mouth, then he wrenched her arms behind her back. The man propelled her toward the smaller automobile.

She worked her tongue around the rag. It wasn't stuck in very far and she managed to get it out of her mouth. It fell to the ground in the dark as he shoved her forward.

A scream tore out of her throat, and he clapped his hand over her mouth. "If you make another sound, your mother is dead. Understand?"

She nodded, and he took his hand away. "Richard?" she gasped. "What do you want? Where is my mother?"

"Get that rag back in her mouth, Jerry."

Jerry? Olivia strained to see the man's face. The sliver of moonlight through the window showed a slimmer, shorter man than Harrison's valet. Jerry and Mrs. Bagley were in on this too?

"I can't find the rag," he muttered. "You have a hanky?"

"No," Mrs. Bagley growled.

Olivia heard a woman moan. The sound came from behind her. "Mother?"

"She's here and if you scream, I'll kill her first," Jerry said.

"Whatever Richard is paying you to help him, I'll pay you more if you let us go," Olivia said. "I promise you won't go to jail."

"Richard?" Mrs. Bagley laughed and shoved Olivia. "That milquetoast nephew of mine has nothing to do with this. He's much too *forgiving* to mete out justice where it's due."

"Nephew? You're Lulu's sister? The one she went to live with after leaving our house?" Olivia struggled to see the woman's face in the dark. "What do you stand to gain if I'm dead?"

"If you're all dead, Richard will get everything. He'll share it with the aunt who raised him. But it's not about the money. It was never about the money."

"It's just revenge then?" Jerry's grip on her arms never slackened. The only way she would be free of him would be if he let go.

"Your father gave everything to you and your sister. He let his wife toss Lulu to the dirt. She went quite mad, you know." Mrs. Bagley's voice rose.

"Mother, don't," Jerry said. "Stay calm."

"Calm?" Mrs. Bagley's voice rose to a near shriek. "The Stewarts are to blame for everything. For the way we lived hand to mouth. For Lulu's death by her own hand. They have to pay for their sins. I've waited and waited for God to do it, but he has let them prosper. So I have to do it."

"But you'll go to jail. No one will believe this was an accident. You'll be found out."

The woman's smile was chilling. "Jerry will testify he saw Frederick Fosberg sabotage the plane. And we also have his gun in our possession. He'll take the fall, not us."

"Fosberg tried to kill us?"

"He tried to kill Harrison. He was convinced Eleanor killed herself because she was afraid of having her reputation besmirched. Of course, Harrison had nothing to do with it—Jerry threw her over the cliff—but Fosberg's rage suited our purposes."

"It was Jerry on the boat," Olivia said. "He tried to kill me."

Mrs. Bagley shoved her. "Enough talk. Let's end it, Jerry."

Jerry shoved Olivia toward the roadster. He wrapped a rope around her arms, then lifted her into the seat and tied the rope to something on the floor that she couldn't see. She opened her mouth to scream, and he stuffed a vile-tasting rag into her throat. From the oily texture it must have been used to wipe grease off the cars.

She began to work the rope but it refused to loosen. Straining to see in the dark, she realized her mother was slumped unconscious against the other door. Olivia's scream tried to work its way past the rag, but all that emerged was a choked gasp.

The next moment she heard something splash. The stench of gasoline choked her. They were going to set the carriage house on fire!

THIRTY-EIGHT

HARRISON SAT FOR a long time just staring into the flickering fire. All his bright hopes for the future were gone. His father was a swindler, maybe worse. He still wasn't convinced his father hadn't orchestrated Mr. Stewart's death. The man he would have trusted with his life had betrayed him. Worst of all, the woman he'd meant to spend the rest of his life with believed him capable of killing her sister and plotting her own death. And she'd deceived him.

"Sir."

He looked up to see Eugene—Richard—in the doorway. The proper response would be to leap to his feet and restrain him until the constable could be summoned, but Harrison couldn't dredge up the will to do it.

"Why, Eugene?" he asked simply. His valet would always be Eugene to him, not this Richard fellow.

Eugene stepped into the office. "I'm not behind Eleanor's murder. I know that's what Miss Stewart thinks. You believed her too. I saw it in your face. That's why I ran."

"The constable is looking for you. Why have you come back?"

"To make sure you know the truth. I had nothing to do with any of this."

"Then who has?" Harrison asked.

Eugene hung his head. He went still, then picked up the forged signatures on Harrison's desk. "What is this?"

"My father forged the paper giving him control of the mine." Harrison rubbed his throbbing head. "If you didn't kill Eleanor, then maybe he did."

Eugene shook his head. "My cousin did this, not your father."

"What? How do you know?"

"It's known in town that if you want a well-done forgery, you go to Jerry."

"Jerry? He's your cousin?"

Eugene nodded. "Your father wouldn't sully his hands by doing this himself."

"And the one from Mr. Stewart to Eleanor? He would have done that one as well?"

"It would make sense."

Harrison frowned. "What would be Jerry's connection to this? Was he simply hired to do the forgery? Why would my father want Eleanor dead? Or Olivia? He forced Eleanor out here to marry me. He had much to lose by their deaths. But you didn't."

Eugene held his stare. "I would not take their money or their lives, sir."

"Then who is behind this? Who else stands to gain from eliminating the Stewarts?" He saw Eugene pale and glance away. "Who, Eugene?"

Eugene put his hands in his pockets. "Jerry himself. When Mr. Fosberg told Eleanor about the new will, Jerry came to me chortling about how life would be different when I possessed all the Stewart money. That we could take over the estate and be as good as anyone else in town."

"That's not proof," Harrison said.

"There's more, sir. A few minutes ago I overheard Jerry in the Stewarts' garden. He was talking in another voice."

"Probably practicing for the vaudeville play he'll be in. The same one he performed tonight at the ball."

Eugene shook his head. "He sounded like my father. I heard him say, 'Olivia, come down here.'"

"Why would he say that? You mean he was practicing to coax her from her room again?" The pencil in Harrison's fingers snapped. "He was the one who lured her outside, then tried to kill her?"

"That's what I suspect," Eugene said. "I came straight here."

Harrison leaped to his feet. "He's in the house with Olivia! I must get to her immediately."

"I'm sure he would do nothing with a houseful of guests." But Eugene followed him to the hall.

Harrison called Nealy, then went directly to his car. He slid behind the wheel of the car that was parked along the street. The engine didn't turn over. "Come on, come on," he said.

"We'd better walk," Eugene said.

Harrison got out and followed his valet as they ran toward the Stewarts'. Nealy raced after them. As they rounded the corner, a red glow lit the predawn sky.

"Fire!" Harrison seemed to be moving in slow motion though his legs pumped beneath him and his chest burned with exertion. "The carriage house!"

The property seemed impossibly far away. As he raced up the driveway, he detected no shouts of alarm. All the guests were probably sleeping off their exhaustion from being up all night. "Fire!" he screamed again at the top of his lungs. He prayed the servants would hear him.

What if Olivia was in that building? Considering the danger she faced, an unrelated fire would be an unlikely coincidence. Horror seemed to encase his legs in ice. Was he never going to arrive? Panting, he reached the end of the house and ran for the backyard, shouting for the servants as he ran. He rounded the back corner.

The carriage house roof was in engulfed in flames. Embers shot into the air and fell like the falling stars they'd seen that night he first kissed her. He ran for the door and tried to open it, but the doorknob was scorching hot. He took off his shirt, wrapped it around his hand and tried again, but it was locked. With his hand still encased in his shirt, he punched his fist through the glass, reached inside and unlocked the latch, then managed to get the door open.

Smoke and heat poured out of the doorway. He screamed her name above the roar of the flames. Stepping into the inferno, he choked on the smoke and peered through the hideous scene straight from a nightmare. "Olivia!"

Someone touched his shoulder and he looked back to see Eugene in the blazing building with him. "She has to be in here!" Harrison yelled. Holding his arm across his nose and mouth, he began to kick at the flames.

He wouldn't find her alive. The inner conviction nearly made his knees buckle, but he refused to give in to despair. Nealy began to bark. The dog grabbed Harrison's pants and tugged. He let the dog drag him forward. "Olivia!" he called again.

A movement caught his eye in the seat of the roadster. He leaped to the automobile and found Olivia, her eyes half closed and her head lolling against the seat. Her mother was beside her.

"Eugene, here!" He tried to pick her up, but she was tied. It took precious moments to loosen the rope, then he raised Olivia in his arms and ran with her toward the exit. "Get Mrs. Stewart!"

Fire crackled overhead. Burning timbers began to rain down on their heads, and the doorway seemed too far away. He leaped over a blazing rafter and felt the heat of it on his legs as he reached the other side. Looking down, he realized his trousers were on fire, but he felt no pain. He didn't stop to beat out the fire but rushed for the clear air he could now see outside. He burst through the space into the yard where a group of guests were huddled together watching the blaze.

Laying Olivia on the grass, he made sure her clothing wasn't on fire. It was only then that one of the guests took off his jacket and smothered the flames on Harrison's trousers. Harrison caught a glimpse of burned flesh and wondered when the pain would start.

He spotted Mrs. Bagley and Jerry watching the blaze from the porch. Her face fell when she saw Olivia on the grass. She grabbed Jerry's arm, and they disappeared inside.

Eugene exited the carriage house with Mrs. Stewart in his arms. The hem of her nightdress was smoldering, and Harrison tossed the jacket to Eugene, who beat at it until the fire was out.

Olivia seemed unhurt. He cradled her in his arms and took the gag from her mouth. Her eyelids fluttered and she swallowed.

"Water!" he called to the shocked crowd. "Shh, don't talk," he told Olivia. "I've got you." He held her close. "I can't lose you, Olivia." He rocked her back and forth.

"I prayed you'd come," she said, her voice hoarse.

He pressed his lips to her forehead and thanked God they'd been in time.

❧

Her lungs burned with every breath she drew. Olivia opened her eyes and coughed. She tried to sit up, but gentle hands pushed her back. She realized she was in her bed. The scent of smoke still clung to her even though someone had removed her smoky clothing and replaced it with a clean nightdress.

"Lie still, darling." Harrison's face shimmered in her vision.

She blinked and his face came into focus. "Mother!" She tried to rise again, but his hands on her shoulders held her down.

"She's fine. Eugene got her out." Time enough later to tell her about her mother's burns. They weren't life threatening and would heal without disfigurement.

"Richard didn't try to hurt me," she said past the pain in her throat. "It was his aunt and cousin."

"Eugene told me."

"Where are they?"

"In custody. Brown caught them fleeing town. Jerry is telling the constable everything."

She clutched his forearm and drew it away so she could take his hand. "Harrison, I'm so sorry. Can you forgive me?"

"I already did, the second I realized I might lose you." He raised her hand to his lips.

"There was no excuse for how I acted."

"I'm not without blame. I was too proud to make you listen to me. I believed the worst about Eugene too, and I was wrong." He slid his hand under her back. "I'm going to raise you up. Ready?"

She nodded, and he lifted her to a seated position. Her vision swam again, then cleared. "I need to see my mother."

"She's resting. I spoke with her. The doctor is with her now."

"Did she have many burns?"

He shook his head. "Mostly on her ankles, but they will heal. He was concerned because of her age. He wanted to check out her heart and lungs, but he said he thought she'd be fine. He treated your burns and the one on my leg."

She coughed, her lungs still hurting. "You were burned?"

"Just my leg. I'll be fine."

"What's going to happen to them—the Bagleys?" she asked.

His lips flattened and his eyes narrowed. "They'll be tried for your sister's murder. And for trying to kill you and your mother."

There was a tap on the door, and he turned. "Come in."

His valet poked his head into the room. "I wondered if I might speak to Miss Olivia?"

Richard stepped into the bedroom when Harrison nodded. Olivia stared at him. In the daylight he looked even more like her father. And he was her brother. She struggled to wrap her mind around that fact.

"I wanted to personally apologize," Richard said. "And to assure you that I had no idea what was happening until this morning when I heard about the forgeries. I really thought Eleanor killed herself."

"I don't understand," she said.

Harrison smoothed her hair. "Eugene says Jerry is the person to go to when someone needs a forgery."

"So he forged my father's signature onto the agreement with Bennett?"

Harrison nodded. "And he wrote the letter we thought was from your father."

"Why would he tell Eleanor to cut off all ties with the Bennetts?"

"The constable said Jerry was trying to cozy up to Eleanor. He had hopes he could win her. He didn't know of her relationship with Fosberg," Harrison said. "When he found out, she had to die to prevent the attorney from laying any claim to her money."

"What of hearing my father's voice? Was that you, Richard?"

He shook his head. "I went to talk to my cousin Jerry early this morning as the guests went off to bed. I found him in the garden practicing speaking in your father's voice."

"I don't understand," Olivia said. "Jerry was the person I heard?"

Richard nodded. "He's always been good at mimicking voices."

"He did an excellent job in the play," she said. "All this for money." She would have given the Bagleys all the money they wanted if they'd only spared her sister's life. Olivia rubbed her head. There were sore spots. Burns most likely.

"They wanted revenge more than money," Harrison added.

"She hated our family so much," Olivia marveled. "It seems extreme."

Richard nodded. "My aunt had a hard life that was made even harder after my mother died. When your father built the grand house here, the only job she could get at the time was as his housekeeper. The more she saw the differences between his life and the life we lived, the more deranged she became. I often heard her say she could do a better job running the estate than the Stewarts did."

"Did they have anything to do with my father's death?" She had to know.

Harrison shook his head. "If anyone did something wrong there, it was my father. He maintains your father's death was an accident and I tend to believe him. But even if that's true, he took the opportunity to swindle your mother. I found evidence in the books that the diamond mines are producing millions of dollars, and my father is paying only a fraction of that into your accounts."

It was all so overwhelming. "Now what?" she asked.

"I told Father he has to fix it. All of it. And turn himself in."

"Will he?" Richard asked.

Harrison's jaw hardened. "If he doesn't, I will."

Olivia stared at her new brother. "Now what, Richard? We need to get to the bottom of the will."

He shook his head. "The document makes no difference to me. I'm not going to take your money. It's not right."

"I think Father wanted to right a wrong," Olivia said softly. "It's clear that you will never let my mother want for anything. You're a good man. I believe we can trust you."

He swallowed hard and looked down. "I can't take your money."

"I'm going to talk to our attorney. Will you accept whatever just settlement he suggests?"

He raised his eyes and stared at her. "If you insist, Miss Olivia."

"Just Olivia," she said. "You're my brother, and you saved my life tonight." She tightened her grip on Harrison's hand. "You and Harrison."

A sheen of moisture gleamed in Richard's eyes. He bowed. "I'll take my leave now, Olivia, and let you rest."

"Wait!" She held out her hand. "I want to know why you don't hate us like the rest of your family."

"I used to," he admitted. "After my mother hung herself."

Olivia squeezed his hand. "I'm so sorry."

His Adam's apple bobbed and he blinked rapidly. "Thank you. I got into trouble as a teenager. Petty theft, breaking windows. A cop in the San Francisco suburbs caught me, but instead of arresting me, he made me go to church with him."

"And you came to know Jesus," Harrison said.

Richard nodded. "That changed everything. I couldn't harbor bitterness like that. So I just . . . let it go. I was free. Bitterness binds you. Look at my aunt and cousin."

She shuddered and released his hand. "Don't go too far. I want to get to know my brother better."

A ghost of a smile flitted across his face. He nodded and closed the door behind him.

"I did the same thing to him that you did to me," Harrison said. "Even though I'd known and trusted him for years, I believed he had duped me."

She tugged on his hand until he sat on the edge of the bed. "So are you still going to marry me even if I'm poor? *And* a Stewart?"

He grinned. "I thought you *were* poor until I saw the accounting books. I'd rather support my wife myself. Are you sure you still want to marry me knowing we are going to have to work hard to make a go of the business?"

"Trying to talk your way out of it?" she teased.

He leaned down until his face was just inches from hers. "Not a chance, darling. I'm not letting you get away. When will you marry me?"

"Today?" she suggested.

"I'll get the preacher." His eyes were serious.

Heat settled in her cheeks. "We could make it soon," she whispered. "But just a small wedding after everyone is gone. I'm done trying to impress people."

"We'll have it on the beach at night. Right where I kissed you under the falling stars. If we're lucky, it will happen again."

"There are enough fireworks when you touch me that we don't need falling stars," she said, pulling him down to kiss her.

ACKNOWLEDGMENTS

IS IT POSSIBLE that *The Lightkeeper's Ball* is my eighteenth book with my Thomas Nelson family? They are truly my dream team! Publisher Allen Arnold (I call him Superman) is so passionate about fiction, and he lights up a room when he enters it. Senior Acquisitions Editor Ami McConnell (my friend and cheerleader) has an eye for character and theme like no one I know. I crave her analytical eye! It was her influence that encouraged me to write a historical romantic mystery, and I'm glad she pushed me a bit! Marketing Manager Eric Mullett brings fabulous ideas to the table. Publicist Katie Bond is always willing to listen to my harebrained ideas. Fabulous cover guru Kristen Vasgaard (you *so* rock!) works hard to create the perfect cover—and does it. And of course I can't forget my other friends who are all part of my amazing fiction family: Natalie Hanemann, Amanda Bostic, Becky Monds, Ashley Schneider, Andrea Lucado, Heather McCoullough, Chris Long, and Kathy Carabajal. I wish I could name all the great folks who work on selling my books through different venues at Thomas Nelson. Hearing "well done" from you all is my motivation every day.

Erin Healy has edited all of my Thomas Nelson books except one, and she is such an integral part of the team. Her ideas always make the book better, and she's a fabulous writer in her own right. If you haven't read her yet, be sure to pick up *Never Let You Go* and *The Promises She Keeps*.

My agent, Karen Solem, has helped shape my career in many ways, and that includes kicking an idea to the curb when necessary. Thanks, Karen—you're the best!

Writing can be a lonely business, but God has blessed me with great writing friends and critique partners. Hannah Alexander (Cheryl Hodde), Kristin Billerbeck, Diann Hunt, and Denise Hunter make up the Girls Write Out squad (www.GirlsWriteOut.blogspot.com). I couldn't make it through a day without my peeps! Thanks to all of you for the work you do on my behalf, and for your friendship. I had great brainstorming help for this book in Robin Caroll, Cara Putman, and Rick Acker as well. Thank you, friends!

I'm so grateful for my husband, Dave, who carts me around from city to city, washes towels, and chases down dinner without complaint. Thanks, honey! I couldn't do anything without you. My kids—Dave, Kara (and now Donna and Mark)—and my grandsons, James and Jorden Packer, love and support me in every way possible. Love you guys! Donna and Dave brought me the delight of my life— our little granddaughter, Alexa! Though I tried my best to emulate her cuteness in the scenes with Jennie, I'm sure I failed!

Most importantly, I give my thanks to God, who has opened such amazing doors for me and makes the journey a golden one.

READING GROUP GUIDE

1. Do you ever feel you are insignificant and nothing you do matters? Why or why not?

2. Do you have a dream you have been too intimidated to pursue? Maybe even too afraid to name it? What is it?

3. Name characteristics of some of the true friends you have had. How important is it that they point you back to God?

4. Have you ever altered your behavior because of others' expectations the way Olivia did? What allows you to be yourself?

5. Do you know anyone who has allowed bitterness to fester? How can you help that person forgive and let go?

6. Family expectations were very different for children a hundred years ago. What would you have found the most difficult about growing up in that era?

7. Society at the turn of the last century was also preoccupied with appearances and impressing other people, much as we see today. What can you do to keep from falling in the hole of materialism?

8. What do you want badly enough that might tempt you into compromising your integrity?

9. Olivia was wrong for keeping her secrets from Harrison. At what point should she have admitted her identity?

10. God sees us as we are inside. Does this comfort you or intimidate you?

Libby arrives at the Tidewater Inn hoping to discover clues about her friend's disappearance. There she finds an unexpected inheritance and a love beyond her wildest dreams.

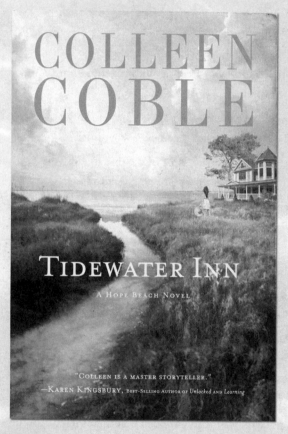

The first novel in the Hope Beach Series

AVAILABLE IN PRINT AND E-BOOK

ESCAPE TO BLUEBIRD RANCH

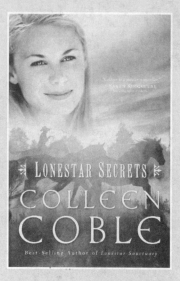

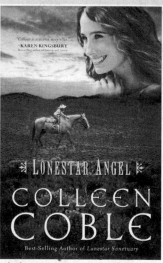

AVAILABLE IN PRINT AND E-BOOK

*F*our friends devise a plan to turn Smitten, Vermont, into the country's premier romantic getaway—while each searches for her own true love along the way.

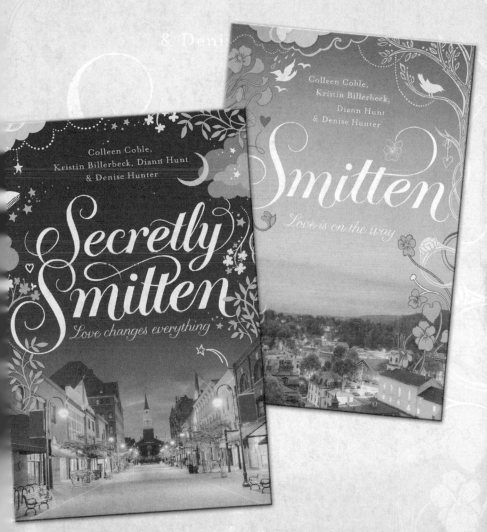

AVAILABLE IN PRINT AND E-BOOK

THOMAS NELSON
Since 1798

THE ROCK HARBOR MYSTERY SERIES

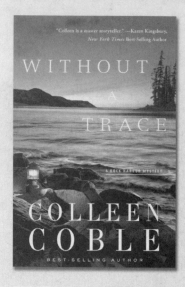

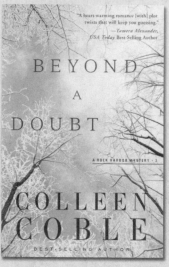

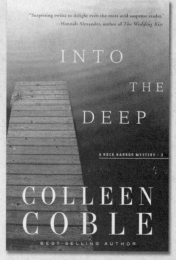

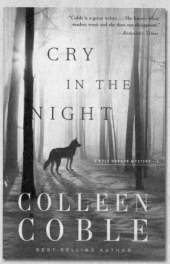

AVAILABLE IN PRINT AND E-BOOK

THOMAS NELSON
Since 1798

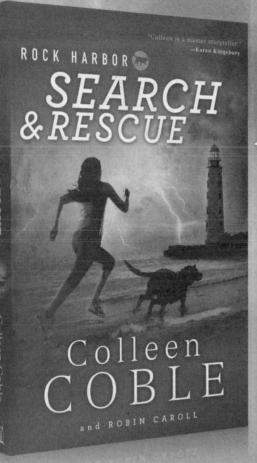

About the Author

AUTHOR PHOTO BY CLIK CHICK PHOTOGRAPHY

RITA finalist Colleen Coble is the author of several bestselling romantic suspense series, including the Mercy Falls series, the Lonestar series, and the Rock Harbor series.

Visit ColleenCoble.com